Tír na nÓg

Vaughn F. Keller

This is a work of fiction. Names, characters, businesses, places, events, locales, and incidents are either the products of the author's imagination or used in a fictitious manner. Where data is used, it has been taken from public records.

©Copyright 2022 by Vaughn F. Keller
All Rights Reserved

Paperback ISBN: 9798362899936

To Melody

Who brought me to Georgetown

TITLES BY VAUGHN F. KELLER

FRANK KELLY MYSTERIES

    Behind the Neon
    The Unwilling Pawn
    Dirt

COLLECTIONS (Short Stories, Essays, Poetry)

    Glimpses
    The Corner of My Eye

Chapter One: The Extension

The kitchen radio was on to the news station. Two United States F22 Raptors had intercepted two Russian Tu-95 bombers and two Su-35 fighters somewhere off the coast of Alaska. I shook my head and kept scrubbing the refrigerator. I had done that in 1964, in F-102 Delta Daggers. Fifty-five years later and the United States and Russia were still playing the same insane game of 'chicken.'

My grouchiness was interrupted by my cell phone. It was Rachel. I was always surprised when Rachel called. I usually called her; she didn't call me. But when she did call, I was rarely surprised by why she called. Inevitably, she was either in trouble or needed something. Hannah had always cautioned me to be patient and kind. "Rach has had a hard life," Hannah would admonish me. When I shot back, "Who the hell hasn't?" it led one more time to the 'Maybe we could have done more' talk. I hated that talk. With Hannah gone now for four years, I did my best to internalize 'the talk' and cut my forty-three-year-old daughter some slack.

This was a "favor" call seasoned with a bit of trouble. We completed the "how are you's?" the "fines," and finally got to her asking, "Have you moved from the farmhouse down to Tír yet?" 'Tír' was Tír na nÓg, our summer home on Heron Cove in Georgetown, Maine. I told her, "Almost. You caught me in the middle of cleaning out the refrigerator."

The troubling element, when it came, was tepid compared with all the other troubles Rachel had been through. And then, as I knew it would, came the favor part.

"Dad, remember I told you Wendy changed majors?"

"Yeah. Vaguely." I said, "Sociology to history, right?"

"Yeah, history. Now she's talking about maybe wanting to teach. Don't ask me why history. Anyway, in the middle of the semester, her boyfriend broke up with her, and she took it hard. She sort of bottomed out."

"How bad?" I immediately thought like mother, like daughter. Rachel knew what I was thinking.

"She's okay, Dad. Don't worry." Her tone was just on the edge of acerbic.

"Okay" was shorthand. We both understood it. So, Wendy wasn't on drugs, alcohol, or pregnant. So, 'bottomed out' meant what?

Then she changed her tone and became matter of fact: "She couldn't get it together enough to focus. She was able to get by in most of her courses, but she ran into trouble in this one history course. She didn't finish the major paper. She didn't even start it. And the course is a prerequisite for two of the courses she wants to take next semester. Her professor has given her an extension until the end of the summer. So, she's got to have the paper in before the fall semester begins. They're holding spots for her in the courses she wants to take, but she has to get this paper done. Anyway, we were wondering if she could spend the summer with you at Tír and work on the paper there? You know how much she loves Tír."

I said, "I suppose so, but I'm surprised she'd want to come here. She hasn't been to Tír in four years, and she'd have to drive a half an hour or more to get to a decent library. I might be able to get her a summer pass at Bowdoin. But she'd need a car."

"We talked about that. Maybe she could use Jesse's motorcycle. It's still there, isn't it? Or maybe your truck when you aren't using it. You still have mom's car, don't you? You've been driving that most of the time, right?"

I think I kept my voice level and at least somewhat free of piss-off-ed-ness. This was going to get complicated. I said, "Jesse's bike is here, but you'd have to ask him about using it. She'd have to go through a course and get a motorcycle endorsement to use the bike. And yes, I still have mom's car." I hesitated. Then I added, "I'm sure we could work something out."

"Thank you, thank you, thank you."

"What's the paper on?"

"She has to do a history of the place she thinks of as home."

"But she doesn't live here. So why doesn't she stay in Brattleboro where they'll have source documents?"

"I know. We talked about that. Actually, though, Georgetown is better for her. We've only lived in Brattleboro for two years, and most of that time, she's been away at school. She doesn't think of it as home. Given how much we've moved, Georgetown is the closest thing she says she has to home."

I withheld everything I wanted to say about Rachel's multiple moves, boyfriends, and two husbands. But, at the same time, when she told me Wendy thought of Georgetown as home, it closed the deal. It was everything Hannah had ever wanted, a homestead for her children and grandchildren, a place to return. The framed piece of needlepoint Hannah picked up at a yard sale still hung in the farmhouse kitchen. The quotation was from Frost's *Death of the Hired Man*: "Home is the place where, when you have to go there, they have to take you in." And if I were honest, I would welcome Wendy's company. My children and grandchildren rarely came anymore, not since Hannah died. And, for research, the Georgetown Historical Society might have everything she needed. If she required Wi-Fi, though, she was out of luck. "Does she know there's no Wi-Fi down at Tír?"

"She can go poach at the library, or maybe down at Five I." 'Five I' was the local abbreviation for Five Islands, a tiny village named after the cluster of five small islands at the end of Georgetown, which was also an island. Five I was home to a couple of shops, a take-out restaurant with picnic tables, and a lobster pound.

"Sure, why not?"

"Dad, thanks. I appreciate it. I'll drive over this weekend if that's okay with you. Would Saturday work?"

"I suppose so. I should be down at Tír by then if I hustle."

"Super. She can help you move. Oh, one more thing. Wendy's now a vegetarian. I've told her that she has to fend for herself when it comes to food. Oh, and I know this is asking a lot, but can she bring Charlie with her?"

"Charlie, too?"

"Oh, come on. You like Charlie. He's completely housebroken, and he's an absolute love muffin. You should get your own dog for company. Having Charlie around will be a good trial run. You haven't had a dog since Monster died."

"Fine. Charlie, too. Where are you going to be this summer?"

"Here. Where else? I'm flat out. I have a new boss, and she wants to do all new events this summer. She was a cruise director on some ship and doesn't understand that summer people and locals want the same thing every year. You understand. You know, that's what summer's about. The Chamber of Commerce is going along with her, though, so I don't have any choice but to try and make it happen. It's late to be lining things up, so I'm on the phone all day long. She's decided she wants more 'adult' events, whatever that means. I don't think she gets that the adults love going to the events for the kids."

"Do you think you'll be able to spend any time up here?"

"Maybe one or two days. Maybe after Labor Day."

"How about when you pick Wendy up at the end of the summer?"

"Probably not. She'll have to be back in school by the end of August."

"Okay. So, I'll see you Saturday."

"Thanks, Dad."

I finished scrubbing the refrigerator with a solution of vinegar and water, unplugged it, emptied out the ice cube trays in the sink, and left them on the counter to dry. I'd come up from Tír and reverse the process a day or two before the farmhouse tenants came the first week in June. That way, they'd have ice, a cold refrigerator, and a welcoming bottle of chilled champagne when they arrived.

These tenants were new people, referred by regulars, as was usually the case. Hannah and I hadn't paid to advertise or deal with a broker in years. This couple had taken the only open week I had left, the first week in June. I warned them that it might be cool and foggy, but they didn't seem to care. People 'from away' think of Maine as an endless summer from June to September first with nothing but sun, lobsters, and blueberries. I always told my renters, "There's fog, people. Fog. It blocks the sun, and it can be chilly and damp." The regulars knew it and came anyway. I always supplied lots of dry, seasoned wood for the fireplace, and I could tell from the years of guest book entries that the foggy days were spent reading, cooking, or going on excursions to Bath, Brunswick, or the stores down in Freeport. First-timers always had to go to LL Bean. Actually, most of the regulars did as well, a kind of annual pilgrimage.

These people were newlyweds. Maybe fog's exactly what they wanted here: a gray cocoon protecting them from the outside world. Who knew? Being a newlywed isn't what it used to be when I was their age. They could use the canoe and the kayaks if they got some nice days. I had told them the farmhouse was big, but they wanted it anyway. Maybe they planned on having a lot of guests. A honeymoon with guests. When you've already been living together, it might not matter much.

The house was certainly big enough. It was about as classic as a center chimney colonial could get. The original house had four rooms on the main floor and four rooms upstairs. The stairway between the floors was narrow and changed directions three times. Every one of the original downstairs rooms had a fireplace. There was a bee-hive oven in what was the original kitchen and even a root cellar in the basement. The floors in the old section were the original wide pine boards cut from local timber. A barn was attached by a room that now functioned as the kitchen. There were no more sheep in the barn, but tenants loved thinking that where they now parked their cars, livestock use to live.

Painted white, close to the road that crisscrossed the island, it would forever be 'The Convey Farm' no matter how many generations of Buckleys had lived there. Every generation had added its own touches from indoor plumbing to central heat, and more recently, Hannah and I had set about restoring the house to its colonial roots.

I knew every inch of the house. I had painted it, swore at it, and slept in every room, including the kitchen, attic, and basement. I had only lived someplace else when I was in the Air Force and again when Hannah and I first got married, and that was only for a couple of years. I love this old house. I know it's too big for me and I don't care.

I got busy and carried the box of refrigerated items I was taking with me out to the truck. It contained everything from mayonnaise, random bottles of mustard, and an assorted selection of jams and jellies to perishables – milk, eggs, cheese. I put the box in the back and returned to the house to do a final check before locking everything up.

As I did every year, I started in the attic. Every old house has an attic smell. It's a dry smell, an old smell. The unpainted wood had absorbed decades of scents, old cardboard boxes, old and new plywood from the roof being redone or repaired, mothballs from trunks, wet clothes hung up to dry before washing machines and driers made their way into the basement, worn rugs on the floor collecting dust, rarely vacuumed except when someone couldn't stand it anymore and said, "That's where the kids play." There was the smell of dead pine needles that had stuck to ornaments in the Christmas boxes.

My grandfather Will had moved into the farmhouse when he was in his twenties. His sea trunk was still here in the attic. It had its own smell. I took a minute to sit down on it. It was my trunk now, and I used it to hold my changes of clothes from season to season, coats and jackets in the summer, bathing suits and shorts in the winter.

Grandpa Will used to say he grew up here. His trunk still had the name of great-grandfather Jamie's schooner, *Treasa,* stenciled on both ends. Grandpa Will used to say leaving his father's schooner was the best and worst decision he ever made. He'd laugh and say he thought farming and building ships would be easier than hauling granite in the hold of a two-masted wooden sail-powered antique. Stonington down to New York City and back in every kind of weather. He used to say, "When I started farming, I found out worrying about the weather was just as hard as sailing through it." He would always add, especially if she were in the room, "But becoming a sheep farming landlubber with your grandmother was the best decision I ever made."

The house is larger now than when he lived here, but the farm is a bit smaller. My dad sold off two acres. He would have sold off more if my mother had let him. He allowed one pasture to return to wood. Now, I've leased our pastures to George Marshall. He summers his flock of sheep here. The summer tenants love it. They get to say, "We'll be spending—whatever their lease says—on a sheep farm in Maine."

I could see Grandpa Will's grass landing strip from the attic window. It's still intact, as is the barn he built as a hangar. The name *Buckley Airport* on the side of the barn is fading, and I need to repaint it. I had just mowed the grass, and the strip was in good shape after all these years. It takes a bit of work to keep it that way, but I still use it, and I love having it there. Sometimes my flying friends also use it.

My grandfather got the flying bug when some barnstormers came through Brunswick. He decided he was damned well going to learn how to fly. Much to my grandmother's consternation, he did. Then, after WWI, he decided he was going to have his own plane and his own landing strip. And he did. "I've got the only close to flat piece of land on this island, and I'm going to take off and land on it," he told my grandmother.

It wasn't completely flat, so he dug a fire pond and used the fill to make it as flat as he could. My grandmother worried it would attract mosquitoes, but when fire hit the island in 1934, she was glad it was there.

My grandfather taught his sons how to fly, and my father taught me. Only one of my four offspring wanted to fly, and by the time Joel was ready, lessons from an approved school with a certified instructor were necessary. I drove him back and forth to Brunswick. He was licensed to fly before he was licensed to drive.

My dad extended Grandpa Will's strip to accommodate the planes he used for business. During the non-snow, non-mud months, he flew out of 'Buckley Airport.' The rest of the year, he rented hangar space in Brunswick and kept whatever was the current plane there. Over the years, he had four in all. When he died, I traded his last plane in on the one I now fly, a turbocharged Cessna 206 Stationair. I follow the seasons the same way he did. I love flying in and out of the farm.

Flying cost us one life and almost one more when I include myself. One of my uncles died in WWII at Midway. I almost died twice in Vietnam. The armed forces liked having pilots who already knew how to fly and weren't overly careful. That was the Buckley men and airplanes, not too careful.

I checked the screening around the attic windows to ensure it was intact and no critters could get through. It had taken months, but I had finally won my battle with the squirrels.

There were fewer boxes to shove back under the eaves than there used to be. I'd been cleaning things out since Hannah died. The kids didn't seem to want anything, so they went to Goodwill or the dump. I held on to the old photo albums. Hannah was the keeper of the albums. No one created albums now. They took pictures, showed them on Facebook, and that was that. Maybe someday, one of my kids or grandkids will want these. Even when I offered to let them go through the Christmas boxes, there were no takers. My four children have all been movers. They haven't been planted the way Hannah and I were. My oldest, Ruth, always quoted some organization expert about 'if you haven't worn it or don't love it or something or something, get rid of it.' I was not getting rid of the four boxes of photo albums nor the three Christmas boxes, even if it meant only looking at them twice a year: when I got ready for summer, like now, or when I returned from Tír in September. I should probably get rid of some of the old tax returns and legal stuff, but there is a lot of room in the attic, and one never knows.

There was no way I would get rid of the files that contained years of every article I'd ever written for the newspapers where I'd worked. Most of them were news articles, some political commentary. Three boxes were filled with *Home Town Boy*. The paper published my column every Friday for years. There are also boxes of the three books I wrote years ago. People want one once in a great while, and I always leave a copy of each one out for tenants and invite them to take one. Several boxes of rejected manuscripts are waiting to be redone or edited or something or other. Many of them are typed, still waiting to be scanned into my computer. Then there are boxes of work started but never completed.

All was in order, so I went down to the second floor, locking the attic door on the way. The attic was off-limits to tenants.

I went room by room. I had already vacuumed the floors, and all the scatter rugs. I looked for any stray wisps of dust I had missed. I again felt a pang of guilt at the gray painted pine floors. Hannah hated the painted floors, and I had promised her I would 'restore' them like we had done on the first floor. We should have done it when we did the downstairs, but we didn't have the money at the time. I said I would do it myself, but I never got around to it. The truth is I wasn't sure I could do a decent job, so I kept putting it off as though somehow, by magic, it would happen—pride doth goeth before the 'anticipated' fall.

I made sure all the windows were locked, and the screens were down onto the lower panes. I only locked the windows because tenants tended to be city types, and they liked their locks. I can't imagine living with that mentality all year long.

After checking the kids' rooms, I went into our bedroom; it would always be 'ours.' I folded up our pictures and put them into the carton I had left there—children, grandchildren, and the two of us. Tenants didn't want to see my pictures. Besides, I wanted them with me down at Tír. Hannah and I had moved them every year since we started renting the farmhouse. They'd be back in place come September.

Ours was the largest of the bedrooms, part of the addition we had put on. The kids thought we were nuts putting an addition on when they had left home, but Hannah wanted bedrooms for grandchildren and holidays. We couldn't afford the addition until they had all graduated and were out on their own. Hannah also wanted a bathroom on the second floor, so of course, we put in two, one for guests and one for us. Ours is immense and has a big tub with jets. Because it faces the pastures away from the road, Hannah wanted a big window next to the tub so she could look out. There are no blinds. When her sister asked her about it, she said, "No one can see me, and, at my age, I don't care."

I carried the box of pictures downstairs and left it in the hall while I checked the first floor. I made sure the guest book and the instruction book were in place on the kitchen counter, left a note next to the fireplace that the damper was closed, checked the locks on the windows, picked up the box of pictures, and went out the back door. I left the tenant key under the rock next to the granite steps. It was in the same place it had been for all the years we had been renting the farmhouse during the summer. I put the carton with the bedroom pictures on the truck's passenger side and drove down to our cottage, our Tír na nÓg. Another summer had begun. On the drive down, I wondered what Wendy would be like. I had not had any time alone with my granddaughter since she was young, and I'd taken her sailing. 'Bottomed out' was kind of vague. I wondered if this was a good idea.

Chapter Two: Shopping

She was already an hour late. With Rachel time is often elusive. So, I took my coffee, went out, and sat on the porch swing. It was time to replace the batteries in my hearing aids. I had finished one and was working on the second when I heard a car come down the dirt road to the cottage. It was in a hurry. Rachel, I thought. I had just finished closing the door of the right battery compartment when I heard the car stop on the side of the house. I put my hearing aid in, got up, and heard a bark. Charlie. Why did Rachel think I liked Charlie? Charlie was almost as much a stranger to me as my granddaughter.

I walked around to the side of the cottage. Seeing me, Wendy rushed over, arms open. "Grandpa. Thank you so much for letting me come!" I was always taken aback by how red my granddaughter's hair is. There was a family debate about whether it was her father's Ashkenazic blood, or my mother's Celtic. I hugged her. The effusiveness continued. "It is so good to be here. You have no idea." Obviously, I didn't. Charlie was jumping on me, also wanting recognition and affection. I ignored him. Wendy continued, "I love, love, love it here." I refrained from saying, "So why have you stayed away for the last four years?"

Rachel opened the trunk of her ancient Camry, a hand-me-down from Hannah, and shouted, "Wendy, come here and get your things." My youngest walked over to me. "Dad, thank you for doing this. I know it's a lot to ask, but I didn't know what else to do, and she really wanted to come."

"It's fine. Don't worry about it. It'll be good for me, too."

"She'll take care of herself. She's pretty self-sufficient. Sometimes, a little over the top, but basically a good kid, and she'll take care of Charlie. So you don't have to worry about that."

"I hadn't planned to. But I do have a couple of questions."

Wendy approached us, hauling a suitcase, a duffle bag, and wearing a bulging backpack. I said, "Need any help?"

"No. I'm good."

"Upstairs bedroom, one on the far right facing the harbor."

"Great, I love that room."

While Wendy headed towards the house, I escorted Rachel towards the pier going out to our floating dock. "How are you doing?" I asked.

"Don't worry. Sober as a church mouse. Still going to AA meetings. I'm good, Dad. I have been since Mom got sick."

"I know, I'm sorry."

"It's okay. I understand. You're always going to worry, and I love you for it. I think the move to Brattleboro has been good for both of us. And before you ask, no men. Not for the two years we've been there. Even with Wendy away at school, I'm doing well on my own. Mom would be proud of me."

"I am, too."

"I know. I also know it's harder for you. And guess what?"

"What?"

"I'm back in school."

"Seriously?"

"Seriously. Just one course this summer. It's mostly online."

"In what?"

"Recreation, Park, and Tourism Management. They've accepted all of my basic courses from years ago because of my work experience, so I just have to do the courses in the major. I should be able to finish up in three years."

"Honey, that's wonderful, but how are you…"

"Affording it? Frugality and loans."

"Wendy?"

"Jerry picks up all of her tuition, room, and board costs. He's a prick, not much of a father. But he's got the money, and she's going to a state school. He's been pretty easy to work with, believe it or not."

"That's new. What's changed?"

"New girlfriend. She's nice. I like her a lot. So does Wendy. I'm happy for him. I think he did well this time. It's sure made life easier for us. I talk to her, not him."

"Think it'll last this time?"

"He's different since he's been with her, so I think it might."

"So, you're good with it?"

"Yeah, I am."

"And…"

"Julien? He's good. Glad to be back home in Chamonix with his kids. Wendy and I both miss him at times, but it was the right thing to do. He stays in touch with Wendy, which is nice. They talk skiing."

"And you?"

"I miss him, at times, a lot. I have no interest in dating and even if I did, let's just say Brattleboro is not the best place to meet interesting men who are educated and single. Or boring and uneducated, for that matter. Truthfully, I'm content with my life right now. I have friends from my meeting to do things with and I've a pretty active social life. No complaints."

I looked at her and saw she meant it.

"There is one thing I did want to tell you."

"What?"

"I've changed my name back to Buckley."

"Really? That's a surprise."

"Yeah. I didn't have Greenberg or Guay long enough to get used to them. Don't you dare laugh. I talked to Wendy about it. It was fine with her. So, I'm Buckley for life no matter what happens."

"Wendy didn't mind?"

"No. When I told her what I was thinking it led to quite a discussion about names and identity. She's growing up."

"I can see that. With that red hair…"

"She's a knock out. I know."

"Takes after her mother. You're looking good."

"There's fifteen pounds less of me. I feel good."

Rachel was beautiful as a teenager and as a young woman. Alcoholism took its toll and for several years she looked tired all the time and bloated. That started to change when she joined AA and the transformation was now complete with the weight loss.

We started heading up the pier towards the house. Wendy was now busy unloading shopping bags from Rachel's car. Rachel said, "She brought some food with her for a day or two."

"Oh. I still have to shop this afternoon to get supplies for Tír."

"She'll help. She's going to need more stuff, anyway."

Charlie was sniffing around. Every once in a while, he would lift a leg to let the world know he had arrived.

No one would ever say Bath, Maine, was a shopping Mecca. There was only one proper supermarket, Shaw's. Since it was the anchor for what is grandiosely advertised as the Bath Shopping Center, that's where we headed. Down on Front Street, Brackett's was the IGA in town, but Shaw's was cheaper for extensive shopping. We took the truck. I have a roll-up tonneau cover for the back, so I wasn't worried about rain.

There's only one road leading off Georgetown Island, Route 127. As we drove toward Bath, I thought about Wendy handling my truck. When you live in Georgetown, you drive a lot. You have to, to get off the island. I knew all the timing down to the minute. From the farmhouse to Shaw's is twenty-one minutes, Tír na nÓg to Shaw's is twenty-nine minutes. Although it was a reasonably predictable half an hour in winter, Brunswick was always an unknown because of traffic. Wendy would probably be driving a lot this summer.

I've never bought a new car or truck—stupid waste of money. I always buy a loaded vehicle three to five years off the market—low mileage, and you can usually get a good deal. My truck's now five years old, a Toyota Tacoma Sport, single cab. Four-wheel drive, of course, and I love it. It's pretty big, though, and Wendy's only about five foot five. Somehow, she and the truck didn't seem to fit together.

That left Hannah's Subaru Outback. The only problem with that was it had been Hannah's car. I use it when I drive into Portland or Boston because parking the truck can be a pain. My problem with Wendy driving it, though, was that it was still Hannah's car. That left Jesse's motorcycle, a fifteen-year-old Honda Shadow. It wasn't a huge bike, as bikes go, 750 CCs. It ran fine. I took it out every once in a while, but still, the damned thing weighed five hundred pounds. I wondered if Wendy could handle a bike that big? Rachel had been no help. Jesse said his niece could use his bike, but bikes are dangerous. Rachel had okayed the motorcycle and put this plan in motion, but I felt responsible for Wendy already, even if she was twenty.

So, I withdrew from transportation decision making and asked her about the course she was taking and the paper she had to write. That was, I thought, an innocuous query to get us talking to one another.

She said, "It's a dumb assignment. It's supposed to be a history course."

"Why is it a dumb assignment?"

"Who cares about the history of the place where you grew up unless you live someplace like Boston, New York, or Philadelphia where the real history that matters was taking place?"

"Brattleboro or Georgetown don't make the cut, huh?"

"Exactly."

"How did your professor explain it?"

"She's only an assistant professor."

"Oh. On the younger side."

"And thinks she's so cool."

"But she did explain it?"

"Yeah. Of course. She said the history of where we have lived contributes to how we experience ourselves and how we experience the world. She says we inhale this history when we're young, from stories people tell us and even from where we went to school as a kid. But, according to her, we rarely reflect on these stories because no one ever asks us to. Here's the biggie: often, the stories are inaccurate. I think she wanted to be a shrink, and this is her way of working it out."

"Oh, did she give any other reasons?"

"She wants us to, as she puts it, 'do history.' She wants us to do what a historian would do and use the tools that a historian would use. I have absolutely no interest in ever becoming a historian. Zilch. Nada. Maybe teach history. I'm not even sure about that."

"But she wants you to learn historical methodology. Perhaps she thinks you'll be in a better position to judge the work of historians if you…"

"Did she call you and tell you what to say?"

"I'm sounding like her?"

"Exactly."

"What's the title of the course?"

"Historical Methods."

"Oh."

"What do you mean, oh?"

"I think it sounds like a great course, and the two rationales she has provided make all the sense in the world to me."

Wendy laughed and said, "Mom warned me."

"About me?"

"She said you should have been a college professor."

"You know I have taught journalism classes from time to time."

"No, I didn't know that."

"I have a hunch there may be quite a bit about your family you don't know."

"I'm sure, but Georgetown, Maine. Really Grandpa, whatever happened here? People fished, farmed, and worked at the Bath Iron Works like Grandma."

"And your great-grandfather and your great-grandmother."

"As I said, doesn't sound very exciting."

"Or do you mean very important?"

Wendy didn't say anything. I added, "So you think that your family and the people of Georgetown are boring? What do you know about the generations of your family who have lived here and all the other people who have lived here as well?"

"Okay. Nothing."

"And your professor, who I am getting to like more and more, wants you to find out."

We crossed the bridge connecting the island to the mainland. I asked, "Have you ever read Howard Zinn's book, *A People's History of the United States*?"

"Not the whole thing. I was supposed to read it last semester. Do you have a copy?"

"You didn't bring yours?"

"No, I forgot."

I took a deep breath. I had a hunch I would be taking a lot more of them this summer, "Yes, I do, but you need your own, so you can make notes. We'll order it tonight."

"Isn't there a Kindle edition online?"

"I'm sure there is, but how do you write in the margins of an online book?"

"Oh. It's easy. You just keep a word file going and toggle back and forth."

"Oh. And that works?"

"Sure. Oh, she also wants us to find primary sources for our paper. Actual documents. How on earth am I going to do that about Georgetown?"

"I'll introduce you to the folks at the historical society. They'll point you in the right direction. I also may have some things in the articles I've written over the years that will be helpful."

"That would be great."

"So, you have to finish the Zinn book. Any other reading you have to do this summer?"

"Unfortunately. Pre-reading. One for each of the courses I'm taking in the fall."

"They are?"

"*Mayflower.*"

"Philbrick. Great book. You do know, though, that we had a colony here before Plymouth."

"You're kidding."

"Nope. What else?"

"Something about the Roosevelts and time."

"*No Ordinary Time.* Doris Kearns Goodwin. Won the Pulitzer."

"You've read both of these?"

"I have."

We had almost reached Route One, that historical road stretching from the Canadian border to Key West in Florida, when Wendy asked, "Are they long books?"

"What books?"

"The ones I have to read."

I was looking to make sure I could sneak out into the endless Route One summer traffic. But, once I got into the stream, I answered, "Just the right length for the summer."

She did a barely audible, "Humph." That was followed with, "Thanks a lot, Grandpa." I took another deep breath. It was going to be a long summer.

It was Memorial Day weekend, and the parking lot at Shaw's was crowded with SUVs. Some of them carried bicycles on roof racks.

Others had bumper hitches and carried them in the back like metal bustles. RVs and cars with boat trailers took up double spaces. We had to circle twice to find a decent parking place.

Shopping with Wendy was a novel experience for me, an exercise in adaptation. Not only was Wendy vegetarian, but she also avoided gluten. She had never been diagnosed with a disease that would require being gluten-free, but she considered it to be a preventive measure. It took us forever. Every label was scrutinized. She said, "Mom shops for me at home and everything in the food court is marked at school."

I didn't comment. My shopping is ritualized. I could be in and out of Shaw's in fifteen minutes if there was no line at the checkout. I knew what I wanted, where it was, and I was irritated when they changed product placement. It always took longer in the summer when the hoards arrived. They had arrived. We were there for an hour between Wendy's dietary precision and the checkout lines.

As we crossed back over the Sagadahoc bridge that connects Bath to Woolwich, Wendy looked out the passenger side window to Bath Iron Works. This shipyard has dominated the area's development and history.

"What's that?" she asked. "It looks like that ship from the James Bond movie."

I knew exactly what she was referring to, a four-billion-dollar Zumwalt class guided-missile destroyer with a stealth shape. I told her all I knew about the ship and then added some information from an article I had read about the first one launched, "Do you know the name of the first captain?"

"No."

"James A. Kirk."

"Sure, and the first officer was Mister Spock."

"No. But, the name of the first captain was James A. Kirk, not James T. Kirk."

"Are you a Trekkie, Grandpa?"

"No, just read a piece about it."

There was no response from the passenger side of the car.

As we crossed Back River that separates Arrowsic from Georgetown, Wendy asked, "Did you write any articles about Georgetown?"

"Many. Not just Georgetown, the whole area. Every Friday, for years."

"Do you still have them?"

"Yes. Some folks have suggested I select the ones I like best and turn them into a book. I never got around to it. Why?"

"I'd love to read some of them."

"Uh, you wouldn't be looking for a shortcut, would you?"

"Seriously? No. I'm interested."

"Okay. They're at the house, up in the attic."

"Could we stop and pick them up?"

"There are a lot to go through."

"That's okay. I have all summer."

"You might want to start with your required reading."

She didn't respond.

Chapter 3: The Visitor

When we got down to Tír, there was a handwritten sign taped to the door: *Wendy, call me on my cell!!! Rina 202.387.2457.* I shouted back to Wendy, who was getting our groceries out of the truck, "Note for you! Looks like Rina's here!"

"She leave a number?"

"Yep."

Wendy started moving faster. I held the door open for her so she wouldn't have to put her load of groceries down. As she went by me, she stopped, kissed me on the cheek, and said, "Hot damn, the kikes on bikes are back in town. Watch out, Georgetown."

I shook my head. "God help us."

Rina Fishman lived two cottages away. This is what Hannah always wanted. Rina and Wendy had spent every August together here on the cove and over at the yacht club from when they were little kids. It ended the summer Rachel went into rehab, and Wendy spent the summer with her father, who refused to let her come to Maine for August. This summer was her first time back for longer than two or three days at a time.

Rina's great-great-grandparents were one of the first families to build a place here on Heron Cove after my grandfather started selling off parcels back between the wars. My grandparents welcomed the Fishmans. Others did not. Some people ignored them; some shunned them. The Fishmans had committed two sins. First, they were summer people, so the locals disapproved. Second, they were Jewish, so the yacht club people disapproved. Grandfather Will thought the only thing strange about them was they didn't eat lobster, and that was not August Fishman's doing but his wife's. She told my grandmother, "I make an ersatz lobster salad for him from haddock, but it's never enough with this man. He wants the real thing, not some Jewish imitation."

Maine was not a welcoming place for Jews. As late as the 1950s, two-thirds of the resorts in Maine, the highest of any state in the country, refused to accept Jews as guests. Likewise, Maine colleges like Bowdoin and Bates didn't want them. Colby was the standout. August's son Bernie had fallen in love with his summers in Maine, and when he came back from the war in the Pacific, that's where he wanted to go to college. So, Colby it was. He loved it, and that's where his son, Judd, went. "I'm probably the first Jewish legacy in Maine," Judd would brag.

I grew up with Judd Fishman, and my kids grew up with Judd and Pat's children. I had never known a summer without Judd, or Judd and Pat, except when I was in the Air Force. If Rina was here, Judd and Pat might be here, too. Like mine, their children didn't come for more than a few days at a time anymore, but the grandkids might come for a week, sometimes two or more, to get 'Grandma and Grandpa time.' Rina's parents were both physicians. Their vacation idea was a Caribbean cruise in February and as many extended weekends as they could manage throughout the year. Patty complained, "I get my son up here for one long weekend a year. I love my daughter-in-law, but I wish she had not decided to pursue academic medicine. All she does is write grants and then worry about getting them." Judd would remind his wife that they did get one weekend a year at Heron Cove, and they were always invited to go on the cruise with them. "I hate those big monsters with thousands of strangers," Pat would say.

Wendy and Rina had been as inseparable as youngsters as Judd and I had been. Wendy's father, Rachel's first husband, Jerry, was Jewish. Wendy was Wendy Greenberg. The girls used to go back and forth to the yacht club on their bikes, so they started calling themselves the 'kikes on bikes' one summer. They liked to think they had integrated the Eroscohegan Yacht Club. Of course, they hadn't.

Their parents' generation had.

Acceptance hadn't happened in time for Judd and me. We were in our twenties before enough of the club members had evolved and dropped their 'restricted' thinking and screening. Their blinders had never stopped me, my sister, or my parents from inviting the Fishman's to join us at all the yacht club events. Judd's parents never came, but Judd and his sister did. Most of the members were too civilized to be openly rude to a couple of Jewish kids coming to club square dances and crewing on sailboat races with their goyim friends.

When Judd's dad, Bernie, was finally approached about joining the club, he politely told the three people on the membership committee to go fuck themselves. Bernie already belonged to the New York Yacht Club and was racing with some of the best sailors on the East Coast. He told my father, "Jack, the Eroscohegan Harbor Yacht Club crowd is a collection of pretentious academic assholes with their round-robin cocktail parties, calling their cottages by kitschy names like "Seaduced," and people by absurd nicknames like 'Bunchy' and 'Dunce.' You Buckleys," he'd say, "are the exception, because Tír na nÓg means something and you truly are Irish." Actually, the current Buckley's are watered down Irish. Old Walter Convey, my maternal grandmother's father, had some Brit blood in him, and then I went and married a mixed breed.

By the time Wendy and Rina came along, no one at the club gave a damn about your religion, just what prep school or college you had gone to or where you were currently enrolled. Nevertheless, Wendy and Rina had heard the stories of the days of restriction and rejection. The names 'Greenberg' and 'Fishman' bonded them and set them apart from the 'WASPS,' who continued to make up most of the club's membership. So, proudly they proclaimed themselves 'kikes on bikes' and that's how the other kids referred to them. Some of the parents at the club thought that was horrible and gave lectures to their young ones about antisemitism which, of course, went in one ear and out the other. "But that's what they call themselves," the youngsters would argue. The nickname wore out after a couple of summers and was dropped, except between Wendy and Rina.

Seeing that note from Rina was good for Wendy and good for me. I just hoped Rina was here for more than a weekend, a lot more than a weekend. I also hoped it meant that Judd and Pat were here, maybe even for the entire summer.

I went about putting groceries away while Wendy ran down our pier to get privacy and better phone reception so she could call the number Rina had left. I watched her jump up and down and spin around once or twice. Again, I smiled. Rina was here. Wendy was happy. I was happy. Rina would keep my granddaughter busy.

Charlie barked. I opened the door, and he ran down the pier, down the ramp, and onto the dock where a Great Blue Heron had been seconds before. Three flaps of the heron's wings and the magnificent bird was in the water, safe from the noisemaking miniature poodle claiming ownership of our waterfront. Wendy took the phone away from her ear and shouted at Charlie to stop barking. He ignored her, and she ignored him. Finally, he stopped when he appreciated that he had established his place as 'King of the Waterfront' and the heron was not about to intrude on his domain.

Everything stowed, I went out onto the porch and sat in one of the rockers I had placed in the same spot it occupied every summer for three generations. It had survived who knows how many coats of paint and touch-up jobs—always Benjamin Moore Cool Aqua Blue. Fog was starting to come in from the Gulf of Maine, up the Sheepscot River, and into the cove. A light breeze was helping the fog along. My wonderfully young, vibrant, red-haired granddaughter soon became muted into the mist.

The mist. One night, during our third summer together, when my memories of dropping bombs and being shot at over Laos were beginning to fade, Hannah and I sat here in the fog, and Hannah told me about the name. "Tír na nÓg. 'Land of the young' is the literal translation. It was the mythical heaven of your ancient ancestors, the 'Otherworld' of perpetual youth, abundance, and happiness. Home of the gods."

She was pregnant and uncomfortable with Ruth and had spent our two-week vacation reading Celtic mythology rather than sailing or playing tennis. She read to me:

> *A hero set out on a quest, and a mist descended upon him. A beautiful woman from the Otherworld emerged from the mist and sang to him of this happy land, Tír na nÓg. If he fights her battles, she will love him forever. She offers him an apple, and he follows her into the mist. They travel across the seas and are never seen together again. The hero eventually returns to his own world and is forever changed by his knowledge of the Otherworld and the woman who loved him.*

I remembered reaching for Hannah's hand and holding it. She squeezed it in return. I didn't have to tell her she had forever changed me.

When we first met, Hannah knew nothing about the Irish or Celt mythology, and I didn't know much. So, she decided we would learn together. "You can't have a place called Tír na nÓg and not know anything about it."

"It was called that even when it was a lobster shack," I told her. Of course, it wasn't true, but it was fun to say it.

"Your point being....?"

I had no reasonable point to make. "Nothing."

My Tír na nÓg on Heron Cove is a house of dreams. It is a dream handed down from my grandmother to my mother to my Hannah. It's a dream of family and summer, of children squealing when they jump off the dock into the cold Maine water. It's a dream of clambakes, sailing, and picnics at the lily pond, where the water's warm by August. It's a dream of everybody coming to visit at some time during the summer, or at least every other summer. It's a dream of everyone wanting to be here. It's a dream of puzzles that everyone builds on, Monopoly games that go on forever because no one is rushed, square dances and steel drum bands, and a man who plays the spoons. It's a dream of time to read and have private talks. It's not of the Otherworld; it's a dream of this world. The women have made the dream happen, but the men have shared it. With Hannah gone, I didn't know how to make it happen.

Wendy skipped up from the pier, led by Charlie. She rat-a-tat-tatted sentences as she came: "Rina is here until the end of August. Her grandparents are here 'til after Labor Day. Mrs. Freeman said to say hello. She wants you to come up for breakfast tomorrow morning, at about nine. Call her. Can Rina come here for dinner tonight? I'll cook."

I took a minute to process the flood of information. "Sure. I'll give Pat a call about tomorrow. But, first, let's get some firewood in. It's going to be cool tonight, and call Rina. Remind her to bring a flashlight with her. It will be dark with this fog, and I don't want her hurting herself going up the path after dinner."

"Grandpa, she's been going up and down that path her entire life. She could do it blindfolded."

"Please, just call her."

Judd sent Rina down with two bottles of excellent Sauvignon Blanc. One disappeared with dinner. Seeing these two young women sitting on opposite sides of the dining room table, I was struck by the differences. Rina's olive skin and black hair contrasted with Wendy's red hair and freckles. Rina was a little taller than Wendy, chunky, where Wendy was athletic. Wendy looked like her father; Rina looked like her mother. Neither of them looked like their grandparents.

I don't think I've ever bought tofu in my life. I've made fun of it, probably eaten it without knowing it, but certainly never cooked it. To my astonishment, my granddaughter knew what she was doing with it in the kitchen.

I listened as they talked. There were many 'have you heard from?' questions about people they knew in common from the yacht club. There were memory recitals from when they were young. They created a list of things they 'had' to do this summer.

After dinner, I started to clear the table, but the two young women ordered me to get out of the way and go build a fire in the living room. Wendy was insistent. "Come on, Grandpa. It's our turn." Feeling old and close to the edge of obsolescence, I obeyed.

We called it a cottage, but it was bigger than the farmhouse, even after the addition. The cottage was my grandma Nell's idea. She had two older brothers who had 'deserted the farm' and moved to Worcester to become 'big shot industrialists.' Nell was left behind with her parents to run the farm until my grandfather came along. She never forgave her brothers, and neither did her father, which is how the farm came to be handed down to Will and Nell. Actually, old Walter Convey, Nell's father, sold it to Will and Nell for far less than it was worth.

Each of the Worcester 'deserters' had married and had a bunch of kids. Nell could have cared less about her brothers or their wives, but she wanted a place for her nieces and nephews to visit in the summer and get away from the heat and stink of Worcester. So, after the war ended in November 1918, my grandparents were feeling flush. Double shifts building warships at the Bath Iron Works and selling wool for uniforms brought in more money than either had ever known. Grandpa Will started buying property on Heron Cove. No one else wanted it. My grandmother made a deal with him. If he was going to buy that "worthless piece of rocky waterfront" on the cove so he could get into "that ridiculous lobstering business," he was going to build her a summer place big enough to house her family. He said he would if she would let him build a grass airstrip on the farm and buy an airplane. She agreed. He didn't know how to fly yet.

By December, he and a group of friends had built a pier of giant granite blocks out to deep water in the cove. It was a good deal for everyone—they helped him build the pier; he let them keep their boats there. He also built himself a shack to hold his fishing gear. Seeing what was happening, my grandmother quickly provided him with a plan she had sketched out and told him to get to work on the cottage as soon as the weather warmed up. According to my father, who witnessed the goings-on between Will and Nell, that winter was spent revising her original plan, which looked more like a small hotel than a 'cottage.' Apparently, the two of them alternated between calm discussions and "Come on, Nell," and "No, Will, you come on."

She knew exactly what she wanted. The kitchen was to be on the small size. "I am not putting out fancy dinners in the summer for a bunch of kids." There was to be a bedroom and bath on the first floor. "I climb stairs all winter long. Not in the summer." There were to be four big bedrooms upstairs, each big enough for multiple beds, plus a bathroom. A central stone chimney with a big fireplace would take the chill off on cool summer nights and mornings.

There was no insulation, and the upstairs rooms were divided by single layers of vertical boards rescued from a torn-down barn in Richmond. Consequently, sexual carryings-on at Tír na nÓg had to be very, very quiet. The other problem was that a noisy snorer could be heard between rooms. A boisterous one was referred to as a 'two-roomer.'

Grandma wanted angles. Lots and lots of angles with a big porch wrapped around the back and two sides of the house. Where it wrapped around the kitchen, it was screened in for meals. She cut pictures out of magazines and presented them to my grandfather with "Like this, Will." Gray shingles with green trim and a shed finished off her dream. Damned if she didn't get it all.

The fire was going well when the girls came in from the kitchen. "Grandpa, we're going to head down to the clubhouse and play ping pong; see who's there," Wendy said.

"No one will be there. The club doesn't open for another month. You know that." I said with authority.

"I want to see if anything's changed."

"You are joking," I replied.

Rina laughed, "We know. If anything changed, the entire world would become unhinged."

Wendy said, "I want to look at the bulletin board and see what the dates are for the Rum Regatta."

"Wendy," Rina said, "It's always the second weekend in August."

"Okay, already. I just want to go down to the clubhouse."

"Enjoy, but…."

"They're right here." Wendy held up two flashlights.

"Do you have…?"

Rina held up two paddles in one hand and a ping pong ball in the other. The table was still inside the clubhouse. I hadn't set it up on the porch yet. As one of the only club members who was a year-round resident, I kept an eye on the place as my father and grandfather had before me. Sometimes I think that's why they allowed us in as members. We came cheap. "Aren't you forgetting something?" I asked.

"Keys?"

"Hook next to the door."

After they left, I made sure our outside front door light was on. Of course, Wendy had turned it on as they left even though it was still dusk.

The Rum Regatta was one of the several inviolate Yacht Club events. I was surprised Wendy had forgotten when it was. The Anglo founder of the town of Georgetown was John Parker. He, to his credit, actually paid a hogshead of rum and a few pumpkins to Chief Mowhatawormit for the whole island and the islands around it. So, Parker got a good deal.

Hundreds of years later, in 1925, the yacht club members decided the real estate deal should be celebrated by hosting an annual regatta. Obviously, it had to be called the Rum Regatta, and the Saturday night party after the day's first races should be conducted with a plethora of drinks derived from rum. This was in the middle of Prohibition, but they knew where they could get rum—my grandfather. They asked him if he could supply a 'hogshead' of rum, sixty-four gallons. Unable to do so, he provided a barrel, thirty-two gallons, with a spigot. That barrel made it through more than one regatta. The content was reserved for that singular event and improved with age. When Grandpa Will retired from his illegal entrepreneurial endeavor, they kept the tradition but had to refill the barrel from other sources.

Thinking about the regatta, which I have never won, I realized I might have enough crew to race this year. Winning the Rum Regatta had never been my aspiration, but the idea of an old man winning in the open cruising boat class had some appeal. The winners—there were more than one—had their names inscribed on little copper plates that were then tacked on to the 'Barrel.' Eventually, the barrel would have to be replaced. But the barrels were never thrown away. The current 'Barrel' resided on a table in the center of the main room of the clubhouse. The other barrels from previous years were positioned around the main room. I can't imagine what Jamie Buckley, my great Grandfather from Carna, Ireland, would have thought about The Rum Regatta.

Thinking of him, I glanced up at the granite mantlepiece over the fireplace. There were models of three different schooners Grandpa Will had made. The biggest was the *Phoenix,* the boat that had brought my great-grandfather to Brooklyn, New York.

January 3, 1980
HOME TOWN BOY by Michael Buckley

When my editor brought it up, we were each on our second beer at the Sagadahoc Bar and Grill in Bath. It was late Friday afternoon, and the Sagadahoc was, as usual, packed, smoky, and noisy. I had to ask him to repeat himself. I wanted to make sure I had heard him correctly. He said he wondered if I would be willing to write some occasional pieces for the Friday edition of the paper. Friday was always a slow news day, and he would be ready to add a little something to my paycheck every time I wrote a piece.

Newspaper reporters in Mid-Coast Maine are not noted for acquiring wealth. Our middle name is 'supplement.' Lobstering is one way, farming—in my case, raising sheep—helps, and marrying a wife who makes a good income is still another. I have managed to do all of these. Being a reporter for a small Maine newspaper is not exactly a hobby, but the paycheck sometimes implies that it is. Not wanting to appear overly enthusiastic, I said, "Let me think about it." He then added, "You can write about whatever you want. Sort of like *Talk of the Town* in the New Yorker. Just make it interesting."

I love and am proud of *The Bath Bugle*, and my editor is a very nice, if somewhat frugal, man and a good editor and publisher. But, mentioning our paper in the same sentence with the New Yorker is quite a stretch. Even in my most arrogant and pretentious moments, the closest I come to the writing ability of E.B. White, who wrote *Talk of the Town* for many years, is that we both live in Maine. However, it sounded like a compliment, so I said, "I've thought about it and, yes, I'd enjoy that." He also said I could call the column—it had moved from occasional to column—anything I wanted.

At the same bar, a week later, I found myself sitting next to George Parker. One of George's claims (he has many) is that he is a descendent of the original Parker family that settled out on Popham

Beach a few years before the Pilgrims left the Netherlands. I have reminded him that if his family had just stayed put and not gone back to England after a year, our area would be "America's Home Town" and not the town founded by that radical cult down in Plymouth, Massachusetts. If those Popham Parkers only had someone like Tisquantum (Squanto to the Plymouth folks) to help them through their first winter, then they might have stayed, and Plymouth, Massachusetts would be one of the towns you drove through on your way to Cape Cod from Boston.

Now his clan did manage to set up an actual colony out on Popham Beach in 1607. And they built a boat, *Virginia of Sagadahoc*, in their spare time. So, George and his clan can rightly lay claim to being the first shipbuilders in what was a New World for the English. I'd give him that.

George ignores the Spanish who settled in Florida and built St. Augustine in 1565, making that fair city the oldest continuous settlement founded by Europeans in America. The founder, Admiral Pedro Menéndez de Avilés, is not exactly a well-known name in our history books. So, from the Spanish point of view, perhaps the Parker clan was 'from away.' I'll remind George of that the next time I see him. Of course, this is all good-natured joshing, and he usually comes back with, "You say that because you're 'from away.'" The ultimate Maine condemnation.

So dear reader, assuming you have gotten this far, a question for you: When does someone stop being "from away?"

My father and I were both born here. We did both marry women 'from away,' I will grant you that. My paternal grandfather was admittedly from quite far away—Brooklyn, New York, to be precise—but he married a woman from Georgetown. Her father had been born in Georgetown, as had her grandfather and, we think, great-grandfather. I don't know beyond that. With that lineage, in no way do I think about myself as being 'from away.' In fact, my editor hired me because he said I was 'A hometown boy.' I have lived here my whole life except for the years the United States Air Force had other plans for me: Texas, Alaska, and in a Quonset hut in Southeast Asia, all with a bunch of other pilots.

Georgetown, Maine has always been my home, and I am a 'Home Town Boy,' regardless of what George Parker thinks, and thus the name of this column. I plan to explore and comment on different things that come to mind, sometimes at length, sometimes briefly, and I hope you have as much fun reading as I will writing.

In the meantime, though, let me know how you define 'away,' and who is right, my editor who calls me a 'home town boy,' or George, who insists I am 'from away?'

Knowing you have a place where you feel known, accepted, and belong are powerful experiences, and while George and I have a great time poking fun at one another, there are deeper, often hidden, meanings at work here. It is about having a place in the world where you feel at home. For me, that has and will always be this wonderful area we live in. But, on the other hand, my spouse is definitely 'from away.' She grew up in Brookline, Massachusetts. George and I agree about this; she is definitely 'from away.'

Chapter Four: Leaving Home

The blight and hunger returned. Historians would eventually refer to it as the 'Mini Famine.' However, in 1879 people had no way of knowing how devastating it would become, and they were once more terrified. Whatever hope was left from the time of the 'Great Famine' had disappeared. It had only been thirty years, and memories of death, decay, and loss had not receded. Back then, one million died, then, and another million left to go wherever they could: Britain, Australia, America, and Canada. Remaining in Ireland? The country was still decimated, and here it was coming at them again. Options were scarce.

The farmers were still tenants and destitute, but the British owners kept increasing the rents and evicting the tenants. This allowed the owners to consolidate their lands under tenants who could pay the higher rents. Moreover, the English Parliament had passed the Encumbered Estates Act. When a British owner had mortgages on his property, but he couldn't pay his debtors because the Irish tenant farmers couldn't pay him, speculators could buy the property, evict the tenants, and establish larger, more profitable farms.

Jamie Buckley's mother was born four years before the Great Famine began. She survived, but barely. She told her son stories about the British landlords exporting cattle and grain from Ireland while the farmers and their families starved to death. She told her son stories of hunger and sickness, of her brother and two sisters dying while she watched. She told her son about her cousins lying in their own waste from dysentery and cholera while their parents and grandparents, both the living and the dead, shared the same floor, the living too weak to bury their dead. Jamie Buckley heard the stories repeatedly from his mother and others and could tell them as knowingly as if he had lived through the horrors himself.

Some things had changed. Charles Parnell had formed the Irish National Land League and was working to make it possible for tenant farmers to own their own land, but the reforms were years away. No one knew how the British would react this time. Would they be so callous as to ignore world opinion and engage in still another genocide? Many of the same people were still in power in England, as were their attitudes. Charles Trevelyan, the British Colonial Minister, had seen the Famine as a "…mechanism for reducing surplus population." For Trevelyan, the famine was also an act of God:

> *The judgement of God sent the calamity to teach the Irish a lesson, that calamity must not be too much mitigated. The real evil with which we have to contend is not the physical evil of the Famine, but the moral evil of the selfish, perverse and turbulent character of the people.*

Jamie Buckley hated the English. His mother wished she hadn't told him the stories. She was afraid he would say the wrong thing to the wrong person at the wrong time and be punished for it.

Jamie had been christened James, after his father, on July 7, 1862, in the Church of the Assumption in Tullamore, County Offaly. His world was the bog country of mid-lands Ireland. His father was a 'bog man,' and in the summer, when school was out, Jamie would go with his father to the family's turf bank and help him cut peat which they sold for heating and cooking throughout the town and county. Jamie loved the summer and feeling useful. When he got big enough to handle a shovel, he didn't mind shoveling the horse manure from the small barn that housed their two horses. What he loved most, though, was sitting with his father on the seat of the wagon they used to deliver the peat. Sometimes his father would even let him take the reins.

His world changed on his tenth birthday when his father died of consumption, and his mother had to send some of her six children to live with relatives. Being the oldest, Jamie was the first to go. He was sent to live with his mother's remaining sister, his Aunt Maude, and her husband, Liam.

He went to the West Coast, to the area north of Galway known as Connemara, to the town of Carna, where they spoke the Irish language called Gaelic. Knowing only English, Jamie was forced to learn the language quickly to survive in this new strange, barren land. He was used to the lushness of the land along the Grand Canal that wove its way through Tullamore. He was used to walking the lowlands of bogs. Where he had been a Buckley in Tullamore, now he was an O'Buachalla in Carna. The sounds were as strange as the land. At night, Uncle Liam told him stories of Irish heroes and a land to the west, Tír na nÓg, a magical place of eternal youth.

Jamie learned that Carna was once bigger than Tullamore, but death and emigration had taken their toll. It had never recovered. What had been a town of eight thousand was now home to only two hundred people. Houses and barns had collapsed from dis-use. Nothing new had been built.

His Uncle Liam raised sheep in the hills around Carna. His Aunt Maude made the clothes they needed, and there was food from both her garden in the growing season and from the root cellar in the cold months. They were tenants, though, and had to pay rent. They had built their home with only one window because the British taxed every window you had. Their window faced South. The front, and only door, also faced South and was split in two so the top could be left open to bring the sun in on warm days. It was a way of cheating the government in London while getting more light into the main room they used for cooking, eating, and relaxing. Jamie slept in a loft over his aunt and uncle's bedroom. As Jamie grew older, he worked with his uncle during the day and went with him to the pub in the evening. As a formal effort, schooling ended in his thirteenth year when the teacher left, and they could not replace her because there were too few children in Carna to warrant a teacher.

Aunt Maude took on the task of educating Jamie. It consisted of having him read every night, write a letter to his mother every Saturday morning, and solve arithmetic problems that had to do with items like sheep, people and the different foods they ate. History was taught at the pub by his uncle's friends. He learned that some of them claimed to be descendants of the survivors of the Spanish Armada. He learned that when violent storms destroyed the Armada in the sixteenth century, some of the survivors made it to the Irish shore and never left. He learned that Carna was a thriving town before 'the hunger.'

St. Mary's Church was the grandest church Jamie had ever seen. Built before the famine for a much larger town, there used to be three priests in residence. Now there was only Father Walsh. Newly ordained, he had come to St. Mary's in 1847 when Father Kelleher died of typhoid and Father O'Connor became so despondent from the famine, he left to go live with his sister in Clifden.

It was Father Walsh who introduced Jamie to the world outside of Carna. The priest had been to Rome, New York, and Boston. Being the most educated man in Carna, Father Walsh became another source of education outside the home. In addition to administering the sacraments, he taught the catechism classes, provided counseling to the troubled, and helped organize the community to address its problems. For Jamie, Father Walsh became many things: a friend, older brother, tutor, and guide to a world outside of Carna. Father Walsh told Jamie about his own teacher, John Henry Newman, who had started the Catholic University of Ireland and had just been made a cardinal. He told him about the war England was waging against the Zulu in Africa, and Jamie could tell that Father Walsh was hoping the

Zulu would win. He told him about the rebellion that certainly would be coming in Ireland and that it was only a matter of time. He also helped Jamie understand why he was so frightened by his feelings for Treasa de Burca and why, when she kissed him, his world changed, still again.

Treasa had helped him learn the strange language when he first came to Carna, and it was Treasa who didn't make fun of him for being sent away to live with his aunt and uncle. She was taller than Jamie at first, but as they entered their teen years, their bodies changed. Jamie grew tall and broad. Treasa's body also changed as did their teasing, wrestling, and glances at one another. When her grandmother died, Jamie rowed Treasa out to the island in the harbor they had held as their private place. Treasa cried and told her friend stories of her grandmother, her máthair mhór. Then, a year later, it was on that same island, their island, that she kissed him.

When he could, Jamie would help out his friend, Colm Folan. Colm and his father were fishermen, and in their red-sailed Galway Hooker, they would be on the water every day they could. Depending upon the season, they fished for pollack, sea trout, mackerel, and cod. They would take their catch to Galway, and Jamie loved the days when he would join them. While Colm's father negotiated the sale of the fish and acquired goods to be returned to Carna, Jamie and Colm would leave the dock to explore Galway.

At first, Colm's father let the boys take turns skippering the boat on the return trip if the weather was not too bad. As they grew older, the boys handled the boat both ways on the Galway trips. These days were not work for Jamie, and he and Colm dreamed about having their own boat someday. Colm hated fishing the way Jamie hated sheepherding. Their boat would transport goods along the Connemara coast from Galway to Westport. They would bring necessities to all the islands and towns along the way. They would arrange barters for people and take shares as a price for their transport.

When the blight returned in some of the counties, Colm and Jamie stopped talking about having their boat. The infestation killed spirits as well as crops. Jamie knew what he was going to do, what he had to do.

As much as he loved and enjoyed his uncle's company and his stories, it was his Aintín Maude who talked to him about living. Usually, he would listen to her and on occasion he would talk to her. On his seventeenth birthday, in 1879, he told his aunt he was damned if he would live his eighteenth birthday being hungry and watching her and Uncle Liam waste whatever food they had on him. On his eighteenth birthday, Jamie O'Buachalla would be in America or Australia working and sending money home to them as their sons had done before they had their own families. His cousins were both in Australia, but Jaime didn't care where he went, America or Australia, or maybe Canada.

At Sunday Mass Father Walsh encouraged the congregation to pray for those who were hungry and losing their land. He then asked them to pray that the blight would only last for one season. Next, they prayed for the bishop, the pope, and the souls in purgatory. Finally, Father Walsh added a prayer for the Prime Minister, Benjamin Disraeli, that he be sympathetic to the plight of the Irish people. After Sunday Mass, Father Walsh gave Jamie a birthday present, a book, *The Adventures of Tom Sawyer*. "I think you'll like this, Jaime. It's about a boy who lives with his aunt. Just don't get any ideas from it that Maude and Liam will blame me for. Promise?"

A week later, when they returned home after Mass, Jamie told his aunt, "I'm going Aintín Maude. There ain't nothing left here for me, and you may not have enough food for you and Uncail Liam. You shouldn't have to feed me when I can go someplace else."

"Give Parnell a chance, Jamie. We survived it last time. We will this time. Things are going to change."

"No. I can't wait. I need to go now while I still can."

"Jamie, please. You're talking foolish."

"Don't you understand? I've got to do this. There's no other way. Can't you see that? I'll get a job, make money, and send for you."

"Oh Jamie, we aren't to be going no place. We'll be dying here, won't we? Just like our parents. And those before them."

"If you want to stay, stay. I'll go to America, and I'll join the Fenian Brotherhood, and we'll come back and get rid of the fuckin' Brits. We'll bucket down shite all over them till they leave."

"You're not about to join the Fenians, you eejit," Maude said. Her tone offered no compromise.

"I will if they'll have me," Jamie said as he walked out the door.

Jamie didn't know whether Uncle Liam was sympathetic to a young man striking out on his own, as his own sons had done, or he was concerned about feeding the three of them. Whatever his reasons, he didn't discourage Jamie from the idea of leaving. He didn't even discourage the idea of joining the Fenians. When Maude would say, "Jamie's too young to be on his own," Liam would say, "The boy's as big as a barn and strong as a horse. He's a man. He does a man's work."

When Jamie was off in the boat with Colm, in the hills with the sheep, or finding places to be in private with Treasa, Liam and Maude fought about Jamie's leaving. It wasn't an argument; it was a survival fight. The end would mean change, forever change. They both knew it and tried to protect Jamie from the depths of their war. Maude rarely cursed, and never had she thrown anything at her husband in all their years of marriage. However, her devastation at Jamie's leaving was complete, and the words and more than a few dishes flew in Liam's direction.

The angrier she got, the less it became about Jamie. The disappointment in her own sons was a knife in her heart. "They said they'd write. They never write. They said they'd come home. They never come home. I don't even know if they're married or if I have grandchildren. Jamie stays. He's the only son I have left."

Liam argued. "He's not your son. It's not your decision. He has a mother. It's not even her decision. It's his."

"Get out of here. You're a fuckin' monster. Go to your pub like you do every night and leave me alone like you do very night. Go. Go. Get out of here. Leave me alone." And he did.

It went on this way for over a week. Finally, they didn't even speak to one another. Neither spoke to Jamie. Liam stayed late at the pub. Maude cleaned up after dinner and went to bed. Jamie didn't know what to do. Finally, he couldn't take it any longer and asked his aunt what was happening. It was Saturday night after church. There was more talk of hunger coming.

Jaime didn't know how to ask in an easy way, so walking back from church—Liam had gone straight to the pub—he couldn't contain his discomfort and blurted out, "Are you and Uncail Liam fighting?"

Maude stopped walking. Rather than look at Jamie, she looked towards home. She realized that they had been scaring Jamie. He was being abandoned once again, if not physically, emotionally. "We are, Jamie. I don't want you to leave, and he thinks you should go."

"Why do you want me to stay so much? You heard. People are already starving in Mayo, and it's coming our way."

"We'll have food. We don't grow potatoes. It won't be like last time. We'll make the garden bigger, and people always be needing wool."

"But not be havin' money to buy it."

"It won't be like last time. It won't. Parnell…"

"Can't do a bloody thing to stop a blight."

"You'll be safe here. I promise."

"I'm not worried about me. People who left are sending money back. That's what I want to do. I want to go to America."

"Oh, Jamie. Those people be livin' horrible lives."

"They used to be. Things are better now. Uncail Liam said New York City be havin' an Irish mayor. A William Grace."

"And how does he know that?"

"Someone told him."

"He just wishes we had gone when we had the chance. An Irish mayor. He's dreaming."

Jaime knew he was never going to convince her and said something he hadn't dared to say before. "Aintín Maude, I'm bored here. Every year's the same, and I don't want to wind up raising sheep and paying rent to some Brit who doesn't even live here and would let us starve and not think about it. Colm and I wanted to get a boat but with the hunger coming, we don't talk about it anymore."

"What about your mother and your brothers and sisters?"

"When was the last time I saw my mother? My brothers and sisters? I don't even know where they are. I never see them now. Wouldn't be any different. I go or stay."

"You could try and find them."

"And then what? We could starve together?"

Slowly Maude accepted that, like her sons, Jamie would leave her. Slowly, the silence between her and her husband eased into pleasantries, and Liam started coming home earlier. Both of them knew that Jamie would go, but they would remain. The two of them were out of dreams. They held their mourning close inside to spare Jamie.

They started to help Jamie prepare for his departure. Jamie would wait until after lambing season. Maude would write to her cousin in Galway and ask if Jamie could spend a night with them on his way to Cork City. She would also write to Liam's sister, Siobhan Callahan, who lived in Cork City to ask if Jamie could stay with them while he worked and saved up money to pay his passage to Canada, America, or Australia. Maude insisted that Jamie write his mother and tell her about his plans to leave Ireland.

Jamie would travel by boat, public cart, and train. The first leg of the journey would be on his friend Colm's boat, from Carna to Galway. He asked, begged, Colm to leave Ireland with him. Colm said he couldn't. He had to stay and help his father. Colm tried to get Jamie to stay. They argued about it. Finally, Jamie told Colm, "I have to go now. If I don't, I'll never go."

"You know, you'll never be comin' back."

"Yes, I will, but it'll just be to visit. Maybe you'll come and visit me, wherever I land."

"Visiting each other? You're a dreamer O'Buachalla. Da and I'll take you to Galway but it'll be the last time we see each other."

"No, it won't. You'll see."

From Galway, after spending the night with Aunt Maude's cousin, Jamie would travel by public cart to Bantry. From Bantry he would travel by train to Cork City and then to the Callahan's. A lot would depend on Liam's sister and her family in Cork City. Maude acknowledged in her letter that they didn't know how long Jamie might have to stay with them before he could save enough money for passage on one of the new steamships that sailed out of the harbor. If Jamie went to New York, perhaps he might look up her son and his family who had emigrated there a few years ago.

The afternoon before he left, Jamie went to visit Treasa. He asked her to go with him. "Come with me. It'll be a grand adventure."

"Are you out of your mind," she answered. "I can't just leave."

"Why not?"

"You can be such an eejit sometimes. We're not married. We're not even engaged, an' you donna know what's before you."

"I know I'm leavin' tomorrow. An' I do know. I'm goin' to Cork and get work and then goin' someplace where the Brits don't control everything and I donna have to worry about starving."

"I know, Jamie, but I canna go with you. Not now. My parents…"

"Would understand. My Aintín Maude and Uncail Liam do."

"You're a boy. It's different."

"I'm a man."

"I know. It's just different."

"Will you come when I get settled?"

"What do you want me to say?"

"That you'll come."

"Yes. You terrible big gobshite. I'll come. You better write."

"I promise."

Chapter Five: Cork

The first thing Jamie saw when he got off the train in Cork City was two men carrying signs: 'Work or Bread.' People were still starving in Cork. Whatever commercial or industrial zeal the city had before the Great Famine was now gone. When Jamie arrived, it was a city of tenements that were barely fit to live in, a city of widespread disease, a city with little hope. And to Jamie, a young man raised amidst the smells of bogs and mountains, Cork was a city of the putrid smell of death and decay. A smell that made him gag.

The plan they formed at the kitchen table in Carna with Aintín Maude and Uncail Liam was the plan of dreamers. Cork presented a different reality. For Jamie, Cork quickly became a place to get in and out of as quickly as he could. He would plow ahead, he thought to himself. He'd soon be out of this place.

Although Cork had lost people since the beginning of the famine, others had come in from rural areas. So, when Jamie arrived, over 78,000 people were trying to make their way there. Jamie was overwhelmed. He had never seen so many people in a street at one time, even during a parade in Tullamore.

His train ride from Bantry was noisy and dirty and thrilling. It was dusk when he arrived, and the gas street lamps were just being lit. He had never seen anything of their kind before. He didn't take time to examine them. He was hungry and he wanted to get to the Callahan's as soon as he could. He had the names of two streets but no map and no house number.

Cork was a city of rivers, islands, and bridges. It was a city of churches, hospitals, jails, monasteries, and convents. There were military barracks and theaters. There was even a park and a college. Jamie had no idea where he was going and wandered from place to place, asking directions. People tried to be helpful, but he found himself coming back to the same place over and over again as conflicting instructions confused the big seventeen-year-old. He was sure people gave him directions as if they knew the streets he was looking for, but they really didn't. He also had a hard time understanding many of them. The English they spoke was different from the English of Tullamore, and only on rare occasions did he encounter someone who spoke Irish, and even that was different from what he had learned in Carna.

People would ask him what parish he was looking for, but he had never lived in a town with more than one Catholic church. The idea of more than one parish meant nothing to him. He didn't know what parish the Callahans lived in. He knew to ask for Barrack Street, but it was one of the oldest streets in the city and it was long. He walked its length several times. He was looking for a street two blocks off of Barrack, but there was a maze of lane after lane after lane. As it became close to ten o'clock, he still hadn't found the street he was looking for. It started to rain.

He had seen the spires for Saint Finbarr's Cathedral and began to use them as a landmark during his wandering. Finally, needing shelter for the night, he headed for the cathedral, thinking he would find some from the overhang at the entrance. When he arrived, he saw three entrances. The two smaller ones were already fully occupied by people and whatever belongings they possessed. He saw an empty spot under the central entrance. This entrance was wider than the others but offered less shelter. Several people had already beaten him there, and the lucky ones had pushed into the back corners where they could use the walls to block the wet breeze. The older, sicker, more desperate huddled in the center. He headed for a space close to the road and started to move people and bags to create room for himself. With his youth and size, there were a few grunts of complaint, but no one challenged him. He sat and leaned up against a woman behind him. She didn't seem to mind since he blocked rain from falling on her. He put his bag on his lap and tried to sleep. The cold, hunger, and stench from his companions didn't matter, and after a while, he dozed off.

Morning came, and the rain stopped, but not the mist. People started to stir and gather their things together. A man tried to grab Jamie's sheep hide bag that held all of his possessions. Jamie kicked him away and swore at him in Irish. The man swore back at him in English. The man pushed Jamie down with one hand and tried to grab his bag with the other. Jamie grabbed the man's arm and pulled the man down on top of him. He wrapped his legs around the man's waist and squeezed as hard as he could. He started to strangle the man with his free arm until he let go of Jamie's bag. The man tried to pry Jamie's arm from his throat, making it possible for Jamie to use his other arm. Jamie squeezed his throat as hard as he could. The man started to gurgle. Jamie didn't care. He was crying and kept pressing. The woman who had been behind him began to yell at him to stop, "You're killing him. Let him go." Her interruption brought his mind back to what he was doing, and he released the man and kicked him away. The man rolled off, fighting for breath. Jamie got up, picked up his bag, and looked around.

He was used to pissing and shitting out in the fields or hanging off the side of Colm's boat. At home, he used the outhouse. The pub in Carna had an outhouse, as did the church. In Cork, he didn't know where to go. He couldn't see any outhouses. He asked a man who had been next to him, and he pointed down the street, "Get away from here, or they won't let us stay here."

"Is there an outhouse down there?" Jamie asked.

"The street, you fucking gobshite."

Jamie walked. He couldn't stay where he was, and he didn't feel ready to meet people he didn't know, even if the Callahan's were somehow related. He had already forgotten how.

They were related, they were expecting him, but it didn't matter. He had to get out of Cork, but he didn't know how. He didn't know which way to walk. He wanted to leave, now. He didn't care how.

He relieved himself in an empty alley. A woman leaned out her window and threw the contents of a slop pot into the street and just missed him. She shouted at him, "Get outta here, you fuckin' gobshite." Coming back onto Barrack Street, Jamie walked by a pub where the owner was opening for the day. He was sweeping the floor out onto the street. Jamie asked the man where the harbor was. "Which one?" the man asked.

"Where the ships for America and Australia sail from."

"You mean Queenstown?"

"I guess."

"Hope you got enough money."

"I just want to see the ships."

"Dreaming, are you?"

"No. I'm going."

"Now?"

"Soon."

"The bleeding state of ye. Ye might want to button up those pants and clean your face."

Jamie turned and started walking back towards the cathedral. The pubkeeper yelled at him, "Wait a minute, ye dumb pup. You're going the wrong way. Come here."

Head down. Jamie returned to the pub. "What's your name?" the man asked."

"Jamie Ó Buachalla."

"West Coast. Where?"

"Carna. North above Galway."

"Donal Lynch." The man held out his hand. "When was the last time you ate something, Jamie?"

"Yesterday morning."

"I have some bread from two days ago and a few other things. Come on in. You can get that face of yours washed, get something to eat, and I'll point you to where you want to go. I'll draw you a map. It's a tricky harbor with bridges and roads that don't seem to go anywhere."

"Thank you."

Donal led Jamie into the pub. "You want Queenstown. Brits changed the name just because the fuckin' queen visited. Vic the bitch comes during the famine, people dying, and all the Brits care about is changing the god damned name of our harbor. Steal our food and our names. But, Cove is Cove, and it will be again," Donal said. "Sit. Eat something."

"I don't have much money."

"Yesterday's food. Go ahead. You don't, I'll give it to somebody else."

"I be most grateful."

"Where you staying?"

Jamie told Donal about his trip from Carna, the Callahans, and his search for the address. Donal said, "I'll draw you a map for there, too. You'll need it."

Jamie left with a full stomach, buttoned trousers, a clean face, and two maps. Donal told him it would take the better part of a day for him to walk to the harbor area called Cove now known as Queenstown.

Jamie felt much better with food in him, thanks to the hospitality of Donal Lynch. Donal told him he would be walking for the entire day, but Jamie didn't care. He was used to walking and figured he had enough food in him to last until supper time without spending the small amount left after paying for the cart to Bantry and then the train to Cork City.

He reached the harbor about noon. The first ship he saw was the

Arizona. Father Walsh had told him about the boat. "It's so fast that it only takes seven or eight days to go from Cork to New York. Can you imagine that, Jamie? Seven to eight days, and you've crossed the Atlantic Ocean."

Jamie gawked at the ship. He had never seen anything like it. It was four hundred and fifty feet long, made of steel, and powered by steam and sail. He was so awed he couldn't move at first, and then he decided to walk its length to see how long it would take. So, he started at the bow. When he got to the stern, he saw a three-masted schooner, it was only a quarter the length of the *Arizona*. It was tied to the wharf right behind the behemoth. Two men were unloading lumber and putting the square-cut logs onto a long wagon. Four horses stood patiently, waiting to pull the wagon away. A driver with another team and wagon waiting to be loaded was lined up behind them.

"Hey you, boy!" a man shouted at Jamie from the cockpit of the schooner.

"You mean me?" Jamie answered.

"You see anybody else?" the man asked. "You want to work. I'm down a man, and I need the help. You look big enough. I pay. At the end of the work. No waiting. You want it?"

"Sure," Jamie said. He walked to the end of the schooner, past where the men were unloading.

"What's your name?"

"Jamie Ó Buachalla, Buckley."

"Pissant doesn't know his own name," one of the loaders shouted.

"No matter," the man said. He was clearly the one in charge. He was about the same age Jamie's father would have been. He was smaller than Jamie, had a cropped gray beard, and spoke in clipped sentences. "You work with me. Put your bag here in the cockpit." Jamie hopped down onto the schooner, dropped his bag behind the wheel and binnacle, and waited for instructions.

They unloaded lumber for the better part of the afternoon. As they worked, Jamie learned that the *Phoenix* sailed out of St. John in New Brunswick, Canada. It carried lumber from St. John to Cork. Its return voyage would be to Tenerife, Barbados, New York, and then back to St. John. It was called the *Phoenix* because it had sunk and been refloated.

Jamie was strong enough to do the work. But he was exhausted from lack of sleep, and as they were unloading one of the logs, he tripped on the starboard railing and dropped his end of the log, almost causing his partner at the other end to fall. "Sorry," Jamie said.

"Better be. Don't do be doing that again. You okay?"

"Yeah. I'm fine."

"Another ten, and then we'll be done."

The four of them gathered in the cockpit after loading the last log onto the final wagon, and the driver had driven off. Another man emerged from the schooner cabin and joined them. His right arm was in a sling, and Jamie could see the splints holding the arm together where it was broken. He was the oldest of the group. He was squat, and Jamie thought he looked like a barrel with a short neck and head attached.

The leader introduced Jamie to the three other men. The first mate was Tommy Hynes. The man with the broken arm was Gordon Puddester, who went by Pudd. The final man, not much older than Jamie, was Stephen Chaffey. They called him Fogo after Fogo Island, where he was born. The leader, the schooner's master, was Jacob Lyver.

Jamie thought Tommy looked at him in a strange way. It made him uneasy. Tommy was probably about the same age as Jacob but looked out of place somehow. Tommy's face was wrinkled and looked like his nose had been broken and never reset.

Jamie learned they were all from Newfoundland, but two partners in Quebec City owned the *Phoenix*. He found it strange that the boat sailed from New Brunswick with a Newfoundland crew and was owned by people who lived someplace else. The crew members spoke English, but it sounded strange to him. It wasn't like the Irish who spoke English, and he wondered at times what they were saying to one another.

Pudd went below to fetch biscuits and a bottle of whiskey. Jamie was surprised by how well he managed with one arm in a sling. Jamie was more than happy to be invited to stay, but he said he had to go.

"Where you going with that bag of yours?" Jacob asked him.

Jamie told them about his trip from Carna, his plan to go to America, Canada, or Australia, and his staying with the Callahan's while earning some money to buy passage. He told them about sending money back to his aunt and uncle. He even told them about Treasa de Burca but used her English name, Therese Burke.

"The boy's got a dolly already," Tommy said. "You shave yet, you oversized pissant?"

"You want to go on one of those coffin ships? You out of your fucking mind?" Jacob said.

"I don't know. I just got to get out of here. There's another famine coming."

"I doubt it," Jacob said. "Too much disgust with the Brits from last time. They won't do the same thing twice. America and Canada loaded with Irish who will send money. Won't let it happen."

"Maybe. I still want to go."

Jacob asked, "You know how to sail?"

"Yes, sir. I sailed and fished with my friends up in Carna. My friend Colm and I were going to get our own boat and do trading. Then we heard about the crop failure, and the hunger had started up in Mayo. I wanted to leave; Colm decided to stay."

"Sailing. It all be the same," Jacob said. "Fogo can't sail for shit, but we still be bringing him."

"Because he's your cousin's son be the real reason. He doing okay, sometimes," Tommy said.

"Thank you for sticking up for me," Fogo said.

"Don't push it. You still can't steer a course to save your bloody life," Tommy said.

Jacob interrupted the banter, "Jamie, would you go on up forward for a couple of minutes. I want to talk to my crew."

Jamie walked up to the boat's bow and sat down on the deck, looking out at the harbor. He could hear the voices coming from the cockpit, but they were low, and as hard as he tried, he couldn't figure out what they were saying. Occasionally, he could understand Tommy when he raised his voice and complained that Jamie was 'green.'

After a couple of minutes, Jacob called to him, "You can come back now." Jamie did so. When he reached the cockpit where the others were seated, Jacob said, "Relax. Sit down." Jamie did as he was told. "So, after Tenerife and Barbados, we're going to New York City and then back to New Brunswick. We been talking about taking you on. That suit you?"

"Yes, sir."

"We're down a man 'til Pudd's wing heals, so you can come if you're willing to work and learn."

"Oh, I am."

"We got room for ya. We'll take ya and feed ya for your work, but no shares. So you won't be making any money. You understand?"

"Yes, sir. No shares."

"Okay. As I said, I'll pay you for today, but that's it. Be here early in the morning."

Chapter Six: The *Phoenix*

The Callahans didn't seem to mind much when Jamie showed up at nine that night. They knew he was coming and had a rough idea of what day he would arrive, but nothing more. He was exhausted from eight hours of walking and five hours of unloading lumber, but he couldn't contain his excitement about his good fortune running into the crew of the *Phoenix*. He told them, "I can't hardly believe it. I'm only here a day, and I've made some money and been offered free passage to America. All I have to do is work as a crew member."

Patrick Callahan let him go on. When Jamie finished, he said. "You out of your mind, boy. You think it's that easy? Fucking Brits. They'll work your arse off, but they're not going to pay you for crewing for them?"

"They're not Brits; they're Canadians."

"No difference," Patrick said.

"I told ya. I know they not be paying me to be crew. I'm working my way to New York. I'm not an eejit."

"You sure they're okay? This bunch? Some Irish been sold into slavery that way," Nora added.

"They paid me today. They're not slavers."

"Sure." Patrick said. "But then they get you over there and say you owe them passage. So, you wind up working for them for free for years because they say you got a debt. Who's going to listen to you over there, huh? A boy or a ship's captain? Who do you think?"

"They're not going to be doing that. They need me. One of 'em is hurt. Another of them, Fogo, is only a couple of years older than me, and he's not as big. He's happy enough."

"How would you know? Maude wrote you was a dreamer boy, and we had to look out for you. So, we're doing just that."

"Leave him be," Nora said. "We can talk about all that tomorrow.

You eat anything today?"

"Not much. Man at a pub not far from here gave me something to eat this morning. Tonight, I had some biscuits on the boat before I left."

"You weren't here this morning," Nora said. "Where'd you sleep last night?"

Jamie told them about his journey from Carna, trying to find them, and sleeping on the steps of the cathedral. He omitted almost killing the man who had tried to take his bag.

"Jesus, Mary, and Joseph. Dinner's all gone, but I can make you up some porridge. Put yourself and your things in the back room."

When he got to the room in the back of the small house, he slid his bag under one of the two beds and lay down on it. It was too short for him, but it didn't matter. When Nora went in to get him and saw he was asleep, she decided the porridge could wait until morning.

Jamie didn't hear Patrick leave for work the following day. The first thing he knew, Nora was shaking him to wake up. "I got that porridge for you if you'll be having some and some bread, and I have a little jam. Will you be wanting tea?"

"Oh, no. What time is it? I'm due at the dock."

"A little past seven. What's your rush? You have to eat something."

"Seven. The tide. I gotta go. I have to be there by one."

"One? You have time to eat, then."

"If I be quick. Thank you."

The walk to Queenstown was easier with a good night's sleep and a full belly, but it was still four hours. The strangeness of Cork and the awful smells were still there. He was grateful when he got closer to the harbor, and the smells changed to the more familiar and more pleasant ones of salt air.

Now, he paid more attention to the city as he walked towards the harbor. He passed lane after narrow lane of small two, and three-story houses butted up against one another. They were all as gray as the cobblestones on the streets. They looked the same to him. Lines for hanging clothes to dry stretched across some of the lanes. People were up and about, and he heard shouts and cries of children. He found himself missing the familiarity of Carna, his friends, his aunt and uncle, and especially Treasa. He swore he saw her when a young woman with black hair appeared, walking in the opposite direction. Maybe she had followed him to Cork. When he saw it wasn't her, he felt tears forming and quickly wiped them away.

His longing for Treasa and his old life didn't leave until he crossed over into Queenstown. He felt himself tensing up. Fortitude. Father Walsh had preached on the virtue of fortitude. The idea of fortitude consumed him as he approached the harbor. He would do this. He would go to America. He would send money back to Aintín Maude and Uncail Liam. He'd find work for Colm, too. Or maybe they could be shipmates like he and Fogo. He would send for Treasa, and they would marry and raise a family in America, or maybe Canada.

Everyone was already on board when he reached the *Phoenix*. "Nice of you to join us," Tommy said.

"Am I late?"

"No, you're fine," Jacob said. "Tide's almost half in, and we can turn the boat soon. Got to get her bow in. We'll offload the hold today. Tomorrow, we clean out the leftovers, and stowaways."

"Stowaways?"

Fogo laughed, "All the bugs that come with the lumber."

Jacob said, "Cargo's supposed to start coming in the afternoon. We'll load the next day if it's on time, and we'll leave on ebb tide Friday."

"And when has it ever been on time?" Pudd asked.

"Shut your face, you one-armed Crip," Tommy said. "Why do you give a fuck. You ain't got to lift a finger anyway."

"What will be carrying?" Jamie asked. He was afraid Jacob might say people, people paying to go to America.

"Pork and butter to the Brits in Barbados," Jacob answered.

"I thought we were going to New York," Jamie protested.

"Jesus. And you call me stupid," Fogo said just under his breath to no one.

"You sure you want to take this pissant?" Tommy said.

"Don't let 'em get to you," Pudd intervened. "We'll get you to New York. Never you worry. See, it's like this: we follow the trade route because that's how the winds and currents go. First stop is Tenerife in the Canaries, off Africa. We get supplies there. Then we cross and go to the Caribbean. For us, that's Barbados. We offload the pork and butter and get loaded with rum. Then we sail North, pick up the Gulf Stream, and head for New York. New York, we trade the rum for cotton and take it to Boston. Who knows from Boston? Whatever we can get."

Fogo added, "We head South 'til the butter melts. Then we take a right. Ain't that right?"

"I taught you that, and by the time we turn right, the Crip here should be ready to work again," Tommy said.

"I'll be outworking you when we unload in Barbados," Pudd said.

"How long it gonna take us?" Jamie asked.

"How long it take you to sail from Galway to, where was it you from?" Tommy asked

"Carna. Depended on the wind."

"It depended on the wind," Tommy mocked.

"Cut your shit. He's a green kid," Pudd said. Then, he turned to Jamie: "If everything goes right and we got wind, and nothing breaks like caused me this broken arm, we'll be in La Palma in two weeks or so if we can stay the hell out of the Azores high."

"Azores high?"

"No fuckin wind, you dumb mick," Tommy said.

"I'll explain it to you later," Jacob interrupted. "We'll be in La Palma for a day, possibly two, to provision. Another three weeks to Barbados. We'll be there, again if everything goes right, for three or four days, then another two weeks to New York. Figure two months in all. Good time a year you picked, Jamie. May, June. After Northeasters and before hurricanes."

"We won't get there by June twentieth, will we?"

"What's June twentieth," Jacob asked.

"My birthday."

"Aw, it's his birthday. How old will you be? Fourteen?" Tommy said.

"I'll be eighteen."

"He'll be fuckin' eighteen. You want we should throw you a party?" Tommy said.

"Enough," Jacob said to Tommy before turning to Jamie. "You know how to row?"

"Sure."

"Let's get to it then. You and Fogo launch the dinghy."

Jamie and Fogo hooked up lines to both ends of the dinghy, where it was stowed upside down on the cabin top. They raised it, turned it right side up, and lowered it into the water. They climbed down into the dinghy and rowed around to the bow, where Tommy and Jacob carefully lowered the anchor down to them. They rowed out into the harbor and dropped the anchor overboard when they were opposite the bow of the *Phoenix*. Jacob and Tommy released the stern and spring lines of the *Phoenix*, threaded the anchor line through a block and tackle system, and started to pull the stern out towards the anchor so the bow would face the wharf. Fogo and Jamie rowed back to the schooner, fastened the boat alongside, and climbed on board.

"Fogo, you and Jamie take the dock. The first wagon's here. Wave him forward," Jacob ordered.

The boys hopped off the bow and onto the dock. The wagon driver saw them and got the two horses moving until the end of the wagon was opposite the bow of the *Phoenix*. Fogo called to the boat that they were ready. Pudd leaned down into the cabin and repeated the message.

Jamie was surprised to see hatch doors open on either side of the bow. Soon the first piece of lumber was sticking out. Jamie realized that what they unloaded yesterday from the top of the boat was only a fraction of the lumber the boat was carrying. These pieces from the hold were longer and heavier, and unloading them was more brutal than anything Jamie had ever done before. Jacob and Tommy would push a piece out until Jamie and Fogo could grab it. Then they would pull it out, across the side of the wharf, lift an end up onto the wagon, and push it all the way up.

An hour later, Jamie didn't know how long he could keep it up. He didn't say anything because Fogo didn't say anything. The driver of the wagon sat there reading a newspaper. Jamie hated him. They kept at it until the wagon was full and the driver pulled away. Jamie saw there was another wagon just waiting to pull up.

"How many wagons?" Jamie asked.

"Too fuckin many," Fogo replied.

They unloaded lumber for four hours. After that, they started taking breaks between wagons, but Jamie was pushing himself to move at all when the last wagon left.

"Okay, you two, let's get the anchor up and swing her back," Jacob commanded after the last wagon had left. Jamie and Fogo looked at each other and shrugged.

When they got the boat back alongside the wharf, Jacob gathered them in the cockpit and had Pudd break out biscuits and whiskey.

Exhausted, everyone but Pudd fell asleep sprawled out on the deck within a half an hour. Pudd let them sleep while he went below to cook dinner. When he finished, he woke them up, and they went below to the small galley and crew's quarters.

Jamie still had a four-hour walk ahead of him. He didn't know how he was going to do it. Jacob had been thinking the same thing and told him to sleep on board because the next day, they had to clean out all the debris and bugs from the lumber and give the *Phoenix* a good cleaning, or the pig broker wouldn't clear the ship to be loaded with the barrels of bacon, ham, and butter.

Jamie didn't argue. Jacob paid him his day's wages, and they all headed for their berths. The *Phoenix* had been laid out for six crew members, so Jamie tucked into one of the two empty berths and fell asleep. Again, it was too short, and he silently thanked Uncail Liam for having built a long enough bed for him back in Carna.

No cargo had arrived by three o'clock the next day. The boat was clean enough to be inspected, but the broker had not come. So, Jacob told Jamie to go home but be back early the next day. "Plan on staying on board. Don't forget your oilskins."

"I don't have any."

"Jesus H. Christ, Jacob! This pissant's so green he wouldn't know what hole to put it in," Tommy said.

"Fogo, come with me and the greenie," Pudd said. "Bring your money, kid. There's a chandler a block from here. We'll get you set up, and Fogo can carry it back and stow it. Me and Jacob's going to go do some serious drinking while Tommy goes bugger his favorite moll and makes believe she loves him even if he's at the end of the line to get in."

"Go fuck yourself, you Crip. That the hand you use? The one in the sling. What you gonna do 'til you can use it again? Gonna have your new friend here, do it for you?"

"Go bugger your bitch and get shite-faced, you stupid ass."

On the way to the chandlery, Jamie asked, "What'd I do to him?"

"You're Irish," Fogo said. "He hates the Irish. His wife left him for an Irishman four trips ago. Then she moved to Boston with the guy and took Tommy's kids with them," Pudd explained.

"Oh, great."

"Tell him the rest," Fogo said.

"Doesn't matter," Pudd said.

"Tell that to Tommy."

Pudd waited a minute while they kept walking before he said, "The *Phoenix* used to be called the *Louisa May* after the owner's daughter. Tommy was first mate when they were hauling Irish during the famine. Some people were sick before they even got on board in Queenstown. On one of the trips, there was this girl. Her parents both died within a week out. They prayed some prayers and threw them overboard. The girl was maybe thirteen or fourteen when she saw her parents go into the sea. So, Tommy decides he's going to marry her. I guess she said yes. What else she gonna do? No parents. Don't know no one on board the boat or in New York.

"Anyway, Tommy gets her pregnant on the way over. When they get to St. John, he sends her to stay with his brother and his family up in Newfoundland. He rents himself a house in St. John after she delivers. Moves her down there, and they have another kid. She meets some people there and settles in.

"Tommy stays with the *Louisa May* and is onboard on the trip when the boat goes down."

"It sank?" Jamie asked.

"Yep. Tommy says they were coming into the Gulf."

"St. Lawrence," Fogo added.

"Thank you, Fogo. Anyway, Tommy says they had a stiff breeze, so they were flying. Because of all the lumber boats coming in and out of the Gulf, you have to be careful cause some logs always go overboard. They must have hit one. Tommy says they started taking on water, and the pumps couldn't keep up, and the people below decks were going crazy.

"Anyway, they try making for Sydney on the end of Nova Scotia. It's getting dark, and they run into a fog bank. Now, they're on a dead run, and wind is still blowing like shite. On the way into Sydney, they run up on the South Bar. Wind pushes the boat broadside onto the bar before they get the sails down and pins her to the bar. Tide's coming in. Big tide there and fast. So, they're still taking on water from the hole, and now the boat's stuck on the bar. But the boat's so damned stuck, water just comes in over the side rather than floating her. Seventy some odd Irish in the hold. They all drowned."

"Jesus," Jamie said.

"So, Tommy finally gets home, tells his wife about what's happened, and she's real upset. Tommy tells her he doesn't understand why she's so upset. They got the passage money ahead of time. That makes her more upset, and Tommy says something about them being only Irish, and she goes nuts.

"Well, Tommy goes back to the *Louisa May* to help them get it off the sand bar where it been for a month. He finds out it's got a new owner who wants nothing to do with being a death ship. Renames it *Phoenix*. Gets himself a new master, Jacob. Eventually, they get the boat off, fix the hole, get all the sand out, get a load of lumber, and head out. After his first trip with Jacob, Tommy goes home, and his wifey and kids are all gone. Never seen them again after that."

Fogo added. "He blames the Irish for everything bad happens to him. He also makes less money now 'cause there was bigger money moving Irish than moving lumber."

"He's a really good seaman, though," Pudd said. "Reason Jacob keeps him on. Damned good navigator. As good or better than Jacob. Great at the helm, too. Straightest wake you ever seen. You can learn a lot from him."

"Just don't talk to him," Fogo said. "He's a mean son of a bitch and enjoys it. Especially when he's swilling."

When Jamie announced his plans to the Callahans, Nora insisted that he spend the evening writing a letter to his Aintín Maude. Jamie also wrote a letter to Treasa de Burca, to Colm, and still another to Father Walsh. He told them he would be going to New York and finding Nora and Patrick's son, Harry. If they wanted to send him a letter, they could send it to Harry. He ended each letter with the address for Harry that Nora provided. Nora promised to mail the letters for him.

Patrick again told Jamie he was out of his mind and that Canadian or not, they would try to get the better of him and to watch his step.

Jamie didn't tell Patrick about Tommy Hynes.

Chapter Seven: Tenerife

The breeze was barely enough to fill the sails when they pushed off from the wharf on the morning of April 30, 1880. Tommy was at the helm; Jacob was at the bow shouting instructions; Fogo and Jamie ran from sail to sail, adjusting the lines as Jacob dictated. Once away from the wharf, Jacob went below to make the departure entry in the ship's log. Jamie would see him make a log entry three times a day for the length of the voyage: date, time, barometric pressure, longitude, latitude, sea conditions, wind speed, distance since last entry, course, and any circumstances that he deemed noteworthy. Tommy would do the same for his watches. If there was cloud cover and they couldn't use the sextant, they would estimate their latitude and longitude.

When they passed Spike Island in Cork Harbor, they started to ride the outgoing tide, and their speed increased by two knots. The wind bounced off the land, though, and Fogo and Jamie had to adjust sails each time the wind shifted. Then the wind started coming into the harbor, and they had to pull the sails in tight and begin to tack back and forth to make headway. Jamie was used to tacking Colm's boat with its single mainsail and two jibs. Tacking the *Phoenix* was an entirely different matter. With three jibs, a foresail on the first mast, a mainsail on the second, and a mizzen on the third, tacking was a major operation.

Pudd had told Jamie the *Phoenix* was a 'Tern Schooner' because all three masts were the same height. The sails were bigger than anything Jamie had handled before. It took him a while before he got used to how fast he had to move as they tacked all the sails every time they came about. It became clear to him how useless Pudd would have been with only one good arm. Jamie realized Jacob wasn't doing him any favors bringing him onboard; Jacob needed him.

It wasn't until they passed the bluffs at Fort Carlisle and made it out into the Celtic Sea that the wind direction steadied, and Fogo and Jamie could relax. Jacob didn't say anything when he came on deck from the cabin. Pudd whispered to Jamie, "You did good for your first time. Not like sailing your Galway Hooker, is it?"

"No, it sure isn't. How come Jacob wasn't on deck when we left? I thought he was the master."

Pudd smiled. "He is. But what we just did was easy. Jacob trusts Tommy like I told you. After he worked on the log, he checked the hold again. Made sure everything was fastened down tight before we hit the Atlantic swells and start to get bounced around a bit. We get the wind behind us on a run with swells coming in just aft the beam, and this boat swings its butt end around like a drunk dancer in a French whorehouse. You'll see. You'll be holding on to something most of the time."

It was starting to get dark when they reached Fastnet Rock. The cast-iron lighthouse reached ninety-one feet into the air and was the tallest building Jamie had ever seen. Its white light blinked steadily every couple of seconds, and Jamie couldn't keep his eyes off it. Father Walsh had told him about the name given to the jagged rock island during the Great Famine, "Ireland's Teardrop." It was the last piece of Ireland that would be seen by those who were leaving. Pudd saw Jamie leaning against the rail, came up to him, and nudged him in the side with his one good arm. "Think you'll ever come back?" he asked.

"I don't know. I really don't."

Jacob joined them in the stern. He had a device with him that Jamie had never seen before. Pudd sensed the young man wanted to ask a question but didn't want to reveal his ignorance, so Pudd stepped in. "It's a taffrail log. It will measure how far we've gone through the water. Here. Take a look."

Jacob handed the device to Pudd. "See this propeller at the end of the line. It's going to spin when we move through the water. This dial at the other end of the line we attach to this here rail, the taffrail." Pudd eased the device into the water. "Now watch." Jamie couldn't see the propeller spinning at the end of the line as it eased away from the stern of the *Phoenix*. Finally, the dial attached to the taffrail started to respond. "You see? That's all there is to it. Simple enough, huh?"

"That's it?"

"Yep. Each watch will record how far we've traveled through the water."

Jacob headed towards the cabin. "If you be through teaching, you gonna feed us?"

Pudd laughed, "Aye aye, Captain."

With all sails full, the *Phoenix* left Ireland in its wake.

The previous evening, while they were drinking at the Roaring Donkey, Pudd told Jacob that it would be best to keep Tommy and Jamie separated from each other for the time being. Jacob agreed. "Probably best. I also want to keep a close eye on the kid and see what he can do. Tommy's right about one thing; the kid's green as they come."

Pudd said, "Yeah, but I think he's a speedy one when it comes to learning. You watch, a lot faster than Fogo. You teach him, and I think you got yourself a good hand, there. The kid's big, and he's strong as a fuckin' ox team."

Jacob laughed, "You see the shoulders and arms on him? He grows anymore, and we won't be able to wedge him into a berth. Already hanging over the side when he stretches out. You gonna have enough food to feed him?"

"I added more when I provisioned yesterday. We'll be fine."

"You think he's gonna learn?" Jacob asked. "Hasn't said anything about wanting to be a seaman. Just wants to get to New York and make money."

"Well, I guess we'll find out, won't we? He's young. Other than money, I think the only thing he knows for sure is he wants his dolly."

That evening they began the system of watches. Jacob and Jamie would stand watch together, as would Fogo and Tommy. Tommy and Fogo would have the watch from eight to midnight as they made their way out through the Celtic Sea to the North Atlantic.

Jacob and Jamie would have three watches each day, as would Tommy and Fogo, four hours on and four hours off. Jacob and Jamie would take twelve to four in the morning, eight to twelve noon, and four to eight in the evening. One would be at the helm while the other tended the sails or did other chores. If they ran into a storm, they would wake up the others to give them a hand with the sails. In addition to the jibs and the three gaff-rigged sails on the masts, the *Phoenix* flew smaller sails, topsails attached to each gaff's top, and still two other sails, called fisherman staysails. With his arm still in a sling, Pudd didn't stand watch. He barely managed to do his other job, which was cook.

Jamie was nervous about the complexity of the rig and all the different names. After dinner, he helped Pudd clean up. When they were done, he asked Pudd to take him through every sail and line on the boat. Jamie took out his pen and the paper he had brought to write letters during the trip. With Pudd sitting next to him in the small galley, Pudd had him draw out a diagram of the boat and the sail plan. He then had him write the name down for every sail and line. Pudd quizzed him repeatedly until he felt Jamie had some mastery of the rigging. Then he told Jamie to go up on deck. "I want you to start up forward at the bow and work your way aft to the stern. You take this drawing and make it real. Now get going."

"Shouldn't I get some sleep?" Jamie complained.

"After. You'll still get some. You don't want Jacob to be telling you to do something and you acting like an imbecile and having to ask a lot of questions. Now get going."

Jamie did as he was told. He went up on deck with his diagram and started at the bow. As he worked his way aft, he tested his memory of the sail plan and the name of each sail and line. He followed each line from where it was attached to the other end and figured out its function. If he couldn't figure it out, he would try to get Fogo's attention and ask him. Tommy was at the wheel, and Jamie stopped asking for Fogo's help as he approached the stern of the boat. It was eleven o'clock, an hour before his watch began, when Jamie crawled into his bunk.

Jacob wanted to see how Jamie would handle the helm, so at midnight on his first day at sea Jamie Buckley found himself steering a one-hundred and fifty-foot schooner towards an island off the coast of Africa. Standing next to him was a man he had only known for a couple of days and whom he now depended upon to get him to his dream.

Slowly Jamie got used to steering the boat. He had never steered anything with a wheel before. The Galway Hookers used tillers and were very responsive little boats compared to the *Phoenix*, which Jamie felt took forever to turn. Jamie also realized he had never sailed at night before, and, in almost all of his sailing, he was in sight of land. While Colm's father's boat had a small compass kept in a box under one of the seats, it was rarely used. So now Jamie was steering by compass alone. It was set in a large binnacle right in front of the helm. Jacob gave him the course to steer. It took the novice seaman a while to get used to watching the compass and steering so the way the boat was headed was precisely lined up with the pointer on the compass rose. More than once, Jacob told him to move the wheel slowly and give the boat a chance to turn. It seemed to Jamie that it took forever for the compass to move to where he wanted it to be. Before long, he realized it was the boat moving around the compass, not the other way around.

The swells didn't make it any easier. The compass floated, and the boat danced. Jamie began to feel his stomach do things he had not experienced in years. Jacob must have sensed it because he asked, "How you doing?"

Jamie lied, "Fine."

"If you start to get the wobblies, look out at the horizon until they calm down. And stop looking at the compass so damned hard. Just glance down at it every minute or so. Feel the boat. Feel the direction. You'll be fine. You're trying too damned hard to be perfect."

Slowly, Jamie relaxed into the movement of the boat, the compass, and the waves lifting and turning the boat. By the end of his first watch, his confidence had grown, and Jacob was saying less and less to him. Jamie took Jacob's silence as the highest of praise.

Over the next two weeks, Jamie stood behind the helm of the *Phoenix* for one hundred and seventy hours. Jacob would be close at hand when they ran into squalls, or the wind shifted, but never next to him or behind him. What had been specific instructions during the first couple of days became, "You might want to head up a bit," or "Try easing off a tad." By the second week, Jacob would sit, lean up against the mizzen mast, and doze while Jamie steered the boat towards the Canary Islands.

Once in a while, Jacob would get bored and take over the helm and have Jamie tend to the sails or perform some other chore. Jamie came to know every term for every line and sail like he had been on the boat for years. When he was off watch, and they ran into a squall, and Tommy and Fogo needed help, he knew what to do to strike a jib or a topsail or put a reef into one of the gaff-rigged sails. He was the strongest man on board and was getting stronger every day from the work. He was the one who was asked to handle the mizzen, the largest of the sails, when it had to be reefed.

He became curious about the mysteries of the sextant and the charts that Jacob used. On the Sunday of the second week, he asked Jacob if he would teach him to use the sextant. Jacob was brusque in his response. "One thing at a time. Maybe after we leave Tenerife, but I'm not promising."

When Jacob told Pudd about the conversation, Pudd said, "What'd I tell you? Kid's smart, and he wants to learn."

"I teach him how to navigate, and Tommy's going to shit a fuckin' pig."

"Let him. We're not paying the kid. He's holding his own. The least you can do is teach him."

"I'll think about it."

Jamie loved the midnight to four watches. Pudd, Fogo and Tommy would be asleep below. Jacob would be dozing, and the *Phoenix* belonged to him. The sea was his; the stars were his, and every sound of the boat was his. He could change the sound of the *Phoenix* through the water by changing course one or two degrees and then bringing it back. Since they were heading downwind most of the time, it wouldn't require the sails to be trimmed differently. Then he would come back a couple of degrees in the opposite direction to compensate. He knew Jacob would object, but he was asleep. Once in a while, he would drum on the wheel with his fingers remembering a tune. By the end of two days, his stomach was fine, and so was he. He was finer than anytime he could remember except when he and Treasa were lying down, holding each other in the hayloft of her father's barn.

Fogo had gone forward to take care of a jib sheet that had gotten wrapped around the capstan when he saw Pico del Teide. Rising over twelve thousand feet into the air over Tenerife, the volcano could be seen from miles away, long before the island itself. "Tenerife!" Fogo shouted.

"Right where it's supposed to be," Tommy replied.

From below, Jamie scrambled out of his berth, threw his clothes on, and rushed up onto the deck, almost knocking Pudd over who was cooking breakfast in the galley.

"Easy boy, it'll be hours before we get to the harbor in Santa Cruz. We've got to go all the way round the end of the island. Ask Fogo if there's any snow on old Teide whitey."

"Snow? How? It's hot!"

"Not up there, it ain't. That thing's four times taller than anything you got back there in Ireland. It snows up there."

Jamie wasn't listening. He was rushing up the galley stairs to get on deck.

Santa Cruz, the main harbor on Tenerife, had cost Lord Horatio Nelson an arm when the British tried to take the Canary Islands from the Spanish. When Pudd told Jamie the story of the Spanish defeating the British at Santa Cruz, Jamie was amazed. It was the first time he had heard of the British being defeated at anything, and he was delighted. "No shit. They lost. Father Walsh told me there's a statue of Nelson up on a pedestal in the middle of Dublin. We get free of the feckin' Brits, that'll come down."

"Jesus, Jamie. Easy there, boy. You want to be careful with that stuff, especially when we get to Barbados. And keep that mouth of yours shut around Tommy."

Santa Cruz was bustling with ships loading and unloading. Many had stopped to add to their provisions before continuing their voyages to other places. Pudd was in charge of provisioning. He went about negotiating for water, foodstuffs, and some delicacies with the two young men in tow in anticipation of the next and longest leg of their voyage to Barbados. Pudd added a keg of Madeira wine to their provisions. "Damned stuff lasts forever," Pudd told them.

Tommy left the boat the minute all lines were made fast to the wharf. "There he goes," Fogo said.

"Where's he going?" Jamie asked.

"To get his pipes cleaned if his pego doesn't turn into a lobcock because he drank too much first," Pudd said. "You'd think the arse would know better at his age, but he don't. So, Fogo, you want to go with him after we get this stuff on board?"

"Not with him and the places he goes," Fogo said. "I'll wait 'til Barbados. I know a good place there. What about you, Jamie?"

"No."

"Jesus. I'll bet Jamie's a fuckin' virgin," Fogo said to Pudd. "I'll bet on it."

"I am not," Jamie said.

"I'll bet you are. What say Pudd, we help him get a three-penny upright tonight? You ain't got enough, I'll spot you the money 'till we get to New York."

"We ain't paying him nothing. Remember?" Pudd said.

"Forgot. I'll give you the money then. Just for an upright, though."

"Leave him be, Fogo. Let's get the stuff we need and get back to the boat. Then, I'm taking you lads to Calle de la Noria, where Jacob's going to meet us. We'll have a real dinner, and our lord and master will be doing the paying."

They pushed off the wharf at dawn the following day. Tommy stayed in his bunk. Jacob was at the helm while Fogo and Jamie took care of the lines and got the sails up. Once outside the harbor, Pudd offered to take a turn at the helm. He said his arm was better, and he could handle it. Jacob said no. Pudd argued. The morning breeze was still light, so Jacob finally said okay. That left Jamie to make the porridge and tea for everyone. He did so as quietly as he could to avoid waking Tommy.

Chapter Eight: Barbados

Sailing in the trade winds was new to Jamie. There was little to do. He started to measure time according to the four-hour watches they kept. When he was not on watch, he would write letters to Treasa and Aintín Maude. Day after day, the trade winds remained steady. They followed the few clouds downwind, and Jamie watched them form, dissipate, change shape, and re-form.

They were making good time, and on the third day out of Tenerife, the wind was so steady they did not make any adjustments to the sails. The course was simple. Sail south-south-west until they were about two hundred and fifty miles northwest of the Cape Verde Islands and then stay with the winds and head west for Barbados.

Jamie loved hearing Pudd tell stories about past voyages and ports and the members of the crew. He learned Tommy had been at sea since he was fifteen and had run away from a father who had beaten him. He learned Jacob was married and had seven children. He learned Fogo was trying to save money to buy a boat with his brother, but he kept spending it as fast as he made it. Jacob now held back a quarter of each of Fogo's shares for him. He learned Pudd's wife died three years ago, and he lived with his oldest daughter and her family when he wasn't at sea. Pudd told Jamie he planned to sail as long as his body let him. Jamie learned about Newfoundland and Corner Brook on the Bay of Islands, where Pudd was born. It had been six weeks since he broke his arm, and it was healing well.

Pudd told Jamie to be careful when they got to Barbados. When Jamie asked why, Pudd told him about the history of the Irish on the island. "Before the Brits brought darky slaves to do the sugar cane, they brought a lot of Irish slaves; some say as many as fifty thousand. Descendants are still there. Somewhat free now. They call 'em

Redlegs 'cause a sunburn. Real poor. Worse than Ireland if you ask me. So, you run into some, don't be surprised. They all second, third generation. They never been to Ireland. Brits still be treating 'em like shite, though, so they stay to themselves. Brits on the island think Irish and Africans should still be slaves and treat 'em that way. Law is Brit law, but England a long way away. So, they do whatever they damned well want. Just keep your Irish mouth to yourself; you be fine."

There was little breeze coming across the deck with the wind behind them, and the days were hot. No one wanted to be below decks until the sun started to go down. Off watch, they'd find some shade from the sails and doze on deck. Jamie was at the wheel on the four to eight watch on the fourth day out of Tenerife. Jacob surprised them when they gathered together in the cockpit to eat the evening meal. "No topsails tonight. Barometer's dropping, and I expect we may be in for a blow."

"What you be thinking?" Fogo asked.

"Been watching after the barometer for the last couple of hours. Still going down and going faster. Don't like that line of clouds over there." Jacob pointed in the direction of Africa. "We're still too far north for a big one, and it's only June…"

"Don't matter," Tommy said. "Gonna come, gonna come. Can't be doing shite about it now."

It came fast. Tommy and Fogo had just started their watch when the wind changed direction, and the rain started. Tommy was at the helm and told Fogo to get everyone up on deck. Where they had been on a run with the wind almost directly behind them coming over the starboard quarter, they now pulled the sails in to meet the new wind coming over the port beam.

Jamie hunted for the oilskins he had packed away and put them on. Jacob was already on deck; he started shouting orders, "Fogo, strike number one jib! Jamie, you're with me. Tommy, maintain course for now!" When Pudd started to come on deck, Jacob shouted at him, "Get below! I'll holler if I need you."

Jamie and Jacob went to the aft of the boat. Jacob let the mizzen halyard down to the first reef point and made it fast. Next, Jamie began tying the reefing lines under the boom, reducing the sail area. Jacob joined him until the sail was smaller than it had been. Next, they repeated the process for the mainsail. By the time they got to the foresail, Fogo was able to help them.

With reduced sail, the *Phoenix* didn't heel as much, and Tommy reported he could hold course without too much of a problem. Jamie and Jacob returned to the cabin. "Gonna be a long night," Pudd said from the comfort of his bunk, swaying in its gimbals with the increased motion of the boat.

Jamie crawled into his berth but couldn't sleep. An hour later, Fogo again shouted below. Jacob and Jamie crawled out of their berths, pulled on their oilskins, and went back on deck. The waves had built, and the wind was causing a loud whining in the rigging. The *Phoenix* was sailing broadside to the wind, and the spray was coming up over the side, rolling down across the deck and out the scuppers. The lee rail was now buried in the water.

"Can you hold her?" Jacob shouted to Tommy.

"Barely."

"Luff her up a bit. We'll get more sail down."

Jacob had to shout to make himself heard to Fogo and Jamie. "We're going to strike the mainsail first and see how it goes."

The boat was heeling badly, and they had to fight to keep their balance. Fogo was helping to tie the gaff down to the mainsail boom when a large wave hit them. Fogo lost his grip and the rush of water from the onboarding wave swept him down the deck. He had to scramble to get one hand onto the starboard mizzen stay so he wouldn't be swept overboard. Jacob was too busy to say anything.

The boat heeled a little less with the mainsail down, but the wind and the waves were still building. "What do you want to do?" Tommy yelled to Jacob.

"Fuck. Wait 'til we get the mizzen and foresail down and then head off. We'll put a drogue out and run off under bare poles. Fogo, tell Pudd to hand you up the drogue. Tommy, wait 'til the sails are down and the drogue is in the water before you head down."

Fogo disappeared below deck. When he came back up, he carried a six-foot wooden pole that had three discs of differing sizes attached to it. There were three or four small holes in each one of the disks. The device was connected to a long line.

Jacob and Jamie got the mizzen down and were tying the last reef in the foresail when Jacob shouted, "Fogo, make the drogue fast to the mizzen mast and lead the line through the port chock. The minute we start to head downwind, throw the drogue over. Then we'll get the jib down." Fogo did as he was told. As soon as the drogue was ready, Jacob waited for some smaller waves. Then, seeing two coming, he shouted to Tommy, "Now! Head off now. Drogue overboard. Now, Fogo! Get the damn drogue overboard, and don't let that line get fouled."

Ten minutes later, all the sails were struck and lashed down. Tommy tied the helm down so the rudder was amidship and wouldn't break swinging from side to side in the oncoming waves.

They all went down into the cabin. Jamie and Fogo used the pump to empty out the water that was sloshing in the bilge. Jacob checked the cargo to make sure nothing had come loose from the pounding. When everything was squared away, the crew members went to their berths and tried to get some sleep.

"She be making like a cork," Pudd said from his berth. After he said it, an enormous wave came up and over the transom and crashed onto the deck, causing the boat to shudder.

"Some fuckin' cork," Tommy said. Then, to Jacob, he said, "Why didn't we ride this heading into the wind with a sea anchor? Easier on the boat."

Jacob didn't say anything. Jamie got the feeling this wasn't the first time Tommy had questioned Jacob's judgment. When another wave crashed down on them, Jacob struggled in the boat's confused motion to get into his oilskins. Rather than go topsides through the aft hatch where an onboarding wave could wash into the cabin, he went forward to use the hatch in front of the foremast. A couple of minutes later, he returned to report that everything was holding together as far as he could tell, and the drogue was doing a good job slowing them down and keeping them from broaching with the on-coming waves.

"How big?" Fogo asked.

"Half a mast. Maybe more."

"Jesus," Fogo said.

"Shoulda gone bow in with a sea anchor," Tommy said.

Again, Jacob didn't respond.

Hour after hour, the *Phoenix* continued its corkscrew motion pushed by the waves. Every time a big wave crashed over them, Jamie shuddered along with the boat. In his head, he knew that they were safer in the cabin than they would be on deck, but he felt trapped and started to wonder what he would do if they capsized or one of the masts broke. He thought about his escape route and realized it wouldn't matter. At least his stomach didn't betray him.

The storm passed by noon the following day, the sun came out, and the regular trade winds returned. Large swells from the storm remained, but the *Phoenix* handled them easily, and the crew relaxed. Jacob scrutinized the boat to ensure nothing had broken and no lines had frayed and needed to be replaced. When he got out the sextant to take the noon sight, he asked Jamie to join him. "You want to learn how to do this?" he asked.

"Oh, yes. Do you think I can?"

"Can what?"

"Learn how?"

"I wouldn't be asking you if I didn't think you could."

Fogo was at the helm, and Tommy was dozing with his back against the mizzen. When he heard the conversation, he asked, "Why we need three people to know how to navigate?"

Jacob didn't answer him. The next time the watch changed, Tommy told Jamie, "You be careful, pissant. He just being nice. We don't need you. Pudd get better, you be gone."

For the remainder of the voyage, Jamie studied navigation under the tutelage of Jacob. He learned how to use the sextant, how to use the Nautical Almanac, and how to plot courses. In addition, he learned how to read the charts that were on board. By the end of two weeks, Jacob had Jamie doing all the navigating and log entries for their watches. Jacob checked his work less and less as they approached Barbados. Jamie became more comfortable asking Jacob questions and less anxious when Jacob would quiz him. Every time Tommy said something to him out of the hearing of the others, he ignored him.

With his arm healed, Pudd now started taking a turn in the watch rotation and would spell Jacob or Tommy on one or two of their watches each day. Jamie pressed Pudd for more stories about ports in America and the kinds of boats and cargoes that sailed in and out of them. He learned about schooners carrying ice and granite from Maine to New York and farther south. He learned about carrying coal and cotton from the South to New York and New England ports.

During the storm, Jamie had wondered whether his fantasies about being a seaman were just that, fantasies. He never wanted to be that scared again. But, as they approached Bridgetown in Barbados, the lazy days and nights in the trade winds and his growing confidence as a sailor, and now as a navigator, erased the memories of the storm and his fears.

Jamie was on the twelve to four watch with Pudd the last night out from Barbados when he asked Pudd about the storm and the disagreement between Tommy and Jacob. "Were you worried, Pudd?"

"That storm? Naw. Been in much worse. *Phoenix* be a good boat and most of our cargo below deck, so weight keeps her on her keel."

"What was going on with Tommy?"

"Tommy after his own boat. Thinks he knows more than Jacob. We could o' headed into the wind and rode it out on a sea anchor like him wanting to do. Would a been fine that way, too."

"What's a sea anchor?"

"Same thing as a drogue. Same idea. Only boat's bow into the wind. It's a tougher ride like a horse buckin' but less risk to rudder—both work. I'd rather run off like we did. A hell of a lot easier on the body. Less noisy, too. Easier to sleep."

"You slept?"

"Sure. What else you gonna do? You get scared?"

"A little."

"Down below? Trapped?"

"Yeah."

"Safest place to be. You'll get used to it."

"It happen a lot?"

"Storm like that? Hell no. First one like that in probably ten or twenty trips. Relax. You did great. You ready for Bridgetown?"

"Guess so."

"Bridgetown's big. Not as big as Cork or New York, but big. And rum, lots and lots of rum. Shitty harbor, though. Swells come in and make it rolly as all get out. We'll use the wharf to load and unload. Other than that, we'll hang on a hook in the harbor. Row back and forth. Fogo loves the place. Knows it inside out. Stick with him, and he'll make sure you have a good time. He'll probably take you to Nelson's Arms. He loves that place. You ever drunk rum?"

"No."

"Best rum in the world, and cheap here. You stick with Fogo. He likes you. He'll take good care of you."

They anchored out in the harbor the first night, and no one went ashore. Then, early the next morning, a steam-driven tugboat pulled alongside. Jacob and Tommy tended the lines while Fogo and Jamie raised and stowed the anchor.

Jamie had seen pictures of steamboats and had seen a couple of them in the harbor in Queenstown, but those were paddle wheel boats. This tug didn't have any paddle wheels. "How's it move?" He asked Pudd.

"It's got a thing called a propeller that's attached to a shaft. Engine turns the shaft. Shaft turns the propeller."

Pudd's explanation left Jamie wholly bewildered. Shaft, he understood, but how did a propeller work? He knew he would have to see it and have someone else explain it to him. He wondered if Pudd knew how a propeller worked. Maybe Jacob did.

With no sails to raise, they were alongside the wharf within thirty minutes. The wagons were already there, and they immediately started unloading the barrels containing the pork and butter. The barrels were much easier to handle than the lumber had been, and by mid-afternoon, the *Phoenix* was empty, except for the keg of Madeira.

Jacob went to the end of the wharf to talk to the agent and sign the papers. Each barrel had been opened and inspected during the unloading, and everything was in order. When Jacob returned to the boat, he told them they would be in Bridgetown for three, possibly four nights before they could take on their cargo of rum. "Seven boats ahead of us. He wants us to get off the wharf now. Tug's not available, so we'll warp off and drift out to where we'll anchor. Wind's with us.

"Jamie, you and Fogo launch the dinghy. Tie up to the bow while we drift out in case we get a wind shift, and we need you to do a bit of pulling. Be a human tug you two. Get going."

The sun still had a couple of hours to set when the five of them tied the *Phoenix*'s dingy up to a floating dock at the far end of the wharf, close to the main street of Bridgetown. The road alongside the waterfront was busy with horse-drawn wagons carrying different goods to the schooners lined up bow to stern loading or unloading. The workers were primarily Black, and Jamie couldn't understand what they were saying to one another. As they climbed up the ramp from the dock, he asked Fogo, "What language's that? I thought Barbados was British."

"Banjan. It's a kind of English. Whites don't speak it. Africans use it. Drives Brits crazy."

"How come you know so much about Barbados?"

"Got stranded here for close to a year after me boat got sold out from under me, and the new master wanted his own crew. I probably coulda found another berth but decided to stay awhile. Got a job working sugar cane doing the counting for the field manager, making sure Africans and Irish kept up. Made good money but right boring and hot. Got lucky and signed on with Jacob when he come through over a year ago. You ready to have some fun?"

"Sure. What you got in mind?"

"Surprise, Jamie. Gonna be a surprise. You after liking it for sure."

Jacob gathered them together at the top of the ramp. "Before we split up, back here by midnight. You not here; you're on your own tonight. Dinghy goes with me. Back in the morning to pick you up, you not here when I go. You ready, Pudd?"

"Ready as ever," Pudd said.

"Come on, Jamie," Fogo said. "We be going before things get too crowded. Lot a crews here."

"Where we going?"

"You'll see. Tonight, you become a man. Got to get you all taught up for your dolly, so you don't disappoint her, and I know just the wagtail to do you. First, though, to Nelson's Arms. We be getting some of the best rum on the island into you."

Fogo didn't warn him. Jamie was thirsty and gulped his first swallow of 'the best rum on the island.' He tried not to show Fogo the agony he was in as the rum burned his throat and started his eyes watering. Fogo was watching him and started to laugh. The bartender also saw what was happening and brought over a glass of water and half a lime for Jamie to suck on. Fogo was laughing hard by this time. "First time," Fogo said to the bartender, who was also smiling.

"You need to take it easy, Jamie."

"How can you drink this stuff?"

"Heh, wait a minute. I saw you drink whiskey the first night on the boat, back in Cork."

"Yeah, but that was good Irish whiskey, and I knew enough to sip it. I thought this was like a beer or something."

"You gonna be learning a lot tonight. We be trying this a different way."

Fogo had the bartender bring over some limes, sugar, and water. Then, Fogo showed him how to mix it. Three drinks later, Jamie said, "Yeah. It's good this way. Yeah. I like this."

"Told you. Good, and now it be time to be on our way."

"Where we going?"

"Great place. Best women on the whole damned island."

"Oh, shite. I don't know if I can do this, Treasa…"

"She be grateful that you be experienced and know what to do. You doing this for her, after all. Got to remember that."

At the time, Jamie and the rum thought Fogo had an entirely reasonable point of view. So the two of them left Nelson's Arms and walked up Broad Street.

Her name was Adanna, and she was lighter than the other women Jamie had seen on the streets on the way to the 'best guest house in Bridgetown.' Adanna greeted Fogo warmly when the two young men walked into the parlor. She kissed Fogo on both cheeks. He hugged her and turned to say hello to the other women sitting scattered about the room. "Told you we smart to come early," Fogo said to Jamie. Then he whispered something to Adanna and again turned to Jamie, "She after taking real good care of you."

Adanna smiled at Jamie, reached out, took his hand, and led him upstairs and down a hall to a bedroom on the back of the house. She opened the door and guided Jamie inside. She walked over to the bed and sat down. Then she patted the bed next to her and said, "Here, sit. Let's talk."

Fogo was in the parlor talking to two of the women when Adanna came down the stairs leading Jamie by the hand an hour later. When they reached the bottom of the stairs, Adanna turned, held Jamie's face in her hands, kissed Jamie on both cheeks, and said, "I hope you come back soon. I'd love to see you again."

Jamie smiled at her and said, "Maybe tomorrow. We're here for a couple of days."

"That would be wonderful. I'll look forward to it. You're adorable." Then she turned and looked at Fogo, "Thank you for bringing your friend."

Fogo paid Adanna with money that Jacob and Pudd had given him. There was enough left for Jamie to return the following day, but only for a half an hour.

No one had seen Tommy for the three days the *Phoenix* hung on her anchor in Carlisle Bay. On the fourth day, the tug was available and pulled them into the wharf. The wagons were waiting, and with

Tommy still missing, the four of them started loading the barrels of rum onto the boat. There were also barrels of molasses. The loading went quickly, and the tug again pulled them out into the harbor, where they anchored the boat.

When they rowed back into the dock, Pudd was in the bow going over his list of the provisions that they still needed to get on board for the crew. He asked Jacob, "What you think? I figure him in?"

"Yeah. Arse want his voyage shares; he be here."

When they reached the top of the ramp, Tommy was standing there. "Thought we was loading tomorrow."

"Fuck you," Pudd said.

"You said you wouldn't be a crip no more, and you got the Irish brat. You didn't need me."

Jacob didn't say anything to Tommy. He just looked at him. Tommy ignored him. "Come on, Pudd. Let's get the supplies. Everybody back here in three hours. We leave soon as everything's aboard."

Jacob and Pudd climbed onto the waiting wagon they had hired to help them with their shopping. Barbados was big and spread out, and they didn't want to be carrying things from one place to another.

When Jacob and Pudd left, Tommy turned to Jamie and said, "We don't need you no more. Row out and get your things. You're staying here with the Redlegs."

"No, I'm not," Jamie said. "Jacob didn't say I was staying here."

"Jacob didn't say anything about that," Fogo said. "You sounding crazy, Tommy."

"Not your business, Fogo. You keep still."

Tommy walked up to Jamie and pushed him in the chest. "You heard me. We don't need you. You staying. I'm the first mate and navigator. Get it. Now go fetch your things, you good for nothin' Redleg Irish pissant." He pushed Jamie again, harder than he had the first time. It was a mistake.

The rage that had been contained for weeks exploded. Jamie slugged Tommy in the stomach, and when Tommy bent over, he socked him on the temple. Tommy toppled to the ground. Jamie jumped on top of him and started hitting him in the face and head as hard as he could. He was crying and hitting. He couldn't stop. He didn't hear Tommy's nose breaking or see his lips split. He didn't see the welts form on Tommy's cheeks or the blood under Tommy's left eye. He didn't feel Fogo trying to pull him off. He just kept hitting and crying and shouting, "No!"

Two men came over to help Fogo pull Jamie off. As they did so, Jamie started kicking. He didn't know his right foot broke two of Tommy's ribs. The three of them finally wrestled Jamie to the ground and pinned him there. Tommy lay next to him, unconscious.

When they let Jamie up, Fogo told him, "Get in the dinghy. I'm rowing you out and then coming back. Jacob will figure this out."

One of the two men asked Fogo what he wanted to do with Tommy. "Let's lie him down on this bench. Our skipper will handle it. Be back in a couple of hours."

When the *Phoenix* left Barbados on June 12, 1880, Tommy Hynes was in his berth. He had bandages wrapped around his middle to keep his ribs in place. His face had been wiped clean of blood. His nose was twisted worse than it had been, and one eye was swollen shut. Pudd had him sip some broth and Madeira through his split lips. He told him, "You're a lucky bastard. The kid would've killed you if Fogo didn't stop him. And Jacob? Jacob could a left you there to rot. He be feeling sorry for you, I guess. I don't know why. You're one dumb son of a bitch. When Fogo told us what happened, I thought Jacob beach you sure. I'd keep my damn mouth shut for the next two weeks if I was you."

They were on a broad reach now with the wind steady over the starboard side. Fogo was at the helm, and Jamie and Jacob were sitting in the cockpit. No one was talking. After an hour, Jacob said, "You want to go to New York? Up to you to get us there. You be doing the navigation. I'm going to sleep. Don't wake me unless the wind changes."

Jamie was on the midnight to four watch when he became eighteen. No one mentioned it. Jamie had forgotten about it until he made the log entry at the end of the watch and wrote down the date.

Fifteen days later, Pudd saw the sails of three schooners and the stacks of a steamboat all headed in the same direction. He called everyone on deck. The wind was coming out of the Southwest, and it was hazy. They couldn't see the shore. "Sandy Hook?" Jacob asked.

"Not yet. Hazy as hell. Damned smoky southwester."

"Jamie, what you think?"

"They're further in and on the same bearing we are. So, they may see it."

"Stay with it then."

An hour later, they saw the lighthouse. Fogo shouted, "Brooklyn, here we come, and we got some rum."

Jacob said, "Pudd, you and Fogo go forward and keep a lookout, would ya? It'll start to get crowded coming into the harbor."

"We're miles out," Fogo said.

"Come with me, lad. " Pudd said, "Your eyes are better than mine," and whispered, "He wants to talk to Jamie. Alone."

After they moved forward, Jacob came and stood alongside Jamie. "Me and Pudd been talking 'bout you. Know you want to go to New York, but you also want to make some money. What if you were to stay with the *Phoenix* for a few trips, maybe even a year or two. Pay you same share as Fogo.

"Tommy be seeing the last of this boat when we get to Canada. Too much trouble. I could use another navigator, and you got real good at it."

"You serious? Really?"

"Why you always questioning when I say something to you?"

"I'm sorry. I've had my heart set on New York so long I haven't thought about nuthin' else."

"I'll need an answer before we leave in a couple of days."

"Okay, sure" Jamie paused before saying, "Thank you, sir. Means a lot to me, you asking."

"One other thing. Know you didn't expect to make anything on this trip. Just wanted free ride, but we decided you should get a quarter of Tommy's share. I already told him. Told him he was leaving, too."

On Sunday, June 27, 1880, eighteen-year-old Jamie Buckley climbed up onto the wharf in Brooklyn, New York, with money in his pocket.

July 2, 1999
HOME TOWN BOY by Michael Buckley

"The summer people will buy anything if they think it's made locally." Thus proclaimed my younger sister, Maude, when she was twelve years old. "I don't get it. When they're home, they brag about buying imported stuff, but when they're here, they want local things. They're confusing."

One day she was out in the pasture next to the road that goes by our house. She was walking the fence line to make sure it was still intact after a windstorm. Sometimes a limb or a tree would fall on the fence, a post would break, and an opportunity would be created for one or more of our adventurous sheep, usually rams, to explore the outside world.

As usual, she had Twerp with her. Twerp is a Border Collie, and, in addition to our sheep, he has been herding Maude for years. Twerp was the runt of his litter and thus his name. Though small, he knew his herding job—children and sheep—and did it well. He was also fearless. The biggest ram was no match for Twerp's speed, bark, or a nip or two if needed. Twerp and Maude had a lot in common and were best friends. Our Great Pyrenees guard dog, Monster, tagged along twenty yards behind.

While perambulating the pasture fence, a car slowly drove by with all the windows open. Summer sightseers. The way Maude tells it, a young girl was hanging out the back window and excitedly shouted, "Look, Daddy! Sheep." With that, Daddy dutifully pulled over to the side of the road, and his passengers exited the car. They crossed over to where Twerp and Maude were. "Can I pet one?" the little girl asked Maude.

"Sure," Maude said and went and collected a lamb away from its momma, who, after a mild protest, followed them over to the fence. Monster was not too happy with this situation. He let it be known and positioned himself between the strangers and his charges, but Maude told him to be quiet and lie down, which he did. The little girl reached through the fence, petted the lamb, oohed and awed, and asked her mother, who was busy taking a picture, "Can we get one? He's so soft."

According to Maude, it was apparent that "he" was a "she." It was also clear the little girl was oblivious to the size of the momma sheep who was standing right there and was the future size of the adorable little creature that the little girl was now in love with.

"Oh, honey, we have no place to keep him." Mommy wasn't very observant of sexual apparatus either. This blatant ignorance of such matters irritated Maude. Farm kids learned the differences early.

The youngster was clearly disappointed, but the mother offered an alternative that was to change Maude's life. She said, "Perhaps we could buy some yarn from these nice people, and I could make you some mittens or a scarf."

I am very proud of my sister for what she did not say. She did not say that they could buy lamb meat from our farm at the Island Market. On the other hand, the mother did not understand the ten or more steps it takes to get wool from the back of a sheep to yarn that is ready to be used for knitting. So, Maude lied and said that some of the yarn in the Woolworth's store in Bath was from our farm. Who knows? It might have been.

However, the conversation did give my entrepreneurial, 4H member, kid sister an idea. Over the following winter, she learned everything she could about processing fleece. She even tried shearing once but lost that battle to an unhappy, very large wether. Wethers are castrated males. They are more docile than rams, but they can be imposing, and this was an older gentleman who had been sheared many times and did not want to be experimented on by a rank amateur.

Still determined, Maude begged my parents, they relented, and soon we had all the necessary equipment or had made arrangements where she could use someone else's equipment. Finally, my father agreed to give her some fleece at shearing time.

The following summer Maude was open for business. No lemonade stand for Maude— she was in the yarn business, and most importantly, it was locally made. She put up a sign on route 127 that I am sure was illegal. It directed people to our farm for "Locally Made Yarn." But heck, she was only a thirteen-year-old kid and wasn't this all very cute?

She sold several skeins on the first Saturday of the grand opening and was glowing, but she had a problem. At dinner, she asked, "What's the name of our farm?" My father said, "Convey Sheep."

"That's the name of our sheep, not our farm."

"People call it the Convey place or the Convey farm, but we sell the sheep as Convey Sheep," my mother clarified."

My father added, "It's been Convey Sheep ever since Angus Convey started it…"

"I know the story," Maude interrupted, "And then Grandpa Will inherited it, but since nothing ever changes in Georgetown, it's still the Convey Farm even though you are the third generation of Buckleys to own it. I need to have a farm name for my wool. Maybe I'll call it 'Buckley Farm Wool' or 'Maude 's Wool.' I like that, 'Maude's Wool.' Thank you." And with that, she left the table and spent the rest of the evening writing *Maude 's Wool* in every possible way until she found one that suited her. She now had a logo. The copier in the corner of the living room that served as the office for Convey Sheep was used to turn out wrappers with the *Maude's Wool* logo for the skeins.

Well, that little stand grew and grew over the next couple of years. First, she conned or talked my father into having dedicated sheep for *Maude's Wool*. Then, she talked or conned her friends into helping, and a business was born.

Seeing the emerging interest in "locally" grown wool, she added products. We always had chickens and a sizable vegetable garden. Our eggs, tomatoes, beans, and zucchini started appearing as *Maude's locally grown produce*. Maude's stand was becoming quite popular. However, product extensions ended when my father had to go into Bath to grocery shop for un-local eggs and vegetables for our family one Saturday. He put his foot down. Enough was enough. Reluctantly, Maude accepted that but then tried to sell him on the idea of cutting down some of our trees and selling 'local' firewood to the summer people. That was a non-starter.

Careers get started in the most unexpected ways. Today *Maude's Wool* is alive and well as a thriving yarn shop down in Portland. Our herd has shrunk over the years while her business has grown. I know she hasn't washed out a piece of fleece in years, and her yarn comes from all over the world. Every once in a while, though, there is a knock on our door from someone who visited Georgetown years ago, and they want to know if we are still selling our locally grown wool. They do use the word local. Maude was right about summer people; sometimes they are confusing. She tries to be accommodating. Some of the yarn she sells in Portland is labeled *imported*; some of it is labeled *local*.

Chapter Nine: Memorial Day

When I woke up Sunday morning, I was anxious. Years ago, in the dark time, my therapist taught me to call it free-floating anxiety if I couldn't immediately pinpoint the source. "Don't fight it, Mike," he told me. "It's just a feeling. Check for actual threats, physical and emotional. If there are none, see if you can detect any clues about what triggered it. Ask yourself, why now?" The sources will emerge over time, he would say. Anxiety was an old friend by now, so I didn't get overly disturbed when it came visiting. I knew it would resolve, and I knew I'd figure it out if I didn't try too hard.

An hour later, I sat on the bench at the end of the pier with my second cup of coffee. The sun did its best to dry up the morning fog. The light dispersed through the pines on the other side of the cove. I sat, sipped, and watched the fog dissipate.

I knew what was bothering me. My sister, Maude, was coming today; tomorrow would be Memorial Day. Maude and I would argue, yet again, about whether or not I would go to the Memorial Day parade in Bath. We've been having that argument every Memorial Day since Hannah died. Maude lost the argument every year, and Maude rarely lost an argument. I would stay home.

There was no wind. The cove was a perfect mirror reflecting everything above the water's surface—boats, empty moorings, pilings. The only sounds were a few squawking gulls circling Marv Blastow's dinghy as his son Matt rowed them out to Marv's lobster boat. They would only pull a few strings of pots this morning. After that, they had to get back in time to make Matt's band rehearsal before the parade. Matt was in his last year at Morse High School in Bath and played the trumpet.

Everyone in the Buckley family used to go watch Maude and my father march in the parade. Maude had been a majorette in high school and spent hours practicing with her baton during her first couple of years at Morse. When she saw that the cheerleaders got all the attention, she gave up twirling and went out for the cheerleading squad. She made it and spent hours practicing cheers. Now she was an entrepreneur, a small business owner, and a fixture in two communities.

Maude's Yarn Shops in Portland and Freeport were always busy on holiday weekends, so for years, she never made it up to Tír until after Labor Day. However, things changed when she hit her sixties and decided that she did not have to oversee every minute detail of her empire of fifteen employees and two stores.

It's only an hour's drive from Portland to Georgetown in regular traffic. Maude's an early riser, so I was not surprised when I heard her Land Cruiser coming down the hill at seven-thirty. I got up and walked towards the cottage. She opened the back of her car, and her Border Collies, Fire and Ice, bounded up onto the porch. They stopped short when they saw a strange miniature poodle curled up in the sun. Slowly, they approached Charlie, who got up and stood still. He let them do the first sniffing before he returned the greeting. Greetings done, Charlie barked and ran off the porch, trying to entice them into a game of tag. The two collies weren't interested and came over to get some attention from me as I was heading to greet Maude.

"What the hell is that?" Maude asked, nodding towards Charlie.

"Charlie. Wendy's dog."

"Wendy's here already?"

"For the summer."

"Yeah, I know. Hot damn. Where is she? I can't wait to see her."

"Still asleep."

"I'll go wake her up."

"No, you won't. Rina's here, too. They were up late last night."

"Oh, alright. You good?"

"Yeah. You want coffee?"

"Bags first."

Maude never married, or she married her empire, or her empire married her. Hannah and I would go back and forth about which was which and whether there was a difference or not. Maude could be controlling and featured herself as the wise elder in the family even though she was my junior by a few years. My offspring had a love-hate relationship with her. She could be the most generous person alive. When the kids were young, Maude showered them with presents and attention. She took them on trips to Disney, Washington, D.C., and on a cruise to Alaska.

She showed up for events: recitals, games, graduations. She was godmother to all four. Maude also had a habit of telling them how they should run their lives. On several occasions, I had to remind her that they were our children, not hers. Being Hannah, Hannah would remind me that 'She means well, and she doesn't have kids of her own.'

Over the years, Maude has had many relationships with many men of various measures of unsuitability or unavailability. Two of them got to live with her—one for two years, one for three. No one ever made it to four. Eventually, she settled down with a succession of Border Collies, whom she found to be much more obedient than her male companions.

When she traveled on buying trips, we became convenient pet sitters, which was fine with us. Her dogs were always more well behaved than whoever our Great Pyrenees of the moment was. Maude always had intact males, and we always had spayed females so that they would get along most of the time. Her Border Collies would ignore our Great Pyrs, probably thinking they were stupid dolts by comparison. They were.

Maude competed in sheep trials with her dogs. She was one of the few female handlers on the circuit. It was at competitions where she often found her male companions. She would bring them around from time to time when she was in her twenties, thirties, forties, and even into her early fifties. She was always excited about the newest potential, although the excitement levels decreased with age until she settled for the collies. We were always polite and welcoming to the male novelty she would bring, but our excitement also decreased with age. Would this one make it through a year of holidays? Our kids started placing bets.

Maude was as fit at seventy as she was at thirty. Her hair was the same color white as mine, and there was no question that we were siblings, according to everyone who knew us. My mother said if we weren't separated by age, we would look like twins. As we got older and the age difference became less noticeable, I guess we did. I didn't see what everyone else seemed to see, but I took their word for it. I had a good six inches of height on her, and she was stockier than I was.

When Maude was at Tír, she always stayed in the same room. She had grown up in that room and was not about to give it up. It was at the opposite end of the hall from where I could hear Wendy and Rina stirring. Given that the second bottle of Sauvignon Blanc was empty and the wood next to the fireplace was depleted, I knew they had been up late.

I had cut out the Memorial Day event notice in the paper and put it under a magnet on the refrigerator door. I knew Maude would want it, and I thought Wendy might. I felt very considerate getting it for them since there was no way in hell I was going. I didn't want to fight Maude about my going or not going but knew that it would at least be discussed.

> *Several groups will perform services at Bath cemeteries Monday morning, mostly at Oak Grove Cemetery. The Sons of the Union Veterans will hold a service at 8 a.m., followed by the Women's*

Auxiliary at 8:15 a.m., the Sons of the American Legion at 8:30 a.m. and the American Legion at 8:45 a.m. A wreath will be laid at Waterfront Park at 9:30 a.m.

The parade will begin assembling at 10 a.m. at the American Legion Post 21 headquarters and start at 10:30 a.m. The route continues to Lincoln Street, pausing for a wreath-laying ceremony at the soldier's monument on Centre Street, and concludes at Library Park.

With Fire and Ice in tow, Maude brought her bags upstairs, and I could hear her talking to the girls, but I could not make out what they were saying. When she came back down, I said, "So much for letting them sleep. Have you had breakfast?"

"No. What you got?"

"I'm going up to Judd and Pat's. You want to come?"

"Michael Buckley. Your granddaughter just arrived yesterday. This is her first morning here. Shouldn't you be here for breakfast?"

"There's stuff here for the girls. They'll be fine."

"Sit," she ordered.

"Now what?"

"Just sit." I did as I was told.

"I love you, brother, but sometimes you are just plain dumb. You've told me over and over again how much you want to keep Tír as the sanctuary for your family. You say it's one of the most important things in your life. Ritual, my dear brother. Ritual. What does one do at Tír on the first day anyone comes?"

"I suppose blueberry pancakes."

"You suppose? God, are you thick. It's always blueberry pancakes. Where have you been your whole life?"

"Come on; it's too early. No native blueberries until the end of July."

"So, you get the imposters from New Jersey and make a big deal out of them not being as good as the ones they'll have in July."

"Jesus, Maude, who gives a shit?"

"People who are trying to hold their family together. Call Judd and Pat and ask them to come down here and tell them why. You know they'll come. Do you have any bananas?"

"Yes."

"Pancake mix?"

"Gluten-free for Wendy."

"Yuk. When the girls come down, make a big deal about bananas rather than blueberries."

"But Wendy knows I was invited…"

"Be sweet and loving and say it is her first morning at Tír, and that is more important. I'm going up to unpack. Ice, Fire. Come."

The two dogs followed her back upstairs. I called Judd and Pat. Pat said, "Of course. We'll bring our stuff down. First pot luck of the summer. Love it."

I started preparing breakfast. I was going to cook bacon for everyone even though Wendy wouldn't eat it. At least I could make a big deal out of the maple syrup being native and from thirty miles from here, the Goranson Farm in Dresden. For years we'd drive there every March to replenish our supply. I hadn't gone this year. Living alone, I still had plenty left from last year's trip. I figured that we should have plenty of food with whatever Pat was bringing. I poured out the rest of the coffee into the big carafe and started another pot.

Judd and Pat arrived with bagels they had bought in Portland when they landed yesterday as well as fresh orange juice, fruit, and a jar full of Bloody Marys. I had told Pat I was doing pancakes, so she didn't bother bringing eggs, but she did bring lox, a red onion, and capers to go with the cream cheese and chive mixture for the bagels.

She knew that was my favorite breakfast.

Everyone was full of catch-up. It was spontaneous, rambling, and disorganized. We'd circle back with questions we had forgotten to ask. Judd and Pat were supposed to be retired, but both had consulting contracts with their former employers. Judd's ad agency had climbed out of the recession, and they were back on their feet. Pat's lobbying firm had gotten a new contract from the Costa Rican Ministry of Economy, Industry, and Commerce. She was concerned about whether they would be able to help much. "This administration doesn't even know anyplace exists south of Mexico except to stir the pot in Venezuela and praise a dictator in Brazil."

Rina told us about her semester in Scotland and demonstrated her new accent. She loved St. Andrews and was thinking about returning and possibly doing a Ph.D. program in collaboration with Ghent in Belgium after graduating from Duke. Her focus would be International Relations. I immediately became comparative and judgmental. I had a hard time imagining Wendy talking like that.

Eventually, the talk turned to Memorial Day. "I can fit everyone and the dogs in my Land Cruiser," Maude announced when we finished breakfast and got dishes stacked. "No need to bring two cars. Parking's going to be hard." I started to say I would not be going, but when I looked around the table, I saw Maude looking at me, daring me to say I wasn't going. I kept my mouth shut. I didn't want to start an argument in front of everyone, especially Wendy and Rina. I didn't want to go. But that look. We would all go in Maude's car.

My father always marched in his Navy uniform. It always fit. My mother would make sure it was freshly pressed and that the ribbons were all in the right place. When I came back from Vietnam and got discharged, it was assumed that I would march and that Dad and I would march together. It was the last thing I wanted to do, and I begged off. No one pressed me to march, but I did go. The war was still on, and Memorial Day at home was anything but a celebration of

Vietnam vets.

My first year home, there were demonstrators with signs: "Baby Killers," "Bring Home Our Boys," and "War is Senseless." A few shouted things at those in uniform, especially at the marchers my age. Some demonstrators chained themselves to trees where the march ended in Library Park. The war had done enough damage to me without people piling it on at home. Fuck'em. They hadn't been there. They had no idea. No way would I ever march.

My father was furious at the protestors. The year I got home, he left his position in the parade and threatened two of them. A friend pulled him back into the parade. That night he said, "I'm going to march in every damned parade they have in that god-damned town, and when I can't march anymore, I'll ride." He did, right up until he died, and his uniform never had to be tailored to a changing body.

When Hannah and I got together, she insisted we at least go. At first, it was for my father. Then it was for our family and eventually for me. She never asked me to march, but she commented on the changes as attitudes towards Vietnam vets changed. The attitudes might have changed, but the damage hadn't. I had gotten rid of my uniforms as soon as I was discharged, and I wanted to get rid of my medals, but my mother confiscated them and then turned them over to Hannah. So now they were in a small hand-made wooden box on the fireplace mantle in Tír. My son, Jesse, had made the box in the woodshop at school and had carved my initials into the top. He had made it for me for my birthday and was so proud of it that there was no possibility of it not being used for its intended purpose.

I knew Hannah was behind our son's effort. She thought John Kerry was an idiot for encouraging Vietnam vets to get rid of their medals. She had also encouraged me to join the A1 Skyraider Association and go to their reunions. A doctor at the V.A. had also mentioned it to me, perhaps to Hannah as well. I never did. It seemed sick to me. Why would I want to get together with a group of guys I didn't know and spend a weekend eating and drinking too much? For what, to celebrate that we all flew the same WWII airplane together and bombed the hell out of villages and people we didn't know and rarely saw? Golf was always on the agenda, and I didn't play golf before, during, or after Vietnam. It was all a bunch of 'hurrah' bullshit.

Memorial Day was the next day. I didn't have to face it yet. By noon the fog had cleared. Wendy and Rina took off to go shopping with Judd and Pat. There was still a chill in the air, but Maude said she wanted to go for a sail. The *Redhead*, the family schooner, was still in the boatyard at Robinhood, but Sonas, our Herrshoff 12 ½, was bobbing on her mooring in the cove. The boat was ready to go, so I said sure. Neither of us was hungry after all the food we had put away at breakfast. Maude made sure there was enough water for the dogs, and I grabbed the sails from the shed.

Judd says that when you row towards or away from your boat, you should be able to pause, look at it, and relish how beautiful it is. Nat Herreshoff was sixty-six when he designed the 12 ½ in 1914. The boat is so beautiful, so perfect, it is still being built. It's just under sixteen feet of sailing elegance –twelve and a half feet on the waterline. Perfect proportions. My grandfather bought ours for a few bucks from a summer person who was wiped out by The Depression. Grandpa Will had done it as a gesture of kindness. There is no way he could have predicted we would be rebuilding and racing that boat for eighty-five years.

Our cove, Heron Cove, is formed by a peninsula that juts out from the east coast of Georgetown. The entrance to the cove faces south and is relatively narrow. That means the cove is well protected, but for a sailor, it often means having to tack back and forth through this narrow opening until you get out into the mouth of the Sheepscot. From there, it's clear sailing. In a small, responsive boat like the 12

½, there's nothing to it. In a larger sailboat, it can be a challenge. But, returning with the wind behind you is easy for any boat.

Maude took the helm, which was fine with me. I could sail *Sonas* whenever I wanted to. I would also skipper *Sonas* in the Erascohegan races on Wednesday nights and Saturday as well as Sunday afternoons. Once Maude and I cleared the nun at the entrance to the cove, we headed out into the Gulf of Maine. We would have about three hours of good wind if the weather gods behaved.

We didn't talk much. It was nice to be together, be on the water, and be on a boat we had both grown up on. The wind stayed steady at around nine knots, with an occasional gust up towards fifteen that would heel us over and get us up on the windward side.

As we returned to the cove late in the afternoon, Maude asked, "Lobster tonight?"

"Wendy's a vegetarian."

"So?"

"There's nothing down at Five I she can eat."

"Corn on the cob, French fries, red potatoes. Have you been down there yet?"

"No."

"Mike, I love that child, but it is my first night here, which means lobster at Five I."

"We could bring them home. We could eat here where her food is."

"Michael. You are very accommodating. What has gotten into you?"

"Maybe I'm learning to channel Hannah."

Wendy's response to the plan was, "I have some leftovers from last night. I'll bring them with me, and I could live on corn on the cob and French fries. Besides, there's ice cream."

Monday morning, Maude again played the 'Wendy Card' when I

told her I was rethinking my attendance at the parade. So, on Memorial Day morning, she made sure we left on time, found a good parking place, and got situated with chairs in the middle of the parade route, where the bands almost always played.

The police and their motorcycles with their blue lights flashing started things off. They were followed by several firetrucks. Next came political people, then vets walking and riding in cars depending on which war. Classic cars with drivers and passengers dressed in period garb were next. Then came the first band.

It was the high school band. I stood up with the others. Maybe it was seeing Matt Blastow with his trumpet. They stopped right in front of us. The drum major turned, blew his whistle, and held up three fingers. He blew the whistle again, and the trumpeters raised their instruments. When the command came to begin, it wasn't a military march; it was the trumpet fanfare from the movie *Rocky*. Matt was playing his heart out. People were clapping. We all stood. The majorettes were waving at people to start singing with them, "Getting strong now." Wendy, Rina, Judd, Pat, and Maude joined in. I started softly, almost a mumble. Maude took my hand, turned, and sang right at me. I couldn't look at her; it was too intense. I turned back to the band and sang a little louder.

Chapter Ten: Rachel and Wendy

It was early Tuesday morning when I carried Maude's bag out to her car. The sun had brightened the sky without showing itself. Between the breeze and the early morning chill, I wished I had thrown my jacket on. Maude had gone back upstairs to wake Wendy and say goodbye. She seemed to be taking forever. Fire and Ice stayed with Charlie and me.

I had a headache. The previous evening, we had eaten with the Fishman's. Memorial Day: simple BBQ food of hamburgers, veggie burger for Wendy, and a couple of salads. Rina had baked a shortcake and had submerged it with June-bearing strawberries and whipped cream.

There had been lots of wine, and I had picked up a large bottle of Baileys to go with the inevitable games. Last night it was Code Names as usual with the Buckleys against the Fishmans. The Fishmans won more than their share. Maude and I had a hard time figuring out Wendy's clues. Rina suggested we switch around so she and Wendy were on the same team. It became evident that our problem with Wendy's clues was generational. Rina had no trouble with them. Aided by Pat, they destroyed Judd, Maude, and me.

When Maude finally came downstairs, she headed for the pier. "Where you going?" I asked. "Thought you wanted to get on the road. It's cold out there."

"So, get your jacket and come with me. I want a last look."

She waited while I got my jacket and all of us went, including Charlie.

Grandpa Will had built two benches facing one another at the end of the pier. Maude sat down on one and motioned me to sit opposite her. "You know you've got to snap out of it."

"What are you talking about?"

"You're morose. Sometimes you're sour; sometimes, you're sullen. You can be irritable as hell. You know there's a reason people don't come the way they used to, and it has nothing to do with Hannah's death. It's you."

I stood up, "Enough."

"No, not enough. I'm not through. Sit down for Christ's sake. Wendy's here, and she needs you and deserves more."

I sat back down. Maude continued, "I've seen you go into a death spiral before. When you first came home from Vietnam we didn't know if you would ever pull out. You were damned lucky you met Hannah. You still had enough life in you that she thought you'd be okay, and she was willing to take a chance on you. I don't want to see you go down into that pit again. This time you'd have to crawl out on your own because Hannah's not here."

"Thanks for reminding me."

"Mike. Come on. I know how much you miss her. I wish I had found someone to love as much as you loved her, and she loved you; God bless her. But you're still alive, and your family needs you, especially Wendy. Do you think it's an accident she's here? She could have gone to her father's or stayed in Brattleboro. But she came here. I talked with Rachel. Wendy wanted to come here."

"She came here to play. She doesn't want to do any real work."

"God, you can be thick. Yeah. Maybe she did. Who wouldn't? It's a great place. But it's also you. She has no father she can depend on. Rachel's doing okay, but she's still white-knuckling it at times. This new boss is giving her fits. You're the one rock Wendy can hold on to right now. So, deal with it. Did you know Rachel sat her down before she came and went through a very involved and detailed process of making amends?"

"No."

"Well, she did. She needed to do it as part of her program. But she also didn't want Wendy hearing any stories up here from you or anyone else. It was probably too long in coming, but Rachel finally did it, and, from what she tells me, it went well."

"Why didn't she tell me about it?"

"Come on, Mike, how available have you been? Besides, you haven't exactly been as supportive as you might have been to your youngest."

Maude got up, came over to me, and kissed me on the top of my head. "Call me if you need to talk. I have to get going. One more thing, though."

"What now?"

"Remember what you said you would do when you retired?"

"I'm sure you're about to remind me."

"You know, you can be a real pain in the ass. Alright. I will. You were going to write. Have you? No. You have mastered moping and feeling sorry for yourself, though. Let me suggest something."

"What?"

"Sit here for a minute or two, three or four, or whatever it takes. Just consider what I've said. I know you think Hannah did all the work holding this family together, but it's not true. You both did it. You're a pretty smart guy, brother. Figure out what Wendy needs this summer and make sure she gets it. You may not get another chance. And write something. Don't hound Wendy about her paper. Be a model for her."

Maude looked up and down the cove. She breathed in deeply. "God, I love that smell. Come on, boys. Not you, Charlie."

I took hold of Charlie's collar so he wouldn't follow.

I was angry that Rachel hadn't told me about her conversation with Wendy. Was my relationship with my youngest daughter that dysfunctional? Should I call Rachel? Should I say something to Wendy? Should I do nothing? Hannah and I used to call it "Dilemma Mountain Time." We'd always worked it out together. I sat there running 'what-ifs' in my head. No clarity.

Memories flooded back. Wendy was older now than Rachel had been the summer that had changed everything. Nineteen ninety-six was not a good year for the Buckleys.

The Olympic Summer Games were on in Atlanta, Georgia; the Yankees were having a great year, and young kids were obsessed with Pokémon. Monica Lewinsky was giving blow jobs to Bill Clinton in the Oval Office, and Rachel was doing the same thing, and more, to the steward at the yacht club. Monica Lewinsky was twenty-two, Bill Clinton was forty-nine, Rachel Buckley was sixteen, and Timothy Stark was twenty-three.

I was on the yacht club search committee that had hired Stark. He seemed perfect. He had been on the sailing team all four years at Colgate. He had been a camp counselor teaching sailing for two summers while in college. He was a graduate student studying Atmospheric Sciences at Cornell, and he lived in Boston, so we didn't have to pay any travel expenses. One of our members interviewed him over the Christmas break and said he was great. No other applicants came close.

Attached to the clubhouse was a small studio efficiency for the steward to live in during the summer. It was supposed to be off-limits to everyone else so the steward would have some privacy. For the most part, people respected that. The steward got one day off a week, Mondays, but was inundated with people almost every other day. He was supposed to have evenings free, but it rarely turned out that way with everyone around. We didn't pay much, but we never had any trouble getting people who would take the job for two or three years in a row, usually college or graduate students. Tim Stark came right out of the mold.

The steward at Erascohegan Yacht Club—it was always a young male—had several roles. The biggest was sailing instructor: young kids in the morning on Beetlecats, older kids on Blue Jays every afternoon except Wednesday, and women only on the 12 ½'s Wednesday afternoons. The steward also helped the race committee Wednesday evenings and Saturday and Sunday afternoons. In addition, he had to keep the clubhouse and bathrooms clean and stocked with toilet paper and paper towels. Given the size of the clubhouse, that was a two-hour-a-week task at most. He also had to make everyone smile a lot, have the kids love him, and convince everyone they were having the best summer of their lives.

At the start of the summer, because of Tim Stark, Rachel thought she was. In July, she often said, "This is the best summer." We smiled. We were happy she was happy.

That summer, Rachel worked as a nanny five mornings a week for the Harveys. That gave her a lot of free time to hang out at the club in the afternoon. Steward Tim started asking her to help him out with the afternoon classes. She'd operate the skiff while Tim stood in the stern and barked suggestions to the student sailors through his bullhorn.

By the middle of July, Rachel started disappearing every Monday after finishing up at the Harvey's. At first, we didn't think much of it. Hannah was still working every day at Bath Iron Works. On her way to work, she would drop our sons, Jesse and Joel, off at Robinhood Cove Marina, where they were pumping gas and helping out on the docks.

Our firstborn, Ruth, was away for the summer. She had just finished her junior year at Skidmore and was a senior counselor at Camp Four Winds up in Sargentville. I was in and out with reporting assignments for the Bath Bugle and trying to finish a book I was working on. Rachel was, well, sort of ignored that summer. Except for Ruth, we were all down at Tír from June to September as we always had been. Hannah and I never gave Rachel's free time a second thought. The kids always had free time when they were young.

Jesse picked up on it first. A couple of the teenagers, including

Rachel, had talked Stark into driving them over to a steel drum street party in Wiscasset. Rachel had asked permission to go; we knew who she was going with and didn't think anything more about it. The following day it took some doing to wake her so she could get off to the Harveys. On the way to Robinhood, Jesse asked Hannah if she had seen Rachel when she came home the previous night. Neither one of us had. We were usually in bed by ten. Jesse told Hannah that Rachel didn't get home until eleven and that she had been sitting outside in Tim's car for a long time. He said that when she came in, she was weaving and didn't say anything to him when he asked her if she was okay. Apparently, Jesse had decided to sleep on the porch swing, and Tim's car lights coming down the drive woke him up.

Hannah and I asked Rachel about it that night after dinner as she was about to head down to the yacht club. She said, "Me and Tim were just talking about colleges, and time slipped away. He was telling me about different schools." Rachel had just finished her sophomore year in high school. She had done very well, and we had been talking about colleges, so that didn't seem that unusual to us. Hannah specifically asked if she had been drinking, and she said no. She was telling the truth. They hadn't been drinking. Much later, we found out they had been smoking marijuana. The drinking was reserved for later in the summer to go along with other drugs, tangible and emotional.

Remembering that summer, I felt myself sliding into the pit Maude had warned me about. I couldn't help it. Charlie startled me by pawing at my leg. He wanted to be fed. I got up off the bench and started walking back toward the house. I was furious that Rachel hadn't told me about her conversation with Wendy. It was one thing for her to tell Maude it went well. It was another for Maude to say to me that Wendy might be fragile as a result. I was also angry that she had made no attempt to make amends to Hannah or me when Hannah was still alive. Hannah had died knowing her daughter was in a program to stop drinking, one we didn't have to pay for, but she died not knowing whether or not it was working this time—finally. Hannah had died with that heaviness, with the bitter question of, "What could we have done differently?"

The hell with it. I decided to call Rachel. It was still early, and I might wake her up, but so what? She answered on the third ring. Seeing who was calling, her first question was, "Dad, is Wendy okay?"

"She's fine. I'm not."

"What's wrong?"

"Why didn't you tell me?"

"Tell you what? Do you know what time it is?"

"Yes, I know what time it is. Why didn't you tell me you had talked with Wendy before she came and 'made amends,' whatever that means?"

"What did she say?"

"She didn't say anything. Maude told me."

"Maude. Jesus Christ. That woman can't help herself."

"So?"

"So what?"

"Why didn't you say something to me? Maude says she's upset, and I have to be extra careful with her."

"Oh, Dad. I'm not awake yet, and this is not a conversation I want to have right now. We will, but not right now. I'm sorry I said anything to Maude. Wendy is fine, and Maude is getting in the middle of something and making all sorts of assumptions. Trust me, Wendy's fine. It was not one conversation, it was several, and they've been going on for quite a while now."

"What have you told her?"

"Jesus, do you really want to do this now?"

"Yes, I do. She's here for the summer. I want to know what she knows so I don't put my foot in it."

"Okay." Her voice changed. Patronizing. Patient. "When her boyfriend broke up with her, she crashed. I told you that. She wanted to leave school. I said absolutely no way. So we negotiated she would stick it out to spring break. When she came home, we started talking about breakups, and as we talked, she started asking questions about everything."

"What do you mean everything?"

"Dad. Enough. Why are you so angry?"

A wound had been poked. Again. The Rachel wound. It had never quite scarred over where it was protected to the point where I didn't feel it when someone pushed on it.

"I just want to know what she knows."

"Dad, she's been sitting on questions for years. Until a few years ago, I didn't even know the answers. I knew the facts but not the answers. She wanted to know both. It wasn't just about breaking up with her boyfriend; it was about my life and her life. Apparently, Stephen had asked her about her past…"

"Who's Stephen?"

"He's the boyfriend. He's a good kid. He's a psychology major, though, and he started playing shrink with her…"

"Is that why she broke up with him?"

"God. You're all over the place. First, he broke up with her. He told her she wasn't serious enough about her life. He's a year ahead of her and works his butt off, and that's not Wendy. She wanted to play; he wanted to study.

"She was devastated. When she came home for the break, she wanted to know everything about my life and her life, all the things Stephen had asked her about, and a lot more. So, we started talking. It was way overdue. My AA sponsor helped me with it. Wendy asked me questions. I would answer her, which led to more questions. I told her everything. I didn't leave anything out. There are no secrets between us. You don't have to worry about accidentally saying anything."

"Everything?"

"Yes, Dad, everything. There is something else you should know. When she went back to school, I arranged for her to see a therapist. She also joined an Al-Anon group on campus. So, she's got lots of support. She's doing fine, Dad, really."

I waited a minute before asking, "Why did she really want to come here this summer?"

"How many reasons would you like? In some ways, that's where her life actually began because it's where I started to lose mine. She wants some roots, deep ones, and you're one of those. So is Tír. Remember, she spent summers there when she was young, but I was in shitty shape, and she was always worried about what would happen next. So, she wants a fresh start at Tír. And, she does have this paper to do."

"Everything." I couldn't let go of the word.

"Yes, Dad, everything. It's okay, Dad. It really is okay."

"Maude said you made amends."

"I started doing that when I got sober. It's not a one-time deal."

"How the hell did Maude get involved in all this?"

"My fault. I called her to ask for her advice about a shawl I'm making. She asked about Wendy and what she was doing this summer, and one thing led to another. You know Maude. She's a pit bull."

"So, Wendy's fine?"

"She's still hurting about Stephen, but, basically, she's fine. Are you okay?"

"I'm better now."

"She may have questions for you, too. I'd be surprised if she didn't."

"Oh, great."

"She's a good kid, Dad." She chuckled, but it was warm. "She just wants to know about her life. You sure you're okay?"

"I'm better now."

"Good. How was the parade? When I talked to Wendy last night, she said the Fishmans are there for the summer, and you all went."

"Yeah, we all went."

Chapter Eleven: Riding A Bike

Wendy was sitting on the porch swing when I came back up to the house. Her legs were tucked under her, and she was eating what I assumed was her breakfast from one of the large handmade bowls from Georgetown Pottery. She was wearing jeans and a University of Vermont hoodie sweatshirt. The hood was up, and I could barely see her face. I didn't know what to say to her.

"Morning, Grandpa. Mother Maude get off okay."

"Mother Maude?"

"That's what Mom calls her sometimes. Uncle Jesse, too."

I chuckled. "I guess she can be a bit maternal."

"You think? I love her to death, but…"

"I get the picture. What's on your agenda for the day?"

"I was wondering if you could teach me to ride the motorcycle. If you teach me and I take and pass the test, I won't have to pay the three-fifty for a class."

"Oh. I hadn't thought about that. Sure. Why not? You've got your regular license?"

Wendy looked at me as though I had insulted her. "Since I was sixteen. Vermont, but I can drive anywhere. You know that."

Of course, I knew that. I wasn't thinking. What did I know about her life or think much about it? Maude was right. For four years, nothing had seemed real or meant much. I got through the day and settled for that. I recouped with, "Of course. Sorry. We can start this morning if you want."

"That'd be great."

"You know how to drive a stick shift?"

"No."

"Okay." So, we'll be starting from scratch. "When was the last time you were on a regular bike?"

"All the time. That's how I get around at school."

"Of course. Sorry. A motorcycle's very different from an automatic in a car. You'll have to learn how to master the clutch."

"Do you still ride?"

"Yeah, once in a while. Mainly to keep Jesse's bike up and running so he can ride when he's here."

"Do you still fly?"

"Sure."

"Would you teach me how to fly?"

"Oh, no. For that, you need a lot of ground school hours and then a licensed instructor for flight time."

"Didn't your father teach you how to fly?"

"Yes, but that was a different time."

"I thought you taught Uncle Joel."

"Not really. He had to do ground school and take lessons like everyone else. I helped him, and he got a lot of practice time with me, but that was it."

"Can we go flying while I'm here, and you teach me something about it?"

"Sure, that we can do. I thought you had to focus on your paper, though."

"I do, but I'm not going to be doing it twenty-four seven, and I think I'd like to learn how to fly someday."

"You would, would you?"

"Yeah, I think so. Not every family has their own airport."

"Hon, it is a grass strip and a barn."

"Well, not every family has a grass runway and a barn-hangar with a plane inside. I'd be the fifth generation, wouldn't I?"

"You would."

"And your grandfather started it all."

"He did. He was an ambitious man with big dreams. When he built the landing strip it was before he owned a plane or knew how to fly. He built the barn to house his airplane, the one he didn't have; he didn't hold back. I have no idea what he was thinking, but you could put two planes, even three, in the barn he built."

"It's enormous. I remember playing in there as a kid. It had everything in it."

"That's for sure. It's housed tractors, cars, boats, and motorcycles. You name it."

"Tell me about the planes that have lived there."

"Well, right after World War One, Grandpa Will bought a surplus JN-4, a Curtis 'Jenny.' Two of his sons, Brian and my father learned to fly on that plane. It was a very popular biplane they used for everything from wing walking…"

"That must have been insane."

"It was. Anyway, after World War Two he sold the Jenny and bought another plane used for training, a Stearman Kadet, another biplane, war surplus, of course. That was the plane I first learned to fly when I was a teenager. My father also dipped into war surplus and bought a two-engine Cessna Bobcat, which he used for work. They kept the Stearman flying until my grandfather died in 1963. My dad sold the Stearman for four times what my grandfather paid for it. It was considered a 'classic.' My dad also sold his Bobcat and bought the first Cessna 206 when it came out in 1964. He kept trading one 260 after another as Cessna modified them over the years. He bequeathed me the last one when he died. Still flying it. It's got up-to-date Avionics, a rebuilt engine, and is as good as new.

"Only your Uncle Joel took to flying. Unlike the rest of us, he learned at an actual flying school. Your mom would rather ski than fly. Jesse's the sailor. Ruth lives to golf."

"I should learn to fly."

"I thought skiing was your thing."

"Only because I don't know how to fly."

For Wendy, Jesse's Honda was a great beginner bike. It looked like a traditional motorcycle with fenders and comfortable seats. It was not fast, at 750 CCs, but perfect for paved and maintained dirt roads. A highway bike it was not, and it wasn't sprung, or high enough, for off-road riding. But, for just riding around and basic transportation, it was great.

Jesse had two helmets, and the small one fit Wendy. I began by explaining how everything worked and then took her for a ride and explained what I was doing every step of the way. When we came back to the barn, I told her to straddle the bike and lean it from side to side so she could feel the balance points and understand just how heavy the machine was. Then I had her move it forward and backward in neutral. Finally, I had her get on and off, use the kickstand, start the engine, use the turn indicators, and set the rearview mirrors.

Finally, we got to the hard part: get a feel for the clutch. Start. Stop. Over and over in first gear until it was smooth. Then I had her go through the gears, clutch in, without moving. Then I sent her off, shifting through the five gears and then back down again. Stopping. Starting. Over and over.

We did all that without ever leaving the farm. We turned our landing strip into a motorcycle training ground. I found some old lobster buoys in the barn, used them as obstacles, and had her go around them. She learned quickly and surely. She was strong, with long legs, and the bike did not intimidate her in the least. She was a natural. The last time she came back from the end of the runway, she asked, "Okay, I got this. Now, how do I do a wheelie?"

"I haven't the vaguest idea. It's your uncle's bike. If he wants to teach you, that's up to him. On my watch, don't even think about it. Besides, you still have paper learning to do before you're ready for the test."

I had her practice some more for another hour. On the way back to Tír, we stopped at the library so she could access the Wi-Fi. She downloaded the manual for the Honda and all the do's and don'ts of riding a motorcycle that she could find online, from videos to instructional books. We were back down at Tír by noon. She brought her computer out to the porch and started studying. At one o'clock, I asked her if she wanted me to make her an egg salad sandwich. She said sure. When we sat down to eat, she announced, "I'm ready."

"That was quick."

"No, seriously, I am. I've got this. I texted my friend Nathan, and he said I could use his bike to take the test. I have an appointment Thursday."

"Where? When?"

"Thursday at three. Brattleboro. I can take the bus down and back from Bath if you drive me and pick me up. I'll go down tomorrow. Take the test Thursday. Pass with flying colors. Spend the night at Mom's and take the bus back on Friday."

"Someone's letting you use their bike?"

"He's a friend from Brattleboro and from UVM. He'll pick me up and bring me back to the bus. Give me a chance to ride his bike before the test. He's got a small Harley."

"When did you work all this out. I didn't hear you talking to anyone."

"Text."

"Oh. Right. You said that. Sure. What time is the bus?"

"Nine forty-five. Works perfectly. Coming home, I'll have to wait a bit."

"How long is the bus trip?"

"The whole friggin day each way. There's no easy way. Zip. Nada."

I looked over at her eating her sandwich and said, "That's ridiculous. Why don't I drive you? Or, better yet, if the weather's decent, why don't I fly you down and back." I had no idea where that came from.

"Seriously? Would you? That'd be amazing. You can meet Nathan. He's a great guy."

"You're really anxious to do this, aren't you?"

"I hate being without my own wheels. I always have."

I didn't say anything. I understood. Too many times, Rachel either forgot to bring her someplace or to pick her up. Too many years of not knowing what she would face when she got home. Who would be there? What condition would Rachel be in? Transportation was freedom. Running towards, running away. It didn't matter, as long as she could run.

After a few minutes, I said, "Down and back in one day, flying or driving, sounds better than two days on a bus."

She put her sandwich down, walked around the table, got behind me, leaned down, put her arms around me, and kissed me on the cheek. "Thank you. You are the best. I was dreading this trip."

Thursday morning came, and we were socked in. The forecast was for the fog to continue throughout the day. We took Hannah's car. Charlie was in the back. Two cups of coffee were in their cupholders. Wendy had a folder together. She had taken the registration and insurance information from Jesse's bike when we put the bike away. She had her license, student ID, passport, and who knows what else. She wouldn't need half of it, but there was no way that she was going to be denied the motorcycle endorsement because of some paperwork she didn't have with her. We allowed five hours for a four-hour drive. Her idea.

We had just passed Bath when Wendy started talking about Rina, how good it was to see her, Rina's semester in Scotland, and then she asked, "Grandpa, do I disappoint you?"

"Disappoint me? Why on earth do you ask that?"

"Just wondering. I know Mom disappointed you and Grandma with her drinking and not getting her life together."

"You're not your mother. Have I said anything to indicate I'm disappointed in you?"

"Not specifically, but I saw how interested you were when Rina talked about Scotland and going to graduate school. I know I disappoint people."

"Like who?"

"Stephen. My ex. I know Mom told you about him. He thinks I'm intellectually lazy and that I run away from everything."

"And what do you think?"

"That's he's probably right, but maybe it's just who I am."

"That sounds fatalistic. Everyone changes or has the potential. Look at your Mom. I guess it depends on what you want." I paused and was thinking about Maude's less than flattering description of me before I remembered to come back to Wendy. "What do you want?"

"To feel less screwed up. When I look at Rina, I feel shitty. Her life is so normal. I'd die for normal. My shrink says that's often the way ACOAs feel."

"ACOA?"

"Adult Children of Alcoholics. We all want normal and are afraid we can never have it. I thought I could have it with Stephen, but I blew it, and I don't even know how."

"You've talked with your mother about it?"

"That and everything else." There was that word again. "That's all we do is talk. I understand that her AA program is important to her, but sometimes I think she's in love with 'her story.'"

I didn't say anything for a few minutes. Then, when I did, I said, "You don't disappoint me." I meant it. For the first time, I saw and understood Wendy's resilience.

Chapter Twelve: Rachel

I'm a trained journalist according to Boston University. They did teach me to separate fact from analysis and analysis from interpretation. I knew Rachel's story would change over time depending on her audience. I also knew my 'Rachel Story.' It was her father's story and was different from her mother's. Neither, of course, was in complete alignment with Rachel's story. I had no idea what story Rachel had told Wendy or how Wendy had retold it to herself. I only knew mine, and it was not the 'facts only' filing of a reporter. My 'Rachel Story' was not a pretty one, and it hurt.

It wasn't until much later, after the infamous summer of nineteen sixty-six, that Hannah and I even knew how it began. Understanding it was another matter. To this day, I'm not sure that I fully comprehend it or what my role in it was. I know that the yacht club steward, Tim Stark, flattered Rachel endlessly about how special she was, how mature, how different from all the other teenagers. He also treated her differently. He asked her to help him, to function as his assistant, if not his peer. He 'adulted' her that summer, if there is such a word.

In a couple of months, she became addicted to attention, love, sex, and alcohol. We would ask her where she was going, and she would answer, "I'm going to help Tim." She had just turned sixteen and had never had a boyfriend, not a real one. She was like a bingo card, and he was filling in all the squares. What plagued Hannah and me was that we had left the squares blank.

She fell madly, passionately, blindly in love and relished the feeling of being wanted, even adored. She was 'special.' Later, Rachel told Hannah that the sex flowed out of that in a gush. She told Hannah she didn't know whether it was a slipped condom, the times they were drinking and didn't get to it, or just the odds of condom failure given how much sex they were having. She was pregnant by the end of the summer but didn't know it until her junior year in high school had begun.

Rachel did know that she went to see Tim one night at the end of August, and he wasn't in his room. So, she waited for him down at the end of the yacht club dock. She started walking back up to greet him when she saw headlights approaching. She stopped when he pulled in front of his apartment, and she saw there was a passenger in the car. Tim ran around to open the car door for the passenger; he got a suitcase out of the back seat and led her into the apartment that was 'Rachel and Tim's private place,' the place where Tim had made love to her night after night and sometimes during the day.

Tim didn't see Rachel run home crying. She stayed in her room for the entire weekend while Tim introduced everyone to his fiancé.

Two weeks after Labor Day, I was sitting at the kitchen table making a list of chores to close up Tír when Hannah came from upstairs and sat down opposite me. She said, "We have something we need to talk about."

I continued list-making and said, "What?"

"Michael, look at me."

It was a command. I looked up and repeated, "What is it?"

"Rachel's pregnant."

I said the stupidest thing I could have said. "How?"

When she told me about Tim, my first response was to go up to Cornell and beat the shit out of the slimy bastard. I was filled with rage, blame, and, yes, shame. Guilt came quickly and then recycled back among the other feelings. Hannah was a rock. She settled me, and she settled Rachel.

Ruth, Jesse, and Joel were already back in their respective colleges. It was just the three of us who were still in Georgetown. We talked. Rachel cried. She wanted Tim. She wanted to drive to Ithaca and tell him. We said absolutely no way. We kept reminding her he was engaged. She didn't want to believe it. Finally, against our wishes, she called him and emailed him. He didn't respond. Ever so slowly, she accepted he was gone, and she had a decision to make.

Hannah and I worked very hard, perhaps too hard, to let it be her decision. We told her what we thought but tried not to push. Finally, as the time approached when the choice would be more difficult, she decided. Hannah drove her to the clinic and stayed home with her for a couple of days after the abortion procedure.

Afterward, Rachel would cry periodically. There was no anger. In retrospect, I wish there had been. Instead, resignation replaced innocence. Tír was closed up for the year, but she would go down and sit on the porch steps for hours just looking out at the harbor. My youngest was no longer young.

Although Wendy wouldn't come into the world for several years, what happened to Rachel that summer affected her future daughter as much as it affected her. Rachel was right. Wendy's life began at Tír na nÓg.

That fall, the self-medication began, and alcohol was the drug of choice. Rachel built a moat around herself, and the drawbridge was raised. We were denied no matter how often Hannah and I asked to be let in. Rachel had locked her soul away in a dungeon of shame. The only time she lowered the drawbridge and came out was to search for men who would give her attention, and if she couldn't find one, she'd use alcohol. Therapy was offered and refused. She was sure everyone at her school knew. But, of course, no one did. Her siblings were all cocooned in their own lives and had no idea what their sister was going through until Jesse started commenting on her drinking when he was home one weekend from RISD. She told him to mind his own business. We told him we were aware of it and had talked to her about it.

Her grades fell during her high school junior and senior years, but she got into Northeastern thanks to her high SATs and Hannah's father's pull at the college, where he was a faculty member. We hoped going off to college, the new setting, and new people would bring about other changes. It was wishful thinking on our part. She scraped by her first year. On weekends she worked, sort of. She would say she was working in the Food and Beverage Industry. What she was doing was waiting on tables and having sex with bartenders. She was fired twice for drinking on the job.

She met Jerry Greenberg in Rutland, Vermont, the summer after her first year. A Rutland friend from Northeastern invited her to work at a resort in Killington. Jerry's father owned a group of car dealerships in and around Rutland. He hosted midweek staff picnics at the resort where Rachel was waiting tables. Jerry was taken with her, pursued her, and she welcomed his attention. She never returned to school. She dropped out of Northeastern and moved in with Jerry. They were married the following spring. She became pregnant with Wendy, stopped binging, stopped waitressing, and worked at one of the family dealerships as a bookkeeper until she gave birth to Wendy in March.

Jerry wanted her to stay home with the baby, and she did. Jerry was and is a very ambitious man. He was determined to prove to his father that he was more intelligent and more dedicated than his older brother. The success of the family business was his mission in life, and he worked endless hours to prove it. However, Rachel was alone in a strange town with a new baby. All of the attention that Rachel craved disappeared, and her drinking reappeared. When Jerry came home one night, Wendy was still up, and Rachel was asleep on the couch. A glass of bourbon was next to her. That got Jerry's attention.

I'll never forget the phone call. There were no preliminaries. "How much do you know about Rachel's drinking?" Then he told us what had happened. He blamed us. I don't know whether he blamed us for her drinking or because we were supposed to warn him about it, and we hadn't.

Rachel went into the first of three different in-patient month-long rehab programs with lots of guilt and shame. Jerry wanted it to work. Hannah and I were hopeful and encouraging. What we had tried to bring about and were unable to, Jerry and this toddler had accomplished. Rachel wanted to get better. Things went well for a while, but Jerry never really got it about Rachel's loneliness and need for attention. Eventually, he was able to oust his brother from the family business, though. Now he was the chief operating officer and was riding high. Wendy was sure he was also riding someone at work.

Four years later, they were divorced. Rachel went back to work at the resort in Killington and the cycle of the next thirteen years began. Different men, different jobs, two different rehab programs—we paid for these. Wendy would come with us for at least a month every summer. We saw less and less of Rachel except in brief snatches of time.

Jerry got remarried, had a new family, and rarely saw Wendy, although he did send Rachel every child support payment precisely on time. He then repeated himself. His new wife divorced him because he was never home. I told Hannah, "That man is great at providing lots of attention upfront and terrible after getting someone to take care of his household for him. All he wants is a maid, lover, and mother to his children—not a mate."

Hannah ignored my rant. Rachel said, "He tried to help me, Dad. Don't forget that. And he's a lot better than what a lot of women go through with their exes."

After the divorce Hannah and I tried to stay close to Rachel and Wendy. They were always invited to come and be with us. It wasn't just family events; we asked them to live with us. Sometimes Rachel would show up at events; sometimes, she wouldn't. We got used to it. One time we drove out to Killington at her invitation to find out she had left with a new boyfriend for the weekend. Wendy was home with a babysitter. We paid the babysitter, sent her home, and spent the weekend with Wendy.

We would look for clues that Rachel was doing better, find them, and then be disappointed. Rachel was right. There were a lot of disappointments. I had settled for being disappointed. Hannah never did.

However, something changed one night when Rachel came home late from an evening shift. She went to find her bottle of bourbon and couldn't find it or any of her other bottles. Eventually, she did, all empty, all in the trash can where Wendy had emptied them and then broken the bottles. Shards, a pile of shards, was all that was left. Rachel called us that night. She was hysterical. She was furious with Wendy; she hated herself for being a terrible mother. She was going to get sober. She'd make it this time. Wendy was in middle school.

Enter Julien Guay, ski instructor, French, handsome, divorced, with a family back in Chamonix where he had left them to come to America and carve out a new life. At first, Hannah and I didn't know how or why they got together, but they did, and they got married. Rachel started showing up for family gatherings consistently, on time, with Julien and Wendy. She wouldn't drink when she was with us because we never served alcohol if she was around, but she wasn't sneaking out to get something either. We knew something was different this time. We gave Julien credit.

Julien appeared to care about them both. He did things with them. One night a week, Wednesdays, he was never home. It was only much later that we learned Julien had been in recovery for several years and had met Rachel at an AA social. We didn't even know she had joined AA.

Julien was offered a job as head of the ski school at Jay Peak in what Vermonters call the Northeast Kingdom. He took it. They moved, and Rachel got a job in the sales office for the resort. For Wendy, it was another change in school systems: she had gone to elementary school in Rutland, middle school in Woodstock, and now high school in Newport. However, Wendy seemed happy when we saw her even though she stopped spending much summer time at Tír. Her mother was not drinking; she liked Julien, and, thanks to him, she had fallen in love with skiing and was getting good enough to compete in local events. Julien said she was a natural. Perhaps most importantly, Wendy was making friends.

Two completely unrelated events changed everything. First, Julien returned to France; then Hannah got sick.

Julien wanted Rachel and Wendy to move with him to Chamonix. He wanted to get to know his children as well as he knew Wendy. Rachel said no. She had only been in AA for a short time and was still struggling. She didn't dare leave. So, he went by himself. It wasn't sudden. It wasn't harsh. It wasn't out of spite. They had talked through part-time here, part-time there. They had considered every possible permutation of what they referred to as "a modern relationship." Rachel even spoke to us about it.

Hannah's ongoing struggle with pancreatic cancer added another pull to stay in the United States. Rachel wanted to be close to the mother she had disappointed. So, she drove from Jay to Georgetown whenever she could. Julien's departure and Hannah's illness were hard on Rachel and Wendy.

Rachel was determined that Wendy complete high school in Newport. So, after Julien left, they stayed there. As he had promised, Julien stayed in touch with Wendy. Skiing became the focus of Wendy's life for a couple of years. For Rachel, it was AA

A consulting company led the resort through an exercise in 'right-sizing' during Wendy's senior year, and Rachel was 'right-sized' out of a job. She sent out resumes and obtained the event planner position for the Brattleboro Chamber of Commerce. The two of them moved, Rachel found an AA community, and that Fall, Wendy enrolled at the University of Vermont.

Now my granddaughter, this strange young woman sitting next to me, wanted to know if she was a disappointment to me. She said her mother had told her everything. Had Wendy concluded that her mother had passed to her some strange disease, 'disappointing people,' like some bizarre gene?

Maude had said Wendy needed me, and she needed roots. I had no clue how to do that. I was going to screw it up. I could teach her how to ride a motorcycle; I knew how to drive her to Vermont so she could get her endorsement, but beyond that, what the hell good was I?

March 23, 1984
HOME TOWN BOY by Michael Buckley

My friend George told me he was going to get a new car. We were having our usual end-of-the-week second cup of coffee at Maggie's Diner. So, of course, I asked him, "What'cha gonna get?"

"A Ford, of course."

It was the 'of course' that caught my attention. "Why 'of course?'" I asked.

He turned and looked at me as though I was demented. "What else would I get?"

Foolishly, I took this as a challenge demanding an answer. "Well, you could get a Chevy, a Dodge. I've been driving a Volvo, and I like it."

He didn't shake his head, but it was clear I had now convinced him I was demented. He said, "My grandfather was a Ford man, my father was a Ford man, I'm a Ford man, and my son will be a Ford man. You can bet on it."

Now, George does not own a Ford dealership, and, as far as I know, no one in his family does, either. Yet there was this lineage of loyalty to old Henry T. Ford that I find remarkable. Remarkable, but not unusual. I have had similar conversations with Chrysler men and Chevy men. I need to mention that I have never heard such automobile brand loyalty exhibited by any women I know. You may know a Ford woman or two, but I don't.

In my family, past, and present, we have no such loyalty. I have a distant cousin who even drove a Studebaker, and, believe it or not, he bought it in Maine, second hand, of course. When I mentioned this to George, he said, "That's because your people don't care about cars. To you, they're just transportation."

I agreed with him. But then he piled on. "You care about boats. They've got to be old, and they've got to be wood which makes no sense. What's wrong with fiberglass?"

I told him, "Nothing, except fiberglass isn't wood." How's that for an answer? Profound. I began to have an inkling that if I had asked George what was wrong with a Chevy, he would have given me an equally simple, "It's not a Ford." But, if I pressed, he could go beyond that and provide a detailed comparative analysis, and of course, I could do the same with wood versus fiberglass.

In my family, boats are made of wood. More than that, the Buckley men are schooner men. For those of you who are unfamiliar with the variety of sailboat rigs, a schooner always has at least two masts and often more. Schooners come in all sizes and have been built with up to five or six masts. The sails of a schooner are usually fixed to a boom and are hoisted up the mast, unlike a square-rigged ship where the sails are dropped down from yardarms. Schooners also require less crew to sail.

Our Mid Coast Maine boatyards produced many of the biggest schooners ever built. Several large ones were made on Georgetown Island, where I live. The yards in Bath were also noteworthy for building big schooners.

Schooners were the commercial workhorse rigs of sailing vessels from the time of the square-riggers until the advent of steam engines. They were essential all the way back to the American Revolution because they were smaller and more maneuverable than the British 'Man of War' vessels. There is no sea or ocean where a schooner has not ventured.

Our Maine-built schooners have carried lumber, ice, granite, and other goods from Maine to places south and across the Atlantic. Our boats went down below the Mason-Dixon line and fetched coal, and brought it up to New York City and elsewhere. They also were used as fishing platforms along our coast and out into the Atlantic. A square-rigged vessel could never do what our schooners did.

Unlike square-rigged ships, schooners can easily tack into the wind. So, they were perfect for coastal commerce out of range of the trade winds. It is also easy to set and lower sails in a schooner compared with square-rigged ships, and, should a storm come up, dropping a sail or two was not an awe-inspiring feat of gymnastics as it was on a square-rigged vessel.

Other sailing rigs have more than one mast, specifically ketches, and yawls, but those rigs have never carried much more than people who refer to themselves as yachtsmen; schooners are for seamen. There is a world of difference here. That is not to say that a well-turned-out schooner might not be the rig of choice for a wealthy yachtsman who wanted the best. In fact, the first America's Cup race against England was won by a one-hundred-foot schooner named *America*. From the first America's Cup race in 1851 until 1881, all the races were sailed in schooners. Now the America's Cup is raced in boats that belong to the twelve-meter class. These boats are all about seventy feet long and have only one mast. Until last year, 1983, Americans had held on to the "Auld Mug" for 132 years. Then the unthinkable happened. Australians won and took it home to Perth. The United States yachting world became unhinged and swore that it would never happen again. Maybe if they were still sailing schooners, it would not have happened.

Every once in a while, someone asks me why I still sail a schooner, and a wooden one at that. A sloop (one mast) is indeed less work, and a yawl or ketch (two masts with the aft sail smaller than the mainsail) would perhaps be more practical. However, the schooner provides a romance and a connection to history that none of these other rigs can manage. This connection to those who sailed schooners is important to me. My father, grandfather, and great-grandfather were all 'Schooner Men.' It is because of schooners that I find myself in Georgetown, Maine. My great-grandfather, Jamie Buckley, left Ireland as a crew member on a schooner as a young man. He eventually got his own, a schooner built in Bath. His son, my grandfather Will Buckley, crewed for great-grandfather Jamie ferrying goods up and down the Eastern seaboard. A need for repairs is how Grandpa Will wound up in Bath and eventually Georgetown.

When my father, Jack Buckley, decided he wanted a boat, he built a schooner. Named for my mother, *The Redhead* is now mine and has taken me and my family up and down the coast of New England and across the Atlantic and back. So, I am definitely a "Schooner Man."

Wood versus fiberglass is a whole other topic. This is Maine, though, and we are one of the last bastions where fantastic wood boats are being built and repaired. We have a magazine, *Wooden Boat,* and the Wooden Boat School up in Brooklin to prove it.

I do understand George being a 'Ford Man.' However, I'm not sure he understands wood and schooners. But I will keep on trying. We agree that it's good to have something in your life that carries on from generation to generation, even though it may be impractical and even a little bit silly. I'm not sure George would agree about the silly part, but I can always remind him about the Ford Edsel or Pinto. Knowing George, though, I'm sure he'll have an answer for that.

Chapter Thirteen: Five Points

Jamie was anxious to meet Harry Callahan and find out what it would be like to live in New York City. As soon as he was able, he took the ferry across the East River from Brooklyn to New York. Back in Cork, the Callahans had given him the address for their son. When Jamie arrived on the New York side of the river, he asked the first person he met how to get to Mulberry Street.

The man was old and smelled of urine and dirt. His shirt had a rip on the shoulder, and Jamie could see the bones protruding through the thin skin. The man didn't answer right away. It was as though he were trying to focus and pull his thoughts together. Jamie was getting ready to walk away when the man said, "You just off the boat?" Jamie could smell the alcohol on his breath.

Jamie ignored the boat question and said, "Trying to meet up with a relative. Lives on Mulberry Street. You be knowing where it is?"

"It's in Five Points." The man's voice was hoarse. "Used to live there. Nowhere now. Easier that way."

"Can you be telling me how to get there?"

The directions sounded simple, so Jamie started walking. If Cork had seemed desperate to him, lower New York City was worse. The farther he got from the river, the more he felt himself walking in a make-believe land. People didn't seem to be going anyplace as much as wandering with no place to go. They walked with their eyes down, not looking at one another. A young child came up to him with one hand out, begging. The other hand held onto a naked toddler. Jamie walked around them without stopping.

He passed a few men wearing top hats and suits walking and talking to one another. They seemed out of place, from somewhere else. Jamie wondered who they were. He had to give way to a man pulling a cart loaded with household items. A woman and three children walked behind the cart. The woman spoke to the children in a language Jamie didn't understand. Flies were everywhere, as was the stench. He had to be careful to avoid the horse manure in the street.

Two more sets of directions later, he found his way to Mulberry Street and began looking for street numbers. If he ran into someone, he would ask directions again because there were so few numbers. Eventually, he found the right door. He knocked. A young girl, maybe five or six, opened the door a crack and stood behind it, peeking her head around. Jamie said he was looking for a Mr. Harry Callahan.

"Da not home," she answered.

"Do you know where I might find him or when he'll be back?"

"Maybe he'll be back. Maybe he won't. Who wants to know?" A woman opened the door wide. She was smoking a small pipe and carrying an infant.

"My name's Jamie Buckley. I just arrived from Cork. Harry's father said I should look him up when I got here. I'm wanting to move here, to New York. The Callahans said Harry would be able to help me get situated."

The woman just stared at Jamie and said nothing. The baby squirmed a little. The young girl held onto her mother's dress. The woman looked Jamie up and down and finally rested her eyes on his face. "Situated?"

"That's what he said. Maybe help me get started. I don't know anyone here, and this is the only name I have."

"You have any money for rent and food?"

"Some."

"Maybe we can help you, then. This ain't no free boarding house. Where your things?"

"On the boat I came on. It'll be here for a couple of days."

"You left your things on the boat that brought you. You out of your mind? They'll long be gone."

"No, no. You see, it's okay. I'm a crew member. It's a schooner out of New Brunswick. I came on board when it was in Cork."

"They get rid of you?"

"No. They offered me to stay as regular crew."

"Then why don't you? No work here. Not for our kind. That is unless you…"

She was interrupted by a man who had come up from behind Jamie. The man put his hand on Jamie's shoulder and roughly spun him around. "Wha'cha want here? What you doing talking to my wife?"

"I'm looking for Mr. Harry Callahan. My name's Jamie Buckley. I just got here from Cork. His father said I should look him up."

The woman said, "Your Da sent him. Said we would help him get sit-u-a-ted." She drew the word out in a snarl.

"The fuck you say. He actually said sit-u-a-ted. My Da? You come with money?"

"I got some."

The woman said, "The eejit is crew on a Canada boat, and he wants to come here. He wants to come to New York."

"New York. Jesus." The man paused before saying, "Okay, Buckley. You got money. You come and buy me a drink, and we'll have a little talk about our helping you get sit-u-a-ted."

Harry Callahan turned and started walking. Jamie followed him back down Mulberry Street towards the Five Points, where a group of roads all came together.

"My friend here is paying," Harry said to the man behind the bar. "We'll do local." Harry turned to Jamie, "We got a brewery here. Why the hell you want to come to New York?"

The beers arrived in pint glasses. Jamie took a long sip and said, "Be another famine starting. Living with my Aintín Maude and Uncail Liam up in Carna, north of Galway. Sheep farm. They didn't need another mouth to feed, and I wasn't going to stay and watch them die, and I saw no reason for me to die."

"So, you come here to die. Real smart of you, boy."

"Why you say that?"

"Cholera. Sweeps through here every couple of years and kills people off. Makes room for more, though, only now it's the fuckin' I-tal-i-ans who are comin'. Used to be the Coloreds, but they moved uptown to Harlem after we made it clear they weren't wanted here."

"Cholera?"

"You shite your brains out, and then you die."

"Have you known people who've died?"

"A few. Last big one was '66. I got here in '67. The real big one was '32. Almost wiped out the city. Just be time before we get another big one. Like a fuckin' volcano. Never know when it be blowin'. Spread sickness all over the place."

"So, you're saying it's starving there or get sick here."

Harry finished off his beer and motioned for a second one. "About it. Starvin' takes longer. At least you can see it comin' like you did."

"Why do you stay?"

"Like it here. Make some money. Don't work hard. Lots of women."

Jamie ignored the comment about women. "What do you do?"

"I'm a head knocker for Hoggy Byrne."

"What's that?"

"Hoggy runs bets, especially boxin'. I make sure everyone pays up. They don't; I settle the score. The bigger the score, the bigger the hit, the more I get paid. Up to twenty bucks now for a broken arm. Broken nose is ten and a hundred for lights out if someone tries set up their own game. He gives me lots of work, doesn't take much time, and I make a good buck. I do some bettin' myself. Only when I know who's goin' to win."

"How you know that?"

"Jesus Christ. You're just off the boat in more ways than one, aren't you?"

"You're saying the fights are fixed?"

"Sometimes. You just got to know when. I do."

They both drank quietly for a while. Harry went on to his third beer while Jamie was still on his first. Towards the end of his third beer, Harry asked, "You're a big kid. Ever do any boxin'?"

"No."

"You like to fight? I can get you trained up."

"Not really. I get too mad."

"Too mad! You gotta killer instinct, do ya? Can use that lots a ways." Harry laughed, "You wanted ta box, I could get you sit-u-a-ted. My Da said 'sit-u-a-ted?' Didn't know he even knew the word. I can probably help find you something with Hoggy. I'll do some askin'. You can pay us money for rent and food 'till you get sit-u-a-ted. Think about boxing. Ya any good, ya make a lot of money; ya do what you're told."

Jamie finished off his beer and said, "I'd best be getting back to the boat."

"When you come be with us?"

"Not sure. Got more work to do there. They're not leaving for a few days."

Jamie was glad he hadn't brought his gear with him. He walked as fast as he could towards the Fulton Street Ferry that would take him back to Brooklyn, the *Phoenix*, and its crew. He was out of breath by the time he reached the ferry. He didn't have to wait long.

No one was in the cockpit when he reached the *Phoenix*, which was berthed towards the end of the Empire Wharves. He climbed aboard and looked inside the cabin. Seeing no one, he got off and walked past other vessels loading and unloading: animal hides, sugar, molasses, coffee beans. The smells weren't pleasant, but they were far better than Mulberry Street.

Men were working up and down the wharf pushing carts and leading horse-drawn wagons. Crews that were waiting to load or unload hung out on their boats or with other crews. Jamie was impressed with the sense of industry and purpose after what he had seen in Five Points.

He found Jacob, Pudd, and Fogo hanging out with the crew of a two-masted schooner from Boston. "Back so soon?" Jacob asked.

"Yeah."

"Couldn't keep away from us," Fogo chimed in. Pudd didn't say anything but studied Jamie's face.

"Jacob, could I have a word?" Jamie asked.

"Sure," Jacob answered and climbed off the boat and joined Jamie on the wharf. "Let's walk."

The two of them walked in silence down the wharf. Jacob waited for Jamie to begin. When he did, Jamie pointed to the construction on both sides of the river. "What they building?"

"It's a bridge. They build these towers; then they hang the bridge on wires from the towers. Call it a suspension bridge. Been at building it awhile now."

"Will a boat be able to sail under it?"

"Oh yeah. No problem. It be real high. Be able to carry lots of things across. No more ferry that thing get finished."

"Really?"

"Really."

They walked some more along the water and then turned and started walking inland. "Brooklyn's not like New York," Jamie said.

"It be okay," Jacob replied. "Not as nice as St. John, though."

"You want me to stay with the *Phoenix*, don't you?"

"It'd be okay if you did."

Jamie stopped walking and looked at Jacob. Jacob kept on walking. He went a few steps, turned around, and said, "You said you wanted to talk, so talk, and I ain't about to beg you to stay with the *Phoenix*. I asked you once, and that should be enough."

Jamie caught up to him and started talking. He told him about the Five Points, meeting Harry Callahan's family, and then his time with Harry at the bar. "I donna want to box or hurt people for a livin'. I donna know what to do, though. I've had my heart set on New York and bringing Treasa here, and I feel like a fool. I thought it'd be different. Not like this."

"Oh Jamie, you only be talking to one person, now, and seen only a sliver of that city. It's not all like that."

"But he's the only one I know. And work? He says there's little to be had."

They had reached a street with trees and double-decker houses. There were gardens, and the houses were well kept. They had only been walking for about half an hour. Jamie hadn't been paying much attention to the contrast with Five Points until Jacob pointed it out to him. "How you like this? A lot of Brooklyn like this. Different town. Not as pretty as St. John, of course, and nowhere near as pretty as Newfoundland. Jacob pointed to a well-appointed double-decker. "Can you imagine you be livin' inna place like this someday?"

Jamie looked around for the first time. It reminded him of parts of Galway. Some deep longing started to ache at him as he thought about Treasa and the two of them living on a street like the one they were on. "I could never afford anything so grand."

"Maybe not at first. But you be a seaman, and you could live like this. If not here, for certain in St. John. Think about it, boy. You're good at it. Get a berth anywhere. You've already got one with us. Stay on board with us tonight. Oh, and so you know, Tommy's gone. I've wired the owners to let 'em know, and I've leave to hire crew to take his place. So, I'm going to hire. You, or someone else."

"Oh. I understand."

As they walked back to the *Phoenix*, Jamie asked Jacob about Newfoundland, New Brunswick, St. John, and Canada in general. He also asked questions about other kinds of crew possibilities and the kinds of goods going in and out of New York, Brooklyn, Boston, and other places on the Eastern Seacoast.

As they reached the river and started walking back up the wharf, they stopped and watched a three-masted schooner unloading large granite blocks where the new bridge was being built. "How does it carry that much weight?" Jamie asked.

"We could do that, too," Jacob answered. "We got almost that much weight in rum on board now. That granite comes from Maine."

"Where's Maine?"

"On the way to Canada. Figure 500 miles or so north and east, depending on where you going. When you're easting, sailing is easy. Wind with you. Fuckin' bitch coming back and they do that fully loaded. Them blocks better be locked down tight. They shift while you're heeling goin' inta the wind and you capsize. Happened to more than one. Good money, though. City is building and needs lots of it."

"Why don't you do it?"

"Owners don't want to. Canadian boats compete with American boats? Americans not likely to be agreeable to it. Not worth it. Too much trouble."

When they got back to the *Phoenix*, Jacob said, "Think on it tonight. Noon tomorrow, I start lookin.' Day after tomorrow, we be ready to go."

The next day was beautiful. A gentle breeze came up the river and kept the smell of the warehouse to a minimum. There were no watches to stand, and no one had roused him. Jamie had slept ten hours straight. Pudd, Fogo, and Jacob were sitting in the cockpit eating: eggs and bacon with coffee, biscuits, and some Madeira if you wanted it. Jamie saw that Pudd had left him a sizable portion of everything. He filled his plate and went up to join the others in the cockpit.

He said good morning and started to eat. Pudd and Jacob looked at one another, anticipating more. They didn't get it. When he finished, he said to them both, "I want to try it here, and at the same time, I want to stay with you. The only thing I'm sure of is that there's no way in hell I'm going to go boxin,' hittin' people over the head, and maybe killin' someone. And I'm not going to count on Harry Callahan to help me make my way here. I'm going to try and get a crew job on one of the coastal boats. I've got one day to do it. If I can't do it, and it's still alright with you, I'll stay with the *Phoenix*."

"You know I've got to still look, though," Jacob said.

"I know. I know I'm taking a chance and can wind up flat on my arse."

"Long as you know."

Jamie spent the morning going up and down the Brooklyn waterfront talking to whoever he could find. When noon came, he was still without a berth and was starting to feel desperate. He wondered if he shouldn't just head back to the *Phoenix* and hope that Jacob's offer still stood and that he hadn't found someone else to replace Tommy. He was heading that way when he saw the schooner that had been unloading the Maine granite get pushed into the wharf by a steam-powered tugboat.

He helped them make the lines fast to the wharf. Once the boat was made fast, he said to the man behind the wheel, "Could I have a word, sir?"

"You selling something or begging."

"Neither."

"Okay, come aboard."

Jamie talked fast and told the schooner's skipper why he was in

New York, his voyage on the *Phoenix*, and his dilemma. When he finished, he waited for the skipper to say something. When he didn't, he started to turn away."

"You always talk this fast, boy? Where you going? I ain't said nothin' yet."

Jamie turned back to him. "Guess I been gettin' a lot of no's all morning."

"I'm going to give you another. I don't need no one."

Jamie started to turn away again.

"Will you stop that, for Christ's sake," the skipper said. "I don't, but I know who does. Smaller boat. Be just the two of you sailing her most the time. Owner's a good man. Fair man. Had an I-talian for crew last trip. Damned wop just wanted to get home to New York from mining up in Maine. Hard to find steady crew these days. So many boats and not enough crew to go around who know a sheepshank from a bowline."

"I know my knots, and I know navigation. You can talk to Jacob, the skipper of the *Phoenix*. He'll tell you."

"Not me taking you on. I could give a shit what you know. Man you want to talk to is Edward Ladd. Ship is the *Mary B*. Boat's only two years old. Had her built up in Bath to haul granite and ice."

"Ice?"

"Yeah, ice. You don't know much, do you?"

"Know how to sail and navigate."

"Take you at your word. Laddie's unloading on the other side of the river right now. Be back over here late afternoon if all goes well. You can see his boat from here."

"Thank you. I can't thank you enough."

"Mind ya, I'm trying to help Laddie out. He's getting a bit long o' tooth and needs a strong back. You might work out fine." He looked Jamie up and down like he was inspecting a farm animal. "Young, look strong enough, and you've at least one long voyage behind you. Gotta tell you. Laddie's got a Colored for a cook. He's old too. Not much help with the boat, but Laddie's had him a long time, and he's partial to him."

"Don't bother me none."

"Got a place to stay?"

"No."

"Probably let you stay on the boat if you want. With Isaac."

"Isaac?"

"The darkie."

Chapter Fourteen: Granite and Ice

Jacob was as gracious about Jamie leaving the *Phoenix* as Edward Ladd was enthusiastic about having him sign on to the *Mary* B. A young, robust, and knowledgeable sailor with a dream didn't come along very often. Ladd's wife, Rose, who fretted about her husband's health, was thrilled when Ladd told her the news about his new crew member. Not having children of their own, it wasn't but a few months before Jamie had a bedroom at the Ladd's house whenever the *Mary B* was in Brooklyn. The word adoption was never used, but to their friends, the Ladds now had a son.

They did not charge him room and board, and Jamie was frugal in his spending as he looked forward to the day when he could send for Treasa to come join him in America. In the meantime, he wrote to her daily, whether in port or at sea. He couldn't wait until the *Mary B* returned to Brooklyn to read the letters Rose would leave on the bureau in his bedroom.

From Treasa's letters, he learned that the famine Jamie had dreaded spared Carna, although it had ravaged other parts of Ireland. The country had been better prepared this time; England provided some support, and money flowed in from some of the Irish who had begun to prosper in areas of the United States.

Before he heard from his Aintín Maude, he learned from Treasa that his Uncail Liam had died a peaceful death, and Aintín Maude planned to do something she said she would never do. She would leave Ireland and join her sons in Australia. Selling all their household possessions and what remained of the flock would pay for the long voyage and help her settle. When Jaime heard this news, he started exchanging letters with his aunt as well as with Treasa. Not communicating with his mother or siblings bothered him only on rare occasions. His aunt no longer knew where his mother or his brothers and sisters were living. His aunt wrote, "I'm sorry, Jamie. I wish I could tell you, but I can't."

Thanks to his time on the *Phoenix*, Jamie was already on his way to becoming a competent sailor and navigator. But, under Edward Ladd's, now Laddie to him, tutelage, Jamie became more than a sailor; he became a skilled merchant seaman. He learned how to negotiate with brokers, harbormasters, tug captains, dock masters, loading masters, and other people who had their hand out for a portion of profits that the *Mary B* brought in from hauling granite and ice from Maine.

Everyone wanted granite and everyone wanted ice. Cities were expanding and building grand monuments, bridges, and all of the other architectural manifestations of a new culture and civilization. The builders needed granite, and Maine had an ample supply. People were moving into the cities, and ice merchants needed ice for the giant ice silos that could store the precious frozen commodity for months on end. Fresh meat and produce had moved from delicacy to necessity for the emerging middle class. They wanted ice all year long. Affluent people began to have iceboxes in their own homes. Maine winters provided an ample supply.

The skipper who had referred Jamie to Edward Ladd had told the truth. Captain Laddie was a fair man. He recognized that Jamie was taking on increasing levels of responsibility and compensated him well for his efforts. On the other hand, Isaac simply got to stay onboard the *Mary B* and receive a meager allowance. "Can you believe it?" Laddie said one day, right after Isaac left to visit a sister in Harlem. "Twenty-five years ago, that man was a slave. Look at him today. No one beating him, owning him, or selling him. He can stay with me as long as he can carry his weight as cook. Good man. I like him. Some don't see why I have a darkie on my boat. I think they're nuts. Trust him more than the last I-talian I had."

It was still 'granite season' when Jamie joined the *Mary B*. Sailing back and forth to Stonington, Maine was very different than the voyage from Cork to New York. Rather than steady trade winds, they had to sail up Long Island in fluky Southwesterlies, past Block Island, and around Nantucket and Cape Cod. From there, they headed straight for Matinicus and on to Isle Au Haut Bay and Stonington. Four hundred miles, eight days if the weather was cooperating. If they were carrying cotton from the warehouses in New York to the mills of Massachusetts, it would make the trip two to three days longer by the time they sailed into Quincy or Boston, unloaded their cargo, and got back out to sea.

It was always longer on the way back from Maine. They would be heavy with granite and heading into the wind. A trip up and back could take close to a month including time loading and unloading. Then they would be home for a week before they started all over again.

The sailing was more demanding than what Jamie had experienced during the voyage from Cork. There were no steady winds, and the navigating, both celestial and dead reckoning, had to be precise. There were small rocky islets, shifting sand bars, and other boats to be concerned about. Over a thousand boats could be sailing the same route at any point in time. In fog or rain, and there was often fog and rain, collisions happened. Sailing past Cape Ann was especially hazardous. Hundreds of fishing boats coming from Gloucester would cross their path as fishermen made their way to the fertile grounds offshore. Laddie thought the "damned Portugees" were crazy. "Their boats always going down. I hear they're losing two hundred, three hundred boats a year. Never catch me using *Mary B* for fishing. Too god damned dangerous."

The *Mary B*'s trips would be shorter in the winter ice season but far more difficult because of the weather. Northeasters would blow for days on end. The *Mary B* would get covered with snow and ice that had to be chipped away. Occasionally Laddie would say, "Enough of this shit," and they would pull into one of the many New England ports until a Northeaster blew itself out. In places like Nantucket and Sag Harbor, they might lose a day, sometimes two, but warm pubs made it worthwhile. Isaac would come with them. People might stare at Isaac, but they would let him be after a few glances at Jamie's size.

At eighty feet long and twenty-three feet wide, the *Mary B* wasn't as big as the *Phoenix*. She only had two masts, and the mainmast was taller than the foremast. Laddie's commission to the Kelley, Spear, & Company shipyard in Bath, Maine, was to build a schooner that two able seamen could handle. Laddie believed he could make more money by building a smaller boat than the other boats he was competing with. He would need less crew and could manage to get in and out of more ports without the help of a tug. Competent crew was getting difficult to find and keep, and he didn't want to be held up with crew problems. He wanted to be on the water moving cargo, not spending his time trying to find still one more boat hopper who would move about always looking for a few more dollars.

He also wanted a boat that would sail well and was built to haul heavy cargo. He had ice and granite in mind from the very beginning of his plans for the boat. "That's where the money is," he explained to Jaime. "If you can move it fast and safe, your only problem is working your men and your boat too hard. Ice and granite like gold right now. There's a lot of money to be made."

As 1881 came around, Jamie's nest egg had grown to where he was ready to consult with Laddie and Rose about asking Treasa to come to America. They both thought he was too young to get married and should wait another year. Politely, he said he'd think about it.

Late one afternoon that December, after they had finished unloading ice on the New York side of the river, Laddie stayed ashore to conduct some business with the broker for the ice house he supplied. A freezing wind was coming down the river as the steam tug pulled the *Mary B* to the Brooklyn side of the East River. Jamie was at the wheel, and Isaac was standing next to him. Isaac said, "This goin' be your boat."

"What are you talking about?"

"It is. You goin' be her master soon enough."

"Why on earth would you say such a thing?"

"Cap Laddie not doing so well. Sick with something."

"Seems fine to me."

"Remember last time we come home and Miss Rose here. Remember what she said?"

"Bout what?"

"She goin' on about how glad she is you sailing with Cap Laddie and how much they like you and depend on you."

"Yeah. Rose was just bein' nice. That's her way with people. She's a real nice lady."

"More en that. Those two got plans for you. I tellin' you. This goin' be your boat, and soon, too."

Three weeks after this conversation, they headed back to the Kennebec for ice, but first, they had a load of cotton on board they had to unload in Boston. From there, it would be sent to mills up in Lowell. From Boston, they'd sail empty until they got to Bath and then take on a load of ice. It was their first trip of the new year, and no one on board was anxious to make the trip after relaxing for a couple of weeks over the holidays. As they rounded Nantucket Shoals, they felt the wind change direction from the East to the Northeast and stiffen. The sky ahead darkened. It was still early in the afternoon, and Jamie thought they could easily stay on a tight reach until they cleared Cape Cod, and then they could ease off and head for Boston. He was surprised when Laddie said, "We're going in. It's going to be a big one. Let's get ready. Strike the jib and reef the mainsail."

Jamie was huddled out of the wind and was about to say he thought they could make it when he looked at Laddie and saw he was wincing every time he moved the wheel. Jamie got up, put the reef in the mainsail, and went forward to drop the jib. With less sail, the boat moved more easily. They headed off, and Jamie started looking for the Nantucket Light on the island's northern end. They would have to stand offshore to clear the shoals and then jibe to head back up the island's western shore until they reached the harbor entrance marked by the little Brant Point lighthouse. Jamie offered to take the helm, "I can take her if you'd like."

"No. I'm fine," Laddie said. "Just twisted the wrong way. We should be able to make it in through the cut without tacking. I'll need you to tend to the sails and get the anchor down when we make the harbor."

Laddie seemed fine by the time they got to the Water Street Tavern. He ordered himself a hot rum toddy and appeared to be settling in for the evening or longer. "Damned shoulder. Been acting up for over a year now. Especially bad when the weather is cold and frosty damp. What ails you, Isaac? You're older than I am."

"Not much, Cap'n. Been lucky that way. Knees still work, and that's the main thing far as I'm concerned. Knees work, you good."

"Wish my god-damned shoulder worked. Rose says I'm too old to do this anymore. What do you think, Jamie? Am I too old?"

"My Uncail Liam used to say you only as old as you think you be."

"Ain't he the one who just died?"

"Yes, sir, but he was fifty-one."

"Had a good long life, then. I'll be forty-four next birthday, and all my friends are already dying out. Comes too soon, Jamie. Got to make the most of it."

"Sure do, Cap'n," Isaac said.

"You, Isaac. You don't even know how old you are. You could be a hundred and one, and you wouldn't know it," Laddie said.

"That's the truth, for sure."

"How come you don't know how old you are?" Jamie asked.

"Never knew his mommy or daddy to tell him," Laddie answered for Isaac. "Daddy was sold, and his mommy died soon after he was born. Then he got separated from woman who took care of him. Isn't that right, Isaac?"

Isaac didn't say anything for a minute then asked, "You want another drink, Cap'n?"

Darkness had come early, and the wind had the harbor erupting in short, steep, white-capped waves. By the time Isaac rowed them back to the Mary B., Jamie had to sit in the stern holding on to Laddie so he wouldn't fall overboard.

Chapter Fifteen: Captain Buckley

Brooklyn was still a fiercely independent town in 1882. While there had been talk of Brooklyn joining New York City for several years, it wasn't until 1898 that it became part of the city, as a borough that looked across the East River to Manhattan. The vote to consolidate was very close, and for decades the losers would refer to it as 'The Great Mistake of 1898.'

Brooklyn city records in 1882 indicated the sale of a schooner, *Mary B*, to one James Patrick Buckley. Also recorded was the death of Edward Jonah Ladd and, several months later, the marriage of James Patrick Buckley to Treasa Ann de Burca.

Laddie knew something was wrong with his health. In anticipation, and to provide for his wife, he had struck a 'fair deal' with Jamie, and formal paperwork had been drawn up by a lawyer so there would never be any doubt about his intentions. The agreement stipulated that Mr. James Buckley would buy the, *Mary B*, over time from a share of the profits generated by the *Mary B*'s activities as a merchant vessel. When Mr. Edward Ladd died, Mr. Buckley would continue to pay Mrs. Edward Ladd (Rose) the agreed upon share as long as she would live. Upon the death of Mrs. Edward Ladd, any remaining debt would die with her, and the boat would belong to Mr. James Buckley free and clear.

After the papers were signed, Laddie said to Jamie, "So now I crew for you."

"Oh, no. You still be her skipper as long as you want."

"Jaime, you're the owner now."

"Then I be hiring you as captain. How much you be wanting?"

Laddie laughed, "I'm too old to do the worrying. Your boat; your worries."

Jamie couldn't believe his good fortune. He was the master of his own vessel. The day the papers were signed, Jamie wrote to Treasa and asked her if she was ready to come to America. "I'm as settled as I can possibly imagine. I have more than enough money to pay your fare, believe it or not. We can get married as soon as you get here." He told her they could stay with the Ladds until they found a place of their own. He went into great detail about the *Mary B.*, and what a fine vessel she was. He didn't wait for a response; he wired her the money for the fare.

She didn't write back; she just came. Jamie, Laddie, and Isaac were on their way to Maine when she arrived at the doorstep of the Ladd household in Brooklyn with all of her belongings in two bags.

Rose opened the door when Treasa knocked. Rose was not expecting her and was taken aback by the young woman who stood before her. Tall, slender, exhausted blue eyes contrasting with black hair, Treasa managed a smile, but just barely.

"I'm Treasa de Burca. I'm looking for Mr. Jaime Buckley. Am I in the right place?"

"You certainly are. Please come in. Let me help you with your bags. I'm Rose. Jaime isn't here right now. They're on their way to Stonington."

"Do ya know when he'll be back?"

"Probably three weeks, but come in."

"Three weeks. I shouldn't have come. I'm such an eejit. I didn't think. Of course he's not here. What do I do now?" She was crying when she asked the question.

Rose answered, "You come in, I'll put the kettle on, and we'll have a nice talk. We have lots of room, and I want to get to know you. How was getting through immigration at Castle Garden? Did everything go okay? Was the wait terrible? I've heard of people waiting for more than a day to get processed. Did you have any trouble finding us?" Treasa was exhausted from her journey and worked to stop crying so she could answer Rose.

"Oh my," Rose said. "I need to stop shooting questions at you, dear. Here, I'll show you to our spare room. You take your time and make yourself at home. Come down whenever you're ready."

As Jamie had said to Isaac, Rose was a kind woman, and that was her way. Within twenty-four hours, Treasa was surprised at how welcome and safe she felt. Rose wasn't Irish; her ancestry was Dutch, and she was a protestant. Nevertheless, Rose did not fit all of the stories Treasa had heard about how Americans treated the Irish. It was also apparent that Rose was very fond of Jamie and that he had found a home with Edward and Rose Ladd.

Rose started making plans for a wedding. She began to introduce Treasa to her friends and every new person they met had ideas about where and how the wedding and reception should take place. When Treasa suggested they wait for Jamie to return, Rose said, "What on earth would he know about how to put a wedding together?" Planning proceeded.

"I suppose you'll be wanting a Catholic wedding?" Treasa had not anticipated the question. Jaime had never mentioned the Ladds were not Catholic.

"Yes," she answered. "Jaime and me, we're both Catholic."

"Yes, dear, I know. I just wanted to make sure. It will be St. James, then."

As they walked back from St. James after discussing possible dates with the monsignor, Rose asked, "Since your father has passed, would you welcome the notion of Mr. Ladd giving you away? He is so fond of Jamie, and I think he would be pleased beyond belief to do so."

"Would you mind terribly if we waited 'til Jamie got home? Things are happening so fast. They're going ahead of me thinking."

"No, of course not."

Things were moving at a speed beyond Treasa's imagination, and she had yet to even set eyes on the man she was marrying. She had only known through letters for what had seemed an interminable time. Then, one evening, after they finished dinner and cleaned up in the kitchen, Rose said, "I am so excited. I never thought I would ever plan a wedding for a daughter. Please pardon my enthusiasm, Treasa. It is so nice to have a young woman in the house, and I know I must seem like a horrible busybody to you, but…"

"I understand, I guess. But all I care about is seeing Jamie again. I haven't even been thinking much about marriage and weddings and things."

"Do you want to get married?"

"Yes, of course. I just ain't given it much thought. You know, a wedding and all."

"Oh my. And here I've been assuming that's all you'd been thinking about."

"Maybe I should have, but I haven't."

"Your letters?"

"No. Just writin' about our days and how much we miss one another."

"Oh."

Laddie did not live to give Treasa de Burca away to James Buckley. When the *Mary B* arrived in New York and delivered its ice to the broker, some ice remained on board. It was being used for the deceased body of Edward Ladd. Isaac said it had been a heart attack. Jamie said he didn't know. His report to Rose was, "He was sittin' there in the cockpit not saying anything when suddenly he tried to stand up, said 'Oh God, no,' and keeled over. I didn't know what ta do. All I could do was just stand there and watch him die." He repeated "I didn't know what ta do" several times before Rose finally told him to stop blaming himself. "There's nothing you could've done, Jaime. I know that."

They buried Laddie at the Flatbush Reformed Church. People

from the church and the neighborhood visited and brought food for close to two weeks. Not many people knew Laddie because of his seafaring, but everyone knew Rose. She was an integral part of the community she had grown up in. She was a Venderbeek and proud of the lineage of her Dutch ancestry. Although neither she nor Laddie had any family ties left, Rose was very well-liked and respected for her work in the community and as a church member.

The tragedy of the household subsumed the joyous anticipation of the young couple. Jamie took long walks by himself. Treasa helped Rose. There was no talk of a wedding. Isaac came to the funeral and stood outside the church.

Rose made it clear that there was to be "no hanky-panky" in her house until they were married. Jamie and Treasa didn't know how long they should wait after Laddie's death to set a date for the wedding. In the meantime, Jamie had trips to make, and Treasa had a neighborhood and culture to get to know. However, they did find that when the *Mary B* was at the wharf, the boat's cabin provided sufficient privacy for the two of them to explore one another in ways that only a few years before would have been thought unthinkable. "Aren't we but horrible sinners," Treasa said on a Sunday morning while Rose was at church and the two of them were on the boat.

"Would you rather be at Mass? We can do that if you'd like."

"And have to listen to that old monsignor drone on and on. He says the slowest Mass in history. I don't want him to marry us. I want the young priest, Father McCormick. I hope the monsignor gives us a choice. Father McCormick calls him 'the boss.' The bishop isn't around much. We're too low class for a bishop anyway."

"You might be. I'm not. I own me own boat."

"You mean you and Rose Ladd, don't you?"

"You know what I mean. I'm goin' ta change her name soon as I feel it's right."

"To what?"

"*Treasa*, of course."

"Oh, Jamie. Are you really?"

"I am. *Mary B* was Laddie's mum."

"What was her full name?"

"Baynham. Mary Baynham."

"Will it be the *Treasa B*?"

"Nope. Just *Treasa* unless you want the 'B,' or we could go full out and call her the *Treasa de Burca*."

"No, no. She's not big enough for all that."

"You're saying I should get a bigger boat?"

It turned out to be a June wedding, and Father McCormick married them. Setting the date, though, was a logistical storm. Neither the bride nor the groom had any family or friends in Brooklyn, and Jamie said he wasn't sure about even asking the Callahans, although Treasa finally talked him into it. The Callahans, although family, didn't come. "Probably didn't want to have to pay for a wedding present and the ferry," Jamie explained when Treasa wondered why they didn't come.

Jamie was determined to have the wedding when the *Phoenix* was in port so Jacob could be the one to walk Treasa down the aisle. Fogo and Pudd would be there as groomsmen, and they would invite the new crew member, whoever he was. Rose pointed out how ridiculous that was because they could never plan when the *Phoenix* would be in Brooklyn. They didn't know if the boat was even doing the same route anymore.

Rose was a planner, and she wanted it to be a big wedding so she could invite all her friends. "Children, it's my only chance to give a wedding, and I want to do it the right way." She didn't say anything directly about how much the Ladds had done for them, but there was a not-so-subtle implication that they should both feel guilty if they did not let her do this for them, or her.

The young couple relented. Close friends of the Ladds supplied a bridesmaid, best man, flower girl, and a father to walk Treasa down the aisle. Rose had insisted that the newlyweds live with her. "The house has plenty of room, and it makes no sense whatsoever for you to go paying rent someplace when you can live here. Besides, it will be yours someday. My wedding present will be deeding it over to you when I die. I had thought about leaving it to the church, but you two are my family now, so it will be yours. The church may not like it, but it's mine to do with as I see fit. I've done plenty for them over the years, and they know it."

It was not a good time for a newly married young man of twenty, with meager business experience, to be going out on his own. Even though the country was in a depression, railroad lines had quadrupled during that time. Rail now connected New York City to Portland, Maine, and railroads were quicker and could haul more ice than schooners. Ice was now being 'manufactured' in New York. It had yet to make inroads into the ice trade, but some schooner owners were worried about it.

Jaime wasn't. "That manufactured stuff isn't real ice," Jamie told Treasa. "They have to use gases and all sorts of expensive equipment to get one block for Christ's sake. With all its ponds, lakes and rivers Maine's never going to run out. Winter comes, it's cheap to saw the blocks out of a pond. Our problem's going to be the fuckin' railroad, but not yet."

Jamie's immediate problem, though, was crew. The newly named *Treasa* was too big for one person to handle, Isaac was too old to do more than cook and take an occasional stint at the wheel, and Jamie found it hard to get crew who didn't try to cheat or steal from their young captain. If it were not for his size and his growing reputation as an angry young man who would throw you overboard while underway if you gave him a problem, Jamie would never have been able to survive. Jamie went from crew member to crew member for six months before deciding to wire Colm Folan to ask him to come to America to help Jamie out with the *Treasa*. He prayed that Colm still considered him a friend even though it had been a few years since the two had communicated with one another. To his surprise and delight, Colm said yes. Depression had reached Ireland as well. Members of the Irish National Invincibles had killed the top two British appointees to Ireland, and there was more talk of rebellion. Colm wanted no part of it. He wanted out.

For Jamie, it would mean crew he could depend on, but it would also mean 'another mouth to feed.' "That'll be five people I'm responsible for, Treasa. Five. And you wanting to get pregnant. I can't do it. Not now. Please. We have to wait 'til things start looking up." He then said something that he wanted to take back the minute he said it, "Maybe Rose will die, and we won't have her share to pay out from every trip. That would be a big help."

"Jaime Buckley, don't you dare start to thinkin' like that. I'll get a job. I'll find work, but you stop talking like that. You wouldn't have a boat, and we wouldn't have a place to live not been for Laddie and Rose."

"I know, but you not be workin'. No wife o' mine goin' to work over here." This conversation took place when they went to New York City to see the new electric lights in lower Manhattan.

"So, I'll work over there," Treasa said, pointing towards Brooklyn.

"You'll not be working, and that's final."

"You're a gobshite, Jamie Buckley. I'm bored beyond belief. I have no friends. You be away most of the time. We need money, and I need something to mind while you're gone, don't I?"

"No."

"Then take me with you. I'll cook. Isaac's too old to be much help anyway. When Colm gets here, it be like we was in Carna. Be fun. Why not? Give me one fuckin' reason why not? Just one. Don't be a fuckin' gobshite. It's a brilliant idea, and you know it."

"Women and boats don't mix. I'd be laughin' stock of every broker, dockmaster, and sailing crew from here to Canada and back. I get enough of that as is."

"Jamie Buckley, you may have a big body, but you don't have a big brain. You stay right here, and don't you dare follow me. I'm goin' back to Brooklyn and maybe to Carna." Treasa walked towards the ferry. Jamie stood still for a full minute, watching her walk away. When he understood she might be serious about Carna, he followed her as quickly as possible.

Treasa only made one trip on the boat named for her. At first, she and Jamie assumed she was throwing up because of seasickness. Isaac assured Jamie that this was not the case. Colm thought it was all very funny until he saw how distressed his two friends were.

Treasa lost three pregnancies over the next four years. Finally, they became convinced she could not have a child. Although he continued to argue against it, Treasa did get employment, at The Lotos Club in Manhattan. It called itself a gentleman's club that catered to gentlemen who were interested in the arts. Treasa made very little money, but it gave her something to 'mind.' Cleaning, dusting, making beds, and tidying were not beneath her, and she stopped talking about returning to Carna.

She overheard conversations about poetry and novels at the club. These discussions fascinated her. She started to spend time writing in a journal she had purchased. She also started to read more than she ever had before. In addition to her work at the club, the writing and the reading gave her something to 'mind' when Jamie was away. Through conversations with members of the club, she was able to borrow books, many of them written by members. She devoured everything she could get her hands on, and several club members took an interest in Treasa's reading habits, especially one of the founders. "Mr. Clemens always brings me books when he comes, Jamie. Some are his, but he has been bringing me books by women as well. Do you want to read some of them?"

Jamie evidenced little interest in her literary pursuits, and Rose thought she was being a 'silly young woman' who should have been spending more time on religious matters. To be polite and mollify her, Treasa accompanied Rose on several occasions to revival meetings that were the all rage in and around Brooklyn. Treasa considered these outings a matter of kindness and duty rather than interest.

Meanwhile, Jamie was getting to know the Maine Coast intimately. He and Colm would often spend an extra day or two exploring when the weather was good, and spending more time would not jeopardize their commercial commitments. With more than four thousand islands, the coastline of Maine was longer than five thousand miles, and the two young men imagined themselves explorers at times as they sailed the *Treasa* into one small harbor after another for the first time.

The country was changing, and religious movements were gaining traction, but worse, in Jamie and Colm's eyes, they were also gaining political influence. Parallel to what Rose called The Awakening of America, a temperance movement was underway. The young men both thought the temperance movement to be one of the silliest things they had ever come across.

"Can you imagine them trying something like that in Ireland?" Colm asked one night when they were at anchor in Stonington.

"Tar and feather for the politicians that tried it," Jamie responded. "Just a lot of talk."

"I don't understand it. These eejits say it's immoral. Do they even read the fuckin' bible? There's wine all over the place. How the hell they say it's immoral?"

Still, as the movement became more serious throughout the United States, especially in Maine, where all but cider was already banned, the two young men saw another service they could add to replace the ever-dwindling ice trade. Canada was not that far away, and Jamie 'knew some people' who could get him started with a new cargo.

However, even in Maine there was relatively little interest in rum and whiskey from Canada. Alcohol was readily available in private clubs through secretive but robust channels. Enforcement of 'The Maine Law' was lax and, as Jamie was to say many years later, "We were ahead of our time."

The need for coal, though, grew as New York grew, and Jamie began looking south to Philadelphia. The new railroads could not keep up with the demand, so schooners were needed. New ones were being built just to haul coal. Some of them were enormous, four and five-masted behemoths, but there was still room for those of the smaller size like the *Treasa*. Maybe the new machines could make ice for New York, but no machine was going to make coal or granite, and New York needed both. "Flexibility," Jamie told Colm and Isaac. "We need to be flexible."

"We be damned dirty boat we start hauling coal," Isaac said. "You wind up being black as me. See how that suit you."

May 26, 1990
HOME TOWN BOY by Michael Buckley

The beaches will be opening soon. When I walked down Main Street in Bath earlier this week it seemed every store window had advertisements for beachwear, beach toys, beach towels, beach chairs, and beach umbrellas. And don't worry, if you don't get downtown, the advertisements will find you via the mail you get at home.

Some items don't seem to change over time. Sand buckets and shovels are good examples. They come in different sizes and colors but the basic designs have stood the test of time. This is not the case with beachwear, specifically bathing suits. Covering up has become less of a priority as the years have gone by, especially for women. However, it is my observation, and a generalization, that men's bathing trunks seem to be getting longer while bikinis are shrinking. I am ignorant of the dynamics of appropriate beach nakedness that control such things. It is merely an observation.

We are lucky hereabouts. We have two glorious beaches close at hand. Years ago, old Walter E. Reid bought up a big chunk of Georgetown, well over a thousand acres, and then gave a piece of it to the State. I guess he didn't need all the land he originally bought. At one point, the beach at what is now Reid State Park was used for bombing practice and marine landings. I'm not sure the birds and turtles approved of such goings-on, but I doubt they were given much consideration. The time hadn't come yet, to worry about the planet and habitat destruction.

The beach out at Popham is not as big but it is as delightful, and you can visit Fort Popham if you get tired of the sun.

In addition to enjoying beaches, we need them and their dunes. Yes, they provide us with places to tan and play, but they also act as barriers to protect us from storms.

Each beach has a unique personality but, sort of like people, they are constantly changing. That can create all sorts of problems for us. So, we construct artificial barriers to keep these natural barriers in place: seawalls and breakwaters. We also break up these natural barriers and dredge holes through them to keep our channels open since we don't trust the tides and shifting sand to put the openings where we want them to be and then keep them there.

Beaches also create political problems for us. We say they are priceless, but if you have enough money, you can buy your own beach and keep others off it, or at least keep them from getting to it. So, beaches aren't really priceless; they are just pricey. Older states, like Maine, have more of a problem with that than the younger states of the West, where public access is built into deeds.

It gets a bit dicey in Maine when the summer people leave. The locals come out and use the beaches and pretty much ignore the 'access' problem. Clamming and some fishing require access. No one thought much about beach access before summer people or rusticators as they became known in the 'Gilded Age.' For one thing, the idea of a vacation of any sort was not an aspiration most locals had, especially during the summer, what with fishing, boat building, and farming and all.

The rusticators could afford to take a month or a summer off, and they started buying up beachfront. While they liked the locals well enough as a steady labor supply for cleaning and repairing, they did not want them on their 'priceless' beaches during the summer months. So, beach access became like the freshwater pumped to their summer homes. When the rusticators turned off the water at the end of summer, the locals turned on their access to the beaches and vice versa. Water goes on; local access gets turned off. Water goes off; locals head for the beach. It's a steady rhythm, sort of like the tides or phases of the moon. Most of the time it works pretty well as long as the rusticators don't start erecting a lot of locked gates, and the locals don't damage the empty summer cottages.

Down in Florida, people name their cities and towns after their beaches and make sure they stay open to the public all the time: Miami Beach, Deerfield Beach, Palm Beach, Vero Beach, Daytona Beach. People go to these places for the beach. Back up here in Maine, the only town we have named for its beach is Old Orchard Beach. It's not that we don't have a coastline; we have more than Florida; it's just that our ancients weren't that impressed with the attractive power of beaches. It is also true that our beaches aren't nearly as impressive in size, and, of course, there is the water temperature, you have to like cold water—a lot!

On the other hand, our beaches have things that those southern beaches do not. Tidal pools are a gift to the scientific education of our young ones. You make a mistake in your sandcastle, don't worry. The tide will erase your mistake, and you get another chance in twelve hours. It's true, we don't have a lot of days for baking in the sun, and swimming is for the hardy—my father would say the foolhardy. However, we have the advantage of a new surprise every day as the weather changes, and a new beauty appears, one that is a bit different from the day, or even the hour, before.

I'm glad beach weather is coming. The days will get longer and so will the line of cars waiting to cross the Davey Bridge in Wiscasset.

Chapter Sixteen: Comparisons

I heard Jesse's motorcycle come down the driveway. Wendy was riding faster than I would have liked, but no faster than I was used to Jesse riding when he was here. I may have been a bit envious. I've gotten much more careful over the years and ride less and less. Rina was on the back. At least they were both wearing helmets. Maine does not require helmets for adults, but if you are within a year of getting your learner's permit, you have to wear one, and so does your passenger. I still wear one when I ride. I see a lot of idiots who don't, but then Maine breeds a lot of idiots who ride motorcycles and believe they have stepped out of a comic book and are immortal.

I was sprawled out on the porch swing. Their arrival interrupted my note-taking for a short story that I would never write. Still, I would have the notes if someday I decided to get serious about actually writing again. I had been once. I had the rejection slips and letters to prove it. I had been toying with an idea for a new novel for years now but had nothing to show for it. I was turning into that pathetic creature in Henry James's short story, *Madonna of the Future.* My creative masterpiece was always just around the corner. If I had been more realistic, I might have accepted that whatever writing juice I had was already expended.

Wendy parked the bike next to the shed and the two of them joined me on the porch. Charlie pawed at the screen door to be let out so he could greet them. Wendy let them out and said, "Grandpa, can we borrow the truck? We were thinking of going clamming and …."

"I thought you were a vegetarian."

"I am, but I take a vacation once in a while and become a pescatarian, and I figured if I was going to be in Maine for the summer…"

"You didn't have lobster when Maude was here."

"I snuck a little. I had forgotten how good it tastes."

"Where you thinking of going?"

"The Bay."

"Where're you going to park?"

"Indian Point. Most of the Indian Pointers aren't here yet, and we'll only be there for a couple of hours. Rina's got to be back and start work on a project she brought with her."

"Oh. She's working on a project." It wasn't subtle, but it was the best I could do. Wendy just looked at me. She didn't say anything. It had been a week since Rachel dropped her off, and I had not seen her do any reading or writing. Neither had she asked me to help her get a pass to the library or introduce her to people at the historical society. Maybe she was testing whether or not she could disappoint me. If she was, she was learning that she could. I said, "You can take the truck, but if someone down there says something, be polite and leave. For God's sake, don't say that you didn't know. It's my truck, and I'm not exactly a stranger around here."

"Thank you. License?"

"On a lanyard in the hall. Clam rakes and buckets are…"

"In the shed."

Of course she remembered where they were kept.

Wendy was very proud of the Pasta Alle Vongole she served the two of us for dinner that night. She had a right to be. When I asked her about it, she said, "NYT Cooking. I use it all the time. I save recipes I like, and it's all online. No paper recipe cards covered with junk the way Mom's are. I use my tablet. By the way, you should get internet down here. How do you live without it?"

"I've got it at the farmhouse."

"You need it down here."

"I do, do I?"

"I might be able to set up a hotspot even though the cell service stinks. I can set it up easy-peasy."

"Do you have to pay extra by the month?" I thought it was a legitimate question.

She laughed, "No, of course not."

"Sure. Why not, then? Speaking of the internet, I wondered when you wanted me to make the calls to the library and the historical society for you. You ready to start on your paper yet?"

"What does that have to do with internet service?"

"Well, you said you could do a lot of your reading online." I stopped talking and looked at her. "Okay, I'm curious. Are you planning on doing the paper? If you are, do you need any help?"

"Are you asking me now because I said Rina has a summer project?"

I was taken aback by her directness. "I guess I am, in part. I was under the impression that getting the paper done was important to you, and that's why you're here for the summer."

I never expected the explosion that followed. "My being here isn't enough for you? Why does everyone want more from me? You sound just like Stephen!" With that, she raced out the door, and a minute later, I heard the motorcycle come to life and then the sound of gravel flying off the rear wheel as she headed up the hill.

She was back in twenty minutes. I timed her. I didn't know her well enough to know whether she would come back or not. I debated just letting her head for her room but rejected it. I thought about the conversation with Maude. When she went through the living room and headed for the stairs, I said, "Wendy, please, come sit. Tell me what's going on. I'm not your enemy."

She hesitated but came over and sat down on the couch opposite me. Then she got up, went into the kitchen, and got a can of soda from the refrigerator. When she sat back down, there was no preamble. "No offense, but I wasn't supposed to be here this summer. Stephen and I were going to spend June in France with Julien and then bum around

Europe for the rest of the summer. Then the shithead breaks up with me because I'm not good enough for him. I still could have gone and stayed with Julien, but now everything's all screwed up because of this lousy history course. I thought if I came here, everything would be fine, but it's not. It's like being right back in school and having an assignment to do. And now you're comparing me to Rina, just like always."

"Whoa, whoa, whoa. Where's this coming from?"

"Be honest. Aren't you?"

I was. But there was a paper to be written. I didn't know about her previous plans for the summer. Would she believe me if I denied it? Probably not. If I confirmed it, would she pull away?

I said, "I didn't know about your plans for the summer and how disappointed you must be. I have been focused on your paper, and in that regard, when you mentioned Rina, I was wondering when you would start working on it." I waited for her to say something. She didn't.

She pulled out her cellphone, and started fiddling with it. "Wendy, can I have your attention?" She looked up. "Let me tell you something. When your grandmother and I used to get into a fight, and it wasn't going anyplace, one of us would say to the other, 'okay, let's start over.' What do you think, shall we start over?"

She didn't say anything, so I asked again, "Would you like to?"

"Do I have a choice?"

"Yes. You do."

I think my answer surprised her. She mumbled, "Okay."

"You seemed excited when you first got here, Rina being here, learning to ride Jesse's bike. Have I done something to change that?"

Her answer was a protest, "No!"

"Help me out then; what's going on?"

She didn't say anything. She patted the couch next to her. Charlie jumped up to join her and she started to pet him. "It's Rina. Her life is so damned perfect, and mine is so shitty."

"Why do you say that?"

"Look at my parents compared to hers. My mom's an alcoholic who can't get her life together. As far as my father's concerned, I'm a check he mails to the college. My mom goes through men like her bottles of booze, and now she's spewing her history on me all the time, so I 'won't be surprised by anything.' Also, Julien left us to go back to his 'real children.' That's just for starters. Rina told me all about her great boyfriend when we were clamming, and she has this interesting research project she's working on for one of her professors. I'm stuck here for the summer doing a lousy make-up paper I could care less about, and the only boy I've ever really cared about broke up with me because I didn't have my act together. How the hell does he expect me to have my act together given my family?"

I chuckled. I couldn't help it.

"It's not funny?"

"Oh, Wendy. You remind me of myself at times. I've circled the drain so many times. You're going to be fine, kiddo. Your mom is trying. She may not be doing it perfectly, but she's trying."

"She's 'trying' alright."

"Question: did Julien want you to come this summer?"

"It was his idea."

"So, you're pissed at him for leaving, but he wants you in his life. Seems to me like both are true."

"I guess."

"Now you're going to get pissed at me. If you had done the paper, where would you be right now?"

"Chamonix."

"Even without Stephen?"

"Yes."

"You know all this. That's got to hurt."

She didn't say anything. She sat there petting Charlie. I waited.

She said nothing. Finally, I said, "Okay. What are you thinking?"

"Nothing."

"I don't believe that for a second. What are you thinking?"

"I'm fucked up. So is my life."

I watched her push Charlie away and crawl into a ball on the couch. "Maybe that's the problem. Thinking that way. Your grandmother would never approve of the language I'm about to use. Nevertheless, here goes: you may have fucked up last semester. You didn't write the paper, there were consequences and you're pissed about it. That doesn't define you or your life. You're smart. You've connected the dots. If you had done the paper, you'd be in Chamonix. Hon, a person who's fucked up can't connect dots. Julien went to be with his children and wanted you and your mother to come with him. It didn't work out for some excellent reasons. Pay attention. He stays in touch and wanted you to come this summer. He wants you in his life. You know how to connect all of those dots. Your mom is learning new ways of being your mother—perfectly, no. Again, you know how to connect the dots. Stephen, I don't know about. He sounds a bit pompous and judgmental to me. The relationship was important to you, though. Losing it sucked, and you couldn't hold it together. The connection of those dots makes all the sense in the world to me. If that makes you fucked up, so am I."

She didn't say anything. She sat up, and patted the couch. Charlie jumped onto it, and she started to pet him. She leaned down and nuzzled the back of his neck. He stretched his head back and tried to lick her face. I asked her again, "What are you thinking?"

"You don't think I'm weird?"

"Weird, yes, fucked up, no."

"Thanks a lot."

"You're welcome."

"Oh shit. I forgot to feed Charlie." She got up and headed for the kitchen; Charlie followed close behind. She returned; Charlie didn't.

When she sat back, she tucked her legs underneath her and asked, "Do you miss Nanna?"

"Every day, every hour, every second."

"So do I. I wish people didn't have to die."

I didn't know what to say that wouldn't be trite, so the two of us just sat there. The fire was dying down. Soon there would be nothing but embers. I started for the kitchen to close up for the night when Wendy said, "Grandpa, I don't know where to begin."

I stopped and turned back to where she was sitting. I could see the top of her head above the back of the couch, red hair glowing in the last of the firelight. "Begin what?"

"Getting my act together. My life. The paper. Take your pick."

I walked back in, leaned over, and kissed her on top of the head. "You'll figure it out."

"I don't know how."

I looked at her huddled on the couch, holding Charlie. All I could think of was Rachel huddled in the same place so many years ago. "Let's talk in the morning." She didn't say anything. I went over and sat next to her and put my arm around her shoulder. "I love you. Maybe we can figure this out together."

Chapter Seventeen: The Work

Finally, the work on *Redhead* was finished. The boatyard called at 7:30 in the morning to let me know that the new transceiver for the radar had arrived. "The boat should be ready by noon, Mike. Maybe earlier if we don't run into any problems. I'll call and let you know when we're done."

"Thanks."

"You gonna need any help bringing her over?"

"No. My granddaughter's here. I'm all set."

The boat had been in the water for a week. When the yard put her in and tested everything, they discovered the radar wasn't working. They diagnosed the problem as a bad transceiver. So, of course, a replacement had to be ordered. It couldn't be avoided. The transceiver is the guts of a radar system, and radar on a Maine boat is like air conditioning in Central Florida. You can live without it, but you'd rather not. GPS will let you know where you are on a chart, how fast you're going, what direction you're heading, and a lot of other things, but it won't show you anything not on the chart, like other boats, freighters, or aircraft carriers you might just bump into when the fog is thick. For that, you need radar. So, for the past week, the *Redhead* had been sitting on a mooring in front of the boatyard.

The service manager knew I would be up at 7:30. That's when their day began, so any boat owner waiting for their boat would be up, too. I hadn't seen Wendy yet, so I assumed she was still asleep. There was no need to wake her.

I poured myself a cup of coffee, walked to the end of the pier, and sat down. From upstairs in the bed with Wendy, Charlie must have heard me leave and came down. He barked at me from behind the screen door, so I went back to the house and let him out. He immediately headed for his favorite tree, paused, lifted his leg, and went off into the woods. He was a modest young gentleman and believed his morning and evening toilets should be performed in privacy. He had no such qualms about where he peed. His ritual completed, he joined me at the pier and found a place with no shadows to interfere with his enjoyment of the morning sun.

Some mornings the coffee tasted better than others, even though I never varied how I made it. It had to do with my mood and the weather. Sometimes I felt those were one and the same. This morning was sunny and brisk, Maine June brisk. The coffee tasted especially good. This was also my thinking time, which was not always good for me. The weather would affect that as well.

Wendy called from the house, "Charlie, breakfast!" Charlie did not need any encouragement. Within five minutes, both of them were headed in my direction. Charlie did not dine; he inhaled his food. For the hell of it, I timed him yesterday. Just under a minute from start to moving the empty bowl around. Wendy had a cup of coffee in one hand and a coffee carafe in the other. She was wearing flip-flops, sweat pants, and her UVM hoodie, which was covering her head and a good part of her face.

As she got to where I was sitting, she said, "More coffee?"

"Thanks. I didn't know you were up."

"Couldn't sleep. Decided to get some work done." She sat down on the bench opposite me.

"Oh."

"Don't be that surprised. I downloaded all three books yesterday at the library."

"How? It wasn't open."

"Their Wi-Fi stays on. I poached it from outside. Do you know how many pages I have to read this summer?"

"Well, given what you've told me, I assume a lot."

"Try one thousand, seven hundred, and fifty pages. It's ridiculous. That's three books. And that doesn't include any research reading I'll have to do to write the paper."

"Unless I'm mistaken, one of those, the Zinn book, is from last semester."

She looked at me over the cup of coffee she was holding to her mouth. "You hate me."

I couldn't tell if she was serious or not, so I decided to treat it as non-serious commentary on my part, pointing out a simple fact, not fake news. "I wouldn't dare hate you. You cook too well. I'd be risking delicious dinners. No way I'm going to risk giving those up."

"How will I get it all done plus write a paper?"

"One word at a time, I suppose."

"Grandpa, that is not helpful."

"Perhaps not, but it's true. Just set a reading schedule for yourself. For example, let's assume you have sixty working days this summer. If my math is right, that's around thirty pages a day. Doable, don't you think?"

"I gave myself sixty-five days, and it's less than thirty."

"You already figured it out. Put in some time…"

"Two hours a day on the paper. Three to four hours of work a day in total. I know. It doesn't sound like much. Told you I couldn't sleep. I kept figuring it out. Also, can I borrow your library card for Bowdoin? If you give me a note saying I'm living with you, I can get my own card for fifteen dollars."

"You sure?"

"That's what it says on their website. I looked that up, too."

"Wow. You have been busy."

"This is my problem. I start every semester getting organized this way, and then it all falls apart. I get behind and then wind up not giving a shit after the first couple of weeks. After that, why bother? There're too many other things to do."

"You mean having fun."

"It's not just having fun. It's all sorts of things."

"Like?"

"I don't know. Hanging out with friends. Skiing. Playing bridge. Just things."

I didn't say anything. The two of us just sat there with Charlie stretched out in the sun between us. I didn't know what to say. My hunch is she didn't either. So finally, I said, "Yard called. The transceiver arrived, and they're installing it this morning. Want to help me bring the boat around?"

"You see. That's exactly what I mean. Things always come up."

"Okay, I can bring her around by myself."

"No, I'll help."

"You sure? I'll be fine. Done it a million times."

"I know, but..." She stopped talking. "I want to help. You want more coffee?"

"Please." She filled both of our cups, and we again retreated into silence. She turned and looked up the harbor where a lobsterman was pulling his traps. He didn't have a stern man, so it was twice the work and twice the time.

Without turning, she said, "Maybe I could become a lobsterwoman like Linda Greenlaw."

"Don't expect me to be your stern man like her father was."

"What an amazing woman. First swordfish, then lobsters, and now she's writing. Did you ever see *The Perfect Storm*? She can keep the sword fishing."

"Scary movie. Book scared me more. I didn't need to know that much about the physiology of drowning." Did it bother her? I read the book and saw the movie. Why was I walking on eggshells? Damn it, Maude. Again, there was silence.

Finally, Wendy asked. "Did you know what you wanted to do when you were in college? I have absolutely no idea what I want to do when I get out of school. Rina knows—graduate school and then become an academic. She's got her life all planned out. Did you?"

This felt like a trick question, another disappointment maker. I answered her honestly, though. No more damned eggshells. "I did. I knew in high school. I was going to be the next great investigative reporter."

"Mom told me some story about you getting suspended or something."

"I did not get suspended. It was just threatened."

"What happened?"

"I was working on our student newspaper in my junior year, and I saw teachers smoking in the teacher's lounge. Students would, of course, get suspended for smoking. I thought this was blatantly unfair. Talk about a double standard. Teachers could; students couldn't."

"Did you smoke?"

"Nope. Never did. Anyway, I started hanging out around the door to the teacher's lounge, and every time someone went in or came out, I would look in to see who was smoking. I'd jot their names down. I was getting ready for my big expose in the school paper about who the smokers were. Well, one day, I saw the French teacher come out, and she was looking a little disheveled. I saw the coach through the door, and he was buckling his belt. There had already been rumors about the two of them, so I knew I had a real scoop. Anyway, I wrote this article about hanky-panky in the Teacher's Lounge. Actually, it was more like a gossip column with lots of questions and innuendo. Needless to say, the faculty advisor to the newspaper, Mr. Etchell, was not too eager to print it. Being sixteen, I was incensed and gave him a lecture about free press and censorship. He didn't find my lecturing him to be endearing. I told him I was going to publish it on my own. He said if I did, I would probably get suspended, or possibly expelled. He called my father. My father was not pleased, and said he was in absolute agreement with Mr. Etchell. He wanted to know what on earth I was thinking. I proceeded to give him a lecture about freedom of the press. He was no more impressed than Mr. Etchell had been. So, I considered mimeographing it and handing it out around the school."

"What's mimeographed?"

I took a deep breath and shook my head, "That was an ancient way of doing what copy machines do now."

"Did you do it?"

"No. I made the mistake of telling Maude what I was going to do. She told my mother, who took me aside and described the horrid consequences that would befall me if I were that stupid."

Mockingly Wendy said, "Mother Maude sold you out?"

"She did. It was not the first time, nor the last."

"So, you knew what you wanted to do even before you got to college."

"Yeah, sort of. My father wasn't happy about it, but my mother convinced him to let me major in journalism if that's what I wanted to do. Dad wanted me to become an engineer and go into business with him. I had no interest whatsoever in engineering, so what did I do? I married one. He loved that, and it became a standing family joke.

"Once I got to B.U., I became serious about journalism. Watching McCarthy get taken down by journalists like Edward R. Murrow was heady stuff. I. F Stone became my hero, and I started reading the *I.F. Stone Weekly*. I saw journalism as a way to make a difference in the world, and I loved it. I also loved that many of the writers I admired started out as newspaper journalists: Twain, Hemingway, and of course, E.B. White. Did you know Stephen King wrote for his high school and college papers?"

"No. I didn't. Who was I. F. Stone?"

"Probably the greatest investigative journalist of all time. Politicians hated him. I wanted to be like him. I wanted to be a great investigative reporter and sometime novelist. So much for planning."

"What happened?"

"How did you describe it, 'things always come up.' All sorts of things."

"You did work as a reporter, and you've written novels."

"Approximations. Bath is not exactly Boston or New York." I paused before I said, "Forget I just said that. Excuses are easy. I think I never got serious enough to make the sacrifices I would have had to make. Luck also enters. There's always luck—unfeeling, uncaring, luck."

That was a conversation stopper. And we stopped talking for a few minutes. When I broke the silence, I asked, "Why change your major to history?"

"Who knows? I needed to declare a major. Sociology didn't turn out to be what I thought it would be. I liked history in high school. So, it was sort of a 'why not?'"

"Interesting. Probably as good a reason as any. I've always loved history. I just remembered something I hadn't thought about for a long time. I had a professor at BU, Edward Dietrich. He drew a link between journalism and history that I love. He was pushing us to be fanatically accurate and to provide context, no gonzo journalism allowed with this guy. He would say, 'People, you are leaving the crumbs for the historians to follow. When they open up their microfiche readers, it will be your words they will be reading. You are recording history as it happens. Never forget this. You have to get it right, and you have to do it every single day. Imagine that some historian will be reading your words a hundred years from now.' Dietrich would also say, 'Reporting is writing the first draft of history.' I still love that."

Wendy asked, "What's microfiche?"

The *Redhead* was named for my mother. She didn't much like the name, but my dad didn't want to go with a traditional *Margaret O* for Margaret O'Neil. *Peggy B,* for Peg Buckley, was in the running for a while. My grandfather often referred to my mother as 'the redhead' as in asking my father, "So, Jack, how's 'the redhead' doing?" When Dad settled on the name, he was not moving from it. When the boat was passed on to me, no consideration was given to a name change. I would have faced a family rebellion at the suggestion of a name change.

My father knew exactly what he wanted when he had her built. The famous naval architect, John Alden, had set out to perfect the schooner as a boat you could race and use for a family cruise. Alden would build one, race it for a year, learn from it, and then build another one the following year. He designed fifteen in this series starting in 1922. Dad knew, he didn't just think, that the second—Malabar II—was the most beautiful of the lot, and he was determined to have one when he got out of the Navy at the end of World War II. He said that thinking and dreaming about it when he was in the Aleutians helped him to get to sleep at night. Finally, five years after the war ended, he had enough money to do it.

Ribs of white oak, planks of white cedar, trim of black walnut, spars of spruce, *The Redhead* is a sculptural masterpiece of wooden boat building. Over the years, we've replaced almost every piece of her, including the motor three times and the sails many times. She now has the most up-to-date electronics, but the original binnacle and compass remain. The bell from the *Treasa* is also there.

The *Redhead* turns heads wherever we sail with her bright red hull, white cabin, and varnished trim. When we tie up to a dock, people wander over to ask questions about her. She's not enormous, a little over 41 feet, including her bowsprit, but she's very comfortable. Four can sleep in the main cabin on facing settees and pilot berths. Another two can sleep forward in the V-berth. My mother used to say Hannah and I had four kids because we didn't want to waste any space.

One of the most important things about her is that the people at the boatyard treat her like she is a fine piece of art, which she is. A picture of the *Redhead* under full sail is on their website. In addition, pictures of her have appeared in magazine articles about Maine. Once in a while, I become a little anxious about sailing her because of the way other people treasure her, but only once in a while. I've been sailing on her since I was ten years old.

Wendy wanted to take the motorcycle over to the boatyard and leave it there. Once we brought the boat back to Heron Cove and put her on the mooring, I would then drive her back to the yard, and she would head into Brunswick to get her library card. I said her plan was fine with me. When I went to get on the motorcycle, though, she stopped me. "Uh, uh. I'm driving. You get the 'bitch seat,' Gramps."

I have never ridden on the so-called 'bitch seat' of a motorcycle in my entire life. I was terrified. Perhaps not terrified, but it took a deep breath, maybe two, before I climbed on behind her. Fortunately, the ride over to Robinhood was only fifteen minutes. I relaxed after about five of those. I had taught her well.

The service manager was tied up with another customer when we got there. I checked to make sure the fuel tank and both water tanks were topped off. I checked the oil, the batteries, and the tension on the engine belts. We waited. I turned on all of the navigation equipment. It worked. Finally, I turned on the radar. The image returns were sharp through all distance ranges. I was ready to go. We waited. I turned on the radio and went to the marine weather station. Nothing had changed. The day was beautiful, with wind from the southwest at 9 to 10 knots.

Finally, the service manager appeared, jovial as ever, clipboard in hand. He apologized; he saw I had the radar on, and I said I was pleased. I signed the paperwork, we got the lines on board, and left. We had been waiting there for an hour, but with the feel of the boat underway, forgiveness came quickly.

We had the sails up and drawing before we got to the Sheepscot River. The day was so beautiful we decided to head out into the ocean and circumnavigate Seguin Island before bringing the boat around to Heron Cove.

The wind was gentle, and I asked Wendy if she felt comfortable taking the helm. She said, "Come on Gramps, it's just like riding a bicycle." She came over to the leeward side to get a better view of the sails and settled in. I started up forward, stopped, turned to her, and said, 'Gramps.' Really?"

"Grandpa is too formal for a whole summer."

"Oh." I turned and went up forward. I sat on the deck and leaned back against the foremast. I loved this perch. I could watch the gentle rising and dipping of the bowsprit against the horizon. 'Gramps.' Yeah. If I were 'Gramps' for the summer, that would be okay.

The conversation on the pier was gnawing at me like a sore tooth. I had been very quick to give advice, "One word at a time." With all of my started, but not finished, writing projects, when did I stop finishing things? It was long before Hannah died. Her death, my usual excuse for my malaise, didn't work. Whatever happened to that young wannabe investigative reporter-novelist? It had been more than a dream or an aspiration. It was going to happen; then it didn't. Still, I held on to those 'someday' boxes up in the attic.

From the stern, Wendy shouted, "Ready about! Duck your head, Gramps!" I scrambled to the side of the mast so the staysail boom could come across and I wouldn't be thrown overboard or get hit in the head. "Hard alee." The boat came across the wind smartly and settled on the opposite tack. From the stern, Wendy released the jib and winched it in on the opposite side for the new tack. I moved back to my perch in front of the foremast.

So, Wendy didn't know what she wanted to major in. History was a default choice. Maybe I forgot why I majored in journalism. It seemed so long ago. "One word at a time." I had said that. That applied to both of us. What a pair we were: a twenty-year-old with no dreams and a guy in his seventies who had given up on his—a long time ago.

Chapter Eighteen: The Attic

The young newlyweds who had rented the farmhouse were city folks from New York. They didn't own a car and had rented one for their honeymoon, a two-week adventure on a sheep farm in Maine. I had not met them except over the phone. She, her name was Miranda, was the niece of people who had rented from us many times before. So, I felt comfortable renting to them, sight and credit report unseen.

To help our renters, Hannah, ever the engineer, had put together the most detailed house book one could imagine. It described in minute detail where everything was and how it worked. It included addresses and telephone numbers for everything from churches to hospitals. I updated everything every year and added the latest brochures for local and not-so-local attractions. It was rare that renters ever called us unless there was indeed an emergency. When that happened, it usually had nothing to do with the house. Consequently, I was surprised when I got a call from the new husband, Barry, saying the BBQ grill wasn't working and that it had stopped in the middle of their grilled salmon the previous evening.

I asked if he had checked to see if there was propane left in the tank. He asked how he would check. I told him that there were marks on the side of the grill where the tank hung. I explained that as propane was used, the tank became lighter and rose on the sprung hinge so you could tell how much propane was left in the tank. He must have turned away from his phone because I heard him say something to Miranda. When he returned, he said they had not done that. I was about to tell them about the spare tank in the barn when I decided it might be best if I went up and changed the tank myself if it was out of fuel. All of this is carefully explained in the 'House Book,' but either these city folks didn't know how to read, which I doubted, or they were used to calling for help when things didn't go as planned, which I believed to be the case. I wondered if they had ever grilled outside before. That was probably part of their Maine adventure.

When I arrived at the farmhouse, I was greeted with thanks and apologies. Miranda, the new bride, acknowledged that she had consulted the 'House Book' that morning, and it was all clearly spelled out and that Barry, the groom, had retrieved the spare tank from the barn and was out back trying to replace it. I smiled my owner's 'no problem' smile and went out back to assist Barry. I was concerned that he might be having some difficulty with the mechanical task that had fallen upon him to perform.

I was right. He had gotten the old tank off and was looking at the new one. He was seated cross-legged in a yoga position in front of the grill. I asked if I could give him a hand. He looked up from his position and, with a somewhat plaintive voice, asked if I would tell him what to do. I was gentle. "First time, huh. No reason why you should know how to do it." I guided him through the replacement process and showed him the marks on the grill where the weight was measured. With the new tank in place, it registered full. I assured him, "That will last most of the summer, but I'll take the empty with me, get it refilled, and put it back in the barn. Why don't you test this one out and make sure everything's working okay?"

He did. The grill worked. I picked up the empty tank and was headed back to the truck when I stopped and turned to him and asked, "Would you mind if I took a minute to get something from the attic?"

"No. Not at all. And thanks for helping me with this."

"No problem. Any other things you need?"

"No. We love it here. It's so quiet, and it's cool seeing the sheep."

"Well, they can get noisy at times."

"Actually, we like hearing them."

"Good. I'll just be a minute, and then I'll leave you folks alone."

I went inside, climbed upstairs, and unlocked the door to the attic. I knew exactly what I was looking for, my box of old 'Home Town

Boy' articles. I had done several historical pieces over the years, and I was feeling kindly toward Wendy. I thought she might be able to use them. Perhaps the personal touch of knowing the author might help increase her historical curiosity and get her work done. I probably wanted to show off to her as well. Two typewritten pages a week, forty-eight weeks a year—I took off for vacation and holidays—and fifteen years all led to close to 1500 pages. If she read them all that would be close to as much reading as she would do for her course. What the hell, she didn't have to read any of them, let alone all of them. But they'd be there, just in case.

I knew they were neatly cataloged by year, each year in its manila folder. I got the box and put it aside at the head of the stairs. I was about to head down when a thought hit me, and I turned back to retrieve another box. It contained a book I had started about a labor strike in Jay, Maine, in 1987. When I was working on it, I thought it was the best work I had produced. Then it became my best 'I'll finish it someday' work. Then it became a box at the bottom of a pile of other boxes in the attic, sequestered away beneath photo albums, old clothes, and assorted unacknowledged junk.

The 'Jay, Maine' box was filled with detailed notes, also filed away in manila folders. I knew exactly where it was, dug it up out of its grave, blew some dust off it, sneezed at my stupidity, and put it with the 'Home Town Boy' box.

I took the boxes down to the truck and put them in the front seat so nothing would blow away. Then, driving back down to Tír, I felt a strange combination of pride and foolishness.

The dining alcove at Tír is large and has windows on three sides. One side looks out over the porch to the cove. The only furniture is a huge old wood table painted yellow, ten chairs that don't match, and an ancient buffet that my mother bought at an estate sale for thirty dollars. All the windows were open, and Wendy was sitting at the far end of the table looking at her computer screen. A large mug was close at hand. Neither brush nor comb had found its way to her hair. She looked up, "Morning, Gramps. You were out early. I heard the truck leave."

"Renters needed some help with the grill. Since I was there, I got some stuff from the attic."

"What'd you get?"

"Old copies of 'Home Town Boy,' the column I mentioned. The one I wrote for the *Bath Bugle*. I did some historical pieces over the years, and I thought you might find them interesting, maybe helpful."

"Wow. Thank you. BTW, I've started reading the Zinn book. It reads like a novel. It's not dry at all."

It took me a minute to register that BTW was text speak for 'By the way.' "Glad you like it. It's a very different perspective on American history."

"That's an understatement. Columbus was a horrible human being. That we celebrate Columbus Day is absurd. He was evil."

"Winners get to write the history. And, that's what most of us are taught."

Jesus, what was this kid doing to me—'One word at a time,' 'winners write history?' I was saying things to her I should have been saying to myself for years. I asked, "Do you mind if I hijack this end of the table? I want to look through some of the stuff I brought back with me."

"Course not."

So, there we were. Opposite ends of the table. Working. How many times had this happened over the years? Different people—parents, grandparents, children, grandchildren—had sat here eating and tasking. There wasn't a desk to be found at Tír, just the dining room table. When it was just Hannah and me, we would leave our work spread out and eat at the small table in the kitchen. When there were more people, our work would get moved to the top of the buffet. If we needed the buffet, our work would wind up on the floor unless there were toddlers with us. That required a move to the bedroom—usually on the bed. No one ever thought about bringing a desk into Tír. It wouldn't be fitting. It wasn't that there wasn't room; it just wouldn't fit.

I opened the box marked 'Jay, Maine.' I took out seven manila folders and put them on the table. Just looking at them made me cringe from the memory of what happened there. International Paper had been as corrupt as Christopher Columbus. The story had never been entirely told, in my judgment. Labor academics had dissected it. There had also been a play and a book by the union organizer. However, I didn't think the people who were involved had told their side of it. I spread the files out. Some contained transcriptions of interviews; some had documents in them, and some had chapters that I had started writing or had completed.

Wendy looked up and asked, "Whatcha working on?"

"Sorry, will I disturb you if I work here?"

"No, just curious. Besides, I need a break. I'm going to get some more coffee. Want some?"

"No, thanks. Maybe a glass of water since you're going to the kitchen."

"Sure."

As she came back in, mug in one hand, a glass of water in the other, she said, "So tell me."

I realized I wasn't enthused about telling her. It wasn't the story that was holding me back; it was that I had never finished it. I was embarrassed. "Oh, it's just something I was working on years ago."

"Tell me about it."

I paused before responding. "Well, you know the way you said reading Zinn was like reading a novel?"

"Yeah."

"Well, I wanted to write a non-fiction novel."

"What's a non-fiction novel?"

"Basically, just what the name implies. It's using a narrative form, like a novel, only using real people and events to tell the story of what happened. Usually it takes place in current or recent times while it is fresh in people's minds."

"Like?"

How much did I want to talk about this, and what my aspiration had been? Do I give the long answer or the short answer? I decided to go someplace in between. "Well, the first one I ever read, and the one that became quite famous, was *In Cold Blood* by Truman Capote. I read it when I was in college and became fascinated with it. Not just the story or the history, but how he brought it to life. It combined the elements of good storytelling with the factual focus of good reporting. It made the events and the people more available, easier to read, and more real."

"What do you mean, 'more real?'"

"More emotion, meaning, not just facts. I think people understand more through narratives, stories, rather than bare facts."

"Huh. Interesting. What's *Cold Blood* about?"

"*In Cold Blood*? It's about the murder of a family of four in Kansas in the late fifties. Capote and an author friend of his, Harper Lee, went to Kansas and interviewed people, including the murderers, the investigators, family members, and townspeople. Then Capote took a long time to write and rewrite the book. Something like six years."

"Harper Lee. Who's Harper Lee? The name rings a bell."

"*To Kill a Mockingbird.*"

"Oh, yeah, sure. So, you wanted to write something like *In Cold Blood*."

"Tried. Twice. Two different stories. Never finished either one."

"How come?"

"Who knows?" That wasn't true. I did know. I knew exactly what happened: four young children, two working parents, sheep to be taken care of, a sick mother-in-law, and a constant state of exhaustion. My commitment to take on the marathon of writing a research-based novel didn't survive. Other, more immediate obligations of family, work, and maintaining a farm were stronger.

Wendy wasn't going to let go. I think she was honestly curious. "What were your books going to be about?"

"You really want to hear this?"

"Yes. History, right?"

"Okay. Both were based in Maine. The first was about a horrible labor strike in Jay, Maine. The second was about a man who poisoned people in his church in New Sweden, also Maine."

"You're kidding? He poisoned people? At Church?"

"Yep. Far as anyone could tell, he put poison in the coffee. One person died. Several got sick."

"God. Sounds horrible. How come you didn't finish that one? Sounds fascinating. TV show or movie, kind of."

"Someone beat me to it. She wrote what she called a non-fiction novel or tried to. She didn't do a good job as far as I'm concerned, but she got it out there. There was no room for two."

"What was wrong with hers?"

"She imagined conversations between the detectives and wrote about them as if they were real."

"So, she lied."

"Well, yes and no. The whole idea behind a non-fiction novel is that you don't make stuff up. If you're imagining things, trying to fill in blank spaces when you couldn't get real information, you make it clear to the reader that it is you, the author, who is imagining what might have happened, or might have been said. I don't think she was clear about that some of the time."

"Got it. You said there were two books. And the strike?"

"In nineteen eighty-six, up in Jay, the International Paper

Company set out to destroy the union and succeeded. It did incredible damage to the town, the union, and individual lives. That's the one I have here. I might look at it again and see if it's worth doing any more work on it."

"Really?"

"Well, we'll see. I thought I'd read over what I had done. You sure I won't disturb you if I work here?"

"No. It's neat. Sort of like studying in a library."

We didn't say anything more to each other until it was time for lunch.

Chapter Nineteen: Jay, Maine

When I was working for the *Bath Bugle*, there were always deadlines. When I was working on my novels, deadlines didn't exist, which is why they took me so long to finish. I never had a contract with a publisher with a promise to deliver a manuscript on a given date. When I'm honest with myself, I was a hobby writer. Sure, there was always the hope that one of my efforts would catch on and I would become well-known—rich, too. I was lucky enough to have a small local publisher who enjoyed my tales of families living on the Maine coast and their struggles with everything from lobster wars to losing loved ones at sea. Judy Reddin, my publisher, didn't seem to mind that they never made either of us a fortune. Typically, they would do well in the summer when they would be displayed in the 'local authors' section of the bookstores along the coast. As Amazon took over and more and more people read on Kindle, some local stores have closed down and Amazon doesn't have 'local' sections on its website. Sales have dwindled.

So why on earth was I considering opening up my attic boxes and thinking of writing again? Something about this labor story, though, had never been told. It was a David and Goliath story: union versus management. It was a story about a company with record profits demanding wage givebacks.

Within the town of Jay, people were divided between union supporters and union detractors. When I had gone there during the strike, fear was palpable, as was distrust and hate. It had been a national story because of the actions, or inaction, of the national union. It was also a story of the decline of an industry and of unions in general. I knew the story was still going on, but I had stopped telling it. So had everyone else.

So, a week after bringing the box down to Tír and going through my files and making notes, I found the story of the strike gnawing at me, an uncomfortable hunger. If I could lecture Wendy about going 'one word at a time' in her reading and writing, I could damned well do it myself. If she was going to work three or four hours a day, so could I.

She was doing it. It had only been a week and a half, but she was following through. When Rachel called Sunday night, Wendy spoke to her first. When they were finished, Wendy handed her phone to me and said, "Mom wants to talk to you. She probably wants a report card."

I didn't say anything in response to Wendy's comment. When I got on the phone and said, "Hi," that's exactly what Rachel wanted. "How's it going?" She asked. "She getting any work done?"

"It's good," I answered. "We work in the morning. Most afternoons, she's off with Rina, or Rina is over here. They've been sailing a few times, played tennis over at the yacht club."

"The net's up already?"

"I went over and helped them put it up."

"You said, 'We work every morning.' 'We?' What's that about?"

"I might resurrect a piece I was working on years ago."

There was a qualifier in my answer, 'might,' but somehow, even saying that brought me closer to committing to doing it.

"Wow, Dad, I'm surprised. A new novel?"

"Not sure. Possibly non-fiction, historical piece, or maybe even a non-fiction novel. I'm not sure how far I'll go with it, but I'm looking at old files about a labor dispute in Jay." So much for my commitment: 'Not sure how far I'll go with it.'

"And Wendy's doing well? Buckling down?"

"Far as I can tell." Even that statement had the ring of qualification. 'Gramps' had best get on board. "She's going to get this done, Rach. I'm sure of it." There, take that for being definitive.

"And you two are getting along?"

"Like two peas in a pod. I'm glad she's here."

"I can't tell you how relieved I am. Thank you, Dad."

"She's a good kid, Rach."

"I know. It's just...."

"That you're a mother, and you worry."

"Yes."

We chatted for another ten minutes or so, mostly about her trying to please her new boss. I was impressed with how clear headed her problem-solving was. Then she said, "They've decided to give me Mondays off in June. So, I might drive up on a Sunday night and then come back early Tuesday morning. I won't be able to do that in July and August, though. Okay with you?"

"Of course."

"So, we'll talk next Sunday, and I'll have another report card ready for you."

"You're terrible."

"That's what Wendy tells me. Love you."

"Me, too."

When I got off the phone, I went into the living room where Wendy was curled up under a blanket reading. Charlie was snuggled up next to her. Hearing me come in, she asked, "Report card?"

"Yep. Gave you an 'A.' Could have been an 'A+' but I wanted her to think there was room for you to grow."

"Thank you."

"Don't thank me. You're the one doing the work. By the way, do you have any plans for tomorrow afternoon?"

"No."

"Want to take a road trip with me?"

"Where're you going?"

"Up to Jay. There's a paper museum there. I've never been. Technically it's in Livermore Falls, right next to Jay. About an hour and a half drive. I called and made an appointment for us to visit.

They're only open a couple of hours on Saturdays in the summer, but they'll open up if you call. When I told the person what I was working on, she was delighted to have us come."

"Sure. Why not? Get my head out of Zinn. By the way, I have an appointment in the morning with the lady from the Historical Society. She sounded thrilled that I was interested in the history of Georgetown. And, I've started reading that book you suggested."

"*Ancient Sagadahoc?*"

"Boring. Tedium on steroids. Names, dates, and blah. Everything I hate about history."

"Hmm, 'tedium on steroids.' I'm afraid I'm having a difficult time with that imagery."

"You know what I mean."

"Well, if communication is an exchange of meaning, then yes, I did understand you. However, perhaps my grading was a little too generous. If I take attitude into account…"

She ignored my comment. "What time do you want to get going tomorrow? I have work to do in the morning if I'm going to be available."

"Touché. One o'clock fit into your schedule?"

"I can manage that."

Rina agreed to come down and let Charlie out and feed him if we decided to grab dinner on the road. We took the truck. For some reason, I always take the truck if I'm driving in Maine.

Wendy and I chatted for the first half an hour of the drive up to Livermore Falls. She had decided to read the Zinn book first and then go on to the Roosevelts later in the summer. Her judgments about the Chandler book, *Ancient Sagadahoc*, were ones I could not disagree with. I found the information to be interesting but the presentation to be sterile. When I told her this, it led to a discussion about writing. It didn't take long before I found myself going into one-way lecture mode about the craft of writing. She was shutting down, so I shut up.

We rode in silence for about fifteen minutes. We had just crossed over the Maine Turnpike at Sabatus when she surprised me and said, "Did I tell you? I talked Rina into riding out there with me last week."

"Out where?"

"Popham, remember? I told you about it."

"You did. Sorry."

"I wanted to see where the Popham Colony was. It's weird; in all the summers I spent at Tír, we never drove out there. So, Rina and I wandered around Fort Popham for a while. Can you imagine living there in the winter during the Civil War? And those people in the Colony in 1607? I would have gone home to England, too. And the fishing camps were even before then. Talk about roughing it."

"It wasn't easy, that's for sure."

"We came across something exciting."

"What's that?"

"We ran into some grad students from U Maine, Orono. They're spending their summer camping there while they work on a dig. Apparently, we don't know if the Abenaki had permanent settlements there or if they only came down summers."

"Really?"

"Yeah. We stopped and talked to them for a while. Fascinating stuff."

"Not like the Chandler book?"

"Okay, Gramps. Yes. Some of the information is the same. More fun talking to people who are…"

"Your age and doing something rather than writing about it."

"For sure."

We chatted a bit more, imagining what it would have been like to live the way the Abenaki had or those first settlers and how ill-prepared we were to do what those people had done. Finally, we talked about how amazed those people would have been if they were dropped into our world today.

Quiet descended again. It sounded to me like Wendy was beginning to engage. Taking Rina out to Fort Popham with her was something I would not have expected. In our discussion, she referred to facts from both the Zinn and Chandler books. She sounded curious. Meeting the graduate students and talking to them about their work had pulled her in. She said, "What a great way to spend a summer and get credit for it."

When we passed the Riverbend Campground just before Leeds, I realized one of the reasons I was having such a hard time committing to work on a new book. Hannah and I had picnicked at Riverbend when we took a trip to Androscoggin Lake searching for the Cattail Sedge.

The lake is the only one in Maine where the Cattail Sedge grows, and Hannah wanted to see it and the lake. So, on a Sunday in September, when every one of the kids had something to do, we put our kayaks in the truck and went looking for Cattail Sedge. According to the article in *Downeast Magazine* that Hannah had read, in all of Maine the Cattail Sedge only grew in Androscoggin Lake. The explanation was that although large, the lake was only fifteen feet deep and was warmer all summer long than most of our Maine lakes. She had become fascinated with it, so she packed a picnic, and off we went.

Crossing over the river, I remembered that day. I remembered Hannah. I remembered Hannah editing and encouraging me as I worked on the novels. She wasn't my muse, but she was an integral part of the environment in which I felt safe to write. How could I write without her telling me what was and was not working? Without her, I didn't trust myself. I felt the same way about being a grandfather to this young woman sitting next to me. Without Hannah..... I didn't want to complete that thought and instead told Wendy the story of our trip in search of the Cattail Sedge.

"Did you find some?" She asked.

"We did."

"Why did Nana want to find them?"

"I have absolutely no idea."

We drove for another fifteen minutes before Wendy asked, "What are you looking for at the museum?"

"I'm not sure. I thought it would be a good place to start getting my head back into the dilemmas the strike brought on for the people associated with the mill. I'm also curious if some of the people I interviewed are still here or still alive. I'm also wondering if I am as fascinated with the story today as I was when the strike occurred."

"What grabbed you then?"

"Oh, wow. That would take a book."

"Yuk, yuk. Very funny, Gramps. How about the Stark Notes version?"

"I really couldn't do that until after the book is finished."

"Why are you being so secretive?"

"I don't know. Okay, here are some headlines. I've been thinking about focusing on families I interviewed in 1987 and 1988. In one family, both husband and wife worked at the mill and had for a long time. In another family, the husband was a scab and drove quite a way to work. Most of the scabs commuted to the mill at first. However, International Paper eventually hired them as full-time replacements, so it wasn't long before they started moving into town.

One family owned a hardware store and was hurt financially during the strike. The strike went on for sixteen months. Over a thousand workers were out on strike. That's a lot of reduced income to be spent in local stores. Everyone was hurting. In another family, the husband was a supervisor. The other two families had workers at the mill who were on strike.

"Here's the issue in a nutshell. The company was making record profits. Over the years, they had increased wages for the workers so that the pay scales were out of whack with any other jobs in the area. So, the company decided they would reduce the wages for the union workers, make them pay more for their health care, not pay double for overtime on Sundays, and no more paid vacations—including Christmas."

"Did they reduce the wages for managers, too?"

"Of course not. Just the union workers. So, when the strike took place, the company brought in scabs who were more than happy to work for lower wages. First, they locked the strikers out; then, they fired every single one of them. It got vicious. When some of the strikers crossed the picket lines and returned to work, they had their houses shot up in drive-bys. The scabs were also pretty violent. One striker was threatened with being shot for shouting at one of the scabs."

"So, the company made even more money."

"Yes."

"And the rich get richer…"

"And the poor get poorer."

"America's brand of capitalism. Labor is a commodity. Look at it today. Three men have as much wealth as fifty percent of the people in America."

"You sound like Stephen."

"Do I now?'

"Yeah."

"Do you want to talk about him?"

"No."

"Well, if you ever…"

"No."

The museum was housed in an elegant early nineteen-hundreds Victorian that had, at an earlier time, been occupied by a mill manager. The old oak woodwork and stained-glass windows were striking, as were the large rooms filled with displays. Unlike city museums, this one was homegrown by people whose lives had been shaped by the paper mills and the strike. It was still staffed by volunteers who were devoted to its existence. They had collected artifacts, and each one was labeled with an explanation of how it had been used. Hundreds of pictures adorned the walls with labels describing what the picture was depicting and the year the photograph was taken. There was a hands-on area where you could make paper under the tutelage of a docent. There were videos of interviews with people who had worked in the mills. Some of them were homemade; some were the work of professionals. I was surprised to learn that the museum contained the union's archived documents from the time of the strike.

While I worked my way through some of the videos and looked at the index of the strike documents, Wendy learned how paper was made. I noticed she was having a conversation with the docent on duty after her papermaking lesson.

Three hours later, we thanked the docent and headed for the car. On the way, I asked, "Want to grab dinner here before we head back?"

"Sure."

"The docent..."

"Her name was Penelope. She said to try La Fleurs."

La Fleurs was a typical small-town family restaurant: extensive menu, plastic table cloths, knotty pine wainscoting, specials on a blackboard, pictures of local scenes and people scattered around on the walls, large clock over the cashier's station you could see from any-place in the dining room. Dependable, but not fancy. A place where men kept their caps on and people pushed tables together for birthdays and showers.

After we had ordered, Wendy showed me the paper she had made. "It was really fun. I had no idea how paper was made. Penelope was so nice. I told her about the project I'm working on, and she had a great suggestion."

I picked up the small piece of paper Wendy handed me. "Which was?" I asked.

"She said I should go to the Maine Maritime Museum in Bath and talk to someone from the history staff."

"Great idea. I should have thought of that."

"No biggie. I didn't know museums even had historians. Penelope said her museum is too small, but many of them are sort of amateur historians about that area and the mills. That's so cool."

We chatted a little on and off as we ate, mainly about the food. After we ordered dessert, two different pies from a wide selection, Wendy asked, "Did you always know what you wanted to do, I mean, really?"

I knew we had already had this conversation. So, what was she asking? Did she think I was bullshitting her before? Really? What was this about? I used her own words. "Yes, I really did." Then, I made it even more specific. "I wanted to be an investigative reporter for the Boston Globe, the New York Times, or the Washington Post. I didn't care which. Now remember, I was in high school when I was thinking these grandiose thoughts. By the time I graduated from BU my lofty ambitions had mellowed a bit, but not much. I thought I might have to work for a smaller newspaper first.

When our pies arrived, I asked, "What's bothering you? You know many people don't know what they want to do at your age."

"You did. Rina does. Aunt Maude did. Uncle Jesse did. Uncle Joel did."

"Ruth didn't. I'm not sure if she knows to this day. Wen, what's stirring this up?"

"I don't know. Majoring in history was sort of a 'what else am I going to major in' decision. I haven't thought about what it might lead to other than maybe teaching in high school or something. I never knew historians worked at museums. And meeting those grad students from Orono. They seemed to love what they were doing. So, I went on UVM's website and started looking around. Archeology is in the Department of Anthropology. The courses sounded interesting. I don't want to change majors again. I'm just really confused. I don't want to screw up."

"Could you minor?"

"I suppose. What do you think?"

Hannah and I used to talk about moments like this with our kids, the moments the questions were true, vulnerable, and far-reaching. The moments you had to dig deep as a parent and be equally vulnerable and humble.

"I will think about it, but my immediate reaction is that you're coming across ideas and possibilities that you have not encountered before and having some difficulty just letting them sit with you and mull about. You want closure rather than feeling free to explore. People change careers all the time, Wendy. It doesn't mean they made a mistake. Usually, they integrate the learning from the first career into the second. I have one thought, though, of which I am very sure."

"What's that?"

"Comparing yourself to others is not going to be helpful. Just be you. If this is a time for you to explore, then be an explorer."

The minute I said those words, I knew I would write my book.

March 21, 1980
HOME TOWN BOY by Michael Buckley

Yesterday was the vernal equinox, the first day of spring but being Maine, there were snow flurries as I drove to work this morning. Some folks away from the coast may be getting up to a foot of the white stuff. The weather in Maine doesn't pay much attention to seasons or astronomers.

I remember my science teacher, Mr. Sullivan, showing us his models of the planets and the sun, and how on the vernal equinox the sun crossed over the celestial equator and was now in our Northern Hemisphere. So yesterday, the sun rose due east and set due west, and night and day had equal time. In some places, Pagans celebrated the feast of Ostara. My father used to say that it was the beginning of mud season in Maine.

Seasons are important, whether they are mud or otherwise. As everybody knows, there are more than the four seasons of the astronomers. My mother had boxes in the attic to celebrate the seasons. There were far more than four. There was a winter box, Valentine's Day box, Saint Patrick's Day box, Easter Box, Fourth of July box, Thanksgiving box, and Christmas boxes of every shape and size. Each year, all the Christmas boxes were taken out whether or not everything in them was used. Each of her boxes contained decorations appropriate to the 'season.'

My seasons were different than hers. There were ice hockey, basketball, hunting, baseball, fishing, and football seasons. I had assorted equipment and clothing for each of my seasons as she had boxes for hers.

Living on a farm, the livestock chimed in with their seasons, as did the vegetables in the garden. Out in the ocean, the migration of whales was seasonal, as was the spawning of herring. The government piles on by delineating what fish we can catch and what we are allowed to hunt during what time periods, all marked off as seasons. Maine residents get a special one-day season, October 30, when only residents can go after deer. November is open to residents and those 'from away.' Seasonal licenses add to the State coffers.

If we ever plotted the beginning and end of everybody's seasons on the calendar that hangs next to the refrigerator, there wouldn't be much room for birthdays, doctor appointments, school openings and closings, and the comings and goings of family members.

On a deeper level, there is Ecclesiastes 3,1-8:

> *For everything there is a season, and a time for every [a]purpose under heaven: a time to be born, and a time to die; a time to plant, and a time to pluck up that which is planted; a time to kill, and a time to heal; a time to break down, and a time to build up; a time to weep, and a time to laugh; a time to mourn, and a time to dance; a time to cast away stones, and a time to gather stones together; a time to embrace, and a time to refrain from embracing; a time to seek, and a time to lose; a time to keep, and a time to cast away; [7] a time to rend, and a time to sew; a time to keep silence, and a time to speak; a time to love, and a time to hate; a time for war, and a time for peace.*

Seasons are about a time to do things, a call out to pay attention, to engage. They are about change. We take some things out and put others away. And at the same time, they are about continuity. We can count on Christmas being December 25 every year. I know the decorations from years of memory.

Neither the vernal nor autumnal equinox cares a hoot about any of this. They preceded our existence on this planet and will continue long after we're gone, unless some other change comes along and tilts our planet a different way. Some of us do care about these astronomical events, though. Our ancestors built stone circles and created rituals to measure and mark these changes. Now, we set our clocks back and forth depending on whether our days are getting shorter or longer.

Soon mud season will be over in Maine, and bats and gloves will come out of the closet, seeds will germinate in window boxes, and, on our farm, we'll get ready for lambing. Change will be in the air, as will the permanence of tradition to mark the changes. Change and permanence, two sides of the same reality. We need both. We have both. I find that comforting. I hope you do, too.

Chapter Twenty: A Different Marriage

When Treasa told Jamie that March of 1888 was the worst month of her life, her husband didn't know what to say. She would repeat it many times over the years. He understood some of it, but only some. Their son, Will, had been born on January 19th. After all the miscarriages, they were both in awe that he was alive and healthy. At times, Treasa's joy overwhelmed her, and Jamie would ask her what she was 'blubbering' about. She told him it was hard to explain. She tried. She told him she loved how her infant son would stop crying when he latched on to her breast. She told him his gurgles were the most beautiful sound in the world. One evening Jamie heard her laughing in the kitchen where she was bathing Will. When he came out to ask her what she was laughing about, she said, "Would you believe what he did? Here I'm drying him, I lean down to kiss his beautiful bare belly, and he pees all over me. He's definitely your son, Jamie Buckley. Look at that thing on him."

Jamie and Treasa came back together in a new way, one they had lost in the years of trying to conceive a child and then giving up on the idea of ever having a family. February turned out to be a month full of wonder for them both. Jamie had planned to stay home for the first few weeks after Will was born, but he couldn't leave them. So instead, he kept extending his time in their home in Brooklyn. He asked Treasa question after question about their infant son. One time, when he asked her another 'why' question, she said, "This is my first time, too, Jamie. How the hell am I supposed to know why he does some of the things he does?"

The country was just emerging from a deep economic depression, though, and Jamie had to return to sea. When he finally left Brooklyn on the fourth of March, a deep sadness descended upon Treasa at his going and leaving her alone with a newborn. Jamie was at sea, and Will was just shy of two months old.

On March 6th, Louisa May Alcott died. Alcott had been Treasa's inspiration to write, and Treasa was devastated. She had read everything Alcott had written, even the books she wrote as A.M. Barnard. When she heard the news, she put Will down for a nap and got out her well-worn copy of *Little Women*. The minute she started to read; tears came with an intensity she had never experienced. She did not understand the tears. Sometimes they just came, but she could count on them returning every evening when it got dark. She was alone. She and Will were alone. She did not know where Jamie was. She knew he would return; he always did, but knowing that did not help. She knew he wouldn't be sympathetic to her reaction to Alcott's death.

Jamie didn't understand Treasa's literary interests, any of them. To him, they were a harmless hobby. Since she started working at the Lotos Club, Treasa had been writing poetry, short stories, and had even started on a novel. Writing and reading had become her passions, and she had consumed the novels of women writers. Jane Austen, the Brontës, George Eliot, and others were now in the bookcase beside the fireplace in the Buckley parlor. Jamie told her, "All you do is read, woman. You keep adding books at this rate, and we'll have to add a room."

The year before Will was born, Treasa came across *A Vindication of the Rights of Woman* by Mary Wollstonecraft. It amazed her. It led her to explore a different kind of literature. She consumed the essays, and books emerging from the suffragists. She saw parallels between the struggle for freedom taking place in Ireland and the demands of the suffragists. "Women are like the Irish, Jamie. You men are like the fuckin' Brits. You never let us have anything of our own."

"Are you out of your mind? What do you want you can't have?"

"You want the whole list?"

She read the *Seneca Falls Declaration of Sentiments and*

Resolutions by Elizabeth Cady Stanton and *On Woman's Right to Suffrage* by Susan B. Anthony. She even attended a lecture at the Brooklyn Library.

Alcott spoke to her most directly, and Alcott's death was like the death of a close relative, even though she had never met the woman. "She was only fifty-six, but she accomplished so much. Such a waste," she wrote in the journal she kept. Treasa had a hero, and she had just died. When Treasa would hear one of the members at the Lotos Club say something negative about her hero, Treasa would jump to Alcott's defense. Some of the Club members, especially Whitelaw Reid, who edited the *New York Tribune*, would say things to get a response from Treasa. When she told Jamie about it, he said, "Let it be, Treasa. They're just trying to get your goat."

Jamie didn't know what to make of the 'fuss' his wife would make from time to time about women like Stanton and Anthony. He was far more concerned about the rise and fall of the price he could get for ice and what buildings would need granite. The only time he became aware of her growing commitment to reading the work of the suffragists, was when dinner was delayed or she tried to tell Colm about the plight of women.

The several miscarriages had led Jamie to conclude that her writing and reading were good for her as a way to keep busy without children in the household. She seemed to be less depressed when she was writing, and she reduced her hours at the Lotos Club to write. Jamie thought the support she got for her writing from Lotos Club members was unusual, but he didn't think much about it. He rarely read anything she wrote.

Now, with her focus on young Will, she only wrote in her journal and read very little. She said she was deliriously happy, but there were days when she would cry periodically. Neither one of them understood what the trouble was.

After Alcott's death, March became even worse for Treasa. Five days later, the entire East Coast was shut down by a blizzard. Fifty-five mile an hour winds and close to forty inches of snow closed everything from the Chesapeake to Maine. The wind was so strong that there were snowdrifts fifty feet high out in Gravesend near Coney Island. When Treasa went to open her front door, a wall of snow greeted her. She couldn't see out any of the windows on three sides of their house. At the back of the house, there was no snow for a good twenty feet where the wind had whipped around the house, but then there was a high drift that went over the fence that separated their home from the neighbor's. Treasa was more scared than she had ever been in her life. She had lost all means of communication to the outside world. She felt encased in a white tomb. What if Will needed a doctor? Would they run out of food or fuel? What if something happened to Jamie? Where was he? Without Jamie, what would they do?

  Treasa and two-month-old Will survived. Treasa moved them downstairs to the parlor. She was grateful they had a coal-burning stove, and she only had to bank it two or three times a day to keep it going. She would only start the cooking stove in the kitchen once during the day. She was relieved they just had a delivery of what she was now thinking of as 'black gold.' In the dark nights of the following week, she imagined scenario after scenario of what she would do if she couldn't get out for food or if Jamie would never come home.

  She didn't know it, but close to five hundred people had already died in the storm. Two hundred ships had been destroyed at sea, and more than a hundred sailors had lost their lives. Those who were rescued were battered, and some died later from their injuries. Yet, unknown to her, 'the boys,' as she referred to her husband and his crew, managed to make their way to the island of Matinicus. While she was shoveling coal into the furnace, they were shoveling the heavy snow off the *Treasa* to keep her afloat and not have to jettison the ice packed away in the hold.

When Jamie returned, Treasa told him she hated Brooklyn, hated the United States, and was ready to return to Ireland. She told him, "It may rain there, but we never have winters like this. Will and I will not go through this again, Jamie. What if something happened to you? I didn't realize how much I be missing everybody and Carna. You're never here. I want Will to know his grandparents and his aunts and uncles. I want him to grow up with his cousins. It's just Will and me here, and I'm alone day in and day out with no one to talk to."

Rose had been gone for barely a year when Will was born. As much of a busy body as Rose had been, Treasa missed her. It would have been easier if Rose had been with her during the storm. Rose always knew what to do. "She would have loved Will and spoiled the hell out of him," she said to Jamie one night when they were bathing him. "She would have been the grandmother of grandmothers."

"And she would have been tellin' you what to do every minute," Jamie reminded her.

"And we would have worked it out. I miss her, Jamie. I'm alone here with Will. I been thinking we should go back to Ireland."

"To that mess? Balfour's imprisoning people for nothing. Tenants have nothing and those who do try to change things wind up in jail. Go back to that? Never. I'm doing good here. Don't let this storm get to you. Never happen again. It was the worst ever, and everyone sayin' so."

"T'is not just the storm. I was scared for you, and I felt so alone. Maybe when I can get back to work, I won't be feeling this lonely and…"

"What you be talkin' about, work? You not be goin' back to work."

"Not till I stop nursing, but then I am."

"No, you're not. Who be takin' care of Will?"

"I'll find somebody. Only two, maybe three days a week. I miss it. I miss the Club."

Jamie thought it was best to postpone the decision, or at least the argument, with a declaration of "We'll see."

Two weeks later, on March 22nd, things changed. An extraordinary thaw did away with most of the snow. Days were warm, and their basement hadn't flooded out, something many of their neighbors couldn't say. Deliveries were again reaching homes, and Treasa looked forward to reading the newspaper every day. It also helped that Will was only getting up once in the night to be fed. Jamie was glad to be home after the storm. They had been delayed for a few days, but the boat was fine, and they got their price for the cargo.

The thaw, and neighborly shoveling, made the sidewalks clear enough for the two of them to walk Will in his carriage. After that, it became a morning ritual: breakfast, newspaper, go for a walk. On the fourth day of the thaw, one article got Treasa's attention, and when they walked that morning, she said to Jamie, "I want to go to Washington, D.C. We can take the train."

"Why on the earth would you be wanting to go to Washington? You're still exhausted, and Will's far too young to travel. And what the hell would we be goin' to Washington for?"

"Will's healthy as can be. I'm a strong Irish woman, not one of these prissy uptown American types. I want to go."

"Why?"

"You've heard me talk about this woman, Susan B. Anthony. In Mr. Reid's *Tribune* this morning, I read that she's leading a conference on Women's Rights. It's in Washington. It starts this coming Sunday, and I want to go. So, I'm going to go. With you or without you."

"What about Will?"

"I'll bring him with me."

"He's a baby, for God's sake."

"People take babies on the train all the time."

"Even if you got there, they wouldn't let you take a baby into a hall where they be speaking. What if he started crying or you had to feed him?"

"They're women. If he cries, I'll take him out. Most of them women will have nursed babies. They won't care to see a woman feeding an infant."

"Why? Why would you risk taking an infant on a dirty train to Washington? Where would you stay? How long would you be gone? You know I can't go."

"Jamie Buckley. Women are coming from all over America to this conference. Maybe even the world. The world, Jamie. Think of it, all over the world. I want to be part of it. Things will change, you eejit, and you'd best be seeing which way the wind's blowin.' You're a sailor, and you'd best be trimmin' your sails. You'll see. I'll be votin' before I die, and I'll be makin' as much money as that stupid valet at the Club."

"You vote? Come on, now. You lost your mind? Women don't know enough to vote, and why on earth would you want to? I vote for both of us."

"If you're here to vote. And that's not it, you gobshite. I know more than you do about what's going on in the world. I read. I read everything. What do you know? Maybe how to sail a fuckin' sailboat back and forth to Maine. I read everything. I talk to people at the Club. You just talk to Colm and Isaac, and Colm's a fuckin' eejit."

"You're not going."

"You commanding me now?"

"You heard me. You're not goin.' That's it."

"Like hell, I'm not. So, you not be tellin' me what I can and can't do."

Jamie found his way to Jack's Bar and Grill, leaving behind a slammed door with a shattered window, a furious wife reading information about transportation to Washington, D.C., and a marriage that had just changed forever.

Treasa went to Washington and took Will with her. Jamie sailed to Stonington for a load of granite to be used to construct a pier in New Jersey.

When Wyoming was admitted to the Union in 1890, its State Constitution gave women the right to vote, the first State to do so. Treasa wanted the family to move to Wyoming. Jamie said, "You'd be moving by yourself, wouldn't ya?" It took many months, but gradually Jamie adjusted to his new marriage. He would occasionally ask Treasa what she was reading and even brought some of her writing with him on a trip. When she asked him about it when he returned, he said, "I like the poetry. Your stories are about us, though, and you got a lot of it wrong."

"You write about what you know, Jamie. It's fiction, though; I make things up. I ask myself, 'what if,' and I go from there."

"Sure sounds like us."

"You don't get it."

They never talked about the suffragist essays she gave him to read.

Treasa went back to work and continued writing and started spending more and more time attending meetings and rallies.

Jamie hated Brooklyn becoming part of New York City in 1899; Treasa thought it was a 'brilliant' idea because Brooklyn was backward compared to New York. When Jamie wasn't at sea, he wanted to stay home; when Jamie was home, Treasa wanted them to travel. Treasa became increasingly active in the suffrage movement, which added to their disagreements. Treasa marched, went to meetings, wrote letters, went to meetings, handed out leaflets, had meetings at their house, and stopped writing poetry and short stories. She did not become less passionate about reading and writing; she added a passion. Lotos Club members had enjoyed mentoring their employee in her writing. However, they did not enjoy her lectures about patriarchy, and eventually, Treasa was invited to leave their employ. Jamie was not disappointed with her firing. However, she now spent more time with 'those women.'

One evening while Jamie was home, Treasa announced that her son would attend Boy's High School and then go to college when he was old enough. Jamie's response was, "Why on earth would you be thinking of college for him? Neither of us went."

"That's the whole point. I want a better life for him."

"He'll have one. By the time he's that age, he can be sailin' with me, learning his craft so he can take over. He'll own a good boat free and clear. Won't be owing nothin' to no one."

"No! He's goin' to college, Jamie. College. Imagine that. Our son goin' to college."

Jamie looked at her and shook his head. "Let's not get started on that. It'll be one more thing to fight about."

"Damn. You can't, can you? Why is it so hard to imagine that your son can be educated?"

"That's your god damned Club people talking. Them and them women you hanging out with. You and all your reading and writin' and wantin' to vote. You just remember what's makin' it possible for you even to do those things."

Jamie was ready to storm out again when Treasa stopped him and said, "Please close the door softly on your way out this time. Will's takin' his nap, and I'm tired of replacing the glass."

Jamie caught himself before he reached the door. He turned around, looked at her, shook his head, and summoned a fake smile. He walked towards the door on tiptoe. Before he reached the door, he turned and said, "My son be helping me on the boat summers when he's old enough."

Treasa shouted, "If he wants to."

"He will. You'll see."

When he was a toddler, Will was given over to the care of Rose's friend, Lina Janssen, who had been Treasa's maid of honor. That freed Treasa to go to meetings and organize new groups of women. When he entered school, Will went to the Janssen's at the end of the school day.

In high school, Will told a friend he was an orphan. Left to his own devices, the teenager developed a vivid imagination that not infrequently brought him to the attention of the police. Will created a shy, secretive, cunning persona for himself. He found it helpful for stealing from local stores while portraying himself as a sweet little lad. Some older boys in the neighborhood observed Will's talents and invited him to join them in some of their escapades in Irishtown. Will became adept at various tactics for relieving people of watches, wallets, and whatever shopkeepers did not keep under lock and key. With others to help, it was easy.

Irishtown was close to the waterfront and home to multiple small distilleries owned by gentlemen who did not believe in paying taxes for their entrepreneurial ventures. The distilleries were a source of pride and jobs for the local residents. Will's capacity to observe, honed in his shoplifting experiences, became prized by two distillery owners. He had a unique ability to spot the presence of tax collectors as they got off the ferry and approached Irishtown. The distillery owners offered to pay Will for his skills in observation, deduction, cunning, and running.

The teenager set about learning every alley and street near the waterfront. Running as fast as he could, he would warn his employers so they could close their shutters and entrances and look to all the world like boarded up warehouses innocently abandoned in the middle of the poverty that was Irishtown. The tax collectors would search in vain for distilleries they knew were there. When they tried to bribe Irishtown neighbors for information, what they received was distorted beyond recognition.

Will's new occupation was more lucrative than stealing from stores and people on the street. Besides, running through the streets was not a crime. As after-school and weekend employment, it was a way of making his 'private money.' When Treasa was home and would ask him where he was going after school or on Saturdays, he would say, "Playing stickball with some friends." Treasa saw a son doing well in school, having friends, and behaving well at home. She was proud of him.

Jamie, on the other hand, felt distant from his only child. Will didn't like sailing with his father. "It's boring," he would complain. So, summers, Will continued his part-time business, and his reputation as a trusted lookout spread to two other distilleries. He chose his clients well and was never caught, never even interrogated.

Jack's Bar and Grill was their place. Jamie and Colm would go there on the night before they left on a trip to discuss the challenges they had ahead of them. Then they would go there the night they returned to brag or complain about the profitability of the trip. Visits to Jack's was one of those rituals that was best kept secret. One evening, after discussing the tides for the following day, Jamie complained to Colm, "Now she calls herself a 'Suffragist.' What the hell is a fuckin' 'Suffragist?' I don't know her. Who the hell is this woman?"

"Same woman you used to sneak off to that island with when we were kids. She was a rebel then; she's a rebel now. Why you acting so surprised? You loved her then; you love her now."

"She acts like I'm her enemy. You should hear her sometimes, the way she talks about men. I'm a man, for Christ's sake. Doesn't she know that?"

"It's a phase. She had her writing phase; this is her, what's the word, 'Suffragist' phase. She'll be on to something else in a year."

"I don't think so. You should hear her. Now she wants to go to Boston. She went to Washington for that big meeting. Why on earth does she want to be going to Boston?"

"Listen to you. That meeting in Washington was years ago. You want to chain her to Brooklyn? Jesus, Jamie."

Treasa had told Jamie, "I want to see what's happening in Boston with 'the movement,' and I want to visit my cousins." She was excited about taking the train and felt comfortable that Lina would look in on Will periodically to make sure he was okay. She only planned to be gone for a couple of weeks. "After all," she said to Jamie, "Will's in high school and almost as tall as you. He never gets into any trouble. He can fend for himself until you get back from Philadelphia. You said it was a short trip."

"I don't want you to go. Not now. You read the papers. You know there's a pox outbreak up there. I don't want something to happen ta you. So why don't you wait until it's over?

"And when will that be, a year, two years? No, me cousins have just come, and I remember what it was like when I first got here. They need a friendly face."

"It's too risky."

"I'm healthy."

"Healthy people can get the pox."

"Darlin', I'm going to be just fine."

It was Treasa's first trip to Boston, and she spent the better part of a week deciding what she would bring—packing, unpacking, and then packing again. Approaching forty, this was her first trip since she had taken the infant Will to Washington, D.C. It would take her the better part of the day from when she left Brooklyn until she arrived in the Irish-dominated city where her cousins now lived. She made sure she got a window seat. She wanted to see everything, and she rode with her head pressed to the window as the train made its way up the coast through Connecticut before turning inland at Providence.

At the end of her first week, she wrote a letter to Jamie.

> *Jamie,*
>
> *You should see this place. It's smaller than New York by half, and they have a strange way of speaking English. There are Irish everywhere, and Eileen was right. It's almost like being in Galway, but much larger.*
>
> *I went to a meeting of the group here, but it was as disappointing as their rally. New York is much further along than Massachusetts, and the women are not as well informed.*
>
> *Eileen and I have been walking all over the city, and I feel safe here. Eileen agreed to go with me out to Concord, and we saw the different houses where Louisa May Alcott lived. I wanted so much to go into them, but we couldn't. We also went to Walden Pond.*
>
> *In Boston, we went on, or in, a train that runs under the streets of Boston called a subway. It is very strange, and I don't think I like it. I know they are starting to build them in New York, but I prefer our elevated trains that run over the streets.*
>
> *I will be home in plenty of time for Thanksgiving and have invited Eileen and Joseph to come to join us with their two young ones. Please tell Will that Matthew can't wait to meet him. He's younger than Will but I think they will*

get on well together.
Your loving wife,
Treasa

Treasa never made it home for Thanksgiving. On the twenty-sixth of November, she died of smallpox in a quarantine facility on Gallops Island in Boston Harbor. She had been there for a week. Jamie and Will had not seen her since the day before she left for Boston. Jamie was not allowed to bring her body back to Brooklyn for burial. Will dropped out of high school and joined his father as a crew member on the *Treasa*.

Chapter Twenty-One: Will At Sea

The *Treasa* had been battling a headwind and a foul current for three hours. They had just tacked away from Nantucket shoals when Colm yelled below to tell Will to come on deck and stand watch. Will, warm in his bunk under layers of wool blankets, swore to himself, "What the fuck am I doing here?" His father was asleep in the bunk opposite him

Will still had his pants and shirt on to stay warm. Unhooking the lee cloth that kept him from rolling out of his bunk, he swung his legs onto the floor, bracing himself against the boat's heel. He put on a sweater, a jacket, and oilskins to help keep him dry. He found his sea boots and stuffed his double-socked feet into them. He put on his wool watch cap and then his oilskin hat on top of it. Grabbing the overhead handholds, he made his way to the companionway stairs. Once on deck, he was greeted with cold spray coming off the windward side of the boat.

It was December 17th, 1903, a little more than a year since his mother had died, and Will was miserable. He missed home, hated sailing in the winter, and longed for the freedom to wander around Brooklyn and Manhattan. He wanted to be back home making and spending the money his parents didn't know about. He missed being appreciated for his sharp eyes and swift feet. He missed his life.

When Will took the helm at ten in the morning, he didn't know that thirty-five minutes into his watch, Orville Wright would be flying twice the length of the *Treasa* in a self-propelled heavier-than-air flying machine. Neither did Will know that Wright's twelve seconds in the air would change Will's life and the lives of his sons, grandsons, and great-grandsons.

Will just knew he was cold and angry at his father for not letting him stay in school and at home in Brooklyn. He liked school. During the rare times when she was available, he had enjoyed talking to his mother about school and what he was learning. But, on the boat, he felt trapped. It wasn't just the confines of the boat; it was the lack of freedom to do what he wanted. He thought it was stupid to bring ice from Maine to New York to store it until the weather warmed. He thought it was stupid to hold on to a big empty house in Brooklyn when they could have an apartment in Manhattan, where the action was. Basically, Will thought everything about his life, and especially his father, was stupid. So, when a larger than average wave crested and sent water rolling down the decks and the icy spray splashed into the cockpit, hitting him in the face, he shouted, "Fuck you, you stupid son-of-a-bitch."

Nathan, Isaac's nephew and replacement, had been asleep when Will had come on deck. He was surprised, then, when Nathan opened the companionway hatch, stuck his head out, and shouted above the noise of the wind, "I've got coffee on. Grits to come. Want anything else?"

"Yeah, nigger. I want you to come up and take my watch."

Nathan didn't say anything. Instead, he turned back to cooking on the stove, which stayed relatively steady in its gimbals as the boat moved around it. When he sat down on his bunk waiting for the water to boil, he looked across to the other side of the cabin and saw Jamie looking at him. Jamie said, "I'll handle it." Again, Nathan didn't say anything.

Because of the strong headwinds, it took them two days before they rounded Rockaway Point and could ease off onto a reach into New York Harbor. After they unloaded the ice in Manhattan, one of the small steam tugs towed them across the East River to their home wharf in Brooklyn. They gathered in the cabin to talk about what was next, but Jamie asked Colm to go up to the house where he, Will, and Colm lived. He told him, "I'll brief you later. Wait for us there. Maybe we'll go to Jack's. I don't know what's there to cook."

After Colm left, Jamie looked at his son and said, "I don't know who the fuck you think you are, but you be apologizing right now."

"To who, for what?"

"You don't know?"

"No."

Jamie didn't say anything. It took a minute with the three of them sitting in silence for Jamie to grasp that Will didn't know. He realized his son had been left to bring himself up alone and develop his own moral code, one that was forged in the racism and criminality of Irishtown and the prejudices of his Dutch caretakers. Finally, Jamie said, "Nathan, why don't you be goin' home. Be back day after tomorrow in the mornin', late, close to noon."

Will got up to leave. "Not you. Sit," commanded his father. "You got some serious listening to do."

Will would never forget that afternoon. It began with the story of a young man sent to live with his Aintín Maude and Uncail Liam in Carna to avoid starvation. It continued through the good luck of meeting up with some Canadians at the dock in Cork and learning seamanship from a wonderful man named Jacob. Will knew a little of the story of the *Treasa* and Edward Ladd. He knew nothing of the story of Isaac's grandmother, who had been brought to Charleston, South Carolina, from the Kongo Empire as a slave. Slowly and barely, Will saw that his father and Isaac had been more than shipmates; his father looked up to Isaac. It started to register that Isaac's nephew, this Nathan, was a paid member of the crew and was to be treated as such.

It was a long story with many pauses as his father retrieved memories. Will didn't say anything. He let his father talk. Finally, when Jamie finished, he turned to his son and said, "Where on earth did you get the idea that you're better than anyone else? You never got that from your Ma, that's damned sure. And you sure didn't get it from me. So where?"

Now Will began talking. Slowly at first. Occasionally he would stop and say, "I don't want to talk about it." Jamie would ask a question. Will would continue to talk. He talked about being angry that he wasn't like the other kids because his dad was always away and his mother was a 'nutcase suffragette.' He never used the words 'abandoned' or 'different,' but his father understood that's what he meant. When he said that he told his friends he was an orphan, Jamie stopped him.

"Why? Why in heaven would you say that?"

"Might as well have been."

"Jesus, Will. Were we that bad to ya?"

At one point, he became sarcastic about how his parents didn't 'get' what life was really like in Brooklyn. When he said that, Jamie told him to "Watch it." Finally, Will talked through tears about missing a mother who was gone too much of the time. Then Will got angry at Treasa for not caring about him, and all that mattered to her was the damned voting shit. "Who cares if women vote? Why's it such a big deal?"

Jamie absorbed the pain and let him talk. When he stopped talking, Jamie said, "Let's go home, get Colm, and head out for a good meal." Jamie locked the Treasa hatches and climbed up onto the wharf. As they started walking to their home, Jamie put his arm around his son's shoulders.

They were a block from the house when Jamie said, "Now, about Nathan, you know what you need to do."

"What?"

Jamie stopped walking and turned to Will. Will saw the look in his father's eyes and said, "You're kiddin' me."

Jamie didn't say anything. Will said, "You want me to apologize?" Jamie still didn't say anything. Will said, "Do I have to?" Jamie still didn't say anything. Will said, "If I have to." Jamie still didn't say anything. Will said, "Okay, I'll do it. Can we go now?"

They started walking again, and Jamie returned his arm to where it had been around Will's shoulder.

When spring came, and the weather warmed, Will's acceptance of his new life also changed. Nathan teased him about being a 'fair weather sailor. Increasingly, Will came to enjoy the older men's company and took pride in taking on the responsibilities of a crew member. The trapped feeling started to wane. He stopped thinking about his being onboard the *Treasa* as a convenient solution to the problem of not having anyone at home to look after him. He learned his new trade, somewhat grudgingly, no matter how his father tried to get him as excited about it as he had been when he first shipped out on the *Phoenix*. Will became competent, if not enthusiastic.

When summer came, Jamie announced that they would take a week off in mid-July—an entire week to do nothing. Christmas week, they were used to, but this was something new.

'Nothing,' to Will sounded terrific. He decided to spend his time hanging out with his old mates in Irishtown. When his father asked him if there was anything he'd like to do, Will provided an oblique and guarded, "Just hang out." Jamie decided that they should spend time together. "You know, your mother always after me to spend time gettin' to know Manhattan, and you always tellin' me I know nothing about Brooklyn. Maybe we could go see some stuff."

"What stuff?"

"You tell me. You're the one tellin' me I don't know."

"Thought you liked just stayin' home."

"I do, normal times."

"This ain't normal?"

"Yeah, but. Oh shit, Will. You want ta do it, or not?"

"You serious? You want to go ta Manhattan?"

"Yeah. Time may be for you to put up."

"Okay, where ya want ta go?"

"I be leaving it to you, ain't I?"

"Ya mean it."

"Christ, Will. Yeah, I mean it."

The two of them became tourists. They went to the Statue of Liberty; they went to see the Flatiron Building, which had just been completed; they went to the circus at Madison Square Garden. Towards the end of the week, they visited the breweries in Irishtown. Jamie had insisted on meeting some of Will's mates, which led to conversations about how he knew them, and piece by piece, Jamie extracted from Will the background of his exploits in Irishtown.

Will was reluctant, stubbornly so at first, to introduce his father to the two brewery owners whom he had worked for, but he did so. At each stop, Will hung back and stayed out of the conversations. Finally, he became aware that his father was doing more than just chatting the owners up; he was gathering information. Jamie wanted to understand the liquor business. Where did they get their supplies? Who did they distribute to? How did they avoid taxes and the law? He also asked for their assessments on the anti-liquor crusades popping up around the country. Maine was not the only state to be 'dry,' even though no state had been able to close down access to liquor completely.

When Will asked him about it after they left the second brewery, Jamie said, "It's the damned machines making artificial ice right here in the city, and it's that bastard Charles Morse. He's puttin' a stranglehold on the ice business. It's become a damned monopoly. You haul for Morse, or you don't haul. He got the backin' of that Tammany Hall bunch. Couple years ago, remember when it got so hot?"

"Yeah."

"Morse and his bunch get Tammany to let him jack the price of ice to the fuckin' moon. No reason to. He just wanted money. Got caught, though. It stirred things up. Didn't matter none. He still the fuckin' 'Ice King.' Some shite of a king.

"Been tougher to get people on the Kennebec to sell to us. We still got small groups willin' to do it, but for how long? At this end, I can only sell to restaurants with their own lockers. That's all we got. I give em a fair price, and they don't need Morse. And now these machines."

"We could do coal."

"No. We ain't bout to breathe that dust into us. The only people they get to crew on those coal boats are darkies 'cause they can't find no other work."

"You thinkin' liquor?"

"Maybe someday. Granite's still good. It's still faster shippin' with us than getting it in from the coast to the rails and then down here."

"Da, you sure about liquor?"

"Why you ask?"

"I've heard stories."

"Like?"

"Murders. Beatings."

"Worried about your ol' man, eh? I can take care of myself. Sides, just thinkin' and talking."

On the way back home, Will asked, "You ain't been to Coney Island, have ya?"

"Nah. Why would I want to go there?"

"It's fun."

"You been?"

"Couple a times. Ya want to go?"

"Oh hell, why not?"

"Great. It's real easy. Train takes us right out there. It's quick. We could go this afternoon."

It was quick. Jamie had seen it from the water many times and had never been interested in going there. Once there, he found it was more exciting than he had anticipated. There were several amusement parks, a rollercoaster, and every type of food he could imagine. The place was crowded. Jamie found himself getting caught up in the excitement. "I wish I could see The Elephant," he said to Will.

"What elephant?"

"It was this great big elephant built on top of a hotel. It was the first thing I saw when I came into the harbor on the *Phoenix*. I seen it from the *Treasa*, too. Then it burned down. You could go inside the thing. Laddie told me all about it. Your ma wanted to come out here, but we never got around to it. Must have been something. See a wooden elephant on fire. Would've loved to 'ave seen that."

"Want ta go on the rollercoaster?"

"Alright. Don't look very high."

"It's fun. Come on."

They did and continued to wander around, going from stall to stall. Occasionally they'd play a game. They had just come out of one amusement area, and Will was leading them to another when they saw a big crowd. "Wonder what that's all about?" Jamie asked?"

"Probably just some speaker. Seen one here last time."

"Come on. Let's go see."

The two of them walked over to the crowd and started making their way through. Jamie asked a woman what was going on. "It's Mother Jones and her Children's Crusade. They've walked all the way from Philadelphia."

"Who's Mother Jones?" Jamie asked.

"You don't know?"

"Nah."

"She's marching those kids all the way to Oyster Bay. She wants to get Roosevelt to pass laws about children working. They got leaflets up there. Tell you all about it."

"Come on, Dad. Let's get going," Will said.

"Let's go listen for a minute. Just a couple of minutes."

When they got closer, they encountered a woman handing out leaflets. Jamie picked one up. It was labeled "March of the Mill Children." There were pictures of young children going into and coming out of mills in Pennsylvania. The leaflet said that the children worked sixty hours or more a week and couldn't go to school. The march was to bring attention to these children who just wanted to go to school.

As they got closer to the speaker, they saw the children first. They were carrying signs, 'I want to go to school,' 'I want to play.' Then, when they got closer, they could see and hear the woman who was talking. "She's old," Will said.

"Guess she's not too old to walk here from Philadelphia," Jamie replied. "Different life, you could a been one of those kids. Makes sailing for a livin' look pretty good, eh?"

"No way you getting' me inta one of them mills."

"Don't worry. Never let it happen."

"Can we go, now? There's more to see."

"Sure. What's next?"

Chapter Twenty-Two: Logs

Jamie said Will inherited his mother's interest in books. His son read everything and was curious about everything. Will had been on board the *Treasa* for a year before discovering that the newly opened Pratt Institute Library was only two miles away from their home in Brooklyn. Whenever the *Treasa* returned to its homeport, Will would head off to the library to return books, catch up on newspapers and magazines, and check out more books.

There were some things Will did not mention to his father about his reading. He didn't tell him that his reading on their voyages up and down the New England coast was how he avoided the boredom that came over him. Reading kept him occupied. Once he learned his craft as a merchant sailor, he found the tasks repetitive and often tedious. The challenges of weather, competition, railroads, and steamships he left to his father to worry about.

Will came to know the library well. By the time he was twenty-one, he had read every newspaper and magazine article the library had about flying and ballooning. Jamie didn't believe him when he told his father that the Wright's newest plane had stayed in the air for over an hour. When Will said that someday flying machines would be used to haul cargo, Jamie told him he was dreaming and should get back to reality.

He didn't tell his father he always went to the library late in the day to meet Pauline DeMarco, who worked at the circulation desk. They were physical opposites. Will was tall, broad, and ruddy with light hair; Pauline was small, dainty, and dark-skinned. One evening when the library was closing up, Will asked her about her accent. She took him over to the globe next to the front door and showed him where Catanzaro was in Southern Italy.

Theirs was a relationship marked by voyages. At first, they talked on the front steps after the library closed. A few trips later, he started walking her home. A few trips after that, their relationship became physical. They were each other's 'firsts.' Without a place to go, they found amazement in the back seat of Pauline's family's car, which was parked in the driveway of her home. Even though it was a new Model T Ford, it squeaked when they became too energetic, and Pauline was sure her younger sister could hear them. Her bedroom was on the first floor next to where her father parked the car.

Will confided in Nathan. He described the ecstasy and uniqueness of their love for one another. Nathan stifled a laugh, but barely. When Will asked him about it, Nathan said he had something stuck in his throat. Eventually, Will told Nathan about how much he loved the shuddering that convulsed Pauline's body when she would have an orgasm. He wanted to know if all women were like that. He was disappointed in Nathan's response: "Some do; some don't." Later that day, Nathan asked, "You know what you're doin' boy?"

"Whatcha mean?"

"You be careful now, not get that girl in a family way, have to get married. You bein' careful?"

By the end of the voyage, Will benefited from sexual tutelage based on Nathan's extensive experience. He also had information about where he could obtain the latest rubber condoms. "You don't go usin' those old skin kind. May feel better, but they break too easy."

While Will's relationship with Pauline had taken time to develop, it accelerated quickly with the addition of 'protection' and Nathan's tutoring. For Will, voyages now lasted forever, and reading didn't help. When they were home, every day in Brooklyn was a library day. He would get there early and come home late. When Jamie asked him about his late hours, he said, "Meetin' friends for a pint." Since Will never displayed any distressing after effects the following day, Jamie was not concerned.

The relationship ended abruptly. In February, a month after his twenty-first birthday, Will went to the library to discover Pauline no longer worked there. When he knocked on the door of her home, her father answered. When Will asked to speak to Pauline, her father replied, "We don't want you a comin' round here."

"Why?" Will asked.

Pauline's mother was watching them from the kitchen. She shouted out, "You shanty Irish drunks. No goin' fool with my daughter."

Will didn't know what to do. All he could think to say was, "I'm not a drunk. I work hard. I love Pauline." He was shouting to a closed door.

They were getting ready to leave for Stonington when Will told Nathan what had happened. Nathan said, "Fuckin' WOPs don't even know the difference. Believe me, boy, you no shanty Irish. You as lace curtain as they come, what with your Da owning his own boat and a house."

Once underway, Will stopped talking. He grunted responses when asked questions. Colm teased him, "Better seasick than lovesick, my young pup. At least when you're seasick, you can do something productive like throwing your guts up."

"Go fuck yourself," responded the young pup.

When Jamie asked Will what was bothering him, his son responded, "Nothing." Jamie had to ask Nathan to find out what was causing his son to be so quiet. "First love. Your son's got it bad," Nathan said. "He'll be alright. Just got a bad case of lovesickness."

"I'll talk to him."

"Good luck."

The following day Jamie and Will were on watch together. It was a beautiful day, and the wind was good. Jamie asked Will to take the helm. "Nathan told me what's eatin' at you. Says you cared about this girl and her parents wouldn't have none of it cause you ain't Italian. Sorry. Her loss. They're bein' stupid. Plain fuckin' stupid. Shit like that."

Will didn't say anything. Jamie didn't expect him to. "You're a good man, Will. A real good man. You got a future, too."

Again, Will didn't say anything. Jamie continued, "It's hard missing someone you love. Damned painful. I miss your ma, something awful at times. Wish she could see you now. She'd be real proud of you, especially with all your reading. I know you miss her, too. And now this girl. That's a lot of missing."

Jamie was standing next to his son, looking forward. He heard his son's sniffles. He didn't look at him. Instead, he put his arm around his son's shoulder and squeezed.

After that trip, Will went to the library less frequently. The new librarian at the circulation desk was older and married.

Will was below in his bunk and had almost finished reading *Two Years Before the Mast* when the fog bank enveloped them. The wind was from behind, from the southwest, at eighteen knots. Every sail was up and they were sailing at hull speed, close to twelve knots. Colm was at the helm. He shouted, "Will, you and Nathan better come up. I need more eyes in this shite." Jamie looked up from his bunk, where he had remained for the last two days with a fever.

"Now," Colm shouted from the cockpit.

"Damn it," Will said. He wanted to finish his book. It was the second book he had read so far on this trip. He had three others stashed away in his locker.

"Will, Nathan, now!" Colm shouted again.

When he got on deck, Will saw why Colm was worried. The fog was thicker than he had ever seen it. At times he couldn't see the front of the boat. The fog would lift for a few seconds; then, they would be back in it and lost in a world of gray. Everything was wet from the thickness of the fog.

"We need to slow down," Colm said. "We hit anything at this

speed, and we're in trouble. I'm going' to head up so you two can strike the topsails and the main. Then get the jib down, and we'll run under foresail and staysail."

"Where are we?" Nathan asked.

"Close to the mouth of the river. Sometimes I can hear the horn on Seguin."

"Oh, great. Logs," Nathan said.

Colm had just thrown the helm over when they hit them, three of them. Someplace up the Kennebec River, logs had gotten away from a log boom. The escaping logs had made their way downriver on the outgoing tide. When Colm threw the helm over to head into the wind, the *Treasa* picked up speed and slammed into three twenty-foot logs riding low, the tops just touching the surface. Two glanced off after doing their damage, but as the boat turned, they hit again. They drove right onto the third log.

"Shite," Colm yelled.

"What happened?" Jamie hollered from below.

"Dad!" Will shouted and went below decks to check on his father and the damage. Water was coming in from where the two logs had broken ribs and seams between three planks. Farther forward, though, the third log had smashed planks into splinters, and water was gushing in.

"Tell Colm to leave the sails up and head for the river." Jamie was out of his bed and stuffing blankets into the hole to slow the amount of water flooding into the boat. "Get Nathan on the whale pump. You dig out the tide table for the mouth of the river and look at the chart. We need to ground her. Find us mud or sand. Lots of it. We'll have to patch her from the inside."

Will ran up the companionway stairs. "Leave the sails up and head for the river. Nathan, whale pump." He came back down and dug out the tide table. "Four hours to slack."

"Good. Find us a place and give Colm a course."

"I don't know where we are."

"Shite. You work on the hole, and I'll figure it out. Grab the number one jib, fold it into layers so it'll cover the hole, and tack it into place over the blankets to hold them in place. Then you start pumping."

Will took the toolbox from under the chart table and grabbed the jib from the forward sail locker. The water was up to his ankles and climbing. He grabbed the hammer, a handful of short nails, and started tacking the sail over the blankets. "It's not helping," he shouted at his father. "Water's still comin' in."

Jamie paid no attention to him. He was busy plotting a course on the chart with his parallel rules. Then, when he was satisfied, he yelled up to Colm, "Can you see Seguin?"

"Not yet, but the fog's starting to lift a bit. Wait a minute. I think I see it."

"I hope to hell you're right. Steer sixteen degrees. It'll take us east of Pond Island. I want to get around the Fort, and we'll ground her up in the bay."

"Sixteen degrees," Colm confirmed.

"You and Nathan switch off steering and pumping."

Will pumped away on the hand pump, sending water through the hose out into the cockpit and down the scuppers back into the ocean. Jamie got a bucket and started scooping water out of the cabin and throwing it into the cockpit. The two of them had to establish a rhythm so Jamie would not hit Will, who was standing at the companionway stairs.

The water was knee-deep when they rounded Fort Popham and headed into Atkins Bay, and ran the *Treasa* aground in the thick mud. Jamie, Will, and Nathan kept pumping and bailing while Colm took the sails down so they wouldn't go so deep into the mud that it would be impossible to get them off. Finally, when Jamie started coughing uncontrollably, Will told him to get back into his bunk.

As the tide went out, the water stopped coming into the *Treasa*. They had most of the water out of the boat within an hour. Leaving his father below, Will went on deck with Colm and Nathan. Colm said, "We need to get the dinghy over the side. Will, get me the small hook from the anchor locker. Take the chain off it and bring it back to me. I'm going to fix the main halyard to it and row it out broadside so when the water goes all the way out, the boat'll lean over on her good side, and we'll get a look at the damage. While he's doin' that, Nathan, get the main anchor from the bow and bring it back here. I'll come back and row it out towards the river so we can control how far forward she goes when the tide comes in. If we can slow the damn leaks, we may be able to float her and get a tow upriver to Bath and get her hauled at one of the yards."

Two hours later, the *Treasa* was leaning over on her starboard side. The waterline on the port side was now exposed, and Colm went over the side to inspect the damage. Planks had been broken where the first two logs had hit. The third log had stove in the port bow at the waterline. Back aboard, Colm went below. He pulled gear away so he could inspect the boat's ribs. "We've got real problems," Colm told Jamie, who had remained in his bunk at Will's insistence.

"How bad?"

"Nothin' we can fix here. We need haulin' and a yard. Need to replace ribs and a lot of planks on the port side. We were damned lucky we were close in and light. We been loaded, and farther out, she'd be on the bottom. I'll be leavin' Nathan and Will to keep workin' on the damage. I'm goin' ashore and see if I can get a lift into Bath. Come back with a tug when she floats free, and we'll tow her in. Any luck, one of the yards has some empty rails, and we can get her hauled. Worst thing happen, we strap her to a wharf, and I get a crew to bail and pump while we slow the leaks with canvas and boards. We also gotta find a hotel for you. You not be stayin' on this boat tonight. That's for damned sure."

"I'll be okay. I'll stay on board."
"Like hell, you will. I'll carry you off I got to."

There were no boatyards that could haul them that day, so they tied the *Treasa* in tight to a wharf that catered to smaller boats and had very little water at low tide. The *Treasa* would be sitting on the mud when the tide went out, but she wouldn't heel over away from the wharf. At low tide, the water would be below the damage, and they could get caught up on the water that had made its way into the hold and bilge. Colm recruited two men to help them with the pumping, and he deposited Jamie in a boarding house on Front Street.

The three able crew members stayed on board the *Treasa* that first night. They gathered around Jamie's bed the following day at the Pinewood House. He was still a bit feverish but was getting good care from Clara Wilson, the owner. Already, she had gotten the doctor in to check on him. "Three days in bed for you, lots of fluid, keep Vapo Rub on your chest, lots of sleep, and you'll be good as new," was the physician's prescription. "It's not pneumonia, just a nasty cold. Clara'll take good care of you." Clara—no one calls me Mrs. Wilson—brought Jamie pancakes, ham, and toast for breakfast.

"You lookin' good, ol man," Colm said when the three of them walked into the room where Jamie was in bed.

Will had never seen his father look like this. He noticed how gray his father's beard and hair had gotten. His face was pale. Jamie was still tall and big, but he didn't look as strong lying in bed with the covers pulled up to his neck. "Da, how ya doing?"

"Feel like shite, but I'll be okay. What's happening?"

Colm described what they knew about the damage and told him about the plans to haul the *Treasa* the next day. Nathan told him about the temporary caulking and internal and external planking they had done. "Still leaks, but we can keep up with it, no problem."

Colm said, "Got a boat surveyor comin' this afternoon when the tide's out. We'll know more then. We'll be haulin' at Percy and Small. Got their foreman comin' as well. Be a while before they can do anythin,' though. Everyone up and down the river is full out with new builds."

Jamie swung his legs over the side of the bed, trying to get up. "Shite. I wish Blaisdell still owned that yard. He be the one built her. He'd get to her fast."

Colm put his hand on Jamie's shoulder. "You get back in bed, boy-o. We be lucky to get her hauled. Wait till you see what's goin' on out there. You should see the size of the boat they're building at Percy's. I never seen anything so big."

Will said, "For Christ's sake, Da, we're lucky we're here at all, and you be bitchin'? I'm just glad we're on land no matter how long it take to fix the damned boat. We could be out there somewhere in the fuckin' dingy freezing our arses off with nothing to eat or drink."

"Real optimist, this one," Colm said.

Jamie said, "Alright. Enough. Let's wait and see what the surveyor and foreman have to say. I donna care what the fuckin' doctor says. I'm not staying in this bed for three god damned days."

The news from the surveyor was not good. Jamie and the crew already knew about the ribs and planks that would have to be replaced. Colm had asked the surveyor to go through the boat from stem to stern, from keel to masthead, and find out if there were any other problems. There were. The *Treasa* had worked hard for thirty-one years, carrying heavy loads, primarily granite and ice. The surveyor's report included sixty-three separate items that should be addressed when she was hauled. Looking at this list and knowing what else they were working on in the boatyard, the foreman said it would be several months before all of the repairs were made, and the *Treasa* was ready to get back to work. The yard would take care of the hull issues first, but then she'd have to go on a mooring while they worked on the others. When Colm objected, the foreman said, "I'm sorry. But look around. Where the hell would we put your damned boat."

Two days later, Jamie went to the yard office to talk to the foreman about the estimate that had been prepared. Thinking he'd be able to negotiate downward, he was taken aback when the foreman said, "I don't need the work. I'm doing you a favor. We'll get to them as we can but you got to understand, we've got deadlines to meet on the boats we're building. I don't give a damn that she was built here. This isn't Blaisdell's yard anymore, and we've got all the new builds we can handle without having to do repair work. I can't get enough men as it is. Take it or leave it." Jamie hated not having a choice.

That night when they had dinner together, Jamie described the situation. Colm had predicted what was going to happen and talked to people in different yards up and down the river. Will and Nathan had also been talking to people.

Will was ready when Jamie said, "You know what's goin' happen, don't ya? They never have time to work on the *Treasa*. Never get to her to finish up once they get her in the water and on a mooring."

Will jumped on it. "So, I stay here. I already talked to one of the supervisors working on that monster they building. He said he'd hire me right away. So, I stay here and watch out for the boat and make sure the work gets done. Mrs. Wilson says I can take this room when you leave. Pay's good at the yard. I'll be fine."

Colm waited a minute before he said. "If you be wantin' to, there's a boat upriver that has a new owner. Bigger than *Treasa*. He's adding to his fleet. Doesn't have a skipper or crew yet. Wants to get the boat working right away. Told him we might be able to help him out. He said he would need at least a year. Said he'd pay us in shares."

"What's he want ta be doin' with her?" Jamie asked.

"Setts, granite setts from Stonington. Also, feldspar, from the other side the river in Georgetown. Take the feldspar down to New Jersey."

"Maybe. I guess worth talking to the man. But a god damned year. *Treasa* be ready in what, four to six months at most. Maybe we agree to six months. We did that, I could keep an eye on *Treasa* the times we're in here, and Will can stay with us."

"Nah, Da, I think it'd be best me staying here in Bath so I can watch out for *Treasa* full time."

"You sure that's what ya want to do? You don't know no one here."

"Yeah. I'm sure. I'll make sure the work gets done; I'll be learnin' some things, too. I'll see you when you're here for the feldspar. Six months, we'll all be back on the *Treasa*."

July 4, 1986
HOME TOWN BOY by Michael Buckley

Ten years ago today, we celebrated two hundred years of experimentation with self-governance. We're still working at it. That's good news, and we will celebrate it this weekend with fireworks, parades, and lots of speeches, some good, some boring. If the weather is good, and maybe even if it isn't, we will BBQ all sorts of food and consume tons of potato salad, Maine potatoes, I trust, and of course we'll swill down a wide assortment of spirits of various degrees of hardness.

Twelve years ago, we saw how strong we are at conducting this experiment. A President tried to mess with our voting. A couple of young reporters, Bob Woodward and Carl Bernstein knew something was wrong and were determined to find out what was going on. For months they worked to uncover the truth. Against a lot of odds.

It was a tumultuous time. The Nixon White House denounced the reporters, the Washington Post, and the New York Times. Many other newspapers published articles saying the stories were false. Eventually, it was the offspring of immigrants, one a prosecutor (Leonidas Jaworski), and the other a Judge (John Sirica) who helped bring the sorry mess to an end. At the time, forty percent of the citizenry did not trust the media, mainly because Nixon told them not to.

I have to admit, as a reporter, I was proud of my profession. Woodward and Bernstein did what I was taught to do when I was in journalism school back in the sixties. Get the story. We need a free press and people like them if we are to have a democracy. Democracy is something you work at.

Today, in the Northern part of Ireland, they struggle with what democracy means. There are riots, murders, and people don't feel safe to live their lives. In South Africa, the idea that "all men are created equal" is still a dream. Apartheid reigns in politics, and violence reigns on the streets. Democracy, this concept we celebrate today, is tough to bring about and tough to hold on to.

I wonder what old John Parker and the folks he hung out with would think about our experiment. They got here and built a colony before that bunch of radicals down in Plymouth, and if they had stayed put for a few months longer, no one would have heard much about the people down in Plymouth. But, alas, they went home. However, let's not forget that during their second winter in Plymouth, those folks were starving again and had to be bailed out by our Maine fishermen.

To the best of our knowledge, no one had a revolution on their mind—yet. When they finally got around to it and the colonists decided to revolt, they needed a plan for how they would govern themselves They'd need a full blown constitution, once they removed the yoke of the oppressor. There was a lot of fighting and fussing during the construction process, and it took them four years to work it out. The work started in 1787. The first drafts, though, did not talk about the people. They spoke of the branches of government and what each branch could do. The "Federalists" thought that was sufficient. The "Anti-Federalists" were displeased. They wanted some rights included for the people. Jefferson argued for them; Madison took to writing them. The very first one provides the context within which Woodward and Bernstein could do their work:

> Congress shall make no law respecting an establishment of religion, or prohibiting the free exercise thereof; or abridging the freedom of speech, or of the press, or the right of the people peaceably to assemble, and to petition the government for a redress of grievances.

Over the years, we have developed a whole library of laws and interpretations of what this sentence means, and we are still at it. When dictators, or would-be dictators, want to run things without respect for the people, these are usually the rights they go after first: religion, speech, assembly, press, redressing grievances. It's all there. It's hard to be a dictator if people have these rights.

Nevertheless, sometimes politicians and others who want power try to do away with them. We fight back. Sometimes it gets messy, but usually, common sense prevails, and this sentence's wisdom emerges in the end.

Our revolution was not simply one of leaders and battles. It was not merely to throw off the yoke of a king who wasn't right in the head. It was that, too. But, more importantly, it was a revolution of thought, of how we view ourselves as human beings, and how we choose to govern ourselves. So, as we clap for our bands, girl scouts, and all of the others who parade today, and as we enjoy the company of family, friends and the wonderful food, let's take a few minutes to ponder that first amendment. As a newspaper person, I always give silent thanks to Mr. Jefferson and Mr. Madison for recognizing that if we are to remain free, people like Bob Woodward and Carl Bernstein need protection from a would-be dictator.

Two hundred and ten years. It is worth a parade.

Chapter Twenty-Three: The Yacht Club

The Erascohegan Yacht Club, and the homes associated with it, is a summer affair. Only a few club members arrive before the middle of June when the weather warms up, and there is less fog. Some more dribble in right after schools and colleges let out. Grandparents, aunts, uncles, cousins, and friends start to show up in July, and by the first week in August, everyone who is there to stay for any length of time is present and accounted for. August is the big month for events: tennis tournaments, regattas, and cocktail parties.

Because we lived in Georgetown, Hannah and I were a permanent fixture at the club. The week before opening, we helped the summer steward get things ready to welcome members; the week after Labor Day, we helped pull the floats as well launch and ready the clubhouse to hibernate for the winter.

Over the years, we got used to the social ritual of being asked about our children, grandchildren and when they would be arriving. More recently, I got used to making excuses for why they were not coming. I don't know if club members ever interpreted my rationales as excuses, but that's what they felt like to me. Of course, Maude's weekend appearances of late helped.

Before he became a husband and stepfather, I could depend on my third born, Jesse, being present on weekends. Jesse loved to sail. Of our four children, he had done the best in sailing class. He loved to race and thought going for a day sail was boring. However, the challenge of an ocean voyage was a different matter. That earned his approval. He was only fourteen when we sailed to Europe, and he handled the *Redhead* better than any of his siblings.

When he graduated from high school, we were not surprised when he decided to apply to the Rhode Island School of Design. He wanted to be a graphic designer, and RISD met his biggest nonacademic requirement—they had a sailing team. In the summer, he raced at Erascohegan. In the spring and fall, he raced on the sailing team at RISD. When he moved to Boston after college, he would drive up to Tír late Friday night and head back to school right after the last race on Sunday. He even planned his vacation time around regattas. His focus on racing came to an end over spilled milk.

We were beginning to wonder if Jesse would ever get married. Then he met Naomi. As my mother had done with Hannah and me, Hannah and I started dating things as BN and AN—before Naomi and after Naomi. Before Naomi, Jesse had adopted a 'work hard, play hard' Boston lifestyle. This included multiple women, none of whom were ever invited to Georgetown. There were ski trips to Aspen and Vail. He would say, as though it were obvious: "Who wants to ski on New England ice when you can climb on a plane and be skiing on powder the next day?" In April, there was crewing on a client's boat during Antigua Race Week: "It's the wind, Dad. There's always wind." At one point, he commuted to Milan on a project: "Dad, it's the design center of the universe. I never thought I'd be doing what I am doing back in high school, and Mr. Rhodes told me I was a good artist." Jesse never lacked enthusiasm. He approached Naomi the same way.

Jesse and Naomi would say that chocolate and milk brought them together. Jesse was working on a project for one of the Mars brands, Dove. It was a packaging assignment, and there had to be a photograph of milk flowing into chocolate. Jesse needed a food photographer, one who could shoot milk and chocolate and make the product look real, fresh out of the freezer, 'sweaty,' and irresistible. The design agency sent Naomi, and Jesse found her 'absolutely irresistible.' That she was a Black, divorced mother with two daughters, one ten and one twelve, didn't faze him. "Instant fatherhood with no diapers or sleepless nights. It's a deal." Hannah and I just looked at one another when he said that to us. They married, and Jesse moved in with his 'ready-made family.'

It took about two years filled with many dramas and sleepless nights for the four of them to adjust to one another. Still, with multiple therapists, together and individually, they managed to create a family. It was complicated. Naomi and her ex-husband worked together in a photography studio they had started before they were married. Raymond, the ex, came out as a gay man shortly after the girls were born. He was now married to Alex, a jazz pianist. The six of them celebrate holidays together. Maude's assessment: "Very modern." I like Raymond a great deal, but Alex is a pompous pain in the ass.

I love Naomi. I love her and Natalie and Miriam. Even though she now lives in Boston, Naomi was and remains a Manhattan person. She grew up there, Upper West Side, to be specific. The pejorative word, 'citified,' does describe Naomi. She knows everything about every New York City borough, from subways to museums to restaurants. So, when she met Raymond, and he lured her to Boston, she was reluctant to leave. To this day, when she refers to 'the city,' she means Manhattan.

While she has come to love Tír, sailing is an unsolvable puzzle to her. Black kids from the 'Big Apple' don't grow up learning and loving the feel of a sailboat. The idea that this invisible force called wind propels a vessel through the water is a mystery to her.

One spring, with Jesse's encouragement, she did try to learn. She took lessons at Steve Colgate's sailing school on City Island while Jesse enrolled in a racing clinic. Jesse loved his clinic; Naomi hated her class, especially after her boat collided with another boat. Jesse knew better than to persist. Natalie and Miriam were a little more open to sailing. Still, when they were on board, they were more interested in sunbathing and reading—they would complain when a sail hid the sun.

It's not a long drive from where they live in the Jamaica Plain section of Boston to Georgetown, Maine. With no traffic, it's under three hours of kids asking, "How much longer?" But, of course, in the summer there is always traffic. Cape Cod beaches are closer, and, as independent entrepreneurs, neither Jesse nor Naomi can patch together more than three or four days of consecutive vacation time to make the trip to Maine worthwhile. When the kids were younger, Disney World and Caribbean Resorts were a plane ride away, nonstop. As the girls got older, their interests and schedules created logistical chaos. Natalie was now twenty-two, and Miriam was a few months younger than Wendy.

Everybody has always loved Jesse. He was and is 'that kind of guy.' Naomi added even more to his likability. Wendy has adored Jesse since she was a youngster, and he would take her sailing. Once, when she was fourteen and disgusted with her mother, she left home and headed straight for Jesse and Naomi, who, with Rachel's permission, gave Wendy sanctuary for a couple of days. She also thought it was neat that two of her cousins were Black and city people.

Wendy was in the kitchen doing the dinner dishes when Jesse called. He didn't call me; he called Wendy. I heard her end of the conversation, "Yes, yes, yes! When? Everybody? Everybody-everybody?" Then there was silence on her end. Then, "Gramps is going to be in seventh heaven." Silence. "I love it. Thank you so much. Rina and I are going all over the place on it."

When she hung up, she came into the living room, went over in front of the fireplace, and did a pirouette holding her cell phone out in front of her like a microphone: "I am pleased to announce that the Boston wing of this family will be gracing us with their presence from Thursday evening, June 27th, when they arrive, until the following Tuesday morning when they leave."

"Are you serious?" I responded.

"I am. Uncle Jesse said he wanted to be here the weekend the club opened and said that Sonas had better be in good shape because he intended to kick some WASP butt and win the races on Saturday and Sunday. He also asked," she now did a bow in my direction, "if I would crew for him."

"Obviously, you said yes."

"I did, and he wants to know if you and Mother Maude would take Naomi, Natalie, and Miriam out on the *Redhead* to watch the races."

"To which you said…"

"Yes, of course. He said he was going into a meeting and he'd call you tomorrow."

"He's going into a meeting, now?"

"He's in Denver."

"I'll be damned. We're going to have a house full."

I immediately counted heads and beds. Wendy could stay put. Maude could have her usual room. Jesse and Naomi would take the room at the end of the hall, and the girls could have the room opposite them. The only bathroom on the second floor would get a workout. The clipboard where you signed up for shower time was still hanging on the wall next to the door, although I'd have to replace the sign-up sheet from the last time it was used. The linen closet in the hall was fully stocked. I knew Jesse would call me tomorrow. We'd talk about food then. By calling Wendy first and recruiting her as crew, he made her feel important and special. I loved him for doing that. I don't know if either of them could explain their relationship. I asked Hannah about it once, and she said, "Who knows? Just be glad it's Jesse she adores."

I asked Wendy, "Did he say how they were getting here?"

"Going to rent a car and drive. It always freaks me out that they don't own a car. Jesse is the only one in that family who drives. Blows my mind. I'd go crazy if I couldn't drive."

"City people, honey."

Wendy called Rina to tell her. From Wendy's end of the

conversation, I gathered that the two of them were going over the weekend schedule of events at the club and what the four young women were and were not going to attend.

Jesse and Wendy won only one of the four races. Jesse mistimed the start on the first race and they were over the starting line early. He never recovered after he had to circle back around the committee boat and re-start. During the start of the second race, he got stuck in the middle of the fleet and could not break free. During the third race, he did much better and came in fourth. Watching from the *Redhead*, I saw my son's rust begin to wear away. I also saw his intensity increase. By Sunday afternoon, he was focused. This was no longer a social event. He was back at RISD, determined to trounce nearby Brown University. It didn't matter that they were racing in an old design created in 1912 rather than a modern boat. Jesse had Wendy moving her weight constantly, sometimes asking her to bend by a matter of inches. Onboard *Redhead*, I pointed this out to Miriam who replied, "There's no way I would ever crew for D2." Raymond was D1; Jesse was D2; Alex never made it to consideration as D3.

The celebration after the race was traditional. The silver from a long-ago estate sale had been polished and was used to serve tea. Lemonade was available, as was sherry. A variety of quartered sandwiches and cookies were laid out to ward off hunger until the barbeque, which was still a few hours away. Non-racing males were dressed in Nantucket red shorts or trousers with navy blue blazers. Females wore an array of sundresses that made the club porch look like a late-May flower garden. Everything remained under plastic wrapping until the last racers had made fast to their moorings, been collected by the launch, and deposited on the club dock. Every Sunday in July and August would see the same ritual repeated.

Fortunately, there were no fouls, and subsequent protest meetings for infractions of the racing rules had to be adjudicated by the race committee. Instead, the racers gathered in clumps talking about wind shifts, tactics, and how well their boats moved compared to last year. It was always the boat that changed, never them.

Maude and I were talking to the new Commodore when Judd and Patty came up and joined us. A few minutes later, the Commodore excused herself to make her social rounds. Judd asked us, "Have you been out on the porch yet?"

Maude answered for both of us, "No. We came right in for some grub."

Patty said, "Well, get ready to be surprised. The Lands are here."

"Kitty and Warren?" I asked.

"No," Judd said. "Nan and Joe."

"You're joking," Maude said. "They haven't been here in what, fifty years."

"Fifty-three, to be precise," Patty said. "Joe's in a wheelchair and is in pretty bad shape. He had a stroke a few years ago and now has early dementia. Kitty and Warren convinced Nan to leave Palo Alto and bring Joe here for the summer. Apparently, they are afraid it might be Joe's last chance to spend any time at Erascohegan, and Joe said he wanted to come back one more time."

I listened to the conversation but didn't say anything. Nan had been my first true love, and I had been sure we would get married. We weren't quite engaged, but we were a couple and were looked upon as the 'club sweethearts.' Warren was Joe's younger brother. Kitty and Warren lived in Concord and came to the Land cottage every summer. I would hear about Nan and Joe's life from Kitty. I never said much or asked many questions.

After I graduated from BU, Nan and I wrote daily the first month I was deployed as a new Air Force Second Lieutenant. In July, the letters became fewer and fewer. Finally, at the end of August, when I was suffering through the heat of Texas learning to control F-102 interceptors, the last letter came. She and Joe had been together that summer in Maine, he had proposed, and they were getting married the following year in New Canaan. The Erascohegan Yacht Club had new 'club sweethearts' to celebrate.

It had been almost textbook "Dear John." No phone call, just a letter. It was not like I was unreachable; I was only in Texas, for Christ's sake. The hurt of Nan's rejection followed me through training and through my first deployment flying F-102s in Alaska. The pain of rejection wore away, and was eventually replaced with dread and disgust when I was sent to drop bombs on Cambodia and Vietnam. When I finally got back to the States, Nan and Joe had settled in Palo Alto, and there was Hannah to pick up the pieces and put me back together. Still, over the years, I accepted Kitty and Warren's 'Nan and Joe updates' with benevolence if not enthusiasm. And now, here they were, intruding upon my perfect weekend, and I was pissed about it.

I was more pissed when Nan found me an hour later. I was busy corralling my gang and herding them to head home when she came up to me and said, "Mike, it's Nan, Nan Wilder. Kitty said you were here. God, it's been a long time. I'd love to chat. Get caught up."

Like I didn't know who she was. I was polite. "Sure. I can't right now, but we'll find a time." As I was saying that, Wendy appeared with Rina, Natalie, and Miriam. Wendy said, "Gramps, we're going to start back. We'll get supper started. Take your time."

"Okay. You leaving now?"

"On our way." The girls started walking.

"Is one of those your granddaughter?" Nan asked.

"Three of them are. The one on the far right is Judd and Patty's."

From her reaction, I deduced that Kitty had not told Nan everything about my life and my children's lives.

Chapter Twenty-Four: Perceptions of Age

I have not awakened to an alarm clock since Hannah died. A good night's sleep has been a sometime thing for a while now. However, I keep to my morning ritual when I wake up, and it doesn't vary. It didn't even change Monday morning, with a house full of people. When I walked out to the end of the pier and sat down, Charlie came with me and my coffee.

The cove was still. The tide was in, covering our little pebble beach. There was no need, yet, for the seabirds to do anything but float in the quiet water. Their food would become available later when the tide receded, exposing the creatures that lived below the tidal line. Nothing moved. The sky was clear. Golden. Even Charlie knew that noise would be out of joint with the morning.

I sat facing the mouth of the cove. Beyond it, the Gulf of Maine was still. The only motion was my breathing. When Maude came, she came quietly, and sat beside me—no greeting. She knew. Occasionally we would sip our coffee. She held hers in both hands for warmth against the morning chill. Ice and Fire joined Charlie at our feet.

An eagle left its nest at the top of its pine tree and, with three flaps of its wings, reached soaring height and began to circle at the end of the cove. I pointed to it in case Maude hadn't noticed. She acknowledged by leaning against me.

We stayed there, still, until the sounds from the kitchen reached us as others began to wake up and start their day.

"I suppose I should think about packing and get on my way," Maude said.

"Sure you don't want to stay and leave tomorrow when the rest of the crew goes?"

"No, I've got some vendors coming in." She got up and turned to face me. "What a weekend of surprises. Jesse and his bunch here. And then, Nan Wilder."

"Yes, Nan Wilder Land. Talk about... surprises. She wants to 'chat.'"

"Do you want to 'chat?'"

"I suppose."

"Have at it. By the way, congratulations, Gramps."

"On what?"

"Gramps. I love it. Wendy's having a good summer, Mike."

"I think so."

"Believe me, she is. And I understand you two write and read every morning."

"We do."

"And you've been up to Jay three times."

"I have. Once with Wendy to the museum, and twice to conduct interviews."

"I'm excited for you both. Give me a hug and I'm on my way."

I stood up and did what I was told. I watched her walk back up the pier with Ice and Fire obediently behind her. Watching her leave, a feeling of loneliness descended even with the house still full of people. They were the wrong generation. I sat back down.

Two of my children were missing. I wondered what they were doing this morning. Ruth, in Pearland, Texas, would still be asleep.

Joel. Be safe, Joel. For God's sake, don't take any unnecessary chances. It would be close to five in the evening in Afghanistan. Would he have flown today? So far, no C130 Js had been shot down. So far.

I wanted him home. I wanted him at Tír. It didn't matter that he was forty-two, incredibly competent, and doing what the Air Force had trained him to do. I still wanted him home and safe.

Safe. I couldn't keep Hannah safe. I can't keep Joel safe. I can't keep anyone safe. Would Joel have wanted to go to the Air Force

Academy if I hadn't decided to do Air Force ROTC? Was Nan right, after all? Had my decision to accept a commission been 'ridiculous?'

So, Nan wanted to chat. Our relationship had taken place like a two-act play. We had grown up together. Her parents had been among the earliest of the summer people to settle on the peninsula. Her grandfather was one of the founders of the yacht club back in 1924. Their house was one of the first, a typical Maine summer cottage with gray shingles, dark green trim, and a wide porch looking out on the Sheepscot River.

At first, there was no clubhouse, just a bunch of guys who wanted to race and agreed that the Nat Herreshoff designed 12 ½ was the perfect boat. Eventually, they built a clubhouse, and Nan's grandfather was the first Commodore.

Nan's dad was a nice man whom everyone liked. On the other hand, her mother was an alcoholic who was in and out of treatment programs for a while before she refused to go anymore. Eventually, everyone in the family and the club members just accepted that no change would take place. Nan's older brother finally left home and was brought up by an aunt and uncle. Nan stayed with her parents.

Nan and I took sailing lessons together, crewed for one another in races, and had a puppy love summer between sixth and seventh grade. She was a summer fixture in my life. She would hang out at Tír with me, Maude, and Judd when she couldn't stand being at home with her mother.

A year older than me in age, Nan was quite a bit older than me in dealing with life struggles. When she was in her junior and senior high school years, she was dating and bedding college students. She never did so at Erascohegan and managed to keep up the Wilder 'good family' façade every summer. No one believed it, but she and her father tried.

I had just finished my junior year in high school, and Nan was on her way to college when she suggested we go out to the *Redhead* one afternoon in mid-August. When we got on board, she went down into the cabin and told me to follow her. She hopped onto the V berth and asked, "So, Buckley, you still a virgin?"

I stammered, "Yes, but I've done everything else."

"Everything else." She paused and smiled at me. "Okay. The chances are that sometime in the next year or two, that will change. I'm not going to let that happen with someone else. I'm going to be your first. This afternoon. Here and now. I want to make sure you get broken in right."

I had never felt so embarrassed, excited, or scared. Immediately, I had an erection.

"Do you have the cushion filler for this thing?" she asked, pointing to the gap in the V berth.

I didn't answer. I scrambled to get the cushion from where it was stored, Nan moved over, and I put it in place, converting the V berth into almost queen size at one end. While I was doing that, Nan was removing her clothes. When she finished, I just looked. "What are you looking at, Buckley? Never seen a naked lady before? Your turn."

That afternoon was the first of several afternoon visits to the *Redhead* before Nan left for college. None of our parents, siblings, or friends seemed to notice. Nan always had condoms. By the end of the summer, I felt well broken in. Then she left for her freshman year. I missed her terribly when she left. Looking back, that was the end of Act One of the Nan-Michael drama.

Nan did not return to Erascohegan after her freshman year or sophomore year. Neither did her parents. The Wilder home was rented both summers to a family with young children. No one knew why the Wilders were absent, at least not then. When they returned the third year, it was without Nan's mother. The Wilders had gotten divorced, and Nan's father now had a new woman with him, younger, sober, and pregnant.

I was thrilled to have Nan return. Two years of maturity and a girlfriend during my first college year added to my confidence as both a sexual partner and mate material.

Nan had also changed. Now when we talked, it was a very different kind of talking. She spoke openly about her mother, her brother, and the new woman in her father's life. She spoke about her real estate aspirations. She said she wished she had gone into architecture, but sales and development were an excellent second best. We went out to dinner together, inexpensive places in Bath and Brunswick. By the end of the summer, we were making love and saying we loved one another.

We visited each other during the next school year. She would come into Boston from Bentley University in Waltham, or I would go out there. When she graduated, she got a job with an architectural firm in Boston and a studio apartment. I spent more than a few nights there and used my dorm room primarily for studying. I was happy; Nan less so. As things became increasingly serious, we discovered two problems, at least according to Nan. First, I was going to become an Air Force officer. She thought that was ridiculous. It was the year of the Bay of Pigs absurdity, the Cuban missile crisis, and things were heating up in Vietnam. "You'll be away a lot. Do I follow you from base to base? Do I live alone and wait, hope, for you to come home in one piece?"

Second, I was going to be a reporter after the Air Force, and that was equally ridiculous. "Reporters don't make any money." By this time, Nan's mother was sober but without marketable skills; she was having a rough time living on her alimony. Nan was adamant that she would never find herself in that position. Money had become very important to her.

As my graduation approached, the tension between us began to rise. I was going to Texas for training and had no idea where I would go after that. I graduated and left. No Tír for me that summer. Act

Two ended with 'the letter.' My parents, Maude and Judd were subdued about the news. To me, they said they were sorry. To each other, they said, "Thank God." Years later, my mother said, "I knew you would never end it. Good for Nan. She knew what she needed and went after it. She could never have given you what Hannah did. It wasn't her fault, Michael. She didn't have it to give."

Jesse and Rachel invited me out to dinner Monday night. Naomi took all four girls into Brunswick to see the movie *Yesterday*.

I knew something was up. I was unprepared for what it was, though. Jesse wanted to eat at the Bath Brewing Company. He had done a packaging project for one of Boston's myriad micro-breweries and had, according to Naomi, become obsessed with finding the 'perfect' ale. So, he ordered a 'flight.' Rachel and I had Diet Cokes. Initially, I was disturbed that Jesse had suggested we eat at a brewery. But, when Rachel saw my reaction, she pulled me aside to say that it was okay and not to say anything to Jesse.

After a shared collection of appetizers, Jesse asked, "Dad, have you given much thought to the future?"

So, it was time for 'the talk.' It opened with as much nervousness and circumspection as parents having 'the talk' about sexuality with their teenagers. In both cases, 'the talk' usually occurred long after information had already been ingested and decisions considered. I was determined, though, not to make it easy on them.

"Yes, I have. In fact, I have been obsessing over it. The current administration is so anti-science that we have to depose this would-be dictator and his like before they destroy the planet." I chose to torture them: "We could lose Tír if the planet's temperature keeps warming and melting the ice caps. Some people in Orono have worked on projections for sea-level rise and what it would mean for our coastal communities."

Rachel laughed, "Your future. By the way, I love that Wendy has decided to call you Gramps. Right now, you are being a 'Gramps.' So, Gramps, what are your plans for when the old bod starts to slow down."

"Are you suggesting that I am getting old?"

"Older."

"Thank you, my dear daughter; I hadn't noticed. I appreciate the two of you pointing this out to me."

"So?" Jesse said.

"So?" I said back to him. I was enjoying this much too much.

"So, what are your plans?"

"To live and die in Georgetown. Sounds like a good movie title, doesn't it?"

Jesse now tried a patient tone of voice, "Come on, Dad. We just want to know what your thinking is. Ruth is concerned."

"If my oldest daughter is concerned, why doesn't she ask me? She might call me once in a while rather than my calling her. And, she might even consider visiting to see for herself how her decrepit old father is doing." So, this was Ruth's idea, and Jesse was the messenger. I asked, "And your brother? Joel? Is he on this?"

"Dad," Jesse said, "no one is in on anything. But I did talk to Joel. He said, "Sure, go ahead and talk to you, but do so at my own risk. He predicted you would get pissed, and he said you'd talk to us when you were good and ready."

"He was right. About both." I took a long drink of my ale and let them stew. "He still at the Bagram airfield?"

"I assume so. It wasn't a long conversation. I forgot how big the time difference was, and he was going to bed."

"I wish he'd come home," Rachel said.

"When we talked a couple of weeks ago, he told me he'd be out of there by October," I replied.

"Can we talk about this, Dad?" Jesse asked.

"Okay. I'll stop busting your chops. What do you want to know?"

"Do you have any plans?"

"I do." I waited.

Rachel laughed, "That's it?"

"I answered his question."

Jesse shook his head and looked up at the ceiling. "Mother, give me strength."

Rachel said, "I think Jesse is asking if you would share with us what they are so we can understand them and then communicate them to your other two children."

I smiled at them and took another drink of my ale. "Okay. Do you want to take notes?" This was fun. Rachel stuck her tongue out at me. "Oh, alright. Maude and I have talked about it at length, plans for both of us. She wants to retire next year. She plans to stay in Portland. The farm will be home base for both of us long term. If she gets sick or incapacitated, she moves in. The same if I get sick or incapacitated; she moves in. If care becomes an issue, we hire someone to help. We have the room if we need someone to live in, so that's not a problem. We would both like to be living on the farm when we die. We're also both very aware that there are all sorts of things we cannot predict, and making any definitive plans beyond a couple of broad brushstrokes is a waste of energy. That's the plan."

"And Tír?" Jesse asked.

"We rent it out when family members aren't there."

"And the land?"

"What about the land?"

"Are you going to sell any of it off?"

"Why would I? I need the pasture rental income to be eligible to pay only the agricultural taxes on it. We start selling land off, we lose all that. And for what? Neither one of us needs the money, at least not at this point."

"Well, Ruth was thinking..."

"What was Ruth thinking?"

Jesse took a deep breath. "She and Harold have run into some financial difficulties. She didn't want to ask you for money but she thought you might consider selling off some land, and since you've told us we're to inherit it when you die, you might be open to selling off some of it now."

Rachel looked at her brother with a look I had never seen from her before. "You did not tell me that Ruth's crap was what this was all about. She called you, didn't she."

Jesse immediately went on the defense. "Well, yeah, but it started me thinking about Dad's future, but it's not just about Ruth." I might as well have been in another room.

"So, you need money, too?" Rachel said.

"No. I do not need any money. We are doing just fine. It is also about Dad and…"

I interjected, "His becoming old, and 2F—fragile and feeble."

Jesse was still in defense mode, "I didn't say that."

Rachel was back at him, "You might as well have."

"Both of you, stop it. What kind of jam is Ruth in?"

"It's Harold," Jesse began. "He's broke. He owes money. From what I understand, a lot of money."

"How?" Rachel said. "I thought he was the oil tycoon in the family. The one who made the big money."

"From what Ruth told me, when he left his uncle's company to go out on his own, he invested heavily in his new company, remortgaged the house, borrowed, and then everything started shifting away from oil to natural gas. In addition, things moved away from shale drilling. He wasn't diversified, and now the loans are due. He has nothing left to use as collateral.

"He had talked his father into investing in the new company, and dear old dad has no interest in helping him out, and neither do his sisters. He's already been down that road, according to Ruth. Hal still has two years to go at Baylor, and he's not exactly scholarship material."

"Spoiled brat is more like it," Rachel added.

"Stop it," I said.

Now Jesse was getting irritated. "So that's it. Ruth said we were going to have to talk about your future plans at some point, so why not now when one of us needs help."

"What did you tell her?" I asked.

"That she was right; we should know what your plans are."

"And about selling off land so she could get some of her inheritance now?"

"That's on her. I told her I'd be a reluctant messenger. When I told her to call you herself, she said you didn't like her, and I was your favorite. So, I was the best person to talk to you."

"Oh, Jesus. She didn't really say that?" I asked.

"Yes."

"Well, you are," Rachel said.

"Hardly. Joel is."

"And you agreed to be the messenger. Why pray tell?" I asked.

"Because I'm stupid, and she pleaded."

"Jesus, Jesse. Sometimes you can be an absolute dunce," Rachel said.

I ignored them. I knew the back and forth about whether Jesse or Joel was the favorite son was a somewhat teasing skirmish that had gone on for years. The truth was, though, I did not like the person Ruth had become. When she married Harold Nokart I was not impressed with his cowboy boots, Stetson hat, and bolo tie. I told her so. Hannah was furious with me for saying something. My retort had been, "I wish my father or mother had said something to me about Nan." Hannah didn't honor my defense with a reply.

Ruth had met Harold when he was completing his MBA at Harvard, and she was a senior at Emerson. It didn't take long before he whisked her off to Houston to meet his family of oil people. They got married right after graduation and set up housekeeping in Pearland, outside of Houston. Thanks to Harold's parents, my Georgetown, Maine daughter now belonged to a country club where the initiation fee cost more than I made in a year working for the newspaper. She played golf. She joined the Junior League. She got pregnant and had Harold Junior, Hal. She voted for George W. Bush, John McCain, Mitt Romney, and Donald Trump. She knew better than to talk to me about it.

When she was in high school, she had said she wanted to get out of Georgetown because it was a "Hick community of farmers, fishermen, and welders." So, she moved out alright, way out. I didn't know her anymore, not that I ever did. Hannah stayed in touch. She went to Pearland when Hal was born. She went to Pearland when Ruth had her gall bladder out. She went to Pearland and helped Ruth pack when they moved into a larger house and then into a much larger house that you could fit both Tír, and the farmhouse into and still have room for a boat or two.

The Nokarts had come to Tír twice in twenty years. We would arrange to see them at least once a year, usually in Pearland. Harold would make brief, ghostlike appearances when we were there, as would Hal. Only Ruth and Hal came to Hannah's memorial service when Hannah died. They stayed for two days. I hadn't seen her in four years and talked to her maybe every other month. Now she wanted me to sell off farm property because Harold had fucked up. Like hell I would.

On the drive back to Tír, Jesse asked, "What should I tell Ruth?"

"Nothing. I will send her an email telling her if she wants to talk to me, she can call me. I'll give her a couple of optional times. You stay out of it."

There was no more conversation for the rest of the drive. Finally, when we got home, we said good night to one another and went to bed.

Rachel left early the following day as planned. I didn't hear or see her go. It was raining, not hard, just drizzling. The house was cold and damp. When I got up and went into the living room, there was a fire in the fireplace, and Jesse was sitting there sketching.

"Coffee's ready," he said.

I went into the kitchen, got 'my' mug out of the dishwasher, filled it, returned to the living room, and sat down.

"Dad," he said, "I'm sorry. She sounded terrified. You're right; I shouldn't have gotten in the middle."

"If she wants to talk to me, she'll have to call me herself. What time are you leaving?"

"As soon as everyone gets up and packed. We'll grab breakfast on the road."

"You sure? We've still got a lot of food."

"Yeah. The girls want to stop at Winnegance. We'll stock up on some scones to eat on the road. You and Wendy want to follow us in?"

"No, it's back to work for both of us."

We sat quietly for a couple of minutes before Jesse said, "I'm glad we came."

"So am I."

"Rum regatta? Eggemoggin Reach? Maybe even Castine and Camden. You up for them?"

I smiled. "If I have crew."

"I think that can be arranged."

Chapter Twenty-Five: Square Dance

I tried once to take a picture of the opposite side of the cove. Actually, I tried several times, but I could never capture what it looked like to me. In the morning, with the new sun coming through the pines, it's a shade of green that only exists for an hour. It's the oaks and maples standing so strong and tall, sheltering. It's the rocks on the shore, dark, without light yet. All of this in random layers, colors, and shapes. A beautiful chaos. Sitting on the bench at the end of our pier is the perfect place to be during this hour before it becomes something else, something different, still beautiful, but not this beauty, not this gift, not this reason to live. "Take me there, Mike," Hannah would say when she was too weak to walk there on her own. I'd help her get out of her hospital bed in the living room and into her long coat, protecting her against the morning chill. She'd have to lean on me as we walked out onto the porch. She'd sit while I took the wheelchair down the steps and unfolded it for her. It was a bumpy ride down to the pier, and she would scold me for being a poor driver. It was our hour. One morning, just before it was time to return to the cottage, she said, "I want to live, Mike." She didn't say, "I don't want to die." "I want to live." That was Hannah. She always wanted 'to live.'

That last summer, that time on the pier was our hour before the drives to chemotherapy and doctors and exhaustion and a return to the hospital bed at Tír na nÓg. Tír na nÓg, the land of eternal youth. It didn't feel like the 'land of eternal youth' that final summer. It hasn't any summer since then, until now, in moments. I'm starting to think of those as 'Wendy' moments.

Wendy and I have developed our own ritual. I always wake up before she does, and I make the coffee. Then, I take my cup down to the end of the pier for my hour to watch the sun come up. Later, she comes down to join me, bringing a cup for herself and the carafe to refill mine.

One morning, when she came down, she had something clenched in her mouth so she wouldn't drop it while she carried her cup in one hand and the carafe in the other.

I asked her, "What do you have in your mouth?"

She put down her cup of coffee on the opposite bench and showed me a tiny book. "Something I found in a drawer in the table next to the fireplace when I was looking for a rubber band. Look how tiny it is. It's by a Buddhist nun. Her name's Pema Chödrön. I have no idea how to pronounce it with those dots over the 'O's.' She's weird looking."

"It was Nanna's." I always used the 'grandmother name' when talking to my grandchildren about Hannah. Given that her name was Hannah, it was never in doubt that as a grandmother she would be a 'Nanna.' "Her sister gave her that book when Nanna was sick, and Valerie came to be with her."

"Aunt Valerie? The one who lives in India? I remember her from the funeral. Unfortunately, I didn't get to spend any time with her."

"That's too bad. She's a good person. Her husband Tarun is, too. Very quiet, but he's a good guy."

"How long has Aunt Valerie lived in India?"

"Yikes. She moved there right after grad school. Close to fifty years."

"Wow. How come?"

"Well, she's sort of the black sheep in the Turner family. Couldn't stand the sciences. Loved philosophy, theology, stuff like that. We thought she might go to Divinity School someday. She went to India as a post doc to study Vipassana meditation with Tarun's father in Varanasi. That's where she met Tarun, and that was it. They adore one another. They've made a life there. At first, they would come to the States for a couple of weeks every summer, but it became every other year as their kids got older. Now it's just for events, but not all of them."

"How many times have you been there?"

"Five or six times over the years."

"What's it like?"

"Different. Different in more ways than I could even begin to tell you."

"I'd like to go someday."

"I know you'd be welcome."

Silence. This had become our pattern—short conversations followed by silence. I never knew what the silence meant. Finally, she put her coffee down and leafed through the tiny book. After a couple of minutes, Wendy asked, "Why'd she give this to Nanna? It's all short things."

"Valerie and Tarun are Buddhists, Tibetan Buddhists. I think she thought it might be helpful to Nanna when she was dying."

"Why? They don't look like prayers."

"I don't know. I've never looked at it. Nanna would take it with her when she went for chemo."

"Okay if I borrow it?"

"Of course." Then I said, "I'd like to keep it in that drawer when you're done. That was the table we put next to the hospital bed."

Nan came alone to the square dance on Friday night. She was still slim, and her hair was now auburn, made that way, I am sure, by a regular visit to a salon. It was down below her ears and ended in small flips out to the side. This was not the young woman with long straight black hair of my memory. She wore glasses now, and I could see age in her neck. She looked tired even though she smiled as she walked over to me. She expected a hug and received one. Hugs are measured in beats like music. This one was two beats too long. I knew the smell, her smell, 'White Shoulders.' Christ. She was still wearing 'White Shoulders.' She broke the hug by kissing my cheek and stepping back, but leaving her hands on my arms. She said, "I was sorry to hear about Hannah."

"Thank you."

I was about to say more when fiddle music started, and Wendy came skipping over to me in time with the rhythm. "Okay, Gramps. Let's do this."

I introduced Nan, "Wendy, this is Nan Wilder."

"Nan Land," Nan corrected me.

"I'm sorry," I said, feeling like an idiot.

"It's okay," Nan rescued me. "He's all yours, Wendy. Have fun, you two. Maybe I can get one later. But, if we don't, at some point, we need some 'catch up' time."

We never did find ourselves in the same square. Nan left about an hour later. Her in-laws arrived about ten minutes after she left. Kitty Land came right over to me. "Michael. Nan said you were here. She's gone back to the cottage. We're taking turns staying with Joe. He finds it hard to be alone when he's not in his own house. I'm happy you're here. Warren and I have a favor to ask. It's a biggie."

"I'm listening. Will if I can."

"Joe is failing quite rapidly. He's gotten more frail over the past six months, and his memory is going fast. We hoped that being here would be nice for him and help with his memory issues. You know, give him some variety. He seems to perk up when he and Warren talk about their time when they were young and lived in New Canaan."

"Makes sense."

"Well. Here it is. We'd love to get him out sailing, but it would be impossible to do it on our Herreshoff. Might it be possible for you to take him out on the *Redhead*, just for a couple of hours? I know it's a big ask."

Of course she knew it was possible. Everyone had seen me wheel Hannah down to the dock, help her get on board, and take her out for a sail. Maybe this was becoming a new role for my beloved schooner in the club's life. There was no way to say no, and even if there were, I wouldn't have. I said, "Of course. Glad to. I'm racing on the weekends, so I'd rather do it during the week. It would be best to leave and come back on either side of high tide, so the ramp from the pier to the floating dock will be easier to navigate. I learned that the hard way."

"You are a sweetie. Thank you so much. Do you think there's any chance it might be possible to do it next week? Warren has to return to Concord the following week, and he'd love to make it a brother thing."

I wondered why Warren hadn't asked me himself. I said, "I'm sure we can find a good time. I'll figure out the tide and keep an eye on the weather. Might have to be short notice. I'll give you a buzz."

She laughed, "Anytime would be great. We aren't going anywhere. And again, thank you so much for doing this. We knew you'd understand."

"I do."

Tuesday at one o'clock turned out to be a perfect time. The weather would be clear; a twelve to fourteen knot breeze was predicted, and high tide would be at two-thirty. That would give us a few hours when the ramp wouldn't be too steep from the pier to the floating docks. I didn't want to interfere with Wendy's reading time, so I asked Judd if he would crew for me. Kitty told me that Nan would pack a lunch for everyone. So, Nan was coming, too.

Rowing out to the *Redhead*'s mooring, Judd said, "You're a good man, Charlie Brown."

"Not a big deal."

"By the way, my conspiratorial wife thinks this adventure was Nan's idea, not Warren's."

"Does it matter?"

In a mock Irish accent, Judd said, "Me wife just be looking out for the welfare of me oldest mate."

I answered in like manner, "And you and your wife be out of your feckin' heads."

He bantered back, "Don't be so sure. You got gob smacked by that wench once and, according to the fair Patricia, when Nan made her entrance last Friday, she made straight for you like an old nag heading for the barn."

I dropped my faux Irish accent. "Old nag heading for the barn? Where the hell did you get that from? And if Nan's an old nag, what the hell am I?"

"Well, she is a year older than you."

"Jesus. You two are certifiable. Besides, she's married."

"And..."

"And nothing."

Warren, Judd, and I were able to get Joe on board without any difficulty. Once we cleared the cove, Judd and Nan worked together to get the sails up. Judd had to remind her about a couple of things, but fifty years later, she still remembered how the sail plan of the *Redhead* worked.

I hadn't paid much attention to Joe while getting him on board. Once underway, looking at him, I was struck by what I saw. The stroke had taken away one side of his body. His face sagged, and his arm and leg were useless. His speech was difficult to understand, and his head tilted to one side. It was hard to see the robust man that Nan had married. She was attentive to him when she brought out lunch. He could still feed himself but he had to be careful because the left side of his mouth didn't function effectively. Nan had packed a special lunch for her husband, anticipating the difficulty that a boat in motion might bring about. For Joe, she had packed finger food; she had packed lobster rolls for the rest of us. Watching Nan, I saw myself attending to Hannah.

We sailed out of the Sheepscot River into the Gulf of Maine. The wind was as predicted, and we moved along smartly. I asked if there were any preferences for where we should head. There were none. That meant taking them on the 'scenic route.' We would head southeast until we cleared Damariscove Island, then easterly past Pumpkin Island. Leaving Pumpkin to Port, we would head north past the White and Inner Islands. We would then head west. Depending on how well the wind was holding, we'd dip into Boothbay Harbor before heading back to Georgetown and Heron Cove. Lots of islands to see up close on every point of sail before the trip was over. I had taken people on 'the scenic route' more times than I could remember. It was always a crowd-pleaser. Whale sightings were common, and there were always seals.

After lunch, I offered the helm to Warren as we sailed off the wind heading for Damariscove, but he demurred. When he did, Nan asked if she might take the helm. I said yes, and she came up to stand next to me. I moved aside, told her what to aim for, gave her a compass course, and pointed out where we were on the chart plotter above the binnacle holding the compass. She handled the boat well, and I relaxed. Judd went below and retrieved the binoculars. He said, "I'm going forward to look for whales. Let me know if you need me."

"Will do," I answered.

Joe started to nod off with the motion of the boat. Warren helped him to lie down on the cockpit bench. In a couple of minutes, he fell asleep. "I'm going up with Judd," Warren said to no one in particular. "Keep an eye on him."

Except for a sleeping Joe, Nan and I were alone. I asked her what I wanted to ask at the square dance, "How are you doing?"

"It's hard. It's hard for both of us. But, fortunately, we have enough money and good insurance, or we'd be broke."

"Kitty kept me somewhat up to date."

"I'll bet she did. That's Kitty, the communicator."

Nan didn't say anything for a couple of minutes. Then, when she spoke, it was to fill me in. "Mike, it seems like it's been forever since you and I've talked. A lifetime ago."

"It has been."

"Amazing how life throws things at us. You with Hannah's cancer. Joe's stroke. You're never ready for these things. We never had children, so we never had a post-retirement bucket list. We wanted to do something; we just did it. Joe's law firm did well, and I did okay in real estate. When we were working, we lived in separate orbits. If I felt like we were drifting apart, Joe's answer was to get away to someplace exotic. Then, when we would travel or have an adventure of some kind, we'd come back together. It was sort of strange, but it seemed to work for us. The stroke, though, has meant we are together all the time. We don't get a break from one another."

"Do you get any time away? You know, for yourself?"

"A few hours here and there. Joe gets scared easily. So, I try to stay close. Neither of us has any family close by, so it's just me."

"Tough."

"Being here with Kitty and Warren is a help. I've started reading a novel. As the summer goes on, I hope I'll be able to do more. Maybe even go for a sail."

"No reason why not. Their boat's up and running. Warren's racing it."

"I suppose. It's been years, though, since I've sailed by myself."

"Oh, it'll come back."

She didn't respond for a minute. Then she said, "It's been a long haul. How'd you manage?"

"I guess it was different for us. It was only a little more than a year from the time she was diagnosed until she died, and we had done everything together anyway, so being together wasn't different. We just had to do different things."

"You were lucky."

I wanted to say, "You don't know how lucky." But all I said was, "Yeah, I was."

From the bow, Warren shouted, "Starboard, about two o'clock. You see it? Just spouted."

We turned to look. Warren's shouts woke Joe up. Judd and Warren hustled back to the cockpit. "Judd said, "You want to jibe her and go take a look?"

I answered, "Sure, why not?" I took the wheel from Nan and said, "Judd, you get the main. Warren, would you haul in the foresail? We can let the staysail jibe herself." When the sails were in, we jibed and headed for where they had seen the whale. Joe was now fully awake, and Nan helped him to sit up.

We headed for where they had seen the whale. Every couple of minutes, we would see the condensed air spout from the top of the animal's head. "Humpback," Judd said. "Look at that thing. Might be others."

A couple of minutes later, we saw two other whales farther out. Warren turned to his brother, "It's a pod, Joe. Want me to describe it to you?"

Nan gave her brother-in-law a look that said, 'He's not blind, for Christ's sake.' Warren got the message and came over to his brother and tried to hold the binoculars so Joe could see through them. Joe grasped them with his good hand to steady them, but between the two of them, they couldn't make it work, and Joe pushed the binoculars away. None of us said anything, and the excitement of seeing the whales was gone.

The remainder of the sail was uneventful. We saw seals, commented on different boats that we passed, and sailed parallel to the schooner *Eastwind* that took people out on daysails from Boothbay Harbor.

Other than the expected 'thank you's from the Lands when they left, very little was said during the trip back to Heron Cove. After helping Warren get Joe off the boat and onto the yacht club dock, Judd and I took the *Redhead* out to her mooring. "He's in rough shape," Judd said as we sat in the cockpit, finishing the thermos of coffee we had brought with us.

"Getting old sucks," I answered.

"Sure does. Make a deal with you."

"Okay. What do you have in mind?"

"Let's not get old."

August 13, 1993
HOME TOWN BOY by Michael Buckley

Friday the 13th. It is a legendary day for bad luck. There are several different stories about how we went about adopting this belief, but our British cousins clearly influenced it. It is not the same all over Europe. The number 13 is unlucky for the Spanish, but they think it is Tuesday the 13th rather than Friday the 13th that brings a foul wind. The Greeks agree with the Spaniards, but for different reasons. On the other hand, the Italians think the sky may fall on the 17th, although Friday is fine with them. Regardless of these cultural vagaries, it is always a day on which legend tells us we should be 'waiting for the other shoe to drop.' But, of course, that 'other shoe' has a history of its own.

Scientists tell us that this can be serious business. In fact, upwards of twenty million Americans suffer every Friday the 13th. Doctors even have a long unpronounceable name for it: 'Triskaidekaphobia.' I don't think I have it, and I hope you don't, but I am aware of Friday the 13th every time it rolls around. Perhaps we need things like Friday the 13th to keep us on our toes, to remind us that we are not in control of everything as much as we might try to believe otherwise. Legends are good that way.

Last weekend there was a wonderful concert in Bath. It was a beautiful August evening, one of those times when the locals and the summer people mingled together in the park and just enjoyed being alive. The songs, robustly performed by a group from nearby Brunswick, featured ballads about legendary people. These people had either overcome obstacles with heroic might or had been Friday the 13th characters with shoes dropped on their heads over and over again. Paul Bunyon and his ox Babe were provided with an upbeat remembrance. Johnny Appleseed made an appearance, as did Robin Hood. The Friday the 13th crew included old ones like 'Sweet

William' and more modern ones like Bob Dylan's 'The Lonesome Death of Hattie Carroll.'

Out here in Georgetown, we have two legendary characters. I wonder if either of them would be a good subject for a ballad. Walter Reid made wads of money, bought a lot of land, built a big hotel, and then bequeathed much of his land to the State for a park on the ocean. It's not ballad material, though. He didn't rescue any maidens in distress, slay dragons, or drive steel like John Henry. Entrepreneurs don't seem to make the grade when it comes to ballad singers.

However, we do have a Friday the 13th character who I think might fit the bill, Chauncey McKinney. Shoes didn't simply drop on Chauncey; they rained on him. To be fair to those dropping the shoes, Chauncey was a bit eccentric.

Our man raised sheep out on Rogers Point—now Indian Point to attract the rusticators. The land out there is pretty rocky and not much good for farming, but it's okay for sheep. Although he built some stone walls, Chauncey would use natural barriers and islands to keep his flock in check. Removed from shipbuilding and other sources of civilization, Chauncey was a hermit with a flock. Of course, establishing causation is always a problematic enterprise with human beings, and it is hard to know whether isolation led to his eccentricities or his eccentricities led to his isolation.

Chauncey did not want to lead his beloved sheep to slaughter, so he slaughtered them out in the fields. The image of Chauncey walking across the fields with blood dripping from his blade made for wonderful bedtime stories for the Island's young. It's been told that more than one mother said to a disobedient child that they would be left to wander among Chauncey's sheep if they didn't behave.

Perhaps the more eccentric aspect of Chauncey's eccentricities was his belief that little men lived under the ground and were responsible for the trees growing. They pushed them up. I don't think he ever described the science of this to anyone, but it is certainly consistent with what the Irish know of the 'little people.' This aspect of Chauncey's view of the world became sufficiently well known, that people came from as far away as Bath to dig around his trees looking for pots of gold that they were sure Chauncey or the 'little people' had buried there.

Now for a bit of shoe dropping. A summer person, Frank Thompson, wanted to buy Chauncey's farm because it had a substantial waterfront. Chauncey refused to sell. So, Thompson hatched a scheme. You see, Chauncey cut his own wood to heat his farmhouse. One day Chauncey felled a beautiful maple, and to repay the 'little people' for their kindness in making the tree grow, he put some silver coins into the hole. Seeing this, Thompson and the local postmaster, Clem Todd, claimed that the tree was on Todd's land, and Chauncey owed Clem fifty dollars for the tree. Chauncey was a solid citizen and consulted the boundary markers. He didn't want to take something that belonged to someone else, but he also didn't want to be taken advantage of. A surveyor and a lawyer were brought in by Todd and Thompson. They ruled against Chauncey. Being without the fifty dollars, Chauncey was informed that he would have to give up some land.

You can imagine how crestfallen Chauncey was. His eccentricities became more pronounced. Bats in poor Chauncey's belfry were mentioned. Todd then called upon the local authorities to come and take our Chauncey away, which they did. Men in white coats arrived by boat for Chauncey. Before they could take him away, though, Chauncey screamed to the heavens, "I utter a curse on the people who have taken my land from me and on those who will live here after I go." It was around 1901 when Thompson and Todd laid claim to Chauncey's land.

Apparently, the new owners were not shepherds. Thompson and Todd brought in a man and his wife from Scotland to tend the sheep. While out in his boat one day, the man's boat was caught in a tide rip.

The boat pitched over, and the man drowned.

Years later, it was the summer people who got hold of Chauncey's land, and they have it to this day. I am told by someone who should know that a few of them even dig holes around Chauncey's trees, just in case. Given what they have to pay for land out there, they might just need some of that gold.

Anyway, we need to find a good balladeer to honor Chauncey, a true Friday the 13th man.

Chapter Twenty-Six: Nell

In Ireland, as young people, both Jamie and Treasa were Catholic. Catholic, that is, as many Irish are, with a healthy dose of nonchalance and a wink to many of the prescriptions of the Irish Catholic Church. They continued that way in Brooklyn. Both of them had been befriended by priests, so their attitudes were not antagonistic. Since neither of them was interested in theological explorations, there was no skepticism involved; their practice of Catholicism was just a familiar comfort with rituals learned in childhood. They were not involved in the life of the Brooklyn parish where they lived, what with Jamie being away as much as he was and Treasa's working in Manhattan.

Their son, Will, was baptized and confirmed, of course. After that, the family would never miss Mass on Easter or Christmas. Sometimes, when Jamie was away, Treasa brought Will to Mass on Sundays and made sure he went to catechism classes to make his first communion and, then again, so he could be confirmed.

Treasa's relationship with the church began to shift in direct proportion to her involvement with the suffrage movement. At the time of her death, no one in the family had any relationship to Catholicism. Whatever had been there had been organized by Treasa. Treasa didn't 'fall away,' she moved from nonchalance to rejection. The Catholic Church fiercely fought everything 'the movement' demanded. The church position was simple: women will not vote and women will not work. The Church did more than provide 'guidance.' It worked to impose its 'will' on the political process that was developing. For Treasa, it was an easy equation. The church rejected her as a woman; she rejected the church.

Jamie and Will had never received much from the church. For them, fading away was neither a conscious decision nor an important one. If asked, each would have called himself a Catholic, and, after Treasa died, Jamie would take the two of them to Midnight Mass at Christmas. In part, it was because they had nowhere else to go.

As a young man in protestant Bath, Maine, Will never gave church a thought, not any church. He was not against religion; he just didn't think about it.

The *Treasa* was back in the water with several new ribs and planks by the end of October. They had also replaced the foremast, which is when they discovered dry rot where it was stepped on the keel. Will attentively made sure every item the surveyor had discovered was addressed. Between his work at the yard and fulfilling his responsibilities on the *Treasa*, he was now a skilled shipwright.

With little to distract him, he studied the plans of other ships being built along the Bath waterfront. Then, on Sundays, when the shipyards were dormant, he would wander from yard to yard examining the boats in various stages of completion.

The six-month contract that Jamie had signed was now up. With the completion of the work on the *Treasa*, Jamie, Colm, and Nathan were once again sailing her up and down the Northeast coast between Maine and New York and, sometimes, Philadelphia. Jamie was surprised and irritated that his son did not want to join them.

However, for seven months, Will had been working on the *Wyoming,* the largest sailing ship ever built. He didn't want to leave Bath until the *Wyoming* was launched and on her way. "Christmas, Da. I'll just stay 'til Christmas, New Year's at the latest." Already behind schedule, the yard was pushing to finish her and get her in the water. It was heading towards winter, and New York needed coal from the mines in Pennsylvania. The owners needed the *Wyoming* in the water and working as soon as possible.

Things for Will were fine until the *Treasa* left Bath, and the weather became increasingly cold and often dreary with rain and snow. Will wondered if he had made a mistake not joining the others when he had the chance.

By November Will's life was consumed with loneliness. Most of the men at the boatyard had families and disappeared on their days off. The first six months in Bath had been exciting: being on land, exploring the area, taking day trips on the train to Portland. A couple of his workmates had even invited him to clambakes during the warm summer months.

In November, though, darkness came early and stayed late. Sundays, when there was no work, were especially bad. He stopped his pilgrimages to the various yards along the river and confined himself to his room, reading and drinking. Although Maine was doing more to shut down the supply of alcohol, it was still available if you knew where and how to acquire it. Gathering with his mates from the yard to drink at the end of the workday was not possible on Sundays. He came to dread Sundays.

On a Saturday in December, he would remember it was the fourth, and he was complaining to one of his workmates, Dennis Irving, a man his age, about the coming Sunday. Dennis said, "When was the last time you got laid?"

Will said, "I can't hardly remember; it's been so long."

"Tomorrow's Sunday, and you have no plans, do ya? That sucks."

"Tell me about it?"

"You Catholic?"

"Raised."

"Come with me to Mass tomorrow morning. There's a church Christmas bazaar afterward. They do it every year, the first Sunday in December. The thing runs all afternoon. You can buy Christmas presents that the church ladies make. They got stupid games, spaghetti dinner, and bingo at the end of the day. People come from all over, Catholic or not. Main thing is, lots of horny unmarried women show up. I know a lot of 'em, and I know who does and who doesn't. So don't worry. I'll point you in the right direction."

"You serious?"

"You kidding? No problem. Guaranteed. Got ta get your pipes cleaned, Buckley."

"Ya got someone in mind?"

"Maybe."

It might have happened the way Dennis said it would if Will had not been attracted to the table with sweaters, scarves, and other knit goods. He needed a new sweater. The one he had was patched at the elbows, and as much as he appreciated his land-lady's efforts with needle and thread, she was not a great seamstress, and one of the patches was pulling away.

He sorted through the display, picked one out that was a deep blue, and held it up to see if the size might be right. The woman behind the table smiled at him and said, "It will look good on you. Brings out the color in your eyes. Why don't you try it on?"

He did. It didn't feel quite right, and he said, "What do ya think?"

"I think it's a little small. You've got broad shoulders." She turned around and spoke to a younger woman who was bent over, taking sweaters out of a box. "Nell, see if we have one like this, only bigger." The woman called Nell stood up to see what her mother was talking about. She looked at Will. She came from behind the table and walked around him, looking him up and down. Finally, she reached up and pulled the sweater out at the shoulders. "I think this one is fine. He just didn't have it on right."

It was her touch. He loved her touching him. When she walked around in front of him to admire her handiwork, he looked at her more closely. She was the perfect size, a little bit taller than most girls, but given his height, that was as it should be. Her hair was perfect, brown coming down to her shoulders. Her face was perfect, pretty. Just right. Blue eyes. She was about to turn and walk back behind the table when he collected himself and said, "I don't know. Maybe, but let's try on a larger one just to be sure."

Four sweaters later—any of them would have worked—Will chose the first one. "I think I'll wear it," he said. He didn't know that it was the first of many sweaters he would wear made by Mary Ellen Convey, known to everyone as Nell. In addition to the sweater, he bought scarves for his father, Colm, and Nathan.

He knew it would be impolite to hang out at the Convey table, but he prolonged his shopping long enough to ask questions of mother and daughter. He discovered the Conveys owned a sheep farm on Georgetown Island. In addition, he found out Nell was in her last year of high school, and she stayed in Bath during the week with her aunt so she could go to high school there. Fridays, after school, she returned to Georgetown. She had two older brothers who decided they were not farmers and were 'making their way' elsewhere, someplace called Worcester.

Rather than move on to other tables, Will looked for Dennis. When he found him, Dennis was talking to two young women. Although he didn't want to interrupt the conversation, Will found it difficult to just stand there and act interested after Dennis introduced him. So, when he sensed a pause in the conversation, he said, "Den, can I ask you something? Sorta private."

Dennis smiled and excused himself. When they got to the side of the room, and no one could hear them, Dennis said, "I told ya, didn't I? Who is it, Ruth or JoAnn?"

"Neither one. Ya know Nell Convey?"

"Sure. Went to school with her brothers."

"What's she like?"

"What da you mean?"

"I don't know. What's she like?"

"Christ, Buckley. This I can tell ya. Forget it if you're thinking you're going to get her to go to bed with ya. She's more Catholic than the fuckin' pope."

"No. Not that. She seems nice."

"I guess she's nice enough. Great tits, but you ain't getting your hands on 'em. Not that one. I know someone who tried."

"No. I just mean…"

"What do you mean? I don't get it. I thought you wanted to get laid."

"I do, but…"

"But what?"

"She seems nice. So, you think she is?"

"Sure, if you want nice."

Will managed to sit next to Nell at bingo. He tried for dinner too, but she sat with a group of her girlfriends. He tried to speak to her after dinner, but she was busy helping her mother pack up the woolen items they had not sold. A man was helping them. Will assumed it was her father.

On Monday, Dennis came up to him on their lunch break. "Nell Convey, huh. Good luck with that."

"What da ya mean?"

"Hey. If that's what you want, go for it. You know where she'll be every Sunday morning, at least."

Will went to Mass the following week. He arrived early and wore his 'Convey sweater.' After Mass, he found Nell and told her how much he loved his sweater. She said, "Looks good on you. There's more where that came from if you need another." She also commented she had not seen him there before.

"No, it's my first time. I haven't been in Bath long."

"Oh. Where you from?"

Will took that as an invitation for him to start talking. He didn't realize how much he wanted to until he began. He told her about his life in Brooklyn, his mother's death, his time on the *Treasa*, and his coming to Bath. She listened. She asked some questions. After a while, he said, "Oh, God, I'm sorry. I've bored you silly."

"No, not at all." Her voice changed, "So, you're leaving after the *Wyoming*'s finished?"

"Not sure," he answered.

He was back at Mass the following Sunday. He sat right behind the Conveys to make sure he didn't miss her after Mass. He followed them after Mass was over. Nell excused herself from her parents, turned to him, and said, "Are you following me?"

"I guess I am. Is that okay?"

Nell smiled at him and said, "So how was your week, Will Buckley?"

He was thrilled she remembered his name. "Really good. I wanted to ask you something. We're scheduled to launch the *Wyoming* on Wednesday. You want to come down and watch? It's goin' to be something."

"Can't. School."

"Shite, too bad."

He saw her react to his use of the word. He moved ahead. "Biggest wooden ship ever built. Right here in Bath. Going to make history. Six masts. They even have steam engines to haul the sails up."

"Are you going to sail on the boat? Is that how you're leaving?"

"Nah. Nah. She's built for coal. They'll hire a bunch of Coloreds, cheap. I wouldn't want to sail on her, though."

"How come?"

"Thing's going to flex all over in a storm. You wait and see. Those seams are going to be opening and closing. I wouldn't want to sail on that thing. They're going to be pumping all the time. They hit a bad storm; thing might come apart."

Nell did come to the launch. Everyone in the high school came. The whole town came. Will felt very proud when he joined all the other workers for a group picture with the *Wyoming* in the background. He didn't get to talk to Nell, though. She stayed with the other students from her class, and they all returned to school after the launch.

The day after the launch, when he returned from work, he found a telegram taped to his door. It was from his father. They had run into problems with a granite broker in Philadelphia, and the *Treasa* wasn't going to make it back to Brooklyn in time for Christmas. They'd be back for New Year's, though. All of Will's plans for taking the train down to New York to be with his father and Colm were destroyed in a few words.

When he went downstairs, Clara was in the kitchen. Hearing him, she shouted, "Everything all right, Will?"

"Trip home for Christmas is off. My Da is stuck in Philadelphia."

She came out of the kitchen to talk to him. "Oh, I'm so sorry. I know you were looking forward to that."

"Yeah, I was. Oh, well. Problem with hauling cargo. Between the weather and the brokers, you never know."

"Does this mean you'll be here for Christmas?"

"Suppose so."

"Well, then, you'll have to come with us. I'll talk to my daughter. There's always room for one more. She does Christmas, and she always makes a big fuss."

"I couldn't."

"Yes, you can. I insist."

On Sunday after Mass, Nell asked, "So, Will Buckley, what's next, now that the *Wyoming* is floating in the harbor. Are you going back to Brooklyn?"

"I don't know. I was goin' to go home for Christmas, but my Da is stuck in Philadelphia, so he's not goin' to get home until New Year's. I'm supposed to join them back on the *Treasa*, but I'm not sure it's what I want to do. I'm kind o' tired of sailing and never being able to depend on things. He didn't get here for Thanksgivin' and now Christmas."

"Oh, that's terrible. So, where are you going to be for Christmas?"

"My landlady's invited me to go with her to her daughter's."

"You don't sound excited about it."

"I suppose I'll go, but I won't know no one there 'cept her."

"That's a shame." Nell paused before saying, "I've got an idea. Now you stand right here, and don't you move."

Nell left Will standing alone on the bottom step of the church while she went over to where her parents were talking with some people. Five minutes later, she came back and said, "Okay. You're welcome to come to our house out in Georgetown for Christmas if you'd like. We won't be coming in for Midnight Mass, but we'll be here Christmas morning. You can come out with us, and then my aunt and uncle will bring you back Christmas night. Or, if you want, you can sleep on the couch, and you'll come back with us when we come back for Mass on Sunday."

"It's the next day, isn't it?"

"Yes, silly. Mass two days in a row. We'll all be very holy. So? Any questions? Oh, and my mother said, 'Your presence is present enough.' Don't even think about trying to figure out Christmas presents. I know you don't know us, either—well, you know me a little—but we'd love to have you. So, what do you think?"

"You serious? Thank you. I'd… I'd love to."

When he told Clara about the invitation, she said, "Oh, isn't that nice. I know them. They're very nice people." When he told Dennis, he said, "They asked you for Christmas? You haven't even kissed her yet, have you? That's big. She must like you—a lot."

"No. I haven't kissed her. So, you think she likes me?"

"God, are you dense? She invited you for Christmas. What are you going to bring? How you gonna shop for people you don't know?"

Will didn't know what to do. Dennis was right. He didn't even know who would be there other than Nell and her parents. He mentioned it to Clara. "Oh, don't go being silly. You go and bring a big box of cookies from the bakery. That'll be fine."

"What kind of cookies?"

"You tell Minnie I said to fix you up with a big assortment of Christmas cookies. She'll know what to do."

On Christmas morning, Will packed a bag to take with him so he could spend the night. When he walked down to the church to meet the Conveys, he was cautious with the box of cookies he carried. At Mass, he sat with Nell and her parents.

After the Christmas meal, the Convey family distributed presents. Nell gave Will a watch cap she had knitted to match his sweater.

Chapter Twenty-Seven: Father and Son

They only worked a half day on New Year's Eve at the shipyard. Will had brought his bag to work with him, and the minute the whistle blew, he grabbed his bag and walked to the railroad station in Bath. It would be a long ride to New York City with changes in Portland and Boston.

He couldn't get Nell and Christmas at the Conveys out of his mind. He took out a pencil and started writing 'Nell Buckley' in the margin of the newspaper he had picked up. Then he tried it as 'Mary Ellen Buckley.' He decided he liked the sound of 'Nell Buckley,' but liked the way 'Mary Ellen Buckley' looked on paper. When he finished, he took out a copy of *With the Night Mail* by Rudyard Kipling that he had borrowed from the library the previous day. He tried reading, but his mind was otherwise occupied.

It was almost daybreak by the time he reached his home in Brooklyn. He had slept a great deal on the train so was not terribly tired when he opened the door and yelled out, "Happy New Year."

From the time he watched the Conveys leave Bath after Mass the Sunday after Christmas until the train arrived in New York, he thought about little else but Nell, the Convey family, Christmas, and the farmhouse. When he walked through the parlor and into the kitchen in Brooklyn, he knew what he was going to do. There was no Christmas tree; there were no decorations of any kind in the house. He realized there hadn't been since his mother died.

He found his father and Colm having breakfast in the kitchen. His father got up and came over and held his hand out to shake it. "You're home. Grab a chair, and I'll make you some breakfast."

"Glad you made it, laddie," Colm said. "We were beginning to wonder. Now that you're here, I'm going go up and pack."

"Where you going?" Will asked.

Jamie said, "Colm finally got himself a steady woman. Only problem is she lives up in the Bronx. She tolerates him, though. So, he says it's worth the trip."

"It is indeed," Colm said. "And now I'll be leaving this den of confirmed bachelorhood to get a few real home-cooked meals an' wake up with a warm rump next to me. See you in a couple of days, Will."

"Wait. I've got a present for you." Will went back into the hall, opened his bag, took out three carelessly wrapped presents, and brought them into the kitchen. He gave one to his father and one to Colm. Then, holding up the third, he said, "This one is for Nathan. He around?"

Jamie said, "See him next week. I'll make sure he gets it."

The two men opened their presents, and each took out a scarf. Will said, "I know the woman who made these."

"This is beautiful, Will," Colm said, wrapping the scarf around his neck. "It sure looks like it'll be good and warm."

Jamie gave his son a puzzled look. "You know the woman who made these?"

"I do. I met her at a church bazaar. I bought this sweater I'm wearing from her. She gave me the cap as a Christmas present. Her name's Nell Convey. Her mother and father asked me to spend Christmas with them."

Colm said, "Thank ye, Will. I truly love it. Sorry to say I didn't think about a Christmas present for you, but I'm goin' to take care of that before we shove off. How long you here?"

"A few days."

"Good. See you before you go." Colm left the father and son standing in the kitchen.

"That was right generous of 'em. Take ye home for Christmas." Jamie said.

"They're wonderful people, Da. They have a big sheep farm out on Georgetown Island. It was great doin' Christmas with them. Amazing food. I've never seen anything like it. They started with oysters and clams. Then had something called consommé, which I'd never had before. After that, they had a goose they'd raised just for Christmas dinner and three different kinds of pies for dessert. Mrs. Convey told me Nell made the pies."

"Who's Nell?"

"I just told you. The daughter. A little younger than me. Real nice. Pretty, too. I really like her."

Jamie didn't say anything for a minute. Then, when he started talking, he said, "Ya know I was raised on a sheep farm. Awful smells, those things. Gets into everything. Their house smell?"

"No. Not at all. Smelled fine."

"Doesn't matter. You know you won't be gettin' to Bath much now that the *Treasa*'s in good shape."

"Da, I'm thinkin' 'bout goin' back to Bath and workin' at the Bath Iron Works. They got these Navy ships they're building out of metal. That's the future, Da. Boats like the *Wyoming* thing of the past. Yard's already built a battleship and two smaller ships. You should see those things."

"I did when I was there. I'm not impressed. Maybe good for fighting, but not for hauling. Too expensive."

"You just wait. Few years, not goin' to be any schooners left."

"Come on. That's bullshit. Wind is free. Always has been, and it always will."

"Yeah, and when there is none, you sit and wallow. Everythin's changing, Da. Di' ya' know there's even an airoplane going to be used by the army? It's called the Wright Military Flyer."

"Where is ya getting all this stuff?"

"Ain't nothin' to do at night but read, and I'm only two streets from the library. Papers come up from Boston every day. Reading this interesting book right now. Takes place in the future, but…"

"Jesus. You're filling your head with nonsense."

"It's not nonsense, Da. It's happening—now. And I'm right there in the middle of it."

"You're in the middle of nothin', Will." Jamie turned back to the stove and started cracking eggs into a frying pan. When he adjusted the flame, he turned back to Will. "So, you don't plan on comin' with us, eh. Is that it? I got that right? What is it, the girl?"

"No, it's more than that. You know I never liked sailing the way you do. But yeah. I'm hopin' Nell likes me. I think she does."

When Will finished eating, Jamie said, "Come with me." The father led the son into the parlor. "Sit down. I got something to tell you." When they settled into chairs facing the fireplace, Jamie said, "I'm ready for you to start takin' the *Treasa* on your own trips. Get your own crew. I'm almost fifty. Probably only got maybe a couple more years to live. That is if I'm lucky. *Treasa* be yours, then. So's the house."

"What about Colm? Why Colm not takin' her?"

"Colm's ready to stop now. He's stuck on this woman. Wants to be with her all the time."

"What about Nathan?"

"Oh, sure. Can ya imagine that? A Colored man running a schooner? Makin' deals with brokers? You out of your fuckin' mind? It's you or no one."

"You're not sick, are ya?"

"No. I'm fine. Don't have the energy I used to, but I'm doin' okay."

"So why ya talkin' like this?"

"Jesus, Will. I'm not goin' ta live forever. Always told ya, ya be takin' over the *Treasa*."

"I know, but …"

"So, now it's time."

"But…"

"No buts. It's time. You're ready now as you'll ever be."

"But, Da, what if I don't want to?"

"What do ya mean? 'If I don't want to?' Not want to? You don't have a choice."

"Yes, I do."

"Like hell ya do!"

By the time they were through, they had shouted themselves out. Will picked up his bag, slammed the front door behind him, and checked to make sure the return ticket to Bath was in his pocket.

Colm thought it was hilarious when Jamie told him about the argument and how it ended with Will storming out and slamming the front door. "Well?" Colm said.

"Well what?"

"Did he break the glass?"

"No, he didn't break the glass." Jamie went back to carving up a block of cheese for the two of them to have with their beers.

Colm laughed, "You woulda broke the window."

"You think it's funny? He's gone. Who's goin' take over the *Treasa*? You be bailin' on me. Nathan sure as hell can't do it. I be depending on Will ta do it."

"Jesus, Mary, an' Joseph. You're bein' a fuckin' eejit, Jamie. You were younger than he was when you left Carna 'cause you didn't want to die on a sheep farm. So now he's leavin' home and may wind up dying on a sheep farm if this Nell gets her way with him. And you don't think that's funny? God, you're getting' old."

"He's my only son. Who's goin' to…"

"You sure you don't have any spares you haven't told me about?"

"You're bein' a complete arse. Go ahead an' laugh. If you had a son, you sure wouldn't be actin' like it was nothin'."

"If I remember rightly, you left your Aintín Maude and Uncail Liam in the same position, didn't ya now?"

"They had sons."

"Who was in Australia and not 'bout comin' home."

"And there was a famine comin'."

"Which never reached Carna. Come on, Jamie. He's not a seaman. Ya said so yourself lots of times. And, it sounds like the lad's head over heels in love. You think freezing your arse off on the water haulin' granite from Maine to New York's goin' to compete with that? Yourself ought to think about gettin' a woman while you still got the chance. Come on. Do what I done. Settle down."

"Settle down. How can I do that without someone run the *Treasa*?"

"Oh, Christ. Sell the fuckin' *Treasa* while she'll still fetch a good price."

"Like hell I will. I ain't dead yet, and neither is she."

"God, if you could only hear yourself. You're a good man, and I love you like a brother, but sometimes you can be a fuckin' eejit."

Will's train ride back to Bath was filled with fury and emptiness. First, his mother left him for her damned movement, then she died. Now his father wanted to chain him to the god damned boat. He remembered the freedom he felt wandering the streets of Brooklyn as a teenager. By the time he reached Bath, he was determined to go his own way. He'd create his own family, one that was his and would stay put. And he would stay put. No leaving his family. No, he wouldn't do that.

When he met up with Nell after Mass the following Sunday, he asked her for a moment in private. Nell told her parents she wanted to talk to Will for a couple of minutes. Will led her down the street from the church. When they stopped, he said, "I been thinkin' about this all the way to Brooklyn and back. I know we aint but knowing one another but a short time, but you seem to like me and…"

"What are you trying to say?"

"Would you marry me? We could get married right after you graduate. I've got a job and the pay's good for around here."

"You're joking, right?"

"No. Don't you like me?"

"Of course I do. Oh, Will. I admit I've imagined it, but… Will, have you talked to my father?"

Will had not even thought about talking to Walter Convey. "No, I haven't. I didn't think…"

"That's obvious."

"Are you sayin' you don't want to marry me?"

"No. I'm not saying that but this is awful sudden, and I need to talk to my parents and think about it." She kissed him on the cheek. "I'll see you next week." Then, she walked quickly back to where her parents were chatting with friends.

"What did Will want?" her mother asked.

"I'll tell you later," she whispered in reply.

Over dinner dishes in the kitchen, her mother said, "Well? Are you going to tell me?"

"Will proposed. He wants to get married right after I graduate."

"Absolutely not! You hardly know the boy, and you've just turned eighteen. Do you even know if you love him?"

"I think I do."

"Thinking's not enough. You need to get to know him. So do we. But now? Absolutely not. That's final. The boy's welcome to come around and maybe if you're doing more than 'thinking' come Christmas next year, and it's still what he wants, then…"

"Then…"

"Then maybe, and just maybe, that might be a good time to get engaged and maybe get married in the spring and have a proper wedding, not something thrown together in a rush. Have you said anything to your father?"

"Do you think I should?"

"Yes. And now would be a good time so I don't have to keep it a secret between us. Now go in and tell him."

"Now?"

"Good a time as any."

When Nell talked to her father, the discussion was brief. "No, you're both too young." Will was devastated when Nell told him about the conversations the following week; Nell was not. "A year from June, Will. It will fly by. My parents are right. We need to take some time, don't you want to know me first? You may not like me."

The time was well spent, and Will survived his enforced celibacy. He caught up with Nell every Sunday after Mass and spent more and more time on the farm, often helping Nell's father. When lambing season arrived, he took some time off from the shipyard and stayed with the Conveys. They got engaged at Christmas, and wedding plans became serious. Although Will was not yet married to Nell, he had become a member of the Convey family by the time his second lambing season came around. After an exhausting night waiting for lambs to drop, Nell said, "You be careful. You get any closer to my parents, and they'll adopt you, and then I can't marry you."

When they did marry on June 18, 1910, Jamie and Colm were there. Will insisted that Nathan be invited, but Nathan didn't come. Instead, he sent a present with Jamie and Colm for the newlyweds. When Will voiced his disappointment to his father, Jamie said, "Will, it'd be too dangerous for him. They're havin' KKK meetings all over Maine. Who knows how these people you're marryin' into feel about that?"

Chapter Twenty-Eight: Big Money

Will and Nell Buckley threw a party for their son Jack on Labor Day weekend in 1920 to celebrate his fifth birthday. Their son Brian was seven already, and Connor, their youngest, was two. Jack's birthday wasn't until the fourteenth, but they wanted Jamie, Colm, and Nathan to be able to come. Jamie came with Nathan. Colm declined because of his age and severe arthritis.

Nell's brothers came from Worcester with their families. Nell's parents came. They now lived in downtown Bath in what became known as 'the Bath House.' In addition to being in Bath, the house had three bathrooms. "Don't you dare call it 'the bathroom house' Nell's mother admonished." Children Jack and Brian's ages came with their parents. Neighbors came.

The decade since they first met had been good to the young couple. Nell had insisted Will not enlist in the military during the 'Great War,' the one to end all wars. She said, "My father's too old to manage the farm, we have the boys, and you're needed at the shipyard." All of this was true. What was also true was that Will had no desire to spend day after day in a trench in France in a war that President Wilson had said was not America's affair. When German submarines and a 'secret' pact between Mexico and Germany changed Wilson's mind about America's involvement, Will and Nell held firm in their isolationist beliefs. Of course, it helped that the military had no interest in him with his job building ships for the Navy and his young family.

The war effort was highly profitable for the young couple. Between multiple shifts at Bath Iron Works and the sale of wool to the mills to produce clothing for the troops, the young couple made a great deal of money. Nell would later say that it was a good thing Brian and Jack were easy babies, because they did not get much attention when they were infants and toddlers during the war years.

They waited until after the war to have Connor. Nell decided some things about being a 'good Catholic' did not make any sense to her, like the prohibition on birth control. She told Will, "You barely glance at me, and I'm pregnant. I'll be damned if I'm going to wind up with ten kids like my Aunt Agnes." Will had no objection. However, after Connor was born, one night after the boys were in bed, Nell suggested that she would like to have a daughter. "Can't you Buckley's produce anything but boys? I would love to fuss over what a little girl would wear. I'll never get to plan a wedding, Will. I want to plan a wedding. Just one." A year later, they buried an infant, a girl, who was 'stillborn.' They named her Elizabeth and buried her in the Convey-Buckley cemetery on the farm. After that, they didn't try again.

As a community, the town of Georgetown was not doing well. Farmers and fishermen had left to go into the service or to work in Bath, where they could make more money. In addition, the photography school that had brought artists to the island did not survive the war, and closed after five years. Summer people still came on the steamship *Virginia*, but the war years had taken a toll with 'summer people,' as well.

In 1920 only four hundred and twenty-nine people lived year-round on the Island. Fifty percent of the Island's population had left or died since Will first came to the Island. During a walk after the party, Will told his father, "The island'll come back, Da. Hard to tell when. Everybody's been sellin' out, and I been buyin.' Timing's been good to me. This rich guy, Reid, he been doing the same thing. He owns fifteen hundred acres now. I got no idea what he's goin' to do with it all. That hotel he built is a dandy. We'll take ya there sometime. Ya ought to sell the house in Brooklyn and move up here. Ya get a good price for the house in Brooklyn. Maybe try your hand with lobstah. Coming thing. Be home in your own bed every night."

"Lobster? You crazy? I'm doin' just fine. Legs still strong. *Treasa*'s good, and there's money to be made."

"You're fifty-eight, for Christ's sake. When you gonna stop? Nell's dad is just a year older than you, and he sits, reads, eats, and sleeps. All his friends have died already."

"You sound like Colm. Do I look like I'm ready to die?"

"No."

"Good. I'll be sure to let you know when the time comes. You finish that place down on your cove?"

"Yeah, you want to see it?"

"Sure do. What's it taken ya, two years?"

Will took his father down to Heron Cove and walked him around the land he had bought, and showed him how he had carved out plots for future development. He took him into Nell's pride and joy. Jamie walked from room to room, out onto the porch, and finally out onto the pier anchored at each end with granite foundations. He said, "You could house five families in the damned place she had ya build."

"Not hardly. But it's going to be great for the kids. Nell's nieces and nephews, too."

"Right about that. Since you're so rich, now, you ought to give it a name. Thing is big enough."

"What, like those Newport places?"

"Sure, why not? You built it for all the kids, right?"

"Yeah, that was Nell's idea."

"And they'll grow up and have kids and so on, right?"

"I guess."

"So ya ought be callin' it Tír na nÓg."

"You're joking me."

"Nah. Your farm's always going to be 'The Convey Place.' Like no Irish live here."

"We own it."

"Don't matter. Name'll never change. Convey's granpa built it.

It'll stick. So, you get to call this place whatever you want. Call it Tír na nÓg. Can't get much more Irish than that. Nell know what it means?"

"Doubt it."

"You?"

"'Course I do."

"So, teach her."

"Maybe better if you do. You know she can't say no to you."

Nell loved the idea, and the next time Jamie came to visit, he brought a hand-carved wooden sign with the name spelled out in Gaelic.

The States ratified the Eighteenth Amendment to the United States Constitution in 1919. Prohibition would go into effect in January of 1920. It was expected. There was now a great deal of money to be made. Will wanted some of it; Nell was hesitant. Jamie was not. He wanted his share, and when 1920 began, Jamie started making trips to Canada, where he filled the *Treasa* with crates of liquor. He had done some construction work on his boat. What looked like solid granite blocks were thin slabs covering empty spaces underneath. Even a careful view would not lead one to suspect that anything was amiss. If asked to remove the granite by the Coast Guard, Jamie would laugh and say he would be glad to once they reached the wharf in New York or Philadelphia and had access to a crane. Jamie and his new crew would unload their wares into speedboats off the coast of Long Island, get paid, and head straight back to Canada for more liquor.

When everyone left after the birthday party, father and son talked at length about what the amendment's passage meant for their fortunes, long-term. They did so out of the hearing of Nell and the three boys. Then, after an hour, Jamie said, "We need to do this when we've had less to drink."

The next day, Jamie and Will went fishing. In addition to their fishing gear, they brought a bottle of Canadian whiskey that Jamie claimed was the best there was. With their lines in the water, they now got serious about the impact of Prohibition on their future and fortunes. Will again brought up the idea of Jamie moving to Georgetown. "Why on earth would I want to move up here? Now? You crazy. I'm makin' a fortune haulin' liquor, and I'm goin' to make a lot more. This Prohibition thing ain't goin' to go on forever. I give it a year at best. I'm gonna make as much as I can while it's there to be made.

"I don't want you to think it's good for you, though. You should stay away. You doin' great as 'tis, you and Nell. You make good money at the shipyard. Just keep at it. Get rid of the damned sheep, though. I don't get the sheep. Makes no sense to me. Why the hell you keepin' them? War's long over. Nell says market for wool's way down."

"Convey tradition, Da. No way Nell givin' them up."

"Conveys are livin' in town. They don't even live here anymore. Farm's yours. You bought it. Yours to decide."

"I know, but the truth is, things startin' to slow down at the yard. Sheep farmin' is a safety thing for Nell. We grow a lot of our own food now, and we own everything outright. We ever have to, we can make it here on the farm without my job. Hell, we could eat 'em all if we had to. Got just 'bout everything we need right here."

"I suppose."

"I still need to have somethin' else goin'."

"Like what?"

"You not be saying a word to Nell."

"About what? You haven't told me anything."

"I'm buyin' an airplane. Should arrive any day now. Comes in a kit. Fifty bucks. A Curtiss 'Jenny.' The latest, the number 4. War surplus."

"Ya don't know how to fly."

"Got it all figured out. I got a guy in Brunswick who'll teach me. I've already laid out plans for a grass strip. I'm ready to go."

"Ready ta go where? Oh shit, Will. You're not thinkin' you gonna fly alcohol? Jesus, Will. Too fuckin' dangerous."

"Nah. Not the way I got it figured out. Ya can't tell Nell, though. She knows about the plane and the airstrip and me learnin' to fly. She doesn't know that I plan to fly back and forth to Canada. This Jenny I'm gettin' will cruise sixty miles in an hour and has range of a hundred and fifty miles. I'd only have to make one stop for fuel between here and the border, and I've got a plan for how I'm goin' to do it."

"And how much can the damned thing carry?"

"Not a lot."

"And you get stuck in bad weather?"

"You can land these things anyplace. You set it down in a field…"

"And get your wheels caught in a furrow and get flipped over."

Will smiled at his father. "Gotcha goin' didn't I. Aw, Da, I know all that. I'm only half serious about this. I am goin' to get in the business, though. I've also ordered a new lobsta boat. Incredible design by Will Frost. I've even ordered an airplane engine for it."

"So? You goin' be fishing for lobsta?"

"With an airplane engine in the boat? Fishing? Not hardly. This boat's goin' to fly across the water. Government not have anythin' to catch it."

"Shite. You better be damned sure ya know what the hell you doin.' It's goin' be dangerous you connect to the wrong people. You sure about this? You got a supplier?"

"Not yet."

"I hate ta see you do it."

"I'll have the boat in two months, Da. I'm gonna do it."

"I don't like it, not one damned bit."

"But it's okay for you?"

"I don't have a family to support."

"Yeah. And that's why I'm goin' to do it. Put money away for bad times."

"You not be thinkin' we work together."

"Nah. You be way offshore on your run, and it'd be too unpredictable where you be. You're goin' all the way up to St. Pierre. Makes no sense you havin' to come in close enough to shore for me to reach you."

"Will, you gotta be careful. This gonna open up, and all sorts of people gonna get involved. I been making trips once or twice a year to Canada and selling some in New York to people don't wanna pay taxes. This is different. Now liquor's gonna be illegal; lot more at stake than taxes. Could turn nasty. You doin' well as t'is. Not worth you takin' the risk."

"Oh, Da. You're worried 'bout me? You get pissed, though, when I say I get worried 'bout you and want you come live with us."

"Live on a fuckin' sheep farm? No, no, no."

"Least you not goin' ta Ireland no more. You're not. Are you?"

"Once in a while."

"Shite, Da. That's crazy. You get caught carryin' guns an the fuckin' Brits 'ill kill ya."

"I'm careful."

"Rebellion's done, Da. It's done. Can't you see that? Easter Rising was five years ago. Nothin' come of it 'cept jail and killin' and…"

"Don't want ta talk 'bout it."

"Oh shite! You're still at it. Christ, Da. You're outta your mind. That where your money goin'? I knew there was somethin' didn't make any sense. That's it, isn't it?"

Will outfitted his semi-displacement lobster boat with a motor big enough for two boats and began 'lobstering.' He named the boat *Mary Ellen*. Since most lobster boats are named after wives and mothers, he thought this would add to the disguise, for his wife if no one else. In the *Mary Ellen*, he would be outside the three-mile limit, loaded up, and back in Heron Cove in less than two hours. He would transfer his 'catch' to a waiting truck, collect his payment, be back in bed, and be well-rested for work at the shipyard the following day. If they knew about it, no one in Georgetown seemed to care, and if they did care, a special gift bottle was all that was needed to maintain discretion. But, of course, one of the benefits of people leaving the island was fewer bottles had to be distributed. Like others, it didn't take Nell long to figure out what was going on. At first, they argued, then they negotiated the number of runs he would make. Eventually, she agreed they were building a nice little nest egg for themselves that would be available if any of the boys became college material. She was sure they all would.

It all went well until 1923 rolled around, and the Internal Revenue Service received money to enforce the law. One of the first things they did was order high-speed boats that could match those that had been defying them for three years. On a cloudy July night, one of them had been following a schooner operated by William, 'The Real McCoy,' McCoy.

The government 'revenuers' on board their new high-speed boat could do nothing outside the three-mile international limit. They operated without lights and followed the schooner at a safe distance waiting for a transfer.

Will was waiting patiently for the schooner to appear. When it did, the schooner dropped its sails and hoisted its price list; Will brought his boat alongside. He was a steady customer and had the routine down, so the transfer took place in minutes. After he was loaded, he left the schooner and headed back to shore. The government boat followed at a distance. The minute Will reached the three-mile limit, he called upon all the speed he had paid for and headed his 'lobster boat' for Heron Cove. Glancing behind him, he saw the high-speed wake of the government boat. Weighted down with his cargo, Will's boat was not a match for the government vessel. Seeing this, Will started dumping his cargo into the sea. Dollar after dollar in the form of cases of liquor were strewn out behind him. By the time he reached the cove, his boat was empty, and there was nothing the 'revenuers' could do except bask in the knowledge that they had just cost Will a great deal of money, as much as he would have earned in two months working at the shipyard.

When he tied up at his dock, the government boat circled at the mouth of the cove, but not knowing where the channel was, did not follow him in. When he got into bed, Nell was not sympathetic. "Enough is enough," she scolded. "You think this is some kind of game. You're going to get yourself killed one of these days." Will was reluctant to stop, but this encounter with a government boat was sufficient for him to decide that it was indeed time to end his evening trips out on the Gulf of Maine.

Jamie's problems were not with the government. He never came within the three-mile limit. He had always worked for himself and did not want anything to do with the collaborative ventures taking over the liquor import business. There was a war going on for control of the industry. In all of the New York boroughs, there were winners and losers. Eventually, consolidation took place, and there was one consolidator, Salvatore Luciano. By 1925, Salvatore Luciano was known as Charles 'Lucky' Luciano, and he controlled the distribution of alcohol in New York and its suburbs. His rule was simple, you became a part of his distribution system, or you went out of business, one way or another.

The independents, like Jamie, were brought into the Luciano supply chain. If they balked, they would be convinced, physically. If they continued to be obstinate, they would be eliminated. Jamie had been approached to sell his wares to Luciano and only Luciano. Believing he was too small an operator to matter to Luciano, Jamie kept on business as usual. Also, he was slowing down and didn't want any pressure from Luciano to make more trips and have a quota hanging over his head. He was even thinking of moving to Georgetown, where he could teach a thing or two to his grandsons.

At Colm's request, Jamie had come into port for a few days so the two of them could go to a Yankees ball game. Since he had left the *Treasa* and moved to the Bronx, Colm had become a baseball aficionado and had season tickets to Yankee Stadium. Colm told Jamie, "This could be the night. The night the 'Bambino' does it." And he did. On Friday, September 30th, 1927, Babe Ruth set the world record and hit his sixtieth home run in one season. New York City went wild. It took Jamie hours to get home. He wanted to get an early start the next morning, so when he reached Brooklyn, he stopped at a speakeasy he supplied and called his new crew member, Jory Daley. Jamie told Jory that he was going to sleep on board the *Treasa* and for Jory to come down to the boat early the next morning.

Jamie was sound asleep when gas was poured on the decks of the *Treasa*. Once lit, there was no way Jamie could escape the inferno that developed. By morning there was nothing left to save or to bury.

Chapter Twenty-Nine: Depression

Even though there was no body, Nell insisted they arrange for a Funeral Mass for Jamie. Initially, Will thought it was a ridiculous idea. "He didn't care a thing for religion and wouldn't have wanted one. Would have said it was silly." It took a couple of days before Nell convinced him that they had to do it for the boys, if for no other reason. "They need to be able to say goodbye, even if you don't. You also have to think about Colm and Nathan."

"What are we goin' to bury, a piece of burnt wood? And, where the hell we goin' to bury that? Whatever's left of him is in the mud at the bottom of the East River. It's right where it belongs."

"Will."

"He was too old to be runnin' booze. Shoulda moved in with us like I told him. He'd still be alive and not at the bottom of the fuckin' East River."

The priest at the Catholic church in Bath refused to have the funeral there since Jamie was not a parish member. Nell tried other Catholic churches in the area but got the same answer. It had to be at St. James back in Brooklyn because the Church would need a baptismal record showing Jamie was a Catholic. St. James had them from when Jamie and Treasa were married. Nell made all of the arrangements. She also told Will, "When we get back, we will get two headstones, one for your father and one for your mother. We will put them side by side in the Convey plot right here on the farm. It's 'bout time she got one, too."

"Your parents goin' to be okay with that?"

"Of course they are. There are a lot more than Conveys buried there now."

Fortunately, Father, now Monsignor, McCormick was the rector at St. James, and he guided Nell through the process. He remembered the young couple he had married. He knew about Treasa's death and asked if a Funeral Mass had been said for her at the time of her death. Will said it had not. The priest asked if Will and Nell would like a service for both of them. He explained that it would not be a funeral service but a 'Memorial Mass' because there were no bodies. He assured Will and Nell that it would hold all of the sanctity and blessings of a traditional funeral. He avoided discussing whether Jamie or Treasa had been practicing Catholics or not.

Because neither Nell nor the boys had ever been outside of Maine, Nell suggested they make it into a family trip. In addition to the Memorial Mass, Will wanted to talk to the police about what had happened. He also planned to put Jamie's house on the market to be sold. Nell wanted to show the boys where their father had grown up. She also wanted to see it herself.

The day after the Memorial Mass, Nell took the boys into Manhattan to sightsee. Will put a 'For Sale' sign on the house. When he met with a police detective, the detective said the fire was an accident, and the police had no intention of opening an investigation. When Will said that was ridiculous, there was no way it could be an accident, the detective said, "Look, Mr. Buckley, you know what business your father was in. There are close to a hundred thousand speakeasies in this city and at least thirty-five gangs competing for the liquor business. There are killings all over this city every day. All we know for sure is that your father's boat caught on fire. No one saw anything. What the hell do you want me to do? My advice to you, go home. Just go back to Maine and stay there. Think of it as an accident; it probably was."

"Like hell, it was an accident. That's impossible. There was nothing on board that would cause a fire like that."

"What about gas? Maybe he started up the motor, and there were fumes in the bilge."

"Jesus, the boat didn't have a fuckin' motor, for Christ's sake. The fire was set. He was deliberately burned to death."

"What do you expect me to do about it? Come on. Be realistic. Do you even know who would want him killed, anyway? Maybe setting the boat on fire was just someone sending him a message. He didn't usually sleep on board, did he?"

"No."

"See what I mean. Maybe someone was after the boat, and your father was in the wrong place at the wrong time. Come on. Leave it at that. We still don't know that it wasn't an accident."

"I can't believe you. It was no fuckin' accident."

"Okay. You want to play this out; we'll play it out. So, who knew he was going to be on board?"

"His crew: a new guy, Jory something."

"He want to hurt him?"

"Never."

"How can you be so certain?"

"Jory's just a kid."

"So, who would want to hurt him?"

"Maybe this Luciano guy. My father wouldn't sell to him. He wouldn't go along with Luciano."

When Will said the name Luciano, the conversation ended. The detective just said, "There's nothing I can do. I'm sorry for your loss. I am. Hell of a way to go, but there's nothing I can do. There isn't. You should just head home."

That evening they sat down to dinner in Jamie's house with Colm, Colm's girlfriend, Lucy, and Nathan. After Nell put the boys to bed, the adults gathered in the parlor, and the five of them started telling stories. For the most part, Nell and Lucy sat and listened. Finally, after a couple of hours, Nell said she was exhausted and headed off to bed. Colm said, "We'd best be goin' too, but Nathan and I have somethin' for you, Will, before we do. We thought you'd like to have it. Took a while to find it, but we were able to fetch it at low tide. It's in me car. Nathan, would you go out and get it?"

Nathan came back with a box and handed it to Will. When he opened it, Will saw it was the ship's bell from the *Treasa*. At first, he couldn't say anything. He just held it in his lap. Nathan finally said, "Will, I hope that's alright. If it's not…"

"No, no. Thank you. I appreciate it. I just hadn't thought about it." Will looked at the bell and said, "God damn you, Da. Why couldn't you leave well enough alone." Then he looked up and said to the others, "He didn't have to do this anymore. I told him. I told him he had a place to go. I told him to come live with us in Georgetown. I shoulda tried harder."

When he went to bed, he told Nell that he would stay for a couple of days and make sure everything with the sale of the house was in order. He also had to figure out what to do with the furniture and everything else in the place. He told her she should leave the following morning so the boys would not miss any more school. He asked her if there was anything in the house she wanted to get shipped to Maine. She said, "I'll take a look in the morning. I think I'd like that set of silver. I've never had anything like it."

"It belonged to the Ladd's. I think there's an 'L' engraved on it."

"There is. I looked last night. I don't care. It's beautiful. Also, that tea service is silver. I know we could sell it all, but I can't imagine us ever buying things like that just for us. Wouldn't we be something at the holidays? Imagine, a couple of sheepherders with silver. Am I being terrible?"

"Nah. Anything else?"

"Not that I can think of, but I'm going to take a closer look tomorrow before we go. We'll do it together. There may be things you want for yourself. I know it sounds ghoulish, but it's what people do."

"I know. We can also think about things the boys might want when they get older. Also, I'd like to do something with the money from the house when I sell it."

"What are you thinking?"

"We're doing just fine. I'd like to split it three ways between us, Nathan, and Colm. I think Da would have liked that."

"Sometimes I just love you to death, Will Buckley."

The following day Will watched Nell, and the boys get in a taxi and head for the train station. They'd be back at the farm by nightfall, if there were no delays. He and Nell had put together a list of things to pack up and ship to Bath. He'd carry the silver with him on the train when he left. He also had a list of tasks he had to get done before heading home.

He was going to wait on those tasks. He didn't tell Nell how he would spend the rest of the day. Right after they left, he headed for the area of Brooklyn where he had been a runner for the breweries when he was a teenager. He wanted to know who was responsible for setting fire to the *Treasa* and murdering his father. He was certain his former bosses would know who would have done it.

He was surprised to find that what had been a solid Irish neighborhood was now mixed with Italians. One of the men he had worked for was shot leaving his house the previous year. When he found the other one, Timmy Boyle, he was greeted warmly.

"For Christ's sake, if it isn't Will Buckley. Look at you all grown up. You're taller by half, boyo, and at least three times the weight. How the hell are you? Want your old job back, do ya? You were the best of the best, ya know. I was sad to lose ya when your ma died. The business has changed with this Prohibition. For the better for some of us. Now I'm an importer. A lot easier. What the hell ya up to now?"

Will told him about his father, the *Treasa*, and the fire and why he was there. When he finished, Boyle said, "So, the cops don't want to get involved. Scared to's why. Most are being paid off by someone or other. Not goin' ta bite any hands and all that, ya know. Can't says I blame them, either. Who ya got an eye on? Anyone in particular?"

"Da was havin' trouble with someone called Luciano. Da was wantin' to slow down and just supply to some people he was already workin' with. Da told me someone from Luciano told him he had to sell to Luciano."

"Oh shite, Will. You need to stop right there. Don't even think 'bout askin' questions. I could get my hand cut off even talkin' to you just this little. I like you boy, but I not be helpin' ya, and I think it be time for you ta go. Now. Too many eyes. Too many mouths. Sorry. Go home. Now." Boyle turned around and walked away from Will. He stopped, turned around and said, "I mean it; go home. There is nothing here for you. Ya got ta leave it alone."

Will had nowhere else to go for information. He started back to the house he had been brought up in, but detoured and walked to Jack's instead. Because of prohibition, it was now a 'restaurant.' There was no longer a bar and no bottles were on display. He settled himself down at the table where he, his father, and Colm used to sit, and ate his lunch. Some people recognized him, came over, and said they were sorry about the fire and his father. One of them offered him a password and an address if he wanted to drink. He thanked him.

By the end of the week, the house was in the hands of a lawyer. Nathan and Colm took the few things they could use that Nell didn't want shipped to Georgetown. The rest went to the church. When Will left for Georgetown, he was loaded down with boxes of carefully wrapped silver and the bell from the *Treasa*. His plan was to hang it next to the backdoor of the farmhouse. Eventually, he thought, there would be a boat worthy of it.

Many months later, Nell laughed when she read about the twenties being called the 'roaring twenties.' She said, "Sure didn't roar in Georgetown; didn't even whimper." However, some things had changed over the years. Nell was now able to vote. This led to heated arguments with her brothers about whether women should have been 'given' the right to vote. According to them, their wives had not voted and never would. Two Thanksgivings of arguments were enough for Nell, as well as for her parents. Finally, after her older brother told her she wasn't smart enough to vote, her father told him to get out. Her younger brother said, "He goes, I go, too."

Her father said, "Okay, both of you can leave." With that, the two families packed up and drove back to Massachusetts. After that, neither of them came for the holidays, and only Nell's mother missed them. However, Nell stayed in touch with their wives. As she had planned, her nieces and nephews came to Tír na nÓg for a month every summer.

The care of the elder Conveys was left to Nell, and she was attentive and competent in making their lives comfortable in their home in Bath. The Buckleys had lunch every Sunday after Mass with the Conveys. Nell's parents adored their grandsons, although it was clear that Brian, being the oldest and most outgoing, was their favorite. Since Treasa and Jamie were deceased, anything the boys knew of grandparents was supplied by the Conveys.

Will became increasingly political as he watched poverty grow in Maine. He could not believe what was happening in the country, especially in Maine. The rise of the KKK made him furious. Because of Isaac and Nathan, he took it personally. When fifteen thousand clan members met in Waterville, Maine, Will was ready to do battle. The group made it clear that Maine did not want any Jews, Negros, or Catholics—Kikes, Koons, or Katholics—to consider themselves welcome. In addition to 'niggers,' French and Irish Catholics were again put on notice. By 1924 there were close to one hundred and fifty thousand members of the 'Invisible Empire' in Maine. The 'Empire' burned crosses on lawns in cities all over Maine. Terrorized French-Canadians and Irish Catholics were sometimes the targets.

In a phone call with Colm one night, Will told him, "There are no Coloreds in Maine to speak of, yet these fuckin' hillbillies waltz around in their fuckin' worn-out sheets and think that makes them important." When he would talk to Nell, she would listen politely to his ranting until one night he said, "Maybe we should go to Boston or New York where the Irish control things."

"And what are you going to do there, Will Buckley?"

"Something. I'll find something," he ranted.

When he brought it up again, she said, "You need to talk to my father. At least they're not killing us and burning our churches down the way they used to. It wasn't that long ago, Will. My grandfather lived through that. They hated Catholics then, and many of them still do, but it's better than it was. At least now they're focused on the Jews and the Colored people rather than us."

"You know that's not so. Tell that to the French Catholics up in the County. Besides, what Jews? You mean Jews like the Fishman's? You think it's okay to go after them? You want to tell that to August? Or what about Nathan if he was living here? What would you say to Nathan?"

"No. I didn't mean that. We know them."

"So, if we know them, they're off-limits. They're good kikes and koons."

"No. I'm not saying that. I just mean... Oh, forget it."

The contrast between rural Maine and the coastal cities in the 1920's was stark. Advertising and consumerism had developed quickly after the end of the war. Department stores like Macy's were becoming more common. Music had changed, and new dances had entered the culture along with it. Flappers and flamboyance grew, and while some people in Maine's cities were making a lot of money, that was not true in Georgetown.

The Bath Iron Works went into receivership in 1925 and was sold at auction, leaving Will without a job. More Georgetown natives left to find work elsewhere. A year later, the quarry closed, and the Italian workers, who had been living in grass hovels, left. In 1929, only three hundred and sixty-one people called Georgetown home. In 1880 there had been well over a thousand.

The people from 'away,' those who still had money, came in the summer and started buying waterfront property. Will and Nell were lucky they had property to sell. Will divided his land around the cove and began to sell lots. They went slowly at first but gathered speed. "I'm selling the damned things for nothin,'" he complained.

"At least we have something to sell," Nell would reply.

"And what do we sell when they're all gone?"

"We'll be okay. God will provide."

"Like He's doin' for those who are already starving?"

"We won't starve. We live on a farm."

Soon the summer people around the cove created the Erascohegan Yacht Club on the three acres that they bought from Will and Nell. A small corporate group from 'away' bought Rogers Point the following year. They renamed it Indian Point because it sounded more exotic. They started selling off lots as well. Real estate people began to call the land along the ocean Seguinland and advertised it to the rich. The economic gap between the summer people and the local people grew.

Without employment, Will pieced things together. He used his lobster boat to actually fish for lobster. He joined the yacht club for ten dollars a year, bought a Herreshoff 12 ½ from another member, and learned how to compete in club races. He told Nell their involvement in the club was a good investment, and it was. The yacht club people bought their lobsters directly from Will in the summer. During the other three seasons, he repaired their cottages. Brian and Jack got summer jobs cutting the grass and hauling the garbage for club members. Will also put his plane to work. He went to fairs and carnivals and took people on rides in his *Nelly*. At home, he would buzz a birthday party for a small fee.

For Nell, the farm had always been the stable economic ground in her life, never more so than now. The farm's vegetable garden grew. What they didn't eat, she canned for the winter. She added pigs along with more chickens. They now had three cows. The boys became farmworkers as well as students. Even the youngest, Connor, had chores assigned to him. The price for lamb and wool dropped, but there was still a market. With all of this industriousness, the family needed a second truck. The grange became as much a center of their life as the parish had been.

"We're a lot better off than most people around here," Nell would remind Will when he got down on himself for relying on the shipyard. But, he'd complain, "I should've seen it coming. War ended. Orders stopped. Simple. Any idiot could have predicted it."

"Be glad we got the farm, your boat, and your plane. So, we're out of lots to sell, but we're doing well compared to everybody else we know."

"But…"

"Oh, stop it with your 'buts,' Buckley, or I'll make that your new nickname, 'Buts' Buckley."

"I'm fed up with feelin' stupid. Depending on the yard was just plain stupid. So I'm goin' make sure the boys never find themselves in that hole."

"And how are you going to do that?"

"They're all goin' to know how to fly. Not everyone can do that. Being a pilot's a skill that no one can take away from them, and it's always goin' to be needed."

"Always going to be needed? To do what? Take people on rides at fairs like you're doing."

"You'll see. They're delivering mail in planes now. Army and

Navy are using planes. It's the fastest growin' thing on the planet besides telephones."

"Your father was right. You're a dreamer. People need to talk. They don't need to fly."

"You're wrong; you'll see. Before you die, people will be flyin' across the ocean every day. Maybe you'll have flown to England or France, or Ireland. Yeah, Ireland. We'll fly to Ireland."

"You're crazy."

"Let me teach you ta fly. You'll see. It's an amazing feeling. You're in total control…"

"No one's ever in total control of anything. Haven't you learned that yet?"

"Come on. Let me teach you."

"No way. I'll ride with you once in a while, but that's it. We'll talk about teaching the boys when they get older and the time comes."

When the stock market crashed in October, 1929, Brian and Jack already knew how to fly. However, Connor was afraid of flying, so he never learned. While his older brothers loved to fly and sail, Connor was the farmer in the family. "His name is supposed to mean 'lover of wolves,' but I think it's the sheep he loves," Will said to Nell one morning after Connor had rushed out after breakfast to see how the new lambs were doing.

"We need one farmer to keep this place going. Nothing wrong with that," Nell answered.

"You favor him."

"Of course I do. He's my baby. Nothing wrong with that either."

Chapter Thirty: Fire

Nell was thrilled that Brian and Jack were home for the summer of 1934. Even though she had been to the University of Maine campus in Orono several times, it continued to feel like a distant planet to her, and she was glad the boys were sleeping in their own beds at Tír na nÓg. Both boys had chosen to enroll in the engineering program, much to her disappointment. She had hoped they would go into agriculture and eventually take over the farm. Although he was still in high school, Connor promised her he would.

Finished in 1927, the Carlton bridge that connected Bath to Woolwich had made it possible for the boys to go by car to the high school in Bath. Following the Convey tradition, Nell did not think the boys could get a good high school education on the island. Will, ever the reader, saw college and a degree in engineering as consistent with his plan for his sons to enter 'aeronautical endeavors.' Brian and Jack were already pilots. "Maybe they'll have careers designing new airplanes," he told Nell. She found it hard to comprehend their fascination with flying. Connor, on the other hand, was a mystery to Will. He hoped that his youngest would someday want to learn how to fly, but Connor had yet to show any interest. Will would tell Nell, "He's built real close to the ground, just like you are. The other two are up in the air with me."

Her retort was, "In a lot more ways than one. You three have your heads in the clouds. Some people around here are more sensible."

College, though, was a given. That was never a question for either of the parents, although they foresaw different paths for their sons. In the good times of prohibition, as money poured in over their pier at Heron Cove in the form of barrels and bottles of name-brand whiskies, they set aside money for college. Nell insisted it be in cash and kept in the house, secreted away in the basement where neither a thief nor fire could get at it. Will thought she was being ridiculous. When banks started failing in the '30s, and the stock market came tumbling down, he said to her, "You're a damned witch, Mary Ellen Convey. You smell out danger like no one I've ever known. You're as fey as if you'd been born in Carna."

Whenever Brian and Jack were home from Orono, the talk was always of flying and what they would do when they graduated. On January tenth, 1934, six Navy Consolidated P2Y Flying Boats took off from San Francisco and landed in Hawaii twenty-four hours and thirty-five minutes later. It was the topic of discussion when Brian and Jack came home for Easter. After Easter dinner with the Conveys in the car, the three pilots in the family dissected every aspect of the flight as they headed back to Georgetown. They agreed that the Navy was ahead of the Army in its understanding of aviation. "I want to fly one of those P2Ys," Jack said. "Best of both worlds, a boat, and a plane. Think about it. Flying for twenty-four hours straight."

"I wonder if they pissed out of the plane?" Connor asked. "Can you imagine some guy in a fishing boat minding his own business and all of a sudden…"

Sitting in the middle of the back seat between his brothers, Jack and Brian accosted him with elbows and cries of "idiot" and "stupid." The movement caused the car to sway from side to side until Nell shouted at them to stop it. They did. The talk returned to flying and planes.

When he traded his WWI 'Jenny' for another plane, Nell thought Will was insane. "What are you doing?" She said, "Look at what's going on. People are losing their homes and you're buying an airplane."

"A used airplane."

"I don't care if it is used. What's gotten into you? We shouldn't be spending money on anything we don't need. What if that drought comes East? What would happen to the farm? The farm goes; what would we do?"

Hotter than usual summers had decimated agriculture in the middle of the country. Oklahoma was a 'dust bowl,' and people were migrating all over the country looking for work. People were hungry. Trying to make light of it, Herbert Hoover had said, "Nobody is actually starving. The hoboes are better fed than they have ever been." Soup lines and shantytowns were commonplace. Unemployment affected a quarter of the country. Even when people had jobs, they didn't know how long they would last. Nell had always said grace before dinner every night. Now, it took on a new meaning for the Buckley family. They were fortunate, and they knew it.

It wasn't just the United States. Europe, Germany, Poland, and Austria saw unemployment rise to twenty percent. In addition, in the aftermath of WWI treaties were being re-negotiated or broken. Nell's anxiety about the future contrasted with Will's "We'll handle things when they come, if they ever come." The 'they' covered whatever the newspaper reported that day: the rise of Hitler, Mussolini, and Stalin in Europe; the dust bowls in the United States. Will's approach scared her. Nell would say, "You read all the time. Why doesn't what's going on bother you? There could be another war."

"Okay," he would say. "Worse comes to worst, I go back to work at the shipyard. That's not a bad thing, now, is it?"

"Oh God, Will. What about the boys?"

He didn't have an answer for that other than to say, "Stop worrying. You're driving yourself nuts. You're turning into a 'Nervous Nellie.'"

Neither could have predicted what they would worry about on Monday, June fourth. It was a beautiful early summer day. They had enjoyed a series of them. Brian and Jack were out on the *Mary Ellen* pulling lobster pots. That had been their summer work for a couple of years. Will insisted they take turns as skipper and stern man. The skipper handled the boat while the stern man did the grunt work—opening the traps, taking the lobsters and crabs out, discarding what was too small, rebaiting the traps, and getting them back in the water. Connor was still at school in Bath. Will had driven to Bath to buy a new set of spark plugs and points for the tractor and had timed it so he could pick Connor up on the way home. Nell was in the garden weeding and staking vegetables. She had the hose running because of the dry spell.

Up on Chase Hill, a couple of workmen had built a small fire to heat their lunch. They had been working on a survey tower for the Coast and Geodetic Survey. Will would later refer to them as, "God-damned city people who didn't know how to put a fuckin' fire out."

On the way home from Bath, Will and Connor could see smoke rising from the hill. They went directly there. Others had also gathered. The workers were gone, but their lunchtime fire had flared up in the wind and was now out of control. It had already consumed several acres. Georgetown had no fire-fighting equipment to deploy. By the time Will and Connor arrived, their neighbors were hard at work creating fire breaks, trucking water in, and beating the fire into submission.

Seeing the smoke from where they were on the *Mary Ellen*, Brian and Jack came in and drove to join the others. Men from all over the island had come. By nightfall, it looked like they had succeeded in extinguishing the fire. No embers were seen smoldering, and everyone breathed more easily. They didn't want to take any chances, so the men developed a schedule to have a few people rotate to monitor the area throughout the night. They created a telephone chain to notify others if the blaze erupted again. At that point, no houses had been lost.

The night was peaceful. The following day, they reduced the

number of people who would keep watch on Tuesday. That evening, everyone went home for dinner convinced that the fire was out and there was no more danger.

On Wednesday afternoon, Nell and Will got dressed in black to attend Stearns Scott's funeral at White Cove. "It's going to be big," Nell said as she got in the car. "He's lived here all his life, and everybody will be there. I've known that man all my life."

"And his many wives?"

"Be kind. Grace was only twenty-six when she died. Estelle was... Well, she was Estelle. Bertha…"

"Who he married two years after divorcing Estelle…"

"So, the man liked to be married. Don't you?"

"Only to you."

Nell was antsy during the service. When it was finally over, and they went outside, the reason was apparent. The fire had started up again, and the wind was helping it along. What had once been fields for farming had long been allowed to return to woodland filled with second-growth trees. The woods were now thick, at points impenetrable. Dead wood and leaves from years carpeted the floor. In addition, it had been unusually dry for four weeks. The situation was perfect for a fire, and before long, the fire was marching north along the island and consuming everything in its path.

Out pulling pots, Brian and Jack could again see the glow and smoke from the water and immediately headed back to the Cove using all the engine power that had powered the *Mary Ellen* during its rumrunner career. When they reached their dock, Jack hopped off and ran to Tír na nÓg. "What are you doing?" Brian called after him.

"I'm calling Grandpa. Connor's still at school. Maybe he can stop him before he heads home with the Carvers."

"I'll meet you at the truck. The shovels and axes are still in the back. I didn't unload them."

A southwest wind blew the fire towards the Northeast end of the island. Trees burst as the fire engulfed them. The roar was deafening. More firebreaks were dug, and trees cut down. Men from off the island had come to help. The fire burned through the afternoon and night. Finally, a combination of the firebreaks and a dying wind managed to halt the fire's forward movement. It never reached Soldier or Lowe Points, where a southwest wind would have blown the fire across the narrow inlet that separated Georgetown Island from Westport Island. This time, though, houses were lost.

Any respite didn't last long. On Thursday morning, the fire flared again, but the wind had clocked around and was now blowing from the northeast, heading back down the island moving towards the villages. Again, volunteers came from miles away. Upwards of five hundred men were now fighting the fire.

Houses and cottages along the Little Sheepscot were destroyed one after another. Exhausted, Will and Brian stayed with the firefighters while Nell and Jack used both trucks to help people move valuables out of their homes and bring them to the wharf at Five Islands, where they thought they might be safe.

Thursday night was the worst. The fire was driving south along the shore and headed right for the village at Five Islands. The entire east side of the island, from Robinhood Cove to the Sheepscot, was burning. Sometimes it would die down, and then a breeze would fan it back to life. The fire continued on its march and made it to within five hundred yards of the village at Five Islands while people watched in terror. Then, finally, a wind shift back to the southwest saved them and their homes.

Friday morning, a subdued wind quieted things for a while, but with a fresh breeze, the fire came back to life, and by mid-day, the northeast quadrant of the island was enveloped in smoke. It wasn't until Saturday that the fire had no more fuel or wind to stir it into life. It wasn't until the following weekend that patrols were ended, and all the volunteers went home.

The Convey farm was covered in soot, but the farmhouse and the outbuildings were all intact, and none of the livestock had escaped, although several showed cuts where terror had pushed them into fences. Three ewes had been trampled and had to be put down.

Nell turned to Will during one of their inspections and said, "I wish more people had fire ponds the way we do."

"You mean the one you objected to because I needed the fill for the airstrip?"

"Yes, that one."

"I'm just glad we didn't have to use it."

"But if we had, I suppose I'd have to be grateful you wanted to fly your bloody airplane out of your own airport and using good pasture land to do it."

"Thank you, my dear, for graciously acknowledging the genius of your husband in anticipating all eventualities."

"You are impossible. You do know that, don't you?"

Will took government officials up in his plane to photograph and assess the damage. Neighbors banded together to help those who had lost their homes or whose fields had been destroyed. More people decided to move off the island.

"It's cursed," was the statement of one of the oldest residents, John Porter, as Connor and Will helped him load his belongings onto their truck. He was moving to Portland to live with his daughter. His house still stood, but everything around it was blackened debris. He decided to just walk away. He had a place to go, but that was not true for everyone.

The summer was different than any they had experienced. With the loss of cottages and a blackened island, not all the summer people returned. It wasn't just the fire. Some were now feeling the Depression and conserving whatever money they had accumulated.

For the Buckley's, the loss of summer income was devastating. They had lobsters and no one to sell them to. No one wanted to go on plane rides. For Will, depression was no longer an economic term. It now resided in the very fiber of his being.

There were no parties. The yacht club opened late and closed early. Will didn't chide Nell about being anxious. The five of them now worked on the farm because they had little else to do. They had to conserve gas, so off-island trips were rare except for Sunday Mass.

When July came, Will and his sons found themselves with little to do other than help Nell with the gardens, take care of chores that had been postponed, some for years, and grouse about being bored. Finally, after a grousing session, Nell said, "Get out of here. All of you. Find something to do, anything. Just stop it."

Later that night, she said to Will, "Whatever happened to the man I married? You were so optimistic and now look at you. You're drinking too much, complaining about everything, and acting like the world is against you. Fire didn't touch us. Can't imagine what you'd be like if it had. You can't control this. Accept it. Depression's hit everyone."

"Except the rich. Club is still going while our neighbors don't have enough money to pay for gas and electricity."

"You going to go on about the rich again?"

"Damned rich started this, but we're the ones suffering."

"Not true. Some of them lost everything, including some of our friends at the club."

"Damned few." Will sank deeper into his chair and his glass of whiskey. "Quaint."

"What?"

"Fucking summer people. When I was at the market, two women were looking at the notices tacked up there. This one bitch is talking about Crandall's daughter advertising to take kids on horseback rides, and she says to her friend, 'Isn't that quaint?' Crandall doesn't have a pot to piss in, and his daughter's trying to help out, and this bitch calls it 'quaint.' I wanted to slap her."

Nell continued to knit for a few minutes before she said, "What happened to all your big ideas? You used to have an idea an hour. It's one of the things I love about you. Your mind never stops working. Where's my old Will hiding out? I miss him."

The next day, Will had some ideas. When he told Nell, she said, "You want to spend money? Now?"

"It's an investment. It's not a lot. It makes sense. It's so damned obvious; I don't know how the hell I missed it."

"If it'll keep the four of you busy, it's probably worth it."

The next day Will arranged to buy two horses and a wagon. The following day, the four of them started salvaging trees that the fire had scorched. If they were still around, none of the landowners had any objections. It was as though the depression and the fire had wrapped the island and its people in smoke. The only ones who weren't affected were the summer people on the shore.

Day after day, Will and his sons cut and hauled hardwood and pine to the road. Sometimes they were able to use the wagon. Sometimes the horses would just drag the trees. Once they got the trees to the road, they loaded them onto their trucks and brought them back to the farm. Will convinced Nell that they weren't using much gas and that it was an 'investment.' There was no market, but Will knew that people would be rebuilding and need lumber. It might take a few years, but it would happen. He was sure of it. Nell pointed out to him the irony. "So, you're getting this wood for free. Then, someday you will sell it back to them. And you feel okay about this?"

"Sure. They'll be buying it back as boards. And who knows. Look, a lot of them have their places up for sale now. Do you think they'll all rebuild? I doubt it. But some will. And this island's got a shoreline, and it's not all built on. More summer people are going to come and want to build. Why shouldn't they buy from us? They won't have to go into Bath and pay for getting it delivered out here."

From not having much to do, the four men were now busy every day. Finally, in early August, they took some of their salvage to the mill to have it turned into usable lumber. When they returned, they got about building their own ice house. When Nell asked about the ice house, Will told her it was so they could have fresh meat and fish. "As soon as we get ice, we'll load her up. Brian and Jack'll be back in school, but Connor and me will get us some deer, turkey, and fish. Our refrigerator is nice, but it doesn't hold much, and I'm sick of lamb and chicken. We get enough, we may be able to sell some."

"To who? No one's got any money."

"Maybe we stock up in the spring and sell to the summer people when they come back."

"Better be a good ice house, then."

"It will be."

While Will and the boys were laughing again by the end of July, August was not a good month for Nell. On the fifteenth, her father died of a massive stroke. While some people said it was a "good way to die" and "he had a good life," Nell felt the loss intensely. Then, on the twenty-fifth, driving home after Mass, Brian announced, "I'm going to join the Navy when I graduate. There aren't going to be any jobs for a new engineer right out of school, and since I can already fly, I'm sure they'll take me. Jack and Connor can handle the lobstering in the summer, and with me in the Navy, Grandma can move into my room. She'd like that, and you wouldn't have to worry about her being alone with Grandpa gone."

June 1, 1984
HOME TOWN BOY by Michael Buckley

Next Monday, June 4th, will be the fiftieth anniversary of the biggest fire in Georgetown, Maine's history. It sputtered, flared, sputtered, and flared again for several days. Shifting winds made it difficult to put out. The fire destroyed homes, outbuildings, crops, and even some livestock. Fortunately, no one died. My grandfather and grandmother told me stories of people staying up all night to keep watch and of the help the island received from neighboring towns.

My grandfather, an avid reader, said the fire proved that the words of John Donne were accurate. They're worth remembering:

> No man is an island entire of itself; every man
> is a piece of the continent, a part of the main;
> if a clod be washed away by the sea, Europe
> is the less, as well as if a promontory were, as
> well as any manner of thy friends or of thine
> own were; any man's death diminishes me,
> because I am involved in mankind.
> And therefore never send to know for whom
> the bell tolls; it tolls for thee.

The fire showed that while we might live on an island, we are not alone. Neighbors helped neighbors, and the neighborhood expanded to towns miles away that sent people and machines to help contain the fire. No one got paid anything. It was volunteering at its best.

The fire led to the formation of a robust volunteer fire department that has done its best to protect Georgetown Island residents and their property ever since that fateful week in June fifty years ago. Since I returned from Vietnam, I have been a proud member of the department.

An outfit such as ours requires many different skills. There are various positions to be filled. Some of them have titles, but one of the most important ones does not. It is that of recruiter. Our current 'Recruiter in Chief' told me a story recently that demonstrates just how vital his role is.

Like many others in small communities, our department suffers from an aging process. Many of our younger folks have left the island for greener pastures, and replacing our older volunteer firefighters has become more difficult. Our 'RIC' (Recruiter in Chief) is always on the lookout for new blood. He's got a sharp eye and a keen nose, and when a prospective target comes into view, he enters into a well-honed stalking mode before he pounces for the kill.

Well, a few years ago, he learned about this fellow, summer type, who decided he was going to try his hand at living here all year. Now, he hadn't sold his home in Boston; it wasn't even on the market, but he had purchased a year-round home complete with insulation and an oil-fired furnace, so our 'RIC' was cautiously optimistic. His optimism increased when he heard that the newcomer had two children who would be entering our school come fall.

The stalking began. He made his first move at the Georgetown General Store, where our 'RIC' just happened to engage his prey by reflecting on his newness to the island, throwing in a welcome and, "I hope I'll see you around."

During the second encounter, names were exchanged casually. "By the way, I'm Bill (not our RIC's real name)." Name acknowledgments and hellos followed two to three times, then came the pounce. This one took place while looking through the mail in front of the post office. "You know, I've been thinking about you, and I thought about how you might meet some folks here in town. Okay if I come by and talk to you about what I have in mind?"

Well, Newcomer thought that was just fine, and a date and time were established. On the appointed date, Bill showed up at

Newcomer's home and was introduced to Mrs. Newcomer and the two little Newcomers. They settled around the kitchen table with coffee, and Bill began his pitch. "Just wondering, when you were a little kid, did you ever dream about becoming a fireman? Wearing the hat, riding on the truck, and racing off to a fire?"

"No, I don't think so."

That threw Bill. What kid doesn't at some point dream of becoming a fireman? However, Mrs. Newcomer piped up, "I did. Does that count?"

"Well, it sure does," Bill said.

Bill explained that while people are used to having professional fire departments in the cities, out here in Georgetown, we rely on volunteers to protect lives and belongings from fire. And it was a great way to meet people and become part of the community. By the time Bill finished, Mrs. Newcomer had signed up as one of the ladies who would provide support at fire sites. However, Mr. Newcomer had multiple reasons why he couldn't do it. He kept throwing up excuses, and Bill tried batting them away, but it was clear Bill wasn't getting anyplace. Finally, Mrs. Newcomer said, "Well, I live here, and you can count on me."

And we have. She has been a wonderful addition to our team, and last I heard, Mr. Newcomer was getting the message. So, we'll see if he shows up.

Of course, showing up and being counted on is what volunteering is all about. Feeling like you belong to something bigger than yourself or your family is important to most of us, and when it is something as dramatic as fighting fires, it can get the juices flowing. I'm betting that Mr. Newcomer will show up someday, if not to fight fires, then to do something else.

Fortunately, we have never had to fight a fire as big as the one my grandparents did fifty years ago. I know, though, that if we did, we would have lots of help just as they did. Donne was right; no man is an island. The same is true of communities. We are all neighbors and we are at our best when we act that way. It's too bad that sometimes it takes a fire to remind us of that.

Chapter Thirty-One: Drifting

I didn't sleep well Tuesday night, or I slept worse than usual. Images came and went, not dreams, just images that wouldn't go away: Nan reaching down to help Joe sit up so he could see the whale; my struggling to help Hannah up onto the *Redhead*'s deck after she had to go below to use the head; the smell of Nan's perfume when she hugged me; holding Hannah on a Sunday afternoon after making love with the breeze coming in over our naked bodies through the *Redhead*'s open hatch; the devastating emptiness when I read the letter from Nan telling me she was now with Joe, and it was all over between us.

Looking out the window as the bedroom brightened, I could see the sky, gray and cold. It was raining. I turned over and tried to get back to sleep but couldn't. I lay there watching the window and the water beads as they raced down the glass. There would be no coffee on the pier this morning. The weather had turned, and the house was chilly and damp. I praised myself for closing the windows last night.

I got dressed and went into the living room. Wendy had started a fire, and I could see her in the kitchen cooking. Hearing that I was up, she shouted from the kitchen, "Morning. Oatmeal? I made enough for both of us. Coffee's ready."

"Fire going, coffee ready, and oatmeal coming. You do good work, kid."

"Anything for you, Gramps. BTW, how was your sail yesterday? You didn't say much last night."

"It was good. I think they enjoyed it. We might do it again." I joined her in the kitchen.

"Rina filled me in on the sordid history between you and this Nan person. I don't think I like her very much, ditching you like that."

"She's okay. And if she hadn't..."

"You would never have married Nanna, had my mom, and I wouldn't be here."

"True, true, and true. Let's eat in front of the fireplace."

"But of course." She dished out two dishes of oatmeal while I cut up a banana.

"Banana?" I asked.

"Please."

We settled in front of the fire. We had our regular spaces now. Wendy had claimed the right-hand side of the couch facing the fireplace. The rocker next to the couch was mine. Everyone knew that. An end table with a standing lamp gave us both enough light to read. It was another Grandma Nell yard sale acquisition, as was my padded rocking chair. "It's mission style," Hannah had told me once. "We should get one to match it." Unfortunately, we never got around to it.

"Think there'll be a race tonight?" Wendy asked.

"Probably. Rain's supposed to stop around noon." I had a small NOAA weather channel radio that I listened to every morning. It hung in the bathroom next to the window. I turned it on while I shaved. I had done it for years and had been teased about it for years by my wife and children. It's essential, though—the weather. Every sailor and pilot pays attention to the weather. The weather isn't something apart from you. You live or die in the weather. You don't control it, but it can sure control you.

Wendy asked, "Would you mind terribly if I didn't crew for you tonight?"

"No, I can handle the Herreshoff alone, or someone else might want to join me. What's up? You and Rina doing something?"

"No. Someone else asked me to crew for them."

"Oh. Who?"

"Archie Howlett. I met him Friday night at the square dance. He told me he's staying at the farmhouse and has been coming here for years. I don't remember ever meeting him."

"The Howletts come in July. You always came in August. They've been coming for, oh God, it's got to be twenty years now."

The sound of the rain changed. A wind had developed and was now driving it across the porch as far as the living room windows. I didn't close upstairs last night. "Would you ...?"

"On it." Wendy ran upstairs, and I could hear her moving from room to room. She came back down a couple of minutes later. "Everything's closed up tight. I locked the windows so they wouldn't rattle."

"Thanks. So, you met Archie Howlett."

"Yep. What's he like?"

The yacht club has always had a slight over-representation of academics and ministers, professions where people have the summer off or at least a month. Because the club is old and has always been volunteer to its core, it's a low-cost enterprise. Academics and religious types can afford it. The Howletts were both. Jay taught high school social studies in New Haven, and Olivia Lane-Howlett (she always used her hyphenated name) was the Unitarian Universalist minister in nearby Stratford. Word of mouth brought them to Georgetown. The summer they first came, there were no rentals along the cove, so they rented our farmhouse for the month. They've been coming back ever since. It was 1999. I remember it because it was the year that John-John Kennedy crashed his plane off Martha's Vineyard. Liv and Jay wanted to know all about my take on it and how it could happen. So did everyone at the club. As the pilot in residence, I was suddenly an expert commentator at the post-race tea the Sunday after the accident.

I had watched Archie and his younger brother, Gabe, grow up. I knew Archie had followed his father's social studies interests and was working on a master's degree in history at Princeton. I knew Gabe had followed his father's passion for cooking and dropped out of college, much to his parent's chagrin. He was enrolled in a culinary school in Colorado. Christmas newsletters. We had exchanged them for years; that is, Hannah had. I didn't keep up with our end of it after she got sick.

Starting the first year they rented the farmhouse, Hannah and I had a standing invitation for dinner on the Friday night before they left at the end of July. Jay would cook, and it would always be a four or five-course menu of recipes he had practiced during the month. It was always exquisite, truly fine dining coming from our kitchen. They maintained my invitation after Hannah died, and I was grateful. That's the kind of people they are.

The Howletts had a Beetlecat that they towed back and forth each summer from whatever town where Liv was serving as a minister. Over the years, Liv had served three different congregations. Archie didn't need crew to race the gaff-rigged Beetlecat. I knew that. Wendy knew that. And now she wanted me to 'tell her' about Archie.

I had no idea what to tell her about Archie. I hadn't paid much attention to him. He was the Howlett's son. He was here for a month each summer. I never heard about him getting in any trouble. He had to be smart enough to get into Princeton for graduate school. Beyond that, I didn't know what to say. Hannah would have; I didn't.

I could tell her much more about Jay and Liv. I could have told her that Jay was a gourmet cook and one of the things he loved about the farmhouse was its kitchen and its appliances. If we didn't have a kitchen tool, he bought it and left it behind. We wound up having one of the most tooled-out kitchens for miles around. I didn't know what some of them were used for. I could tell her that Jay was easy-going, fun, and one of the most incompetent sailors in the club. He always came in last or next to last in every race. Once, he came in third because he was so far back that he caught a wind shift that no one else had. He was able to ride it right to the finish line. We showed him our appreciation for this feat by throwing him in the water when he reached the dock.

I could tell Wendy that Olivia Lambert-Howlett was serious,

earnest, read a lot, and knew how to make you feel welcome. I could tell her that Liv was caring and was very good to Hannah that last summer. I could tell her that when Valerie was here from India, the three women would spend hours talking on the porch. That first year after Hannah died, I could count on a monthly call from Liv to find out how I was doing.

Archie, though, he was Jay and Olivia's son. What else did she want to know? Was he a decent guy? Of course. He was Jay and Olivia's son. Could he sail? Probably better than his dad, but that wasn't saying a lot.

The front moved through, and the afternoon sky was cloudless and windless. The race was going to be a competition looking for the slightest breeze. Archie would have been better off without Wendy's additional weight, but off they went in the twelve-foot Beetlecat to join the other Beetlecats gathering together for the start. The Herreshoffs would start ten minutes later.

I grabbed my sails and was headed for the dock when Nan intercepted me and asked, "Need some crew?" Several others heard her question.

Racing at Erascohegan is not a serious business for most of us, especially the Wednesday night races, which attract fewer boats. Many of us sail solo on Wednesdays, and we don't use spinnakers because of the lack of crew. Given the absence of wind, having Nan on board would slow me down, but saying 'no' would embarrass both of us. So, I said, "Sure, why not." I could think of several 'why nots' but left them unsaid.

On the way down the ramp, she said, "Just like old times." I didn't answer. It may have been my imagination but I was sure everyone was watching us and would provide commentary to one another as we rowed out to get *Sonas* underway. We got the sails up, Nan unhitched the boat from its mooring, and we sat there. The only air that moved was from talking and exhaling. The tide was going out, and we started to drift very slowly with it.

I saw the Steward head the club launch over to *Allegro*, the Herreshoff owned by Moe Allen, the chair of our race committee. I didn't quite pray that they would cancel the race because of a lack of wind, but I was close. I hate drifters at all times, but a drifter with Nan felt unbearably awkward and confining.

I was in luck. The Steward got on the bullhorn and shouted, "Race canceled due to lack of wind." The tide had only taken us about fifty yards from the mooring, so I got out the paddle and handed it to Nan. She went forward, leaned over the bow, and started to paddle. I guided us back to the mooring; we lowered the sails, put the cockpit cover on, and rowed back to the dock.

I looked around to see where Archie and Wendy were. Their sail was down, but they were sitting in the cockpit. I could hear Wendy's laughter come across the water. At least they were having fun. When we reached the dock Nan said, "It's still early. Do you want to come up for a drink and some nibbles?"

I responded, "Thanks for the invite, but I'm going to wait for Wendy. Maybe another time. Raincheck?"

"Of course." She knew, I know she knew, I was feeling uncomfortable around her. She walked away along the shore in the direction of their cottage, *Land's End*, where Joe was waiting for her.

I walked up the pier and onto the clubhouse porch to wait for Wendy. I took a chair next to Moe. He asked, "You okay?"

"What do you mean?"

"Just checking. I saw what happened with Nan."

"I think she needs a friend."

"I'm sure. Old friends are the best kind."

I looked at Moe and shook my head. "Are tongues starting to wag?"

"Hey, it's Erascohegan. Would you expect less?

"Oh, great."

"Don't worry about it. Everyone survives."

I didn't respond. I thought about Rachel, 'Not always.'

I saw Wendy and Archie rowing in. "Got to get going."

"Too bad we had to cancel," Moe said. "See you Saturday."

I walked down to the end of the pier to wait for the two of them. "Dad, can I borrow the truck and drop Archie off? He rode his bike down."

"Sure. How you doing, Arch?"

"Good, Mr. Buckley. You?"

When I returned to Tír, the light was blinking on the answering machine. I went over and pushed the play button. It was Ruth. This was one of the times I suggested we talk. I called her back.

She said, "Dad, thanks for getting back to me. How's the summer going?"

"Great."

"Look, I know you talked to Jesse. I'm sorry. I should have called you myself."

"I would agree with that."

"You're angry."

"I would say more disappointed than angry. But here we are. Why don't you fill me in on what's going on. All I know is that the two of you are in financial trouble, and you want me to sell some land to help get you out of it."

"Wow! You really are upset. Maybe I shouldn't have called."

"I'm listening. Go ahead."

"You sure?"

"Yes."

"Okay. As you know, Harold has always wanted to have his own business."

I had not known that. She may have mentioned it. But, if she had,

I didn't remember it. It was certainly not something I had ever given a second thought.

She continued, "Three years ago, when Trump was elected, Harold decided this was the time to leave his uncle's business and strike out on his own. His thinking was that the new administration would loosen all of the ridiculous regulations on the oil industry, and there would be room for the small operators to take advantage of it because they could move quicker than the large companies. I just thought he knew what he was doing, and it all made sense. So, he talked his father and a couple of our friends into investing money, and off he went. To be honest, I didn't pay a lot of attention to what he was doing. I just knew he was excited and seemed more alive than he had been for years."

I did not know any of this, but it was her story, and I let her tell it in her own way.

"Well, we had some savings, but we had just bought the new house. The mortgage wasn't that big, and based on his income from his old job, we could afford it. So, we used our savings and took out a second mortgage to get the new business up and going. He was convinced that rigs in the shale area would produce and that oil would again be competitive with natural gas. He was sure that we would become multi-millionaires quickly because once the rigs started producing, he could sell out to a big company, and we would retire."

"So, what happened?"

"It took forever for the deregulations to go into effect that would help people like Harold. As a result, natural gas has stayed strong, the price of oil did not go up, and we are in debt up to our necks."

"So, what are you going to do?"

"I don't know. We have college tuition to pay, and Baylor is not cheap. We can't pay the two mortgages. We have borrowed money from our 401K to have something to live on. Harold's dad is furious with him. His sisters feel like he cheated their father. His uncle doesn't want him back because he feels betrayed that he left. He's out looking for a job, but until he finds one, we are in a real jam, and even when he does get a job, we will have a ton of bills we are just rolling over that we are going to have to catch up on."

"Have you put the house on the market, or are you under-water on it with the two mortgages?"

"We might break even, but Harold doesn't want to sell. We both love it."

"Wouldn't a smaller house cost a lot less to keep up with?"

"Probably, but Harold is convinced we should stay put and that things will turn around in another year or so."

I didn't say anything for a minute. I could feel the rage building inside me: 'Harold doesn't want to sell,' but they thought I should. I did my best to be calm, but even I could hear the ice in my tone, "So you want me to sell off some of the farm."

"You've said that the four of us would eventually inherit the farm when you died, and Harold and I were wondering if...."

"Wondering if, or are counting on?"

"Dad, we are in a real jam."

"But you don't want to sell your house." I emphasized 'your.'

"Not if we can help it."

"I'll think about it and get back to you. In the meantime, you might consider looking for work, too."

"What kind of job could I get?"

"I don't know. I'm sure you can find something."

"Like what? Be a greeter at Walmart?"

"I read they're hiring."

"Come on. Be serious."

"I am."

"Thanks for nothing." The line went dead.

I don't know what Hannah would have done. But I know she

would have told me to take a deep breath and go for a walk and then call Ruth back. In all of our years together, I never went for a walk, even though she kept telling me to do so. Instead, I went down to the dock, climbed in the dinghy, and rowed out to the *Redhead*. I opened everything up as though I was going to take her out by myself. I turned on the radio and listened to the weather report. I turned on the navigation instruments and made sure everything was functioning the way it was supposed to. Then I went forward and laid down on the V-berth, not to go asleep but to think in the privacy of what had become my sanctuary.

After half an hour of having no thoughts worth remembering, I turned everything off, closed up the boat, and returned to Tír. Over dinner, I didn't say anything to Wendy about the phone call with Ruth. Neither of us was talkative. After the dishes were done, I went to my computer and started searching. I found something in Forbes. They quoted some kind of oil industry magazine. It reported that twenty-nine percent of the private operators had stopped drilling. The article concluded that "…any activity stabilization for this group of private companies is likely a sign that better times for the entire industry may be on the horizon. Unfortunately, we are not observing such a signal yet." Harold was not alone in his bad fortune. Still, it was easier to come to me than to sell their house. I wondered whether I was responding to this situation or to the silence when Hannah was sick and all the years of being treated like the poor hick relative from Maine who wasn't worth calling or visiting.

Chapter Thirty-Two: Cocktails

Every family has traditions or tries to have them. When a tradition works, it creates stability in an unstable world, certainty where there is none. You belong when you join in, even if you don't feel like you belong. Your participation is the price of admission; a 'does this person belong' interview. Climbing the five thousand, two hundred, and sixty-nine-foot Mt. Katahdin was an annual tradition for the Howlett family. I never understood this masochism. But then, they never understood my sailing a forty-foot boat across the Atlantic Ocean and back.

The Howletts always 'did Katahdin' towards the middle of their time at the farmhouse. This year it was to be on July 20th. They would camp at the base of the mountain the night before and the night of the climb. You had to make reservations at the Baxter State Park campgrounds months in advance to get a campsite. Consequently, the Howletts never knew what the weather would be. And then there was the mountain. The weather at the campground could be summer wonderful, and the forecast for the day promising. At the top, though, the weather was constantly changing, and it could be snowing and blowing a full gale when you got there. Climbing Katahdin was not my idea of fun.

Hannah and I did go with them once. Hannah loved it. I didn't hate it; I just found huffing and puffing for eight hours to say you had done something to be uninspiring. Yes, the views were terrific, but you were looking down at the trail most of the time, so you didn't break your neck. Sometimes, you had to wait for the people ahead of you—turtles who stopped at every break in the trees so they could gawk at the view and take pictures.

The Howletts invited me to join them every year after Hannah died. I was not surprised, then, when I received a call from Jay with an invitation to join them this summer. I also doubt he was surprised when I thanked him for the invitation but declined. This year, what came next was different: "Do you think Wendy might enjoy it? We would love to have her come along."

So, was it Wendy they were after, or was it Archie after Wendy? It was all very polite but did not take a master sleuth to decode what was going on. I was tempted to give a smart-ass or brusque answer but decided to maintain the code of decorum that had been established. I said, "I don't know. She might. Let me put her on."

I went out to the porch where she was reading, "Wendy, phone. It's Jay Howlett." I didn't say anything more.

"Mr. Howlett?"

"Uh-huh."

I sat down next to where she had been sitting and returned to reading interview notes from my last trip to the paper museum. I expected her to be back in a couple of minutes. Instead, she came out to the porch twenty minutes later and sat down. "It was Archie, not Mr. Howlett. The Howletts want me to go with them to hike Katahdin. It's this weekend. Archie said it's easy and a lot of fun. They do it every year. You don't mind, do you? I wouldn't be able to crew for you Saturday or Sunday, though."

"No. It's fine. Archie said it's easy?"

"Yeah. He said it's just a day hike, and the views are spectacular."

Easy, perhaps if you are young and fit, which Wendy was. Given her athleticism, I was not concerned about it being 'easy' for her. It would have been damned hard work at my age, and I consider myself fit. 'Just a day hike.' Talk about minimalization. I asked her, "So what's the plan?"

"Okay, we're going to leave Friday around ten. Arch said we'll get there late afternoon with a stop for lunch. His parents have reserved a campsite at this place they always go to. It's called roaring something."

"Roaring Brook."

"Yeah. That's it. We'll set up camp and then do the hike on Saturday. Up and down the same day. We will stay at Roaring Brook Saturday night. Then, we'll break camp the next morning and be back in time for dinner Sunday night. Archie asked if I had a sleeping bag and a backpack. He said I could use his brother's if I didn't. I told him you might have some stuff."

"We have both. They're in the attic at the farmhouse. Do you need a tent?"

"No. Arch said they have a big six-person tent. Do you have an air mattress?"

"Attic, where the sleeping bags are."

"Great.

"I take it you're looking forward to this?"

"Oh, yeah. It'll be a good break from the books."

Then, I couldn't help myself. "Looking forward to the hike, or your hiking companions, or should I say, companion?"

"Grandpa! I've just met him."

"So, what happened to 'Gramps?'"

"I only use that when you're being nice to me. Oh, could you take care of Charlie?"

"Yes, I can take care of Charlie."

I have no idea how the 'cocktail' tradition started at Erascohegan, but it is firmly established. Invitations for dinner were rare. However, cocktail parties were one of the essential ingredients that made up the Erascohegan summer. Typically, they occurred on Friday and Saturday evenings, and there were always more than one taking place on any given evening. By the end of the summer, you would have 'cocktailed' with everyone in the club, be au courant on everyone's life over the past year, and equally up to date on what the coming year was expected to bring. For those of us in our seventies and above, the standard content was health, deaths, children, grandchildren, new births, and, for some, great-grandchildren. Serious health discussions were held in small one-to-one conversations on the porch of the host and hostess's house or out on the lawn. Of course, you respected the privacy of these pairings unless you were invited in.

No one worried about driving home because most of the cottages were relatively close together. You knew who was going to drink too much and who never drank or was a 'friend of Bill's—a recent acquaintance or a long time 'friend.' Young children often came with their parents and played outside when they were not dashing in and out to raid the appetizers. But unlike most of the Erascohegan social events, the cocktail parties were primarily adult goings-on.

Of course, there was a dress code. For men, blue blazers were the uniform of the day. Long or short pants were acceptable, but boat shoes were required whether you sailed or not, preferably the dark brown variety with rawhide laces. On the other hand, the women always seemed to me to have more options than the men. Hannah assured me that I only thought that way because I wasn't a woman. However, one year I did observe that every woman in the room had a sweater draped, not worn, around her shoulders. When I pointed that out to Hannah, her response was to sing, "*In the cool, cool, cool of the evening.*" We're not stupid, Michael."

Widows and widowers were always invited. I referred to them as the 'pity' set of which I was a member in good standing. We were not expected to host. After I joined that group, I decided one year to host my own party at Tír. I was looking forward to it. I was in my 'I can do this' mode. I received several "Oh, Mike; you don't have to do this" comments. I did do it, but just that once. People seemed to be too uncomfortable with my attempt to be hospitable.

The most desirable attendees were the twenty and thirty-year-olds. They were the ones who were leading exciting lives, and everyone wanted to know what was going on in their worlds. Wendy and Archie were now in this category. If two people of this age group were seen together several times during the summer, the wondering would begin. Club summer romances leading to marriage were highly valued. For Erascohegan members, 'She was a (whatever her maiden name was)' conveyed endless information about the spouse's heritage to the club cognoscenti.

A divorced person, by contrast, was condemned to invitational limbo. If more bodies were needed because of unexpected 'regrets,' he or she would get a late call: 'Max, if you're not doing anything tonight, why don't you stop by…' However, if there was an attempt at matchmaking in the works, they would receive an invitation that might include a: 'I'd like you to meet…'. Naturally, Erascohegan welcomed these matches, but they did not carry the same value as those of the young'uns.

The bar menu was anything but uniform at these events, and the same was true for hors d'oeuvres. The competition was rampant between some houses. So, when Moe Allen said he would see me Saturday, he meant Saturday evening for cocktails and the Saturday race. Moe was a top competitor in both sailing and mixing. He always had a unique 'drink of the evening' in addition to the standards. Wine and beer would always be available, but the wines and beers would be unusual at Moe's cottage. Even the non-alcoholic punch would be unique. His wife, Telle (from Estelle), tolerated Moe's mixologist ambitions. You could always depend on Telle for a lovely and abundant assortment of hors d'oeuvres, and you never had to worry about preparing dinner when you got back home.

Moe's cocktail feature on July 20th was, he told us, the French 75, which, he also told us, dates back to WWI, and Harry MacElhone's Paris, and New York bars. According to Moe, and I am sure Wikipedia, it was named after the French 75mm field gun because of its 'kick.' Who would have thought of combining gin, lemon juice, and champagne? Bless you, Harry. It was delicious. As

I have aged, my tolerance for alcohol has significantly diminished, but this concoction inspired me to return to the bar for a second French 75. I found myself standing next to Nan Wilder Land. She had just come in and was ordering her first. She was alone. Seeing me, she said, "Hi. I was hoping I'd bump into you here. I wanted to apologize if I put you in an awkward position Wednesday night. You know, asking if you needed crew."

I lied, "No, no problem. It was fine."

"Being at the club, it just felt so natural. God, how many times did we sail together when we were kids?"

"Lots, that's for sure."

We separated into different conversation groups for the next two hours, coming back together in others, then separating again. I found myself looking forward to being together with her as we did this party dance. I liked listening to her talk.

There is a choreography to our cocktail parties. They are from five to seven, and at the end of the two hours, people start to say their goodbyes and meander off to their own homes. I was about to leave my unfinished third drink on the bar when Moe said, "Here, take it with you." He poured my French 75 into a plastic cup, and I headed towards the door.

Nan was standing on the porch. She, too, had a plastic cup in hand. She asked, "Do you mind if I walk with you?"

It was a little under a mile from Moe's cottage to Tír na nÓg, a twenty-minute walk or a thirty-minute stroll, down the peninsula to the head of the cove and then back up to the middle on the opposite shore. The Land cottage was on the way. Nan took my arm as we walked down the porch steps. I didn't mind. It was nice to be touched, and I felt like I was of service.

By the time we reached the dirt road that would take us around the cove, our cups were empty, and Nan's grip on my arm had a different purpose. First, she commented on changes she noticed in one of the cottages we passed and how the dirt road we were on was in better condition than she remembered it. Then, as we approached the head of the cove, she said, "Can I ask you something?"

"Sure."

"What was it like, taking care of Hannah all those months? It's been going on for over two years with Joe, and there's no end in sight. You saw him. Some days I feel sorry for him. Some days I just feel sorry for me. I hate it, but I can't help myself. I can't talk to Warren or Kitty about it. Sometimes I feel like I'm a terrible person."

These were the kinds of intimate questions people asked Hannah, not me. I didn't say anything. She said, "I'm sorry, Mike. I didn't mean to put you on the spot."

"No. It's okay. I guess I did feel sorry for myself at times. It was more anger, though. I didn't want to lose her, especially at first. I was angry at cancer, doctors, nurses, and anyone who wasn't perfect and reassuring in taking care of her. God help you if you said the wrong thing or made a mistake. I was furious. I did my best not to show it to Hannah, but she knew. At times I still feel that way."

"How did you handle it?"

"Hannah. Watching her handle it. She was amazing. She actually set a death date."

"What do you mean a death date?"

"It was Hannah being Hannah. Hannah, always the engineer. At first, she learned everything she could about pancreatic cancer. The average survival time from diagnosis to death, even with treatment, is eight months. So, she chose a date precisely eight months from the day she was diagnosed and said, 'Okay, that's the date I'm going to die.' At first, I was incredulous and got angry at her for being fatalistic. I talked about Ruth Bader Ginsburg, what the doctor had said about some people living for years. It was all bullshit. I just didn't want to think about losing her. She was much more sensible. I remember her saying in her most Hannah-ish way, 'Michael. If we live with that date, we can cope and make the most of our time. Our job is to use every bloody second of it.' It felt unreal. It was like we were working together on a project at BIW, and she was the project manager."

"That's incredible."

"She was."

"Did it help?"

"Yeah. It did. I know it helped me. I think it helped both of us. We got everything; she put everything in order. It was literally like she was going to retire, not die, and she was making sure that the next person who replaced her would know where everything was and what to do. From passwords to her memorial service. Within two weeks, she had it all together. Then she made a list of all the things she wanted to do over the next eight months and scheduled them according to her treatments and when she thought she would be getting sicker."

"You're kidding."

"No. One night when we had just gotten into bed, I asked her if she planned to create a Critical Path for us on her computer. I'll never forget it. She looked at me for a minute, and then she said. 'That's a great idea.' And she did. She created a damned eight-month project plan, printed it out, and hung it up in the kitchen. When Rachel saw it, she was very upset and told Hannah she was being morbid and defeatist. Hannah told her, "Damn it, Rachel, if you could have a birth plan when you were pregnant with Wendy, I can have a death plan."

"That's unbelievable."

"Nope. That was Hannah. So, tell me about Joe."

"Oh, Joe. He's very anxious. He's waiting for the next stroke all the time, and now he's losing his memory rapidly. The doctors are no help. They have no idea how likely it is that he'll have another stroke or how bad it might be."

"That's got to be hard to live with for both of you."

"It is. I think I might be able to handle it if that's all there was."

"What do you mean?"

We had reached the Land cottage. We stopped. She said, "Would you mind terribly if we kept walking. I'd love to see Tír again. I have such wonderful memories of the time I spent with your family there. Remember the way your mother used to take us blueberry picking?"

"Of course. Would you believe we still have the same cans on the same strings that we'd hang around our necks so we could use both hands? They're hanging in the same place in the hall."

"You're not serious?"

"I am. Come on. I'll show you."

We started walking again towards Tír. After we walked in silence for a couple of minutes, she said, "Joe had an affair with a lawyer from another firm. It went on for over eight years. The only thing that ended it was the stroke."

"Oh, shit. Did you know about it?"

"Remember how I told you we led parallel lives? Well, it appears those lives were a lot further apart than I knew. I didn't know about the affair until just before the stroke."

"How'd you find out?"

"His work cellphone. I picked it up to use it one day when we were in the car. We had stopped so he could go pick up his dry cleaning. I had left my phone at home. His phone was plugged in, so I used it to call my office. I saw he had a bunch of text messages. I don't know why, but I opened them up. He, they, were planning a golfing trip. In one of his texts, he said that he couldn't wait to fuck her. The dumb slut had responded with love and kisses emojis. I confronted him about it. He started by giving me a bunch of bullshit about a conference that included golf, and he was just joking with her. I lost it. I took his phone and got out of the car. I was going to head right for a lawyer. A week later, the fucker goes and has a stroke and begs me not to leave him. What was I going to do?"

Nan stopped talking. I put my arm around her shoulder. I didn't know what to say. We walked for a few minutes, and then she said, "Fuck it. Fuck him. Fuck his whole damned family that thinks he's such a saint. And now…now they're trying to put a guilt trip on me for not being supportive enough, because I hire people to stay with him while I try and lead some semblance of a life."

Again, I didn't know what to say. We kept walking towards Tír without talking. I opened the door when we reached the house, and Charlie raced out. I said to Nan, "Come on in. I want to show you." I flipped the hall light switch on, "Voila. There they are. Where they've always been."

Nan went over, took one of the cans off the hook, and hung it around her neck. "Let's go. Let's you and I go and pick blueberries. Tomorrow. Let's go tomorrow."

She looked like she was twelve years old, except she had tears in her eyes. I went over and took the can from around her neck. "Are you sure? What about…?"

"I need time away with a friend, Mike. Just some time. You understand."

"Yeah, I do. Maybe we could do that. In the morning."

"And I can crew for you in the afternoon?"

"Why not? Do you want a drink? I have some wine and beer and a little liquor."

"Hell no. I've had much too much already."

"Something to eat? I can cook us up some eggs or something."

"You know what I'd like? A peanut butter and jelly sandwich and a glass of milk."

"Super crunchy and…"

"Blackberry, I'll bet you've got it."

"I think we do."

It started on the porch on the same swing where we had sat and kissed so many years ago when we were the 'club sweethearts.' But it quickly moved beyond kissing, and Nan said, "You know where this is heading. Are you sure?"

I said, "I am if you are."

She said, "I am."

We went into my bedroom and helped one another get undressed, touching each other's bodies as we did. We said things about the changes in our bodies. We commented on each other's scars, asking how they happened.

Later, when I entered her, she grimaced and stopped me. "Mike, I'm sorry. I can't. It hurts too much."

She started crying, and I rolled off her and asked, "What is it?"

"Age, god damn it. God damned age. I've become a dried-up old tramp."

"Oh, Nan. Come here." She rolled over into my arms, and I held her. A few minutes later, Charlie barked. He wanted to be let in.

Chapter Thirty-Three: Spindrift

Nan didn't spend the night. I walked her home, chastely kissed her good night, and left. On the way back, feelings of guilt began. She was married. Joe had been cheating on her for years, and now she felt trapped. Did that matter? She was still married to him. When I got back to Tír, I poured myself a glass of milk and went out onto the porch. Lights were going off on the other side of the cove as people settled in for the night.

I felt I had betrayed Hannah. I remembered one of our sails on the *Redhead* when she was sick. There was little wind but Hannah didn't care. We had no place to go. The day was on the cool side. I had brought up a blanket from below and thrown it over Hannah, who was stretched out on the lee side cockpit bench looking up at the sky. "This is perfection, Michael. There's not a cloud in the sky."

"Delights of a stationary high," I answered.

"I know. You wish there was more of a breeze. Relax. Enjoy this."

"Okay." I turned on the autopilot and went over to sit next to her. She pulled her knees back to make room for me and then she laid them on my lap after I sat down.

"Do you like being married?" She asked.

"What? Do I like being married?"

"Well, do you?"

"I do, to you."

"You had better say that. But, no, I'm asking something else. Do you like being married? Living with someone day in and day out. You know, the farts and burps test."

"Given my singular experience of marriage, and given my previous answer, I would have to say I like it very much."

"You're being difficult. Let me ask it a different way. When I die, do you want to be a celibate bachelor for the rest of your life, do you want to have multiple girlfriends and spread your wit and sexual charm among many ladies, or do you want to remarry?"

I hated these 'after I die' conversations. "I have no idea, and I have no desire to think about it."

"Well, I do. I think you will be happier being married. So, I want you to marry someone vivacious, ten years younger than you are, a widow herself, who had a good marriage, has some kids and grandkids, minimal baggage, and is an absolute dervish in bed."

"Jesus, Hannah."

"But above all, she has to love you and take care of you until the day you die—the way I was supposed to. That's why she has to be ten years younger. I want you to live a long time. "Hannah was not describing Nan Wilder. Nan did not meet any of Hannah's criteria. I was not supposed to be having sex with Nan Wilder, married or unmarried.

Then there was Wendy. Did my granddaughter need to have her summer confused by me having a 'Yacht Club Affair?' I could imagine her overhearing the busy bodies speculating and judging. That's the last thing she needed. Trying to explain what had just happened with Nan was the last thing I needed. I wouldn't know how to, anyway. I was her grandfather, for God's sake.

Fortunately, the day after my aborted liaison with Nan, Sunday, was windy as hell. It was blowing so hard that there were white caps in the cove. There would be no races. I would not have to tell Nan I would prefer that she not crew for me. I also didn't want to talk to her about Saturday night, and how conflicted I was feeling. Other than guilt, I didn't know. I hated that I was still attracted to her. Her being attracted to me felt wonderful. Our nakedness and the limited sexual attempt had been exciting, and made me painfully aware of how much I had missed sex over the years since Hannah had gotten sick. I was a mess of conflicted feelings. I decided that when Wendy got home from her hike, I would go away for a couple of days. I'd go up to Jay, spend some time at the paper museum, and interview some more of the townspeople who had been affected by the strike. My research for the book was coming along, and I had even finished editing the work I had done years ago. I spent late Sunday morning and early afternoon making phone calls to line up interviews.

I didn't call Nan. I knew I should, but I didn't know what to say. "Thanks for last night, but I feel guilty, and I never want to do that again." What if I said, "I'm sorry, but I want to respect your marriage to Joe. Perhaps we can just be friends." I considered, "I'm just not ready, and you're still married."

Wendy arrived home from her mountain climbing expedition in the middle of the afternoon. "How was it?" I asked.

"Great. I'm exhausted, though. Didn't get much sleep. Four people in a tent is a bit much, even if it's supposed to be built for six. I'm going to take a nap unless you need me for something. I'll tell you all about it when I wake up." So much for the bubbly Wendy distraction from thinking about Nan.

Wendy was taking a nap. Maude called to tell me that she would not be coming up this evening. It was too windy to go sailing. My mind wouldn't let go of what happened Saturday night. I desperately needed a distraction. I knew reading wouldn't do it. So, I decided to do something I had been putting off. I called Ruth to talk to her about their financial situation. Both her home phone and her cell went to voicemail. I thought about going up to Judd and Pat's to 'hang out,' but they had seen me leave with Nan after the party, and I didn't want to answer any questions. I didn't want to tell them the truth, but I also didn't want to lie to them. If I diverted the conversation or told them I'd rather not talk about it, they would wonder why.

I decided to do something that I had never done. I got in my truck, drove to Bath, and went to the Spindrift Sports Bar. I wanted a drink. At the Spindrift, I could get a drink, munch on something, watch whatever baseball game was on, maybe run into somebody I knew, and be back home in time for dinner with Wendy. I left Wendy a note on the inside of the porch door and took off. Halfway there, I pulled over and sent her a text message, just to be sure.

The Spindrift is a typical New England sports pub, a U-shaped bar with two large television monitors on each wall. No matter where you sat, you could lose yourself in whatever game was on and never have to talk to anyone if you didn't want to.

When I walked in, I saw Pete Higgins sitting at the bar. Pete and I had grown up together in Georgetown. As youngsters, we had played boyhood fantasy games—cowboys and Indians, war, and in the summer, when the pond was warm enough for swimming, frogmen. We had all the equipment: cap guns, holsters, rubber knives. Eventually, we graduated to Red Ryder BB guns, with parental warnings not to shoot each other's eyes out. We went fishing, explored the coastline in my dinghy, rode our bikes up and down the hills of the island, and managed not to get hit by speeding cars. As we got older and into high school, Pete and I went our separate ways. Pete got in and out of trouble and eventually dropped out of school and joined the Marines. Everyone said the Marines would straighten Pete out, which was probably true until he was sent to Vietnam. He came back minus a lower leg and developed an addiction to alcohol that survived several stints at various treatment centers. He was a quiet drunk and held down a job as a janitor at a church in Brunswick. He lived in an apartment in the center of Bath and relied on what limited public transportation existed. No insurance company would insure him because of his tickets for driving under the influence. When I would bump into his cousin, I would always ask how Pete was doing. I don't know if Pete asked about me.

Seeing him, I decided to say hello. I walked over to where he was sitting, clapped him on the back, and said, "Pistol Pete, how the hell are you?"

He looked up and said, "Buck the fuck, what are you doing here?" It had been a long time since anyone called me 'Buck the fuck.'

"Good to see you, too."

"Oh, bullshit. Sit down and get a load off, for Christ's sake. What're you drinking?"

"Don't know yet."

"Come on. Let me buy you something."

"What's on tap?"

"They got some fancy-dancy local shit that costs too much. Sam okay?

"Sure."

The Red Sox were playing the Toronto Blue Jays at Fenway. We watched during the innings and then talked between them. First, we talked about the seventeen-inning loss to the Twins. Then, we talked about how long Tom Brady could keep it up and what would happen to the Patriots this fall. Then, we started to talk about politics and Trump. We quickly realized we were on opposite sides of things when Pete began to complain about the 'damned wetbacks' invading his country."

As the game went on, we kept buying beers for one another. It was a high-scoring game, so the game and the beers went on and on. Finally, when I realized it was getting late, almost six, I said goodbye to Pete and the bartender, whom I now knew as Missy.

On the way to my truck, I realized that I had drunk more than I had in years. I didn't think too much about it. I was able to get the keys out of my pocket and into the ignition. The Spindrift and Pete had worked. I hadn't thought about Nan in hours. Now I had to concentrate on getting home. On the road, things were fine for about the first fifteen minutes. That's when a car behind me started honking. I couldn't figure out why until I looked down at my speedometer and saw I was only going twenty-five miles an hour on a stretch of road where I would usually be doing fifty. When we hit a straight stretch, the car passed me. The girl sitting in the passenger seat gave me the finger.

Somehow, I made it to Georgetown without hitting anything or anybody and without getting pulled over. I didn't want to go home and have Wendy see me this way. I went, instead, to Judd and Pat's house and pulled into their driveway, just missing their car but scraping a stone wall. Judd came to the door, having heard the screech of metal on stone. I didn't get out. I just sat there. Judd came over to my truck and knocked on the driver's side window. I opened the door and started to get out, but he stopped me. "You okay?" he asked.

"No, I'm drunk."

He took a minute to let what I had said sink in. "Okay. Let's get you into the house. You sure the truck is in park?" I looked. It was.

I managed to get into the house without tripping or falling. Pat had come to the door and watched me wobble towards the house. Judd said, "He's had a bit to drink."

"I'll start some coffee," Pat said. "Dinner's almost ready. I'll bet he hasn't eaten."

"Probably not."

I said, "Wendy's home. I can't go there. She can't see me like this. Rachel…"

Judd turned to Pat, "Rina home yet?"

"No, she just called to say she's on the way."

"Call her and tell her to pick Wendy up. She's home. Tell Rina I'm treating them both to dinner at Five I, and I'll pay her back later."

"She'll think that's weird."

"Yeah, but she'll live with it. Tell her Mike's having dinner with us."

"Okay."

Slowly, with coffee and food, I returned to some resemblance of the self I was familiar with. Unfortunately, my head did not like what I had done to it, and the Tylenol Pat gave me was barely keeping up. I told Judd and Pat about Nan, my confusion about it, my trip to Spindrift, and my drinking with Pete. When I told them about what Hannah had said to me, Pat said, "She was serious, Mike. She wanted me to be on the lookout. She told me to find someone good enough for you. Although, to be honest, I haven't done a very good job."

"Any job," Judd said.

"True enough," Pat said.

After dinner, Pat said, "I will leave you two to talk. The girls are probably still down at Five I. I'm going to try to catch them for ice cream."

After she left, Judd said, "You know, if you wanted to get wasted watching a ball game, you could have called me and done that here."

"I didn't want to tell you and Pat about Nan. I knew what you'd think."

"Thanks a lot, buddy, for the confidence in our ability to understand."

"I'm sorry, I'm just…"

"Feeling totally fucked up right now. I get it."

"I can't believe I got drunk. With everything Wendy's been through with her mother, what the hell is wrong with me?"

"Besides being human? Look, I have known you forever. You are not a drunk. I haven't even seen you tipsy…since when? Maybe Joel's wedding. Sorry, my friend. You are not a superstar when it comes to drinking."

"Nan Wilder, Judd. What the hell was I thinking?"

"Listen, I have a bat in the garage. Why don't I go get it so you can hit yourself over the head with it? Just don't ask me to do it for you."

"Thanks a lot."

"By the way, my friend, Nan is hot for a woman in her seventies.

I made the mistake of saying that to my dear wife. She was not pleased, although she agreed that Nan has aged exceedingly well."

"She has, hasn't she?"

"Sounds to me that your male hormones have not deserted you. Have you considered that the episode with Nan may have been a gift? You now know that your libido is intact and your plumbing works, even if she had a little trouble with hers. You may need a little work on your impulse control, but hell, you haven't had much need to concern yourself with it for a long time. I'm surprised something like this didn't happen a long time ago. And, just so you know, when Nan made her appearance at the club, and we saw the shape Joe was in, Pat predicted something like this might happen."

"It was that obvious?"

"You are joking, I hope. First, she wanted to crew for you, and then she asked you to take them out on the *Redhead*? You were not alone in this."

"But what about Joe? She's still married to him."

"Yep."

"And Hannah."

"What about Hannah?"

"What she said."

"What, what she said?"

"You know."

"Oh, for God's sake, Mike. Her checklist? Hannah was being very loving, telling you she wanted you to remarry. Her criteria, though? Come on, think about it. How many women in the all of Maine, maybe New England, would fit her criteria? Maybe she did want you to remarry, but she sure set the bar so damned high that no one could reach it."

I laughed. "Yeah. I thought of that at the time."

"Good. So. What are you going to do now?"

"Avoid Nan."

"For the summer? Good luck with that."

"Well, for now at least. I'm going to go up to Jay for a few days and work on the book. Wendy knows I'm working hard on it, so…"

"You're not going to say anything to Wendy, are you?"

"No."

"And when you get back from Jay?"

"I'll have to talk to Nan."

"You know what you're going to say?"

"Haven't a clue. That's why I'm going to Jay. Who knows, maybe I'll get inspired."

"Yeah, good luck with that, too."

"I don't know. Maybe some distance and getting my head around this book and what I need to do will help."

"Can't hurt."

When I went outside, I looked at my truck. There was a long scratch along my left front fender from where I had hit Pat and Judd's wall. If Wendy asked about it, it happened in the Shaw's parking lot in Bath. The person didn't even have the decency to leave me a note. It must have been a summer person.

November 7, 1994
HOME TOWN BOY by Michael Buckley

The entire family calls him 'Cousin Carl,' and I suppose he is. I get lost with the 'seconds' and 'removeds' when it comes to the cousin relationships in my Grandmother Nel's family. I know, if I was interested, someone could tell me just where Carl fits into the Convey relational jigsaw puzzle.

Carl and his wife own a dairy farm up in Charleston. When deer season comes around, Carl invites me to join him on 'Maine Resident Day.' He calls it hunting; I call it hiking. Carl is very serious about his hunting and is usually successful. 'Resident Day' is a special day for the Maine hunting fraternity. The deer have not yet consulted the calendar and chosen to head as far away from civilization as they can get.

It helps that Carl's knowledge of the haunts of deer and his accuracy with a rifle are impressive and contribute to his success. If, as usually is the case, I am not as successful, I will beg off of additional hikes. However, I know we will receive our annual gift of a couple of frozen venison steaks come Christmas.

I enjoy my time with Cousin Carl. He is a good man, and his take on the world situation is always different from mine. As an inland person, he has developed a knack for teasing me about my coastal perspective. The price of lobster is about as foreign to him as the wholesale price of milk is to me.

On our trip last year, we stopped at the post office on the way home, and Carl bumped into a friend of his. They chatted for a few minutes on the post office porch while I waited in the car. When he got into the car, Carl told me he had been meaning to talk to this friend for a while now, and Carl was glad he had 'bumped' into him.

Bumping into people at the post office is an integral part of the social fabric of a small town. Everyone goes there, usually at least a couple of times a week. It's not just to retrieve bills, letters, pamphlets, and magazines, or pay bills and send letters. On our trip, Carl was picking up a part for his toilet that had succumbed to the ravages of age and use. Getting parts shipped in by mail is important in small communities. The local hardware store can stock just so much. Since many of these small-town post offices are housed in or next to the general store, the trips always have more than one purpose. Our next stop was to the general store for paper towels, bread, and a bottle of ketchup.

When we returned to the farm, did what we needed to do with the deer, and washed up in the kitchen, Carl told his wife and daughter that he had bumped into his friend at the post office and recounted the conversation that had taken place. Then he gave his wife the groceries.

You may not be aware of this, but if you live in a small town, the United States Postmaster General can significantly impact being able to 'bump' into your friends. In 1969 President Nixon appointed Winton Blount Postmaster. Now Blount came from a small town in Alabama but had been around Washington, D.C. for many years. Cousin Carl would call Blount, the 'ultimate insider.' Nixon gave Blount the task of changing the post office in big ways. Above all, he was told to make it more efficient.

Even though he was a small-town fellow and should have known better, Blount decided he would close down most of the small post offices across the country. The uproar was substantial, and he didn't get very far. Ever since Winton Blount, though, every Postmaster General has taken aim at small rural post offices. Some have succeeded more than others.

While efficiencies are often given as the rationale, there are other forces at work. Competitors to the post office, like UPS and FedEx, are in there egging Congressional folks on with fancy dinners and donations to campaign coffers. Carl thinks it's all about greed and another example of how urban and suburban folks have no appreciation for life in small communities. When I commented on the small size of the post office, and wondered how long until it got closed down, Carl said, "Damn it, we had a post office here before the town was even incorporated. LuAnn's been our postmistress for over thirty years; she knows everyone in town and knows everything that's going on. You want to know how someone's doing, you ask LuAnn. These asses down in Washington, they don't get it. We depend on having a post office here."

    I agree with Cousin Carl. I can't imagine not having our post office in Georgetown. At one point, we had several on the island, one in each village. Ours is as important to me as Cousin Carl's is to him. Sure, I could leave the flag up on my mailbox to let the carrier know that I had a letter to go out, but I'd rather take it down to the post office. I want to make sure I have the correct postage. Besides, I never know who I might bump into. I might even bump into someone I didn't know I wanted to bump into. That happens a lot, and I'm grateful for it.

Chapter Thirty-Four: Highway Man

In 1933 people were leaving Georgetown. The new president, Franklin Delano Roosevelt, was trying to remake the United States in response to the Depression, but he was fighting opposition hourly. Led by Robert Taft from Ohio, the Republicans in Congress did whatever they could to stop or slow things down. Eventually FDR got his new series of legislative efforts passed, but they came too late for many of the people in Georgetown.

When Will and Nell left their farm on the way to deliver Jack to his freshman year at the University of Maine, Jack pointed out that the roof of the McConnell's barn had collapsed in on itself.

Nell said, "Wasn't Billy McConnell in your class?"

"No. He was a year behind me. Dropped out when they left."

"Where'd the McConnells go?"

"I dunno."

"Barn roof fell in last winter," Will said. "They moved out two years ago, and the place is still vacant. Bank owns it now. No one wants it. Probably couldn't even give it away."

"Shame they couldn't hold on a little longer," Nell said.

"He started to drink. Couldn't take it anymore. Can't blame him. Who the hell knows when things are going to turn around?"

From the back seat, Jack said, "I'm never going to wind up like the McConnells."

"Better not," his father said.

"You won't, dear," his mother said. She turned around and looked at her son. "You'll always have your education."

Jack would later say that it was the sight of the McConnell's fallen roof that started the hunger in his gut. He would succeed; no matter what.

When Jack graduated four years later, he was optimistic. Ever so slowly, employment was coming back but Jack wanted actual work, not Civilian Conservation Corps employment, or Works Progress Administration employment. He was glad he graduated in 1937 rather than two years earlier when his brother had. When Brian graduated, there was no work. Even with his degree, he could not find anything, so he had joined the Navy. "What am I going to do here besides eat your food?" he asked his parents. Will didn't say anything. Nell answered for them both, "You know we have plenty of food."

"I was speaking metaphorically," her educated son said.

Later, when they were out of earshot of their sons, Will told Nell, "I can't believe this."

"What?"

"That's exactly what my father told his aunt and uncle when he left Carna. He didn't want them to have to feed him with a famine coming."

"It's not the same."

"Yes, it is. People left Carna; people leaving Georgetown. So now our son feels like he has to leave."

"People'll be back, and you'll be ready for them with that lumber and all."

"What if I'm wrong? What if they don't come back and try to rebuild?"

With diploma in hand, Jack had no interest in following his brother's footsteps into the armed forces. Jack wanted a job, a real job, with real money. He told his parents, "No McConnell's barn for me. Someday, I'm going to be rich."

Unlike Brian's experience, when Jack graduated, civil engineers could get jobs, and Jack got one with the Maine State Highway Department. A new law had been passed that called for a survey of all of the roads in Maine to assess their condition, traffic flow, economic benefits to the communities they passed through, and anything else that would help Maine formulate a 'rational' highway system. A planning division had been created, and Jack was one of its first employees. He was thrilled to make the fifteen hundred dollars a year he was offered. He immediately went into debt. He got a loan from Kennebec Savings and Loan, and bought a brand-new Ford convertible for eight hundred and fifty dollars. It had an eighty-five horsepower V-8 engine and was painted a bright red. He loved driving it with the top down through the center of Bath. He'd drive down Commercial Street and then back up Front Street waving to people he knew. Jack Buckley had arrived.

"That car cost more than half your salary," his father pointed out.

"For now, Dad, for now. This job is 'til I get something better. You watch."

It was the first time anyone in the family had owned a new car, and it was all his. Then he rented an apartment in Augusta, the state capitol, for twenty-five dollars a month. He felt very mature. He told his younger brother, Connor, "I'm never going to be like the McConnells. I'm never going to be a victim—never. And I'm not going to start acting like one now. Don't you listen to Mom and Dad. The Depression has beaten them down. Look how Dad spends every night working on those *Phoenix* and *Treasa* models. He doesn't even listen to the news anymore. You'd better be like me or I'll break your arm. Go for the gold. I've got a good-paying job, and I make a lot more money than anyone in the family."

Brian came home on leave in mid-June. He arrived too late to attend Jack's graduation but compared to Brian's graduation, little had been made of Jack's. Jack understood. Brian was the firstborn. Brian had been the first in the family to get a college degree. Brian was also the first in the family to enlist in any branch of the armed forces. Jack knew everyone would make a big fuss over Brian; they always did. He knew Brian would march around in his uniform rather than wear civilian clothes, even when he was home on the farm.

Jack drove down from Augusta to see his brother and Brian oohed and ahhed over Jack's new Ford as he was supposed to. One warm summer evening, Jack even let Brian take the wheel of his car. They drove into Bath, and the two brothers made the loop through town. Brian had his uniform on, and people waved to him. Jack told his mother that letting Brian drive was the most profound example of brotherly love that had ever been demonstrated by anybody, at any time, in the history of the world. Connor, who had just finished his first year at Orono, was not invited along for the ride.

Nell shook her head at the interplay among her three sons and at times wondered at the lives she had brought into this world. Will didn't say much when the boys would start to tease one another or talk about their plans for the future. When he did, he expressed his concern that they didn't know what they were up against. "You'll learn soon enough," was his admonishment. The only time Will showed any excitement or enthusiasm was when the talk turned to flight.

With Brian home, there was a lot of talk about flight that weekend. The previous January, Howard Hughes had flown from Los Angeles to New York in seven hours and twenty-eight minutes. In Spain, the Nationalist and Republican pilots were fighting it out in new biplanes that were far superior to anything used in the 'War to End All Wars.' That March, Amelia Earhart had flown a new mono-wing Lockheed Electra from Oakland to Hawaii in just under sixteen hours. It seemed that speed, altitude, and endurance records were set daily.

"Biplanes are ancient history," Brian lectured to the assembled Buckleys over dinner. "All the new fighters and bombers are monoplanes. They're faster, easier to build, and have as much or more lift than a biplane. Can you imagine going up to fifteen thousand feet in that old heap out in the barn?"

"Remember, that old heap has got you where you are today,"

Will said.

"Yeah, yeah. I know, but you've got to see these new planes, Dad."

"What are you flying now? I thought you were still flying a biplane?" Jack challenged.

"Was. Not anymore. I've just been reassigned. That's why I'm home. A break before more training."

"Where are you going?" Nell asked.

"Eventually, I hope the *USS Enterprise*. It's an aircraft carrier. It was launched last year. The 'Big E.' Not commissioned yet. That comes next year, but that's where I'm headed if I get what I want. I think my chances are pretty good. I get my commission in a couple of months, and I've been first or second in all of my classes in training. Mom, the damned ship is over eight hundred feet long. Can you imagine that? That's two and a half football fields, plus some."

"Do you know what you'll be flying?" Jack asked.

"Possibly an amazing new plane, the Douglas TBD Devastator, most advanced airplane ever built. I've seen them. Torpedo bomber. Carry bombs or torpedoes—the Mark Thirteen torpedo, or up to a thousand-pound bomb. Crew of three: pilot, bombardier, and gunner. It's all metal and has a completely enclosed cockpit and the damned wings fold up so you can carry more planes on board a carrier."

"Enclosed cockpit doesn't sound like fun," Will said.

"Jesus, Dad. Who the hell wants an open cockpit at fifteen thousand feet going two hundred miles an hour? You'd freeze your 'you know whats' off in five minutes."

"I suppose."

"It carries torpedoes?" Connor asked.

"Yep. You get one torpedo in the right place, and you can sink a battleship."

"How can a plane torpedo a ship? I get how a submarine does it because it's underwater, and you can't see it, but a plane would be shot down if it got anywhere near a ship."

"Very easy little brother." Brian used his hands to explain, "You come in low, and you're coming in fairly slow to get a good shot, maybe a hundred miles an hour, and you're just off the water's surface. The ship's big guns don't go down that low. The machine guns don't have much range. You're not doing it alone. You've got a flight of five or six planes coming in from different angles. No matter which way the ship turns, it's in trouble. So, you drop your torpedoes pretty far away from the ship and get the hell out of there."

"Have you practiced this yet?" Connor asked.

"No. Not yet, but I will."

"How certain is all this?" Nell asked.

"It's the Navy, Mom. Who knows? I do know I'm off to Norfolk."

As soon as Brian left, Jack returned to Augusta, his apartment, his job, and his pursuit—he was sure he would be successful—of the blond clerk at the A&P down the street from where he lived.

None of his friends, and certainly not his family, would have called Jack promiscuous. Instead, they said he was a 'ladies' man.' Unlike his two brothers and his father, Jack was a throwback to the genetic pool that had given his grandfather Jamie his six-foot-two inches height. Jack had black hair, blue eyes, a thin Errol Flynn mustache, a job, and a new car—a convertible. This combination, plus his outgoing 'I can do anything' personality, made him wildly attractive to the young women in Maine's small towns and cities emerging from the Depression. Young, eligible men with money in their pockets were rare.

His job planning the future of Maine highways took him all over the state. Every place he went, he had four goals. One was to do a far better job than any of his peers so he would get noticed by his superiors. The second was to meet as many people as possible who might someday hire him as a freelance engineer. The third was to be charming and avoid any conflicts. The fourth was to have a girlfriend in every town he visited so he would not have to spend any evenings alone while he was on the road. He told Connor, "Those Navy idiots brag about having a girl in every port, but they don't spend enough time there to do anything about it. I do. And the state is paying me to do it. This job is amazing."

Aroostook County in Maine is the largest county east of the Mississippi, and is larger than either Rhode Island, Delaware, or Connecticut in landmass. Referred to simply as 'The County,' it borders Canada and is as Acadian French in language and culture as it is American. Close to ninety thousand people lived there in the nineteen-thirties, and they didn't travel much because they couldn't. What roads existed were meager and carved out of forests, logging roads for the most part. Houlton, Caribou, and Presque Isle were the only towns of any size, and it took forever to get there from Augusta. But at least they were relatively close together, and, once there, Jack could get to all three in one day if he had to. These three towns were important to the state. They were the trade and shipping centers for the Aroostook valley. Potatoes and timber dominated life. Both had to be transported, though, and that meant roads. Jack spent most of the summer of 1937 planning them.

He didn't mind. There was a good bar in Houlton with decent food, and most importantly, June lived in Houlton. June was a few years older than Jack, had already been married and divorced, was endowed with large breasts, and possessed a very adventuresome attitude towards sex—all attributes that Jack found endearing. June had no interest in committing to anything long-term, was primarily interested in having fun, and liked Jack's car. In addition, Jack liked to dance, and there were not many men in Houlton who did.

June's father had worked on the construction of the United States Army's Houlton Radio Intelligence Station during WWI and, later, on the building of the AT&T Transoceanic Receiver Station. He had become an avid consumer of the 'news' because of these endeavors. He also became fascinated with radio and radio waves. By 1937, when Jack first met him, he had an elaborate short wave radio installation in the attic of the Eaton home and was nightly communicating with other amateurs in the United Kingdom and throughout Europe.

June had her own trailer in her parent's back yard, a remnant of her failed marriage, and that was how Jack came to meet June's parents, Roy and May Eaton—June's older sister was April Eaton. June's ex-husband was in prison for armed robbery, so June's parents were delighted June was spending time with Jack, despite her protestations that she would never get married again. Jack was a 'college boy,' and there were only a couple of them in all of Aroostook County in 1937. Jack was also polite. "He's so well-mannered," June's mother told people when she was asked about the man June was seeing.

In addition to his activities with June, Jack looked forward to May's home-cooked meals and never hesitated to accept an invitation to dine. By the end of July, Jack was a fixture at both the Eaton home and June's trailer whenever he was in the area.

On one of these evenings, July 7th, Roy came down from his perch in the attic and announced, "We're going to be at war with Japan. Mark my words."

"Roy, what are you talking about?" May asked.

"Japan. You'll see."

"See what?" June asked.

"See that I'm right."

"Roosevelt said we wouldn't get involved in Europe. So why on earth would we go to war with Japan?" Jack asked.

Roy, the newsman, was specific. "The Japanese now have fifteen thousand men in China; they just broke a treaty and launched an attack at the Marco Polo Bridge. Watch this blow up. Going to be just like Manchuria."

June said, "Who cares? Come on, Jack, let's go."

"Wait a minute. I'm curious."

Roy said, "Come have a listen. I've got an extra set of earphones. No one else in this family gives a damn."

The story about the Marco Polo Bridge wasn't covered in the newspaper the next day. Nor was it on the news in June's trailer. Jack realized that Roy, with his short-wave radio, was learning things that the American public was not privy to. June soon became distressed that her father had found a 'news buddy;' Jack was beginning to spend more time in the attic with her father than in the trailer with her.

June started to withdraw her invitations, but Jack did not mind. While not as experienced as June, the First National clerk in Augusta, Willa, was learning fast with Jack's coaching. Jack did not feel deprived.

Jack's work was finished in the three-town area by the middle of August. By then he had his own amateur radio system operating from his apartment in Augusta, and he had mastered Morse code. June visited him once but was not fascinated with the radio operation he had created. Evidence of another woman having spent time in his apartment bothered her. Jack reminded her that she was the one who did not want a committed relationship. He discovered that, in June's mind. the lack of commitment to a relationship only applied to her. She chose not to visit him again.

While his relationship with June was over, Jack communicated with her father frequently and through him increased his knowledge of and participation in the short-wave world. On weekends when he would go home, Jack became a source of information for his parents and Connor about what was taking place in the world. He also found a receptive audience at work where he told people what was happening a day or two before it hit the newspapers.

Jack's work shifted towards Portland, where he found a suitable replacement for June. Esther, the replacement, was, according to her, 'somewhat married.' Not able to find work in Portland, her husband was a logger up in The County.

Jack was successfully meeting all of his objectives. When he worked, he worked hard and smart. As a result, he gained the reputation within the department as someone who was both dependable and capable. He avoided disputes with his bosses and co-workers—Jack Buckley was easy to get along with. And in the places he worked, whether for a day or a week, the 'important highway people' in the town or city knew who he was. There were women in place whenever he needed them. By his own assessment, Jack Buckley was doing well.

Chapter Thirty-Five: Peg O' My Heart

Jack worked in a department whose purpose was to plan a road system for the state of Maine. The department had to work with multiple communities and 'coordinate' with their departments of public works. Jack detested the word 'coordinate.' To him, 'coordinate' came to mean too many meetings with too little action. There were a lot of meetings. Everywhere he went, he was either leading or attending a meeting. The mandate to 'obtain local input' required sitting down with whatever collection of local political aspirants were willing to give up an evening of their time. Usually, they met in some struggling restaurant with mediocre food. Each one claimed to have 'award winning' clam chowder. Jack's job was to ask questions and take notes as the 'locals' made their cases for routes, the width of roads, and construction schedules— always favorable to their own personal property. Road placement could mean the success or failure of a business. Occasionally, the needs of the entire town or area were a consideration. Jack's job was to encourage movement in that direction.

Jack was truly curious and engaged for the first few months, but the local priority pleas began to all sound the same. He soon became bored with 'planning and coordinating.' He wanted action. He wanted to start building something, anything. "I'm an engineer, for god's sake," he complained to his parents. "I didn't go to school to learn how to talk to people and take notes." Charming the young women he met was one thing, but having to charm their uncles, cousins, and fathers was something else. He told his brother, Connor, "These people are all related to each other in some of these towns. There are only two or three last names in the entire god-forsaken place. I don't know how they keep who is who straight. I'm supposed to take notes and make sure I've got everyone's name right. It's ridiculous. Who are these people?"

His sanctuary from the endless meetings was his apartment in Augusta with its radio equipment. When he was home, he would spend hours communicating with people in England and Europe. He knew about German plans to take over Austria from an amateur radio operator in England. This operator had a cousin in Switzerland who had a trucking business. The cousin went back and forth between Germany and Austria every couple of days and saw and heard things he reported back to England.

Jack's penchant for the news increased the more time he spent time with his fellow radio operators in Europe. He even replaced the radio in his car with a newer, more powerful one so he could listen to the news as he traveled from town to town.

From his radio friends, he learned about the magazine *Flight* that was published in England. He subscribed. Following every advancement in flight became a passion, and an escape. When 'Wrong Way Corrigan' flew to Ireland rather than California, Jack told his father and Connor that he was certain Corrigan had not done it by mistake. "He's something else," he told them. "Damned Bureau of Air Commerce told him his plane wasn't 'airworthy.' He showed them." Jack told Connor, "Someday I will fly across the Atlantic, or maybe the Pacific, or both." Connor's response was that of the unimpressed younger brother, "Yeah. Sure."

As much as he hated the meetings, Jack knew that coordination with the other New England states was becoming more critical. Except for Vermont, the states shared a coastline, and the ancient Route 1 was becoming heavily traveled and in terrible disrepair. An increasing number of trucks and cars carried people and goods up and down the coastal corridor. Even with railroads, once cargo was unloaded at a freight yard, it had to be delivered to its destination.

Connecticut, Rhode Island, Massachusetts, New Hampshire, and Maine shared this coastal corridor. Because of population density, railroad connections, and the harbor, Boston had developed as the transportation hub for New England. In many places, Route 1 was even called 'The Boston Post Road.' Consequently, when the states met to coordinate, Boston was the natural place to gather.

On September 21st, 1938, the worst hurricane in memory devastated Long Island and marched across Long Island Sound, creating damage in every New England state. Even Maine, usually safe from hurricanes, experienced tidal surges and high winds that upended boats and destroyed roads. In Montpelier, Vermont, one hundred and twenty miles from the Atlantic, there was salt spray on people's windows. In New Hampshire, the wind on top of Mount Washington registered one hundred and sixty-three miles an hour. In Massachusetts, two-thirds of the fishing fleet was beaten to death, and cities along the coast were under eight feet of water. In Gloucester, a fifty-foot wave hit the coast. Connecticut homes were swept into the sea, and one hundred people died.

A week after the hurricane, a meeting was called in Boston of all New England Highway Departments to assess the damage and develop recovery plans. Coordination of repair efforts where roads went from one state into another was high on the agenda. Jack was one of two planning people from Maine dispatched to the meeting.

Jack took the train from Brunswick to North Station in Boston the evening before the meeting began. He traveled with his workmate, friend, and the other delegate from Maine, Trevor Benoit, and the two of them shared a room at the Parker House hotel. The night they arrived, they joined other meeting attendees at the hotel bar after dinner. Later they went with the other state representatives to the host's suite for additional discussion and libations until early morning.

The meeting invitation had said the Massachusetts Department of Public Works would conduct the meeting in one of the larger conference rooms at the State House. Jack had been to Boston a couple of times and had seen the gold-domed building from the outside. Now, the young engineer from Maine felt powerful entering the building. Jack Buckley, of Georgetown, Maine, was there to participate in a high-level meeting. His edginess about meetings was suppressed by the grandeur of the building, the importance of the gathering, and his role in representing Maine. It was heady stuff for a twenty-three-year-old who had been raised on a sheep farm.

He arrived early to find his way to the correct conference room. Trevor, his head suffering from over indulging the previous evening, said he would join him later. There were very few people walking the corridors of the State House that early in the morning, and no one he met knew about the meeting or where it was to take place. The invitation said there would be signs giving directions. Seeing none, he assumed he had arrived before they had been put up. Finally, he found someone who had a suggestion about where the meeting might be. Following the directions that were offered, he found his way to a corridor with numbered rooms. Paying attention to the numbers on the doors, he bumped into a young woman who was carrying a large pile of folders in addition to her handbag. The woman lost control of her burden. As folders and papers spilled on to the floor, Jack noticed how short she was, and how she was dressed—white gloves, black hat, and a green coat.

Simultaneously, the two of them dropped to the floor to collect the folders, files, and contents of her handbag that were scattered across the corridor. Documents had escaped their files and were strewn all over the floor. "Oh, shite," the young woman said. She shouted at Jack, "Don't touch them. Just let them be. I'll do it. You don't know what goes where."

"I'm so sorry," Jack said. "Here, please let me help."

"You can't help. Just leave them where they are. You be going on about your own business." Her brogue was thick.

Jack stood up and nodded towards the door. "I think I'm where

I'm supposed to be."

She looked up, a face of freckles, blue eyes, framed with red hair. "Is it Hurricane Highway Recovery Planning?" she asked.

"Yes, I'm Jack Buckley from Maine." He reached his hand down to her.

She looked up, ignored his outstretched hand, and said, "This is the room. Just go in and sit down. You're early. Meeting won't start for an hour."

"I know. You sure I can't help you?"

"No, you can't. You done enough already." She looked down again and started putting papers back into files and files back into their folders, one folder for each state.

"Do you always wear white gloves to work?" Jack asked, not knowing what else to say.

"Is there something wrong with that?" she asked, not looking up.

"No, I was just wondering."

"Can't you see I'm trying to concentrate?"

"Yes, I'm sorry, Miss…?"

"Miss can't you see I'm very busy."

"Sorry." The Buckley charm was not working. Jack was not at all used to that. He didn't move. He just stood and watched her.

"Will you go inside and stop your staring?"

He did as he was told.

An hour later, the meeting got underway. When Jack received his name tag and folder from the young redheaded woman, he said, "Thank you," and added, "Again, I'm sorry I bumped into you."

She answered, "As well ye should be." She smiled when she said it, and Jack relaxed. He watched her as she completed her distribution tasks.

A man in a dark suit rose and said, "I want to welcome all of you to Boston. My name is Francis E. Kelly, and I have the privilege of being the Lieutenant Governor of the Commonwealth of

Massachusetts. Unfortunately, Governor Hurley can't be with us today to welcome you. He sends his regrets. He's in New Bedford, meeting with representatives of the fishing fleet. As you may know, the fleet was completely destroyed by the hurricane. So, without further adieu, let me introduce John Beal, the Commonwealth's Commissioner of Public Works."

Kelly left the room, and Beal laid out the agenda for the two days they would meet. When he was done, he said, "If you need anything while you're here, don't hesitate to ask my very talented and able secretary, Miss Peggy O'Neil. Mind your manners, though. Peggy's a graduate of Katherine Gibbs, and part of her training included handling louts like us." The men sitting around the conference table gave a polite chuckle.

So, Peggy O'Neil was her name. Jack blanked out the comment about her handling louts. He was sure the warning did not apply to him. His interest in Miss Peggy O'Neil grew the more he looked at her. He wondered what reasons he could create to come to Boston in the future. It was an easy train ride from Brunswick.

When the first day ended, Jack waited until everyone had left before he approached her. "You arrive early and leave late, do you?" She asked when he walked up to her.

"Peggy, ah Miss O'Neil, I was wondering if it might be possible that you were free for dinner this evening?" Jack asked.

"My, my, Mr. Buckley. You should be knowing it would not be appropriate for me to have dinner with someone who is attending the conference."

"Why not?" Jack asked. Her talk about what was appropriate surprised him. His question was a challenge, explain yourself."

He felt her answer to was rehearsed, "I prefer to keep my social and professional lives separate. I'm sure you can see the benefit of that."

He didn't know what to say. The best he could manage was a

weak, "Well, I hope you change your mind."

It took four trips to Boston in late November and early December along with multiple invitations, all without success, before he believed that she was serious about not mixing the two. Finally, after her last refusal, he called her at work and said, "I would like to get to know you. If I come to Boston just to see you, like on a weekend, would that be okay? No business involved."

"I'm not sure that would matter."

"Jesus," he said. "Do I have to quit my job for you to see me outside of work?"

"No, you don't have to be quitting your job. But, Mr. Buckley, did it ever occur to you that I might be seeing someone already, or it might just be you?"

"I. I…" Jack stammered.

"It never crossed your mind, now, did it?"

It hadn't. When he told Trevor over a post-work beer, Trevor laughed, "So, the magnificent Jack Buckley, the gift to all women from here to Canada and back, just had his balls handed to him by a wee Irish lass."

"Fuck you, Trev."

"Ah, poor Jack. She's gotten your number, hasn't she?"

"Go to hell, you damned Canuck."

"Wow. It's that bad?"

"Shut up. I don't know. There's something about her."

"Besides the fact that she won't give you the time of day, and you can't stand it? Yeah, sure."

"No, really, Trev. I've never reacted this way before."

"Really? Let me ask you, though. How would you feel if she agreed to see you? You would have won."

"Nah. It's not that."

"So, what the hell is it?"

"Just a feeling."

When Jack went home to Georgetown for Christmas, he told his mother about meeting the 'woman I'm going to marry.' He told his mother about his unsuccessful attempts to get to know Peggy O'Neil. "I keep trying and she keeps saying, 'no.' I don't know what to do."

"Why don't you try writing her a letter? Tell her about yourself. You know how to reach her at the State House. What do you have to lose?"

Jack wrote his letter to 'Miss O'Neil' the day after Christmas and asked his mother to edit it before he sent it. It took him three drafts before his mother approved. It was simple, informative, almost Victorian in tone. He finally mailed it on New Year's Eve. He wondered if she would reply or think he had lost his mind.

Two weeks later, when he arrived home after a rare three-day trip up the coast to Machias, he nonchalantly collected his bills and flyers and was astonished to see a letter from a Miss Peggy O'Neil.

Dear Mr. Buckley,

I was surprised to receive your letter of December 28. I was intrigued by your background and the similarity to my early years. Like you, I was raised on a sheep farm. My home is in a village called Brinlack. That is in the town of Gweedore, which is at the foot of Mount Errigal in County Donegal, Ireland. The real name of Gweedore is Gaoth Dobhair, but I doubt that you could pronounce it correctly without coaching. As you can guess, I speak Irish and English. Unfortunately, the pronunciation of the Irish language is difficult for most English speakers.

I have never been to Carna, where your grandfather lived when he was young, but I have been to Galway, which is not that distant. I have heard the stories of the "Little Famine" from members of my own family. It must have been a terrible experience for your grandfather. But it appears your family has done well in America.

You are fortunate to have received the education you have. It is difficult for a woman to become educated beyond the primary grades in Ireland. I was blessed to receive tutoring from a wonderful lady, a former school teacher from Dublin who had come to Gweedore to care for her mother and father.

I have only been in America for two years. I came to Boston to help my brother's wife when she gave birth to twins. After my sister-in-law felt comfortable with the twins and did not need me on a full-time basis, I enrolled at the Katherine Gibbs Institute. I found it to be a most rewarding experience. I have now decided to stay in Boston for a year or two, and I hope to see more of America.

If you have the time to drop me a note, I will enjoy hearing from you,

Sincerely yours,
Peggy

(O'Neil)

Two letter exchanges later, Peggy wrote: *"I asked my superior, Mr. Beal, if he thought it would be appropriate for you and me to have dinner together if you were in Boston. He said he thought it would be fine since you didn't work for the Commonwealth of Massachusetts. So, if you do plan to be in Boston at some point and would still like to do that, I would be pleased to accompany you to dinner.*

Dinners began in Boston towards the end of January. Jack started making weekend day trips to Boston in February. In March, their families met. In April, Peg came to Georgetown to help with lambing. In August of 1939, Miss Margaret Mary O'Neil and John Patrick Buckley had their intentions to marry published in their respective parishes in Bath, Maine, and Boston, Massachusetts. When his father wondered if they weren't moving too fast, Jack said, "Dad, I don't want to wait, neither does Peg. We may be at war with what's going on in Europe, and we both want to be together now. Who knows what's going to happen? We can't count on anything."

"Roosevelt's not going to let us get involved."

"That's not what I'm hearing. When I'm on the radio, I hear stories. People have no idea what's going on."

"Like what?"

"Roosevelt's already getting planes to the Brits."

"No, he's not. He can't. It's against the law. The Neutrality Act."

"Well, he's doing it. He flies them up to Houlton and has them pulled across the border into Canada by horses."

"How the hell do you know that? It's crap."

"No. It's happening. Heard about it from my friends up there."

"Hasn't been on the news."

"My short wave."

"You and your damned radio."

"It's going to happen, Dad. Roosevelt's not going to have a choice. *Time* magazine already made Hitler their 'Man of the Year.' He's going to take over all of Europe. Have you been reading the translation of his speeches? He's crazy. Roosevelt's not going to have a choice."

"This is why you want to get married, now?"

"Yes."

"Does Peggy feel the same way?"

"She does."

"Oh, Jack. You're both so young. I hope to hell you know what you're doing."

"We're about the same age, you were."

"Yes, but…"

"Dad. Come on. You know I'm right."

Chapter Thirty-Six: War

When she and her husband returned from their honeymoon on Cape Cod in June of 1939, Margaret Mary Buckley moved to Augusta, Maine. Her husband's radio equipment was moved from the dining room table to a corner of their parlor. Because of her training and recommendations from her superiors in Boston, Peg quickly got a position with the office of the mayor. Jack now spent as little time traveling about Maine as he could without irritating his boss. The newlyweds took weekend trips to the farmhouse in Georgetown or the O'Neil's in Boston. When the warm weather finally arrived in July, Tír na nÓg became their destination.

That summer, everyone was talking about the appropriateness of the Roosevelts serving the king and queen of England hot dogs and beer when the royalty visited the President and his wife at their home at Hyde Park. The New York Times reported that the queen had to be taught how to eat a hot dog. Nell Buckley was appalled. Will thought it was funny. The O'Neils suggested arsenic would have been a lovely condiment for the 'Royals.'

Every evening, Peg and Jack were glued to the radio. Talk of war was constant. They listened to Churchill:

If my words could reach Herr Hitler, as indeed they may, I would say to him – pause; consider well before you take a plunge into the terrible unknown. Consider whether your life's work – which may even now be famous in the eyes of history – in raising Germany from frustration and defeat to a point where all the world is waiting for her actions, consider whether all this may not be irretrievably cast away.

Jack would read the newspaper to Peg every morning while she made breakfast. She didn't understand Jack's passionate response when Germans started passing laws that Jews couldn't buy real estate, stocks, or bonds. Jack told her, "They've lost their minds. They want Jews to give banks a list of everything they own. They're even keeping Jews from selling their valuables. Their own things, for God's sake." Then, on one of their trips to Tír na nÓg, Peg was introduced to the neighbors, the Fishmans. It was the first time in her life she had sat down to a meal with a Jew. She was anxious at first. All of the negative stories about Jews she had been brought up with in Ireland were challenged as the two families told jokes, talked politics, and broke bread together. That night Jack said, "Were you okay at dinner? You seemed nervous."

"I was, would you believe? Especially at first. The Fishman's just seemed so…"

"So what?"

"So normal."

"What did you expect?"

It was a long discussion that night. Was it the Jews or the Romans responsible for the crucifixion of Jesus? Who cared? "The Fishman's are good people," Jack said. Harmony was disrupted, regained, and disrupted again as the Irish Catholic immigrant encountered her a-religious husband whose family had Jewish friends come to their home for dinner.

Before the young couple's arrival at Tír na nÓg for the Fourth of July Weekend, Nell asked Will, "Can we not talk about politics? All you and Jack do is argue about whether Roosevelt will get us into war. The two of you wind up shouting at one another, and you're both so damned pig-headed…"

"I don't shout; he does."

"Jesus, Mary, and Joseph. You should hear yourself. You both do. The last time they were here, Connor had to come in from the boat because he could hear you all the way out at the mooring. He was worried something was wrong. Peg's brother and her family are coming this weekend, and I want them to have a good time. No politics. You hear me?"

"Oh, for God's sake. What the hell are we going to talk about? What else is there to talk about? The weather?"

"Yes, the weather."

"Maybe we can talk about what Ireland will do when full-out war comes in Europe."

"Don't you dare."

Peg's brother Tommy and his wife, Maeve, came for the long weekend. The two-year-old twins remained behind with Maeve's mother and father. In spite of Peg's wishes, everyone talked about politics and the situation in Europe and the Pacific. When Will pressed them, the O'Neils opined that Ireland would remain neutral unless Germany attacked the Republic. Tommy said, "After what we've been through getting the fuckin' Brits off our backs, there's no way in hell we're going to turn around and become a Nazi campground." Jack pointed out that the Prime Minister, Éamon de Valera, said Ireland would be neutral. Tommy responded, "Yeah, we'll see if Éamon will hold to that if Hitler decides to come ashore and use Ireland as a base for going after the Brits. The IRA'll be back at it. Gettin' rid of Fritz'll be much easier than getting rid of the Brits, don't you know."

With the presence of the O'Neils, Jack and Will contained their volume for the weekend. Everyone went clamming on Sagadahoc Bay, and Tommy helped Jack and Connor select lobsters from the Buckley's lobster car that was tied to their dock. "You call them 'bugs,' do you?" Tommy asked.

"Yep. That's what they look like, and they got the same nervous system as a grasshopper," Will explained. "They get hungry enough; they'll eat their young."

The weekend went well, subdued and polite until the evening news reported that Neville Chamberlain, England's Prime Minister, told the House of Commons on Sunday, July 3rd, that a German military build-up had taken place in Danzig in defiance of the Treaty of Versailles. Nell excused herself and went to bed early, as did Peg and Maeve. Jack, Will, and Tommy stayed up talking until the early hours of the morning.

A year later, Peg would swear that it was on the 4th of July that she and Jack conceived their first child. "I wanted an April baby," Peg said. "There was no way I was going through a hot summer big as a bloody house." She had been careful to monitor her fertility cycles, so when she missed two periods, she announced to Jack that they had done it. Her planning had paid off. "I told you it would work," she told him. "Listen to me, John Patrick Buckley. I know what I'm about with this sex stuff. It will be a boy, too, now won't it?"

Nell thought that was hysterical. "So, you planned for it to be a boy?"

"I did, didn't I."

On the day Peg told Jack, "This is the day. We're going to bed early," Franklin Delano Roosevelt gave an Independence Day address to the country:

> *The United States will never survive as a happy and fertile oasis of liberty surrounded by a cruel desert of dictatorship. And so it is that when we repeat the great pledge to our country and to our flag, it must be our deep conviction that we pledge as well our work, our will, and, if it be necessary, our very lives.*

Peg wanted a child. She did not want Jack to go to war. She saw these as interdependent. If Jack had a child and America went to war, surely he would not be drafted. She worried, though, about the way he had been talking. The first of the American Volunteer Group had arrived in China with their Curtiss P-40 fighter planes. They would fly on behalf of the Chinese Government. United States retired General Claire Lee Chennault and his *Flying Tigers* were portrayed in the press as heroes, and Jack told Peg all about the group and its airplanes.

Peg's worry increased when Brian wrote home about the movie *Dive Bomber*. Many scenes of the movie had been shot on the *USS Enterprise* and Brian wrote home that you could see him in some of the scenes that were filmed on the carrier's deck. In addition, Brian reported that his squadron had done several flyovers for the movie. When the movie was released in late summer, everyone in the family went to see it. Will told every friend he had that they had to go see 'The movie our Brian is in.' Will and Nell were not happy when they learned that the movie was about problems pilots were having with altitude sickness and blacking out from 'G' forces when the dive bombers pulled out of their dives. Jack tried to assure his parents that Brian was not flying a dive bomber but a torpedo plane. "It's okay. They're nothing like dive bombers. They're much safer," Jack told them.

Peg was five months pregnant when the Japanese attacked Pearl Harbor. When Jack came home to the apartment in Augusta on December 8th, Peg informed him that Congress had declared war on Japan. Jack left their apartment and said he'd be back in a few minutes.

"Where are you going?" Peg asked.

"I need to think about something. Don't worry. I just need to go for a quick walk."

When he returned, Peg said, "Where'd you go? You're scaring me."

"I just needed to think something through."

"What, on earth?"

"I'm going to enlist in the Navy."

"No you're not. War's for single men like Brian and Connor and your friend Trevor. Don't you even be thinking about enlisting. You're going to be a father. War's not for fathers."

"It is for this one. What kind of father and husband would I be if I let others do the fighting for my family?"

"A live one."

"Don't you get it? They just attacked us. Pearl Harbor's part of the United States. Between the Japs and the Krauts, they want to destroy us. You know that, damn it. We have to stop them before they get to the mainland. The Krauts are already sinking ships off the coast of Maine, for christ's sake, Peg. Any day now you'll see ships burning at the mouth of the Kennebec, and next thing you know, they'll be landing. You watch, we'll be at war with Germany by the end of the week."

It didn't take that long. Two days later, Congress declared war on Germany and Italy. Jack, Connor, and Trevor enlisted in the Navy on December 15th along with hundreds of thousands of young American men. Will had already returned to work at the Bath Iron Works. Now, Nell joined him.

Jack and Connor left for basic training. Peg quit her job in Augusta and moved in with the Buckleys in their farmhouse. With Will and Nell now working in the shipyard, Peg said she'd manage the flock as long as possible. She told Will, "I've done this before. You're down to only sixty now, and that's nothing. You got two good working dogs. I'll need help with lambing 'cause they be dropping and my baby arriving at the same time when spring comes."

She didn't say anything to anyone, but she wondered about her decision to become pregnant. She wondered about the irrational thinking of her husband to enlist when he was about to become a father. She wondered who these people were, these people she was now living with. She wondered if she wouldn't be better off returning to Ireland and her family in Brinlack. She didn't know how on earth she would get there. The North Atlantic was dangerous. The German submarines were treating all ships as hostile. Peg cried at night, wondering how she could have been so stupid to think Jack would never enlist.

One night after dinner, when Nell went upstairs to get a book, she heard Peg crying when she. She knocked on Peg's bedroom door, Jack and Connor's old room. "Come down and sit with us, Peg. Crying by yourself isn't good for you."

"But haven't I created an awful mess?"

"Why on earth do you say that? What have you done?"

"I want this baby. I do, but I thought it would also keep him out of the war. I don't understand you Yanks and the way you think." She started crying again, "I'm sorry."

Nell didn't say anything at first. She just sat on the edge of the bed and looked at Peg. When she spoke, there was an edge in her voice. "We'll be downstairs. *Jack Benny* will be coming on. I think you could use a good laugh."

Peg stayed in her room until she heard Nell come up to bed. The radio was still on, so she knew Will was still downstairs. She knocked on Nell and Will's bedroom door. Nell told her to come in. Peg was crying quietly. "Are you mad at me?"

Nell pointed to the bed. "Come sit." Peg did so. "Peggy, I have three sons who have enlisted. How do you think I feel? I'm scared stiff. I'm petrified I won't see any of them again, ever, or they'll be wounded. I've imagined every worst nightmare possible. I'm sorry I was short with you before. I haven't permitted myself to cry, and here you are going about doing enough crying for both of us. I don't know what you and Jack talked about, having a baby now and all, but I could have told you it would never have stopped him from enlisting if we were attacked."

"I know. I'm being a terrible…"

"No, you're not. You're just scared like the rest of us."

"I don't know what to do."

"Neither do I. I've got to keep busy and somehow feel like I'm supporting them, so I've gone back to the shipyard. Same with Will. I don't know what else to do. We have to do what we can. I don't see any other choice."

Peg started to cry again. "I don't want to support him. I want him home. I don't want to have this baby alone."

"Of course, you don't, and you won't. Will and I will make sure of that." Nell put her arms around Peg. Peg continued to cry. She didn't notice that Nell was crying.

After Jack learned the history of the Navy, how to salute, march, and wear his uniform, he went to Pensacola, Florida, the 'Annapolis of the Air.' He was on his way to becoming an 'officer and a gentleman.' At the end of his first week, he wrote his wife:

> *Pensacola is insane. I've never seen anything like it. There are so many of us here to be trained that they have six of us squeezed into dormitory rooms built for two. We have to line up and wait for everything like simulators, planes, even food. I'm one of the only guys who knows how to fly. Looking at the training we are getting, I'll be surprised if most of them don't crash before they get out of here. Too many people, and it's all going too fast. They're trying to turn out 1,000 pilots every month. They're nuts.*
>
> *Brian was right about the Stearman. She's sweet. I wish they let me fly it the way I'd like to, but everything here is by the book, and it is*

> boring. I have my eye on the PBYs. I always said I wanted to fly across the Atlantic. Brian can stay on a carrier as long as he wants. Better food ashore.
>
> More later.
>
> Love, Jack

Jack knew Brian was on the *Enterprise* when the Japanese attacked Pearl Harbor. Fortunately, the ship was at sea, but it was close enough to Pearl for Brian's squadron of Devastators to go in search of the Japanese ships. They found none. That was not true of all of the *Enterprise*'s planes. Several scout bombers headed for Pearl and ran into the Japanese attack. Seven were shot down by Japanese fighter planes or friendly fire from Pearl. When Brian's torpedo squadron returned to the ship, they couldn't believe the stories of what happened at Pearl and to their shipmates. Brian wrote home that these were men he knew. One was a bunkmate from training. It was the first time he had lost a friend. It was also the first time he considered that he might actually be killed.

The *Enterprise* refueled at Pearl and returned to sea with the task of protecting the other Hawaiian Islands. Then they went to Samoa. The Japanese were now conquering island after island with little resistance. While Jack was learning to be an officer and a gentleman, Brian and his squadron onboard the *Enterprise* saw battle in the Marshall Islands, Wake, and tiny Minami-Tori-shima. Nothing was decisive in any of these encounters. More pilots were lost. The Enterprise received minor damage, and in April, the ship returned to Pearl for some repairs and alterations.

In Pensacola, Jack and his fellow trainees heard no good news. They wanted to get into the action. They wanted to do something. But their commanders kept telling them that they weren't ready. In the Atlantic, German submarines were in control. Ships were torpedoed leaving New York Harbor. On land, the German army was unstoppable. Germany controlled not only most of Europe but the seas around it. In the Pacific, the Japanese conducted one successful invasion after another. Bataan, Dutch East Indies, Burma, Rabaul, and Singapore fell. Malaya was abandoned. At Pensacola the "We'll whip them in a week" talk ended. Jack's letters home got darker and darker as his training progressed.

Jack was in a very dark mood when Will called him on April 5th to tell Jack that he had a son. He couldn't get home. He felt trapped on the base. He felt trapped by the war. Maybe Peg had been right. Back in Georgetown, Peg's sister-in-law, Maeve, came up from Boston to be with her. Maeve brought the twins with her and the three of them stayed for a month. Tommy came up on weekends and helped with the lambing and farm chores.

Will and Nell moved into the Convey house in Bath to be closer to their work at the shipyard. Nell had been assigned to work on the destroyer Strong. Will was working in the purchasing department, hunting for the materials that would eventually lead to the launch of eighty-three destroyers. Six days a week, twelve hours a day, was hard on them, but everyone was doing it. They would go to an early Mass on Sundays before driving to the farm to see their first grandchild.

On April 18th, 1942, Americans finally got some good news. Jimmy Doolittle's bombers launched off the deck of the USS Hornet and bombed Tokyo. Fighters from the Enterprise escorted them as far as they could. Doolittle's bombers did negligible damage, but it changed things for Jack and his fellow trainees at Pensacola. They were exuberant. It didn't matter that they were Army Air Force pilots who had flown the planes. They had bombed Tokyo. Jack, along with his bunkmates, got drunk. It seemed to them that the entire base and city joined in celebrating the news. Jack bragged about his big brother being a pilot on the Enterprise. He called Connor, who had finished training and was waiting to get his first sea assignment. All was right with the world again.

On May 8th, they again rejoiced at the news that aircraft carriers had battled it out in the Coral Sea and American carriers had held their own. It was dubious who won or lost. But, if you were at Pensacola, you were sure that the Americans won. Jack again bragged about his brother even though the Enterprise was not involved in the battle.

Things turned dark again on June 3rd when the Japanese invaded American territory, the Aleutian Islands. Jack had no idea where Dutch Harbor was. Neither did his instructors. The next day, the Japanese attacked Midway Island in the Pacific. It seemed to Jack and his fellow trainees that the Japanese were everywhere and they were invincible. What they had thought of as the tremendous success of the bombing of Tokyo was now viewed as a publicity stunt to make Americans think they were going to win the war.

Jack and his classmates celebrated again on June 5th. The war's biggest sea battle had taken place, and the Americans emerged with a clear victory, their first. The Battle of Midway ended with the sinking of four out of the five Japanese aircraft carriers. Only the carrier Yorktown was lost on the American side. Naval aviators had proven they could do it. For Jack and his fellow trainees, this was a big win, not a small one. Midway showed what the U.S. Navy could do. He told everyone about Brian, his big brother, flying a torpedo bomber, who was stationed on the Enterprise. "Brian," he told his fellow trainees, "was in that battle that just changed the course of the war."

It was a month before Jack learned that Brian's plane had been shot down by a Japanese fighter plane; Brian and his crew members were all dead. The Devastators had not scored a single hit on a Japanese carrier, and most of them were destroyed before they reached their targets. The American torpedo planes had proven to be useless except as a distraction for Japanese gunners. They had been sent on a suicide mission without air cover. In Pensacola, they didn't know any of this.

When he learned of Brian's death, Jack still had three more months of training to complete. Jack was now learning to fly the plane he had always wanted, a flying boat, the Consolidated Patrol Bomber, the iconic long distance record setter, the Catalina. After he learned of Brian's death, Jack desperately wanted to get into the fight. He was angry. He wanted revenge.

Both his letters from home and the letters he sent got shorter. His parents were exhausted, his wife was worn out, and the three of them were all suffering from Brian's death and worrying about the two remaining sons. The only one who was thriving was the infant, Michael.

Chapter Thirty-Seven: The Aleutians

Would it be Midway or the Aleutians? The Japanese wanted the American Navy to agonize over the question and then split its forces to protect both. The Japanese considered both to be strategic launching points for attacks on the American mainland. The Japanese high command did not know the Americans had broken the Japanese communication code. Consequently, rather than splitting their forces, the American carrier task force went to defend Midway. The day before the attack on Midway, June 3rd, a smaller Japanese force, a decoy, carried out its mission and began the bombardment of the Naval Air Station at Dutch Harbor on Amaknak Island in the Aleutian Islands. The Americans were not deceived. No naval force had been deployed to the Northern Pacific.

The Japanese lost more than four carriers at Midway. They lost the Midway as a base from which to strike Hawaii. Consequently, the Aleutians now became critical to the Japanese high command. On June 7th, the Japanese decoy force, with no resistance, invaded the islands of Attu and Kiska. They now had a foothold on American territory. As they did in the South Pacific, the Japanese plan was to island-hop their way across the Aleutians into North America. Controlling the Aleutians would enable them to protect their mainland, make it difficult for the Americans to send any supplies to Russia, and establish naval and air bases to eventually invade America.

Jack, like most Americans, had never heard of Attu or Kiska and knew nothing about the Aleutian Islands except they existed somewhere off the coast of Alaska. Stretching one thousand miles from Alaska to Attu, the archipelago contained one hundred and fifty islands, and thousands of islets. Some of the islets were smaller than an acre in size, but they were large enough to destroy a vessel or seaplane happening upon it in the dense fog which was common. In addition, the archipelago also contained seventy-six major volcanoes—thirty-six were active.

The Aleutians seemed like a faraway frigid planet to Jack and his fellow trainees as they enjoyed the warmth of Pensacola, Florida. None of Jack's instructors had been stationed at Dutch Harbor. They had no information or experience to share. Everyone started to pore over whatever they could find about this strange land of islands and rocks. They were not happy with what they discovered.

In the Aleutians, the Americans faced two foes. One was an experienced Japanese Navy and infantry. The United States had old planes, old ships, and an untested military. In addition, the Americans had made a decision. The war in the South Pacific was the priority, not the Aleutians.

The other foe was the weather, especially the fog—there was always fog. The ever-present fog was produced when the northern arctic air from the Bering Sea collided with the warmer Japanese current from the Pacific. In addition to fog, this cold and warm air collision created frequent and unpredictable cyclonic conditions of rapidly changing winds. Katabatic winds, close to hurricane force, would scream down the mountains and throw the American Catalina flying boats into the rocky pinnacles that could reach as high as nine thousand feet. The weather changed so quickly that a seaplane could start to take off in calm water and be banging into choppy waves before it was airborne. If one wanted to create the worst possible situation for airplanes, one would study the Aleutians. On Attu, the farthest American Island from mainland Alaska, there were only ten clear days a year. The month after the invasion, Navy Patrol Wing Four, flying PBY Catalina seaplanes out of Nazan Bay on Atka Island, lost one-third of its planes to either the Japanese or the weather. Jack told Peg, in one of their weekly phone calls, "If it wasn't ours, they'd be welcome to it."

When Jack graduated on September 12th, 1942, it was ten months after enlisting and five months after his son Michael was born. Jack hoped he would get at least a two-week leave before his first posting as a Naval Aviator. But instead, he got a week. It took him fourteen hours with multiple flights and a train ride from Boston before he got to Brunswick, where he saw his son for the first time.

Peg hugged him; his mother hugged him; his father shook his hand; and then he held his son for a minute before giving him back to Peg. After that, they barely talked on the car ride home. Brian's death at Midway had changed the world for all of them. Jack realized he had not fully understood that Brian was dead. At Pensacola, there had been no one to share it with. The phone calls with Peg and his parents were insufficient to convey the grief each was feeling. In addition, so demanding and consuming was the training at Pensacola that he had done little more than sleep, study, and fly. The more the Japanese entrenched themselves in the Pacific, the more intense the training became.

When the family arrived at the farmhouse in Georgetown, Jack felt like he had entered a world he was no longer a part of. His parents now lived in Bath with his maternal grandmother and both Will and Nell worked long hours at the shipyard. At the farm, Peg was alone with his son. Maeve had returned to Boston with the twins. For Peg, everything revolved around young Michael's schedule and the caring of the livestock she was managing, with the help of a fourteen-year-old neighbor. The garden was now back to depression size and still producing. Peg was canning feverously for the winter. Sugar was rationed, and people were told to prepare for additional rationing, including gas. No one had gone to Tír na nÓg that summer. His old room at the farmhouse, the room he had grown up in, was now Peg's and Michael's. Jack's clothes had been packed away to make room for his son's. Jack did not know where he fit in this new domestic landscape.

He had missed Michael's birth. He had missed his christening. He and Peg had decided that the godparents for their firstborn would be Jack's brother, Connor, and Peg's sister-in-law, Maeve. With Connor now off on the destroyer *USS Livermore*, Maeve's husband Tommy had stood in for Connor. And now Jack had only five days at home to get to know his wife as a mother, and his infant son. He also had to reckon with the death of his brother and the memorial service he had missed. Everyone was busy and exhausted. Peg's bravado that she could handle everything had evaporated months ago. The cheery sounds on their phone calls bore no resemblance to her reality.

The second night Jack was home, Michael was fussy and didn't want to fall asleep. Peg was already asleep. Jack picked him up out of his crib and started to walk him, but his son didn't settle down. Frustrated, Jack woke Peg up. "He won't go to sleep."

"Did you see if he needed a change?"

"No." He started to hand Michael to Peg.

"Jesus, Jack. See if he needs a change and change him if he does."

"I've never changed a diaper."

Peg sighed, getting out of bed, "What feckin' good are you? Here give him to me and watch."

For months all Jack had thought about was making love to Peg and holding his son. He was also looking forward to having some time to relax before his first posting. He hadn't figured on the lives they had been leading while he was gone. He hadn't figured on the darkness of Brian's death that had destroyed the lives of his parents along with Brian's. He hadn't figured on feeling out of place, and at times, in the way, as he tried to help. So instead, he found himself closing down and anxious to leave for the Naval Air Station in Seattle, then on to Kodiak, Alaska, and finally to Nazan Bay in the Aleutians. Once there, he would become a pilot-navigator on a new Catalina

Patrol Bomber—a PBY5. He would be the new kid, the lowest of the low, but very welcome to fill out the depleted ranks of his new squadron.

The plane taking him from Kodiak to Nazan Bay had to circle for over an hour before a break in the fog made it possible for them to land. Once there, his orientation was brief. He was assigned to a tent, provided with the gear needed to stay warm—both on the ground and in the air. Most important to Jack, he was assigned to a plane. The night he arrived, he sat down to dinner in the mess tent with his first of what would be several Patrol Plane Commanders, Lieutenant, Junior Grade, Russell Thew. Thew had graduated from Pensacola two years before Jack and had already flown more than a hundred missions out of Nazan Bay. Stationed initially at Dutch Harbor, Thew had watched his plane be blown up on the runway during one of the first Japanese bomb raids.

The minute they set their trays down, Thew said, "So, Ensign Buckley, welcome to the land of snow and ice. You ever read *The Cremation of Sam McGee* in high school?"

"Yeah. I vaguely remember it."

"Well, the weather here is worse. Don't plan on getting used to it. No one does."

"That bad?"

"Worse. I read your jacket. You must be a whiz kid. You got excellent grades. You'll be navigating for us for a while until you get used to the way we do things here. Then you'll be up in the right seat. You'll have your own plane pretty soon at the rate we're going. Sound okay?"

"Sounds great, Lieutenant."

"We tend to use nicknames here rather than ranks. Too fuckin' cold to be formal. People call me Rusty. What do people call you?"

"Well, just about everyone calls me Jack. My real name is John.

In high school, my football coach called me Buck because he always told me to 'buck' into the line."

"Buck it is, then. You'll meet the rest of the crew tomorrow morning. How much do you know about what we're doing here?"

"Not much."

"Okay, let me spell it out for you. The Japs have been here since June, and they control two islands, Attu and Kiska. Attu's only about eight hundred miles from Japan, so their supply line is pretty damned short. They bring supplies and people in by freighters, submarines, and planes. We spot 'em and sink 'em or get our destroyers and subs to do it. Problem is there's so damned much fog we don't do a lot of spotting, let alone sinking. Our orders, though, are when we spot something, we stay with it until we are relieved, sink it, or run out of fuel and go for an icy bath."

"You're kidding."

"Do I look like I'm kidding?"

"Jesus."

"Yep. Sometimes we go bombing. But, again, can't see shit most of the time, so we have turned these slower than molasses concoctions we fly into dive bombers."

"Dive bombers?"

"Yeah, we circle until we see a break in the fog and then dive through, drop whatever we're carrying, and get the hell out of there."

"You're kidding?"

"Same answer as before."

"These planes weren't designed to do that!"

"No shit. You know all those specs you studied about the Cat? Forget 'em. We're doing things with these birds that would drive the engineers crazy. Finally, we go on 'Dumbo' missions. A lot of them."

"Dumbo?"

"The flying elephant. Dumbo had big ears. We've got big wings. Search and rescue. We do a lot of that. Sometimes for our own guys;

sometimes for Army crews. We're going to be doing a lot more of that. Engineers are putting finishing touches on an airfield at Adak. Bombers and fighters are already coming in. Weather'll get 'em if the Japs don't. Our job is to find 'em, splash down, and pick 'em up if the sea's okay. We stay with 'em as spotters until a patrol boat or a destroyer picks 'em up if we can't."

"Got it."

"That one suits you, huh?"

"I've done several water rescues."

"Actual or practice."

"Practice."

"In the nice warm waters of the Gulf of Mexico with healthy swabbies lolling about in their inflatables."

"Yeah."

"Not the same here. By the way, do you know the freezing temperature of saltwater?"

"Yeah. They taught us that. Twenty-eight degrees if it's still."

"You're going to see a lot of ice. You'll be chipping it off of everything. Remember how hot you were sitting in the plane in the middle of the summer? Well, here you're going to be freezing your balls off the minute we get in the air. Then when we get to five thousand, you're going to think it can't get any colder. Then it does. Don't take your gloves off unless you have to or you won't have any fingers left.

"Come on; I'll introduce you to some of the other crews and the bunch you'll be flying with. Your navigation grades were good. I hope you are."

"I think... I'm okay."

"They tell you compasses and altimeters ain't worth shit up here?"

"Yeah. I heard something about that."

"Good. I also want you to meet the guy who was my last

navigator. He only got us lost a few dozen times which isn't too bad up here. We set down one time, and he rowed ashore and asked a fisherman where we were."

"You're kidding."

"Would I kid you? No. He rowed ashore and asked directions."

Even though it was September, daylight flowed into the tent at 0530 the following day. Jack hadn't slept much. The flight from Seattle, the conversation with Rusty, the new bed, and anxiety about his first mission kept stirring him awake. He was shivering as he stumbled into the 0630 briefing, carrying a coffee and a donut. A mix of snow and sleet made walking from his tent to the mess tent and then to the operations tent difficult.

The meteorologist forecasted fog and scattered clouds over both Attu and Kiska. Jack's plane was headed for Attu, five hundred miles away, with a full complement of five-hundred-pound bombs. There would be six Catalinas. His plane would be number two taking off. In formation, they would be high and to the leader's right. Another Catalina had already left and would stay on station over the target, sending radio reports of the weather back to the flight leader. If the weather over Attu was completely overcast and the ceiling was too low, they would head back and try for Kiska.

When Jack got to the ramp, the beach crew already had the lead plane in the water, and had its engines warming up. When the lead plane moved away, Jack and the other two officers climbed aboard their aircraft. Their engineer, bombardier, and the two waist gunners were already on board waiting for them. Jack settled into the navigator's station, took his charts out, and spread them across the table. He found the parallel rules and compass and placed them on top of the charts. Next came pencils and a sharpener. Rusty had told him that there would be a notebook with all the courses he would need already plotted. He put that on top of the charts. Thirty minutes later, they were in the air.

The Catalina is a slow airplane. Its top speed is only two hundred miles an hour, and it typically cruised at one hundred and twenty-five miles an hour. It was initially designed to be the 'eyes of the fleet.' Because the Catalina was so slow, the Japanese fighter planes, the Zeroes, would destroy them in a matter of minutes. The Catalina's only real defense was to hide in the clouds or go low, skimming across the water where it would blend in with the water and be difficult to see.

Their flight would be four hours to Attu and another four hours back. If they encountered Zeroes, it would be ten to twenty minutes before they reached Attu. If they made it past the Zeroes, they still had to face the antiaircraft fire from the ground.

On board the Catalina, the crew consisted of a bombardier stationed in the front of the plane, the 'eyeball.' He was also responsible for the twin thirty-millimeter guns facing forward. Next came a pilot and a co-pilot in the cockpit. An engineer sat up in the nacelle between the two engines that powered the plane. Jack's station was in the fuselage. He sat back-to-back with the radioman. The Catalina Jack was on, had an observation 'blister' on each side of the fuselage aft of the radioman and navigator. There was a gunner in each blister. Each blister had two fifty-millimeter guns. Even with this firepower, the Catalina was no match for the Japanese Zeroes flying from carriers or land.

When the formation was fully formed, and they were on their way, Rusty came down to check on Jack. "Find everything?"

"Yeah. I think I'm all set."

"Some of the courses will look strange because of the problems with the compasses. Don't lose that notebook whatever you do. These courses have been refined and refined since we got here. All you need is one fixed point, and you can get us home."

"What about the radio beacon?"

"What radio beacon? You see a tower anywhere back at Nazan?"

"No. I didn't look."

Rusty smiled at him and said, "I'm waiting?"

"For what?"

"Aren't you going to ask me if I'm kidding?"

Jack let out a sigh, "No. I'm learning."

"Well, the good news is that there is one at Adak now that the field is operational." Rusty turned to the radioman, who was overhearing the conversation. "Right, Sparky?"

"Yep. I tell them pilots how to follow the yeller brick road to Adak. Then you do your magic and get us home to Nazan. Easy as an old hound dog set out to find him a shoeless nigga."

Four hours later, the plane was in a lazy circle waiting for a break in the low-lying clouds over Attu. Jack's plane was stacked number two above the flight leader. The other four planes were stacked above them. Everything seemed slow and calm. Jack closed his eyes and dozed, trying to catch up on his missed sleep. Twenty minutes later, he heard Rusty say, "Here we go. Hang on tight." The plane went into a steep dive. Everything vibrated. The noise of the outside air was a shriek that permeated the plane. Jack felt the increased pressure in his ears, and started yawning and swallowing as fast as he could to equalize it.

He heard the sound of the antiaircraft guns from below and saw puffs of black smoke all around the plane. Then, twenty seconds into the dive, he heard pieces of metal hitting the aircraft. "What's that!" he shouted at Sparky over the noise.

"Shrapnel. AA shit. We're fine if it doesn't hit the propellers or the wings."

Jack heard and felt their bombs release. Seconds later, the plane shuddered as Rusty pulled it out of its dive. Jack felt the pressure of the 'G' forces and hoped that the plane would hold together. Behind him, he heard the waist gunners firing short bursts from their fifty caliber guns as they began to pull up and reach for altitude. Suddenly the plane jerked to the right and headed for the lowest bank of clouds and obscurity. The antiaircraft fire followed them for a minute and then faded away.

"Those poor suckers behind us," Sparky said. "Now the Japs have their guns trained on that fuckin' cloud gap we went through. They'll be diving right into it."

Chapter Thirty-Eight: Patrol Plane Commander

With the Adak airfield open, Army Air Force B24 and B17 bombers arrived and began to hammer away at the Japanese bases on Kiska and Attu. The Catalina squadrons stopped their bombing runs. Instead, the Navy used the planes for what they had been designed for: air-sea rescue, long-distance patrol, and destroying enemy submarines. For the crews of the Catalinas, the days now seemed endless. The planes stayed in the air for ten to twelve hours, searching for the Japanese ships and submarines that supplied their bases.

While the Army Air Force's endless bombing of Attu and Kiska prevented the Japanese forces from moving to other islands, Japanese troops kept arriving. The flight crews speculated on when the Japanese would attack other islands in the Aleutian chain. Jack and his crew kept wondering when Japanese carriers would appear with their decks filled with Zeroes. So, the crew created a pool. Jack chose his birthday, April 5th. He told Rusty, "Daylight, they need more daylight, but not much more." Rusty bet on April 29th, Hirohito's birthday. "After Midway, Japs figure they owe the emperor one for the home team."

Throughout the winter, the Catalina Squadrons lost planes and crews, primarily to weather, accidents, and mechanical difficulties. Jack wrote home that it was the worst four months of his life. There was no light. Full gales were constant, and the long high wings of the Catalinas made landing and taking off in the choppy waters hazardous. The patrols were endless.

In the air, it was too cold to sleep, and normal bodily functions were difficult to manage as they struggled in and out of their gear. The crew was often lost when the radio beacon at Adak was down because the Army planes weren't in the air. When they returned to base, the first thing Jack did was to look to see who was missing.

When they did find a submarine, it was now much more difficult to attack it. The Japanese submarines had begun to copy the tactics of the German U-Boat commanders. Running on the surface, when a submarine saw a Catalina, the submarine commanders no longer ordered their boat to dive. They knew what a difficult target they were for the Catalinas. They also knew how poorly armed the Catalinas were. So instead of diving and hoping a Catalina's depth charges wouldn't hit them, they stayed on the surface and deployed their deck guns on the planes. Moving slowly to line up a shot on a difficult target, the Catalina's 30 caliber machines guns didn't have the range or the power to compete with the deck guns of the Japanese submarines. The Catalina commanders learned to stay out of range and call for destroyers to come and take on the target. If there were no destroyers nearby, the Catalina commander had a difficult decision to make: lose the submarine, or lose his plane.

In early March, Rusty was promoted to commander of Jack's squadron. Rusty had more missions than anyone else available, hadn't screwed up, and everyone liked him. He was an obvious choice. By this time, Jack had already moved to the right-hand seat, so Rusty simply moved him to the left-hand seat and made him plane commander. Most of the officers got promotions in rank. The squadron crews celebrated Rusty's twenty-fifth birthday two days after his promotion.

In late March, the Japanese sent a fleet of freighters to the Aleutians with critical supplies. They were escorted by a large naval force of both heavy and light cruisers as well as destroyers. On March 26th, the armada was discovered south of the Komandorski Island chain in the Aleutians. A much smaller American naval fleet engaged. The Americans didn't realize the strength of the Japanese force. All-day long on the 27th, while still miles apart, the warships shot salvo after salvo at one another. The Japanese crippled one of the American cruisers and damaged several American ships. The Japanese vessels sustained only minor damage. To the surprise of the Americans, Admiral Hosogaya withdrew his fleet. They assumed he was worried about land-based American bombers appearing from Adak. It was the last naval battle fought without air support during the war. Back home in the United States, the battle of the Komandorski Islands was portrayed as a big success. The propaganda machine proclaimed: 'Japanese Fleet On The Run.' Jack and his crew knew better.

However, for the Catalina crews, the battle changed everything. After the Komandorski Islands, the Japanese stopped using freighters and warships to supply their Aleutian bases. All Japanese supplies for Attu and Kiska were now brought in by submarine. As a result, Jack and his crew now spent all of their time looking for submarines. The Catalinas could cover more area than the Navy's surface ships. Patrols became even longer. They flew lower to spot the wake of a submarine and distinguish it from a rogue wave or surf bouncing off of a rock that was only above water at low tide. Often, a submarine crew could hear the engines of the Catalina before the plane's observers could see the sub. Sometimes, the only way they knew a sub was there was when shells hit the plane. Fatigue increased, eyes were strained, and nerves broke as the danger grew.

April Fool's Day was incredibly long for Jack and his crew. They had been assigned the patrol sector farthest from the Nazan Bay base. Upon their return, they landed in choppy water. Freezing spray coated the plane and soon turned to ice. To add to their misery, the beach crew was having difficulty with an aircraft ahead of them, so they had to wait twenty minutes. When they finally got ashore, mess was long over. The cooks arranged to leave out cold sandwiches to feed the late crews.

By the time he got out of his gear, debriefed, and finally got something to eat, Jack was, in his words, 'one miserable son-of-a-bitch.' Rusty joined him in the mess tent with two strangers.

"Shit day, huh?" Rusty said.

Jack barely looked up at him, "Long, cold, nothing to show for it. Just like yesterday, the day before, and…"

"Got it. I want to introduce you to a couple of people who arrived today. This red-headed guy is Bernie Parisi. He's your new pilot. Just graduated. Putting him in your right seat. You'll be getting a new nav tomorrow."

"Nothing against you guys, but come on, Rusty, two newbies at the same time. Give me a fuckin' break."

"The nav man you'll get is enlisted, but he's got six months under his belt. Patrol in Seattle. You'll meet him tomorrow."

"Ain't that special." Jack looked at Parisi. He looked like a high school kid, younger than his brother Connor. The Navy was so desperate for pilots they had reduced the college requirements to two years and cut training at Pensacola by several weeks. How old was Parisi? He wondered if he had reached twenty-one yet? And he was going to be second in command? The crew was going to make mincemeat of him.

"Glad to meet you, sir," Parisi said, holding out his hand.

Jack put his sandwich down, reached across the table, and shook his hand. He found himself saying the same thing to Parisi that Rusty had said to him, "We're pretty informal here. They call me Buck. What do they call you?"

"Red."

"Where you from, Red?"

"Brooklyn."

"Parisi. You Italian? Where'd you get that red hair?"

"Grandparents on both sides were from Sicily."

"No shit. I didn't know Italians had red hair."

Rusty interrupted them. "You'll have plenty of time to shoot the shit in the air." Rusty turned to introduce the second stranger, "Buck, I want you to meet John Huston. He's going to make a film about us. You ever see *The Maltese Falcon*? He made that. Won some Academy Awards."

Huston interrupted, "Nominated. Should have won, but the Hollywood pricks wouldn't know a good film if it bit em on the ass. Glad to meet you, sailor."

'Sailor.' Jack did not consider himself a 'sailor.' He kept eating. Rusty continued, "Anyway, he wants to have one of his cameramen fly with you for one or two missions."

Huston said, "What I want, lieutenant, is to show the real war and the sacrifices you men make here in this god-forsaken place. My man will stay out of the way. Those observation windows on your plane's side are perfect for getting great footage."

Jack looked up and said to Rusty, "You want to put a cameraman in one of our blisters? How the hell we going to spot a Jap sub?"

He turned to Huston, "Besides, I don't know about any great 'footage.' Most of the time, we're just looking down at empty water or flying in fog where we don't see anything."

He turned to Rusty, "You tell him how boring patrol is?"

"Yeah." Rusty turned to address Huston, "You still sure you want to do this?"

"Absolutely. If boredom is what you face, boredom it is. It might only make up a minute of the film, but the story of boredom and exhaustion needs to be told."

Rusty and Huston continued to talk while Jack finished his second sandwich. After Huston and Red Parisi left, Rusty said, "We, you, don't have a choice here. And look, you're the only one I can trust not to embarrass us. Take the camera guy on some sightseeing along the mountains on the way out and the way back, but don't get him killed. When you get out into your sector, let the destroyers know if you run into a sub, but then you get the hell out of there."

"No tailing? What the fuck. What if the destroyers are too far?"

"Out of there, Buck. You get the hell out of there. Powers that be want to make sure we don't do anything that would get anyone killed or embarrass the Navy. And for God's sake, tell Sparky to keep his fuckin' redneck mouth shut. 'Yes sir, no sir, and, I don't know, sir,' are the only words that I want coming out of his putrid mouth. You with me?"

"Yeah."

That night Jack wrote home that he would be in the movies, just like Brian. After he wrote it, he wondered if he should have said it, but he was too tired to go back and rewrite the letter, so he sealed it. Who knew, maybe Connor would get his chance, too. He convinced himself that there was nothing wrong with writing about his possible stardom. His parents and Peg had said that they had seen some of the movies coming from the war department. His family knew he was in the Aleutians. He saw no reason the censors would care, and they didn't open an officer's mail anyway.

The following day a bearded, middle-aged giant was loading equipment onto his plane when Jack arrived after the mission briefing. The giant stuck out his hand and said, "I'm your 'pain-in-the-ass' today. I'll do my best to keep the hell out of your way. Name's Maurice Zelinski. People call me Tiny. Where you want me to stow my gear and my butt?"

"Put your gear in the galley…"

"You got a galley on this thing?"

"Yeah. Not much of one, but it works. You can sit up in the cockpit. We got a cushion for you. Then, when you want to use your camera, you can ride in one of the blisters or up in the bubble."

"Bubble?"

"Bombardier and nose gunner."

"Thanks. Feel free to tell me to get out of the way anytime."

Jack decided he liked Tiny. He wasn't a pompous ass like

Huston. As they taxied out into the harbor, Jack asked, "Ever been on one of these?"

"No. First time."

"Well, this isn't called a flying boat for nothing. The underbody of the fuselage is designed like a speed boat. When we start off, we plow like hell, and there'll be water all over the place, and it'll seem like we're going under. When we get enough speed up, the hull will raise up on its step, just like a speed boat. That's when we start to go faster, and you begin to think this elephant might fly. It's going to be loud as hell. Hull's aluminum, and it will sound like you're inside a big fuckin' tin drum every time we hit a wave. The hull will start to vibrate like hell, and you'll be sure it will come apart. It'll be that way until we get enough lift to break clear of the water."

"Sounds delightful."

"Once we're airborne, it'll take us a while to get up to cruising altitude. These things are slower than shit. But when we're up there, we can stay there forever. We drew the shortest patrol sector today, probably in your honor. Everything goes well, and we'll have you back in eight hours or so. Ready to go?"

"Let's do it."

Four hours later, they had seen nothing but gray water, clouds, and mountains with snow. The ceiling, though, was high, at ten thousand feet. A good day for bombing. With that weather, Jack knew that several squadrons of Army bombers would hit the Japanese troops at Kiska.

The Army bombed whenever they could, but it was hard to tell if the bombing was having an impact. The Japanese had created warrens of underground tunnels to hide their troops when the bombers came. In addition, antiaircraft emplacements were covered with camouflage nets that were impossible to see from the altitude the bombers flew.

Red was at the controls. Tiny was snoring behind him, and Jack was going in and out of sleep when Sparky called up to the cockpit, "Buck, we've got a Dumbo. Downed B24. We've been diverted. Find it and report. Pick up survivors, wounded, and dead if we can. I've got possible coordinates."

Jack turned around and looked down at his new navigator. The new man didn't look up. Instead, he said, "I'm working it."

"Sparky, give us the beacon. It should be on. We'll start there until we have the coordinates."

The course for the beacon on Adak laid out, Jack had Red continue flying the airplane. He wanted to save his energy and attention until they reached the area of the suspected downing. Tiny came to life. "Where can I shoot from and still be out of the way?"

"Go into the bubble for now."

Tiny made his way into the forward gunner/bombardier compartment. Its former occupant asked, "Where do you want me?"

Jack said, "Get us fed. Who knows how long we'll be looking? I'm going to sleep. After people eat, I want everyone except Red, Nav, and Sparks resting. Fuck the subs."

"What about you? Want something to eat?"

"No, not now."

Two hours later, they began their search pattern for the downed plane. Fighters had also been sent out from Adak to help look for the B24. They had been searching for an hour when Sparky said, "Fighters got him. They'll stay until we get there. Another Cat's on the way in case we need him."

Fifteen minutes later, they arrived where two fighters were circling the wreckage of the B24. Jack took the controls from Red. He dropped the plane down to five hundred feet and circled the wreckage. "Looks like he tried to set it down on the edge of the water and didn't make it. It must have hit that hill. Then it tumbled down. Fuckin' bird's upside down." He said into his throat microphone, "Blisters. See anything moving?"

There were now two men in each blister. "No sign of life" was repeated four times. "Okay, we're going in. Get the inflatable ready to go. Starboard side'll go ashore."

Tiny came up out of the bubble, "Can I go with them?"

Jack didn't look at him. "No. I'm busy. Go back where you were. Stay out of the way."

Red said, "Those swells are pretty big. We going to be able to do this?"

"Yeah. We'll do it. I'm going to need you on the throttles so I can time this. We'll pass over once so I can gauge the swell timing, then we'll go in. I'll tell you exactly what I need. Get the wing floats down."

"Okay."

Jack did one circle and dropped the plane down until it was just off the water. Occasionally, one of the swells rose up and hit the plane. He was flying just above stall speed when he told Red to cut the throttles and settled the aircraft onto a rising swell. Once the plane stopped, the two worked to keep the plane floating as stationary as they could, heading into the wind. When the shore party was ready, two men opened the hatch, launched the inflatable, and started paddling it to shore.

"We're taking on water," one of the remaining blister gunners shouted.

"Can you see where it's coming from?" Jack asked.

"Not yet. I'm looking."

"How bad?"

"Can't tell yet." Then, a minute later, he said, "Found it. Three rivets. Must have been that second wave we hit. Nav, I need pencils."

The new navigator headed towards the back of the fuselage with pencils in hand. He also grabbed the hand pump as he went. The gunner took the pencils and pushed them into the open holes where the rivets had popped out.

Forty-five minutes later, the shore party returned with five bodies. The crew helped get the corpses on board the Catalina. The shore party followed. The boat was deflated and stowed. In the cockpit, Jack had Red begin to work the throttles again. "Watch those pencils," he shouted back. "Don't let em pop out. I don't want any water weight."

The plane began to pick up speed but would plow into a swell and slow down. Then it would get speed again as it passed over the swell. When they finally got up on step, Jack waited until the plane was going up on a rising swell before pulling the yoke back and urging the plane into the air.

Once airborne and headed for home, Jack returned control of the plane to Red and went back into the fuselage. "Only five?"

"Yeah. Pilot and bombardier for sure. Other than those two, we couldn't tell who the others were. It looks like all but the pilot were injured before they crashed. Everyone had bandages on them. Rest of the crew must have bailed out."

Jack looked down at the bodies. "Pilot had injured crew. Probably too hurt to send them out in 'chutes. He was trying to get them all home."

Tiny kept filming the crew, looking down at the mangled bodies. The 'footage' would never be used.

February 24, 1995
HOME TOWN BOY by Michael Buckley

According to the weather lady, it was a 'cold snap.' It was only frigid for four of the past seven days. Hyperbole has definitely entered into the reports of the weather. Back in the nineteen seventies, a 'snap' lasted at least a couple of weeks and cold meant cold. Up in Caribou, it got down to -40 in 1955, and before that, back in 1925, it bottomed out at -48 in Van Buren. Below freezing temperatures for four days hardly constitutes a 'cold snap' in my book. It does for my father, though. He called twice from Florida to give me the temperatures in Miami, where he and my mom are for the duration of the winter.

My dad hates winter. During WW II, he spent four years flying PBY Catalina flying boats in the Aleutian Islands that run from the coast of Alaska all the way to Siberia in Russia. Six months of the year were pure hell when it came to weather, and the other six months were purgatory, only it was cold rather than heat that they suffered. So, my father would quote, whether asked or not, Robert Frost's poem, *Fire and Ice*:

> Some say the world will end in fire,
> Some say in ice.
> From what I've tasted of desire
> I hold with those who favor fire.
> But if it had to perish twice,
> I think I know enough of hate
> To say that for destruction ice
> Is also great
> And would suffice.

And, with a few drinks in him, he would launch into *The Cremation of Sam McGee* and would never miss a word. He would emphasize the lines:

It's the cursèd cold, and it's got right hold till I'm chilled clean through to the bone.

Yet 'tain't being dead—it's my awful dread of the icy grave that pains;

> So I want you to swear that, foul or fair, you'll cremate my last remains.

When I was a fairly young lad, I asked my mother about my dad's attitude towards the cold. She told me that when he was in the Aleutians, he was more afraid of getting shot down, surviving, and then freezing to death than he had been of anything else. When I was older, I tried to get him to tell me about those years, and occasionally he would respond. Still, like many veterans, yours truly included, some things were better forgotten or at least given a good shot of repression. For my father, the cold was an exception to that generalization.

The only reason they did not move to warmer climes after the war was because of family. However, when I started talking about colleges, there was a nudge towards considering schools where he could visit in the winter and get some warmth into him. It didn't work with me. The nudge was just that, a nudge. It was soft and subtle. Boston may be warmer than Georgetown, but it was not what he had in mind. So, when it was my sister's turn, there was no subtlety. Brochures appeared showing campuses with flowers and palm trees. He packed her and my mother in his plane and flew them to Miami during my sister's junior year break from high school. It worked. My sister, Maude, fell in love with the University of Miami. She applied, got accepted, and off she went to major in business. While she was there, my father majored in looking at Miami real estate. When she graduated and the last bills were paid, my parents became the proud owners of a condominium on Biscayne Bay. They quickly became confirmed 'Snowbirds.' On January 2nd, the family plane headed south; on May 1st, the plane headed north.

I confess, everyone in my family, including me, came to appreciate having 'Snowbird' relatives. Spring breaks were often spent camping out in my parent's condominium. No one complained about sleeping on the floor or their trips to Disney World. As the kids got older, my wife referred to them as 'post-Disney' children, we went less frequently. The kids started to make their own plans with friends, and pulling everyone together for a couple of days, let alone a week, became increasingly difficult. Miami became a sometime thing.

His four months a year in Miami was heaven for my father, though. I asked him once why he didn't move there full time. He said, "Do you honestly think your mother could stand any more time away from her grandchildren than she already does? That woman is already sacrificing to let me get my four months in. Besides, I wouldn't have any reason to bust your chops about the weather in Maine if I was down there in July and August. So nah, this works out just fine."

Even though this is not much of a cold snap, I'm glad he is wearing shorts and a T-shirt on his daily walks along Biscayne Bay. When we talk Sunday night, he will be sure to remind me how warm it is in Miami. That is as predictable as his launching into a dramatic version of the trials of old Sam McGee last Christmas. The kids always did their best to act scared, and everyone had a good time. The horrors of his time in the Aleutians may have receded in his memory, but the memories of the cold never did.

Chapter Thirty-Nine: Trouble in Texas

When I got home, it was close to nine. Pat, Rina, and Wendy were playing Scrabble at the dining room table. They were intent on the game and barely acknowledged my presence when I said hello, built a fire for them, excused myself, and went to bed. No questions were asked. I had no idea what Pat said to the girls about my absence. As I headed to my bedroom, I turned and looked back at them. Sitting at the table playing scrabble, the three of them seemed uncomplicated and easy. Two days ago, I would have asked if I could join them.

I didn't sleep well. The combination of alcohol and angst about Nan was not a good soporific. So, I slept for a couple of hours, got up, wandered out onto the porch, went back to bed, slept for another couple of hours, got up, tried to read, went back to bed, and finally slept until nine.

Wendy was sitting at the dining room table with papers piled in front of her when I walked into the room. I recognized the box she had gotten them from, old issues of *Home Town Boy*. Seeing me, she said, "Coffee's ready, and there're raspberry scones we picked up on the way back from the mountain."

"Wonderful. Let me get some, and then tell me about your trip." I got my coffee and scones and took my place opposite her at the dining room table. She looked up, "Gramps, you sleep okay? You look beat."

"Not the best. But tell me. How was it?"

"It was terrific. They are very nice people. The campground was pretty crowded, and so was the trail we took, but other than that, I'm glad I went and got to spend time with them. The views are amazing, and the hiking wasn't that hard. Olivia and Jay are both in good shape. They said they do a lot of hiking and walking at home. Archie is really into fitness, so for him, it was a breeze."

"And you?"

"A cinch."

"Good. I'm glad you had a good time."

"I did."

I was waiting for more. I didn't get it, so I didn't ask.

"You reading some of the *Home Town Boy* pieces?"

"Yes, Olivia said I should. She said they were wonderful. You have a real fan. Did you know they subscribe to the Bugle and get it at home? She said I should read them if I hadn't. I like them. I wish historians would write this way. History would be a lot more interesting."

"Why, thank you very much, but I'm afraid you wouldn't learn a lot of history if they did."

She held one up. "I didn't know you had two uncles who were killed in the war. I thought you only had one uncle, Uncle Tommy."

"Tommy was my mother's brother. My father had two brothers, Brian and Connor. They were both killed in WWII. Brian was killed at the Battle of Midway. He was a pilot on the *Enterprise*. Connor was on a destroyer that went down a year later, the *Strong*."

"How horrible for your grandparents."

"It was. My grandmother said she sent the Navy three sons, and they only sent one back."

"Yikes."

"According to my father, Brian's death was hard, but Connor's death sent her over the edge. He was her youngest, and they were very close. The *Strong* was built here in Bath, and my grandmother had worked on it. Apparently, she was very proud that Connor had been assigned to a ship she had helped to build. When it went down, she quit her job at the shipyard and went into a very deep depression. I was too young to know what was happening, but my mother said it was terrible. Grandma Nell would stay in bed for days at a time. She stopped going to church. Finally, she moved back to the farm and left my grandfather in Bath. Mom said she didn't even start to come out of it until my father came home from the Aleutians."

"He was a pilot, too, wasn't he?"

"Yes. Spent four years in the Aleutians. Hated it."

"He wasn't injured."

"No. Ditched three times, but he was never wounded."

"I hate war."

"So do I."

"Oh, this afternoon, I'm going to take Archie into Brunswick. He wants to go to a museum at Bowdoin, some arctic thing."

"The Peary-McMillan."

"Yeah. That sounds right. He wants to build his own kayak like the natives did, and apparently, they've got examples there."

"Taking Jesse's bike?"

"Of course."

"Sounds like fun. It's an interesting place. I may be gone by the time you get back. I'm going to head up to Jay for a couple of nights. I've got some interviews lined up. Two of them are in the evening. I don't want to drive back at night and have to drive back up the next morning. You okay being here by yourself?"

"Gramps. I'm going into my junior year of college."

"I know. Just asking."

"By the way. Arch has asked me if I'd like to go with him and do the Penobscot River Corridor. He's really into kayaking. I told him I'd never been. He said he'd teach me."

"You want to go?"

"Yeah. Sounds like fun."

"Can you afford the time?"

"I'm ahead on reading, so yeah. I can also bring some *Home Town Boy* articles with me to read on the way up and back."

"Oh. You're being too clever by half. You must really want to go. Is it Archie or kayaking?"

"He's only going to be here for another week."

"So, you like him?"

"Don't push."

"Okay. Just asking."

"Gramps!"

"Sure, you can go. If you go before I'm back, leave me all the details on the dining room table. What about Charlie?"

"Rina said she'd take care of him."

"So, this is a done deal?"

"Sort of. It depends on weather."

"So, when are you going?"

"Tomorrow."

I decided to call Ruth from the car on the drive up to Jay. I waited until it was nine o'clock Houston time. She answered on the first ring. "Hi, darling. How are you?"

"Fine, Dad. I got your message. I was going to call tonight."

"Can you talk now?"

"Sure."

"Why don't you tell me what's going on."

"It's horrible. Harold was sure this deal he put together would be a real money maker. He bought this company with a group he put together, including his father and his uncle. When two investors pulled out, Harold took out a second mortgage on the house and borrowed from his 401K. The company had patented some kind of equipment for oil drilling that was supposed to be a game-changer. But it kept breaking down, and no one wanted to take a risk with it. So, we may lose everything."

"I thought the oil industry was booming."

"It is. That's why he was so excited about it. He was sure he was going to make a lot of money and retire by the time he was fifty. Now, I'm going to have to try and find a job. Dad, I've never had a job. I don't know what I'll do. We may lose the house."

"Didn't you see this as a possibility?"

"What?"

"That introducing a new technology is always risky."

"No. I didn't pay any attention to it. It was Harold's thing. He said it would work, and I trusted him. He's always made big money."

"Working for his uncle."

"What does that have to do with anything? He works hard."

I resisted sharing my perception of the work ethic of Harold Nokart. "Jesse said Harold's father was not willing to help."

"They aren't speaking. His father lost money, too, and is furious that Harold didn't do what he's calling 'sufficient due diligence.' I don't know what we're going to do, Dad. Hal is going into his junior year and we haven't paid his tuition yet. Baylor costs sixty-five thousand a year, and he has two years left."

"Do you have any student loans?"

"No. We were making too much money to get any aid or loans."

"Is Hal working?"

"No. He's in Switzerland for the summer visiting a friend. He doesn't know what desperate shape we're in, and I don't want him to have to worry about it."

"Isn't that a bit unrealistic?"

"I suppose. Can you help us?"

"Jesse said you want me to sell off a piece of the farm. My answer to that is no."

"Why not? Grandpa sold off a piece so he could buy the house in Florida. And way back, your grandfather sold off the land around the harbor." Her voice had changed and had gone from pleading to demanding. Now, she wanted me to explain myself. That was not going to happen.

"First, my father did not sell off any of the farmland. There was one lot left on the harbor, and that is what he sold. Second, this farm has been left intact for several generations of Conveys and now Buckleys. It has grown but never shrunk. I will not be the first to start selling off Convey Farm land. I could tell you all of the reasons why not, but they're neither here nor there."

"Dad, come on. I've never asked you for anything before, and the one time I do, you're turning me down. Mom would have given us the money without thinking twice about it."

She should not have said that. "You have my answer."

"You're not hearing me. You don't care about what we're going through. Do I have to beg? Is that what you need? Okay. I'm begging."

"I may be able to help Hal finish up at school."

"Hal. What about Harold and me?"

"You and Harold are adults and will work your way through this. However, you may have to sell the house, and you may have to get a job."

"Get a job. Doing what? Be a greeter at Walmart?"

"Maybe."

"You're impossible." She hung up.

Immediately, I felt 'impossible' and called her back. The phone went to voicemail. I didn't leave a message. Instead, I started questioning my decision. I certainly didn't need all this land, but I think she probably dramatically over-estimated its value. An acre in Pearland, Texas, and an acre in Georgetown, Maine, are two different worlds. I didn't even know how much money she was talking about. I was prepared to offer to help out with loans for Hal to finish up at Baylor. I could co-sign, and then he could take them on when he graduated. If they were as broke as Ruth claimed, they shouldn't have any trouble getting some student aid for his senior year. It was probably too late for the coming year. He'd still graduate owing less than most kids. I didn't think it was all that horrible if they dumped the 'McMansion' they lived in, and Ruth went to work. She was smart. She'd be fine. It'd be good for her.

I wondered if I should get in touch with Hal and deal directly with him. But then realized I didn't have his email address or a cellphone number. Wendy was the only grandchild I had that information for, and that was recently acquired. If Hannah were still alive, I'd have gotten it from her. I'd have asked Hannah, like I always did.

Baylor costs sixty-five thousand dollars a year. Jesus, that was a lot of money. Hell, he wasn't much of a student. He could transfer to a state school if college was that important to him. I made a mental note to look up how much the University of Texas or the Texas State University system would cost.

Hannah always said I was tight with money. I am. I've never felt apologetic about it. I didn't feel ashamed about it now as I made my way up to Jay to learn more about the strike that had devastated the town. Now those people knew what hardship was all about.

My phone rang. I picked it up, thinking it might be Ruth calling back to apologize for hanging up on me. I looked at the number, didn't recognize it, so I let it go to voicemail. Whoever it was, it wasn't Ruth.

In Jay, there is a high school, a middle school, and an elementary school, not even a thousand students in all the schools. Thirteen percent of them live in poverty. That's low for the United States, but it always perplexes me when I think about it. How could we in America let this happen? But then how could Jay have been so devastated by a company that was making record profits?

I had four interviews lined up, one with each of the families I would use to tell the story of the strike and how it affected their lives over the years since it happened. I had talked to all of the people on the phone and they were more than willing to tell their stories this many years later. I had started out with eighteen possible families. Because of deaths, unwillingness, or moving away from the area, I had settled on these four. I was prepared with a set of questions I wanted answers to, but more importantly, I wanted to prompt them to tell their own stories. I had all new equipment with me: a digital tape recorder, omni-directional microphone, and earphones to hear what the tape recorder was picking up—all purchased from the internet after several hours of reading reviews. In addition, I had releases for people to sign. I knew what a publisher would require if the book ever got that far, so I decided to make sure I had everything in order. When I printed out the releases, I realized I did want it to get that far.

I planned to conduct one on one interviews with people as well as household interviews. In addition, I would have one group interview with whomever would come. I also planned to take photographs with my phone, not only of the people but where they lived and the town as it was today.

The more I got into my notes from years ago, I began to see how geography affected the economy, which affected the people. There would not have been a mill if there had not been a river. No lumber, no mill, and so on. Markets, owners, competition, unions, government regulations, enforcement—or lack thereof—all created the storm which destroyed lives.

I had re-read Capote's *In Cold Blood* and Sebastian Junger's *The Perfect Storm* to prime me for the project. In both cases, I felt like I was entirely inadequate for the task I had set out for myself. All of my 'Who am I to think I can…' feelings emerged. When I told Maude, she said, "Of course, you can't. So what? Just write the damned book the best way you know how. I'll read it, and I'll get your kids to read it whether they want to or not. I bet Judd and Patty will read it. Maybe the Howletts. And those people up in Jay will read it. Isn't that enough for you? Drop the grandiosity and just get to it." Hannah would have been more gentle saying the same thing. Both would have been right.

I had brought my 'Jay box' with me. One stop would be to the museum, where I planned on returning the material I had borrowed from them. I also wanted to re-read Paul Hampton's book about the strike. Hampton had been the labor organizer for the AFL-CIO. He was dispatched to help the workers organize and press their claims. This was their first strike, and Hampton was starting from ground zero.

I had made arrangements to stay at the Lake Inn about six miles outside Jay. My room wouldn't be ready until three, but they said I could drop my bags off, check in, and get my key whenever I wanted. After I did all of that and got back in the car, I checked my voicemail. It was Nan. She had left a terse message, "Mike, we need to talk. Please don't avoid me. I couldn't handle that."

I called her back. I was glad it went to voicemail. I left her a message. "I am away for a couple of days working on the project I told you about. I'll call you when I get back."

Chapter Forty: Ancient History

The towns of Jay and Livermore Falls are separated by less than three miles and not much else. They are both company mill towns spawned by the same industry, and controlled by the same mill owners. Maine's independent pride prevented them from merging, although they do share the same high school. Whatever happened in one town affected the other.

Elm Street is a popular street name in New England towns. Even though the elm trees gave way to disease many years ago, no one thought to, or dared to, change the name of the streets. Mill Street is less popular; mills were not as prolific as elms. Livermore Falls has both. In most of these towns, the more money you made, the farther from the mill you lived—often up a hill and away from the stench generated by the mill.

My first interview was with Rona and John Palmer. I drove halfway up Elm Street and took a right onto Cross Street to get to their home. Husband and wife owned Palmer's Hardware in Livermore Falls. It had been in John's family for three generations, and they had hoped it would be handed on to a fourth. Unfortunately, it didn't work out that way.

When we settled down in their living room, Rona did most of the talking for the two of them. She was a very large woman whose weight had taken its toll. She wore a short-sleeved floral blouse, and flaps of skin hung from her arms down below the sleeves. She found it difficult to move, even in her own home, and used a cane. Rona occupied much more space than her husband, John, physically and verbally. When I asked about the business and how it was doing, she answered for both of them. "About the same as it ever did. We make enough to pay the bills and don't owe anybody anything. Running a small business ain't the way to get rich. Never was; never will be.

We'll sell it when we get ready to give it up in a couple of years. Neither of the kids wants it, which is a shame. Place's been in John's family for generations. We made the mistake of sending my son off to a liberal arts college. Wanted him to go to business school. He'd have none of it. So instead went to UMaine Farmington and decided to become a French teacher. Now he's teaching rich kids at Saint Thomas More down in Connecticut. Even became a Catholic. We don't see that much of him."

"And when you do you, you just egg him on and get him arguing," John said.

"Well. That's his problem. He's the one who turned into a socialist libtard."

I thought it best to move away from her feelings about socialist libtards and asked about her other children.

"Just one. My daughter got married and moved to Portland. She and her husband are both nurses now. Would you believe they've decided not to have any kids? It's all money with them, money and having fun. They make a pretty penny between the two of 'em with overtime and everything. They like to travel. Young people don't stay here. Nothin' for 'em."

"That's not true," John contradicted. "We have more people in town now than we did in the seventies."

"And fewer people than we did ten years ago."

"Oh, come on. Not many. You're giving Mike here the wrong impression of what this town's like."

They agreed on very little about Livermore Falls, today or at the time of the strike. However, they did agree that the strike was ancient history, a kind of two-year interruption of a way of life that had existed since the paper mills had been consolidated into International Paper years ago.

I had scheduled the Palmer interview for an hour, right after their store closed. Rona, though, insisted I stay for dinner. She wanted to talk. John would occasionally provide a footnote to her monologues, sometimes clarifying, sometimes providing a different perspective. It was Rona's interview, though, and she wanted to make sure her opinions were told to someone who was writing a book. She also told me that she had thought about writing a book and her friends told her she should do it.

As she talked, I realized that little of what she was saying had to do with the strike and its aftermath. She assured me that the strike would never have existed if it had not been for outside socialist agitators like Paul Hampton. She said, "Strike got over, and those freakin' outsiders left here and never came back. It was good riddance to them. That was the last labor trouble at the mill that amounted to anything. People learned. You don't bite the hand that feeds you unless you want to get bitten right back. People learned. It's all ancient history now."

No matter how hard I tried to bring the conversation back to the strike's impact, she would move off onto a different tangent. I finally stopped trying and just let her go. After a while, I realized that she always came around to her beliefs about the failure of her town government, her state government, and her federal government. The exceptions were when Paul LePage was governor of Maine and now, with Donald Trump as President of the United States. Rona believed that both were men of common sense who "Don't mince words." 'Mincing words' was a sin of great magnitude in Rona's layers of hell. The more she ranted, the quieter her husband became and the fewer the questions I asked.

After an hour of nodding politely, my watch became my friend. I glanced at it, acted surprised at the time, demonstrated my capacity to yawn on demand, thanked her for a wonderful dinner, and excused myself. John walked me to my truck. "Sorry about that. Once she gets going, there's no stoppin' her. She comes home at night and gets glued to Fox News. I don't dare offer any opinions of my own." I told him it was alright and said good night. Driving the truck back to the hotel, I felt like I was in retreat from a verbal offensive by a superior force.

My interviews on Tuesday were far more productive, but my plans for getting people together for an evening dinner went nowhere. People thought it was a waste of time. The strike was long ago, and they didn't want to get into arguments that were best left dead and buried. I felt my story start to take a different turn. How did a town move on past a crisis that changed things for so many people? What was the process through which it embalmed and entombed its history? Would it have been the same if it had been a natural disaster like a flood or an accident like the mill blowing up?

My final interview for this trip was to be with Helen Graham. I enjoyed speaking with Helen on the phone and was looking forward to meeting her in person. She told me that she had fallen, broken her wrist, and badly bruised her right knee. She also said, "I look like hell. My face and my basement banister disagreed about which was the hardest. The banister won." When I asked her if she would like to postpone, she said, "Hell no. I'm fine. My daughter-in-law's here waiting on me hand and foot. Be good for her to have someone to talk to besides an old lady."

I knew that Helen and her late husband Al had both worked for International Paper before the strike. They had both gone out with the strikers and never returned. They had each worked there for over thirty years at the time of the strike and had been in their mid-fifties when they walked out. Helen survived; Al had a heart attack. International Paper made it difficult for Helen to collect all her benefits because she was a 'striker,' but, Helen told me, "Little Al made them pay up. There was no way my son would let them get away with anything. I was lucky. My son's a lawyer. Some others just got screwed. There's no other way of putting it."

If Elm Street was a likely New England street name, Oak Street was close behind. Helen Graham lived on Oak Street in a modest ranch-style house with a one-car detached garage. There were two cars in the driveway. I assumed the second car was Helen's daughter-in-law. It was a little before ten when I parked in the street in front of the house. When I rang the doorbell, the woman who answered was dressed in shorts and a T-shirt that said:

She Believed She Could Change the World.
So She Became a Counselor

She was sweating. "Come on in," she said. "Sorry for my appearance. Just got in from a run. Mom's in the living room. She's been waiting for you."

"Am I late?" I asked.

She laughed. "No. No problem. Come on in. I'm going to take a quick shower, and then I'll join you. There's a pot of coffee and some goodies on the table. Help yourself."

She left me standing there. Two images remained—the T-shirt and her pure white hair. Helen Mirren popped into my head. Wendy and I had just watched the movie *Red*, and Wendy had commented how much she loved white hair like Hellen Mirren's. "Gramps, I want to have hair like that when I get old." My response was to tell my beloved granddaughter that I had a hard time thinking of Helen Mirren as old. This sweaty white-haired woman who had answered the door did not seem old to me, either. I was to learn that her name was Grace.

Finding my way to the living room meant walking a few steps down a hall and taking a right. Helen was sitting on a couch facing me. I couldn't help but stare at her face. It was a mess of scrape marks over various shades of black, blue, purple, and brown. She had definitely lost her fight with the banister. Her right hand and wrist were in a cast which were held across her chest by a gray sling.

"Oh, go ahead and look," she said. "I'm getting used to it."

"I'm sorry."

"Not nearly as much as I am, believe me. So come on in and have a seat. Grace has been her usual angelic self and set us up with coffee and some banana bread. Fixings for coffee are right there. Help yourself."

I did. I offered to get something for her, but she declined. "Had mine earlier. So, tell me, what can I tell you now that I didn't tell you over the phone?"

I told her I wanted to fill in some gaps. I asked permission to turn my recorder on, received it, and began asking a series of factual questions. The old reporter in me doing my job. Get it right. Are the answers the same as I had gotten from other people? Clarify, clarify, clarify. After my information gathering was complete, I told her I had been wondering how and why people seemed so eager to put the strike behind them when there was so much turmoil at the time. I gave her some of the quotations I had collected without naming names. I said, "It seems to me that the prevalent attitude is: That's ancient history."

"Really, Mike? Why are you surprised? Who do you know that celebrates when they lose one of the biggest battles of their life? Did you expect some whoop-de-doo with statues and plaques? Of course we want to act like it never existed. We're not nuts. What do you think? We're a bunch of hicks up here who couldn't get on with our lives?"

"I'm sorry. I wasn't suggesting…"

"Mom, you love being a hick." Grace had entered the room and went over and sat next to her mother-in-law. She turned to me and said, "Got you, didn't she?"

"Had to spoil it, didn't you," Helen said to Grace.

"Mom, you can be so bad when you want to."

"It's part of my charm."

"Okay," I said, throwing up my hands. "You got me. Everybody moved on, except possibly me, and I don't even live here. I'm curious, though. I'm just trying to understand it."

Helen said, "Grace, tell him your take on it. I said it's 'cause you don't want to remember losing."

"You sure? I think Mike is more interested in hearing your story."

"Oh. He will. But you have an interesting perspective on it as a psychologist."

Grace said to me, "Mike, I'm not a psychologist. I was a school counselor and then a middle school principal for most of my career. You sure you want to hear from me?"

"Yes. I'm curious about the way you saw it. How did the strike affect you?"

"Honestly, it didn't affect me that much, directly."

Helen urged, "Tell him your idea, Grace."

"Okay. I was a young married when the strike happened," Grace said. "Al and I…

"Little Al," Helen added.

"Mom, you know he hates that."

"I'm his mother, and I have certain rights."

"Anyway, my husband at the time, Little Al, and I had moved to Concord so he could go to law school. We had both gone to UNH and had no plans to return to Jay and work at the mill, which many of our friends had done. There had never been any troubles between the union and International Paper. Some people wondered if there should even be a union. Then, and here's what Mom is talking about, IP unilaterally decided to change everything. In other words, the old relationship between the union and the company was killed off. I likened it to what happens in the stages of grief when a relationship is ended. At first, people didn't believe it was happening. They were in shock. It was like losing someone who had been part of your life, and suddenly they were killed, and some monster had risen up to take its place. After the shock, people became angry, really angry. Do you know about Paul Hampton?"

"Yes, I do."

"Well, Hampton came riding into town, a town that had never risen up over anything. Hampton was very good at what he did, and soon there were weekly rallies and a lot of excitement, at times almost like a party. It was fury or fun, depending upon the day. Sometimes both. People felt powerful. It was like Clint Eastwood had entered the town on his horse and was going to save it. They were going to win. They were going to lash out. Get even. They could taste blood, and at times it did become bloody. But they didn't win.

"I know, it isn't a direct overlay. When they went to bargain, though, there was no bargaining with International Paper. The company hired full-time replacements and the strikers had no leverage from which to bargain. All the vendors crossed the picket lines. The strikers went into a deep funk of depression. People stopped talking to one another, and eventually, they just accepted what happened. There was a new normal in which the company had all the power. People went back to work, found other jobs, or moved. Something had died. So, disbelief, pain, anger, bargaining, and depression. Eventually, there was reconstruction, the new normal, and ultimately acceptance."

I absorbed what she was saying. No one said anything. My recorder kept running. It captured the sound of the refrigerator and a dog barking outside. Grace and I looked at each other. I became uncomfortable with the moment's intimacy and said, "Thank you. That makes sense to me." I didn't say, "Too much sense. Too close to home." I knew, though, that in that room with those two women, if I had talked about Hannah, and my understanding of the stages of grief, it would have been okay.

Helen brought me back. "What'd I tell you, Mike? She's smart, this one. She hit the nail right on the head. Now you understand why a lot of people are reluctant to dredge things up. This town was never so together as during that strike. Yeah, there were some who were on the company's side, but most people supported the strikers. The company won; the town lost its soul. It never got it back."

My book was taking on a dimension I had not anticipated. We spent the rest of the morning talking about specifics: people, events, changes. I learned that around two hundred of the strikers had left town and gone to Bath to get jobs at the shipyard. When the strike was over, most of them came back home to lower-paying jobs, but it was home. At one point, Helen said, "I gave my husband to that strike. His heart couldn't take it."

As I listened, our talk turned to other matters. I learned that Grace and 'Little Al' had divorced after ten years of marriage, that Grace had retired two years ago, had worked in the Portsmouth, New Hampshire School System her entire career, and still lived there, as did her daughter's family. She had a son who was a social worker in Seattle and had moved there to be with his 'partner' who worked for Microsoft.

I told them about my family, Hannah's death, and Wendy coming to be with me for the summer. I didn't say anything about Nan or my need to get away after my drinking episode. I told them about my family's seafaring and flying traditions but said nothing about my time in Laos.

After a while, Helen excused herself to go to the bathroom. "We need to leave you to your own devices for a couple of minutes. I find it almost impossible to do anything by myself with this busted wing, including going to the toilet, for God's sake. I'm right-handed, and I struggle to do things with my left hand, even opening doors." Grace looked at me, smiled, and went to help 'Mom.'

When they were gone, I got up to stretch my legs and looked around the room. I wondered how long the wallpaper had been there. There was a spinet piano. The keyboard was open, and a Reader's

Digest songbook was on the music stand. It was opened to *Moonlight in Vermont.* Had the book been opened to that page for a long time, or had Grace been passing the time playing the piano while she was taking care of Helen? On top of the piano were various sized picture frames containing family pictures. Some looked like they were school pictures of grandchildren. There was a wedding picture of a young Grace with a man who must have been 'Little Al.' One picture had to be of 'Big Al' from the age of the print. Grace appeared in so many photos that I concluded that the daughter-in-law, divorced or not, was still the daughter.

When they returned, Helen said, "I have an idea. I know you've already picked out the families you want to focus on, but there's someone else I think you should talk to, my minister, Ted Kingston. He saw the whole thing from a different perspective. Want me to give him a call and see if he's free this afternoon?"

"Sure. Thank you."

"And, if you want to come back and talk some more, we would love to have you. Grace's here all summer babysitting me 'til I get this damned cast off. So next time, make it lunch or dinner and bring Wendy if you'd like. It's only, what, a couple of hours?"

"Only an hour and a half. Thank you for the offer. Not sure about Wendy, but I might take you up on that."

Helen called Ted Kingston, and he said to stop by around one. I decided to go back to Le Fleurs for lunch. As I drove there, I decided Grace Graham did remind me of Helen Mirren with that white hair. I'd have to tell Wendy. I wondered why Grace and 'Little Al' got divorced.

Chapter Forty-One: Good and Evil

I went looking for the Jay Congregational Church and found it without any difficulty. However, it was not what I expected. It was New England Congregational white, but it was small, and there was no steeple. The building had a sharply pitched roof, and there were three stained glass windows in front facing the street. You entered from the side in what looked like a three-story afterthought attached to the main building. The small parking lot was across the street.

Ted Kingston was sitting on the front step. Behind him, in the doorway, I could see a paint can and a roller sitting in a paint tray. He got up and offered me his hand when I walked over to him. He was a short, middle-aged man, balding, with a well-developed pot belly that hung over his shorts. He smiled at me and said, "Do you mind if we talk here? It's a beautiful day. I'm technically on vacation but am hanging around to get some work done. Right now, painting the bathrooms."

"No, not at all." We sat down side by side, facing the street and the town below.

"So, you've met Helen and Grace, great people."

"Yeah. I enjoyed talking to them."

"Helen filled me in a bit. Said you're writing a book about the strike in the eighties and how it impacted the town."

"Pretty much. Although it's starting to head in a direction I had not anticipated."

"Let me guess. People can't understand why anyone would care about what happened thirty years ago. Let bygones be bygones. Right?"

"Seems that way. You were here then?"

"I was. This was my first church. I had been an assistant for five years at a big church in Massachusetts and was thrilled to be going out on my own. My wife was a little less thrilled to be leaving a city and moving to a mill town, and that's what Jay was and is. When we came here, International Paper controlled everything. It wasn't always direct, but it was very real."

"Do you mind if I tape our conversation?"

"No. Go right ahead. But, umm, I may ask you to turn it off once in a while. That okay with you?"

"Sure." I turned on the recorder. "Can you give me an example of how the control was exercised?"

"Well, for example, and this was happening when I first got here, a few people, mostly younger, college-educated, started to complain about how the mill was desecrating the Androscoggin River with its waste. They even got some of the high school kids involved. Made up signs. Started a petition to stop it. The environmental movement was just beginning to take hold. The Love Canal scandal was still getting national press; Pete Seeger had the Clearwater campaign up and running to clean up the Hudson. Here in Jay, we had International Paper dumping their waste into the river. Some teachers started to get involved, and that's when things heated up, and we started to see the power of IP over the town's leaders and the schools. It may have been the shortest environmental effort in history. Parents got to the kids, principals got to the teachers, and those left standing were out there on their own with no support.

"Whatever the issue is in this town, if it affects the mills, it's always 'Don't bite the hand that feeds you.' That was International Paper in this town. The hand that fed everybody, one way or another. He that giveth could also taketh away. And it did taketh away, big time, and that's what started the strike. Not much different today."

"You sound bitter."

"Not bitter as much as resigned. It was my first real encounter with the evils of uncontained power. I was young and had supported a couple of the young people in the congregation who were involved in cleaning up the river. I got slapped down for giving them support and offering the church as a place to meet. I was surprised and didn't know how to handle it. From my youthful perch on high, we were confronting an evil. My wife and I had young kids at the time. I was new here. The rest of the congregation wasn't supportive of the clean-up effort, so I backed off—the first of many instances of my backing away from evil.

"Evil?"

"Remember, this was my first church. I was young. I hoped to be relevant. Remember how we used to use that word?"

"Relevant? I sure do."

"Well. I was sure that IP was engaged in practices that would cause people to become ill and despoil the river and all that meant: fish hatcheries, recreation, and so on. IP knew what it was doing, and people in the town knew. But that was the hand, and no one wanted to nibble at it, let alone bite it.

"The strike came later. Like most people here, I couldn't believe what IP did. What that company did was despicable. I used the language of evil with the environmental issue, but this was of a different dimension. This was a direct attack on the people and their town. IP's decisions were intended to create pain so people would bend to the will of their almighty god – International Paper. It was evil, pure evil."

"I guess I'm not used to thinking in those terms."

"I know. You probably think of things like the Holocaust and slavery when you think of evil. This was every bit as evil. It was conscious. It was deliberately inflicting pain, and for what? More profit when you're already more profitable than you've ever been."

"It's a strong word."

"You bet it is. I lost my innocence during the strike. I also lost the theology I had been taught."

"What do you mean?"

"I went to a liberal seminary, and I belong to a fairly liberal denomination. No fire and brimstone, no devils walking around possessing people, no being saved, or you're spending eternity as kindling down below. Evil and Satan weren't much on the minds of our professors except as metaphors. That's nonsense. Evil exists. It's real, and it was here in Jay, and its name was International Paper. But, again, I was found wanting. I didn't have the experience or the courage to confront it. I also realized that being a parish minister required me to make deals with the devil, or at least ignore him."

"What do you mean?"

"My congregation was split into three factions. One group felt that a religious congregation should stay miles away from any controversy, and the strike was about as controversial as you could get. A smaller group felt that the strikers were being greedy and didn't care about the town. They saw the strikers as well-paid babies who should know when they're well off."

"Was that the language they used?"

"Yes, and worse. The third group was hurting from the loss of income and insecurity, which worsened as the strike went on. Month after month, they saw themselves going deeper into the hole, and then the national union started abandoning them. They wanted me; they wanted their church to do something, be there for them and not with platitudes."

"How did you handle it?"

"At the time, I saw my job as being a calming influence. I preached kindness and acceptance. I dug into every biblical story I could that would calm the waters. I think I alienated everyone at one time or another."

"I can imagine."

"I called up one of my professors to get some perspective. He said I should minister to everyone. Minister to my entire flock? Yeah, sure. I told myself that would salve my conscience."

"Do you regret trying to do that?"

"You bet I do. You know the old labor song, 'Whose Side Are You On?' I was called upon to choose a side, and I failed. What International Paper was doing was wrong. The IP decision-makers were not good people. The only thing they worshipped was the capitalist dollar. Unfortunately, the people in the town had also been called upon to choose sides, and I didn't offer any guidance on how to do that."

"How did you resolve it?"

"I didn't. Some of my people left because I didn't side with the workers. They felt abandoned and that the church was irrelevant. Some in the church thought we shouldn't even do food drives for the workers because they were bringing it on themselves. There weren't many like that, but there were a few.

"I wish I had shown up. I mean, really shown up, maybe even on the picket line. I deluded myself with the notion that my job was to make sure the church existed and was not torn apart. That was nonsense. People were hurting one another. There was physical violence at times. Fortunately, we didn't have any of that within our congregation, but some people weren't talking to one another. Try preaching when you see that kind of hate sitting in front of you. I didn't know how to cope with it then, and I still don't. Churches can be absurd about little conflicts. How's this? There was an argument about whether to paint the bathrooms white or yellow? So now I'm painting one white and one yellow. You give it a big issue to handle, one that calls for moral witness and action, and churches often fail. Their ministers fail. Would you turn your recorder off?"

"Sure."

"That's why I'm leaving the ministry."

"I'm sorry, I didn't know that."

"I haven't told anybody yet. I shouldn't have told you. Only my wife and kids and the people at the conference office know. I plan to leave at the end of this coming church year."

"Why now?"

"It's the same damn thing today. Several of the leaders in my congregation are open Trump supporters and don't want me to preach about anything within a stone's throw of moral decision-making. Again. Evil. Put children in cages, mock people with disabilities, and call people fleeing torture rapists. I preached on Matthew 19, and did that ever stir things up. Again, the same song: 'That's political and shouldn't be talked about in church.'"

"I'm sorry, I'm not familiar...."

"Sorry, it's where Jesus talks about the little children not being banished when he's teaching." Then, Ted's voice changed, and he recited. "Let the little children come to me, and do not hinder them, for the kingdom of heaven belongs to such as these." And now we're putting those little children in cages because their parents want them to live."

"Now I remember."

"Same sermon, also from Matthew: 'Again I say unto you, It is easier for a camel to go through the eye of a needle than for a rich man to enter into the kingdom of God.' Some people thought it was a direct attack on Trump."

"Was it?"

"Of course." Ted smiled. "If evil shouldn't be talked about in church, where the hell should it be talked about?"

I thought for a minute before saying, "I find it hard to admit this. I have a problem with my eldest. She lives in Texas and is a Trumpie. I never thought of her as being evil, though."

"You get a glimpse of my problem, then. How do you love someone who is supporting evil? Imagine living with it day in and day out when your job is to preach and inspire goodness."

"And that was your dilemma then, and it is now."

"Yeah. Going back to the strike, after all these years, I still don't understand them. How does a company, knowing that people depend upon it for food, shelter, warmth, and every basic human need decide that it's going to take some of that away when the company is making more money than it had ever had before? How can it tell people you're not going to have Christmas off, you're not going to get paid for overtime no matter how many hours you work, and we're going to tell you when you're going to work, and you will pay more for your health care? They did this when the company was rolling in money. You have to put this in context. International Paper was bursting with profits and still did these things to make even more money. The only answer I have is the presence of evil. I feel the same way today about Trump and those who follow him. I can't do this battle again. I'm not up to it. I failed once, and I know I will fail again. I'm running away, and I know it. I'm tired of feeling like I'm wearing a damned gag in my mouth. It tastes like you know what."

"Running away sounds a bit strong."

"Enlightened departure based upon reflective discernment. How's that for religious doublespeak?"

I laughed, "Well, it does sound better than running away."

"This has been coming for a while. One of the reasons I've stayed as long as I have is because I'm not sure the congregation will survive me. I'm not being egotistical about that. We're down to sixty members, and most of them are as old or older than me. You should see what happens when a new family shows up for the first time. They are pounced on like they are the second coming. I don't know. Maybe new blood will make something happen here that I haven't been able to accomplish. Burnout is not an uncommon phenomenon with us clergy types, you know."

"I have to admit, never gave it much thought."

"We're sort of like the union was here. As long as everything is going along okay, no one thinks much about their minister."

"Maybe you need a clergy union."

"Not a bad idea."

"I'm still struck by the idea of evil as you are using it."

"You ever read anything by Reinhold Niebuhr?"

"No, I haven't."

"You might want to take a look at *Moral Man and Immoral Society*. Niebuhr was an activist as well as a philosopher and theologian. I've been spending quite a bit of time re-reading his works this summer."

"Is the book heavy going?"

"Weighty but not heavy."

"Okay. I'll take a look at it."

"You might find it helpful when you think about your oldest."

"Interesting. I admit it. I don't understand her, and I haven't spent much time trying."

Ted didn't say anything. There was silence between us. Finally, I broke it by asking, "Any thought to what you might do?"

Ted laughed, "I told my wife maybe I'd become a union organizer. She didn't think that was at all funny. I told her not to worry. The truth is, I don't know." He smiled and said, "This will be a year of reflective discernment." Ted paused before saying, "No matter what I do, I doubt I'll make any less money than I'm making now. I do know it won't be any place where I have to wear a gag."

I had an hour and a half drive to think about Ruth. The more I thought about her, the more I realized that I was furious with her, and it was not about Trump or her asking me for help. I was angry at her for the years of arrogance, the years of us having to go to Texas if we wanted to see her and her family, and the scant interest she had shown in Hannah's illness until the very end. I reminded myself that as little as I knew him, Hal was still my grandson and he had nothing to do with any of that. By the time I was home, I was determined to help him out. I also decided to check out *Moral Man and Immoral Society* from the Patten Free Library in Bath. I was used to thinking in terms of right and wrong. Good and evil, though; were they different words, religious words, or a different dimension? I chuckled at the image of Wendy and me at opposite ends of the couch reading weighty tomes.

I liked Ted Kingston and was sorry that he was caught up in, what? An existential crisis? It was clear that ministers had them, too. I also thought about Helen and Grace. I wondered if they might enjoy coming down to Tír for the day and going for a sail on the *Redhead*. We had room if it would be easier for them to spend the night.

Chapter Forty-Two: Lost and Found

I liked working and interviewing people, even when I didn't like the people I was interviewing. Then there were people like Helen and Grace who just make you feel better about the whole human race. I was glad they suggested I talk to their minister, whom I now thought of as Reverend Ted, because that's what they called him. A good, if troubled, man. I'm glad I met him. Good people.

I should know better than to turn on the news when I am in a good mood. Unfortunately, I did turn on the radio only to learn that Boris Johnson would be the next Prime Minister of the United Kingdom. Really! Boris Johnson? Does the United States have this lockstep political move, some kind of sick waltz with the UK? We elect someone like Trump, so they elect Boris Johnson. I wondered if Trump and Johnson would turn out to have a love affair like Reagan and Thatcher. I turned the radio off. I wanted to enjoy the drive from Jay to Georgetown.

I had already started thinking about Johnson, Thatcher, Reagan, and unions. Trump had unleashed virulent xenophobia on the United States. Had Reagan done a similar thing with unions when he broke the Air Controller Strike? Had he opened up a union-busting dam, and was the International Paper strike one of the tragic casualties of Reagan's anti-union flood? The decline of union membership was steep during and after the Reagan years. From 1980 to 2018, union membership in the United States workforce had declined from twenty percent to six percent. National media didn't seem to care about the ramifications. Neither did politicians, regardless of party. Everyone seemed to be taking it as a given. Goodbye middle class. The only unions people heard about were in the public sector: teachers, police, firefighters. I somehow had to convey this larger context. The people I was interviewing did not exist in a vacuum. There was a story to be told, and the strike in Jay was the perfect fulcrum from which to leverage a much bigger story. I was getting excited, very excited. I knew where the book was going. I knew what the stakes were. I was no longer simply resurrecting old notes or trying to see if I could master the form of the non-fiction novel. I had a story to tell, and it was an important story.

I couldn't wait. I pulled off into Riverbend Campground and called Jennifer Marlow. Jennifer was an old friend and the owner of Lazy Days Press. She's an outstanding editor and had published three of my books over the years.

"Jennifer, it's Mike Buckley. You got a minute?"

"Mike? Of course I have a minute and a lot more. It's good to hear from you. But, God, how long has it been? How are you?"

"I'm fine. I know. We haven't talked since…"

"Oh, I'll bet it's been at least a couple of years. I think it was when you had dinner with us when you were in Augusta."

"Really, it's been that long? Wow."

"So, how are you doing? What have you been up to?"

"Not a whole hell of a lot."

"I'm glad you called. You nearby? Can we grab a bite to eat? Cup of coffee?"

"I'd love to do that sometime, but I'm in the car on my way home from Jay right now. In fact, that's the reason I called. I have an idea for a new book."

"A new book? No kidding. What's it about?"

"Yeah. It's a big one." I spent the next ten minutes talking with very few pauses. Jennifer would occasionally ask a question or say something encouraging like "really" or "I didn't know that." Finally, when I finished, I asked, "What do you think?"

"Well, for one thing, I think it's great to hear you so excited about a project."

That was not what I wanted to hear. It sounded like what a

therapist would say. So I said, "I am excited about it. What do you think of the idea?"

"I agree with you that there is a story here. But I think what you're asking is if it is right for Lazy Days."

"Yeah. It's got the whole Maine angle and everything. I thought it might be perfect for you."

"Well, it does have the Maine angle, that's true."

"I hear a 'but.'"

"Mike. You know what we publish. It's a combination of cozy mysteries, romances, and the kinds of things you published with us before; little known but interesting stories about Maine people and locations. What you're describing sounds like a very serious book that might be a case study in labor economics. Very important, but more suitable for an academic press. You know our audience. People on vacation, or people who wished they were on vacation. Escapist entertainment."

I took a deep breath and didn't say anything. I wasn't going to argue with her. She was right. I knew she was right. I knew what was next. The idea of writing 'query letters' to publishers was the last thing I wanted to do, but I knew that she was going to suggest I do just that. I wanted to tell the story, not have to peddle it.

She broke the silence. "I'm sorry, Mike. Now, I can give you the names of some people that might be interested. Also, this is a real departure for you. You're best known for your 'Home Town Boy' pieces and the books we published before. I hate to bring this up, but you haven't published anything in quite some time. I'm not sure about your current name recognition. I know you're very excited about this story, but it may take you a while to find the right venue. At one point you had mentioned publishing a collection of 'Home Town Boy' pieces. I would still be interested in that."

"Thanks. That's a possibility, but right now…"

"I know. I get it. Your reporter juices are flowing, and you think you're on to an important story. I understand. You know, there is one other possibility."

"What's that?"

"Publish it yourself. We've been helping authors with books that aren't right for us. We edit, do covers, get your ISBN, take care of formatting, and get it up on Amazon. You wouldn't have to worry about any of that. Then, since the copyright would be yours, you might get some publishers interested if they started to see some response. I could also help you out with some marketing ideas."

"How much money are we talking about?"

"Depending on how clean the manuscript is, usually about two, maybe three thousand dollars if there are pictures."

"Eww. I'll have to think about it."

"Mike, I know you're disappointed. Why don't I send you a few names? See how you make out. I know query letters are a pain, but it's how the game's played. What do you say? Sounds like you're at the beginning stages anyway. You don't have to make any decisions right now."

"You're right."

"Okay. I'll get the names off to you tomorrow. Let's get together for lunch. We can meet halfway. Maybe Annabella's in Dresden. It's been far too long. And think about 'Home Town Boy.' I know I'd be interested in that."

"I will. Thanks."

First Boris Johnson and now this, all within an hour. I decided to call Maude and whine. She wasn't available. Just as well. If she were available, she'd tell me to get over myself, again.

By the time I reached Tír na nÓg, I was on a relatively even keel. Maybe I was becoming bipolar. I had dismissed that idea by the time I got out of my truck. Charlie came out to greet me, followed by Rina. "Hi, Mr. Buckley. Wendy's not home yet from kayaking with Archie.

She called, said they'd be late. She asked me to feed Charlie and let him out. I was just getting his food out when we heard you."

"She's going to be late? Everything okay?"

"With them? My hunch is everything is very okay." She smiled.

"Oh. I see. Sure. I'll take care of Charlie. I'm not going anywhere. She give any idea of time?"

"No. She just said late."

Rina left, and I unloaded my bag from the truck and went into the house with Charlie tagging behind me. I fed him and looked at the clock.

I had calls to make, and I didn't want to wait. The first one was to Kennebec Savings and Loan. I got right through to George MacGregor. I explained what I wanted to do and why. He said getting a mortgage on the farm in the amount I was considering would be no problem and that it could be done on an expedited basis. My second call was to Sharon O'Neil. She's the lawyer in the family. I told her what I had in mind. She said that what I was suggesting would be relatively painless. I could loan Hal the money for school. He was old enough to sign the note himself. The arrangement would just be between the two of us. When I told her that I wanted to see if somehow we could make it so that I would pay for 'B's or better, she laughed. "That will take a little bit of work to draw up. Do you think that will have the desired effect?"

"Who knows? It might. He can work it out with his parents as far as who pays for expenses beyond tuition, room, and board. It might even push Ruth to ask something of him."

I was going to call Ruth and tell her what I had in mind but decided not to. Instead, I emailed Hal and sent Ruth and Harold copies. If it was going to be between my grandson and me, I was going to start treating him like an adult. He and his parents would still have to figure out his expenses, but his tuition would be covered. He could pay me back over time at the same rate I'd be paying on the mortgage which would be much lower than if he had a student loan. If his parents wanted to help him out, they could pay him, and he could pay me. I knew it was convoluted and Hannah would have thought I was being overly legalistic, but my gut told me it was the best way to help them all deal with their reality. It was a risk. I didn't know this young man, but was that his fault or his parents? I decided it was theirs and mine. I had never done anything to reach out to him. I did know one thing: my proposal would stir up a shit storm in Texas. The only question was how much of it would blow my way.

    I was sound asleep when Wendy got home. Charlie barked when he heard the car come down the driveway. I wondered if I should get up but decided not to. She was a legal adult, too, like her Texas cousin. How the hell did I come to have grandchildren this age? I didn't ponder that for very long. I heard Archie and Wendy talking in hushed tones in the living room and went back to sleep. They were home safe. I hadn't worried about people coming home in quite some time.
    The following day Archie was stretched out on the couch in the living room. He had a blanket over him, and I could see the corner of a pillow under his head, probably from Wendy's bed. I went into the kitchen and started making my regular breakfast. I was sure that Wendy would not be getting up early, so I fed Charlie and left Wendy a note telling her I had done it so he would not get a double heaping of kibble. It was a beautiful day, so I took my coffee down to the pier. Charlie came with me. Having fed him last night and this morning and letting him sleep with me, I was now his best friend.
    I was a bit surprised when Archie came down and joined me. "What a gorgeous day," he said.
    "It is that," I replied.
    "Sorry, we got in so late last night. Hope we didn't wake you up."
    "Nah, I heard you and then went right back to sleep. Have a good time?"

"Wonderful. Wendy's such an incredible athlete; she took to kayaking like she'd been doing it all of her life."

"I'm glad. I think she's been having a good summer."

"I'll say. She loves being here. She's really into her research project. I can't wait to see it when it's finished. I told her I'd help edit if she wanted."

"Really? That's very generous of you."

"No. I'd enjoy it. All the summers I've been coming here, she's shown me that I don't know a thing about Georgetown. Some fascinating things have gone on here. I love the stories she's been telling me."

"No kidding."

"Yeah. I'm glad she switched to history. She's so passionate about it."

I wanted to say 'really?' again but refrained. Was this the same Wendy who complained about her history professor and the assignment at the beginning of the summer? I thought it best to let the conversation develop however it would. I said, "She's been spending a lot of time on it."

"That's what she told me. She's so disciplined. I wish I could be that disciplined. By the way, she read some of your 'Home Town Boy' articles to me on the way up and back. They're great. I loved them."

"Thanks."

He didn't say anything more. I'm not sure why I said, "Month's almost over. You'll be heading home soon."

He said, "I can't believe we only have a few days left. The month has flown by."

"It can go fast. Hope you've had a good time."

"Absolutely."

Charlie barked. Wendy was walking down the pier. Her hair was brushed, and she had on short shorts and a cut off T-shirt. She was barefoot even though the morning chill hadn't disappeared. Is there a grandparent code, especially a grandfather's, that prohibits noticing that your granddaughter is attractive? No, not attractive, 'Hot.' If such a code exists, I was breaking it. The hottie was coming to meet her hunk in their summer moment. The smiles they exchanged were vibrating with youthful knowledge of one another. So, they had more than paddled their way down the Androscoggin.

Archie said, "Hi, sleepyhead."

Maude was her sensible self when she finally called back. There were a few references to my inflated sense of self-importance and belief that everyone in the world should be as fascinated with Jay and the crisis in the labor movement as I was. But, to her credit, she was also using her problem-solving powers to put a few patches on my punctured excitement balloon. It was pretty simple, her 'one step at a time' approach. It often is, when it is someone else's life and you are not the one doing the stepping. So, step one was I would wait to get the names from Jennifer. Then, in step two, I would send off query letters with a first chapter. Meanwhile, I would keep working on the book. If no publisher was as impressed with the story as I was, step three would be to self-publish. Once published, step four was to approach the unions to see if they would purchase and distribute the book to their members, starting with United Paperworkers International. If that didn't work, step five would be to sell the book at summer farmer's markets next year.

It all made perfect sense, and I thanked her for her wisdom. The truth, though, was that I was disappointed. I would prefer to leave these hoops to other people to jump through on my behalf. I was a reporter. I had a good story. People should want to read it. I told Maude I would draft a query letter and show it to Jennifer. However, Maude had become 'Mother Maude' to the book and said, "I want to see it, too." When I told her that I already had the first chapter in my head, she said, "I've known you to have had many projects in your head. None of them have done much good there. When can I expect to see the first draft?" I felt like I was back at the paper with a deadline.

Wendy and Archie were both sitting at the dining room table when I came back into the house. There were sheets of paper laid out before them. Archie was reading one. Occasionally he would make a mark on the one he was reading. Wendy was just looking at him. I didn't say anything. I went into the kitchen to get myself another cup of coffee. It didn't take much to know he was editing her paper. She was quiet. I needed to be quiet. They were doing serious work.

I took my time. A couple of minutes later, I heard her say, "Really? Do you think it's okay? It's only a few pages so far. I still have to plug in footnotes, and I need to get more quotations. I also want to check some things out with the people at the historical society. There are a couple of pieces I'm not sure I got right. But you like it?"

It looked to me, leaning against the kitchen counter with a cup of coffee in my hand, like I had just lost my role as editor-in-chief. I heard Archie say, "This is very good, Wen. I didn't know all this stuff about Georgetown. It's fascinating. I do have one question. Tell me again what the assignment was."

I could hear papers shuffling. Then she read the assignment. When she finished, Archie said, "You've got all the history down. I think she wants you to also write about how it affected your life. You might want to put more in about that."

"You think?"

"Yeah. I don't know, but... Here, give me the assignment. Let me read it to you. Then, tell me what you think."

Chapter Forty-Three: Finn McCool

I didn't know what to say to Nan. I thought about suggesting we just be friends, but what would that even mean after what happened? We couldn't just rewind that night, like resetting the clocks in the fall. What would our friendship look like; what would it be like, feel like? She had confided in me about her marriage and its emptiness. If there was more time together, confidence sharing, touching, we would be right back to where we were Saturday night. My imagination was empty. I don't think I have ever thought about having a woman as a friend. The women 'friends' I had were all married, and, in most instances, I was much closer to their husbands than I was to them. I loved and admired Patty, but it was Judd to whom I talked. Patty was my friend, but it was different. History makes a difference, and Nan and I had a history, then and now. It couldn't be erased.

Nan hadn't simply popped back into my life; she had erupted out of nowhere, inflamed memories, and now she wanted me to be her lover, and last Saturday night, I wanted her. She may have wanted me for the wrong reasons, but she wanted me. I wanted her that night, and what the hell were my reasons? And now: guilt, lust, and looking and wondering about every woman I saw. It was like I had been to the optometrist and gotten a new prescription for glasses. I started noticing women, married or not, in ways I hadn't done in decades. And now, this new woman whom I had met in Jay, a woman taking care of her ex-mother-in-law, this Grace who lived in Portsmouth, New Hampshire. I wanted to know why she got divorced, if she was seeing anyone, was she—I hated the word—available, and what would she be like to kiss. And, thanks to Nan, what would she be like in bed, my bed or hers. Would she 'want' me? I hadn't asked that question for most of my life. Want. Strange word when applied to people—I want you. But, thinking about it, I began to feel something stirring—I wanted Grace.

Archie and Wendy couldn't keep their hands off one another, and I envied them. I missed being with someone who wanted to touch me, somebody I wanted to touch. Hannah and I were like that when we were young. Over the years it changed. It would come and go, touching, like tides: ebbing, flooding, receding, and returning. Certainty. Hannah and I had certainty. After Hannah's death, I accepted the new certainty that it would never be there again, touching. That was certain. I had become absolutely certain it was gone forever, and then Nan.

There was another 'now' that didn't fit into my life, another upended certainty—the second trip to Jay. People's lives, good people's lives, had been devastated by corrupt greed. Reverend Ted had been right. It was good versus evil, and I wanted to tell the story; I had to tell the story. Certainty.

Hannah had read *Warriors Don't Cry* when she was sick. It was the memoir of Melba Pattillo Beals, one of the Little Rock Nine students who had integrated Central High School in Little Rock, Arkansas. Eisenhower had to send in federal marshals to protect her and the other children from the racist mobs that taunted them daily. Hannah had pointed out to me how vital the reporters were in getting that story out to the American public. I know she was saying to me, 'what you do is important,' boosting me up. However, it had the opposite effect. I felt ashamed. In college, I had committed myself to being a courageous reporter, a 'warrior' reporter. Instead, I had written for a local newspaper and covered Board of Education meetings. Redemption. I wanted redemption for that college kid. I had to write the story about the strike and its aftermath, the human story, even if no one wanted to read about it.

My head was spinning out of control, and I had to stop it. I felt like I was on the edge of screaming, throwing things, or laughing like some demented old man.

It was early afternoon. I had time. I grabbed my water bottle, filled it, and walked down to the end of the pier. Charlie followed me down the ramp to the dock. As I reached down to untie the dinghy, Charlie jumped in. I rowed out to *Sonas*. When I got there, I lifted Charlie on board, tied the dinghy to the mooring line, and climbed aboard. My body was tense. It was a good tension, the tension before you wind up to serve in tennis, or just before you kick the ball in soccer. It was the familiar tension of knowing exactly what you are going to do every second. I hoisted the sails, freed the boat from its mooring, pushed the helm over, and felt the energy as the wind filled the sails; the boat leaned to leeward and moved away from its tether. Charlie settled in at my feet, touching me.

Once settled on the tack that would take me out of the Cove entrance and into the Bay, memories began: Nan reaching her hand behind my neck as she kissed me, touching me, and later guiding me into her. Her taste. Holding her. I laughed. I felt awake. I started singing, "Sailing, sailing, over the bounding main; for many a stormy wind will blow, ere Jack comes home again." My dad used to sing that every time we would take off sailing. He would start with his name and then substitute my mother's name, my name, and then Maude's, depending on who was on board. So, I gave Charlie his due, "ere Charlie comes home again." Hearing his name, he looked up for a second and then put his head right back down again.

I felt awake, truly awake. I started thinking about the times when I had felt this way. Years ago, Hannah and I, along with Joel, Jesse, and Rachel, had gone on a long three-legged cruise. Ruth didn't want to go. She had just graduated from college and was besotted with Harold. The voyage was Hannah's idea. Both of us had a lot of unused vacation time and considerate bosses for whom we had spent many years working. The kid's teachers had been supportive of our plan—once we convinced them we were serious about the kids keeping journals and doing assignments.

Hannah had assignments for the two of us as well. We were to read Irish history, literature, and mythology. When she said she was taking James Joyce's *Finnegans Wake* and two books about *Finnegans Wake* with us, I had less than a favorable reaction, something along the lines of, "No one can understand that book. Why are you bothering to bring it?" Her response was, "It's nothing but a giant literary crossword puzzle of myths, symbols, and legends. Come on; it'll be fun." When I scoffed some more, she countered with, "Think of it as abstract art. Inhale it, don't analyze it. Jackson Pollock meets Salvador Dalí, only in print."

"I don't like them either," I said.

"I'll read it to you," she replied.

Finnegans Wake was, of course, included in the book bag. I had enjoyed some of the commentaries. One, in particular, stood out in my memory. The title came from the legend of Finn McCool, the greatest of the Irish mythological warriors. Joyce played games in the book at times: even the title had multiple meanings, *Finnegans Wake*—Finn again is awake. The book is about death and resurrection, at least according to the Joycean scholars. I would have never known this if had it not been for the companion books Hannah had brought. I did, however, know the legend of the mythological giant Finn McCool. In the myth, Finn has many victories but he is then thought to have been killed. However, he was not dead; he was asleep in a cave surrounded by his followers, the Fianna. When Ireland was again threatened, Finn woke up and saved the land and its people—death and resurrection, asleep and awake.

My white Anglo-Saxon Protestant wife was more fascinated with Ireland than I was. I felt like she was trying to convert me to becoming Irish in more than name. Thank God she never converted to Catholicism. My life would have been miserable.

During the first summer, we sailed the *Redhead* to Ireland. Hannah wanted to see Clare Island, the anchorage used by the Irish pirate queen, Grace O'Malley, and her fleet. But, most of all, she wanted us to visit Carna, my great-grandfather Jamie's home. She wanted to make sure our children, and me, had some appreciation for our lineage. After Carna, we slowly made our way down the west coast and around the southern tip of Ireland to Cork, where we left the boat for the winter.

The following summer, we flew to Ireland and sailed the rest of the great circle route as Jamie would have done on his first trip to America. We sailed down the coast of Europe, past the Azores, and turned East at the Canary Islands. It was day after day at sea in the trade winds. We read, played games, and worked on our 'assignments.' We shared watches; Hannah with Jesse, me with Joel. Rachel was too young to stand watch, although she was sure that it was a misperception on our part.

We left the boat in St. Lucia that winter. Then, we flew down over Christmas vacation and enjoyed a week away from the ice and cold. Ruth and Harold joined us. The following summer, we sailed back to Maine. I was happy then. Alive. Awake.

My mind had stopped spinning. I looked down at Charlie. I had sailed with many dogs over the years. I was coming to like Charlie, and I was glad I had brought him. Being nestled at my feet seemed to be all he wanted. The nice thing about dogs is that you can talk to them, and you don't have to feel weird about talking to yourself. So, I spoke to Charlie: "So, Charles, am I a miniature Finn McCool? I'll bet you don't know anything about him. He was a giant who built this great causeway. He was going to take on a Scottish giant who was bigger than he was.

On the other hand, I have been neglecting my youthful warrior ambitions. It's about being awake, Charles. Given how much you sleep, I'm not sure you would understand."

Nan, and then my trip to Jay, had awakened me from my sleep. It was more numbness than sleep. Twice in my life, I had descended into a cave of numbness. The first time was during and after Vietnam—dropping bombs filled with flaming jelly on women and children. Afterwards, Laotian and Vietnamese spotters on the ground providing bizarre estimates of how many people I had killed—reports for Westmoreland to give McNamara. So many things: Josh Loundes dying at the end of the runway as his ancient WWII Skyraider's engine failed during the climb out; the arrogance of Major Barry Stark wanting to make a second pass because someone on the ground had shot at us. Then having his head scattered all over me; leave time in Pattaya with my friend Pip—numbing, numbing, numbing. Then, it was Hannah, patient, ever so patient, loving me awake, loving me into life. She had resurrected me from the cave of Vietnam. "Death and resurrection, Charlie. Death and resurrection."

When Hannah got sick and died, she shoved me right back into that cave. She left me alone in that cave. I felt as alone as I had when I first returned from Vietnam. Now, Nan and the evil of the strike in Jay, Maine. Finn, are you awake again? Is the 'warrior reporter' awake and going to write even if no one reads what he writes? And what of Nan? Finn McCool's loving wife had been turned into a deer, and he searched for her for seven years before giving up. I had lost Hannah four years ago. I had not been searching. "What say you, Charlie? Am I pushing this whole mythology thing a bit too much?" Charlie had no opinion about Nan, Jay, or Finn McCool.

I eased off the sheets and started reaching across the Sheepscot towards Southport. With the reduced heel, Charlie stood, shook, and put his paws on the gunnel so he could see over the side of the boat. I reached out and grabbed his collar so he wouldn't fall overboard. After a few minutes, he lay back down again. I wondered what he was thinking.

Chapter Forty-Four: Breaking Up

I got back home about four o'clock and called Nan. It went to voicemail. I left a message: "I'm back home. It's about four. I was wondering if you would like to go for a walk." I wanted to walk. I didn't want to be anyplace or go anyplace where neither one of us couldn't run away if we felt the need. People were always out walking the lanes of our neighborhood, so there would be nothing unusual seeing two old friends walking together or one of us walking alone.

She called me back about twenty minutes later. "Mike, I'm so glad you called. I was worried that you wouldn't."

I said, "I told you I would."

"I know, but I didn't know what you were thinking. The other night was pretty intense and unexpected."

"Would you like to go for a walk?"

"I'd love to, but I can't right now. Could we do it after dinner, say about seven or seven-thirty?"

"Sure. Do you want me to come over there?"

"No. I think it would be best if I came over to Tír."

"Okay, I'll see you later."

I was sitting on the porch when she walked down the driveway. Charlie announced her arrival and ran out to greet her. I got up, closed my computer down, and called Charlie. It took two more calls before he decided I was serious. I asked, "Do you mind if we take Charlie with us?"

She hesitated. "No. Sure. Or, we could sit here on the porch."

"It's nice out. Why don't we walk?"

"Okay."

I picked the lead up off the floor next to where I was sitting and put it on Charlie. We started to walk. Neither one of us wanted to speak first. As we left the driveway, Nan finally said, "The only thing I regret about the other night was that my aged body was not cooperative. Next time, if there is a next time, and I hope there will be, I'll make sure that doesn't happen again."

I didn't know what to say. It was not how I expected the conversation to begin. I didn't know what to expect, but whatever it was, this was not it. My silence must have communicated more than I thought. Finally, she said, "Say something, Mike. Don't just leave me hanging out there. Please say something."

I had some of this rehearsed: "Nan. I'm conflicted about the other night. It was really nice, but you're married. I know Joe. It might be different if you weren't married, but you are. There's also something else. We haven't spent any time with one another in years. I have no idea what your life has been like except for what you told me Saturday night, and you don't know me, not now."

She didn't respond. We walked for a few minutes before she said anything. "I understand what you're saying. I've thought about it. I've thought about nothing else for the past three days, trying to figure out how I feel and what I want. I'm too old not to think about what I want. I'm very aware of how old I am. I've lost too many friends and then living with Joe's strokes… who knows?"

"I know. I think about death, too."

"So, I'm going to just put it out there. Please, just let me finish what I have to say before you respond. I've thought a lot about this.

"I should never have broken up with you. We were good together. Very good. I loved you. I did, Mike. I knew the minute I saw you at the club last week that I had made an enormous mistake. In college, I was so young and scared. My mother's alcoholism, my parent's divorce, my father starting another family, all of it. I didn't want to be alone, and I wanted to feel safe, financially safe. You were going off to the Air Force, and I would have been left alone, possibly for months at a time. You wanted to be a reporter. You knew you

464

wouldn't make any money, and you didn't care about money. Then Joe came along. I grabbed at what I thought I needed."

"Jeez, Nan, that was probably the right choice for you at the time. You might have been miserable with me."

"Maybe. But I loved you. I don't think I ever stopped."

"Come on. That was eons ago. You don't know me. How the hell could you? The war. Marriage. I'm a different person. Nan, I know things are hard for you right now. Taking care of Joe isn't easy, but you're doing it. You're married. And your husband is sick, and he's here, and he depends on you."

She stopped walking and turned to me. Her voice changed, "You seemed okay having sex with me the other night."

"You're right. I did, and I shouldn't have."

"Well, I'm glad we did. It was good. I needed it. Didn't it feel good?"

"Oh, God, Nan, of course it did, but..."

"Joe. I get it. But don't forget, I'm married to a man who cheated on me for years, and if he hadn't had a stroke, I would probably be divorced right now. Have you thought about that?"

"Not really, and maybe you would be, but you don't know that for sure."

"Oh, yes, I do. What if I was divorced? What would you be saying? What if I had showed up here as a divorcee?"

"Come on. That's not the situation. You are married."

"No, I'm not. I haven't been married to that man since I found out about his fucking affair. We have an arrangement. I will take care of him and stay with him until he dies. He may have cheated on me, but we have a history and he hasn't always been a complete bastard. I wish he were. It would make my life a lot easier. I can't divorce him now. I'm stuck. What if I was divorced? Seriously, think about it."

I said, "Maybe. Who knows?" I was the one on edge now. "You asked me to wait until you got through saying what you wanted to say. There's something I'd like to say, too. I've also been thinking..."

"I'm not through. Let me finish. I must sound like a real bitch. I hate sounding this way. Just let me finish. Then I'll listen to you. I promise." She paused, reached out, and took my hand. "Here's what I want, really want, and I think it's possible if you're willing. I want to have a wonderful summer, spending as much time as possible with you, in and out of bed. I know we would have to be discreet. Then, I want us to stay in touch when I take Joe back to California. When I am there, I want to hire caretakers so you and I can get away for some long weekends, just the two of us. Go out to Palm Springs, maybe up to wine country. When he dies, which may only be a matter of months—who knows—I want to give us a try, a real try, as adults. I'm too damned old to beat around the bush, Mike. I've thought about it. I've thought about nothing else. That's what I want."

I closed my eyes and sighed. She said, "Please don't say anything until you think about it. Please."

"Oh, Nan." All I could think of was to return to, "You don't even know who I am. I'm not twenty anymore. I'm a different person."

"We don't change that much. And I do know you. I know all about you. I've never stopped asking questions. I know you had a rough time of it in Vietnam. I know you had a good marriage and have a lovely family. I also know what I felt when we were together Saturday night, and I think you felt it, too. I think we would be insane to deny that."

All I could say was, "Let's walk." I had been concerned that she would be upset when I told her I just wanted to be friends. Now I was the off-kilter one. This woman, who I had loved at one time in my life, was offering herself to me. She was also confronting me with my mortality at the same time. What she was suggesting was messy, very messy, but exciting at the same time. No one was at Tír. Wendy and Archie had gone to a concert in Bath. If I suggested we turn around and go back to Tír, I knew she would do so. I knew we would pick up from Saturday night. I wanted to, I so wanted to, but the thought of Archie and Wendy coming home early or somebody dropping by—getting caught. I didn't want to get caught. But that was only part of it. I didn't like the feeling of being part of a betrayal, of lies, of secrets. I didn't want to add secrets to my life. I didn't want lies. "I'm sorry, Nan, I can't do it. I just can't. I could list all of the reasons, but I know you would have an answer for each of them, and I don't want to argue with you about them. That would leave both of us feeling shitty. I can be your friend, but I don't think I can be anything else. I'd like to be friends, but I can't be anything more."

She turned, and we started walking again. Neither of us said anything. Finally, she stopped again and said, "I should have known. Now I feel like an idiot. I think it's best if I head back to the cottage."

I stopped and watched her walk away.

I had just finished the third draft of a query letter when Wendy walked in the door. She asked, "You weren't waiting up for me, were you?"

"No. Just getting some work done."

"It's late. It's almost twelve. I'm going to head off to bed. You want anything before I go up?"

"No thanks, sweetie, I'm fine. How was the concert?"

"Good. Sea chanties. Not my kind of music, but the group was fun. A lot of corny Maine jokes and stories. Some very thick fog patches on the way home. Could barely see where we were going. I'm glad I wasn't driving."

"The Howletts will be leaving in a few days."

"No kidding."

"I'm sorry I didn't…"

"It's okay. I'm really going to miss him."

"I have a thought."

"About?"

"Archie leaving. I've been thinking about doing all three wooden boat races: Castine to Camden, Camden to Brooklin, and the Eggemoggin Reach Regatta. Do you think Archie might be interested in crewing for me? You, too, of course. I know Jesse wants to. He told me when he was here. And then, if I can get Judd and Patty, we'll have a full boat. If he's interested, Archie could stay here at Tír until we leave for Castine."

"Seriously? that would be so cool. When are the races?"

"We'd have to sail to Castine on the 31st. Castine to Camden's on the 1st, Camden to Brooklin on the 2nd, and then Eggemoggin is on the 3rd. We'd sail back here on the 4th."

"Five days on *Redhead*. I'm in for sure. I'll call Archie right now."

She got out her cell phone and headed for the pier to get some reception. I smiled, congratulating myself on being a thoughtful, sensitive grandfather. Of course, Archie would come if he could. Then I remembered that Wendy would be leaving in a couple of weeks. School started on August 26th. I was going to miss her.

I went back to querying. Then, still dissatisfied with my effort, I decided to call it a night. But, before I did, I checked my email. There was one from Hal: "Grandpa, what's this all about?" Another one from Ruth: "Do you know what you've done? Hal didn't know there were any financial problems. You have created a giant mess for me and Harold. I hope you're satisfied."

June 8, 2001
HOME TOWN BOY by Michael Buckley

It's that time of year, again, graduation day. Parents, siblings, grandparents, aunts, uncles, and cousins understand that receiving an invitation implies 'compulsory attendance.' In my day, back in the fifties, high school graduation was a huge deal. Graduating classes were small, and everyone who wanted to could attend. That is not always the case today. The size of high schools has grown dramatically with regionalization, and so have the size of the graduating classes. In some schools, you have to have a ticket to get in. Fortunately, that is not the case here in Bath.

One of the nice things about graduation is the predictability. You can count on some local clergy for invocations and benedictions. The school band will provide some music. There will be some speechifying by a few of the best and brightest students and maybe one by a popular teacher. Then there will be the lineup, the walk across the stage, and hearing the name read out loud—hopefully with the correct pronunciation. Familial and friend applause comes next, then the picture, and, finally, filing back to the seats. At the end of it, all hats will be tossed, hugs will be given to close friends, and there will be a party afterward. The same ritual occurs at high schools across the country with only minor variations.

Colleges and universities add something to the ritual, the granting of honorary degrees. The origin of this process goes back to the Middle Ages. At that time, these were the requirements: the recipient had not fulfilled all of the requirements for his graduation (women did not attend colleges then) before he left the institution; he had moved on into adulthood, where he had become a high achiever; and he maintained a connection to his alma mater. The lofty achievement idea still persists today, although no attachment to the degree-granting institution is required. None other than John F.

Kennedy quipped upon receiving his honorary doctorate from Yale, "It might be said now that I have the best of both worlds, a Harvard education and a Yale degree."

Another group has been added to the mix, the donor. Give a significant amount of money to an institution of higher learning, and chances are you'll get an honorary doctorate. These don't come cheap. The size of the school matters, too. An Ivy League school will cost you more, a lot more, than a small struggling liberal arts school that has never given an earned doctorate to anyone.

Not all institutions give these honorary degrees. MIT, Cornell, University of Virginia, Rice, UCLA, and Stanford, among others, do not. The founder of the University of Virginia, none other than Thomas Jefferson, requested that honorary degrees not be awarded. MIT's founder, William Barton Rogers, regarded the practice of giving honorary degrees as "literary almsgiving ... of spurious merit and noisy popularity."

The award for the most doctorates belongs to the Reverend Theodore Hesburgh of Notre Dame University fame—one hundred and fifty for various colleges and universities. However, you don't have to be human to get one of these. In 1996 Southampton College at Long Island University awarded an honorary doctorate to Kermit the Frog. On the other hand, nine different Universities gave Libyan dictator Muammar Gaddafi an honorary doctorate. From Kermit to Gaddafi is quite a range of 'achievement.' Gaddafi's honorary doctorate clearly devalued Kermit's.

Fortunately, high schools are not confronted with deciding who will get an honorary high school degree. Can you imagine the political mess if this were to change?

Graduation speakers are called upon to be inspirational or funny, one or the other and sometimes both. You can count on the (a) don't give up, (b) give back to society, (c) be true to yourself, and (d) dream big speeches. Of course, there are variations on these themes, but one thing a commencement speaker does not have to worry about it is, "What should I talk about?" The outline is already there. All you have to do is add your own twists and turns. Season it with a bit of autobiography and a dash or two of humor, and you are home free.

There are times when the speeches do soar, and memorable quotes emerge. Gloria Steinem at Tufts University in 1986: "If you have to choose character or intelligence—in a friend or in a candidate—choose character. Intelligence without character is dangerous, but character without intelligence only slows down a good result." There are even times when United States policy frameworks are announced. Secretary of State George Marshall in 1947 at Harvard: "It is logical that the United States should do whatever it is able to do to assist in the return of normal economic health in the world, without which there can be no political stability and no assured peace." No victor in a war had ever done this before.

It's possible we all have a commencement address in us. I am sure we do. Fortunately, we do have an outline to follow. The more important thing, though, is to consider what of our own experiences we would draw upon to inspire the graduates. Would our lessons be drawn from tragedy or triumph? How honest would we, or could we, be? Platitudes or profundity? There is a wide range of possibilities.

Chapter Forty-Five: Homecoming

Jack was in the air headed for the Kuril Islands off the coast of Japan when Japan surrendered on September 2nd, 1945. He and his crew had been flying the same patrol month after month and everyone was bored doing the same thing every day. It was getting cold again, and the thought of being in the Aleutians for a third winter depressed Jack. Tempers were short. Little things became big things. Arguments broke out about everything from the food they were supplied for the flights to who was taking up too much space in one of the blisters.

On these patrols, the crew members saw nothing but gray seas, gray skies, and an occasional fishing boat or whale. They wiled away the time reading paperbacks sent from home. Some books had been swapped so many times that the covers had come off. The two pilots rotated flying the plane and reading or sleeping. Jack also rotated the crew members keeping watch in the blisters and the bubble. On watch, they had the mind-numbing task of scanning the water and the horizon with binoculars. Even though the crew suspected surrender was imminent, when the news came over the radio, everyone on board the plane cheered, laughed, punched one another, and wondered how soon they'd be sent home. Jack requested permission to return to base immediately. His request was denied. "We don't know if every Jap got the word." When he relayed the message to his crew, the response was a collection of curses and groans.

The Japanese had lost the war. They were already losing when the United States dropped atomic bombs on Hiroshima and Nagasaki. Sparky had boasted, "Those bombs were like turning over your fourth ace in poker. There isn't a damned thing your opponent can do. You've got the cards. The stupid ass slants made a stupid fuckin' bet they could beat us, and the assholes lost. It's time to rake in the winnings and get the fuck out of here. Let's turn this goddamned tin can around and go home."

Jack asked, "What'd we win? Remind me."

Two weeks after the surrender, Jack was told the United States Navy didn't need him anymore. He was okay with that. He had been ready to leave for two years, perhaps three. The military already had plans in place, and between 1945 and 1947, the United States discharged ninety percent of the men and women who had been in uniform. Thousands and thousands of sailors, soldiers, and marines were sent home in an operation called 'Magic Carpet.' There were inequities built into 'Magic Carpet,' and soldiers rioted in some places because it took too much time. They were furious that others were home making love to their wives and girlfriends while they were still sleeping in tents or barracks hundreds or thousands of miles away from home. Black servicemen and women were often stranded because the troopships didn't have separate quarters for them. Mixing Black and White troops was inconceivable.

One hundred and ten days after the surrender, Jack was in bed with Peg conceiving Maude. The bed was the same, but not much else. It was four days before Christmas, and there were no decorations up at the farmhouse.

The family had met him at the bus stop in Bath: father, mother, wife, and three and a half-year-old son who hid behind his mother's legs when she asked him to hug this stranger. Jack had knelt and lured the youngster out with a small polar bear he had bought in Anchorage on the way home. When Jack stood up, Michael clung to his mother's leg holding the bear with the other hand. Jack turned away from the two of them, hugged his mother with one arm, and used the other to shake hands with his father. There was coolness that he didn't understand, a formality with his parents that bewildered him, and uncertainty from Peg that troubled him. That Michael didn't want to come to him made sense; his son didn't know who he was. He'd take care of that soon enough.

The ride to the farm was filled with polite questions about his trip home: Was he exhausted? What would he like for his first meal home? Could they pick up anything for him on the way? He felt he could have been anybody coming for a visit. He didn't know how to respond. Ten minutes later, the questions stopped, and they rode in silence. Finally, as they passed the Georgetown General Store and made the turn leading to the farm, his father asked, "Any thoughts about what you're going to do now that you're home?"

From the back seat where she was riding with Peg and Michael, his mother said, "Will. Stop it. He hasn't even unpacked yet. Jack and Peg have a lot of catching up to do."

"Just asking," Will replied.

Jack said, "It's okay, Mom. I've been thinking about nothing else. I want to go back to school."

Peg didn't say anything. Finally, Will asked, "Back to school? Why? I'm sure you can get your old job back."

"Maybe, but it's the last thing I want to do."

"Why on earth would you want to go to school? To study what?"

"Remember how I wrote you about those Army engineers building an airport out of a piece of swamp in Adak. They did it in days. It was a fuckin' miracle…"

"Jack. Language. Michael picks up everything," Peg said.

"Oops. Sorry." Jack turned around and looked at his mother, wife, and son. "Going to have to learn civilian speak again." He turned back towards his father. "I've had a lot of time to think. I want to build things: bridges, buildings, not just roads. I talked with some of the Army engineers up there. They told me structural's the way to go. New materials are being developed, and many materials are being used in new ways 'cause of the war. Aluminum and reinforced concrete, just for starters. People are just learning how to use them. So, I'm going to become a structural engineer. Go back to school. Get a masters. If I have that along with my bachelor's in civil, I'll be hot as a..."

"Please don't finish that," Peg said.

"I was going to say, 'hot as a hen laying a hard-boiled egg.'"

"Where on earth you get that from?" Will asked.

"My radioman was a Texan who had hundreds of sayings like that. So anyway, if I go back to school, the government will pay for it under this new bill and give Peg and me some money to live on. It would only be for a year."

"Peg, did you know anything about this?" Nell asked.

"He mentioned it in a letter, but we haven't talked about it. He's just gotten home, for god's sake."

Jack turned around and said to Peg, "I didn't know the government would pay when I wrote about it. But, now that I do, I can't see why I shouldn't do it."

"Can we talk about this later?" Peg said.

"Sure, honey."

They rode in silence for a few minutes before Jack said, "This country's going to go boom, Dad. You wait and see. I want to be in on it. With a masters..."

"Jack. Please. Can we wait to talk about this?" Peg said.

There was no discussion of Brian and Connor on the drive home. Their names were not spoken until the next day. After dinner, Jack walked his parents out to the car. Will and Nell were still living in Bath. When he said good night to his mother, she hugged him tight and held on until he said, "It's okay, Mom. I'm home." On the other side of the car, his father said, "Come on, Nell. Let's get going."

After he and Peg made love, Jack couldn't sleep. He prowled about the house. Some things had been moved, but not many. He walked into Connor's room and saw it was the same as he remembered it. His kid brother, the farmer, the sweet kid who never hurt anyone.

Rage came slowly and built beyond what he could control. He walked downstairs, grabbed his coat, and walked out the back door. He didn't know what to do. There was nothing he could do. He saw the ax and the woodpile. He walked over to it, picked up the ax, and started swinging. He was chopping, but chopping to destroy. He kept swinging until his arms couldn't take any more.

Farm life is relentless. So are children. Peg had spent her war years in charge of both. Sleep was precious. Peg didn't hear Jack get up and leave their bed after they made love. She didn't hear him return either. She got up the following day at her usual time.

When he finally returned to bed, Jack found it difficult to sleep. He had expected more warmth from his parents, from Peg, too. Was he the only one who was glad he was home? When he went downstairs, Peg was coaxing Michael to finish his cereal. Jack paused in the doorway and looked at the two of them. He didn't move. He wanted to stay where he was, looking, smelling, feeling.

Peg had a fire going in the old wood stove in the kitchen. He was glad his grandparents hadn't gotten rid of it when they put in the gas stove. The coffee pot was percolating. Based on the color, it was close to done.

He knew Peg would have already been down in the basement to add coal to the two furnaces, one for heat, one for hot water. He'd do that from now on. He wanted to. It wouldn't be a chore.

Michael saw him and pointed. Peg turned her head and said, "Here, get your son to finish his breakfast, and I'll make you something. Coffee's almost done. What would you like? Got lots of eggs. Also have ham and bacon."

"Real eggs, real ham, and real bacon. From here?"

"Where else? Of course, they're from here."

Jack sat down with Michael and said, "Come on, little man. Finish up. You need your energy." He said to Peg, "How come there aren't any decorations up? It's almost Christmas."

"We haven't decorated for Christmas since Brian was killed. Michael was too young to know what Christmas was, and your mom couldn't handle trying to celebrate. Then when Connor was killed..."

"So, no Christmas? Jesus. No one told me that. What about Michael?"

"We'd do a small one for him. After Connor, your mother said she wasn't sure she would ever do Christmas again. There was nothing to celebrate. Your mother dreaded every day you weren't here. She didn't know if you'd be coming home. There wasn't much to celebrate. We were all afraid of another shoe dropping."

"But it didn't. I'm here. Is that why everybody's acting so weird? Is that the problem? That I'm here; I made it? Is that it? The least favorite son makes it home while his brothers don't. I can't fuckin' believe this shit. So that's why they didn't act like they were glad to see me. It should have been Brian or Connor that got off the god damned bus. Just not me."

"Jack! Quiet down. You're scaring Michael. And stop talking nonsense. Of course, we're glad you're home; it's just..."

"I'm going for a walk. When I get back, I'm going to start decorating. I'll do it by myself if I have to. I'm home; god damn it. I'm home. I made it."

There was light snow on the ground. There was no wind, and the temperature was just below freezing. The sun was out. The veil of fog he was used to wasn't there. He walked. He walked all over the farm. He noticed where trees had fallen, where fences had broken down and been repaired. He opened the door to the barn they used as a hangar and inspected the 'Jenny' he learned to fly in. His car was up on blocks, so the tires wouldn't get flat spots during his years away. His car. The car he let Brian drive in downtown Bath. Finally, he sat down on the running board and started to cry, then to swear. His big brother, the one who teased him and bullied him, was gone. Connor would never again borrow his things without asking. He was alone.

He found the car jack and, one at a time, removed the blocks and let the car settle onto the concrete floor. He opened the hood and saw the battery had been removed. He'd have to go into Bath and buy a new one. He'd need fresh gas, too. He couldn't wait to drive.

When he got back to the house two hours later, the Christmas boxes were laid out in the living room. Peg was unwrapping the manger scene and putting the pieces on the mantle over the fireplace. He could smell cider mulling in the kitchen. Peg turned when she heard him come in and said, "Don't take your coat off. Give me a minute to get Michael's snowsuit on, and off the two of you go. Take the truck and go get a Christmas tree."

Jack closed his eyes. He didn't want to cry. After a minute, he said, "Okay, we'll go get a tree and I have to get a battery and gas for my car. Peggy, please wait on this. We'll do it together when I get back."

"Alright, I'll just unpack. You'd better stop and pick up some extra light bulbs for the tree, and get a wreath, too. I'm not going to have time to make one."

"Michael and I will make one, won't we, buddy?"

Michael looked to his mother. Peg said, "It'll be fun."

Peg called her brother and sister-in-law and asked them to come for Christmas. She told them, "We're all having a hard time with Christmas. Brian and Connor gone, and now Jack's home. He wants it to feel like it used to and...."

Maeve interrupted her, "Of course, we'll be there."

Tommy got on the phone, "I've been saving something for him. Tell him not to be buying any whiskey."

The O'Neils arrived with the twins on Christmas Eve. With the twins and Michael, it was a child's Christmas morning with endless presents and endless food and drink for the adults. Having helped Peg when Michael was born, Maeve, Tommy, and the twins were at home in the farmhouse. No one had to wait on the O'Neils. They knew where everything was.

When they sat down for dinner, Nell placed empty chairs at the table for the missing Brian and Connor. Will said grace. He added a prayer for the souls of his two lost sons. Tommy suggested they go around the table and say what they were grateful for. He said he would begin and started with, "I'm grateful we are together to celebrate the birth of Jesus, and I'm grateful that Jack is with us and made it home in one piece." Sitting next to her father, six-year-old Siobhan enumerated her favorite Christmas presents and added, "I'm glad Uncle Jack's home." Others followed suit.

It started to snow just after noon. It was coming down steadily by three o'clock, and the wind picked up. Will and Nell left to return to Bath shortly after dishes were done and everybody had dessert. There were hugs and kisses for and from the departing generation. Finally, the children returned to their new toys.

Later, after their wives took the children up to bed, Jack and Tommy were left alone in the living room. Tommy said, "Got something in the car for us. I'll be right back." When he returned, he carried a paper bag. Opening it, he pulled out a bottle. "Bushmills, sixteen-year-old. It's Christmas, me boy, and you are home from that friggin' war. I brought us some glasses."

Jack tended to the fire while Tommy poured the whiskey into two crystal whiskey glasses that he had brought with him from Boston. "We will not insult the drink of the gods by drinking from anything less."

"You're a crazy Mick."

"Ah, yes. But tell me, right now, aren't you damn glad you married my sister?"

The two men talked, drank, and let the fire go down. Tommy

nodded off. Jack covered him with a throw and went upstairs to bed.

Two days later, Will called his son. "I'd like you to come with me this afternoon. Drive down to Brunswick. You free?"
"Yeah. What's up?"
"Have to go to Page. You know, the gravestone place."
"Why?"
"I've been putting it off. Your mom doesn't want to go, and I don't want to go alone."
"Sure, Dad. I'll go with you. What time do you want to go? I'll pick you up. I've got my car up and running."
When he got off the phone, he told Peg about the call. She said, "I don't want you to get upset. They didn't want to get any gravestones until you got home."
"In case they needed three? So what? They thought they'd get a better price on three?"
"Jesus, Mary, and Joseph. You being a total feckin' eejit, Jack Buckley. You'd best be gettin' over yourself and quickly. You have no idea the amount of mourning been done around here. What about you? You lost your two brothers. Has that sunk into your skull yet? You go, and you be nice to your Da. He's a good man and deserves better from you."
"I know. I know."
"Then start acting like it."
"Maybe I'll take Michael with me."
"To pick out gravestones? I think not."
Driving into Bath, Jack realized he had not thought much about the loss of his brothers. He had felt the rage and the pain, but he hadn't thought about what it meant for his parents. He was just so glad to be home, to have escaped, and to have made it back to safety. He didn't know what to think or even how to think about it. The closer he got to Bath, the more he heard Peg. She was right. He didn't know the

mourning that had taken place.

When Jack pulled up to his parents' house, Will was already waiting on the curb. The day was overcast and bitter cold. Will was wearing a long coat, and the ear flaps on his hat were down. He climbed into Jack's car and asked, "You know where it is?"

"Yeah, pretty sure."

"Just head for Brunswick. It's right on the Bath Road. You can't miss it."

They drove in silence. After a few miles, Will said, "This'll make four empty graves, four graves without bodies, my father, mother, Brian, and Connor."

Jack hadn't thought about that. He didn't know what to say. After a while, Will reached over and put his hand on Jack's shoulder and squeezed it as if to make sure he was there. "I'm glad you're home. You'd better not let anything happen to you. You hear? Your mother and I couldn't live with it if anything happened to you."

Will ordered two stones. They were similar to the existing ones for Jamie and Treasa. He also ordered a granite bench with the names Buckley and Convey to be inscribed on the side. "Your mom wants a place to sit when she goes to visit and pray. With her arthritis and her heart, it's getting harder for her to stand up for any length of time."

"She's still young, Dad."

"Fifty-five's not young when you've worked as hard as she has her whole life."

Chapter Forty-Six: Orono

Jack promised Peg they would only be in Orono for a year, and university life would be exciting. He promised her that they would return to the farm weekends, and would go home on school breaks rather than stay in Orono. He also promised her they would go home to have the new baby and he would be there with her. She worried, "Who's goin' to mind the farm if we're in Orono? The garden and the livestock need tending daily."

"Mom and Dad said they'd be happy to move back for a year. They can help with the farm and the new baby."

Peg was concerned about the plan. "Are you paying attention? It's all goin' to fall on your Da. Your ma gets out of breath if she climbs a flight of stairs. You've seen her. You know her heart's not good."

"It's going to be fine, honey. Really. They're going to rent the house in Bath for a year. It's only a year. When I graduate, back to Georgetown we go. You'll see. It'll all work out just fine." He kept pushing and pushing to make it happen. He promised, he cajoled, and he bought presents. He played the role of a dutiful father and husband. Without saying it, he bartered. He adopted an 'I'll do this if you'll do that' strategy. He said he'd help out on the farm on weekends if she and Michael would stay with him in Orono during the week. He was successful.

They moved into a trailer on the Orono campus in June so he could start the summer session. The campus at Orono was chaotic. Veterans who had their education interrupted by the war came home and re-enrolled at the university. Of the 1,848 students enrolled in the 1945-1946 academic year, 928 were veterans. Three hundred of these were married. To house them, thirty-two trailers sprouted on campus, and more than 200 students commuted from where they were being housed at Dow Air Force Base in Bangor. By the fall of 1947, over 2,500 veterans enrolled in Orono, and another 500 enrolled in a satellite campus in Brunswick. The town's population, apart from the University, also doubled as the school and its students needed more services.

Most of the veteran enrollees were starting or finishing their undergraduate degrees. Being both a veteran and a graduate student in the college of engineering made Jack unique. Because of this status, he was given special attention; he loved it. He told Peg he had private tutors for a program he had designed himself. He was on fire and quickly became a star in the college. If his parents' loss of his brothers had made him feel unwanted at home, at Orono he was on his way to becoming a hot commodity for the college to brag about. He was intelligent, ambitious, and had been leading crews while in the Navy, all things the college of engineering valued. He was asked to help tutor undergraduates and got paid for helping one professor on his research projects.

Things were not going as well for Peg. The trailer was cramped with an energetic toddler and two adults. The pregnancy was not as easy as the first one had been. Even with her degree from Katherine Gibbs, no one would hire a pregnant woman. She had grown used to farm chores and the rhythm of the farm, the garden, and the livestock. In Orono, she had little to do but take care of Michael and spend time with other wives who were as bored as she was. Because of the returning vets, there was no room for her to enroll in classes. The veterans got priority. The trailer came to feel like a prison.

By mid-day the trailer was beastly hot, and the space was too small for Michael's energy when she couldn't take him outside because of the weather. Everything was more complicated, from doing laundry to keeping the space organized. She was depressed and couldn't wait for the year to be over. She started staying longer in Georgetown when they would return for summer weekends at Tír na nÓg. Jack didn't seem to mind going back to Orono by himself, which bothered her. By the middle of July, Peg and Michael were living full time at the house on Heron Cove.

Jack was confident that he was headed for great things. As he always had, he made friends easily and established himself as a regular at Oisín's Pub in nearby Old Town by the middle of July. It was an old-fashioned pub and functioned as a gathering place for students and fellow vets. No one had any money, and beers were only a nickel. Everyone was welcome, and every night felt like a party. The war was over. There was a heightened sense of brotherhood among the veterans who were now in this educational enterprise together.

It was at Oisín's that Jack met Marcy Osgood, a junior taking a summer class she had not been able to fit into her fall schedule. An elementary education major, Marcy proclaimed to her friends that she preferred men to books and, as long as the men did not get serious, she liked the company of men more than women. Where Peg was short and had become very serious about life, Marcy was tall and laughed a lot. What started Jack and Marcy off was a couple of beers with mutual friends in a group. It quickly became a flirtatious game. Soon it was a one-on-one relationship in the pub, then in the parking lot, and eventually in Jack's trailer, since men were not allowed into the women's dormitories.

A married veteran like Jack was perfect for Marcy. Jack appreciated the frivolous nature of their relationship as well. He told her he was making up for his celibate years in the Aleutians. "You know those stories about Eskimos sharing their wives," he told her. "I rarely saw any Eskimo women and, when I did, they were old and fat. The guys who stayed behind in the states had all the fun. They had the odds going for them. We did the fighting; they did the screwing."

In his head, Jack was back on the road again, pre-Peg, pre-Michael. Peg and Michael were safe in Georgetown, and he kept telling himself that his playtime with Marcy would end with his graduation, if it even went on that long. This was his year to make up for lost time, and Marcy was a willing and able time machine.

On September 18th, Jack was waiting for Marcy at Oisín. He was sitting at the bar reading the newspaper. As usual, she was late, so he didn't think much about it. Instead, he was lost in an article about the first flight of a new bomber, a B36, that could fly six thousand miles without stopping and deliver an atomic bomb into the heart of Russia.

He didn't notice Marcy until she sat down next to him and said, "We need to talk. Privately. Let's get a booth." She took his hand and almost pulled him off the bar stool as she led him to a booth farthest away from any other patrons.

Marcy looked around to make sure no one was near them when they sat down. Then, Jack asked, "What's going on?"

Marcy had tears in her eyes. "I'm pregnant."

"What do you mean, you're pregnant?"

"You heard me. I'm pregnant. I'm two weeks overdue. I'm always regular. I'm never late. I'm pregnant."

"Are you sure?"

"Yes, I'm sure. I'm pregnant. Why are you acting so dumb?"

"What about your diaphragm?"

"You know I've always used it, but they're not perfect."

"Jesus, Marcy. What the fuck. I'm married. I've got a wife. We're having a baby. What do you want me to do?"

"Want you to do? What am I going to do? I can't tell my parents. I want to finish school."

An hour later, they were at the same table. They had agreed that the only sensible thing was for Marcy to get an abortion, but neither one of them had any idea of how to go about doing that. They had been holding hands stretched across the table when Jack said, "Don't worry about money. I'll pay for it." Marcy pulled her hands away and got up. She said, "I'm going to go pee."

When she returned, she said, "You think that makes everything alright? You'll pay for it?"

They kept talking. Jack kept saying, "Don't worry it'll be fine?" He didn't say what he was thinking: What if something happened to her? He had heard about abortions going wrong and women having to be dropped off at a hospital because they were bleeding so badly. What if she died? Marcy kept saying, "What else can we do? I'm so scared." They walked out to their cars together. When they reached Marcy's car, Jack asked, "Are you sure it's mine?"

"What did you say? Is it yours? Fuck you, Jack Buckley. Fuck you, you son of a bitch."

"Marcy, I only meant..."

"Leave me alone, you bastard. Get away from me." She pushed him away from her car.

Marcy got in the car and drove out of the parking lot, tires spinning. Jack had a momentary wish that she would get in an accident and be killed.

He waited a few minutes thinking about what he had said to her before he got in his car and followed her to her dormitory as fast as he could drive. Finally, he caught up with her and was behind her when she pulled into a parking spot. He pulled in behind her, parked, walked over to the driver's side window, and knocked on it. "I'm sorry, Marcy. This has knocked me on my ass, and I'm all over the place. Come on, roll down your window. We've got to talk."

"Not now we don't. Leave me alone. Just leave me alone."

"I'll call you tomorrow," he said.

Marcy didn't reply. Jack got in his car and drove back to his trailer. He kept screaming, "Fuck, fuck, fuck," and hitting his steering wheel.

Jack didn't hear from Marcy the next day or the day after. He called and left messages for her with whoever answered the phone on her dormitory floor. He drove to her dorm and parked where she usually parked her car, but her car wasn't there. Finally, on the third day of leaving messages, her roommate answered the phone and told him that she had gone to spend time with some friends.

Two weeks later, she called him, and said, "I took care of it," and hung up. The next day she called again. "Put two hundred and fifty dollars in an envelope and slip it into my car through the window. I'll leave it open a crack. And don't let anyone see you."

Jack stopped going to Oisín's and started going home to the farm on weekends. When Peg asked him why he was coming home so much, he said he missed her. He did. He knew he'd miss her even more if Peg ever found out about Marcy. He wondered how he could have been so stupid.

Maude was born on September 27th, a Friday. Jack did not make it home in time for the birth, but he came for the weekend and skipped classes the following Monday. He brought home a large University of Maine mascot, Bananas T. Bear, from the university bookstore for Maude. For Michael, he had a Bananas T. Bear T-shirt.

With his parents living at the farm, Jack felt it was okay for him to return to Orono and Peg told him to go. "We have everything under control here," she said. "I'll see you next weekend." He returned to the trailer determined to be a serious student devoted to his studies, family, and nothing else. He would stick to that throughout the year; he knew he would.

The fall semester went quickly. All through October and the first part of November he worked hard during the week and drove home on weekends. Then, after Thanksgiving, the weather started to make things more difficult. It was a long drive each way. The roads had deteriorated during the war due to a lack of maintenance. In addition, he was increasingly asked to help with undergraduates or work on faculty projects.

In December, he came home for the long Christmas break. The O'Neils came up from Boston, and for a few nights, they had wall-to-wall beds. Tommy brought a bottle of Tullamore Dew with him this time. Will and Nell stayed overnight. Christmas night, the three men, Jack, Tommy, and Will, sat in front of the fireplace talking about Jack's future. Will wanted Jack to go back to work for the Maine Department of Public Works. Tommy wanted Peg and Jack to move to Boston. "City's booming with new buildings, Jack. I can connect you with some people. Hire you in a flash. They like vets. With your new credentials, they'll grab you in a second."

When Jack said, "I don't want to work for anybody. I want to go out on my own. Start my own civil engineering company. Cover all New England."

Will was adamant in opposition. "How you gonna do that? Takes money to start a business and time, lots of time. You got a family. That's too risky. Who knows what's gonna happen with this economy? Look how things have slowed at the shipyard."

Tommy stayed out of it while father and son went back and forth about a post-war economy's relative risks and opportunities. When Jack said, "Soon as I graduate, I'm going to buy a surplus Cessna Bobcat. Dad, you ought to get rid of that old 'Jenny' and pick up a Stearman. They're practically giving these planes away. I'm going to be able to fly all over with the Bobcat. First by myself, then with people who work for me. You can land those things anyplace. I won't be confined to roads. Can land that thing in under fifteen hundred feet. That's half of what we got out there now, Dad."

"What're you going to do in the winter? You can't fly outta here with snow on the ground. You gonna try and plow our strip every time it snows. Yeah. Sure."

"Brunswick. I'll keep it in Brunswick."

"How far can you go in that thing?" Tommy asked.

"Seven hundred and fifty miles. Could fly down to Washington, D.C. on one tank of fuel. Thing cruises at 175, hell of a lot faster than the Catalina I was flying in the Aleutians."

"You got it all figured out, don't you?" Will said.

"Yeah, Dad, I do. I really do. You'll see."

"You two ready for a refill?" Tommy asked.

When Jack shared his post-graduate plans with his professors in the College of Engineering, he received the support he didn't get from his father. He had used his time well, both in class and out. He was seen as a leader, conscientious, very bright, and personable. One of his professors told him, "You're a winner, Jack. You will bring credit to our program."

As his time ended and summer approached, he borrowed money from the bank again, not for a car this time, but for an airplane. The plane cost him less than his car had because of its surplus status. Seeing it arrive at the 'Buckley Airport,' Will decided to sell his 'Jenny' and buy a Stearman as Jack had suggested. Father and son now had something else to argue about, who had gotten the better deal.

What Jack had not anticipated were the job offers he received. The college was graduating a 'hot commodity,' and he was tempted by the salaries and security he was offered. It was clear to him that his assessment of a boom in construction was accurate, and he was in a perfect position to respond. He listened carefully to each offer and was not above leading the interviewers on with probing questions. Most of them asked where he saw the construction sector moving, and the minute they did, he was visionary in his responses as well as how he pictured his knowledge and skills making a contribution. When he would turn down an offer, he always added, "If you need someone to fill in until you can hire somcone, I'm available on a consulting basis."

Buckley Engineering was up and running. Jack's business card featured a logo with a Cessna Bobcat and the words, 'We go where we are needed.' He was needed. Jack had consulting contracts for three projects before the spring semester ended. He was now a subcontractor. When he talked to friends and family members, he omitted the word 'sub.' He spoke of his contracts. He made it clear that people wanted to do business with Jack Buckley, a civil engineer specializing in structural engineering.

At his graduation party, his father approached him and said, "You know, I think you're going to make this work."

"Thanks, Dad."

"One thing, though."

"Oh, oh. Here it comes."

"You're flying high now. You got everything going for you. Beautiful family, starting an exciting career. World by the balls."

"And?"

"It's good, and I'm happy for you."

"So, what's the 'but'?"

"Oh, hell. Just enjoy it."

Chapter Forty-Seven: The Builder

In 1946 five million workers went on strike in the United States. Workers at more than one thousand steel mills went out. Meatpackers went on strike. John L. Lewis called for a nationwide strike by the coal miners. After the conclusion of the war, wages had been cut back while at the same time inflation hovered at eight percent. Workers were squeezed from both ends. The country had never experienced anything like this before. Congress passed the Taft-Hartley Act and restricted what labor unions could and could not do. Truman vetoed the Act, but the Republican Congress overrode his veto.

Owners of companies and investors had benefitted in the post-war economy, and Jack was among them. He wanted to get rich now, not in five or ten years. He was determined to get payback for his time in the Aleutians and the loss of his brothers. Most of all, he wanted to be independent. He told his father, "I'll never get a job where I have to depend on a fuckin' union to fight my battles for me. And I'll never let a union into my business."

"You don't even hire the workers, Jack. Who would unionize?"
"I'm just saying."
"It's a damn good thing Bath Iron Works has unions."
"That's different."
"How?"
"Just is."

Will let the illogic drop. He could not always tell when Jack was 'mouthing off' or when he was reaching a conclusion based upon discernment. As he told Nell, "That son of yours goes back and forth between being smart and being a smart ass."

In Congress, Truman's plans to expand the pie kept getting voted down by Republicans. To add to his problems, there was a severe shortage of housing. The boom that Jack had predicted was happening, but only in a few segments of the economy, with automobile manufacturing leading the way. Jack was right about one thing: where there are cars, roads will surely follow. And where there were roads and bridges to build, Buckley Engineering would be there.

Jack was back in the road business, but at least now he was involved in creating them, not just planning for them. He also had an employee. His former workmate, Trevor Benoit, had returned from the Italian campaign minus three fingers on his left hand. Fortunately, his thumb and forefinger were intact. "I'm a fuckin' lobster now," he told Jack when he came up from Portland to talk about joining Buckley Engineering. A piece of shrapnel from a German grenade had severed Trevor's fingers and part of his hand as the then Lieutenant Benoit waved his platoon to follow him and charge a German position on the beach at Anzio. He considered himself lucky. Over twenty thousand Americans were killed in the Italian campaign. Another ninety thousand were casualties or missing in action.

Trevor had no energy to look for a job when he returned home. Instead, he drank, hung out with friends, and picked up odd jobs. He lived at home, which was fine with his mother, but not his father. Finally, two years after his return, his father said, "It's time, Trev. Three months and I want you out of here."

"Why?"

"Jesus. Do you have to ask that? Why don't you get your old job back with the State or maybe try the post office? They're hiring, and vets are favored."

Trevor knew his father was right. However, he didn't know if he could go through the search process. "Energy," he kept telling his mother. "I've got no energy." Finally, his mother suggested he get in touch with his friend Jack Buckley.

Trevor had no difficulty tracking Jack down to find out what he was doing. His friend talked him into coming to Georgetown for the weekend. Jack picked him up at the bus station and drove him out to the farm, but rather than stopping at the house, he took him out to 'Buckley Airport' and showed him his airplane.

Jack talked non-stop about 'Buckley Engineering' and how things were 'taking off.' When he offered Trevor a job, Trevor questioned whether he could do it with his hand. Jack scoffed at the notion that a couple of missing fingers meant very much in the kind of work that Buckley Engineering was doing. "It's your left hand. You still got your right. We're not shoveling dirt, Trev. We're showing people what dirt they need to shovel. We're engineers, for God's sake." Trevor said he was willing to see if it would work if Jack was. Within a couple of months, Trevor was his old self, and the two of them were having fun flying from job site to job site and making more money than either had ever known in their lives.

While they agreed on most things when it came to work, they sometimes disagreed about other things, both personal and political. Some of their flights included hours of debate about the state of the world. Trevor thought the United States should buy Greenland when United States diplomats floated the idea. 'We need to have bases closer to the commies' was Trevor's main argument. 'It's nothing more than a fucking barren chunk of ice' was Jack's. Denmark, of course, had no say in the matter during their arguments even though Greenland was legally a County of Denmark.

When Jackie Robinson joined the Dodgers in 1947, the two men agreed it was about time. They found that they had to keep that to themselves, though, when they talked with clients. The New England antagonism towards Robinson had become more intense as the 'nigga' kept stealing bases, especially against the Boston Braves.

They also confided in one another. Although they had served in different theaters of the war, there was a bond between them that was not unusual for men who had been in battle. Trevor had three younger sisters and had always wished he had a brother. Jack had lost his brothers. The two men needed one another. Jack told Trevor about his year at Orono, including Marcy and the abortion. Trevor said, "So you want me to be your chaperone? Now I get it. You hired me to make sure you keep it in your pants and don't screw things up? That's why you hired me."

"You got to be good for something, lobster," Jack said.

Trevor told Jack about lying in the dirt at Anzio, so dazed from the grenade's concussion he didn't even know his hand was mangled. "It didn't hurt. It wasn't until I saw a medic wrapping bandages around it that I realized I'd been hit. It was my ticket home, though. Only two of my squad made it. It was the cluster-fucks of cluster-fucks. There wasn't supposed to be any resistance."

The two of them were inseparable. It wasn't just work. Trevor was single and often spent weekends at the farmhouse. "You two are like brothers the way you argue," Peg told Jack one Sunday night after Trevor left to drive home.

"Nah, he's just a friend," Jack countered.

"Whatever you say."

Jack was careful to always return home with presents for Peg, Michael, and Maude. For Peg, it was usually a carton of Pall Malls and a box of candy. Gifts for the kids were typically little trinkets that he could pick up in the towns and cities where he had projects.

Peg and the children had settled into easy domesticity, integrating Jack's traveling into their day-to-day lives. He planned trips so he was always home on the weekend unless the weather was bad and he got stuck someplace. Fortunately for Peg, they now had money to pay local teenagers to help her with the farm, and the kids were happy to get the work. Work was still hard to find for most of their parents. A few folks had returned to Georgetown after the war, and the population was now up to just over four hundred. Some local people got work when Walter Reid donated hundreds of acres of his Georgetown real estate for a state park. Long sand beaches were rare in Maine, and people started to come to Georgetown to visit the park and play in the sand.

While the country appeared to be at peace, it was at war within itself. A million African American men had served in WWII, but they couldn't vote in most of the southern states when they came home. The Ku Klux Klan was active to make sure things did not change.

There was also a growing fear of communism because of the rise of the Soviet Union. It was a constant topic of conversation in homes, on the radio, and in the newspapers. Jack, Peg, their children, Will, Nell, and the O'Neils were at the yacht club on the Saturday of Labor Day weekend in 1949. Trevor and his new girlfriend were also there.

Peg had convinced Will and Nell to join them at the club. When Will objected, Peg said, "Da, Ma can still go out and it's good for her. I know you're worried sick about her, but her heart's not going to know whether she's sitting at home or sittin' on the porch at the yacht club. Jack will come in and drive the two of you out and bring you home."

All the talk was about the Soviet explosion of a nuclear bomb the previous week. Will said, "Now Stalin's got nukes, he's going to be another Hitler. He's already killing his own people. You just wait. Another war's coming and, if it does, we're all going to fry."

Nell countered, "You're a ninny. No one wants to destroy the world. Stalin knows what would happen to his own country."

"You think he cares?"

It went back and forth like that until Maeve finally said, "Can we please talk about something else? This is too depressing, and we can't do nothing about it."

Jack stayed behind when it was time to leave. An hour later, he joined them at Tír na nÓg. "You're already back?" Peg asked. "You fly your parents home?"

"No, I got the Whipples to drive them back to Bath. They were going there anyway."

"That was lovely of them. So, what have you been doing?"

"A little negotiating."

"Okay. What'd you buy now?"

"A Beetlecat for Michael."

"Jack, he's only seven. He just learned to sail this summer. He's too young to have his own boat."

"He'll be eight next summer. He'll do just fine. It was a great deal. Rowlins wanted to get rid of it. He's a cheap son-of-a bitch. Didn't want to have to pay to store it for another year."

"Where on earth you goin' to be keepin' it? Barn's already full with two airplanes and a boat."

"I've got that figured out. I'm going to build a lean-to off the barn. I'm going to make it big enough for both the Herreshoff and the Beetlecat. Then, with the boats out, we'll have more room in the barn."

"For what?"

"I don't know. We'll see. Can always use more room."

The following year, 1951, Peg said they shouldn't go to the yacht club in the summer. "It's a feckin' jinx, don't you know." They were helping to get ready for the opening of the club on June 25th, 1950, when North Korean soldiers swept across the thirty-eighth parallel into South Korea.

Truman said it wasn't a war; it was a police action. It wasn't the United States; it was the United Nations fighting it. Jack and Trevor laughed at the absurdities. The United States started to call up veterans with specific skills to fight in the 'police action.' The military wanted trained pilots. When Peg dared to ask Jack what he was thinking, his response was immediate. "No fuckin' way am I going back in. I've done my bit. Besides, I'm too damned old. I'm thirty-five for Christ's sake, and I'm making good money, damned good money. They're nuts if they think I'm going to re-enlist."

Two years later, Eisenhower was elected in a landslide and vowed to go to Korea. In his speech he said:
Where will a new Administration begin? It will begin with its President taking a simple, firm resolution. The resolution will be: To forego the diversions of politics and to concentrate on the job of ending the Korean war-until that job is honorably done. That job requires a personal trip to Korea. I shall make that trip. Only in that way could I learn how best to serve the American people in the cause of peace. I shall go to Korea. 'to end the war.'

But, as Eisenhower negotiated for peace, his economic policies of cutting both taxes and government spending pushed the country into three recessions in eight years. In the midst of the economic turmoil, atomic bombs kept being tested, and fear of the 'atheistic communists' grew. At home in Bath, Will and Nell said the rosary every night along with the radio and prayed for the conversion of Russia. When they stayed with their grandparents, Michael joined in. Maude was still too young.

Buckley Engineering turned out to be recession-proof. As long as Detroit kept building more and bigger cars, roads needed to be built to accommodate them. For Jack's company, the bonanza came in 1956 with the Federal-Aid Highway Act—twenty-five billion dollars to build 41,000 miles of interstate roads. Jack was ecstatic. "Ten years, at least, Peg. We'll be eating 'high off the hog' for at least ten years. Maybe more. Can you believe this? I'm going to get a new plane and a boat. I'm finally going to build that Alden schooner, the Malabar

II."

"Shouldn't you be waitin' 'til the money's actually in your pocket?"

"The bill passed. It's a done deal."

"How can you be so sure you'll get the jobs?"

"Jesus, Peg. What's wrong with you? Why're you such a downer? I've built an excellent business, and people know me. Course I'm going to get a lot of the federal work. You sound just like a farmer's wife, always worrying. We're not farmers anymore. You're not a farmer's wife."

"Farmer's wife! When the hell have I ever been a farmer's wife? You've never been a farmer. You never gave a shite about the farm or farming as long as I've known you. You're not the farmer. I am. You fly around in your fancy plane and build your roads. What if things change? What if there's another recession and it hits you, or what about a depression? You be damned glad I'm a farmer. You got a bloody short memory, Jack Buckley. During the depression and the war, this farm's what put clothes on your back and food in that growing belly of yours."

"Peg, come on. What's wrong?"

"I'm worried, and you should be, too. Recession, depression. Same bloody thing."

"Okay, you're right. We'll always have the farm."

"And you should be learning something about it."

"What? Why now?"

"Because you may have to run it someday."

"With you as my wife, not a chance."

Things did change for them, but for the better. Buckley Engineering grew. Jack worked out a deal with a boatyard in Rockland that was happy to get the work. A year later, the *Redhead* was launched, and every summer the boat sat on her mooring in front of Tír na nÓg. Jack rarely got a chance to sail her; he was too busy. Peg's brother, Tommy, sailed her more than Jack did. Jack's new plane, a brand-new Beechcraft Bonanza, got a workout as the interstate system grew throughout the country. There was so much work that Buckley Engineering opened offices in three state capitals: Boston, Harrisburg, and Albany. Trevor had married, and his newly formed family moved to Harrisburg to manage that office. Jack managed the offices in Boston and Albany. Where Jack used to be home every weekend, he was now gone for two weeks, sometimes, three, at a time. For several years Christmas meant a new television set for the family. In 1956 Jack bought them their first color set.

Every room in the farmhouse was done over. New electrical wiring and plumbing were installed there and in Tír na nÓg. When it came to the kitchen, though, Peg insisted upon retaining the old wood stove in addition to the modern electric range Jack that bought for them. When Jack suggested they would have more room if they got rid of the old stove, Peg said, "I use it when the power goes out. Besides, I already let you talk me into getting rid of the gas stove. The wood stove stays." Peg didn't know it, but her new range was just like the one Jack's office manager in Albany had. The office manager had also received a new color television set for Christmas the same year Peg and the children did.

Jack was home for the Fourth of July weekend in 1956 when Michael soloed in his grandfather's Stearman. Since Jack wasn't around to teach Michael how to fly, Will had decided he would do it, and he wasn't going to let Jack know. He would surprise him. That was fine with Peg. In her estimation, Jack was always too hard on Michael, and she imagined tears if Jack was the teacher. On the other hand, Maude could get Jack to do anything she wanted.

It was a beautiful day when Will helped his grandson pull the Stearman out of the barn at eight o'clock in the morning. After breakfast, Peg told Jack to head up to the barn; his father had something to show him. When Will saw Jack arrive, he signaled to Michael, who was already in the plane's cockpit with the motor running. Michael started the plane rolling down the grass strip and smoothly took off. Jack stood next to Will, "What the hell's going on? Who's that flying?"

"Your son."

"Michael? Jesus, Dad. You teach him to fly that thing? I wanted to teach him how to fly."

"Well, you'd have to be here to do that, and you're never here. He was ready. You were the same age when I taught your brother and you. So, I taught your son to fly. I'll teach your daughter too, if she wants to learn."

"He going to be okay?"

"Yeah. He's a natural. Reminds me of Brian. Loves it. Flies like he sails. Feels it. Going to be a great pilot. He's a great kid."

"You spoil him."

"I try."

After a couple of minutes of watching the plane gain altitude, Jack said, "You saying I'm away too much?"

"I didn't say that."

"But you think it."

"I told him just to do a circle. Watch him turn onto the downwind leg. Watch him. He's smooth."

"Yeah. He looks good."

"He loves it. Already decided what he wants to do as a pilot. Has it all planned out."

"At fourteen?"

"Of course. Doesn't want to work for any airline company. He wants to become a reporter, have his own plane, and fly all over the country covering stories. He plans to buy his own camera and take movies that they can use on television."

"Where the hell did he get that idea from?"

"Watching the evening news."

"Yeah, sure. Well, he's going to go to engineering school. Join me in the business."

"Yeah. Sure. Of course he is."

It snowed in Albany on Friday, February 20th, 1959. Jack called home at noon to let Peg know he would have to stay over. No one was home.

In Boston, a rheumatologist, Dr. Jerome Whitmore, opened a chart for forty-one-year-old Margaret Mary Buckley, whom he had just diagnosed with rheumatoid arthritis. The doctor told Peg that she had to lose the weight she had gained over the years, and it would help if she cut back from smoking two packs of cigarettes a day. He also told her what she could expect. She learned new terms like flare and synovium. He said he was glad she came in when she did and was surprised that she hadn't seen someone before now, given the pain she had been experiencing.

That night, when she called the hotel Jack usually stayed at to give him the news, no one answered. She left a message with the desk clerk, "Call me when you can." Jack had told her he often took the phone off the hook at night so he could get a good night's sleep.

A year after Peg's diagnosis, Nell Buckley died. With her history of heart problems, it was not a surprise. What surprised Peg was the intensity of the grief she felt. She and Nell had leaned on one another through the war years. Nell had become her surrogate mother, the one person she could always count on. On the way home from Nell's funeral Peg asked her husband, "You ever going to come home? Stop staying in Albany so much? I need to know. I have a right to know. So do your children."

"Oh, come on. I'm home most weekends."

"You need to come home."

With Nell gone, Will returned to Georgetown to live with Jack and Peg in the farmhouse. He rented the house in Bath.

Chapter Forty-Eight: Chaperone

Jack's Beechcraft Bonanza reached cruising altitude. He turned the plane over to his new autopilot and then told Trevor about Peg's diagnosis. Trevor asked him several questions about rheumatoid arthritis. Jack didn't have answers to most of them. Then Trevor changed direction. "Do you remember the question I asked you when you hired me?"

"Come on, Trev. You asked me lots of questions."

"No. This one was different. You told me about your fling with that woman when you were in grad school, and the abortion. I asked you if you were hiring me to be your chaperone? Do you remember? You gave me a wise-ass answer and said I had to be good for something. Remember?"

"No."

"Well, you need one, and it's about time I started doing it."

"What are you talking about?"

"Albany."

"What about Albany?"

"Stop it. You know damned well what I'm talking about. Karolyn Dodge. That's what I'm talking about. Everybody in the Albany office and just about everyone in the company knows you shack up with her when you're in Albany. You've never even tried to be discreet about it."

Jack didn't say anything. The plane droned on as they headed back to Harrisburg after spending two days in Pittsburg. The day was clear, and they had a brisk tailwind. Jack started lightly drumming on the sides of the plane's yoke. "Did I tell you Peg wants me to get rid of this plane?"

"You just going to ignore what I said?"

"She's all freaked out about that crash two months ago. She was a big Buddy Holly fan. Richie Valens. Big Bopper. Some other guy I never heard of." Jack started singing:

> "*Chantilly lace and a pretty face and a ponytail hangin' down*
> *A wiggle and a walk and a giggle and a talk make the world go round*
> *Ain't nothing in the world*
> *Like a big-eyed girl to make me act so funny make me spend my money...*

I wish they'd been flying a different plane. Why the fuck they have to be flying a Bonanza?"

"You're just going to ignore me."

"Yup."

"You've turned into some piece of work, my friend. Your wife is sick. Has that registered yet? You have a seventeen-year-old son you barely know and a thirteen-year-old daughter who worships the ground you walk on."

"I didn't need a fuckin' chaperone then, and I don't need one now."

"Okay. But people in the company know, and if they know, I think you can bet on Peg knowing, and maybe your kids."

"Enough."

"Okay, but it's your funeral if this all blows up in your face."

"I said enough."

"Enough it is."

They didn't say anything more to one another for the rest of the flight. Jack ate at his hotel rather than having dinner with Trevor and his family when they got to Harrisburg. He called Peg that night to find out how she was doing. She said it was one of her better days. He was about to get off the phone when Peg said, "We may have a problem with the school. It's Michael and his reporting for the school newspaper. He's gone a bit overboard on a story, and I will have to deal with it."

"Should I come home?"

"Do you want to?"

"How bad is it?"

"Nothing I can't handle."

Trevor was right; she knew and Jack knew she knew.

When Jack and Trevor met with people from the Pennsylvania State Highway Department the following day, the only words the two men spoke to one another were about the business at hand. After the meeting, Jack headed straight to the airport and did not visit the Harrisburg office. This was unusual, and several staff members commented to Trevor about it. He assured them that nothing was wrong. He told them that Jack had to get to Albany for a meeting that afternoon.

Peg was surprised when she heard the plane fly over the house at six o'clock. The first thing that went through her mind was 'Do I have enough for dinner?' Thirty minutes later, Jack walked in the back door carrying his suitcase and an oversized briefcase. Maude ran in from the dining room where she had been adding a place setting to the table. "Daddy, you're home!" She threw herself at him before he could put his bags down.

Michael clomped downstairs and came into the kitchen, "What're you doing home? Mom tell you to come home?"

"Good to see you, too. No, she didn't. But, given what you've gotten yourself into, I thought it would be a good idea."

"It's all a bunch of bullshit. They're shooting the messenger. I didn't do anything. I just reported what other people were doing. They were screwing in the teacher's lounge. We can't smoke at school; we can't make out. But teachers can fuck and smoke in the teacher's lounge. It's not fair. But can I write that in the paper. Oh, no. It's censorship."

"Watch your language."

"Principal wants to suspend me for telling the truth."

"We'll talk about that later. Where's your mother?"

"I don't know."

"Maude?"

"When she heard your plane, she said she had to go up to the general store to grab something."

"Where's Grandpa?"

Maude answered, "In the living room watching the news. How long are you going to be home?"

"I don't know. A couple of days at least."

"Until they decide to kick me out or suspend me," Michael said.

"You heard me. We'll discuss this later."

Maude said, "You're never home during the week. Is it because of my idiot brother? Everybody in the whole town knows about what he did."

"I didn't do anything. And they didn't publish it. They stopped it," Michael said.

"Yeah, but you told everybody, and that's just as bad," Maude said.

"I only did that after they pulled the article. People have a right to know."

"What? That teachers are having sex? Yuk. In the teacher's lounge? How gross."

Jack stopped them with, "Maude. Stay out of this. It doesn't concern you."

"Yes, it does. Everybody knows he's my brother."

"Do you hear that? It's your mother's truck. Go do whatever you were doing." Jack went out the back door to where Peg was pulling up. The two dogs, Twerp and Monster, started barking and ran over to greet her.

Peg said, "I didn't expect you. Had to pick up a couple of things we were out of." She climbed out of the truck. Jack noticed her wince.

"Here. Let me give you a hand."

"I can manage."

Jack went over to kiss his wife, but she had already started to walk to the other side of the truck to get the two bags of groceries. Jack followed her. He said, "Let me take one of those."

She got the two bags and headed for the back door. Then, over her shoulder, she said, "Get the door, would you?"

Later, after dinner, they sent Michael to his room. Sitting around the kitchen table, Jack agreed to Peg's plan. Michael would lose driving and phone privileges for a month. They agreed that no more than a week's suspension from school was warranted, given that the article was never published. Peg insisted that Michael apologize to the two teachers and promise not to say anything to anyone about the incident. Jack balked at that. "What's he going to say that'll make any difference? Everyone knows already."

"He doesn't have to add to the damage he's already done. He was wrong. He needs to apologize. He needs to acknowledge what he did, that it hurt people, possibly cost them their jobs, and that he is sorry."

"Do you think he's sorry? I don't."

"Well then. You'd better be talking to him about why he should be, and you can take him to the meeting with the principal tomorrow morning."

"Me?"

"You're his father."

Jack was certain that his talk with his son about remorse and regret had no impact. Instead, Michael was more responsive to the idea that he did want to graduate from high school and go to college, and he had better stop messing around and being so self-righteous if he wanted that to happen.

The meeting with the principal and the advisor to the school newspaper was carefully choreographed by the principal. The principal didn't think, given the circumstances, that Michael should seek out the two teachers and apologize to them face to face, although an apology was certainly warranted. Instead, he suggested a letter to each would be an appropriate means of communication. He also thought that a one-week suspension would impress upon Michael the seriousness of what he did. However, Michael would be expected to keep up with all of his school work and would send in assignments with friends. He would take any quizzes and tests that he missed when he returned. He would not be allowed to work on the paper for the rest of the year. In addition, he was to write a carefully researched two-thousand-word essay on journalistic ethics.

Jack had said nothing until the essay assignment was levied. Feeling he was letting Michael down, he said, "What about the teachers?"

The principal answered, "That is a personnel matter, and I am not at liberty to talk to you about it. Is there anything else?"

Jack said nothing. "Well, Mr. Buckley. I appreciate you coming in with Michael. I'm sure the two of you will have a great deal to talk about."

In the parking lot, Michael asked, "Why didn't you say something?"

"You screwed up big time. I'm surprised you didn't get expelled."

"Thanks a lot."

"What did you expect me to say?"

"Something. Side with me. I don't know. Something."

"I don't think you get it. I don't side with you. You were wrong. You didn't think."

"Why's it such a big deal. They're probably going to get married."

"Who?"

"The teachers. Everyone knows it. They think it's funny."

Jack called Trevor that evening. "Trev. Do you think you could handle both Harrisburg and Albany? I think I may just manage the Boston office. Stay closer to home."

Trevor said, "I think you staying closer to home is a great idea. My handling both offices is as bad an idea for me as it has been for you."

"What do you mean? I was doing okay."

"No, you weren't. The Albany staff's been jumping from one emergency to another. You were never there when they needed you, and when you were, you had other things on your mind. Even if you were paying attention, managing both offices is too much for one person."

"Maybe."

"Come on. I'm right and you know it. So, you make up your mind what you'll do about her?"

"Let her go."

"Mistake. Big one. Everyone'll be royally pissed at you if you do that."

"So, what do you think I should do?"

"You're asking my advice?"

"Yes, I'm asking your advice. Don't be a putz."

"Yiddish now. Okay, here's what I think you should do. You know that guy from New York State Highway you're always talking about? Hire him. You like him so much, hire him. It makes sense. Solidifies your relationship with the state. Everyone in the office likes him. Just be sure to talk to his boss before you talk to him. It's a win-win. The Albany staff's happy. The state has someone they know and trust. You get your ass out of there without having to make a big fuss about it."

"What about..."

"She stays put. You say your goodbyes and hope to hell she doesn't go and have a shit fit on you. I hope you didn't tell her that the two of you had some future together."

"No. She knows we don't. She knows I'm not going to get divorced."

"You were clear with her?"

"Absolutely."

"Hope she accepted it."

"What do you mean?"

"She may have said that it's okay, but if you break it off, she may go nuts on you."

"So, you're saying I should fire her?"

"Christ. Fire her; for what? What's your staff going to think? You're a shit? No. You just turn over the reins to the new guy and hope for the best."

His father was loading gardening tools into the truck when Jack came back from collecting eggs. "Where you off to?" Jack asked.

"Goin' up to the cemetery and clean out the crap from the winter. A big branch came down and is resting on the fence."

"Wait a minute. I'll go with you. Give you a hand."

"Okay. Better put your heavy coat on. It's still cold."

"Dad, It's not that cold."

"Yeah, but it's windy up on the hill."

"Alright. Why don't you wait for me in the truck?"

The family cemetery was on the highest hill on the farm. From it, you could see the Atlantic Ocean in the winter when there were no leaves on the trees. A few of the trees had buds, but it would be a while before leaves appeared. When his father parked the truck, he did so facing the ocean. The two of them sat quietly, just looking. The day was clear, cold clear, and they looked out over Heron Cove, across the islands to the horizon.

"You home for a while?" His father asked.

"Yeah, a couple of days at least."

"Then what?"

"I have to square away some things in Albany."

His father opened the door, started to get out, stopped, turned around, and said, "Son, Peg's a good woman."

"I know that."

"Sometimes she's in a lot of pain with this rheumatoid arthritis thing she's got."

"I know."

He left the door open and got back into the truck. "No, you don't. You haven't been here when she has what she calls a flare." Jack didn't say anything. His father said, "She kept the farm going during the war, and I swear she kept your mother alive after Connor died. Since then, she's kept everything going and has been raising Michael and Maude with little help from you."

"I've been working hard."

"No one says you haven't. Maybe just not at the right things."

"What are you saying?"

"Pay attention. Just pay attention to the things that matter. If you don't, you're going to regret it."

The two men didn't say a lot over the following hour when they cut the branch away from the wrought iron fence that surrounded the cemetery. They raked away winter debris and pulled out the remains of the previous summer's annuals that had given their color to the cemetery. When they finished their work, they loaded the tools back in the truck. Jack said, "You go ahead. I'll walk back."

After his father left, Jack looked around at the generations of Conveys buried there and then at the stones for the Buckley's. He wondered if you still called a grave a grave if there was no body buried there. His grandfather and grandmother, Jamie and Treasa, his two brothers. Only his mother's remains were interred here. Interred. Funny word. Formal. Cleaned up word compared to buried. He missed his mother.

He missed his brothers. He thought first and then decided to talk out loud. It felt strange at first, and then it didn't. "Why did you have to go and get yourself killed? I should have been the one who got killed. Not you. Brian, why did you have to go and act like it was fun? Why didn't you tell Connor and me to stay home? Okay, we might have gotten drafted." The illogic rambling ended in tears. He sat down on the bench his mother had wanted so she had a place to sit while she prayed. His father, who knew granite, had chosen each piece of the bench with great care.

Jack sat and looked at the stones of his brothers. Brian and Connor would never have a wedding, never father a child. What would Brian have wound up doing for work? Connor? Connor would have run the farm. Connor would have had five kids and a fat wife. Jack smiled. Brian? Who knew what Brian would have done?

Looking at his mother's stone, he laughed. Tomorrow was Saturday. She would have asked if he was going to drive into town and go to confession.

September 14, 1984
HOME TOWN BOY by Michael Buckley

My family and I try to get away every year for the last two weeks in August. It's some time before school begins, and we have managed to do it for the last eight or nine years. It is one of those family things that everyone looks forward to and counts on, until last year. After I made our reservations, paid our deposit, and was in anticipation mode, my wife pointed out that we would have to return four days earlier than I had planned so our young ones wouldn't miss their first days of school. What nonsense. Everyone knows that school begins the Wednesday after Labor Day. It always has, and it should continue to do so. And it is a half-day.

Well, last year it didn't, and we had to change all our plans. Actually, there weren't a lot of plans, but they had to be changed. I am the one who always makes the arrangements, and if I am being scrupulously honest, I hadn't bothered to look at the school calendar when I made our reservations. Why should I? School begins the Wednesday after Labor Day. We all know that.

Well, I wrote a letter to the Superintendent of Schools reminding her when school begins, and because I work for a newspaper, I sent a copy to our editor, who dutifully published it. It was a cordial letter, but it did suggest tradition had not been given its due and how was a parent to plan. The superintendent, someone I have a great deal of respect for, wrote me that she had appointed me to the district 'Calendar Committee' and hoped I would accept the position. Clever, that one.

Admittedly, I have never thought much about how a school calendar is created. I didn't even know there was a calendar committee which was composed of teachers, administrators, and parents. How could I refuse? She had also sent a copy of her appointment letter to my editor. He printed it, of course. Clever, that superintendent. Now every reader of our illustrious paper knew. An expert had called me out—my respect for her increased.

Of course, I knew that the school year was loosely based on the agrarian needs of our ancestors. It is a pretty loose connection, however. For example, a lot of harvesting takes place after Labor Day and a lot of planting better happen before the first couple of weeks in June. Nevertheless, the need for agricultural families to have their kids around to work during the planting, growing, and harvesting seasons was essential in creating the school calendar. So why change it?

Well, for one thing, it appears we have added a bunch of holidays over the years. We have also added vacations winter and spring vacations for our darlings. Religious holidays have been expanded to be more inclusive, and teachers get some time for professional development. Since the state mandates that students must be in class a certain number of days each year, the intricacy of the school calendar is something to behold. Learning how difficult and important it is to juggle all of these constraints, I soon felt humbled by the complexity of the committee's work.

In other situations, different dates mark out the years. October 1st is the beginning of the fiscal year for the federal government. Our newspaper uses July 1st to mark its fiscal year. Because budgets are set by fiscal years, these are important dates for people whose lives are determined by annual budget allocations. Fortunately for me, the United States Internal Revenue Service and the state of Maine use January 1st for taxes. Those dates have stayed fixed for as long as I have known, unlike the beginning of the school year. If there were a calendar committee somewhere changing those dates every year, I would be in trouble.

I have always felt my year began with the beginning of school. The summer has come to a close, and it is time for a new start. I know that people typically make New Year's resolutions to take effect on

January 1st, but for me, it has always been that first week after Labor Day. It means a new teacher or teachers, a new classroom, and perhaps a new school building for many of us: children, parents, and even grandparents. By contrast, not much changes between January 1st and January 2nd. Here in Georgetown, my chores on the farm remain the same, it is still cold, and the people are pretty much the same. I have to write a different year on my bank checks, which I will forget to do until February 1st. So, that Wednesday after Labor Day has always been a big deal for me. No fireworks or champagne toasts, but a wonderful feeling of new beginnings.

While serving on the committee, I admit I tried to figure out a way to get back to a proper school year beginning. I thought I had it once, but I had forgotten to figure in snow days. Working together we did eventually come up with a calendar that we were quite certain no one would be happy with, but it did meet all of the requirements. I suggested we add an addendum. "Hey folks, we have no control over..." We could then list every last one of them. You don't like ours; let's see you try to do better. We could add, "Perhaps you would like to serve on the calendar committee."

Chapter Forty-Nine: Racing

When my grandparents built Tír na nÓg, my grandmother Nell decided to name the four upstairs bedrooms after United States presidents. "It will be as close as we ever get to the White House and the Lincoln Bedroom," she said. So, there is a Washington bedroom; Adams, Jefferson, and Madison have their rooms as well. My grandpa Will argued for a Lincoln bedroom like the White House but lost. When he asked about the downstairs bedroom, Grandma Nell said, "The queen's bedroom, of course." When Grandpa Will asked if there was one of those in the White House, her reply was, "Yes, there is. You aren't saying I don't deserve a room fit for a queen, are you?" She had the room painted rose, like the one in the White House.

She hung a portrait of each president in his respective room. It was a good thing that each picture was labeled because it was doubtful that any but Washington would have been recognized by most of our guests. The family, of course, became familiar with the likenesses over the years. The picture in the queen's bedroom was of Queen Victoria. My mother replaced that picture with one of Eleanor Roosevelt.

On Wednesday, July 31st every bedroom was occupied in anticipation of a long weekend of sailboat racing. Including a day to get to the races and another day to get back, it would be five days on the water. Wendy and I decided that Archie would be given the smallest of the bedrooms, the Madison. Wendy agreed to shift from the Adams room to the Washington where she doubled up with Maude. Jesse and Naomi got the Adams room; Natalie and Miriam became Jeffersonian for the long weekend.

Judd, Patty, and Rina joined us for dinner Wednesday night. All the leaves were put in the dining room table. The only true oenophile in the group, Patty brought the wine; Judd brought the beer.

Lobster dinner for twelve is messy. When you add clams and corn on the cob you are adding to the mess. It was a two-garbage bag dinner. Jesse and Naomi had stopped to pick up fresh produce including boxes of local blueberries at the farm stand on their way out to Georgetown. Salad and fruit were added to the feast. After we cleaned up, everyone went down to the ice cream shack at the Five Islands Lobster Company.

When we returned, Maude, Judd, Patty and I meandered down to the benches on the pier. 'Code Names' was the game of the night for all the others. Periodically we would hear outbursts of "Yes!" or complaints of "What else could it be?"

On the pier, our generation was busy consuming bottles of a semi-sweet Riesling, courtesy of Patty. It was a beautiful night. At some point, we started telling stories about things we had done in the past. The stories got sillier and seemed funnier as we moved on from one bottle to the next. It wasn't long before people on one of the yacht club's transient moorings in the cove shouted, "Can you keep it down over there?" When we realized they were talking about us, we couldn't help it. We started giggling. We tried to stifle it, but were unsuccessful and finally let loose and started laughing, then calmed down until Judd whispered, "Can you keep it down over there?" That started us up again. Four senior citizens were being asked to quiet down. It was hilarious, ridiculous.

However, we decided it was time to leave our pier perches and take our hilarity to the house when Jesse came out onto the porch and said, "What are you guys laughing about? We can hear you in here." On the way back Patty said, "Hannah would have loved this. This was her kind of night." Judd and Maude agreed. I didn't trust myself to say anything.

I had spent the previous week preparing for the race. I had the rigger come over from the marina and go up both masts to check everything. Wendy helped me buy the dry goods we would need and get them stored. I checked to make sure all of the safety equipment was at hand and fire extinguishers were up-to-date. I had already done most of this when the boat was first launched in the spring, but now I looked at everything as a Coast Guard inspector might.

We brought the bedding down to the boat. Maude and Wendy would share the forepeak; Jesse, Judd, Archie, and I would take over the berths in the main cabin. We put ice aboard Wednesday afternoon along with the refrigerated and frozen goods we would need. Nothing would stay frozen, but at least the frozen foods would last longer. We didn't have to worry about dinners. We planned to eat ashore most nights.

Naomi, Miriam, and Natalie performed angel duty. They got up at four in the morning Thursday and had breakfast ready for us when we rolled into the kitchen at five. They also had sandwiches and snacks all packed in individual bags. We left the mooring at five-thirty. There was no wind. The sea was flat. At least the fog was relatively light. We took turns at the helm guided by the GPS, at times twisting and turning to avoid the lobster pots that the crew member stationed at the bow pointed out to the person at the helm. The last thing we wanted to do was get the lines of a lobster pot wrapped around our prop.

The fog burned off around eleven and a slight breeze came up. We hoisted the sails and turned the motor off. We were running before the wind and with no breeze coming over the bow, it was hot. Archie was at the helm and I was sitting next to him when he said, "Wendy's been telling me about this book you're working on. Sounds interesting. She said you've been interviewing the people who were affected by a paper mill strike."

"Yeah, I have," I responded. "I've been getting some interesting stories."

"Are you going to interview the company people, too?"

"Hadn't thought too much about them other than what cretins they were."

Archie laughed. "I can imagine. I don't know, it might be interesting to know what they were thinking, especially if they lived in the town."

"Could be." We didn't say anything more for about fifteen minutes. As we sailed, I thought about Archie, probably for the first time, in any other role other than as Wendy's summer romance. He was a well-mannered kid, and the son of people I liked very much, but he had also just graduated from college and was on his way to get a master's degree in history at Princeton. Finally, it dawned on me. He wasn't just making idle conversation; he was making a suggestion. He was thinking like a historian. Get all the perspectives. I wasn't sure I gave a damn about the International Paper people and their perspectives. On the other hand, this young man may have something to say, so I started interviewing Archie, "Tell me more about what your thinking is about the paper people."

"I don't know. Just an idea. It might be interesting to think about the strike from a neo-Marxist point of view. You know, things like status differences in Jay as well as the power differentials. I did a bit of Googling when Wendy told me about it. IP was formed by merging twenty different mills, thus consolidating power. So, they formed an oligarchy and eventually exploited the workers. Pretty classic in some ways. So, they all drank the capitalist Kool-Aid and felt that labor was nothing more than a commodity to buy as cheaply as they could. I wonder, though, what happened to the executives and managers who lived in Jay? Were they insular, keeping to themselves, or did they have to deal with their neighbors? Just a thought."

It was a good thought. I kept asking Archie questions. He kept giving me answers. At one point he said, "Status is important. He who has the bread gets to make the rules, whether they are good rules or not. And high-status people never think they got that way because they are lucky. They always attribute it to hard work and smarts. It's a whole system. Is a person who makes a million dollars a year ten times smarter than a person who makes a hundred thousand a year? Do they work ten times harder? It carries all the way through. Look at the status that going to Harvard gives someone."

"Or Princeton," I said.

"Yep. They got the cash so I get a free ride because I went to a high-status undergraduate program. I admit it. The system is being good to me. Now, I get to talk about how corrupt it is. How's that for irony?"

He was smart, knowledgeable. He was tutoring me and I let it happen. By the end of his shift at the wheel, I was aware of a direction the book might take, but not convinced I wanted to take it there. I wasn't writing academic history, theoretical or narrative. I was writing about people who had been shafted.

It was still daylight when we arrived in Castine. We went to the cocktail party hosted by the Castine Yacht Club. I introduced everyone in my crew to Captain Bob Tucker. Everyone called him Captain Bob. He was ninety-one and still skippering his forty-five-foot New York 32 that was built back in the 1930s. After the recognition ceremony, we went to Dennett's Wharf. Archie tried adding a dollar to the hundreds of dollar bills that had been flung onto the ceiling with the use of a quarter. He was not successful. Jesse was. With thirty beers on tap, everyone was happy.

The next day we raced. Jesse got us off to a good start as we headed the twenty-some-odd miles over to Camden. That's as the crow flies. Sailboats are not crows, though. We sailors have to contend with tides, currents, shifting winds, and competitors. Maine, in the summer, has winds that go up and down like a berserk elevator. They also love to change direction and can shift around the entire compass inside of an hour. Guessing where they are going to be and making sure your boat is there to catch them is the task of the navigator. That was me. I guessed right three times and wrong twice. We arrived in the middle of the fleet. Not too shabby for a bunch of rusty sailors who were not used to sailing with one another. Importantly, we didn't break anything or hit anybody. With sixty-three boats in the fleet, that was not always the case.

We did better the following day. The race from Camden to Brooklin took us in and out of the islands of the Penobscot and past some of the most iconic views of the Maine shoreline that one could find. The day was perfect. Sunny, fifteen knots of wind from the Southwest. The *Redhead* was in its element. We hoisted every sail we had. The islands keep the waves from building up and everybody was happy and smiling. We kept saying, "It doesn't get any better than this."

Judd took over the galley with Maude helping. It wasn't long before mugs of hot clam chowder appeared. Sandwiches of various cold cuts followed, all made to order. Patty's brownies were the finishing touch.

As we came down Eggemoggin Reach towards the finish line we knew we had done better than the day before. All boats are given a rating based upon a variety of measures. The ratings and elapsed time from start to finish determine where you place in the fleet. We knew who should be ahead of us and behind us. As we approached the finish line, we couldn't believe what boats were behind us. We came in fifth. That was the best we had ever done. We did wait to open the liquor locker until we were safely anchored in front of the Wooden Boat School, but then Maude took over. In another life, I can imagine her as a professional mixologist. She likes to drink. She hates being drunk, or even tipsy, control freak that she is. But she genuinely loves the endless concoctions that are possible with liquor. If we were doing an S.A.T. test it would read: "Maude is to _____ as Patty is to wine. The only possible answer would be liquor. Without our knowing it, she had made a jug of 'Killer Bees' ahead of time and snuck it on board. All she had to do was add some ice and Selzer and she was ready to serve.

We had planned on eating ashore, but it got late. We had sufficient victuals on board so we dined on a mixture of pasta, canned corn, tuna fish, mayonnaise, all spiced with some curry. Food always tastes wonderful after a day of sailing and there was nothing but compliments for Judd's delicate and imaginative blending of ingredients.

Captain Bob and his crew were anchored nearby. After dinner, they rowed over to join us. All of us gathered in the cockpit sharing sailing stories with varying levels of veracity. Eventually, talk shifted to the race the next day. There would be over a hundred boats racing. The course was a simple one. Rather than racing to a destination as we had done for the past two days we would race out to Halibut Rocks off Swan's Island and then back to where we started in Brooklin. There would be eight classes of boats and we would take off in five starts with ten minutes between starts. Our class would get going at ten after eleven. One of the challenges would be not to hit anyone as all of these boats milled around the starting area waiting to get underway. Over a hundred boats would be racing.

After Captain Bob and his crew left, Jesse's competitive juices emerged. "We're going to do this. Right? With what we did today, we know we can. Right?" At one point Maude said to me, "How did you raise this lad?" Archie chimed in with, "I'm with him. Let's win." We all looked at him as he and Jesse gave each other high fives. Who was this young man my granddaughter had brought on board my boat?

We didn't win, but we came in fourth and that was pure luck. There is little strategy in an 'out and back' race. We are all just playing follow the leader and trying to avoid anyone stealing your wind. The luck was that two of the boats in our class who were ahead of us started trying to steal each other's wind. They were so engaged in their own little dual that we sailed right on by both of them. They didn't care about us. They were having fun in their little match race.

We were back on anchor by four in the afternoon. Maude packed up the bottles we would bring with us for the BYOB party at Wooden Boat. Patty had driven up from Georgetown to join us. After the BBQ dinner ashore and the awards ceremony, she left along with Jesse, Judd, and Maude. You don't get a prize for fourth, and it didn't matter. The three races in three days had been fun. It was a laugh and all-around hugs kind of departure. We were shipmates.

It rained the next day. Not hard, but enough to provide ample contrast with the weather we had been experiencing. Worse, we had to get an early start if we were to make it back to Heron Cove and have plenty of daylight. There was little wind so we went under power. I took the first trick at the helm. Archie and Wendy were below making breakfast. I could smell the bacon and coffee. Archie asked up, "How do you want your eggs, Mike?" As a shipmate, I had authorized the dropping of 'Mr. Buckley' as an appellation.

"Whatever you guys are having," I answered.

"Scrambled, then," Wendy said.

"I'll do KP after we've eaten and Arch takes over the helm."

An hour later Archie was at the helm and I was doing the dishes. Wendy had stayed below and was drying and putting things away. She asked, "Gramps, do you know anything about Rutgers?"

"No. Just that it's in New Jersey."

"I didn't realize it was a state school."

"I think I did know that."

"Archie says it's pretty good."

I stopped washing, turned and looked at her. She saw my look and said, "Just thinking about it. It's only half an hour drive to Princeton. Don't worry, just it's a thought and it's too late to do anything for next semester anyway. Given my grades, I'm not sure they'd want me. It would be nice, though."

Chapter Fifty: Grace and Helen

On Monday, I rowed out to the *Redhead* and spent the morning packing up from the weekend of racing. Sleeping bags, all the partials from the icebox: mayonnaise, mustard, milk, lettuce, half a leftover sandwich, and the remaining dry groceries. Coffee and unused canned goods remained on board. Then I put everything back where it belonged. Racing and living on board with a crew always means things get shifted around. The 'everything in its place' requirement had to be re-instated. Before I left the boat, I called Reverend Ted up in Jay to set up a time to get together. He suggested Tuesday for lunch. Then I called Penelope at the museum. She said she could meet me there in the morning. A call to the Blue Spruce Motel got me a place to stay. By the time I left Tír, it was late afternoon.

On my previous visit to Jay, Helen Graham had said that the next time I came up I should join her and Grace for dinner or lunch. On a whim, I decided to call them and see if we could get together that evening, with them as my guests at a restaurant. Helen had said Grace planned to be there for the entire summer. I found myself hoping this was still the case. I knew I was being presumptuous to invite them this late for a dinner date, but I was feeling reckless. The ladies might be free. I didn't think I would need a reservation at LeFleurs on a Monday night. I was pretty sure they'd be open.

I called from the car as soon as I got cell phone coverage at the top of the driveway. I was delighted to find out that Helen, according to Helen, was doing much better and she did not need any help. Grace, on the other hand, disagreed with her mother-in-law and was still there, and yes, they were free for dinner. However, they would not accept my invitation to take them out because, Helen told me, "Grace is a better cook than any chef within an hour's drive of here." She added there would be no "ifs, ands, or buts" about it. Grace was making authentic Italian cioppino that night and I was joining them for dinner. I thanked her for the invitation and asked what I could bring, perhaps some wine, or dessert. Helen did not hesitate with her answer. "Why thank you, Mike. Grace loves a nice Pinot Grigio. Sadly, I am currently a teetotaler because of these damned medicines, but anything with chocolate in it, and you'll be my friend for life, even if that's not going to be too long."

"Mom, stop it," I heard Grace say in the background.

"Well, it's true," Helen answered her back.

Returning her attention to me, Helen lowered her voice and said, "After you left, we talked about what a nice man you are. So, I'm glad you're coming. It's been a long time since Grace has had a gentleman caller."

I didn't know how to respond to this, so said, "I'm looking forward to seeing both of you." I may have emphasized the 'both' a little too much.

Helen and I talked about what time I should come for dinner, where I would be staying in Jay and the purpose of this trip. After I hit the 'end call' button, I was surprised at how excited I was about our dinner plans. I was even more surprised that Helen used the words 'gentleman caller.' Had I been that obvious? I did find Grace to be attractive, actually very attractive. And bright. And caring. And easy to be with. Apparently, my response to her daughter-in-law was transparent. She might be in her nineties, but Helen Graham was one sharp lady who didn't miss a thing.

So, now I was a 'gentleman caller.' I wondered if Grace saw me that way. Maybe Helen was just having fun with this 'gentleman caller' thing and there was nothing to it. Still, Helen had said they had talked about me after I left and decided I was a 'nice man.' Attractive, though, would have been better.

I knew there was a literary reference here somewhere and I wracked my mind for at least thirty miles trying to remember what it was. If I wasn't driving, I would have gone to Google for the answer. Finally, though, it came to me, Tennessee Williams, *The Glass Menagerie*. Was Helen taking on the role of the mother, trying to find a mate for her former daughter-in-law? Did she see Grace as fragile? That was certainly not my impression of her, but then, I didn't really know her.

My mind went through all sorts of permutations. Did Helen feel guilty because her son had been a lousy husband and caused the divorce? That led to several fantasies about what a horrible human being Grace's ex was. I, of course, by contrast, was a far more decent person with a sterling record as a husband. Recently, I had even refused the advances of a married woman who was throwing herself at me. By the time I got to Jay, I had returned to reality and accepted my ignorance of Grace's marital history. I didn't even know if she used her married name or not.

Dinner was lovely. Helen was correct about Grace's culinary skills which went beyond the excellent cioppino, a recipe from her Italian grandmother, to include the bread she had made for dipping in the broth. She had also made what she called a salad with an 'edge,' because of its endive. I had, for me, splurged on the most expensive Pino Grigio that Hannaford's had for sale. A 'gentlemen caller' wine. Helen was extravagant in her praise of the chocolate cake and double chocolate ice cream—both store-bought—that I had brought for dessert.

At first, the conversation flowed easily: food, weather, all of the safe stuff. Then Helen got to work. She commanded: "Tell us about your family, Mike. All of it. The dirt, too." I thought—it's amazing what you can get away with when you are in your nineties. What followed was an interrogation. She wanted to know everything about me and my family from the time I was born. Or, she wanted Grace to know everything about me. I told them. What did I have to lose? The only time I resisted was when she asked about my time in Laos. I told her, "I've tried to forget it."

She persisted, "What made it difficult, Mike?"

"I don't like talking about it."

She was about to give it a third try when, to my relief, Grace took over with a firm, "Mom, Mike would prefer to talk about other things."

"Okay," she said. "It was just such a despicable war. I'm glad you got home in one piece."

"So am I," I said. I wasn't about to say I didn't get home in one piece. Physically maybe. But one piece? No way.

She didn't give up. "It's sort of like some people around here are about the strike, trying to act as though it never happened. But you can never do that, can you? Whatever happened, happened. Isn't that right, Grace?"

"Maybe, but it doesn't mean you have to talk about it to people you barely know."

"Oh, hogwash. How else do you get to know people?"

"By respecting their privacy among other things." An edge had come into Grace's tone. I surmised they had had this conversation before, and not about me. I changed the focus and said, "Okay then." I addressed Helen, "Your turn, including all the dirt."

"Oh, you don't want to hear about an old lady, you want to hear about Grace. Grace, tell him about you."

"He asked about you."

"I'll tell him about me another time. Now, get on with it."

"Mom, I'm sure Mike would like to hear about you."

I wasn't going to let Grace off the hook, so I laughed and said, "I'd like to hear about both of you. Seems only fair." I wanted to hear about Grace.

Helen said, or commanded, "Grace. Go."

Grace did—with coaxing and coaching from Helen when she was less than specific or minimized her accomplishments.

Grace and 'Little Al' were 'get aways' from Jay. They had escaped, not unlike my daughter Ruth had from Georgetown, not unlike thousands of smalltown kids do when they go away to college or leave for some 'great job' someplace else. Rarely do they return to the town they grew up in. In town meetings, those left behind discuss how they are going to get their children and grandchildren to come back home, or, how will they keep them from leaving. It always boils down to opportunity. Opportunity for work, education, culture, excitement, and a list of reasons that any 'get away' could enumerate. With Grace and 'Little Al', it was education, then employment. They knew each other in elementary and junior high, ignored each other in high school, and then one summer vacation from college they got together. When they graduated, along with their degrees they got a marriage license. 'Little Al' went to Boston College Law School; Grace taught elementary school in Newton. Then came an opportunity for 'Little Al' to join the Boston law firm where he had interned after his second year. There was an opening in the firm's Portsmouth, New Hampshire office.

Everything was going right on schedule. Children came next. Grace stayed at home and since the University of New Hampshire in Durham was close by, she went to school part-time and obtained a master's degree in school counseling. Again, everything was right on track. However, 'Little Al' was given a not-so-subtle message from his supervisor: if he wanted to make partner, he should take the offer to move to the firm's Boston office where he could work on a greater variety of cases and get more billable hours. Grace did not want to uproot the family. They argued. Grace won. 'Little Al' said he would drive the hour commute into Boston. Grace said, "I won the battle and lost the marriage."

Five years of commuting and Al's long hours convinced them that a small pied à terre in Boston made sense. 'Little Al' could stay there on nights he had to work late and they could use it when they wanted to go into Boston for an evening, or even a romantic weekend. Three years later, romantic evenings were being spent in the pied à terre by 'Little Al' and a succession of women he met through his practice. Two years later he met 'the one' and told Grace he wanted a divorce.

At the time, Grace was working as a counselor at an elementary school, loved the work, loved Portsmouth and her sons were doing well in school. She was devastated. Her life was thrown into chaos. Helen was furious with her son and became one of Grace's major supports through two years that Grace described as 'post-divorce chaos." Helen added a few footnotes about how hard it was and amended the word 'chaos' to 'hell.'

Eventually, Grace settled into the hectic, challenging life of a single mother juggling work, 'Dad' weekends, and an ever-changing array of children's classes, teams, and overnights with friends.

A new principal was assigned to the school where she was working. Grace described him as 'retired when he arrived.' A former physical education teacher, he had no interest in curriculum, teaching, or creating a supportive environment for children with special needs. He was only her second principal. She soon learned how important a building principal was and decided that's what she wanted to do. So, again she went back to school part-time for another degree and certification as a school administrator. Seven years later she had her own school.

Along the way, she had two serious relationships—one promising, and one ridiculous, according to Helen. The 'ridiculous' one came first, when Grace was in her forties. Terrence was in one of her classes, recently divorced, very needy, and tried to replace the family he had lost with Grace and her family. He showered her with attention and drama. It lasted eight months. The 'promising' relationship developed when she turned sixty. Cam had sold his dental practice and spent his time studying and doing art, a postponed passion. He had been the family dentist. He was a widower, father, and grandfather. Grace and Cam were together for two years before he moved to follow his daughter's family to North Carolina. They tried to manage a distant relationship for a year but finally gave up. Since then, her life was focused on work, children, grandchildren, friends, family, and community. Now in retirement, she was on three boards and endless committees in Portsmouth.

Helen interrupted with details and commentary as Grace told her story. Helen was selling her daughter-in-law to me, the gentleman caller, and her belief that she had something of high value to sell was apparent. When Grace's story was finished, I said, "Okay, Helen, now it is your turn and I'm not taking no for an answer." Damned if she didn't say, "I'd love to, but it's past my bedtime. We'll have to do it another time. She turned to Grace and said, "I hate to leave you with everything, but I'm sure Mike will give you a hand, won't you dear?"

"Of course. Thank you for inviting me, but I'm going to hold you to your promise. Next time I want to hear about you."

The minute I said it, I realized I had just announced that there was going to be a 'next time.'

After Helen left the room Grace said, "I'm sorry, Mike. She embarrasses me like that all the time. She can't believe I can have a full, happy life without a man in it. You should see some of the men she has tried to fix me up with. She got so frustrated with me at one point, she asked me if I was gay."

"It's clear she loves you."

"And I love her, but I wish she would let it be."

I helped Grace clear the dishes and load them into the dishwasher. I was about to excuse myself for the evening when Grace said, "Want to go for a walk around the neighborhood? I'd love to hear more about Wendy, and the book you're working on. I'm also curious about Tír na nÓg. I'm not familiar with that legend."

Chapter Fifty-One: The Manager

I was curious about which International Paper managers lived in the two towns and rubbed elbows with neighbors during the strike. I planned to get their names from the museum's archives and to ask Penelope and Reverend Ted for introductions. Rightly or wrongly, I assumed that the managers would be reluctant to talk to me, and introductions would be helpful.

When I arrived at the museum, Penelope had prepared a list of the managers at the time of the strike. However, when I asked her who was living in Livermore Falls or Jay during the strike, she said, "None of them."

"None?"

"Nope. All the managers used to live here and be part of the community, but that all changed before the strike. I couldn't prove it, but I could swear the company told them to move out of town, and they did. Some moved to Augusta. I know one moved to Lewiston. Several of them were new to the mill. The managers living someplace else was a big change. This group did their damage during the day and then left town at night. Wives weren't here, kids weren't here, and they weren't here. No one was here to see how badly people were hurt. How's that for you? They didn't want to know, and the company sure didn't care."

I said, "I didn't know that. I didn't have anything about that in my notes from years ago, and I don't remember anybody reporting on that."

"Not sure anyone put it together back then. I know I didn't. I think we were all too shocked at first."

"I assume none of them ever lived here after the strike."

"Not as far as I know, and I think I would have known. It was thirty years ago. Managers weren't kids then. They'll all be retired by now, probably living in Florida or Arizona. Or, dead."

"Probably. Let me take the names, though. I'll try and track them down."

"Bet they won't talk to you."

"Why do you say that?"

"If they stayed with IP, and I'll bet they did, it's IP who'll be paying their pension."

"IP wouldn't be stupid enough to mess around with that. They'd get sued."

"I wouldn't count on it. I think you don't understand how much power these companies have. Look at the Chinese."

"The Chinese?"

"Chinese company, Nine Dragons, just bought one of the old shuttered mills in Old Town. Made a big splash. Parties. All sorts of great press. Things were going to be wonderful. Promised they'd be here for a hundred years. Now, look at them. I've heard they're making the employees work longer hours for the same pay."

"You serious?"

"As a heart attack. Go ask around. You'll see. People have to work."

"Yeah, they do. Seems like nothing has changed. And now the unions are weaker than ever," I said.

"Weaker? This is a non-union shop. These companies treat people like toilet paper. Get the most sheets for the lowest price. We're just disposable to them. A commodity to be bought for the lowest price." It had been years since Penelope had worked in a mill, but she still thought of herself as part of the 'we.'

I went back to the motel and started Googling the people from the list of names Penelope had given me. Only a couple of names came up, mainly obituaries. A suggested 'gift in lieu of flowers' indicated the cause of death for one of them. Another died of 'natural causes,' whatever they were. Two names did come up with pictures because of awards from civic organizations. I paid a month's subscription for one of the internet people-finder programs to get phone numbers and addresses. When I called one of the numbers, the person who answered was a nurse. Her patient was too sick to talk. The other number, though, got me through to Montrose Haig. When I introduced myself, 'Monty' asked me why I was dragging up that 'old strike.'

I told him, "I'm interested in the human story behind the strike. I'm talking to people who were strikers, people who crossed the picket lines, as well as managers at the time of the strike. I'm also talking to people in the town who were not directly involved but were affected, the hardware store owner, for example. So, I'd like to…"

"Well, I'll have to get back to you about that," he said.

"I can call later if you're busy right now. What would be a good time for you?"

"As I said, I'll have to get back to you."

"I promise I won't take too much of your time, and I don't have to use your name if you would prefer that I didn't."

"I'm going to hang up now."

"Excuse me, Mr. Haig. I don't want to put you on the spot here. I'm just wondering out loud. Do you have to check with someone before you can talk to me? As you said, it was years ago." He hung up. I called back. It went to voicemail. I left a message. "We seem to have been disconnected. I would very much like to talk to you. You may have a critical perspective given your position. As I said, I wouldn't have to use your name if you would prefer to remain anonymous." I left my number. I did not expect him to call me back. He didn't.

I was out of names. I had called Reverend Ted before leaving Georgetown, and we had made arrangements to meet for lunch. He was already sitting in a booth at LeFleurs when I arrived. I don't know how I imagined a minister should dress, but this wasn't it. I was brought up with priests in clerical garb, not T shirts, jeans, and, in Reverend Ted's case, a Spruce Mountain High School cap. I wondered how his work painting the bathrooms had gone and whether the color was acceptable to the ladies of his congregation now that it was up on the walls.

We shook hands and were handed our menus by a young man who could not have reached twenty yet. He hovered, waiting for our order. He was not to be denied. Ted already knew what he wanted. Since our young server appeared to be low on patience, I ordered something simple, a tuna fish sandwich with a cup of haddock chowder.

Ted said, "So, you want to talk to the mill's top management, get their side of things?"

"Yeah, I think it might give me a more complete picture."

"Maybe. I have no idea what they'll tell you. They used to be part of the town, know what was going on. I had one in my congregation when I first came here. He moved, though, about a year before the strike."

"Do you think he was told to move?"

"I don't know. Reason he gave was his daughter was going into high school, and he thought she'd get more of what she wanted if she went to school in Augusta. It was a bigger school. I didn't buy it. Kid didn't want to move, leave her friends. I think it was his wife. She was pretty uppity. In her less than humble opinion, we weren't good enough for them. He wasn't that bad, but his wife was a piece of work. I liked him and his daughter, but his wife? I was not sad to see her go."

"You think she was the real reason? Not the daughter."

"I think so."

"I've heard from old-timers that things really changed over the years. Used to be managers' kids grew up with workers' kids. Didn't used to be so much of a class distinction. There was always a pay gap, but the gap escalated over the years. I was told it was big and not just the top man, everyone right under him. You can imagine what that looks like in a small town."

"Yeah. Two-class system. People resented it. I wonder if he'd talk to me."

"I'm quite sure he won't. Died. And, if he were alive, either his wife or the company would have made sure he didn't."

"I'm hitting dead ends. So much for finding that angle on the story."

"Thought about that after you called, and I have an idea for you. How about his daughter? Would it be worth talking to her? She was something of a renegade, and she was very close to her dad. She's stayed in touch with her friends here in town and comes here for services once in a while when she's visiting. She's still on our books as a member. Name's Sage Perkins. Perkins is her married name. I can give her a call. Nothing to lose by asking."

Ted called and left her a voicemail explaining his call. He left my phone number. We finished lunch, and Ted left. I waited. I called and left her another voicemail. I had no idea how long I might have to wait, so I called Penelope to see if she was at the museum. She said that she was, that she had opened up for a graduate student from the Cornell School of Industrial and Labor Relations. I asked, "Can I bring you anything?"

"Some volunteers willing to babysit graduate students would be nice. This character came with a list of questions a mile long and expected me to have all the answers rather than do the work himself. He has his girlfriend with him, and she is bored silly. I set him up with the files he needs, but he is not happy that he's got to do some digging."

"I'll come and hang out if you want. Give you a break if you've got some chores to do."

"Oh, Mike, you are a sweetheart. It would only be for an hour, maybe less."

"Sure. I'm just hanging out, waiting for someone to return my call. You probably know her, Sage Perkins."

"Of course, I know Sage. I didn't think about suggesting you get in touch with her. She'll be a good one to talk to."

When I arrived, Penelope was all packed up and ready to go. Her instructions were simple. "Don't let him take anything. He can make copies, but nothing leaves. I've told him that, but I don't trust this one. He's a 'shortcut' kind of young man. His girlfriend decided to go for a walk, so it will only be the two of you."

"Got it."

I settled in where I could keep an eye on the 'shortcut' suspect. I was being entrusted with thousands and thousands of hours of archival work and who knows what kind of fortune in artifacts and memorabilia. Nothing would leave on my watch.

It was quiet. I looked around. Pictures of people working and mill leaders were on the wall. 'Shortcut,' as I now thought of him, had laid his head down on the table where he had been working and was taking a nap. He didn't snore. The only sound was the hum of a refrigerator. For some reason, I thought about the Ben Stiller movie *Night at the Museum*. I wondered what the people in these pictures might have been able to tell me.

My reverie was interrupted by the vibration from my cell phone. I picked it up and walked into another room to not disrupt Shortcut's nap. It was Sage. "Mr. Buckley, this is Sage Perkins. I got Reverend Ted's message and then yours. How can I help you?"

I explained to Sage what I was doing and why I called her. I also told her that I was at the museum and giving Penelope a break so she could do some chores. My less than subtle subtext was, 'I am one of the good guys.'

"How is Penelope?"

"She seems great. She'd like to have some more volunteers."

"Always. What she has done is amazing. Please say hello for me."

"I will. I know your father died a couple of years ago. I would have liked to have talked to him. Reverend Ted had very nice things to say about him and about you."

"That's nice."

"I'm curious about what the strike was like for your father and your family, during and after."

"Well, Dad and Mom moved us to Augusta before the workers went on strike. In some ways, it may have been a good thing. We had lived in Jay for several years and had friends there. When the directives came down from corporate, my father thought they were ridiculous. It's not as if the company was doing poorly; it wasn't. He felt caught in the middle. As much as I hated moving, I'm glad we did. Living there would have been horrible. He hated facing the people he knew the way things were. To meet them on the streets… it would have been devastating. I don't know if this is true because he wouldn't talk about it, but I think top managers got bonuses for hiring new people as quickly as they did. The mill never shut down. The strike went on forever, but so did the mill.

"So, your father was not in favor of the changes?"

"No. Definitely not. Not all of the managers felt that way, but that's how he felt. He wound up feeling very isolated and disillusioned. He retired as soon as he could."

"It sounds like some of the managers were in favor of the changes that were imposed on the workers."

"Absolutely. Bonuses were tied to the bottom line. In their minds, who cared if the workers were losing out on health benefits, time and a half, and vacation days. Can you imagine, you had to work

Christmas day? What kind of company does that when they are making tons of money?"

"You feel strongly about this."

"You bet I do. People suffered; the town suffered. But, financially, my family did well because of the suffering of others. My parents argued about it all the time when the strike was going on. The wives were tight. My mother knew how the other managers felt and that my father was in the minority. I don't think their marriage was ever the same afterward. Mom wouldn't even go to Jay or Livermore Falls after the strike was officially over. According to her, they were 'spoiled babies' who didn't know how good they had it."

We talked for another fifteen minutes. I thanked her for her time and told her she had been very helpful.

When I walked back into the room where he had been working, Shortcut was packing up his things. "You leaving?" I asked.

"Yeah, got what I needed."

"Penelope said you could make copies if you needed to."

"I took notes. I'm all set."

"She explained you can't take any of the materials."

"Yeah. I didn't."

"Would you care to make a donation?" There was something about his attitude that really bothered me.

"No, that's okay."

What kind of answer is, 'That's okay?' I didn't ask him what was 'okay', but I wanted to. His girlfriend was waiting for him in the passenger's seat of their car. I hoped she'd break up with him.

June 12, 1993
HOME TOWN BOY by Michael Buckley

We are at that time of the year when Volvo and Subaru station wagons sprout in Shaw's parking lot. They are weekenders now: opening cottages, surveying winter damage, hiring local folks to do repairs. Grass is cut every week, so it doesn't get ahead of them when they return full-time after school gets out.

On playing fields, the smack of a baseball hitting a glove can be heard as fathers coach their sons, and sometimes daughters, to follow through and put their whole body into the throw. Schools will soon be out. Gazing out the window and counting the days occupies the minds of more than a few students. Anticipating summer can be a full-time occupation for some.

When I was growing up, June meant my Boston cousins would soon be joining us for their 'Georgetown time.' Twin girls, four years older than me; I looked forward to their visits. I don't know if the difference in our age, or their Bostonian sophistication, led me to bestow upon them an adulation that my parents and their parents found amusing. It all started to fall apart when they reached their teen years and wanted little to do with me, as herds of pursuing boys appeared at our summer home on Heron Cove. I didn't become an afterthought. I was a 'no thought.' Taking them out for a sail could not compete with a pubescent boy who possessed a driver's license.

I always thought of the twins within the context of Boston. They always thought of my sister and me as their 'farm' cousins. All four of us had romanticized versions of how the others lived. It was classic grass growing greener on the other side of the fence or street. In our case, it was one hundred and fifty miles away.

I was young when I fell in love with Boston. It was magical to me. The weekend before Christmas, my family would go there to shop for presents. We would stay with my aunt and uncle and the twins—they did have first names, but they were always 'the twins.' The Christmas lights, store windows, going to see *The Nutcracker* ballet, and shopping at Filene's were the doings of a sorcerer captivating my imagination. It wasn't that I didn't like Bath and Georgetown, but they weren't Boston.

What I didn't appreciate at the time, was that my cousins were having the same experience with Georgetown. They loved helping out around the farm, driving the tractor, collecting eggs from the henhouse, moving the sheep from one paddock to another, and other activities that, to me, were chores and boring as could be. Who would have thought that pulling lobster pots and digging for clams was a cause for elation? Of course, we all laugh about it now.

When it came time for me to go to college, I knew it would be a Boston school. I didn't just want to go to any Boston school, I wanted a school 'in' Boston, not some suburban imitation on the fringe. I considered Tufts a lesser citadel of learning because of its location in Medford. Boston College was first on my mother's list because it was Catholic. Newton might as well have been Worcester as far as I was concerned. Northeastern would have worked geographically, but it didn't have Boston in its name. It could have been in New Hampshire or Vermont. Boston University was where I wanted to go, and that's where I went.

My mother started singing, "How ya gonna keep them down on the farm after they've seen Paree?" She told my father, "He won't be back." Well, she was wrong. After a stint in the Air Force, including a year in Vietnam, I was more than happy to get back home.

One summer, though, the twins decided, absent parental dialog, that they wanted to move in with us. Actually, I think it was a bevy of male admirers from the previous summer that prompted their interest. I don't know how well 'the twins' would have done with farm chores on a dark February afternoon when the thermometer was hanging around five or ten degrees. Their romantic image of farm life was formed by a July 4th to Labor Day set of blinders. It may have been the same with their male admirers. I don't know if 'their guys' would have made it through the winter.

The grass is greener dynamic also affects adults. Most of us who live here full time are used to being asked by a summer person, "What's it like in the winter? I'm tired of the rat race. I thought I might move here full time and slow down." When I am asked, I assure them that it is slower. I then extend my Maine accent and say something obtuse like, "Well now," I begin, "We sorta make our own entertainment. Not much goin' on elsewise. You might not want to sell your house before trying out a winter or two." Some do make the change. But I've noticed they tend to hold on to their city house or get themselves an apartment, a kind of 'just in case' clause.

I much prefer the approach my family has used. Relatives. The twins have stayed in Boston and raised their families there. With separate households, we refer to them by name now. We still visit before Christmas, and it is as magical as ever. More than once, though, I have been known to say on the way home, "It's a great place to visit, but I wouldn't want to live there." I should ask my cousins if they say the same thing.

Chapter Fifty-Two: Boston

In Michael's junior year of high school, four days after his seventeenth birthday, NASA announced the names of the seven military pilots who would go into space, the Mercury Seven. "Gordo" Cooper was an Air Force pilot. So were "Gus" Grissom and "Deke" Slayton. When Michael Buckley saw the news on television, he told his parents he would join the Air Force and go into space. It didn't take him long to have it all planned out. He had already decided he was going to go to Boston University. With his parents, he had visited Boston colleges one weekend in the spring, and, as far as he was concerned, there was only one possibility. Boston University had an Air Force Reserve Officer Training Corps program, and Michael looked forward to becoming a member of Detachment 355, 'The Flying Tigers.' He would do the two years of 'Basic' and then apply to be accepted into the advanced program for his junior and senior years. He never doubted whether or not the Air force would accept him into the program. He knew how to fly; it was a given. Jets first, then space, he told his parents. That was also a given. When his grandfather said, "I thought you wanted to be a reporter." Michael said, "I do, but I can do that later. Who knows? Maybe I'll stay in, do twenty years, and then work for a paper. I'd only be forty-two."

Michael did not know that his grandmother was lobbying against the plan, seriously and persistently lobbying against it. Nell told Jack, "Why on earth would you let him go into the Air Force? You lost two brothers. Isn't that enough? What are you and Peg thinking?"

Jack would counter with, "Mom, he hasn't even been accepted to BU yet. Assuming he does go there, he wouldn't have to make a complete commitment until his junior year. Who knows what will happen between now and then? He's a kid. He could change his mind a million times. So don't be such a worrywart."

What the high school junior and his parents could not predict was that, on July 8th, 1959, fifteen days into his last summer as a high school student, in a place Michael had never heard about called Vietnam, Master Sargent Chester Ovnand and Major Dale Buis would be shot and killed by members of an insurgent group called Viet Cong. The two American military advisors were watching a movie, *The Tattered Dress*, along with other American advisors, and some of the Vietnamese soldiers they were 'advising,' when the Viet Cong fired into their tent. Two Vietnamese guards were also killed.

It was one of Peg's better days. Rheumatoid arthritis is like that, good days and bad days, and the family had gotten used to it. She insisted that she accompany Michael and her husband when they drove to Boston to bring her firstborn to his first-year orientation program at Boston University. Although Jack and his brothers had gone to college, Michael was the first one on Peg's side of the family to attend. No one in Ireland had been. Her brother Tommy hadn't been, and the twins, much to their parents' disapproval, had no interest in going to college and chose to get positions as phlebotomists at St. Elizabeth's Hospital.

Jack was concerned about the trip because Peg tired so quickly, and it was impossible to predict when a flare might develop. She would have none of it. "I've worked bloody hard to get some control over this damned thing. I'm dieted down to my bantamweight, aren't I, and I can tell when things are starting up. We're going to go down a day early. I'll be taking my son shopping for what he'll need as a college man. If I get tired, I'll go to Tommy and Maeve's. I'm going, Jack. Don't think I'm not. We're all going."

"Come on. How will we fit all of us and his stuff into the car?"

"It's simple. You and Michael take the truck with his things. Me and Maude will drive down in the car."

Peg would have preferred a 'good Catholic school like Boston

College' to Boston University. But eventually, she relented. Jack had also given up his push for a school in Florida. Once he was accepted, Peg became enthusiastic. She told everyone, "It's where this wonderful Martin Luther King went and became Doctor King. The University has even given him an honorary degree, hasn't it already?" Peg had been following the newspaper articles about King and was incensed at how a few of the people she knew talked about him, especially if one of his detractors was Irish. She told Michael, "Only an ignorant shanty American Irishman can't see that Colored people are as badly treated in this country as the English treated the Irish for centuries." Since the Buckley family prided themselves on how Jamie and Will had treated their shipmates, Isaac and Nathan, when it was "not the thing to do," Michael had been brought up to share her opinion.

Maude didn't want to go. "I don't want to say goodbye. Mike won't be home 'til Thanksgiving." But she was told she was going, and she went. In Boston, they stayed with Tommy, Maeve, and the twins. Mother and father took their son shopping for clothes and things he would need, and some that he wouldn't. Maude didn't want to go on a shopping trip for her brother, and no one forced her.

The following day the university provided lunch and a tour of the campus for the families of incoming freshmen. While settling Michael into his room, the Buckleys met Michael's roommate, 'Tar' (Thomas Adams Roberts III), and his family. The Roberts were from Malvern, Pennsylvania. After Michael unpacked and Peg made his bed, they went to a welcome reception given by the President, Harold C. Case, and the dean of the Marsh Chapel, Howard Thurman. A few days later, Tar instructed Michael about the Philadelphia Mainline.

On the way to the parking lot to get into their vehicles for the trip back to Georgetown, Peg said to Jack, "Wasn't that the most brilliant day?" Jack put his arm around his wife and said to his daughter, "Maudie, when it's your turn, how about we take a trip to Florida to look at schools?" Maude slept the entire way back to Georgetown. Michael found it hard to sleep that night. There was a lot of noise in the dormitory halls, and he wasn't used to sharing a room with anyone.

Within a week, the differences between the two young roommates emerged. A graduate of St. Paul's School in Concord, New Hampshire, Tar was amazed that his roommate had gone to a public school, had never been skiing, had never been to Europe, and lived on a sheep farm. Tar was supposed to follow the men in his family to Princeton, but he had found St. Paul's to be 'overly serious about everything.' Moreover, Princeton found him to be 'not the right fit' because of his grades, even as a legacy applicant. They suggested a gap year. Tar refused, and applied late to various schools, including Boston University which was his 'safety school.'

Tar soon dubbed Mike his 'Hick' roommate and decided it was his duty to introduce Mike to the finer things in life. He would say, "Come on, Hick, loosen up. This is supposed to be a party school. We've got to do our share to maintain its reputation." By the end of the semester, Mike was 'Hick' to everyone in the old brownstone they shared with other Boston University students. The nickname 'Buck,' acquired in high school, was somehow insufficient at Boston University, at least according to Tar. 'Hick' was, according to Tar, eminently descriptive. "It is precise, Hick. It is denotation to perfection." Along with it came the connotation of acceptance and affection, and Mike came to appreciate his new nickname. It was better than the nicknames many of his fellow freshmen acquired.

By the middle of the first semester, Tar was not doing well academically. He spent most of his time playing bridge and drinking. Even though the drinking age was twenty-one, Tar had established a relationship with a senior who functioned as his broker, bringing Tar and his alcohol together in what, according to 'Hick' Buckley, was an endless supply of gin, vermouth, and even olives. Martinis were, according to Tar, the finest of the finer things in life. He would quote

Hemingway, "They make me feel civilized." Hick did not like them. When mid-semester tests and grades were posted, Michael, the 'Hick,' had gotten all As except for a B+ in French. Tar had Ds, an F, and a C in English composition.

Tar's F created familial battles in Philadelphia. When Tar took the train home for Thanksgiving, Michael was unsure his roommate would return. He did. When Michael asked him how it went with his family, Tar replied, "My mother asked me how you were doing. I made the mistake of telling her what your grades were. You know what she said to me?"

Michael said, "No. I hope she didn't pull the plug on you."

"No. She said that perhaps I had more to learn from my 'hick' roommate than he had to learn from me."

"Seriously?"

"Yes, seriously."

"That must have hurt."

"Damned right it did."

"Sorry."

"It gets worse."

"Oh."

"They're willing to pay you if you teach me how to study."

"Now that's funny."

"What's so funny about it?"

"Come on. You just never study. That's all. Nothing to teach."

"They're not going to pay for a second year if I don't get my grades up. Anywhere. Not even a gap year."

"Oh."

"Can you help?"

"How? You know what to do."

"Just help me get organized and get on my case if I don't do it."

"No way."

"Come on, Hick."

"That's bullshit."

"Please. I'm really in trouble."

"Tell you what. When I'm getting organized, I'll remind you to plan your time out. When I'm studying, I'll remind you to study."

"I'll pay you."

"I don't want your fuckin money. Just don't hassle me when I start acting like your momma."

"I can't promise that."

"You hassle, I quit."

"Okay."

Peg was not at all happy when Michael told her that the day after Christmas, he would be going skiing with Tar. "Why would you be doing that? You don't know how to ski."

"I know. I'm going to learn."

"Where are you going to stay?"

"Tar's parents have rented a place at Stowe."

"Where's that?"

"Vermont."

"How are you going to pay for it?"

"Tar's parents are going to pay for everything."

"Why?"

"They're rich, and they think I'm a good influence on him 'cause I get good grades. They even offered to pay me to tutor him."

"What?"

"Don't worry. I said no. I just get him to study when I study. He's going to do okay."

"Have you told your father?"

"Not yet."

Michael did not tell his parents that Tar's mother and father wouldn't be staying for the entire week that they had rented the chalet. Neither did he tell them that the girl Tar had been dating was also going to be skiing at Stowe, and she was bringing a friend from Simmons with her, Joyce Roskin. She was a New Yorker, Upper West Side of Manhattan. This would be her first time skiing, too. "You can teach each other how to fall," was Tar's encouragement.

Michael and Joyce did fall into the most beautiful freshman year either could imagine. *Moonlight in Vermont* was their song. It was Michael's first serious relationship, and when Michael returned home for Easter, he told his mother, "I think this is the girl I'm going to marry. I want you to meet her. Can she come to Tír this summer?"

"Of course, if it be alright with her parents." Having a Jew at the dinner table was not unusual in Michael's family. Judd was always there in the summer, as his father had been before him. Peg assumed that this Joyce girl might someday convert to Catholicism if they were truly serious. If she didn't, that would be okay too. She would be good for her son if she were anything like Judd and his family.

Joyce's family, however, did not feel the same way. Seeing the intensity of their relationship, her mother asked about the possibility of Michael's converting to Judaism. Joyce felt honor-bound to raise the question with Michael. When Michael told Tar, his roommate laughed. "You, a Jew? Enough you're a hick. She wants you to be a Kike, too?" When Michael mentioned it to Judd during spring break, he also thought it was funny, "So, you'll go from being a lousy Catholic to a lousy Jew. That's going to make your mom real happy."

Joyce and Michael resolved to not worry about either set of parents. Instead, they set about being in and making love with as much enthusiasm as possible. They spent every weekend together exploring Boston. Joyce had a friend, Esther, a senior, from Joyce's neighborhood in Manhattan. Esther lived off-campus. She had acquired a boyfriend who had already graduated and lived in Brookline. Esther's apartment was vacant most weekends, so Michael and Joyce had an available nest for themselves.

Summer came, and Joyce went home to New York. The planned

family introduction at Tír na nÓg never materialized. Michael was not invited to New York or Joyce's parent's rental cottage on the Jersey Shore. After the parental complaints about the costs of long-distance telephone calls, the couple resorted to writing letters.

By the time they returned to Boston for their sophomore year, Esther had already married her love, and the apartment was no longer available. Over the summer, Joyce had met with her rabbi several times and was determined to be a good Jew. Michael was beginning to work on the student newspaper and had less time for romance. Amidst tears and the sadness of longing and acceptance, the young couple was no more by Thanksgiving.

To add to Michael's misery, his Grandpa Will got the 'flu' over Christmas vacation when Michael was off skiing with Tar. By the time he got home, it had turned into pneumonia. Will, the Buckley who had first settled in Georgetown, died the week after Michael returned to school. Nell returned to the farmhouse where she had spent most of her life, and the family rented the house in Bath to a couple of young married school teachers.

In the spring, Michael worked hard. He was determined to make his mark on the journalism department. He spent a great deal of his energy on a paper about the entry of Alaska and Hawaii to the United States. His assignment was to do a background piece on the politics of the two additions. What began as one article turned into four. He was convinced that he wanted to visit both of the new states by the end. When he told his father about Alaska, Jack scoffed, "You want to go freeze your butt off? We'll see how you like it." The journalism department gave him a prize for the series.

Journalism majors at the university were engaged in intense arguments. The new President, John Kennedy, had given a speech to the American Newspaper Publishers Association. He had asked them to support America in its struggle against a 'monolithic and ruthless conspiracy.' He asked them to "consider the national interest in your reporting." Students and faculty took sides, not in formal debates but in arguments that had the vehemence of survival. Michael thought Kennedy was wrong. He had been swept up in his family's and Boston's love for Kennedy. Now he felt betrayed by his hero. From love to hate. First Joyce, now Kennedy. "Sophomore year has sucked," he told Tar when they said goodbye at the end of the semester.

"Come on, Hick, you got into Advanced ROTC, didn't you? What more do you want?"

"Honestly? Among other things, I wanted Princeton to tell you to go fuck yourself when you applied for the transfer. I know; it's your destiny, legacy, and all that shit. Worse, I feel partially responsible for getting you there. So who you going to study with now, Princeton? You better not flunk out."

Tar threw his pillow at Michael. "I'll be fine. Plan on Stowe next year."

"Yeah. Sure. We'll see."

Nan returned to Erascohegan that summer, and within a week, they were the yacht club sweethearts. Since the Air Force had accepted him into the advanced program, Michael decided he would fly as much as possible and get his instrument rating over summer vacation. He fished in the mornings and then drove to Brunswick to do his ground school and get his flight hours in for his rating. The idea of space continued to fascinate him. The United States had sent a chimpanzee into space and retrieved him alive. Yuri Gagarin had made it into space, completed an orbit, and parachuted back to earth when he separated from his capsule still 23,000 feet in the air. Kennedy had said the United States would get a man to the moon and back. Michael wanted to be part of it.

He was determined. He would be the best cadet and the best student the university had ever had. With Tar on his way to Princeton,

Michael requested a single room and got it. During his junior year he wrote for the student newspaper and played intramural football. With Nan close by at Bentley, they would spend at least one day together on the weekends. Junior year came and went in a flash of study, Nan, and extracurricular activities. Tar did invite him to go skiing at Stowe, and Nan came with him. Everyone at home in Georgetown assumed they would get married.

The summer between junior and senior year belonged to the Air Force. Michael was happy with his assignment to Otis Air Force Base on Cape Cod. Otis was the largest Aerospace Defense Command in the United States. Michael felt his assignment was at various times 'destiny' or 'appropriate' depending upon to whom he was talking. On the other hand, Nan thought it was horrible and complained that being at Otis just fed his fantasies about going into space.

There was a hitch. Michael was now deep into his journalism major and loving it, excited by it, and longing to work on 'big stories.' He was now a lead reporter for the school newspaper and pushed limits about stories just as he had in high school. He did a piece on the United Nations condemning apartheid in South Africa on assignment. His professor said it was as good as anything coming out of the Boston Globe. He felt torn between the two careers. But now, he did not have a choice. He had to go into the Air Force.

In May, he went to Nan's graduation from Bentley. His whole family went. That summer, there was a party for Nan and other graduates at the yacht club. Michael, though, was at Otis and couldn't attend. Nan got a job with an architectural firm in Boston. She also rented a studio apartment, but Michael was at Otis and couldn't help her move in. When John Kennedy was assassinated on Friday, November 22nd, Michael was away at an ROTC event for the weekend. Nan was alone in her new apartment. She had no way to reach Michael.

With Tar off at Princeton, the nickname 'Hick' did not survive

Michael's years at Boston University. As Tar became more Princeton, neither did their friendship.

Chapter Fifty-Three: Alaska

It was ninety-six degrees in Big Springs, Texas. The tarmac at Webb Air Force Base had been soaking up the heat for days and then returning it into the air, creating heat mirages. The new Air Force second lieutenants complained about everything from the heat to the food to the non-stop flying. So, one night a group of them did a rain dance hoping to invoke the gods to send severe weather that might ground them for at least a day or two—anything to give them a respite from their training. No one in the training command cared about the complaints or the rain dance. They had heard it all before. The command had trained pilots from WWII through Korea and was still at it.

The young pilots talked about the possibility of a nuclear war with Russia. They had all seen the movies *Fail Safe* and *On the Beach*. They all had images of what such a war might mean. And now there was Vietnam. Which war would it be for them? With twenty-one thousand American 'advisors' in Vietnam, the United States was obviously doing more than advising.

They joked about Vietnam. The Air Force 'advisors' rode along with Vietnamese counterparts on strafing and bombing raids. In the pilots' thinking, and that of just about everybody else in the military hierarchy, the Viet Cong were ill-equipped peasants who would be overcome in months. They were sure the problem wasn't the Viet Cong; it was the corrupt Vietnamese government.

The 'advisor' nomenclature was a joke. Everyone 'knew' that United States pilots were doing the flying. They couldn't believe the Air Force had given the Vietnamese a WWII vintage tail dragging prop plane, the A1 Skyraider, to use against the Viet Cong. Slow, with a cruise speed of less than two hundred miles an hour, the young pilots thought the A1 was a joke. It was even nicknamed the *Spad*, which was a WWI plane.

Michael Buckley agreed with his classmates. He was a jet jockey with aspirations to be a fighter pilot. Trained on the T-33, Second Lieutenant Buckley longed to fly the F-102, the F-104, and maybe even the hottest of the hot, the F-105. The old dream of going into space took a back seat to the excitement of jets. Twice the speed of sound. That was the F-105. It could even carry a nuclear bomb.

At Webb, Michael was bored with the Air Force approach to training. He thought it was too slow, too thorough, too safe. He wrote his father, "I already know how to fly. I may have more flight hours than one of my instructors." He did not make the training command aware of his assessment, directly. However, he was not reluctant to share his judgments with his fellow trainees. Somehow, his commentary made its way to one of his trainers.

Michael had been dressed down before. But in ROTC at Boston University and then at Otis, the dressing downs were more like hazing. Minor infractions and sometimes imagined violations would justify an upper-level student or a training sergeant doing some shouting and using creative insults. All of his classmates received them. No one paid much attention to them, and they knew it was just part of the game they were all playing.

The one he received at Webb was different. The captain who delivered it was from Farnhamville, Iowa. Like Michael, he had begun flying in his teen years and had earned money during college dusting crops. He was not impressed with Michael's flying background and even less impressed with Michael's Air Force training program evaluations. By the end of the hour that Michael stood at attention in the captain's office, Michael was sweating from embarrassment and the Texas heat. The captain's voice had begun softly and never increased in volume. It was a voice used to operating in a direct, declarative manner with no need for pyrotechnics. It came from experience and confidence. It was conttrolled power with full awareness of its potential to determine Second Lieutenant Buckley's future in the United States Air Force.

Michael returned to his room, knowing his time at Webb would be short if he did not adjust his perspective. It was the first time that his attitude had been called into question. He had made mistakes in the past. He had done things that his parents never knew about. He had been caught, on occasion, in a youthful, rebellious action that had gone awry. However, he had never felt his character as a human being was in question. That afternoon an Iowan farm boy provided him with a new experience. He recognized his career was in jeopardy.

A letter from Nan came a week later:

> Dear Michael,
>
> I never expected to write this letter. I am surprised that I am doing it now. You know how important you are to me, and you always will be. However, you know that we have been quarreling this past year about our future and what we want from life. Sadly, I have concluded that we want different things. We talked about this when you were preparing to leave for Texas.
>
> This summer, I went to Georgetown on the weekends. I hadn't planned on this, but I started spending some time with Joe Land. At first, we were doing things as friends. However, by the end of

the summer, it was apparent to both of us that we were developing more than a friendship and wanted to take it to the next level.

I'm sorry, Michael. I will always hold a place for you in my heart. You are a wonderful person, and I have lovely memories of our time together that I will always cherish.

Please be safe.

Your friend forever,

Nan

Michael read the letter on the way to dinner. He stopped, turned around, and headed back to his room. Two F-102s were taking off. The afterburners ignited, and the noise was deafening. He re-read the letter, turned again, and walked back to the mess hall. He went right by it and kept walking towards the airfield. He saw the sentry, turned, and walked towards the base chapel. He didn't go in. He noticed the payphone, went over to it, and called home. His mother answered. Usually, they spoke on Sunday evenings; it was Tuesday. She asked what was wrong.

Two years later, Michael had a new love, the F-102, the Delta Dagger, the 'Deuce.' Supersonic, armed with missiles, it had one job—intercept Russian bombers and shoot them down if they threatened the United States. When Michael called home to tell his father he had been assigned to an interceptor squadron, his father asked, "So where do they have you going?"

"Eielson."

"Where the hell's that?"

Michael was enjoying himself, "Up north."

"Come on, wise guy, where you going?"

"Alaska."

"Oh, for Christ's sake. Of all the places they could have sent you, you're going to some god-forsaken place in Alaska. Do they hate the Buckleys?"

"I guess so. Do you know what the name of the nearest town is?"

"Okay, wise guy, what is it?"

"The North Pole."

"Come on. No, it's not."

"Seriously, it is. Would I pull your leg?"

"Yes."

"It's not that bad, Dad. Fairbanks is only about twenty miles away."

"Is there anything there? Wasn't when I was there."

"Hey. Now it's bigger than Bath."

After a few minutes discussing the weather in Alaska, how much Jack hated it, and how sorry he was that his son was going from boiling to freezing, Jack said, "So. F-102, the Delta Dagger."

"Yep, except everyone calls them Deuces."

"You got what you wanted."

"Yeah. Yeah. I was hoping for the 5, but 'mine is not to reason why.' At least I finally get to do something besides train and train others. Truth is, the Deuce is a good plane. It's like flying an engine equipped with a computer. It's fun, though. I know the damned thing inside out at this point."

"Wait a minute. Your mother's pulling at me. I believe she wants to talk to you. Now she's hitting me. I'd better put her on."

Peg had no interest in the F-102. To her, it was just another airplane. She was just happy that her Michael was going to Alaska rather than Vietnam. Every night she watched the *CBS Evening News* with Walter Cronkite. More than 200,000 American troops were in Vietnam, and Lyndon Johnson had said the Americans would stay until North Vietnam ceased hostilities. Anti-war demonstrations were taking place across the country, and even Dr. King had come out against the war. If Michael couldn't be home, at least he wasn't in Vietnam.

That night Jack told Peg that he wanted to go and visit Michael when he got his first leave time. Perhaps in Seattle, or maybe even Fairbanks. Peg said, "Brilliant. I'll be going with you."

"It's an awfully long trip, honey. It'd be too much for you. I should go alone."

"Absolutely not. I lived through years of you being gone when you were in the Navy. You hated it. I hated it. If we can get to our son, we will go and visit him. We're not going to put him or ourselves through that. We'll go in the summer when Maudie's home from school. She can take care of the farm. There's not much left to take care of now, anyway."

"What if she wants to go, too?"

"If she does, we'll be making a family trip out of it, won't we? We'll hire someone to take care of things here."

"Are you sure the trip wouldn't be too hard on you? It could take up to two days to get there if we have to go to Fairbanks."

"I can be sick here or there. It's not like I'm going mountain climbing."

Their week in Seattle was unusual. They could see Mount Rainier every day from downtown. The Buckley family—Maude had come—took ferries to Bremerton, Bainbridge, Vashon, and Port Orchard. They went to a salmon feast. The week, though, was marred by the news. In August, there were race riots in Lansing, Michigan, and Waukegan, Illinois. In Vietnam, twenty-five F-105s had been shot down in one day. The family did not talk about it. They were there to enjoy one another's company and Seattle. For Michael, though, the news from Vietnam was his first awareness of vulnerability. It was the F-105. How could this happen to the 105? He couldn't understand it.

When he returned to the base at Eielson, he was not surprised that the talk was centered on Vietnam. Most of the pilots wanted to go; they wanted to get into the action. The losses had been from ground fire, and there were endless discussions about the mistakes that the American leaders had made both in Washington and on the field.

The North Vietnamese had created the most heavily defended city in the world, Hanoi. American leaders had allowed the buildup and were now sending pilots to their death. In addition, the North Vietnamese were flying Russian MIGs, and they were destroying the F-105s in dog fights. The American Air Force was getting beaten badly between ground fire and dog fights. Hanoi prisons were filling up with American pilots. In Alaska, Michael felt safe, removed from the dangers of Vietnam.

Since WWII, military planners had seen Russia as the threat. Russian bombers carrying nuclear weapons consumed their imaginations. Consequently, intercepting Russian bombers was the primary mission of the 'new' all-jet Air Force. Air-to-ground combat and dog fights were a thing of the past in their thinking. Michael's F-102 didn't even have a gun, just air-to-air missiles. Michael and his fellow pilots knew that the planes they flew would be of no use in Vietnam.

Instead, Michael waited in ready rooms, flew patrols, or trained day after day. The skies between Alaska and Russia were a different kind of battleground, a battleground of nerves, a battleground of thrust and parry with nuclear warheads. The International Date Line had become a picket line. Russian Tu-95s carrying hydrogen bombs would head towards the United States. American B-52s carrying hydrogen bombs were always in the air heading towards Russia, just waiting for the signal to go and drop their loads on Russian cities. So, it was the Russian Bear, the Tu-95, versus the United States B-52, the BUFF (big ugly fat fucker). Michael's squadron of F-102s was to intercept the Russian bombers as they headed towards the dateline and if they went too far across it and became threatening to the United States or Canada, to launch their missiles and shoot them down. The American B-52s faced the same welcome party at the other end, only from Russian MIGs. Many people thought the whole process was insane and worried that a misstep by either side would destroy the world, the *Failsafe* scenario.

This game of nuclear chicken had been played for many years by the time Michael arrived in Alaska. Leaders changed, planes changed, crews changed, but the game remained the same. When Michael described the scenario to Jack, his father said, "It's as bad as the trench warfare of WWI, only the entire world could be destroyed." Michael let the comment pass.

Michael and his fellow pilots didn't talk much about their role in the aerial game of chicken. What they did was their job. They did what they were trained to do. Once in a while, there was a change-up, a training exercise. Usually, it was to challenge their B52s as they returned from their flights on the Russian-American picket line.

When this happened, they were usually notified in advance that they would be engaged in a training exercise. Some of the F-102s would be armed with 'blank' missiles. They wouldn't know when they would be sent into action, but their readiness, time to intercept, and intercept success would be tested.

Two days after their briefing about an exercise on a November night, Michael and five other pilots were in the ready room. Already in their flight gear, some were dozing, a few were reading, and some were watching Bonanza on television. The call came for two flights of two planes each to intercept two B-52s returning from their picket duty. Four pilots grabbed their gear and headed for their aircraft. Their crews met them there and had the planes ready. They helped the pilots get strapped into their ejection seats and harnesses. The time to beat was five minutes from the call to wheels up. Of course, over a hundred things could go wrong during those five minutes. But, surprisingly, it rarely did.

Another call came in twenty-five minutes later. Michael and his flight leader were scrambled to intercept six Russian Tu-95s heading in past the picket line. It was rare for the Russians to send this many planes at a time, and the difference put everyone on edge. Three flights from the squadron at nearby Elmendorf were already in the air.

Getting to his plane, Michael scrambled up the portable ladder. They were still on the climb out when Michael heard his flight leader say to the NORAD command that had scrambled them, "We don't have anything live onboard."

He heard the response, "Continue as vectored." He knew what it meant. He ran the series of ifs in his mind. If something had happened someplace in the world to light a fire, and if the Russians were actually attacking, and if the flights from Elmendorf were unsuccessful at encouraging the Tu-95s to turn around, Michael and his flight lead were to crash into the intruders. He reached altitude and flew to the right and slightly above his flight leader.

Chapter Fifty-Four: Spads

The standard four-year Air Force commitment did not apply to you if you were a pilot. Time was added on for your initial flight instruction. Then, additional time was added for the training associated with specific planes. Jets required more time than propeller-driven planes. All of this influenced when you could apply for your DOS (Date of Separation). When Peg asked Michael when he would be done with the Air Force, his standard answer was, "It's complicated, Mom."

In the middle of the war in Vietnam, the Air Force announced it would change the commitment time for its pilots from four years to six years. Knowing this was coming, Michael immediately declared his DOS so he'd be out before the change was implemented. It wasn't that he didn't like the Air Force; he had seen enough to know that it wasn't a career he wanted to pursue. The regimentation didn't fit with the crusading reporter image that he had carried with him since high school.

Michael also felt pressure from home. Television news showed disturbing pictures of both the war and the anti-war movement that was gaining energy. There was a direct correlation between the loss of American lives in Vietnam and the amount of pressure Michael felt from his mother and grandmother to get out as soon as he could. When Peg read the news account that one thousand new American troops did not survive their first day in Vietnam, she told Jack, "I'll bloody well kill him myself if he doesn't get out as soon as he can."

What assignments you were eligible for as a pilot was also complicated. Your health, class rank in pilot training, available openings for different planes, and your last overseas deployment dates were all factored in. The Air Force allowed you to indicate your preferences, first, second, and so on, but the needs of the Air Force came first. Gaming the system was a full-time occupation for some pilots. Since pilots were expected to rotate overseas at some point—Alaska did not count as overseas—and Michael was anxious to get out as soon as possible, he found himself in a pool of pilots that did not have much to say about assignments.

Again, it was complicated. In the early days of the Vietnam War, the Air Force F-105s were being shot down at a very high rate, so the Air Force needed F-105 pilots. The Air Force also started deploying F-4 Phantom jets. Training in either of these two jets would have extended Michael's service time beyond the DOS he had requested because of the additional training required.

Before Vietnam, the Air Force had committed itself to becoming an 'all jet' service. The focus was on Russia and interception. Now it found itself in a ground war in Southeast Asia without jet aircraft suitable for close air support. The jets were too fast to be accurate against small ground targets and then there were the surface to air missiles—SAMs—that were deadly against the high-flying jets. They desperately needed a fighter-bomber. The Navy and the Air Force turned to an old WWII propeller-driven plane, the A1 Skyraider. The United States had already given old A1s to the South Vietnamese and, to everyone's surprise, the plane was proving to be an effective weapon against a war of insurgency. The A1s were invaluable as ground support aircraft because they were slow, could carry a wide array of munitions, and could stay in the air for long periods of time. They could be called in by ground troops to suppress the enemy or to provide air cover for downed aircrews while helicopters attempted an extraction.

So, when Michael considered his options, only one did not require significantly extending his time. Since propeller planes did not have the same extension times as the jets—there was less training—he could request prop planes. Michael, though, considered himself to be a fighter pilot, one of the elites. If he wasn't going to fly a jet, he would request an assignment in a fighter-bomber, an attack plane. Consequently, after his tour in Alaska, he found himself at Hurlburt Field in Florida, training on the A1 Skyraider. He was learning to fly the plane he had laughed at when he was a 'jet jockey.' The plan was simple. He would go to Vietnam for at least a year. But then he would be out of the Air Force, and everyone at home would be happy.

Hurlburt Field was home to the Air Force Special Operations Command and the 1st Special Operations Wing. They did consider themselves to be elite. A sign in the officers' mess read, 'Jets are for kids.' Some of the units were even called 'Commando.' All of the planes at Hurlburt had reciprocating engines, and, when Michael arrived, all had the mission of either forward air control or ground attack. He was no longer trained to shoot missiles at bombers he might never see. The air war in Vietnam was very personal. In the A1, you flew close to your enemy. You flew low and slow. Your enemies were antiaircraft weapons, mountains, and sudden storms with high winds and a lot of rain.

Michael didn't tell his parents where he was going until he arrived in Florida. He did call Maude, who was at the University of Miami. Even if brother and sister were still seven hundred miles from one another, Hurlburt, in Mary Esther, Florida, was a lot closer than Alaska. She felt nearby. When he finally did tell his parents, his father started planning.

Two days after Michael told his father where he was, Jack called him and said, "I'm going to fly down. I just bought a brand-new Cessna. It's a 206, new model and it's amazing. This'll be a great break-in trip. I'll go to Miami first, spend some time with Maude, then the two of us will come over to you. Maude can't stay long, so she will take the bus back from Pensacola to Miami."

"Dad, you sure you don't want to go commercial?" Michael asked his father. "Be a lot more comfortable."

"Hell no. This is going to be perfect. I've only got to make one stop on the way down, and no stops from Miami to Pensacola. I'm looking forward to seeing that place again. This is uncanny. You follow me to Alaska, and now you're training a few miles from where I did."

"Mom going to come?"

Jack paused before answering, "No, your grandmother's not doing well. So, your mother's going to stay home. She'd love to come; you know that."

"What's wrong with Grandma?"

"It's her heart. She had a small heart attack."

"Why didn't anybody tell me?"

"What were you going to do about it? Didn't make any sense to give you one more thing to think about."

"Dad. You should have told me. I could have called her or something."

"Well, why don't you do that now? I know she'd appreciate it."

"I will. And, maybe I could send her one of those crates of oranges and grapefruit. Think she'd like that?"

"That'd be nice."

"When you coming? Maybe you could take one back with you. Maybe a couple."

"Sure."

"When y'all get your dates squared away, let me know. Give me as much lead time as you can so I can get some leave time."

"Y'all? Already you're speaking Southern?"

"Can't help it. It's catching."

"Your mother will love that."

Michael was able to patch together two days of crew leave with some weekend time. When Jack and Maude arrived, Jack wore his Navy Veteran's hat. Their first stop was the Pensacola Naval Air Station. Jack proudly showed the sentry at Pensacola his VA identification card. Michael was in uniform. The three of them had no difficulty being admitted to the base, and because of Jack's history with the base, an enlisted man was assigned to them to provide the VIP tour.

They spent three hours touring the base and had lunch at the officer's club. Maude was primarily impressed with the number of attractive men in uniform she saw. "They are all so polite," she said to her father and brother. "They're nothing like the boys at school." Neither her father nor her brother responded to the observation.

That afternoon they went out to Pensacola Beach. They took off their shoes and walked on the beach. At times, Maude would run along the waterline and try to splash them. Then, they would move back out of the way and threaten to throw her in.

About an hour later, Jack suggested they sit at a bench he knew about: "I hope it's still there." Jack was very quiet after they sat down. Michael asked him about his silence. Jack said, "I loved this place. It was the water. It reminded me of home. God, I missed home. I missed you and your mother. I missed Brian. I had a hard time knowing I would never see him again.

"This is where I would come to catch up with myself. We didn't get much time, but we got some. I always swore I would come back here with you and your mother after the war. I never did. Maudie, you weren't born yet. I wish your mother had been able to come to see this place. What do you say? Let's do that as soon as you get out. The four of us. What do you say?"

Michael and Maude both said, "Sure."

In the evening, they picked up dinner at *Joe Patti's* restaurant. The three of them found a table. Father and son shared a bottle of wine. Maude complained about the drinking age and reluctantly settled for a lemonade.

After Maude left to return to Miami, Jack wanted to know all about the 'Spad.' Michael got permission to bring him onto the base at Hurlburt escort him to see a 'Spad.' Jack wanted to fly with Michael in one of the 'E' versions that had side by side positions, but Michael said, "Absolutely no way. I'm not even going to ask. I know what the answer would be. So do you." Instead, they did a walk around together, and Jack asked questions.

"How old are these things? They look ancient. They make them anymore?"

"No. The last one was made in '57. A lot of the planes we're flying are ex-Navy. Some still have tailhooks on them. Damned thing was designed in '44."

"I was in the Aleutians in '44."

"Yeah. This is its third war."

"What's it like to fly it?"

"Nothing like anything I've ever flown before. The engine is so damned powerful the prop torque it generates is immense. You got to practically stand on the right rudder to keep it going straight taking off and on climb out. The stabilizer's offset to compensate, but you still need to stand on the fucking rudder pedal. Then, when you get up to cruising speed and beyond, you have to put in left rudder to compensate for the offset in the stabilizer. You get used to it after a while, but trying to aim this thing in a dive is a trick and a half."

"What's with all the oil on the fuselage?"

"They're all like that. External oil lines and they leak. It takes a lot of oil to keep those eighteen cylinders lubricated. The engine is a beast."

"What are you carrying for ordnance?"

"What would you like? There are six points under each wing and another point under the belly. We can carry just about anything that exists in the whole damned arsenal. We've been told we can carry more ordnance than a B-17 did. We can even carry a nuke."

"A nuke?"

"That's what we're told. It would be a suicide mission. You'd never clear the blast radius; these things are so slow."

"Is there anything you like about them?"

"Yeah. You can see. The F-102 you couldn't see straight ahead for shit."

"You miss the 'Deuce.'"

"Let's just say this is a new challenge."

"You miss the 'Deuce?'"

"Yeah. I do. In some ways, it's fun to go back to basics, but this thing is probably not as well equipped as your Cessna."

"Speaking of which, you want to fly her tomorrow? Show me the sights. I'm curious about what's changed if anything."

"Sure, why not?"

Flying his father's new plane, Michael realized how much he missed the pure joy of flying. Throughout his training and deployment, there was always concentration and tension. Compared to the Spad, the Cessna was quiet and responsive.

They followed the shoreline east with Michael at the controls. After the first twenty minutes of Jack pointing out everything wonderful about his new purchase, the two remained silent for a while as they looked out over the water to the beaches along the coast.

After they turned to head back to Pensacola, Jack asked, "How do you feel about going to Vietnam? You feel ready?"

"Ready as I'll ever be, I guess."

"I wish you weren't going. You could have chosen transport duty, maybe a nice C-47 carrying equipment and people between bases."

"Nah. It's my turn to get my hands dirty."

"That's how you think about it: getting your hands dirty?"

"Just an expression, Dad. Nothing more to it than that."

Michael's final days at Hurlburt were spent on bombing and gunnery practice. They also heard a lot of Spad stories from their instructors. The Spad had heavy armor protecting the underside of the plane. Most had been retrofitted with ejection seats. Losing a plane but the crew surviving was not unusual in Vietnam. Jungle survival was a real thing as far as the Air Force was concerned. However, his instructor told him he would learn "nothing worth knowing" in the survival training he would receive in the Philippines on his way to Southeast Asia.

Michael was astounded by the array of the ordnance that he had to learn. Because everything was carried outside the plane, each piece of ordnance created drag on the aircraft. Then when it was released, the drag went away. As a result, the plane was constantly behaving differently. On one mission, the plane might carry bombs, rockets, and even additional cannons beside the four built into the wings. For night work, flares could be attached to the wings.

Michael realized he was mastering killing people. Shooting down a Russian bomber carrying a nuclear weapon was somehow 'clean,' sanitized. He was keeping the Russians from dropping a bomb. Now he would be the one dropping bombs, and it would be at close range. The bombs came in all sizes. Some were conventional; some were firebombs—napalm. Napalm had been used since WWI but had been perfected over the years. The gas gel would stick to whatever it touched and continue to burn. Sometimes the bombs didn't ignite. So, the pilots had developed a system. Drop regular bombs or 'Willy Pete'—white phosphorus—on the first pass over a suspected enemy. In addition to the destruction, it would create fires. On the second pass, drop your napalm. That way, your napalm bombs would be sure to explode and spread fire where they were dropped. If not, a third pass using your cannons would set them off. An instructor who had recently returned from Vietnam said, "Your FACs (Forward Air Controller) on the ground will let you know how many 'crispy critters' they think you got."

Michael paid attention to every sentence an instructor uttered. He copied every diagram that was put up on the blackboard. At night, the trainees compared notes and prepared questions for the next day. The instructors told them that their planes were old, and the wings should not be overly stressed on their bombing runs. They would dive at a forty-degree angle towards the target and pull up as soon as they dropped their bombs, but they could not pull up too steeply, or they would put too much stress on the wings. They were instructed to monitor the G-forces on the plane and report to maintenance if they had developed too many G's so the aircraft could be inspected when they returned to base.

To add to the difficulty, they could not simply dive straight at their target or simply pull away after completing their run. Antiaircraft gunners would be waiting for them. To make it difficult for the gunners, Spad pilots were told to 'jink' back and forth on their way in and the way out. The instructor said, "Don't go in a straight line. They'll aim in front of you and you'll fly right into their shells. You let them plan on where they think you're going to be, that's where they'll aim."

If they were using cannons and strafing targets, they were told to stay away from the flight leader because they could run right into shell casings spewing out the back of the lead plane's wings.

The training was very different from the intercept training he had received in the F-102s. He knew his experience was about to change as well. So far, in his time in the Air Force, he had never been fired upon. He knew how to deploy the arsenal of missile countermeasures the F-102 carried, but he had never been called upon to use them other than in practice. In Vietnam, in a Spad, he would be shot at. That was a certainty. In Vietnam, his task was to kill people and destroy their ability to move arms and equipment. At times he would see them, and they would certainly see him.

Chapter Fifty-Five: Naked Fanny

The Vietnamese call it 'The American War;' in the United States it is the 'Vietnam War.' It started with United States President Harry S. Truman, and the revolutionary Vietnamese nationalist, Ho Chi Minh. In 1941, Ho Chi Minh was instrumental in creating the Vietminh organization. His goal was to free Vietnam from France's occupation and control. The United States had supported France's colonial claim to Vietnam through several presidential administrations.

WWII changed alignments, at first. France was defeated by Germany in a matter of days. A new government, Vichy France, was instituted and supported by the German victors. The Vichy government, while nominally in charge of all the French colonies, basically ignored their colonies. The new government was attending to the work of persecuting Jews, communists, and any who wanted to do battle with Germany.

Meanwhile Japan attacked the United States and sought to control all of Southeast Asia, including Vietnam. Ho Chi Minh did not want to trade French domination for Japanese domination. He began to fight the Japanese. In return, he received some support from the United States. President Truman, to bolster the support of Ho Chi Minh in his battle against Japan, agreed to support Vietnam's desire for independence once the war was over.

After the war, Ho Chi Minh and the Vietminh did not want France to maintain occupation of their country. Truman was ambivalent. The new French government sought to retain control of its colony, but the Vietminh fought them to a standstill in the French Indochina war. During the war, Truman turned his back on Ho Chi Minh and supported the French, breaking his agreement for an independent Vietnam. In response, Russia and China supported the Vietminh. What emerged was a country divided into north and south by a treaty to end the war between the two factions. The cold warriors of the West supported the newly formed South Vietnam, while the cold warriors of the East supported North Vietnam. Families were separated by the artificial line that was drawn through the middle of the country.

In the United States a new world view was being developed. Under the tutelage of his Secretary of State, John Foster Dulles, Truman's successor, Dwight David Eisenhower, viewed Russian communism as an expansionist ideology. Under the Dulles/Eisenhower doctrine, Russian communists wanted to rule the world and had to be stopped. According to this doctrine, every country that fell under Russia's influence made it more likely to corrupt its neighbor. This 'Domino Theory' became the global world view of the United States. Southeast Asia became the example of the communist threat. Vietnam, Laos, and Cambodia were 'under attack' by communist forces: Pathet Lao in Laos, Vietcong in South Vietnam, and the Khmer Rouge in Cambodia. All of these nationalist, anti-colonial, and anti-monarchy movements were labeled communistic and agents of Russian and Chinese expansionist desires. Eisenhower said, "If Laos were lost, the rest of Southeast Asia would follow." However, within these countries they were more likely experienced as civil wars fought between authoritarian regimes and revolutionary forces. Atrocities were common on both sides.

Eisenhower's successors, the administrations of John Kennedy and Lyndon Johnson, adopted the communist threat lens articulated by Dulles. American policymakers could not imagine that these revolutionary forces were anything other than Godless communists seeking to dominate the world. "Save the world from the Godless communists" was the message of one administration after another. Because of Chinese and Russian involvement, the leaders in Washington had to weigh every American move in Southeast Asia against the possibility of expanding the conflict into

WWIII, and destroying the planet. China was now a member of the nuclear family. It exploded its first atomic bomb in 1964 and then a hydrogen bomb in 1967.

The reality of the war Americans refer to as 'The Vietnam War' was that it was a Southeast Asian war. Thailand, Laos, Vietnam, and Cambodia were all involved. While the United States had allies (Thailand, Australia, New Zealand, and the Philippines), it was fundamentally a war waged by Americans, Laotians, and South Vietnamese against the Pathet Lao, Vietcong, and North Vietnamese.

In Thailand, afraid that the Pathet Lao's revolutionary ambitions in Laos would seep into his country, the Thai Dictator, Field Marshall Thanom Kittikachorn, gave the United States authorization to use several Thai bases.

By the time Michael arrived in Thailand in 1967, there were already five hundred thousand American troops in Southeast Asia. Back home in the United States, the anti-war movement was becoming more aggressive, and clashes with supporters of the war were common. In March, Martin Luther King called the Vietnam War "A blasphemy against all that America stands for."

Michael's plane from Bangkok to Nakhon Phanom was an old Air Force C-47 that creaked and groaned every time it hit an air pocket, and there were lots of them as the hot air rose from the jungle. The plane stopped first at the Udorn Royal Thai Air Force Base close to the Laotian border. American fighter and reconnaissance planes were stationed there alongside the CIA's secretive Air America. There were also American ground troops with the secret mission of suppressing the Pathet Lao from overrunning Laos and turning it into a communist country.

His final stop was Nakhon Phanom, known by the Americans as

NKP or Naked Fanny. It was officially a Royal Thai Air Force Base, but what one saw there were American planes.

Nakhon Phanom had no mountains, even though it was called the 'City of Mountains.' The town and the base sat on the west bank of the Mekong River. On the eastern bank was Laos, neutral by treaty in the conflict between the two Vietnams, but in reality, a battleground. During the 'Secret War' in Laos that no American was allowed to talk about, the United States dropped more bombs on this small country than all of the bombs dropped by all countries in WWII. The debris, deep holes, and burned-out fields and villages were everywhere the Americans thought the enemy might be. Since the Americans did not want their aircraft to land with live ordnance, any munitions not deployed on suspected targets was dropped in Laos before returning to the Thai bases. Bombs that had not detonated upon impact would explode weeks, months, even years later when a farmer's plow might strick one buried in a field. In addition, thousands of mines were dropped to make the network of small roads and paths known as the Ho Chi Minh trail unusable.

NKP was blanketed with a rainstorm when Michael's plane arrived, and it had to circle for half an hour before they could land and bring First Lieutenant Michael Buckley to war.

The weather the month Michael arrived was not unusual. It rained twenty-six out of thirty-one days. Twenty-three inches of rainwater swelled the Mekong River until it was overflowing. The daily humidity was eighty-eight percent, and mold covered everything. Wooden walkways were built between the 'Thai' Air Force Base buildings to avoid walking in mud.

The base was a collection of hastily constructed one-story buildings containing dormitories, repair sheds, administrative and operational centers—everything that was needed to wage war. A variety of bombs, rockets, and ammunition were stored away from the offices and dormitories. Michael's assignment was to the 1st Air Commando Squadron, call sign *Hobo*. The Hoboes called Michael 'Buck' and played with his nickname whenever they got a chance.

Most of his first week was spent orienting himself to the local flying regulations and administrative tasks. Then, on his sixth day at NKP, he flew in the right seat of a model 'E' A1 Skyraider with an instructor pilot in the left seat. It was a combat mission and was completed within three hours. His training pilot was a captain who was in his last month at NKP. Captain Josh Loundes had flown one hundred and seventy-three missions over Laos and had been shot down only once. He had been able to bail out and was picked up within three hours, one of the few times extractions were so quick.

Michael had known Josh briefly when their paths had crossed during F-102 training. Since then, Josh had gotten married and was now a father. He was anxious to finish his last three weeks at NKP and get back stateside to be with his family. Josh talked to Michael about his wife and daughter and their family plans during the flight to and from the target. He described his decision not to extend his Air Force commitment. He told Michael that his wife had already moved the family back to Long Island in anticipation of his tour ending.

They dropped two-hundred-and-fifty-pound bombs in addition to cluster bombs. They also shot rockets at a suspected enemy ammunition depot hidden in the jungle. They didn't see any secondary explosions, neither did their flight leader nor the Laotian Forward Air Controller (FAC) on the ground. "Another waste of time," Josh reported during flight debriefing.

Over the next four days, Michael moved from the right seat to the left seat in the E model A1s. Different instructor pilots flew with him in the right seat. Now he was expected to do everything from the initial briefing with tactical operations to the final debriefing with intelligence. On his last day with an instructor pilot, he flew with Major 'Pip' Rosenbaum. 'Pip slept most of the way to the target area.

This time their FAC was airborne. The FAC to whom they were assigned was an American pilot from Louisiana. He was flying a single-engine light plane, a Cessna. The FAC kept circling, looking for the target provided by intelligence. He even risked going down to treetop level and still couldn't find it. No one shot at him either.

Nevertheless, Michael and Pip dropped their bombs on the phantom target. "Just in case," Pip said. When Michael asked Pip about the drop, his instructor said, "We sure as hell ain't bringing them home. We drop them here or dump 'em on the way back."

When Michael landed, he and Pip went to the intelligence shed to debrief. Upon arrival, they learned that seventy-five miles away from where they had been, Josh Loundes had been strafing a suspected enemy antiaircraft battery when his plane was hit with S-60 antiaircraft shells as he had pulled out of his dive. His wingman following him saw the right wing of Josh's plane disintegrate and then explode as the fuel ignited. The decision was made not to risk a search and rescue mission because the likelihood of Josh surviving the blast was minimal. No parachute had been deployed. Michael didn't know how to react. The news didn't seem to affect anyone in intelligence. It was just news—one less plane and one less pilot for operations to schedule.

After their debriefing, as they walked back to 'Personnel' to deposit their flight gear, Pip asked, "Been to the town yet?"

"No."

"About time you saw our thriving metropolis. I'm taking you. We're leaving in thirty. We'll eat there."

The town of Nakhon Phenom was crowded even though it was raining. As they walked towards the *Shindig*, the bar favored by the Air Force officers from the base, they were approached by women of various ages dressed in very short shorts and skimpy tops. Two had died their hair blond. "G.I., I love you long time. You want long time, not short time," was the sales pitch.

The beer was cheap by American standards, but prices had become inflated because of the influx of United States dollars. As a result, Thai people who did not own a shop, a bar, or a stall were economically left out. "Try the Singha," Pip said. "It's good, a lot better than the others."

The two men found a small table and ordered their beers from an older Thai waitress. "How're you doing?" Pip asked. "Different from Alaska, huh?"

"That's an understatement."

"Training flights going okay?"

"Yeah, good."

Michael didn't want to talk. Pip quickly picked up on it. He knew what Michael was feeling. "You won't get used to it. Don't even try to. I flew with Josh several times when I first got here. He was a good guy."

"Yeah."

"Just put it out of your mind and do your job. It's all you can do."

"Did you know he had a young daughter?"

"Yeah, I know. It's tougher when they're married and have kids. War's for single guys."

"Yeah."

"I'm sorry. You're not married, are you?"

"No."

"Engaged? Girlfriend?"

"No. Almost engaged once. She broke it off."

"Sorry."

They were on their third beer when Pip said, "Hey. You need to get your squadron 'party suit.' On the way back, I'll show you where. Guy's closed now. Hobo's color is dark blue."

Every squadron had its own jumpsuit called a 'party suit' that they would wear to off-duty 'parties' or hanging out. Michael didn't care about getting his 'party suit,' but he knew he'd get one anyway. And

577

he'd put all the correct badges on it just like everyone else did. There'd be one from every place where he'd been stationed and every squadron. He'd be a walking history of his time in the Air Force, a walking résumé.

Four months later, Michael was still 'doing his job.' He was now leading flights and instructing replacements as pilots left, were injured, or killed in action. He had gotten used to planes being shot down and pilots not returning from missions. Some aircraft were from NKP. Others were F-105 and F-4 Phantom jets from other bases or aircraft carriers.

He found 'Sandy' missions to be emotionally draining. These were search and rescue missions. The job of the Sandy A1 pilots was threefold. First, they escorted the Sikorsky HH-3E helicopters, the Jolly Green Giants, to and from the target where the downed aircrew was supposed to be. Once there, one A1 would fly in low and try to draw fire from any hostiles in the area. The remaining three planes would then come in and bomb and strafe to create a protective circle around the downed aircrew before the helicopters would come to pick them up. Often one or both crew members would be injured, which required more time for the helicopter and more time for the A1 pilots to provide protection. Finally, the A1s would escort the helicopters back to base once the downed crew was retrieved. It was not unusual for an A1 or a helicopter to get shot down in the process.

Two days before Christmas, Michael and three other pilots were fully dressed in the 'Sandy' ready room when the report came of a downed Air Force F-4 over the Plain of Jars in Laos. Two parachutes had been seen, and the downed crew's wingman was circling the area. Michael was the flight leader (Sandy 1). Jack Kincaid (Sandy 2) was his wingman. They would be responsible for going in low, finding the downed pilots, assessing the helicopters' landing area, and drawing hostile fire. Sandys 3 and 4 would stay high until Michael called them in. Two 'Jolly Green Giants' were on the way. Michael's flight would protect them on the way to pick up the downed crew.

The Plain of Jars in Laos is a megalithic site with thousands of stone 'jars,' evidence of an ancient civilization. It is also relatively open land consistently fought over between the Pathet Lao and the Laotian government forces. It was difficult to tell on a day-by-day basis who controlled what. In the rainy season, the Pathet Lao would control the area. When it was dry, government forces would push them back.

It was late in the day, and the light was poor when Michael and his flight arrived. Low on fuel, the F-4 pilot descended, flew a tight pattern over where he thought his comrades were and headed back to base.

Michael tuned into the survival radio frequency used by the downed crew and rescue team. He asked if they felt it was safe for them to set off their 'smoke.' The response was a whispered, "No, hostiles close."

Michael said, "I'm going in. Key your mic three times if I am close. Once if I am way off. Here I go."

Jack Kincaid in Sandy 2 followed him. They had to rely on their altimeters in the dimming light because of the lack of definition between air and ground. They heard one click when they reached a thousand feet and pulled up. They made three more passes before they heard three clicks. Close behind Michael, Kincaid dropped a flare to mark the spot.

"You see anything?" Michael asked.

"No."

"We've got light. Let's go."

Michael dove at a forty-degree angle, looking for the downed crew or hostiles. When he reached a thousand feet, he saw muzzle flashes, but it was too late for him to do anything about it. Behind him, his wingman said, "Got 'em," and dropped two bombs where the flashes had come from before pulling up in the opposite direction from Michael.

"Any secondaries?" Michael asked when they regrouped.

"No. I didn't see any trucks, just people. They were shooting at me, but I don't think I got hit."

"Click twice if you can talk," Michael said to the downed crew.

"We don't hear them now," was the reply.

"Can you use smoke yet?"

"We think so."

"Do it."

Michael saw the smoke from the location of the downed pilots and called in the rest of the flight. All four planes started to dive down one after the other. Michael was first and dropped flares so the others could see. Behind him, the other three planes began to use their guns to strafe the area in a circle around the downed crew. Small arms fire greeted them as they went in.

Michael went around and came in for a second pass, jigging as he went. The hostile troops were waiting for him this time, and he answered the ground fire with his wing guns. One of his guns stopped firing. "Jammed," Michael thought. As he pulled away, he saw his port wing was on fire. He hadn't felt any impact. He guessed one of the old WWII shells had misfired and exploded in his wing.

"Shit. I've got fire. I don't think I'm hit. What the fuck's going on?"

"There's fire coming from your port wing. You'd better get out of there."

Michael needed altitude before he dared to try and bail out. He pulled back on the stick and went to full throttle, hoping the engine would not quit on him. He wasn't worried about 'G' forces. When he reached 2,500 feet, he pulled the canopy back and set off the charges that ejected him from the plane. A minute later, he was floating under a white umbrella of nylon. He knew he was standing out against the sky, but so far nobody had shot at him. Below him, he could see the three other A1s making pass after pass where they believed the enemy forces to be.

The wind was gusting and blowing him away from where the other plane had gone down. In the distance, he could see a storm coming his way. When he landed, the wind grabbed at his parachute before he could strike it. It started pulling him along the ground. He tumbled and slammed into a rock. Hitting the rock knocked the wind out of him. The parachute cords had wrapped around the rock, and he wasn't moving anymore. All he could do was lay still for a minute, waiting to get his breath back. When he did, he got out of his parachute harness and watched it catch the wind and start to blow away from him. He followed it, grabbed it and collapsed it into a ball. Shelter. He could make it into a shelter.

He had no idea what had happened to his plane. He could see flares and gun flashes in the distance where his flight continued to hammer away. He turned on his survival radio and listened to the chatter. Kincaid had taken charge.

The storm was coming fast, and he heard them decide to leave and come back in the morning when there would be light. The pilot of the F-4 had hurt his arm, probably broken, but he could walk. The F-4 crew said that they would try to make it to where they had seen Michael land so they would all be together for the night. Michael watched the A1s and the helicopters leave and head in the direction of Thailand. He sat down. He was shaking.

After half an hour, he hadn't seen or heard from the F-4 crew. He was about to head towards them when he heard gunfire from their direction. First, he heard the short individual pops of small arms. It was followed by the louder continuous sound of automatic weapons. Then there was silence. He waited ten minutes and tried radioing the downed crew. There was no response. He waited another fifteen minutes and tried again. Still nothing.

The storm reached him. Between the rain and the loss of light, he could barely see. He sat there. He didn't know what to do. Should he go back and find out what had happened to the crew, stay where he was and wait for them to reach him, or leave the area in case Pathet Lao were heading in his direction? Every option kept running through his mind. He got up as if to move, but didn't know where to go. Finally, he sat back down and tried to think through his options more deliberately.

He decided to move. He put the noise of the gunfire to his back and started walking. The rain was heavy and made the uneven ground slippery. Coming down a small hill, he slipped in the mud and lost his balance. He smashed his leg against a boulder. He started to whimper with pain and exhaustion. "Why can't I catch a break?" he thought.

He got up and started walking with a limp towards a tree line on the edge of the Plain. Every step was painful. He had ripped his pants in the fall, and they were flapping around his bad leg. He could barely see his hand-held compass, but he would look at it every once in a while, to make sure he was going in a straight line. He was headed toward the foothills outside Ban Hai, where he could hide in the trees until dawn. As he walked and slid, he tried to remember the recent intelligence briefings. What was the current status of Ban Hai? What were the recent movements of the Pathet Lao? Was he walking right into the enemy?

By the time he reached the foothills, he was operating on nothing but adrenaline, and it was running out. He only went a hundred yards into the trees before he sat down and opened up his survival kit and drank from his emergency canteen. He risked shining his flashlight on his leg and saw his flesh was ripped, but the tear wasn't too deep. He took a bandage from his survival kit and applied it.

There was nothing left for him to do but to stay away from anything resembling a trail and wait until morning. He tried calling the F-4 crew again, but there was no response. He assumed they were either captured or killed.

It rained throughout the night. He didn't try to use his parachute to erect a shelter. He just wrapped it around himself and laid down. He dozed on and off. He thought about the farm, his parents. Nan was right. He should never have signed up for ROTC. He was stupid. Now he could wind up a prisoner in a, in a… He didn't want to think about it.

He was going in and out of a troubled sleep when the first light came. The sounds of airplanes awakened him, but they were far away. He moved down to the edge of the Plain and started sending out quick distress signals. Ten minutes later, he saw the familiar silhouette of a flight of A1s. Two Jolly Green Giants were with them. He moved out of the tree line, careful to look for any movement from within three hundred and sixty degrees. Relying on sound was no longer an option as the planes started circling in a search pattern. Now he turned his radio on and left it on. He contacted the flight leader within five minutes and moved out to where he could be seen. He told them to fly along the tree line, which was easy to identify. He was spotted a couple of minutes later.

The flight lead dipped his wings and circled him, giving the Jolly Green his exact position. Ten minutes later, he was greeted with, "Welcome aboard," by the helicopter crew chief.

"How about the F-4 crew?" Michael asked.

"No sign of them. We put down and looked. Nothing." Michael started to say something and stopped. "I know," said the crew chief. "We did what we could. Sorry, but they're MIA. You're okay, though. That's a good thing. Right?"

Chapter Fifty-Six: Pattaya

Michael started to make mistakes. He underestimated the drag on the ordnance he was carrying and pulled up too quickly during takeoff on one flight. He was close to stalling when he realized what was happening and corrected, barely avoiding crashing at the end of the runway. On another mission, he was the flight lead. His wingman had to remind him to dump his unused ordnance on the way back to NKP. Once, he started his dive early and went in steeper and lower than was safe. He pulled out so late his flight leader thought he might have been hit. Everyone in the squadron knew about these mistakes, and flying with him became a matter of concern.

His friendship with Pip had grown over the months they had roomed together. The squadron commander asked Pip to talk to his friend and find out what was going on. When Pip asked him, Michael said, "Nothing."

Pip said, "You're acting like you just don't give a shit."

"I don't. Do you? So what?"

"That's not good enough. Some of the guys are starting to talk."

"Fuck 'em."

"Come on. You don't mean that."

Pip kept at him. He asked him if it was about bailing out. Michael said, "Bullshit. Everyone bails out. You've bailed out."

Pip didn't let up. "Come on, man. Something's eating you. We can all see it."

It took Pip about eight tries and a six-pack before Michael finally said, "I should have tried to get to them."

"Who?"

"The F-4 guys. I might've saved them."

"Jesus. Is that what's bugging you?"

"I fucked up. Now, where are they? Dead? Tortured?"

"Give it a break. You saved your ass. You did the right thing."

"I can't cut it. I'm no good here."

"That's bullshit. You got to stop torturing yourself with this crap."

"I just want to get out of here and go home."

"In a body bag. Cause that's where you're headed you keep this shit up."

Pip tried to reassure him that it wasn't his fault, but shame had taken hold, and Michael was having none of Pip's attempts to assuage his feelings of guilt. When Pip reported back to the squadron commander, he was told, "Get him the hell out of here. Now! Both of you. Use your leave time and beat it."

Michael didn't want to go. He didn't want to do anything. If the squadron commander hadn't grounded him until he got his head on straight, he would have flown missions, eaten, slept, and done nothing else. Pip took it upon himself to get his friend onto a plane heading for Pattaya.

Pip was determined to make sure Michael did not become another casualty. He had seen this happen when a pilot started thinking, "That could have been me," "I fucked up big time," or "I got people killed." Sharpness went, attention wavered, and errors in judgment became normal. As far as Pip was concerned, pleasure was the way to get Michael airworthy again. He had to get him 'in the zone.' He knew just the place to make it happen. "My friend," he said, "We are going for the best I&I available to men of our standing. The hell with rest and relaxation; our pursuit is intoxication and intercourse."

U-Tapao Air Force Base in Sattahip, Thailand, was an easy thirty-minute drive to Pattaya. Before the Americans arrived, Pattaya was a simple fishing village. The townspeople of Pattaya did not pay much attention to their exquisite beaches or their lifestyle. What else was there? The buffalo outnumbered the cars. Only a few restaurants and bars dotted the streets. A traveler from Bangkok might stay at a guest house for the weekend, but that would only happen during the dry season. The American base changed all that.

Because U-Tapao was so close to the town and its beaches, the Americans quickly adopted it as the I&I destination of choice. The word about Pattaya soon spread to other bases in Southeast Asia. Within a couple of years, the town became a carnival of bars and women. Sex work and liquor became the foundation of the new economy. Private homes became guest houses. Marijuana was in plentiful supply. But, of course, there were gradations in all of these commodities. Sears and Roebuck advertised items as 'good, better, and best' in its catalog at home in the United States. A knowledgeable person familiar with Pattaya could make the same evaluation for everything the village had to offer. Pip was such a person, and he only pursued the best in all categories when it came to Pattaya.

Money was no issue for Pip, thanks to a grandfather, a father, and two uncles. The family owned several automotive dealerships in Dallas. The brand of car didn't matter to the Piporicchi family. All that mattered was that the dealership was profitable. The United States had become a car-obsessed nation, and Pip's family had become wealthy. Some of the wealth was directed to Pip as a reward for being the hero pilot in the family, a third-generation warrior. Unlike the experiences of his predecessors in the two world wars, the family was determined to provide Pip with an 'enjoyable' war. His buddy Michael Buckley was a beneficiary of this largess.

Pip's real name was Antonio Francesco Piporicchi. His friends gave him the nickname Pip. Unfortunately, his stature also led some to refer to him as 'Pipsqueak.' Pip was five foot six, although he claimed it was seven. His height especially annoyed him since he was the shortest male in the family. He made up for it by pushing limits. He seemed to know exactly how far he could push without getting into serious trouble. Being the youngest in the family, no one seemed to mind.

Pip reserved two rooms for them at the *Joi Guest House*. *Joi* was close to the beach and, more importantly, it was only fifty yards from the *Garden of Rati*. Although a predominantly Buddhist country, Thailand had a small, influential Hindu population. Where Buddhism preached asceticism, Hinduism was sensual, and the *Garden of Rati* was designed to honor Rati, goddess of love, carnal desire, lust, passion, and sexual pleasure. The guest house and the garden were owned by the same people, Mayan Kumari and his wife, Nyra.

The night Michael and Pip arrived, they changed into their 'civies' after being shown to their rooms. Back on the street, Pip guided Michael to the restaurant Aroy in the center of town. The main attraction of Aroy was a circular bar. In the center of the bar was a raised stage that rotated. When Michael and Pip entered, it was occupied by five young women wearing thongs and 'pasties.' The Rolling Stones' *Nineteenth Nervous Breakdown* was blasting away. "Isn't this great?" Pip shouted into Michael's ear.

"I can't hear myself think," Michael shouted back.

"That's the point. We sit, we drink. We watch those lovelies. When they finish their set, they'll come over, hang all over us asking for tips, offer to let us feel them up, which we do, we give them a tip, and then we go get something to eat in the dining room where it's quieter."

A bartender came over to get their drink order. Michael ordered a Singha. Pip corrected the order, "Four whiskey sours and keep them coming until I tell you to stop." He turned to Michael, "Beer is for the base. This is I&I. Tonight, we work on the liquid 'I,' tomorrow we go to the Kumari's Garden of Rati to fulfill our responsibilities for the second 'I.'"

Four drinks later, rather than going into the dining room, they went outside to the temporary patio in front of Aroy, where they ordered dinner. Unlike Nakhon Phanom restaurants, the menu at Aroy was in English. Pip ordered 'Crying Tiger Beef' for them. "It's not as hot as good ole Texas Chile, but it's got some warmth to it. So now we drink beer to keep the tiger under control. You like hot, don't you?"

"Long as it's not too hot."

It was too hot for Michael, but he struggled through it, not wanting to disappoint Pip, who was paying for everything. Every time Michael would start to pay for something, Pip would stop him, and say, "Dear ole Dad's paying for this, I'm not."

"Yeah, but..."

"I'm risking my butt to uphold the family's absurd male lineage of providing fighting men to save the world for truth, honor, blah, blah, blah. I'm nothing more than a fucking family mercenary. Let 'em pay. We're going to use up as much of their money as we can. Think of it this way, when I get my ass blown away, my idiot older brother inherits everything. So, I spend my share now."

"And if you come out of this circus alive?"

"Everybody back home will think I've successfully done my bit to preserve the family story. I will have contributed to the legacy of Italian men fighting for the good ole USA. I'll be regaled as a hero for a couple of months; then, things will go back to normal. My fair-haired older brother will return to his place on the throne."

"Why didn't your brother ..."

"Too old, too married, too chicken-shit. Now eat. Tomorrow we hit the beach and then the garden."

Michael was still sound asleep at ten 'o clock when the Kumari's niece came into his room, sat on his bed, leaned down, and whispered in his ear that his friend was waiting for him downstairs. Slowly Michael stirred. When he realized he was not alone, he sat up, surprised.

"It okay. It time for breakfast. Mr. Pip said wake you. He downstairs now. Wait for you."

"Thank you."

"I do your room now?"

"I need to shower. Where..."

"I show you." She pulled the sheet back and took his hand inviting him to get out of bed. Realizing he was naked, he looked around for a towel. She smiled, "It okay. Sometimes I work in garden." She picked up a towel from the dresser and handed it to him. He wrapped it around himself, and she guided him down the hall to the bathroom.

A half an hour later, he and Pip were sitting on the patio behind *Joi* and eating an 'American' breakfast of bacon and eggs served by Nyra Kumari. They drank Thai milk tea. Michael questioned the bright orange color, but with Pip's encouragement, he tried it and found that he enjoyed it.

"Stick with me, my friend. I will not steer you wrong. How's your head? I didn't think you'd ever get up. We weren't that late last night."

"I know. I feel like I could sleep for a week."

"Probably could. Next is the beach, and you can cop a few Zs there. Then lunch, a nap perhaps, and the pièce de résistance, the Garden of Rati. You may never leave."

"What's this garden all about?"

"Nope. Trust me. Just go with the flow."

Michael wanted to sleep. They went to the beach close to the guest house. He swam for about fifteen minutes, found a place between some palm trees out of the sun, and slept on the beach towel Kumari's niece had provided. Two hours later, he woke up, swam some more, and slept again. It was early afternoon before they returned to the guest house, changed out of their swim trunks, and went to a nearby restaurant. Michael ate a papaya salad, accompanied by a Singha. After lunch, Michael returned to the guest house while Pip went shopping. For Michael, it was time for another nap.

It was four o clock in the afternoon when he joined Pip on the patio. Pip was wearing light weight linen pants and a Thai shirt that flowed down almost to his knees. He had sandals on. He held up a shopping bag. "I took the liberty of buying some things for you. Go change. You even look hot the way you're dressed."

Michael did as he was told and was surprised that Pip had been able to assess his sizes, even down to the sandals which he now wore. They walked the hundred yards to the entrance of the Garden of Rati.

The brass statue of Rati with her male counterpart, Kamadeva, greeted them at the entrance. A young woman dressed in a light weight, almost see-through silk sari led them into the garden. Coconut palms, almond trees, and casuarinas bordered the garden, setting it off from its neighbors. A path led from the entrance down to the beach. Off the main path were smaller paths, each one leading to a simple cabana-type building, eight in all, four on each side of the path. Three of the cabanas were open to the air on all sides. A young woman dressed in a sari sat on a bed in each one. The insides of the other cabanas were shielded from view by opaque gauze fabric that moved in the gentle breeze coming from the beach.

Pip led the way down the central path. Various flowers grew along the way, and the fragrances were rich. Michael had never experienced anything like it before. Pip said, "Take your time," as they walked. "All of the cabanas with the sides up are available. Check out the women. Go up and say hello if you want. They all speak some English. We're here for five days, and we'll be coming back, so take your time. I guarantee that you will have a good time with any of them. I've never been disappointed. I'm heading for that one over there. I love being right on the beach." Pip walked down past two cabanas and walked up the path to the last one before the beach.

Michael stood there, not being quite sure what to do. Then, finally, the young woman from the cabana he was standing in front of came down the path to him and held out her hand for him to take it. "This is your first time in the Garden of Rati?"

"Yes, it is."

"I'll walk with you. Ask me questions if you want."

"Your English is very good."

"Thank you. I try. We all speak some. Aunt Nyra insists."

They followed the path towards the beach where Pip had just gone. The drapes of the cabana he had entered were still up, and they could see him lying nude on the bed. An equally naked woman was massaging him.

"Captain Pip likes to feel the breeze. Soon, she will drop the drapes for privacy."

"You know him?"

"Captain Pip? I do. He comes before, many times." Michael didn't say anything. Finally, she asked, "Does that bother you?"

Michael didn't know what to say. Sharing a woman with his friend did trouble him, but he didn't feel like he should say "Yes." So instead, he said, "No, of course not."

The woman noticed his reticence. She didn't acknowledge it but said, "My cousin is new. Let me introduce you. She is very beautiful. My name is Lata; she is Sarita. How are you named?"

He didn't want to give her his real name, and so he said, "Buck. My friends call me Buck."

"Oh, that rhymes with…"

"I know, 'fuck.'"

"I was going to say, luck."

"Luck? I sure haven't been feeling lucky lately."

"You will be lucky today, with Sarita."

"Lucky?"

"You will see."

Lata walked 'Buck' to Sarita's cabana and introduced them. When she left, she said, "You'll see. Sarita will bring you luck."

Sarita brought Michael into the cabana and told him to sit down on the bed, "Would you like the walls open or closed?" she asked.

"I think closed if you don't mind."

Sarita went around to each of the walled areas and released the drapes. Michael was surprised at how thin they were. He could see out without any difficulty, but when he had been outside the cabanas, he could not see in. It gave him a strange sense of security, even though the fabric was so light that it would move in the breeze from the ocean. When the final material was released and in place, she went to a small nightstand alongside the bed. "Ganja?" she asked, offering him a cigarette. "What do you call it?"

"You mean marijuana?"

"Yes, marijuana."

Michael hesitated and then remembered Pip saying, "This is time away from time, my friend. Anything and everything goes." He accepted the offer of the ganja rolled into a cigarette, and Sarita lit it for him. He took a long inhale and let it slowly out. He offered it to Sarita, who also drew the smoke into her. "Stand, please," she said. She came to him and began to unbutton his shirt when he did. Removing it, she hung it neatly on the back of the chair that was there. She proceeded to unbutton his new trousers and hang them on the back of the chair with his shirt. When she had him completely undressed, she had him sit again on the bed while she removed her sari. Then, standing nude before him, she asked, "Do you like me?"

He wanted to jump up and hold her close, but he knew he shouldn't. There was politeness, a ritual, and she led him through it. Finally, he said, "Yes. I do. Very much." Her skin was a shade of brown he had never seen before. Her breasts were small and firm. She came over and took the ganja from his hand, and took another long inhale. Instead of giving it back to him, she put it out in the brass ashtray on the table. She told him to lie on his stomach.

Her massage began softly. She gently moved from his feet, up his legs, to his back and shoulders. As she did, she leaned close to him. He could hear her breathing and feel her hair against his skin. Her closeness and the ganja opened him to the sensuality of her touch and presence. When she began to move back down from his neck to his back, she used more pressure and, this time, kneaded his muscles. He was surprised at how strong she was. When she reached his feet, she spent time with each one. She began firmly and gradually became softer, ending in a caress. Again, she moved up his body, but now it was gentle. Periodically she lightly drew her nails across his skin and then wiped away the tingling with her hands. He became aroused. She spread his legs and ran her nails along the insides of his thighs. He lifted himself to give her access to his genitals. Gently, she took him in her hands. When he was fully erect, she said, "Turning over, please."

He did so. From the table, she took a condom and removed the wrapper. Placing the condom in her mouth, she moved over and down on him, unrolling the condom on his erection before mounting him.

Two hours later, they were asleep in each other's arms.

Three condom wrappers were on the bedside table. She woke first. "It is time," she said.

"Do I have to go?"

She laughed, "Only for now. You come again tomorrow. Maybe lie with Lata or one of the others."

"I don't want to."

"I'm not here tomorrow. I am going home. You be with Lata tomorrow. I can tell she likes you. You'll like her. She's more, how you say, skilled than I am."

"No one can be better than you. When will you return?"

"Next week."

"I'll be gone."

"Back to the fighting?"

"Yes, back to the fighting."

"You'll like Lata. She taught me. You go with her tomorrow."

He did. He came back every afternoon to be with Lata.

Michael and Pip had their dinners at the 'finest' places in Pattaya in the evening. After dinner, they would sample the bars and sex shows. Michael drank less and smoked more as the week went on. The mornings were spent swimming. His afternoons were spent with Lata, except for one afternoon when Pip said Michael was monopolizing her.

"Come on, bro. Let me have her once before we go back to that shithole." Michael reluctantly obliged and entertained himself with Chara on his next to the last afternoon in Pattaya.

He felt relaxed as they climbed on the plane to return to Nakhon Phanom. However, there was a new kind of numbness that he could not describe. It was pleasant, though, and he mentioned it to Pip when his friend asked him how he was doing.

"Yeah," said Pip, "You're in the zone, man. That's the place. We fight, and we fuck. That's what we do. It's the thinking that's bad for you."

Chapter Fifty-Seven: Major MacGregor

Michael stopped thinking about what he was doing. He did tasks. He flew the airplanes he was assigned. He went where the operations staff and Forward Air Controllers told him to go. He dropped the bombs that were loaded onto his plane, watched for secondary explosions, strafed enemy positions with his wing cannons, and reported the number of people the FACs told him he had killed. He trained replacement pilots on how to do the job, and he took the new pilots into Nakhon Phanom if they hadn't been there yet. He drank beer in the Quonset hut the pilots had commandeered for such purposes and rarely bothered with the officers' club unless he was expected to show up for an event. He wrote meaningless letters home to his parents every week. Often, he would daydream about Pattaya and couldn't wait to return.

He and Pip returned to the Garden of Rati one more time before Pip finished his tour at NKP and left for Florida to assume an instructor position teaching new A1 pilots. The garden felt different to him this time. It was familiar, comforting. He knew people by name. They knew his name. With Pip, and his money, leaving, Michael knew his stays would be much shorter, if at all.

When Pip left, Michael missed his 'why the hell not' attitude. The two of them had gotten in the habit of saying, "Eat, drink, fight, and fuck, for tomorrow is tomorrow." They never used 'die' or 'be killed.' It was always, 'tomorrow is tomorrow." Pip's approach to surviving the war had seeped into Michael's being, and now the disciple had no desire to live any other way. At times, Michael even thought about extending his commitment. 'Why the hell not?'

"I'm thinking of extending," he told Pip on the Tuesday night before Pip was to leave.

"Why?"

"Nothing better to do. Might make a career out of it."

"What would you put in for? Instructor someplace? Administrative?"

"Thinking of here. Do another tour."

"Have you lost your mind? Man, if you're thinking like that, you know you got to get out of here."

"I've gotten used to this place. Let the married guys with kids go home."

"Don't do it, my friend. You're starting to lose it."

"I don't know. Maybe."

"I'm telling you; you're losing it. You start thinking like this, and it's definitely time to get out of here."

Michael started volunteering for night missions. Most pilots didn't like them because it was more challenging to see the mountains at night, and it was easier to get lost and make mistakes. Michael's thinking was that it was also harder for the enemy gunners to see you, and your chances of getting shot down were less. Most of the night missions were to disrupt the movement of men and materials through Laos to South Vietnam along the 'Ho Chi Minh Trail.' Michael liked attacking at night when they couldn't see him coming, at least on the first pass.

They called it a 'trail,' but the singular appellation was inaccurate. It was a spider web of paths and temporary roads that changed daily. You couldn't see what you were trying to destroy most of the time. You trusted your FACs on the ground or in the air to tell you where they saw or heard movement. Occasionally, a FAC in the air would drop a flare and catch a couple of trucks out in the open, but that was rare. At night, the A1 pilots usually depended upon the Laotian FACs on the ground. Often, the FAC's English and sense of direction were not good, and Michael knew he was bombing trees, chickens, and rice paddies as much as he was bombing the enemy.

Still, Michael preferred the risk of running into a mountain to getting shot at during the day. There would be times he was shot at during night missions, but he knew it was more difficult for the gunners to see him. He came to hate it when the night was clear and the moon was full. Being seen was the problem. Some of the squadron's planes had been painted black.

It was on his one hundred and ninety-first mission when the flight schedule called for Michael to do a night check flight with Major Mark MacGregor. A newcomer, MacGregor had already gotten himself a less than sterling reputation in the few weeks he had been at NKP.

Things were usually pretty informal at NKP. Officers used their first names to address one another regardless of rank. MacGregor, however, made it clear that he expected lieutenants, and even captains, to call him Major. That didn't sit too well, especially with his instructor pilots. In addition, according to the check pilots who had flown with him, MacGregor was a lousy pilot. Pip had flown with him once before he left for stateside. He told Michael, "He's a friggin' loose cannon trying to make a name for himself. He doesn't pay attention and doesn't do what you tell him to do. He thinks he knows it all. Worse, he takes stupid risks. He's certifiable. I'm not kidding. This guy's a god damned whack job."

They had different models of A1s at NKP. The two-seat versions, which they used for check rides, came in different configurations. One configuration had matching controls for the left and right seats. Another design only had controls for the left seat. The check pilots hated that configuration because if the newbie screwed up badly, all you could do was bail out, but sometimes they were the only planes available. On the night Michael was to fly with MacGregor, he refused the plane he was assigned because it only had left seat controls. It was the first time he had refused a plane. He didn't care. He would not go up with this guy as a powerless observer.

During the briefing, MacGregor didn't ask any questions. When they got to the plane, Michael asked him if he had any questions about the mission. MacGregor said, "No. I don't know what the big deal is about these night missions. I don't need any more damned check rides. Already done 'em."

"It's different at night."

"Yeah, right."

"You'll see."

Michael watched MacGregor do a superficial 'walk around' of their plane. He followed him and checked everything MacGregor had done haphazardly. When they finished, they climbed into the aircraft with MacGregor in the left seat. They taxied to the end of the runway and sat waiting for the armament specialists to remove the safety devices and arm their bombs and cannons. "They knew we were coming. They should have been ready for us," MacGregor said.

"They'll get it done. I'd rather have them take their time and do it right," Michael answered.

When the ground crew finished its work and signaled that they were 'good to go,' MacGregor's mood changed. "Finally. We've got 'Nape' and 'Willy Pete.' Let's go fry us up some Gooks before breakfast. Give 'em some 'burn baby, burn.'"

They almost didn't become airborne. A small cell of rain enveloped them at the end of the runway. They couldn't see where the runway ended. MacGregor started to pull up before he had the speed he needed. Michael didn't let him. Once airborne, Michael said, "It's harder at night. You can't see shit. Got to trust instruments." MacGregor didn't say anything.

They headed for the Ban Ban Valley. The Laotian FAC, 'Daffy,' had several trucks in sight. Michael and MacGregor followed their flight leader, Dennis 'Flash' Gordon, to the coordinates that Daffy gave them. Flash went in first and dropped a flare. They didn't see anything but jungle. Daffy told them they were too far to the west, by five hundred meters. MacGregor and Michael dove down, heading for where they assumed the trucks would be parked. They dropped two phosphorous bombs. Daffy told them they had gone in the wrong direction. "Fucker can't tell west from east," MacGregor complained.

"It happens," Michael replied.

Flash went back in for another run using the new directions Daffy provided. He dropped two napalm bombs. MacGregor and Michael followed but did not see any trucks or secondary explosions.

"This is ridiculous," MacGregor said. "He's an idiot." Michael didn't say anything. Daffy gave them some new directions.

Flash went down for another pass and dropped a flare. MacGregor and Michael were right behind him. "Nothing," MacGregor said.

"Got 'em," Michael answered. "Two hundred meters out from the flare."

"I don't see 'em."

"Just do it."

"There's nothing there."

"They're there. Two hundred."

"This is bullshit." MacGregor pulled up without releasing any ordnance. As they pulled up over the area where Michael had told him to release his bombs, they saw tracers coming in their direction from the ground.

"Jig right," Michael ordered.

MacGregor froze for three seconds before he moved the stick. The tracers went to the left of them. As they climbed out, Michael said, "That's it. We went way over our 'G' limits. Head home." He was about to notify 'Flash' of their situation when MacGregor turned the plane back towards the target. "What are you doing?"

"They shot at me. I'm going to burn their asses."

"Major. Head to base."

"Shut up, lieutenant, and enjoy the ride."

"Major, as your instructor, you are to do what I tell you to do. Now head back to NKP."

"Screw you, lieutenant, and take your hand off the stick."

Michael knew that getting in a wrestling match would create an inevitable crash. He let go of the stick.

"What's going on over there," Flash asked on the radio.

"We're over Gs..." MacGregor turned the radio off. Michael turned it back on. MacGregor turned it back off. "Lieutenant, I am ordering you to shut the fuck up and just sit there."

MacGregor went into a dive and started firing the wing cannons in the direction of the trucks. Again, they saw tracers from the small antiaircraft gun on one of the trucks coming in their direction. MacGregor kept firing. Then a second gun started firing, and they were bracketed between the two. Ignoring the tracers from the second gun, MacGregor pulled out of the dive and banked hard to the left, right over the second gun. Shells raked the left side of their plane as they flew over it. Michael heard the shells hit. Two went through the left side of the canopy. A third went completely through MacGregor's helmet and almost hit Michael. Blood, tissue, and helmet pieces sprayed all over the cockpit, Michael, and the front of the canopy. A fourth ricocheted off the plane, into the cockpit, and MacGregor's neck. Michael couldn't see. He reached over and felt for MacGregor's hand. He ranked it off the stick and took control of the aircraft. He leveled the plane off and flew low over the jungle away from the guns trying to remember where the nearest hills were. He wiped the blood from his face and from the front of his side of the canopy.

"You okay? What's going on?" Flash asked.

"Plane's hit. MacGregor's dead. I'm flying it."

"Gain altitude. I'll cover."

Michael pulled back on the stick gently, testing the controls. The elevator responded. He wiggled the wings a little, trying the ailerons. The noise in the cockpit was deafening, with much of the canopy destroyed. He kept wiping away the blood, revealing more of the instruments. When he reached four thousand feet, he started heading towards NKP. He had focused on flying the plane; now, he wiped the gore from his instruments. He saw that he was low on fuel and that it was going down rapidly.

"Left tank must have been hit." He said to Flash.
"Dump anything you've got left."
"Here?"
"Yes, here."
Michael released all of his ordnance.
"I'm going to do a fly around. Stay level if you can," Flash said.
Flash reported a couple of minutes later, "Can't see anything obvious. You still have all your hydraulics?"
Michael looked at all of his hydraulic pressure readings. "Yeah. Losing fuel fast, though."
"Controls okay?"
"So far."
"You're going to make it."
"Yeah. Yeah."
"You will. MacGregor?"
Michael looked over. "There's nothing left of his head." Michael pulled the mask from his face and threw up.

He landed the plane and stayed on the runway, waiting for the emergency crews to get to him to make sure there were no fires before they pulled the plane off the runway. He couldn't open the canopy because of the damage. When they got it off, the medics lifted him out. It wasn't until then that he realized his left arm and shoulder were bleeding from the debris of canopy and helmet pieces. It was hard to tell what was his blood and what was MacGregor's.

When he was released from the base medical facility he was still grounded. He had some leave time and went to Pattaya and to the *Joi* guest house. Without Pip, it was lonely. He couldn't afford more than one afternoon at the Garden of Rati, so he spent most of his three days in Pattaya wandering the streets and drinking.

By the end of the second day, he started to experience something he had not known before. He was walking along the edge of the beach where the waves expended their final energy against the sand when he knew what it was. He hated the 'Gooks.' He wasn't angry. They were trying to kill him. He was going to kill them. It was a simple equation. There was no complexity to the knowledge.

He left Pattaya and took the bus to Bangkok for his last day. He got a room at one of the hotels that housed Americans and made a long-distance phone call to Georgetown. When he reached his parents, he told his mother he loved her and asked to speak to his father. When Jack got on the phone, he said, "I'm going to extend for a year if I can stay here. I'm pretty sure they'll let me."

Jack paused at his son's news. "Tell me what you're thinking." Michael did. After listening to his son, Jack said, "I understand but I want you to promise me something."

"What?"

"Don't do anything for a few weeks. Your mom and I have been talking about coming to see you in Bangkok. So don't do anything until after we've had a chance to visit you. Can you do that?"

"I guess."

"Mike, can you promise me that? Just slow down a bit."

"Okay. But I can't wait too long. I have to make a decision pretty soon."

"I know. We'll get there as soon as we can. Will you be able to get any more time?"

"Yeah."

Peg wanted to go, and Jack wanted her to stay home. They fought about it, but Peg's rheumatoid arthritis won the argument. They also fought about Michael being there. "Why didn't you discourage him? Tell him not to join the Air Force?" Peg screamed at him. You lost two brothers. You're responsible for this. If something happens to him, I will never forgive you."

"He could have gotten drafted. Have you ever thought about that? For christ's sake, he could be a grunt on the ground."

"You don't know that. You could have talked him out of ROTC if you had wanted to."

"You could have spoken up more."

"Don't try to turn this back on me."

"He wanted to go. Neither one of us could have stopped him."

"You could have. He would have listened to you."

Five days after they argued, Jack arrived in Bangkok alone. Michael reserved a room for the two of them at the Oriental hotel. Knowing he would be sleep deprived from what would be a twenty-four trip, Jack suggested Michael not start his crew time off until the day after Jack arrived. Michael agreed.

Michael was able to get a flight into Bangkok the following morning, and they met for lunch at the hotel. Despite Peg's argument that he just listen to Michael, Jack had prepared a speech. She said, "Don't you go pushing this. You hear. You just talk about home the first day. Just home. He needs to know it still exists." That wasn't Jack's way. He was an engineer with a problem to solve. It was the only way he knew how to approach the fear he felt for his son's life. He had outlined all of his points on the flights over and had anticipated every argument that he thought Michael would make. For each argument, he had a rebuttal.

Jack reserved a table for them at the Verandah restaurant. He arrived first and waited for his son. When Michael appeared, Jack was surprised at how much weight Michael had lost. He looked gaunt, his uniform hung loose on him, and his face had changed. It was older and hard. When he saw his father walking towards him, his smile was thin-lipped, drawn, forced. Only one thing went through Jack's mind when he saw his son: he had to get him home.

Jack quickly walked over to Michael to meet him and held his arms out to hug him. Michael was surprised. He had been prepared to shake his father's hand. But instead, he let his father hug him, and he followed his father to their table. If he could have, Jack would have taken Michael's hand and led him to the table as he had when his son was a little boy. It didn't matter that he was in his twenties. It didn't matter. All that mattered was getting him home. He had seen this look in men during his war. Seeing it now in his son, he wanted to cry.

He called Peg that night from the hotel. She asked, "How is he?"

"He's lost a lot of weight."

"Come on, Jack, you know what I'm asking."

"Remember when Ron and Deborah got divorced?"

"Of course."

"Remember how detached Ron was from everything but his anger?"

"Yes."

"That's the way Mike is. It's like he got a divorce from life."

Chapter Fifty-Eight: Hannah

In 1955 Noah Mercer heard about the Indian Point development on the island of Georgetown from a client who had just purchased property there. Years before, the developers had accumulated land on a peninsula known in the 1700s as Rogers Neck. For reasons lost in time, the peninsula's name changed to Indian Point sometime in the 1800s. The name meant little to Noah Mercer; he just wanted to build a simple summer home for his daughter Lillian, her husband Charles, and their two daughters, ten-year-old Hannah and three-year-old Valerie.

Noah never entirely accepted that Lillian had married Charles Turner, a young physics teacher at Northeastern University. He wanted her to marry someone like himself, a businessman. It was quite acceptable to him that his daughter chose to become a high school teacher of mathematics; young women became teachers. However, it was not acceptable to him that Lillian returned to teaching before Valerie was old enough for kindergarten. He told his daughter, "If you can't make it on Charles' salary, why did you have another child?" Her response, "I like teaching," was not acceptable to him. Noah was highly proficient in announcing what he found acceptable and unacceptable.

Noah did acknowledge that Charles was a good father to the girls and he treated Lillian with kindness and respect. Nevertheless, Noah wanted more for his only child. Noah's former wife, Lillian's mother, Esther, thought Charles was a lovely man and that Lillian had made the right choice. She told friends, "She was smarter than me. She married someone who doesn't shout all the time, doesn't judge every behavior by some unfathomable code of acceptability, and cares about something other than money."

Giving his daughter what became known as 'the camp' was how

Noah could compensate for his son-in-law's 'poor career decision.' It was indeed a 'camp' during Lillian and Charles Turner's first summer in 1955, complete with a large tent, a lean-to, and a privy. The four acres were sufficiently separated from the neighbors that no one appeared to mind the rudimentary facilities.

Noah had a permanent structure erected over the first winter, and by the summer of 1956, his daughter and her family were sleeping in beds with mattresses. However, the Turner family continued to refer to their summer home as 'the camp' and, to their neighbors, it would forever be the 'Turner Camp.' The name irked Noah. He told his second wife that he regretted deeding the property to his daughter and son-in-law. "If I had just held on to it and let them use it, it would be the 'Mercer Camp.'

Charles and Lillian Turner loved their summers at 'Indian Point' as did their two daughters. Charles would read the academic journals he had been saving during the year. He would also edit the papers he was working on as he climbed the academic ladder at Northeastern.

Charles was not the only academic at Indian Point, and talks on the beach sometimes resembled those heard in a faculty lounge—assorted esoteric speculation and whining about deans and presidents. Lillian would spend time with her daughters and their friends until the middle of August, when she would start to focus on her coming school year. Summer had regularity: clamming in the Sagadahoc Bay at low tide, sailing their third-hand Sunfish off the beach, tubing down Little River, hiking the trails on the peninsula, and excursions to pick blueberries became part of every summer. Evenings were spent with puzzles, games, and always reading. Old friends came; new friends were made.

Noah rarely came. Charles and Lillian improved 'the camp' on their summer escapes from Brookline, Massachusetts. The first was an addition of a comfortable bedroom for Lillian's divorced parents to use when they came. Noah was assigned July for his visits. Esther had August. Charles' family never visited from Idaho. In the summer, their ranch always needed attention.

Noah Mercer slept there a total of fifteen nights throughout the fifties, sixties, and seventies. It became a standing family joke, one that was recorded by a notch into the frame of the bedroom door, one notch for every 'Noah visit.' Noah never seemed to notice the tiny cuts in the frame. His second wife, a woman fifteen years his junior, never came. Her assessment of Georgetown was, "Why would you want to vacation in a place that doesn't have a decent golf course?" Esther came every August and thought the notches were hysterical.

Summer life on the island of Georgetown differed by where you lived. At the Erascohegan Yacht Club, on the other side of the island from Indian Point, life was organized around sailing and many planned social events. By contrast, Indian Pointers were less organized and more private in their summertime activities. Still, people waved as they drove by one another, and seeing a cluster of friends walking along the dirt road was common. There were only a couple of communal gatherings each summer.

In nineteen sixty-four, Hannah chose not to come to Indian Point. The previous year, a friend from Wellesley had introduced her to Richard Goldman, a junior at Brown University. In the spring of 1964, Richard organized students to participate in something called the Mississippi Summer Project. Hannah thought it sounded interesting when Richard described it to her.

Since high school, Hannah planned on joining the newly formed Peace Corps when she graduated from Northeastern. In Hannah's mind, going to Mississippi for the summer to teach children and register voters seemed like a good trial run for her. It took some time, but Hannah convinced Lillian and Charles that a summer in Mississippi working in one of the 'Freedom Schools' would be a good experience for her and wouldn't be 'all that dangerous.' As she told her parents, she would only be in Mississippi for a couple of months.

They could even come and visit her. She added, "Besides, you've both been talking about how something needs to be done about these southern states, Jim Crow laws, and the violence against Black people."

Hannah joined over seven hundred students from around the United States who traveled to Western College for Women in Oxford, Ohio, to train before going to Mississippi. One of the leaders was Bob Moses, Mississippi field director of the Student Nonviolent Coordinating Committee (SNCC—verbally shortened to 'Snick'). Moses believed if 'The Project' could draw attention to Mississippi and make some headway there, it would be a wedge into the South. Mississippi was considered to be the toughest of the southern states. Roy Wilkins of the NAACP had said, "There is no state that approaches that of Mississippi in inhumanity, murder and brutality, and racial hatred. It is absolutely at the bottom of the barrel."

As the training began, there was an immediate cultural clash. On one side were the young, primarily Southern, African American SNCC workers who had already been toiling away at voter registration. On the other side were the inexperienced White college volunteers. During one training session, a film showed a large, White, very obese, registrar of voters. The White volunteers laughed at the man's girth and the way he talked. They could not imagine this person having any power. To them, he was a joke. To the SNCC workers, this man was the person who controlled the fate of the people who they had been trying to register. He was the man who determined who would and would not be allowed to vote. He was the enemy.

Not all SNCC workers thought 'The Project' was a good idea. They wondered if these mostly northern White kids would allow themselves to be led by southern Blacks? Would they understand the dangers, not only the physical ones but the dangers of disrupting the work SNCC had already done? Would these inexperienced White volunteers say something or do something to cause their Black host families to be harmed? And, most of all, were they needed? Some felt having to turn to White college students was an admission of failure. Instead, Moses and the other leaders saw it as a means of getting attention focused on the difficulties of voting for southern African Americans. White parents would pay attention. They would have 'skin in the game,' literally.

The plan was for the volunteers to register African American voters. In the Freedom Schools, volunteers would instruct young African Americans about their constitutional rights and African American history. The White students knew that many obstacles had been erected to prevent African Americans from voting. When the Mississippi Summer Project began, only seven percent of the African American population in Mississippi was registered to vote. The volunteers had followed the television news that covered the Civil Rights movement. They had seen the violence. Intellectually, the volunteers were somewhat aware of the challenges they would face.

During the training, the volunteers were taught that outside 'agitators,' of whom Hannah Turner was now one, were not welcome in Mississippi. She had to be prepared to be taunted, spit at, cursed, and more. "You will be in danger, and we don't want you out walking around alone, especially at night." She was taught how to protect her body in case she was beaten. She was taught to be polite to everyone and not respond when harassed. She was taught the principles of non-violence and how to employ empowerment strategies in education and recruiting.

Hannah didn't know any of this when she joined up with three other volunteers and drove from Boston to Oxford. She had gone to Northeastern because her father taught there. Economically, anyplace else made no sense. She had lived in Brookline all her life. The drive from Boston to Oxford felt like she was leaving home for the first time.

On the trip, the four of them talked about the situation they would face during training and later when they were deployed throughout Mississippi. Hannah was surprised at the differences in their group. She was struck by how little she knew compared with one of their other riders. He would be returning to complete his senior year at Brandeis. She also wondered about the motives of another member of their group. He saw himself as a 'radical' and was prepared to be beaten to death if that's what it took to bring about change. After his interview in Oxford, the SNCC organizers sent him back home as 'not suitable for the work.

As the training progressed, Hannah started to understand the vulnerability of their positions. The volunteers were taught that the federal government had abandoned them. J. Edgar Hoover had said he would not use FBI resources to protect them. Mississippi state and local police were more inclined to beat or arrest them. They were on their own.

During the training, three volunteers left for Mississippi before the others: James Chaney, Andrew Goodman, and Michael Schwerner. They went to investigate the burning of Mt. Zion Methodist Church in Philadelphia, Mississippi. The church had been proposed as a site for a Freedom School. In addition to burning the church, the KKK had also beaten congregation members. Within days, the word came back to Oxford that Chaney, Goodman, and Schwerner had gone missing. Any lightheartedness among the volunteers remaining in Ohio disappeared with the news of their missing comrades. SNCC told the volunteers to call home, talk to their parents, and consider whether they still wanted to go.

Hannah was sent to McComb, about eighty miles south of Jackson. McComb had a history of violence against Black people, violence that was initiated, tolerated and rewarded by the White citizenry. SNCC had tried to register voters there in 1961. The KKK and members of the White establishment escalated the violence and intimidation to make sure the young SNCC workers could not succeed. Finally, it got so bad that SNCC pulled their workers out of McComb, fearing for their lives. Hannah and her team arrived in July, three years later, to register voters and open a Freedom School. They were housed in the homes of local families. Again, the violence escalated. Between August and September, there were eleven bombings of African American homes.

Ronnie Williams, his wife Ethel, and their three children welcomed Hannah Turner and Miriam Peck into their home. Ronnie and Ethel brought their youngest child into their bedroom to create space for the two young women. They gave Hannah and Miriam a room of their own, with a window.

The two volunteers knew little about McComb. They knew it had a violent history, and the singer Bo Diddley had been born there. Neither of them had ever been dependent upon or led by anyone with skin color that was not white. Neither of them had grown up with Black friends. Although Miriam was Jewish, so was her neighborhood of Flatbush in Brooklyn. So, neither of them had any experience being a member of a minority group, eating unfamiliar food, or hearing accents that required them to concentrate to understand what was being said. Neither of them had been trained as a teacher, and neither had grown up with the expectation of violence at any moment. Ronnie and Ethel saw all of this and understood that they had to find a way to help these two young women survive the summer.

On the first day of their classes, Ronnie walked Hannah and Miriam to the Baptist church, where the basement room, usually used for Sunday school, would be their work home for the next several weeks. It was early when they arrived, and the day's heat was beginning to take hold. Walking over, Ronnie kept the talk light. "You be putting me on. You never had grits before? Never? Neither one of you?"

"No, I really haven't," Miriam answered.

"Me, neither," Hannah added.

"Well, by the time you two young ladies ready to head back north, Ethel and me goin' to have you two eating like real southern folk—last thing we do."

As they approached the church, Ronnie asked, "You ready to get goin' with your school?"

"Not really," Miriam answered.

"You do just fine. You know more than the children. You keep that in mind. They lookin' forward to you being here. Be a little shy at first. Never had a White teacher before. That Snick boy, Terrence Smith, he'll help you with whatever you need. He was here before. Know his way around." When they arrived, Smith was already there, along with the pastor, organist, and two women who were introduced as Sunday school teachers.

The room was already set up with twenty or so chairs facing the front where there was a blackboard with a piece missing in the top corner. Smith was at the back of the room talking to the pastor. The three other women were off to the side chatting among themselves. Hannah and Miriam saw the boxes of materials sitting on the floor at the front of the room and went over and started unpacking them. In a couple of minutes, Smith joined them. "Pastor wants to meet you. He'll introduce you to the others. He says it's okay we set up the room anyway we want. Remember, though, it's their building, but…"

"The method is the message," Hannah completed the sentence.

Smith laughed. "Let's get to it." Fifteen minutes later, introductions were completed, and the chairs were now in a circle. Hannah was sure the two Sunday school teachers did not approve.

Thirty minutes later, students of all ages started drifting in. Older siblings guided their younger brothers and sisters. Some parents came with their children, but rather than leave, they took seats.

"We'll have adults?" Miriam asked.

"Looks that way," Smith said. "Pastor said he wants to stay for a bit. See how it goes. Mrs. Ursery, the organist, says she wants to learn some of those 'freedom songs.' The Sunday school teachers; my guess is they're here as critics. Ignore them."

They started the day with one of those, 'freedom songs."

It was more than a little chaotic with all the different ages in the group and attendance varying day to day. Still, by the end of the week, Hannah and Miriam felt comfortable and walked back and forth to school without Ronnie's protective company. They learned to treat each day as a new beginning because they didn't know who would be there. Often new children and adults showed up for the first time. While there was some skill training, especially when it came to reading, Hannah and Miriam depended on stories and literature about African Americans, the civil rights movement from slavery until the present. They provided information about the constitution and voting. They called one day 'Medley in Black' and featured Black poets. All of this material was new to the students regardless of age. Mississippi had forbidden the teaching of African American literature in all-Black public schools. Students were stunned to learn that Langston Hughes was only seventeen when he wrote 'The Negro Speaks of Rivers.'

"You mean I can do that when I'm seventeen?" a twelve-year-old boy asked Hannah after she read the poem.

"No," Hannah said, "You can do it now. You'll just be able to do it better when you're seventeen."

One of the goals of the Freedom Schools was introducing students to the Constitution of the United States and their rights as citizens, including the right to vote. The hope was that some of the students would become leaders and contribute to what was now called 'the movement' long after the summer was over. The obstacle wasn't the ability of students to understand the material that was presented; it was fear about acting upon it. Some of the adults who attended the school in the evening were threatened with losing their jobs.

Under pressure from White parents, Lyndon Johnson ordered the FBI to conduct a massive search for the three missing young volunteers. He even ordered the Navy to get involved and search the rivers and creeks around Philadelphia. It was well known that African Americans were often killed, and their bodies were just thrown into the rivers and creeks of Mississippi. As they searched for the three missing volunteers, several other bodies were discovered. Some were identified; many weren't. It wasn't until August 4th that the bodies of James Chaney, Michael Schwerner, and Andrew Goodman were found. They had been tortured, murdered, and thrown into a shallow grave. It was no secret to any of the volunteers, the SNCC staff, or the host parents that the KKK and the police were responsible. That night, two Molotov Cocktails were thrown at the church where Hannah and Miriam were teaching. Neither homemade device reached the church. When the staff and students showed up the next morning, they found burned grass where the incendiary devices had landed, burned, and been extinguished in an early morning rain.

That evening Terrence Smith pulled the two girls aside and said, "We've been talking. If you want to leave, we'll understand. We want you to call home and talk to your parents. We don't want you to feel any pressure to stay here. We can make sure you get out of here safely if that's what you want to do."

When Hannah called home, she planned to tell her parents she would stay. She expected them to argue with her. But, instead, her father said, "Of course, we want you to come home. Your mother and I are worried sick about what's going on down there. And now that we know what happened to those three boys…"

"They weren't boys."

"You're right. They were young men. Hannah, I'd be lying if I said I didn't want you to hop on the first plane and get out of there. Of course, we want you to come home, but from your calls, we know how important this work is to you. It's got to be your decision."

Her mother was not quite so open, "If I told you to come home, would you?"

"I don't know. Probably not," Hannah replied.

"I'm not going to waste my breath arguing with you about it. If you decide to stay, please promise me you'll stay safe. Don't take any chances. Do you feel safe?"

"For the most part. Yeah. I'd say for the most part."

"Are you sure?"

"Yeah, Mom, they're doing their best to make sure nothing happens to us. We never go anywhere alone."

"Neither did those boys. They were together."

"I know. I'm not going to argue with you about it. Everyone knows we're here, and we're never alone."

Hannah and her mother went back and forth like this for a few more minutes before her father got back on the phone. "Hon, we've been talking to Miriam's parents and some other parents. Miriam has a birthday next week. Her parents are thinking about flying down to help her celebrate. If they do, we're going to try to coordinate and meet up with them at the airport in Atlanta and then fly to Jackson together. We'll rent a car and drive up to McComb. Do you and Miriam need anything?"

"Yes, we do. When you get to Jackson, would you pick up a couple of big fire extinguishers, the old-fashioned kind that use water and you can wear on your back?"

"I know the kind you mean. What do you need fire extinguishers for? Has something happened?"

Hannah paused before answering. "Don't worry, Dad. It's just a precaution."

"You're sure?"

"Yes, Dad, I'm sure. Can you do that?"

"Yeah, of course, we can do that."

"I want to leave one here at the school and give one to Ronnie and Ethel to keep at their house."

"Maybe we can get a couple for each place. Anything else you girls need?"

"You know those big boxes of crayons?"

"Of course."

"If you don't mind, could you bring several boxes? The kids love them, and they disappear, which is a good thing."

"That's easy. Anything else?"

"Not that I can think of offhand."

"Well, call if you think of anything."

"Thanks, Dad."

"We'll let you know our plans. So, lots of crayons and big fire extinguishers. Don't hesitate to add to the list if you think of something. Anything. You hear me?"

"Yes. I hear you."

April 21, 1995
HOME TOWN BOY by Michael Buckley

It is the yellow time of year. Splashes of yellow from forsythias brighten up driveways, and daffodils burst against stonewalls. The gray of winter has been necessary, but it has done its job, and color is coming out to play. Skates and skis, shovels, and de-icer will be stored in their proper places. Snowmobiles will be returned to the back of the barn or nestled in a storage shed.

All of these will be traded for new implements: spades, hoes, lawnmowers, baseball mitts, and bats. Bikes will move up to the front of the garage. Seeds are being started, nurseries are hiring for the big spring push, and sheep farmers are looking bleary-eyed as ewes deliver their offspring. Having been raised with sheep, I know. Lambing season can be exhausting.

It is the color, though. Soon yellow will be joined by the whites of magnolias. Tulips—the ones the deer don't get—will display a palette of possibilities. Thousands of dormant bulbs spring to life.

Taking the tarps off of our schooner has always been the true sign for me that the season has changed. Taking the tarps off doesn't mean I am prepared to do any work on the boat. I say to myself, and sometimes believe it, that the boat has to 'air out' before any actual work begins. Tarp removal demonstrates my conviction that there will be no more snow. The work of sorting and sanding, painting, and varnishing requires warmer days for me and the materials I'll be working with.

It is transition time. The death of winter is giving way to the resurrection of spring. Of course, Easter must be in the spring. All religions know that spring is important. Birth and rebirth have to be celebrated, and the celebrations are ones of life, no madulin stuff here. A couple of wrens have decided that the light fixture inside the barn, the one over the door, is an excellent place to build their nest. We won't use that light for now. When the young ones fledge will be soon enough.

Schools will soon be transitioning their fledglings—one grade to another, one school to another, or out into the world. Fly, young ones. You are on your own now. Of course, we know that is not the case. They'll be back, usually with their laundry.

I find it hard to be in a bad mood when yellow appears. I smile to myself. I often push the season and drive with my window open. I start to look and see if the ice cream shop is open yet. If it is, I know the transition is complete. Winter is out of my mind, and I have changed the jackets hanging on the hook in the kitchen entryway.

My friend Squinty is in charge of getting the baseball and softball fields ready. I have no idea how he got that name. It's one of those names, though, that a family member or the friend of a family member hung on him when he was a little tike, and once it was tightened around his neck, he was a goner, it was never going to let go. I didn't even know his real name was Franklin until he got married and his mother-in-law-to-be put the engagement notice in the paper.

Squinty is an industrious guy. He does everything from fish to drive a snowplow. In the spring, though, he is swamped and is very hard to get a hold of. He is especially attentive to the playing fields. He plays softball in a league, a shortstop. He grooms bad bounces out of the field. He has a vested interest, and fortunately, his interests coincide with those of the recreation commission. He is a transition master. He takes a badly troubled infield full of bumps and bruises from the winter and resurrects it. In his masterful hands, it becomes fit for any major league team that would make its way up the coast to Maine for an exhibition game. I can dream.

For Squinty, it is an act of love for the game. Before he took on his responsibilities, he was playing one Saturday morning in a 'beer game' in West Bath when a hot grounder came his way, hit an uneven chunk of clay, bounced up, and hit him in the old schnozola, a nasty bounce. A broken nose did not keep him from finishing the game, but he swore that would never happen on any field he took care of. It never did.

It might be nice if we all had a Squinty in our lives. I wouldn't mind having someone who poured loving affection into my life every spring and smoothed out all the rough spots so there would be no bad bounces. In the meantime, I have yellow giving the boot to gray, and that will have to suffice.

Chapter Fifty-Nine: The Crew

On the way back from Jay, I decided to stop in Bath to stock up with food for the weekend. It was going to be crowded at Tír na nÓg and very busy. First was the square dance Friday night, and then two days of the Rum Regatta. Maude was coming; Jesse and Naomi were coming. Unfortunately, Natalie and Miriam had other plans for the weekend.

When I got home and went up onto the porch at Tír, I saw a sheet of paper taped to the door; one sentence was highlighted in yellow. I put the first load of grocery bags down on the swing and went to the door so I could read it. It was from Wendy's professor. There were two pages. The first page was a copy of an email her professor had sent to the department chair and two of her colleagues, letting them know that Wendy completed the course, received an A-minus, and her record had been updated. She recommended that Wendy be admitted to the two classes she had requested for the fall semester. The second email was to Wendy. It read:

Wendy, this was outstanding work. I felt duty-bound to deduct half a grade because it was late, but it was 'A' level work. Tír na nÓg sounds like a beautiful place to have spent your summers as a young child. You did a superb job of intertwining your family's story with that of Georgetown and Bath. I look forward to having you in another one of my classes in the future.

I smiled and opened the door to let Charlie out so he wouldn't break through the screen. I shouted, "Wendy!" There was no answer.

It took three trips to bring all the groceries inside. Finding a place for everything was not easy in the small kitchen. I struggled to fit everything into the refrigerator. Whenever we would have a crowd Hannah would say, "We need a second refrigerator. We can put it in the shed." I knew she was right, but it would mean running electricity from the house to the shed. It was one more thing I never got around to doing.

I walked down to the pier to get cellphone reception and called Rachel. She didn't answer, so I left her a voice message in case Wendy hadn't called her yet. I knew she must have, but I called anyway. It was ridiculous, Wendy had done all the work, but I felt this weird role reversal. Here I was calling Rachel to brag about Wendy getting an A minus as though I had gotten the grade myself. Well, why not? Maybe in some small way I had. 'A minus' for summer grandfathering.

I called Wendy, but it also went to voicemail. "Hon, I am so happy for you. You did it. You nailed it. An 'A' paper. You should be proud of yourself." I stood looking out towards the mouth of the cove. I smiled, I chuckled, I even did a seventy-something version of a fist pump.

Back at the house, I thought about calling Grace and inviting her and Helen to come for the weekend. I had one bedroom that was not yet spoken for. I didn't call. It was a bad idea. What were she and Helen going to do, sit on the clubhouse porch while we all went racing? And if Grace came with us, what was Helen going to do? And would Grace have any interest in racing? I decided to call them the following week and invite them down for the day.

Then I saw a note on the kitchen table. I had missed it when I first came in and got busy with the groceries. It was from Wendy.

How's that for a mark, Gramps? I did it. I called Mom and left her a voicemail. Rina and I are down at Five I celebrating with ice cream. Can Archie come up and crew with us this weekend if he can make it?

Of course, Archie could come. The more, the merrier. I liked the young man. I approved, as if that mattered to anyone.

Jesse called and said he wanted to race in the 12 ½ fleet rather than crew for me on the *Redhead*. So I asked him, "Who do you have for crew?"

"Not to worry. I have crew."

"You sure? I don't need everyone on the *Redhead*."

"Got it covered, Dad. See you Friday night."

When I asked Wendy if she was going to crew for her uncle, she said, "No way. Archie and I are with you on the *Redhead*. Rina and her parents are coming too, aren't they?" This was another 'of course.' I had my crew. I wondered if Naomi said 'yes' to crewing for her husband? That would be a first. I had a hard time imagining that. Okay, I wouldn't worry about it, but I couldn't help wondering, "Who the hell did he get?"

Archie showed up Friday morning for breakfast. His explanation was, "I got an early start to beat the traffic." Yeah, sure, Archie. I was polite and told him that I was delighted he could join us for the weekend and asked about his parents, who he assured me were fine. I was tempted to get in a bit of kidding about his early start. As a grandfather, an aged gentleman of many years, I probably could have gotten away with embarrassing him with a wee bit of teasing. Seeing the two of them together, though, and how they were responding to one another, I kept to a politeness motif. I liked him, and I loved her.

In that simple little decision to forgo teasing, I realized that this Wendy was not the Wendy whom my daughter had dropped off Memorial Day weekend. I knew this Wendy, and I loved her. It was no longer the loving of an abstracted grandfather responding to an abstracted granddaughter. Over the summer, I had become connected to this young woman; to her struggles and her happiness. Right now, that happiness was connected to Archie Howlett and his getting up at some god-awful hour so he could be with her. Her response was to run and jump into his arms when he opened the door, and she saw who it was.

Maude arrived by five, complaining about the traffic out of

Portland. Jesse came shortly after but without Naomi. Instead, he brought his crew for the weekend. It was Joel.

My two sons had pulled a fast one on me. If I had been younger and spryer, I might have run and jumped into his arms. I hadn't seen my son in two years. What was supposed to be a one-year deployment had turned into two. Then two had turned into three. He was here now, though, in one piece, and I, again, surprised myself with the sense of relief that I always got when he was stateside. I hugged him and pushed him back, and held him at arms distance: "Damn, it's good to see you. Why didn't you tell me? How long are you here for? Are Sharon and the kids with you? When did you get back from Afghanistan? Are you back in Texas? How long?"

I gave him another hug. He was tan, tall, fit as he always was. Military haircut. Military bearing. Hannah used to say, "He could be an Air Force Academy poster boy." Even in civvies, he looked military.

Jesse answered for him, "We wanted to surprise you. He's here in Georgetown for the weekend. Then he's coming back to Boston with me. Sharon and the kids fly in from Texas next Tuesday."

Joel said, "Thank you, brother. That is the plan. I'm going to rent a car, and then we'll all come up on Tuesday if that's okay with you."

"Of course, it's okay." Then I asked the question that I had been holding back, "Deployments done? That's it?"

"Yeah, and it's unlikely that I'll be going back. I've done my share. I'm back in Texas. It's a new posting. I could be there for a while. I'll tell you all about it when we get some time."

"You bet you will. I can't believe this. You two are impossible. Why didn't you tell me?"

"Blame Jesse, Dad. His idea."

I picked up a pillow off the couch and threw it in Jesse's direction. He caught it and threw it at his brother, "Come on. You thought it was a great idea."

Joel caught the pillow and threw it back at Jesse. "Yeah, but you came up with it."

They were adolescent brothers again, and the pillow went back and forth as they mocked one another about who was responsible for the surprise visit. I reverted to parenting, "Will you guys stop it before you break something?"

Wendy, Rina, and Archie came back from stowing gear on the *Redhead*. When Wendy saw Joel, she dashed from the door and threw herself at him, "Uncle Joel!" I thought, the second dash of the day. Who's next?

It didn't take long to introduce Archie to Joel. Joel returned to military bearing, "Good to meet you." He then went back to being home at Tír na nÓg. "What does someone have to do to get a drink around here?"

Hearing the commotion, Maude came downstairs. Her hair was wet, and she had thrown sweats on. Before she got all the way downstairs, she said, "What's going on down here?"

Joel said, "I'm trying to get someone to offer me a drink."

Seeing Joel, she said, "Will you look who's here? You want a drink; you could show up once in a while."

"Afghanistan's a bit far, you know?"

"Oh, come here, flyboy, and give your aunt a hug." Hug delivered, she turned to me and said, "Get your son a drink for christ's sake." To Joel, she said, "What are you drinking these days, flyboy?"

"Bourbon, rocks."

"Oh, you are so your father's son."

Joel evaded giving direct answers over dinner. He was full of "I don't know" and "Up to the Air Force." The only certainty appeared to be that he would not get deployed again in the near future. Getting the message, people stopped asking questions. I noted that Jesse did not ask about his brother's plans. Something was up, and I had no idea what it was, but it was clear that I would be informed when Joel decided the time was right. I stopped asking questions.

The square dance was what it always was. I don't know how old the caller and his wife were, but nothing seemed to change. He called; she played the fiddle. Kids danced; their parents danced. Aunts and uncles danced, as did grandparents. Rum punch was offered to adults, and kids had their own punch. There were rum snickerdoodles, glazed rum cookies, and my favorite, buttered rum shortbread cookies. It began promptly at seven o'clock and ended precisely at nine o'clock.

Everybody left. A trail of flashlights bobbed back and forth, showing people the way to their cottages. When they arrived, the inside lights went on, and the flashlights went off. When I turned my flashlight on and started to leave, Joel asked if I would stay a bit and sit with him on the clubhouse porch, "It's been a while, Dad. Let's set a bit." We found two rockers and sat down. Maude started to come over to sit with us, but Jesse intercepted her, whispered something, and the two of them followed Wendy and Archie heading for Tír.

When we settled in, Joel said, "Sharon and I've been doing some thinking, actually, a lot of thinking, and talking to the kids. Bottom line is, in a little over a year, I'll have my twenty in. Our kids have been bounced around too much, different schools, towns, and it's taken its toll, especially on Adam. He's ready to start high school. There's no certainty we would stay in Texas if I stayed in, and we want him to be able to start and finish in the same high school."

"You're serious?" I said, "You're thinking about getting out?"

"Yeah. Getting out and settling down someplace so the kids can stay in one school system, make friends, and keep them."

"Wow. Where are you thinking?"

"Here."

"Georgetown? Seriously? That would be wonderful."

"Or Bath. Maybe Brunswick. It makes sense. Sharon and I both grew up in the area. You're here; her parents are still in Gardiner.

They're still healthy, but they're starting to slow down. Shar can work from any place, and she's making great money writing copy for three different ad agencies. They don't care where she lives. She Skypes with clients if they need a face-to-face meeting."

"What about you? What…?"

"I don't know. Some ideas, but nothing definite. Still a year away. Maine Air National Guard is flying tankers, 135s. I could try to hook up with them if they have a spot. I've been flying Herc's so long, I'd welcome a change. I'm going to talk to some folks there. I'd have to go through training, but who knows? It's all up in the air except wanting to settle close by. Sharon thinks I should take a year off and explore."

"Sounds like a good idea."

"I don't know. I think I'm going to need to do something."

"Anything else cooking?"

"Could be a long shot but Lockheed plans on making a civilian model of the 'Herc.' I know that plane as well as anyone. I might be able to get a consulting gig, or even a full-time slot with whatever companies start to buy them."

"They'd be foolish not to hire you."

"It could be a ways off, though. In the meantime, there are a couple of things I wanted to ask you about."

"Sure, what?"

"Well, and remember this is all very tentative and exploratory."

"I'm waiting."

"Okay. Your Cessna Stationair isn't that old…"

"Nineteen ninety-eight."

"And it sounds like you're not using it very often."

"Depends on what you mean by often. I'm still doing the charity work, and I'm always flying people at the yacht club here and there. And then there are people on the island and in town who I help out."

"Okay, well, what if we kept the plane at the airport in Portland

and I started a charter business or hooked up with a company that's already there? Probably more business there than in Brunswick. I'd pay the expenses on the plane and give you a cut on every flight. It would give me something to do while I look around."

"You want to start a charter company?"

"Or hook up with one."

"And use the Cessna?"

"Just a thought."

"Interesting. Plane's in good shape, and I just upgraded all the avionics last year. I'd still want to do the charity work, though, and I'd want to help people out from time to time. So yeah. But yeah, it might just work. Hell, I could fly right seat for you."

"You flying right seat for me? My father the co-pilot."

"Why not? Besides, that way, I'd make sure you didn't wreck my plane."

"I have yet to wreck a plane. So, does that mean I'd have to pay you? Cut into the profits?" He was teasing. I knew it. He knew it. But I actually liked the idea, a lot.

"Why not? I could get my commercial license…"

"You're serious? You'd want to fly right seat?"

"Sure, why the hell not?"

"I guess there's no reason. It just never entered my mind."

"It's a year from now, but…*Buckley Air Charter*. I like the sound. We could start to lay some groundwork this year."

"Dad, let's not get ahead of ourselves here. It's a year away, and it's just an idea."

"Yeah, but it's a good one."

The two of us flying together was something I had never even dreamed about. I hadn't been flying a great deal recently. Talking about flying, I realized that I missed it. The plane was in excellent shape. This might just work. I didn't know if it would work out financially for Joel and Sharon. I asked, "You'll have your retirement pay?"

"At twenty years, it's not much. Around twenty thousand. It goes up with inflation, but I want to bring in additional money. We've been able to save quite a bit thanks to Sharon's income and my perks, but I'd rather not dip into that if we can avoid it."

"Sounds like you two have been doing a lot of planning."

"We have. Retirement is definite. I'm done. Primarily, it's the kids, but it's also the government. I've seen one administration after another make stupid mistakes that make absolutely no sense. Afghanistan has been a major cluster-fuck. Our presence isn't even a house of cards. It's not built that strongly."

"You've been saying that."

"It's true, and it's not about to change. It's not worth seeing people die, especially the civilians."

"Not worth you getting hurt."

"That, too."

"I get it. So, retirement is definite. Anything else?"

"This area. We want to come home, and for both of us, that means Maine."

"I can't tell you how happy that makes me. I only wish your mother was still alive to welcome you home."

"I know. We've talked about that. I wish we could have been here when she was sick."

"You were when you could."

"Not the same, Dad. And now. Well, we want the kids to know their grandparents. They don't. They never really got to know Mom. They don't know their aunts and uncles and haven't spent any time with their cousins. They're all older, but still..."

"They're still cousins."

"Exactly."

"So, what's next?"

"Look at school systems. That's why Sharon and the kids are

coming. We've been doing that online, but we want to do some visits. The schools in this area aren't great. Brunswick is ranked much higher than Bath, so that's where we're going to start looking. We've been looking in the Portland area, too. Falmouth is ranked very high for Maine, and that's a possibility. It's not that far away."

"No, it's not."

"There's something else. It's just a thought, maybe it's not possible, but I did want to mention it."

"What's that?"

"I don't want to get into the middle of anything. We've just been tossing ideas around. Our understanding is that Ruth and Harold have gotten themselves into a financial mess and have asked you to sell off some land to get them back on their feet. Well, what if you sold me and Sharon some land so we could build here on the farm, or you sold us the house in Bath?"

I didn't say anything at first. Joel and his family returning to Maine already had me spinning a bit. I had always thought he would stay in the Air Force as long as he kept getting promoted and liked it. Coming back to Maine with his family had not been even the vaguest possibility. Now, here they wanted to come back and maybe live next door as neighbors, or down the road in Bath in the house we had kept in the family for years as a kind of 'just in case' house. The rent had always sustained it, and it needed little work for an old house. I, on the other hand, needed time to think. I said, "Let me think about it. I'm not sure Ruth's situation has anything to do with it, though. You know I offered to help Hal, and he's accepted what I suggested."

"I know, Ruth told me."

"So, you've talked to her about your plan?"

"Hell no. And it's not a plan, Dad. I just wanted to bring it up to see if it was even possible. I hate to say this, but even though I know there are better schools around, all of us did okay going to Bath schools."

"Yes, you did."

"And the idea of my kids going there and my family living here on the farm or in the house in Bath is, well, it's coming home."

I didn't say anything. All I heard was my son was coming home.

"There's one more thing."

"I'm waiting."

"Ruth."

"What about her?"

"Are you ever going to patch things up with her?"

"What do you mean?"

"Oh, come on. You know what I mean. You haven't seen her since Mom died. You rarely talk to her. I know you two see things differently."

"That's an understatement."

"Okay. I know. She's a Trumpie, but that's more Harold."

"She's got a mind of her own."

"I know. All I'm saying is…"

"Get over it."

"Well, yeah. Sharon and I were thinking. Rather than going to Jesse's for Thanksgiving, come to Texas. We'll invite Ruth and Harold, and Hal…"

"And we'll all make nice."

"Is there anything wrong with that?"

"No."

"You know Mom would…"

"I think you should stop while you're ahead. Let me think about it."

I would think about it. But, beyond that, well, it was a couple of months away.

Chapter Sixty: Whirlwind

It was the middle of August. If there is a 'Maine Summer Season,' this weekend was its 'height.' Saturday morning, the lawn in front of the clubhouse and the docks were bustling with people. Everyone showed up for the Rum Regatta. All the flags were flying. The starter cannon for the races was taken from the storage room of the clubhouse and loaded onto the committee boat. At 0900—military time precision was now in force—all of us skippers assembled on the lawn around the race committee chair, Jay Ivers. When we quieted down, he proceeded to brief us. The cruising boats like the *Redhead* would have a fifteen-minute warning, one blast on the airhorn at 0945; a 'ready' signal of two blasts would sound at 0955; the start with the cannon would be at 1000. The cruising boat course was to circumnavigate Damariscove Island and return to the finish line. It would be up to us which way we would go around Damariscove. He then described the racecourse for the small boats like the Beetlecats and the Herreshoff 12 1/2s.

All of us knew these instructions. They had not varied in years. The cruising boats would circumnavigate Damariscove Island on Saturday and Seguin Island on Sunday. The Beetlecats and the Herreshoff 12 1/2s would race around buoys placed by the race committee: one race in the morning, a second in the afternoon. Saturday night, there would be a potluck party at the club with games for the children and revisiting the day's race for the skippers and crews. Rum, of course, was the preferred drink for the adults. Teenagers did their best to get some for themselves. Awards for the weekend of racing were handed out late Sunday afternoon.

Saturday, we did not do well on the *Redhead*. The wind shifted around a great deal and went up and down like a crazed yo-yo. Schooners like the *Redhead* prefer wind coming from abeam or behind that are steady and on the medium to heavy end of the Beaufort Scale. A force 5, 'fresh breeze,' is perfect for the *Redhead*. Instead, we had force 0, or 1, or 2 all day. We were not last, but only three boats were behind us as we crossed the finish line.

Jesse and Joel were waiting for us at the dock. "Got skunked, huh?" Jesse said.

"Stuff it," Maude replied.

I asked, "How did you guys do?"

"Fifth this morning. Shit for wind. Second this afternoon," Joel answered.

The clubhouse lawn soon became covered with blankets and chairs as crews settled down with the friends and families who had been watching the small boats race. People stopped by our territory to say hello to Joel and how good it was to see him. Two of the men he had grown up with whisked him away to meet their families and find out more about what he had been doing.

After dinner, blankets were folded up and taken to cars or stored in boat bags on the clubhouse porch. The lawn became a place for games. The steward strung up a volleyball net, and Jesse, Rina, Archie, and Wendy joined one of the teams. The old folks, meaning people like me, Maude, Judd, and Patty, commandeered chairs on the porch. Joel was still making the rounds. Everyone wanted 'Joel time.'

It was close to ten when we all returned to Tír na nÓg. Maude brought out ice cream and brownies. Judd opened a large bottle of Bailey's, and the big question was how to have your Baileys. Over the ice cream and brownies, on the rocks, or straight-up were offered as options. But, of course, the purists amongst us assured everyone that straight-up was the only decent way to drink this gift of the gods.

Early the next morning, while we slept, an imprisoned Jeffrey Epstein was found hanging by the neck in his cell. When we gathered for breakfast and learned the news, like many others around the world, we voiced our opinions. Some generated conspiracy theories. Joel and Maude were certain he had been assassinated to protect influential people. Joel was confident it was the work of Trump and his allies. The Clintons were also considered to be involved.

The discussion of Epstein led to a consideration of presidents. First, we agreed Obama would never have gotten involved with Epstein. Then it became, "What if Obama could have run again?" Next was, "Who had the best chance of beating Trump?" Soon the question became, "What happened to genuinely great presidents. Where were they?" That led to, "Who were they?" Answers to that question circulated around Teddy Roosevelt, FDR, and Truman until Wendy said, "Eleanor Roosevelt."

The verbal reaction was immediate and almost universal, "She was never president."

"The question wasn't who the greatest elected president was, but who was the greatest president?" she answered. "Substitute the word leader for president if you want to." She then launched into a lengthy defense of her premise: Eleanor's influence over her husband, her standing with his supporters, her role when he became ill. She provided story after story and fact after fact to support her premise.

We listened. At one point, Rina said, "You go, girl."

Maude said, "I don't agree with you. She may have been important, but she was never president."

Wendy did not give in, "Look at the moral authority she had. Look at what she advocated and what exists today. Eleanor laid the groundwork. She was the influence. Without her and Frances Perkins, the United States would be very different today. FDR may have gotten it done, but…"

"So, you're saying her ideas were presidential," Jesse interrupted.

"No. Not just her ideas. Her influence. Her ability to articulate those ideas and get people, especially her husband, to pay attention."

It was clear she was not about to submit to the wisdom of her elders. Jesse asked, "How come you know so much about Eleanor Roosevelt?"

"I just finished reading *No Ordinary Time* for a class I'm taking next semester."

"Sounds like you did more than read it," Maude said.

"Yeah. I sort of got into it."

"Sort of?"

Archie did not say anything. Neither did I. I don't know who was beaming more as we watched this conversation, me or Archie.

We did much better in the Seguin Island race on Sunday. There was a stiff breeze coming in from the ocean, and we were on a tight reach getting to the island and a broad reach coming back—our kind of wind. We were heeled over and doing close to eight knots for the entire race.

Back at the Herreshoff 12 1/2 races, Joel skippered, and Jesse crewed for him. Joel was out of practice. He got terrible starts; and didn't take his brother's advice, so it was their turn to get 'skunked.' Joel was never the skipper that Jesse was, plus this was the first time he had skippered a race in years. Jesse didn't say much about their two races on Sunday when we assembled later. Neither did Joel.

When all the boats were in and safely moored, the club ladies got out the silver, and tea was served along with finger sandwiches and cookies. There was a non-alcoholic punch as well, supposedly for the children. However, many an adult found the punch an excellent foundation for the rum that was plentiful in flasks brought for the occasion. The punch charade was part of the ritual of the Rum Regatta. If any ingredients other than orange juice, pineapple juice, lime, and grenadine were used in the 'punch for the children,' there would have been an uproar. Some things were sacred.

At 1630, Jay Ivers and the other race committee members called everyone together on the lawn and announced the results. When it was announced that *Redhead* had won second place in the Seguin race, I sent Wendy and Rina up to collect our second-place trophy; a coffee mug with the club's name and its flag pennant printed on the side. The first-place winners would get their names, the name of their boat, and the name of the race they won inscribed on small copper plates that would be tacked to the 'winners' barrel.' With new names attached, the empty hogshead barrel would sit in the middle of the clubhouse lounge until next year. The *Redhead* had yet to get its name on the rum barrel, but maybe next year. We did get to keep the mug.

Joel decided to stay Sunday night. I said I'd drive him to Bath so he could take the bus to Boston Monday morning. Jesse, Maude, and Archie all headed south.

The Fishmans fed the remaining Buckleys as they always did on the Sunday evening of the Rum Regatta. The menu was always the same: lobsters and clams from the pound at Five I, corn and potatoes from the vegetable stand in Arrowsic. Judd took charge of the boiled goods, and Patty made a big green salad. Mid-August is blueberry season, and pies made with Maine's native fruit completed the meal. Rum did not appear. The weekend was officially over with the awards ceremony, so wine and beer were served with dinner. Everyone helped clean up.

After dinner, Joel wanted to go into Bath "to see what's changed." Rina and Wendy went with him. Patty, Judd, and I sat out on their porch looking out over the Gulf of Maine. The night was clear, and from their house up on the hill, you could see the navigation lights of boats out in the Gulf.

"What a weekend," Patty said. "So, Joel's coming home?"

"Looks that way. Possibly Falmouth or Brunswick, but this area."

"Don't have to ask how you feel about it."

"No."

"And Wendy, she knocked my socks off with her lesson about Eleanor Roosevelt last night."

"Me, too," Judd added.

I wanted to say, "Me, three," but instead I said, "She's worked hard this summer."

We talked about the two girls and the summer they were having. After a while, we just sat and looked out over the water. Finally, I said, "You're not going to believe this, but I think I may have met someone."

"As in?" Judd asked.

"As in, an available, bright, very attractive woman."

"Emphasis on available," Judd said.

"Not a Nan, in other words," Patty said.

"Not a Nan."

Judd added, "Nan is attractive, though."

Patty said, "Shush. I want to hear about this woman."

I told them about meeting Grace and her mother-in-law in Jay when I conducted interviews for the book. I told them about my going back for dinner and the walk that Grace and I took. I recounted Helen's description of me as a 'gentleman caller.' I didn't tell them about the fantasies I had been having about Grace.

"She sounds wonderful," Patty said. "Age-appropriate, self-sufficient, intelligent. So, when do we get to meet her?"

"I was thinking about inviting Grace to come down the day after Joel and his family leave. Go sailing, maybe spend the night."

"Only thinking about?" Judd said.

"Judd, shush," Patty said. "Would you invite the mother-in-law?"

Judd didn't give me a chance to answer. "Well, why not just do it? Do you have to invite the mother-in-law?" Judd asked.

"Fishman, sometimes you have no sense of subtlety or

propriety," Patty said. "Yes, he has to invite the mother-in-law."

I answered, "I like Helen. I suppose I should invite her. Of course, I'd rather it was just Grace, but it makes sense to invite Helen."

"Are you concerned that if you just..." Patty started.

"Invited Grace, she might turn me down?"

"Okay, now I get it," Judd said. "It's strategy."

"And propriety," Patty added.

"So, you going to do it?" Judd asked.

"Yes. Will at least one of you come and crew if we go sailing. I don't know how useful either one of them would be on the *Redhead*."

"We will both be there," Judd said. "Patty has to check her out, and I want to watch you in pursuit."

"Judd, stop it," Patty said.

By the time I left, I was committed. I was to call Grace and Helen first thing Monday morning.

I did. I talked to Helen, and we made a date for them to drive down for the day. I didn't mention staying overnight, although I wanted to. The plan was for them to come down the following week, after Joel and the others left. Helen said they would love to go for a sail. Tuesday was best for them, although they could manage Thursday if the weather on Tuesday wasn't good. Grace wanted to know what they could bring. I told her nothing. I knew they would bring something anyway. They were that kind of people. It all felt very formal to me, different from our last conversation. Was this the nature of a first date with chaperones when you are in your seventies? I thought of it as a date. I did not know how Grace thought of our getting together, although I was quite sure that, to Helen, Grace and I were now dating.

The Monday after the regatta, Wendy and I cleaned, did laundry, and shopped. The house filled up again on Tuesday evening with the arrival of Joel, Sharon, and the ABCs: Adam, Barbara, and Casey.

Joel and Sharon swore that they did not realize what they were doing with the names when Casey arrived, and they named her after Sharon's grandmother. Maude started referring to the children as the ABCs, and it stuck.

Sharon's Grandma Casey had been quite the character in Gardiner, Maine. Officially, she was the Town Clerk. But, in reality, she ran the town. She knew everybody's business, and every morning she would head to the A1 Diner, sit in the same booth, and hold court. I wondered if Casey would grow up to be like her grandmother.

I didn't know Joel's children, and they didn't know me. They hadn't known Hannah, and they certainly didn't know their aunts, uncles, and cousins. They knew Ruth, Harold, and Hal somewhat. Because of their proximity in Texas, the two families would occasionally get together for holidays. I knew some of their stories, but phone and Skype calls only go so far. I don't think I ever told Joel I was working on a new book.

The writing was going well. I now had the outline and four chapters ready to show a prospective publisher. I knew where the work was going, and I would stick with it. Even without a publisher, I had committed myself. Work, though, would have to wait. There was hosting to be done. I had some grandchildren to get to know.

Although she was now done with her assigned reading and writing for the summer, Wendy had moved into a new phase. She was reading articles that Archie had suggested to her. With Archie back home, she would put insect repellant on every evening, walk down to the bench on the pier for cell phone coverage, and talk to him, sometimes for an hour or more. She had gone to the library and downloaded two books about archaeology, *When Rocks Cry Out* and *An Archaeology of the Soul: North American Indian Belief and Ritual*. One evening, I walked down the pier, and I could hear her talking to Archie about what she was reading. She was oblivious to me.

During the day, she disappeared after lunch and came back around dinner time. Sometimes Rina went with her. When I asked her where they went, she said they were helping out at "the dig" over at Popham Beach.

After an exceptionally long conversation with Archie one night, she stayed down on the pier. When she finally came up, she caught me dozing on the porch where I had gone to read. "Gramps, can I ask you a question?"

"Sure."

"Did you ever think about changing your name?"

"My name? Michael? No. I would have gotten rid of my nickname if I could have. But, no. I'm fine with Michael."

"I didn't know you had a nickname."

"At school and in the service."

"Oh, you mean 'Buck?' Mom told me you didn't like it."

"Why do you ask?"

"I'm thinking about changing my name."

That got my attention. "Why on earth would you do that?"

"Wendy is a cute name. But I don't want a 'cute' name."

"Oh." Now, I was fully awake. "Cute. I never thought of it as 'cute.' Where is this coming from?"

"It's a little girl's name. Peter Pan-ish."

"Wendy was pretty strong, as I remember her."

"I suppose."

"What would you change it to?"

"Chava."

"Chava?"

"Chava. It's Hebrew. It means life, the first woman. In English, it's usually 'Eve,' but I like Chava better. I'm also thinking about learning Hebrew."

She wasn't asking for my opinion. "Have you said anything to your mother about this?"

"Not yet. Please don't say anything to her."

"I won't."

She came over from where she was standing, leaned down, and kissed me on top of my head. Then, she said, "Sleep tight. I'm going to bed," and went inside. 'Chava?' That would take some getting used to.

Mornings were long and slow that week. During the afternoons, Sharon and Joel, with Adam and Barbara in tow, started making the rounds of schools. Casey asked to stay home after their first day of visiting, and Joel asked if that was okay with me. Of course, I said I was delighted to spend time with her. I had it in mind that I might be able to deliver Casey to the kindness of the sailing instructor at Erascohegan, and I could get some writing done. However, when I suggested that to Casey, she said, "Grandpa, why don't you teach me?" There are some things a grandfather does not refuse. It is a code, a law, a rule. A granddaughter asking you to teach her how to sail is a matter of settled grandparent law.

The Herreshoff 12 ½ is a wonderful boat on which to learn to sail. It is small—the water line is twelve and a half feet and overall it is a little under sixteen feet long—but the boat is stable, responsive, and comfortable for two people. Casey was a quick learner. From her father, she had not only learned about airfoils, she understood how airfoils worked. Casey quickly became fascinated with the idea that sails are airfoils, and they could be shaped in many more ways than the wings of an airplane. After her first afternoon of sailing, she started to teach her father how to sail at dinner. She did remind me of her great-grandmother. Casey was a good name for her unless she decided to change it.

By Friday, I hated to see them leave. They worked hard at their decision. Every night we talked about their findings. They had statistics on each high school: National and State ranking, drop-out rate, college admissions, electives, advanced placement classes. In Maine, Falmouth was consistently ranked number one or two, Brunswick was number nine, and Bath was number twenty. It was clear that the focus was on Adam. He had struggled the most in school: peer group, bad teaching, bad schools. There were many explanations for his poor performance. I had a completely different take on Adam. I thought he was bored, lazy, spoiled, and just hadn't decided whether or not he wanted to learn or wanted anybody to teach him anything. He let his parents do the talking and remained a spectator to the goings-on. When I commented on this to Joel and Sharon one night, they once again returned to poor teaching, schools, and peer groups with low expectations. Sharon said, "Texas public schools are a wasteland."

They also considered the communities, especially the cost of living. Falmouth's cost of living was twenty-nine percent higher than Brunswick's; Brunswick was seventeen percent higher than Bath. These were hard decisions for them. The Air Force gave officers some choices, but the options were limited, and the needs of the service were always first. This was the first time this couple had an open field on which to play. They went at it with an intensity that worried me. Joel had prepared an elaborate spreadsheet; he was his mother's son. Criteria and options were entered and weighted. As they examined the output, they would often reconsider the weighting of the criteria. They were not only learning about their choices; they were learning about themselves and what was important to them.

I understood the process they were going through, but I was concerned that they were not giving themselves the freedom to make a mistake. It was 'as if' a decision could not be undone a year or two from now. I offered my observation that change was possible and was told, by both, "We are not going to change school systems again." At night I could hear them continue their 'process' long after going to their bedroom.

Joel and Sharon announced at breakfast Thursday morning, "We have decided on Brunswick." I don't know what they expected the reaction to be. Casey didn't say anything. Adam didn't say anything. Finally, Barbara said, "I liked Falmouth the best." The next thirty minutes sounded like a business presentation with Sharon presenting. All I said was, "It must feel good to have made a decision." So, the 'Convey Place' would stay intact, and the house in Bath would continue to be rented. Presentation over, Casey said, "Grandpa, can we go sailing?"

Chapter Sixty-One: Grace and Judy

Decision made, Joel and Sharon relaxed, as did Adam and Barbara. Casey remained Casey and just wanted to go sailing. I said I would take the kids sailing so Joel and Sharon could explore Brunswick neighborhoods. I was skeptical about how much help the three young ones would be as crew on the *Redhead*, but I had single-handed the boat when I was younger.

I thought Joel and Sharon might drive around Brunswick, but Sharon wanted more details, so they found a broker who had a free afternoon and was willing to play tour guide, knowing that this Texas couple would be looking in earnest in a year.

Onboard the *Redhead*, Adam surprised me. Away from his parents, he was livelier and did well. When I asked him to take the wheel so I could raise the sails, he kept the boat headed directly into the wind. When I finished getting them up, I realized that in recent years I always had crew onboard managing the sails. Either age was catching up to me, or I had forgotten how big the mainsail was. I made a mental note to look into getting an electric winch.

Barbara wasn't interested in sailing but did as she was asked. On the other hand, Casey was confident she could sail the schooner as well as she could the 12 ½. Of course, she was wrong, but she did her best. Fortunately, the wind was light, and the three of them were on their best behavior. What a difference the absence of parents made. There were no squabbles, and I thoroughly enjoyed the afternoon. I was slowly getting to appreciate what having them within a thirty, to forty-five-minute drive would make in my life. Flying with my son, sailing with my grandchildren—well maybe two of them—and occasional family meals together around a table instead of in front of a T.V.—I assumed they would invite me—were good things.

When we got home around four-thirty, Joel and Sharon were

already there. The laptop was back out. I could see spreadsheets up on the screen, and the two of them were looking intense again. I asked, "So, how was the sightseeing?"

Sharon turned away from where she was leaning over Joel, who entered numbers into the spreadsheet. "I think we may make an offer on a house."

"Now?" I know there was judgment in my tone, but what the hell? He had another year to go.

My son knows my voice tones, and he answered, "Yes, Dad, now. We'll fill you in, but we need to figure something out right now." I know my translation was accurate: "Shut up and leave us alone; we're busy."

"Okay, when would you like to eat?'

"Whenever you want."

"Okay." In a mock whisper, I turned to the kids and asked, "Who'd like to go swimming over at the Lily Pond?"

Adam said, "Sure." Barbara said, "No thanks. I'm going to go read." Casey left to get her bathing suit.

When we returned from the pond, Joel was in the kitchen cooking, and Sharon was setting the table. I went into the kitchen, and Joel asked, "Want a glass of wine or a beer?"

"No thanks. What's going on?"

"We found a house. Actually, we found a plan for a house that's perfect for us. It's not built yet, and they're just getting started. It's a new development."

"New construction? But you won't be here for a year."

"No, but we talked to the developer, and we can make the timing work."

"You're sure?"

"We're talking to the bank tomorrow. But, yeah, we're sure. We get to choose a lot of things because it's brand new. We can get exactly what we want. No settling."

"Have you checked out this developer?"

"What do you mean?"

"Reputation. Does he finish things? Not leaving them hanging forever while he moves on to a new project?"

"Broker we drove around with says he's very reliable."

I knew I was going to check him out. I didn't tell Joel that. Sharon came into the kitchen. "Isn't this wonderful? I can't believe the way we just lucked into this timing. There are only three other lots left. The one we're getting is almost level, and it backs up to an old farm, so we'll have privacy."

"Sounds wonderful." I wanted to say, 'Too good to be true.' Maybe I was wrong. Buying a house was a first for them. Oh, hell. They're both intelligent. They're adults. I stayed with 'wonderful.' Dinner was now a celebration. Everyone was in a good mood. Wendy offered to take the ABCs down to Five I for ice cream after we finished cleaning up. We all went.

When they left the following day, Wendy and I again cleaned the house and did laundry. "Gramps," she said, "We could turn Tír into a B&B. We've got this down pat."

"Good thing Nanna isn't here to hear you say that."

"Why?"

"A B&B? Are you serious?"

"I was kidding."

The weather was 'iffy' when I called Grace and Helen at eight o'clock Tuesday morning with a weather update as we had planned. Helen answered and said, "Rain. When did a little sprinkle ever stop someone from Maine? We'll be there." And come they did, arriving at ten-thirty precisely on time. I offered them coffee and some blueberry muffins that Wendy had made. Judd and Patty arrived a few minutes later. Wendy came down from her room to meet them and then excused herself to return to her room and reading.

I couldn't keep my eyes off Grace. My attraction and subsequent fantasies of the two of us kissing and holding one another made me feel like an awkward adolescent. At one point, I went out of my way to touch her on the shoulder as I passed the plate of muffins to Helen. I watched her interact with Judd and Patty. She was easy. 'Easy to meet,' my old editor would say. I saw her in a new way, as 'with me.'

It was still overcast when we got underway, but at least it wasn't raining. Every sailor has a 'tour' mapped out that guests love. Mine is to go out around Newagen and up into Boothbay Harbor. People get to see islands, usually seals, and, with luck, a whale or two. Sometimes one of the yachts of the 'rich and famous' will be making its way to or from Boothbay, and we can all gawk and complain about the extravagance while wondering what it would be like to be a guest on board. In return, the *Redhead* receives its share of gawking. The old schooner adds ambiance to the Boothbay scene.

Our scenic tour complete, we made our way into the small harbor on Damariscove Island and made fast to one of the courtesy moorings. It was time for a late lunch. I contributed a chicken salad with grapes, Patty and Judd brought a variety of appetizers, and, as I predicted, Grace and Helen brought dessert, sufficient cookies and lemon bars for six crews. Theirs were far better than the store-bought 'Chips Ahoy!' I had picked up at the last minute.

After lunch, I asked if anyone would like to go ashore. Grace said she would love to. Helen said that getting in and out of the dinghy would be too much for her. Hearing that, Patty and Judd said they would stay with Helen, but Grace and I should go. I looked at Grace to see if she was still interested, and she said, "Why don't we? I'd love to get some exercise." Alone time. I would have Grace to myself.

It was still overcast, and the island's bleakness added to a sense of remoteness even though we were not that far offshore from Boothbay. I rowed *Redhead's* dinghy to the stone pier, and we climbed off. Grace said, "I feel like we just landed off the coast of Ireland or Scotland. It's so desolate. Does anyone live here?"

"Yes and no. Most of it is in a land trust now. Part of it is privately owned, but no one lives here year-round. There are some caretakers in the summer, but that's it. At one point, it was thriving. Fishing, dairy farms. It was the first year-round English settlement in America. Before Plymouth."

"Before Plymouth?"

"Yes. At least twenty years, maybe more. It was little more than a fishing camp, but people were here the entire year."

"I didn't know that."

"Most people don't."

"How did Plymouth get the reputation as the first?"

"More people. It grew. And most of all, in the mid-eighteen-hundreds, they launched a publicity campaign that worked. They wanted tourists, even then. Shall we go?"

There are hiking trails on the island, so we left the stone pier and walked away from the harbor. I described the various trails to Grace, and we decided to take the 'pond loop.' It led to the freshwater pond that made the island habitable.

Grace asked me to tell her more about the island as we walked along. I had done a *Home Town Boy* piece on local islands, so I provided her with quite a bit of information about the island, from the early settlements to the wars with the Abenaki. When I told her three hundred or more people evacuated the mainland and came here to avoid being killed, she was surprised. "I have a hard time imagining that many people living here."

"That was in addition to the people already here. The island couldn't support that many. Fortunately, most of the refugees were able to return home before starvation set in." I continued my history lesson until we reached the pond.

When we got there, I took her hand and led her down an incline to some rocks where we could sit. I didn't want to let go of her hand and held it longer than was necessary. "They used to take ice from this pond and ship it as far as New York City."

I became tired of playing amateur historian. What I wanted to do was to get to know this woman sitting next to me. I wanted to hold her and kiss her. She must have sensed something in my silence after the history lesson.

"What are you thinking?" she asked.

Her question surprised me. I didn't know what to say. Finally, I did my best to recover and said, "I was thinking of going back up to the museum in Livermore Falls and wondering if you'd have lunch or dinner with me when I do."

"Just the two of us?"

"Yes. If you'd like to. Or with Helen, if you'd rather."

"I think Helen would probably prefer that it be just the two of us."

"True."

"Mike, can I ask you something?"

"Sure."

"I've had the sense that Patty is sizing me up. What have you told them about me?"

"Not sure what you mean."

"What did you say?"

"I told them I met you, and I'd like to get to know you better."

"That's all?"

"Well..."

"Please, Mike."

"I told them that you are a very interesting woman, and how wonderful it was that you had this great relationship with Helen, and ..." I stopped with the 'and,' unsure of what to say.

"And?"

"And I was attracted to you."

Grace sighed and said, "Wow." She picked up a pebble and tossed it into the pond. "Mike, I need to ask you something. Did you have any expectations about the two of us when you invited us down to Tír na nÓg?"

"No. No expectations."

"Maybe not expectations, but were you hoping something might happen between us?"

This woman was putting me on the spot, and I hated the conversation's direction. It was one of those choice points. Finally, I decided to be honest, or at least somewhat honest. "Possibly. I didn't know."

"Oh, Mike, I hope I haven't said anything that…"

"That what?"

"That led you to think…" She paused. "Mike, this is awkward. If I may use your words, you're a very interesting, attractive man. If I got to know you more, I am sure I would find you even more interesting and more attractive, but that's the problem. It's possible that I might wind up wanting to explore a relationship with you, and I don't want to do that."

"I don't understand."

"You live in Georgetown, and I live in Portsmouth. The one decent relationship I had since my divorce was doomed in large part because of distance. Your life is here. This is your home. Part of your family is moving here. I can't imagine you leaving Georgetown, especially now. Your life is here. Mine is in Portsmouth. It's where my family is, and my life—friends, colleagues, everything. I'm not going to leave that, and neither are you. At our age, I don't think a commuting relationship would work. I know it wouldn't work for me."

"Maybe we could just spend time together, meet halfway…"

"And get to know each other, and what, become frustrated? Mike, that's what I'm trying to tell you. I've done that, and it didn't work for me. I'm sorry. I don't want to try that again."

"Some people seem to do it. Maybe we could just do things together once in a while. I don't know, maybe meet halfway for dinner."

"You aren't making this easy for me. Please understand. Please, Mike, don't try to talk me into something that won't work for either one of us. I'm sorry. I am. Maybe we should head back to the others."

I said, "Okay." I was mad, disappointed, anxious. I wanted to get back to the boat fast, get back to Heron Cove fast, and see them off as quickly as possible. I wanted to be alone. I didn't want to talk to anyone. I wanted Hannah to be alive.

We didn't say anything to one another as we walked back to the boat. We got into the dinghy, and I rowed back. Before we got to the boat, Grace said, "I'm sorry, Mike. I am."

"I understand."

When we got on board, Helen asked, "How was it?"

Grace answered, "Desolate, but very interesting. Mike told me the history of the island." She then gave a synopsis of my lecture while Judd and I got us underway. Even though there was a breeze, I motored the *Redhead* back to the Cove. We were all a very adult, polite bunch. No one asked questions about the walk.

As we watched Grace and Helen drive away, Judd asked, "Did something happen? You and Grace seemed very quiet on the way back."

"She is not interested in pursuing a relationship because I live too far away."

"What exactly did she say?" Patty asked.

I recounted the conversation at the pond almost verbatim. When I finished, Judd said, "Sorry, buddy, I liked her."

Patty said, "I know you're disappointed, but I understand her reluctance. However, look on the bright side. This summer, you had an old flame pursue you, and a very nice woman tell you that if it weren't for the distance, she might welcome you into her bed."

"She didn't say that."

Patty smiled. "Michael Buckley. She did. Believe me. That's exactly what she said."

"I'll take your word for it, I guess."

Judd said, "We need to shove off. We're off to Portland to pick up my cousin Bill."

I went inside and saw a note from Wendy on the kitchen table: 'Publisher Judy called. She wants you to give her a call.'

I called Judy. "What's up?"

"Wondering if you were free for lunch tomorrow."

"Sure. Where do you want to meet?"

"I'm in Rockland for a couple of days. I know it's a drive for you, but would you mind Moody's? Good pies."

"No. That's fine."

Moody's is a diner, an almost one hundred-year-old diner. It sits on Route 1 in Waldoboro and has developed a cult following. I was a member of the cult, and Judy knew that. Famous for its pies, I knew I would finish lunch with a piece of walnut pie and take a four-berry pie home.

Judy was already there when I walked in. No one would ever accuse Judy Reddin of being warm. Brusque, at times to a fault, she is a decade younger than me and has made it clear to everyone who knows her that she will never retire.

With our order in and minimal pleasantries exchanged, she said, "I've read what you sent me and called several people. Bottom line, no one wants to publish a book about a strike that took place back in the eighties. So, if you want to get the book out, you'll have to publish it yourself."

"Oh."

"Yep. No takers, not even a nibble. I even called two agents, and they pretty well laughed at me."

"Shit."

"Tough business. So, self-publish. Cost you some money, but what the hell? You've put all this work in on it. Some people will buy it. Might make your money back. Here are the three self-publishing outfits that seem to do a good job." She handed me a piece of paper with the names. "Many of these places come and go, but these three have been around for a while. Or, if you're willing to do some of the legwork and the formatting yourself, you can put it up on Shamazon." As with most small publishers, Judy hated Amazon.

"I'm not going to learn all that stuff."

"Don't blame you. "Or, my company could work something out with you, but I'd have to charge you."

"You think this is the only way?"

"Yep. Now, I do want to talk to you about *Home Town Boy*. I've got an idea. I'd like to publish a collection of the pieces, call it *The Best of Home Town Boy*. They're all around a thousand words, right?"

"That was the limit. Sometimes a little more; sometimes less."

"And you did them for years."

"Just about every Friday."

"So, pull together fifty of them. We get it out next May in time for the summer. Local bookstores, general stores, B&Bs, gift shops like Moody's. You know, the Maine summer crowd. If they sell, we do a volume two the following summer. Not much work for you, writing's done, you just have to select them. We'll need a biography and an author's introduction. You on board?"

"You're sure about the other project?"

"Absolutely. Mike, be serious. This is an investigative piece about a small town in Maine and a strike that took place years ago. Even if you were a big name like Bob Woodward, I don't think anyone would want it."

"And I'm not."

"A Woodward? Sorry, my friend. Any name recognition you have left is for Maine-based novels, and you haven't published anything in forever. Feel free to do some hunting on your own. Send out query letters. I don't want it, and I don't know anybody who does. Them's the facts. You don't have to like 'em."

"Shit."

"You said that before. Now, *Home Town Boy*. We going to do this?"

"Yes, I suppose so."

"Good. Contract will be out to you in a couple of days."

The rest of lunch was Maine gossip. We both lamented the idea that Paul LePage could run for governor again and probably would. Wind farms, deep harbors, climate change, and the price of lobster were all examined.

Judy picked up the tab. I paid for the pie I was bringing home. I got in the car and left. Two days, two rejections.

In 1827 John Qunicy Adams commissioned the building of the Pemaquid Point Lighthouse. I decided to drive out to the lighthouse rather than go back to Georgetown. I know about the damned lighthouse because I'm a 'Maine Writer' who writes nice stories about Maine. Thanks a lot, Judy. No, I'm not Bob Woodward. Brilliant observation. So, no one gives a fuck about what happened to a town thirty years ago because of greedy bastards. I care, and I'm going to tell the god damned story. I'll go door to door peddling the damned book if I have to.

Then I switched to Grace. Yes, I live in Georgetown, and you live in Portsmouth. I can make it in an hour and a half. So what's the big deal? That's nothing. I'm not asking you to marry me. I then gave Nan her share of verbal abuse for opening me up to even thinking about being with someone.

By the time I reached the lighthouse, I had raged sufficiently to move to self-deprecation. I had taken the easy way. My fantasy about becoming a crusading investigative reporter was surrendered too easily. There were stories in Maine that were never told, and I could have told them. The *Point Reyes Light*, a weekly, for God's sake, won the Pulitzer for exposing Synanon. Maybe if I had done my job, I could have dug deeper than anyone else about the strike and truly investigated what took place. I could have gone beyond *what, when, where,* and *why* to the meaning it had in people's lives. How did it change them, not just how it changed their world, but how did it change them as people? On and on I went with 'What ifs.'

I reached the lighthouse and got out of the car. It was blustery. The tide was in, and every time a large wave hit the rocks spray shot up into the air. Foam gathered where the rocks met the land. I stood and watched for a few minutes, then walked back to the truck, but rather than get in, I leaned against it looking out at the water. I was doing it again, surrendering too quickly. I was taking inadequate work from the past and turning it into something it wasn't. I wanted to interview managers, was rebuffed and gave up—some investigative reporter. I knew what I had to do. I wasn't sure I could do it, but at least I knew the steps I had to take.

Grace was a different story. I didn't know what to do with her rejection but be disappointed. I was taken with her, really taken—a crush. I had developed a damned crush and been rejected. It was teenage hurt, and I found it difficult to let go of. I had seen possibilities; she hadn't. It was that simple. It was that painful. I had no idea what steps to take. There were no steps. She had made that crystal clear.

I got in the truck and started driving home. There was always food. The walnut pie had been good, and I could look forward to the four-berry pie for dinner.

February 14, 1986
HOME TOWN BOY by Michael Buckley

I was rescued today by my eleven-year-old daughter. She was sealing an envelope at breakfast, and I asked her what she was mailing. She shyly told me it was a valentine. I was tempted to ask her who it was for, but her shyness was sufficient for me to say nothing.

Valentine's Day was not a big deal in my family when I was growing up. Even the Catholic Church has downgraded the day associated with Saint Valentine, but florists, purveyors of greeting cards, and chocolatiers have certainly not followed suit, especially the chocolatiers. Like the Mayans, they, too, worship a cacao god, only his name is Saint Valentine. They should. Sixty million pounds of chocolate were sold this week; seventy-five percent of the buyers were men. Perhaps it's not surprising; chocolate has been considered an aphrodisiac for centuries.

But what is a man to do if your loved one does not like chocolate? An acquaintance of mine (we'll call him Norm) is married to a wonderful woman (we'll call her Claire). Claire is one of society's heroes. She works for the Maine Office of Child and Family Services. She's a field worker out on the front lines helping children suffering from neglect, abandonment, abuse, and sometimes hunger and homelessness. It's arduous work, taxing work with long, often unpredictable hours, and Claire does it well. She has never allowed herself to become hardened. It's not a job for Claire; it's a calling.

Maine is a poor state. We along the Mid-Coast have our share of poverty, but Claire works inland where it is very bad; almost twenty percent of the people are poor. Poverty like that is always a breeding ground for drug abuse, alcoholism, and family violence. That is the world in which children are often forgotten, victims of a world that doesn't see them.

Norm is a good husband and is proud of the work that Claire does. He also relishes her qualities as a mother to their three children and her companionship. He admits that he is still in the 'help out' mode of being a spousal partner. His mother never worked, so his expectations for marriage never included a wife who had a full-time job that was so demanding. Nevertheless, he tells me he tries.

For years, he told me, Valentine's Day perplexed him. He reported, "Claire had her sweet tooth removed with her wisdom teeth." So, he tried flowers, but she complained that they died too soon and she didn't have time to trim them and arrange them anyway. She was appreciative of the thought, she would say, but a card was enough. He didn't need to do anything more. So, for several years, he didn't. He took her at her word and always got her a card. However, feeling sub-par as a husband, he started buying multiple cards in various sizes with pop-ups, singing, and every other invention the card manufacturers came up with. Eventually, Claire told him enough was enough, and he was over doing it.

Two years ago, he came upon a solution that worked. He knew Claire loved potatoes, truly loved them, in any form: mashed, baked, roasted, fried. She was not fussy. He told her once, "Claire, your nickname ought to be 'spud.'" She was a Maine gal, after all. His Valentine's Day solution came to him in a bar on St. Patrick's Day where they were serving green beer.

So, when Valentine's Day rolled around, Norm knew what he would do, and he had his surprise all prepared. He told her before she left that morning that he would take care of dinner. That was not unusual, but it usually meant picking up a pizza. Claire liked pizza, so she thought, 'that's nice. I don't have to cook tonight.'

However, the table was set more formally than usual when she got home. A single card was waiting for her when she sat down. The kids were giggling; they were in on the secret. Finally, Norm brought out a dinner of steak, vegetables, and a covered dish he put in front of

Claire. Everyone was smiling. Their youngest said, "Open it, mommy. Open it." And she did. In front of her was a big dish of red mashed potatoes shaped like a heart.

It was a hit. There were leftovers, so Claire enjoyed her present for a couple of nights. I can't speak to whether or not mashed potatoes are an aphrodisiac, but I do know Norm enjoyed telling me the story of their best Valentine's Day ever.

Me? Inspired by my daughter, I did stop at the drugstore and got some chocolates for my wife on my way to work. She's not a Whitman Sampler person. So, I got her the biggest bag of Hershey's Kisses they had. She'd share if I asked, but I won't.

Chapter Sixty-Two: Hannah and Michael

When Michael met Hannah for the first time, she stood in his way. His mother had sent him to the Georgetown General Store to pick up milk and eggs for breakfast. Maude wanted a copy of the Boston Globe. Hannah was standing on the porch of the small store, right in front of the door. She was busy studying the bulletin board with announcements of upcoming events, items for sale, and business cards offering various services. Every general store in rural areas has one of these. Unfortunately, this bulletin board was placed in an awkward location. Michael couldn't get into the store without Hannah moving.

Michael's initial reaction was not favorable. Long, sun-bleached blond hair, headband, tie-dyed shirt, frayed jean shorts, no shoes, and no bra. Summer hippie. Might as well have been wearing a sign saying 'from away.'

"Excuse me," he said impatiently.

"Oh, sorry." She looked at him, smiled, and stepped back so he could go into the store.

That was it. When he came out, she was climbing into the driver's seat of an old Ford station wagon. A younger woman was sitting in the passenger seat waiting for her. Michael noticed the Massachusetts license plate as they drove out of the parking lot. He was right; she was 'from away.' She was sort of cute, though. He stood there watching the car drive away. He thought he saw the younger woman turn around and look in his direction.

When he got home and walked into the kitchen at Tír na nÓg, he put the bag with the eggs and milk on the table and handed the copy of the Boston Globe to his sister. Maude hoped there was an article about the music festival in Woodstock, New York. The television news the previous evening had shown a mile long line of cars trying to exit the highway to make it to the festival. Maude had changed her mind about going or not going a dozen times, but seeing the line of cars, she decided it was just for college kids. "I'm too old. They're a bunch of babies going," she said to Michael.

"Twenty-three. You're right. You're ancient," he said.

It was August 15th, 1969. Michael had been home for two months, and she had promised her parents she'd spend time with him. "He needs you, Maudie," her mother had said.

"What on earth does he need me for?"

"Just to be with him. You're memories. Good ones. You don't have to talk; just be with him."

On Saturday, the following night, Michael said he wanted to go into Bath after dinner. Maude said she would go with him, but she wanted to drive. She had just bought a very used 1959 Chevy Impala. It was bright red with large fins and too many miles, but she loved it. It was supposed to be a Florida car, meaning it didn't have any rust, and, most of all, the price was right. However, the real reason she wanted to do the driving was because the family was concerned about Michael's drinking. He already had one accident when he sideswiped the bridge over the Sasanoa River in Georgetown. Fortunately, his recent discharge from the Air Force provided the sheriff a rationale to give him a warning rather than a ticket.

Michael was having difficulty sleeping. Jack woke up every night when he heard his son moving around the house or he heard the truck leaving in the middle of the night. When Jack asked his son where he went, Michael would become irritable. He became angry at his mother during lunch one day when Peg asked him why he was drinking bourbon at noon. When his father talked to him about it afterward, Michael said, "What's the big deal?" Jack responded, "Talking like that to your mother is a big deal to me." Michael didn't say anything and walked out of the room. He apologized to Peg when she was cooking dinner that evening.

When Maude had arrived at Tír for her summer vacation, Peg and Jack told her about their concerns. Maude promised, "I'll stay close to him while I'm here. I'll keep him out of trouble."

Maude was surprised at how quiet her brother had become. She had to coax him to go sailing. No one had ever had to coax Michael Buckley to go sailing. During races at the yacht club, they exchanged roles. She skippered, and Michael crewed. When she asked him about it, he said, "Who gives a shit about winning a fucking boat race?" If an old friend from high school called, he never needed to be coaxed to go into Bath or Brunswick to drink.

While she was drying dishes one night, Maude said to her mother, "I wish Judd was here. I'm only his sister. He needs a friend. Have you talked to Judd?"

"No. They've got a new baby to worry about, and he's starting his own business."

"So?"

"I don't know if they've even talked the past couple of years. Remember, Michael hasn't been around during the summer since between his sophomore and junior year."

"I suppose."

"We're worried, Maude."

When brother and sister arrived at the Spindrift, it was crowded with local people and the summer folks who had driven into town to hear some music. A young pickup band was doing covers of the Beatles, the Rolling Stones, and Creedence Clearwater. It was noisy, crowded, and a few people were dancing. Michael and Maude said hello to people they knew and headed for the bar. Michael was busy looking around to see whom he knew when he collided with a young woman carrying four bottles of beer, two in each hand. He turned to apologize. It was the same woman he had asked to move out of the way at the general store the morning before. He shook his head, "It's you."

"Yes, me." She laughed, "This time, you're in my way."

"Sorry. You okay?"

"Yeah. No damage. What are the chances?"

"Pretty high. It's a small town."

"It is, isn't it? Well, I guess I'll see you around. My name's Hannah, by the way. I'd shake your hand, but as you can see…"

"Mike. You always a two-fisted drinker?"

"Always. Saves trips to the bar. Good to meet you, Mike."

Maude jumped in. "I'm Maude, the clumsy one's sister."

When Maude and Michael found seats at the bar, Maude asked, "Who was that?" Michael told her about the encounter in front of the general store.

"She's pretty. I did a hand check. No ring. You should ask her out."

"Yeah, right. I'm going to ask a hippie 'from away' to go out with me. Think again."

"I didn't notice you had anything hot going on this summer. Did I miss something? You're so judgmental. I didn't say marry her. I said to ask her out. Get you out of your funk. Have some fun, won't you? She might be fun. She's really cute. Just do it."

Michael didn't respond. They ordered beers. Maude said, "Pete Higgins. End of the bar."

"I'll be right back." Michael walked over to where Pete Higgins was sitting and put his arm around his shoulder, "Hey, stranger."

"Hey, Buck. Heard you were back. Welcome home. You made it. And in one piece."

"Yeah. Sorry about…"

"Yeah. Left something behind over there, but now I got a great bunch of one-legged jokes." Pete imitated a western drawl, "Partner, just call me Hopalong Higgins."

"Jesus, Pete."

"It's okay. Got to laugh, or I'd go nuts. Yeah, it sucks. I manage. Buy you a brewski?"

"No, but thanks. Maude's with me. We already ordered. Just wanted to say hello."

"Give me a call. Catch up."

"Yeah, I will."

Michael started to walk away. Pete said, "Everything's changed, Mike. Even this place. Look at all the fuckin' hippies in here. God damned peaceniks. If I thought I could get away with it, I'd take my leg off and use it to beat the shit out of them. Fuckin' commies."

Michael wasn't about to get into an argument with Pete, who was well on his way to getting drunk. Peg had told him that Pete had lost a leg and had turned into a drunk since he came home. Pete had been one the first to be drafted. The story was that his body had been in one piece for sixty-two days after he reached Vietnam.

No one in Bath would have referred to Pete as a strong person to begin with. Alcoholic father, over-stressed mother, no money, and a learning problem. Bad hand, Peg had said. "Pete's one of those people who was just dealt a bad hand." The corollary was that Michael had been dealt a good hand. "Luck of the draw," she would often say. Before Vietnam, Michael would have argued with her about her Irish fatalism. Not now. Vietnam was all about luck, who had it, and who didn't. Michael wasn't sure which luck was his.

Michael returned to Maude, who was talking to one of her girlfriends from high school. He stood next to them and looked over at the table where Hannah and her friends were laughing about something. One of her friends saw him looking in their direction and nodded to Hannah, who turned and looked at Michael. She smiled at him. He returned her smile and quickly turned away, embarrassed that she had caught him looking at her.

Maude and her friend were gossiping about the people they knew and what they were doing with their lives post-high school.

Commentaries were flying back and forth about the decisions that had been or were being made. Michael stared off into space.

Five minutes went by, and he heard loud voices from the end of the bar closest to the door. Michael turned and looked. A tall, skinny young man with black hair down to his shoulders had come into the Spindrift. He was wearing an army jacket with a big peace button on the left breast pocket.

A man whom Michael recognized as having been ahead of him in high school, Gary Ashland, started yelling, "Okay, everybody. I have a question for you. You all listen up now. This is a very serious question? Do you see this? Is this a man or a very skinny tall woman? Shout out your answers. Now, come on, let me hear you. Don't be bashful. What do you think? Look at that hair. I'm saying it's a girl?"

No one said anything. "Oh, come on." The young man continued to walk over to where Hannah and her friends were sitting. Hannah got up to get a chair from the table next to her that was set for four. Three people were sitting there. Hannah asked if she could take the empty chair. The man at the table said "no" and grabbed onto the chair so she couldn't pick it up. The woman sitting next to him said something, and he released his grip on it. Hannah picked it up and took it over to the table where she was sitting.

Ashland shouted again, "Don't be chicken-shit. Come on. Is this a man or woman?" No one said anything. Ashland walked over, caught up with the young man. "Alright, I'm going to find out. Maybe it's a wig. What do you think?" He grabbed the young man's hair and gave it a yank. The young man spun around and said, "Fuck off, asshole." Ashland said, "Oh, a big tough guy," and pushed him backward. The young man tripped, fell back against the table, slid off, and landed on top of Hannah. Both of them went sprawling to the floor. Ashland shouted, "You god-damned hippies don't belong here!" and started kicking at them, one foot after another. First, he'd kick the young man, and then he'd kick Hannah. Then the young man again, then Hannah.

Michael ran from where he was at the bar. He tackled Ashland, knocked him down, jumped on him, and started wailing on him, punch after punch, as fast as he could hit. One of Ashland's friends ran over and grabbed Michael from behind. Michael threw the person off. He got up and started kicking Ashland as hard as he could. Maude ran over and jumped on her brother's back. "Stop it; you'll kill him. Get off him." Michael stopped. Maude got off him and placed herself between Michael and Ashland. "Look at me, damn it. Look at me. Stop this!" With his sister now in his way and shouting at him, Michael's fury subsided.

The bartender came from behind the bar and shouted, "Get out of here. All of you, before I call the police."

Michael glanced down at Hannah, who was struggling to get up. "Come with me now," Maude screamed at Michael. She turned to the bartender, "We're going. We're going." She yanked on Michael's arm and led him towards the door and outside. Two of Ashland's friends came and helped Ashland get off the floor. He was screaming in pain, "Put me down. Don't move me."

Michael looked back and saw that Hannah, the young man, and their friends were also leaving. No one said anything. Everyone went to their cars. One of Ashland's friends came to the door. "Fuckin' cowards. You're going to pay for this, Buckley. Go run home to Georgetown." Michael started to turn around, but Maude got in front of him and pushed him towards her car.

"Think. For God's sake, think," she screamed at her brother. "They're not worth it. You're home. We've got you home." She was crying. Michael looked down at her and turned around. She opened the passenger door and pushed at him until he got in. Then, they left. They found themselves following Hannah and her friends as they sped away from Bath, across the bridge into Woolwich and onto Route 127, heading out to Georgetown.

"What on earth were you thinking?" Maude shouted as they crossed the bridge. Michael didn't say anything. "You could've killed that guy."

"He was kicking her. I stopped him. So what?"

"You did more than stop him. You lost it."

"So? You want me to ask him politely?"

Maude didn't know what to say next. Then, as they crossed the bridge onto the island of Georgetown, she saw that the other car was still in front of her. "Wonder where they're going?"

"Indian Point."

"How do you know?"

"Guess."

When they drove down the hill past the general store, the car in front of them started to slow down. Finally, they passed the gravel boat launch and took a right onto Indian Point Road.

"You were right."

"Follow them."

"No. We're going to home."

"Just follow them."

"Why?"

"Make sure they're alright."

"What're you going to do if they're not? We're going home."

"Maude, just follow them and stop arguing for christs sake." Maude turned right onto the Indian Point Road.

The road quickly turned to dirt, so Maude slowed down. It had not rained all week, and the dust from the car ahead of them made it easy to follow. The one-lane road twisted and went up and down small hills making speeding impossible. Woods gave way to marsh and back to woods. Occasionally they passed a house they could see from the road. Next, they passed a sign saying *Indian Point Association*. A couple of miles later, they passed a low point with access to a beach. A few cars were parked there. A quarter of a mile later, they took a right following the car's dust ahead of them.

Maude said, "They're heading for the Bay." Michael didn't say anything. "This is a bad idea. We should leave well enough alone."

"I told you. I just want to make sure they're okay."

"And I asked you, what are you going to do if they're not?"

Again, Michael didn't say anything. They followed the car into a driveway then up to a house that fronted on Sagadahoc Bay. The car they had been following was parked on the grass in front of the house. People got out. Seeing Michael and Maude arriving, they waited for them. After Maude parked the car and they got out, Hannah walked over to them. "Well, that was exciting, wasn't it? Thanks for getting that creep off us."

"You okay?" Michael asked.

"More scared than hurt."

Michael nodded in the direction of the young man with the long hair, "How about him?"

"Keith? I think he's okay. He says he is. Why did you follow us?"

"I asked him the same question," Maude said.

"Wanted to make sure you were okay."

"Let's go check in with Keith. My sister's fine. Just scared. Lilly, Keith's cousin, wasn't hit, so I'm sure she's fine. Look at your hands. They're bleeding. They're going to swell. Let's go inside. I'll get you some ice for them. Why don't you go and sit on the porch and get away from these mosquitoes? They're eating me alive."

"No thanks. We need to be getting on home," Maude said.

"No, we don't,' Michael said.

"Someone's probably already called Mom and Dad and told them what happened. They're going to be worried," Maude said.

"You can use our phone if you want," Hannah said. "Call them. Let them know where you are. If you want."

Michael said, "Thanks. Maude, you call. No details. Just tell them we're fine, that we met some people from Indian Point, and we're at their house."

"And if they ask questions?"

"Tell them it was no big deal, and we're fine. And stop acting like you're back in high school and you have to give them an explanation for everything."

"It's you they're worried about."

"Well, they shouldn't be."

"Yeah. Right."

The six of them went into the Turner's house. Hannah detoured into the kitchen to get ice. Maude followed her, and while Hannah put ice and water in a bowl, Maude called her parents and told them where they were. Introductions were made to Hannah and her sister Valerie's parents as they went through the living room where the two Turners were reading.

When they settled on the screened in porch, Valerie, Hannah's sister, offered to get them coffee or soft drinks. When she left with their order Keith said, "Can you believe those animals? Hadn't been for you, they weren't going to stop. I don't get it. What the hell is wrong with those people?"

Maude exploded, "I'm one of those people. I went to high school with those animals. One of 'those people' lost his leg in Vietnam. And it was one of 'those people' who kept you from having your head kicked in. My brother just got back from having two planes blown out from under him. Where were you? Some deferment because you were too chicken shit to go?"

"Maude, stop it," Michael said.

"I will not. I'm leaving. Come on, Mike. This arrogant asshole makes me want to puke." Maude got up and headed for the door leading out onto the lawn. Hannah went after her. Maude opened the door and ran outside onto the lawn, with Hannah following her.

"Maude, please don't go. Keith's mouthing off because he's still scared about what happened. I would really like you and Michael to stay. Please."

"Why? Give me one good reason why we should stay?"

"This may sound lame, but I want to get to know you and your brother."

Maude looked at her and didn't say anything. Finally, she said, "You're serious, aren't you? Why, because we're the locals? You want to brag that you know some of the locals. You..."

Hannah raised her pitch to meet Maude's. "No. Why on earth are you saying that. You don't know me. How about 'cause your brother just saved my butt. And, yes, in part, I want to know some people who live here because if things go well, I'm going to be one of them."

"What are you talking about?"

"I've applied for a job at BIW, and if I get it, well yeah, I'd like to have some friends here. I don't want to get off on the wrong foot with you and Mike because of something Keith said. I'm sorry about that. Please come back inside. You'll see. Keith is going to be apologizing all over the place. I'd really like you both to stay."

When Michael and Maude arrived home two hours later, Michael asked his father if he could use the *Redhead* on Monday. He and Maude had met some people from Indian Point. They'd like to take them for a sail. "No," Maude said, "You want to take Hannah for a sail, and you thought you had to invite all of us. You know I'm right."

668

Chapter Sixty-Three: Healing

The following morning it was chaos in the reception area at the Bath police station. Peg, Jack, and Maude Buckley were all there. Maude had insisted they drive over to Indian Point on the way to Bath to tell the Turners what had happened. All four Turners came, the parents as well as Hannah and Valerie. The cousins, Keith and Lilly, had been called and drove in to join the group. There was a communal expression of outrage that the sheriff arrested Michael because of the fight at the Spindrift. The last one to arrive was Nick Marcus. Marcus was the lawyer to whom the Buckleys turned whenever they needed a will, a contract, or a lease drawn up. Out of sight, Michael was being processed by the sheriff who had arrested him for aggravated assault, a felony charge that carried the potential for ten years of incarceration.

Marcus checked in with the desk officer and was ushered out of the reception area to confer with an assistant district attorney. He returned twenty-five minutes later. He asked Peg and Jack, "Do you know a Gary Ashland?"

They both said, "No."

"Okay. Let's talk for a few minutes; then I'm going in to see Michael as soon as they finish processing him." He led Jack and Peg to a small conference room next to the reception area. "Here's what's happened. This Ashland wound up in the hospital with a broken nose, some chipped teeth, and bruises on his legs and sides. He says Michael attacked him, beat him, and kicked him and that he had done nothing to provoke Michael."

Peg said, "That's nonsense. The man was beating up on some friends, and Michael stopped him. They're outside in the reception area right now. They'll tell you what happened."

"Well, apparently, some people are corroborating Ashland's version of the story."

Jack said, "Who? Ashland's friends? Of course, they would."

"Folks, there may be a problem. They say Michael kept beating and kicking Ashland after he was defenseless. If that's the case, the charge of aggravated assault may not be an over-reach. It will all be up to the district attorney."

Peg said, "Oh, no. Nick. This is ridiculous. You know Michael. What can you do to stop this?"

"I'm going to do whatever I can. Right now, I'm going back to see Michael where they're holding him. But, you both understand, Michael will be my client, assuming he wants me to help him. If he does, confidentiality will prevail, and I'll only be able to tell you what Michael wants me to."

Jack said, "Of course. Nick, my son just got home. He went through hell over there. He gets home, and this happens because of a lousy bar fight. This isn't right."

"Let me see what I can do."

Peg said, "Thank you."

Small town justice is relational. Michael 'Buck' Buckley had played football in high school. He went to Vietnam as a pilot. He was shot down and almost died. He had just returned home. Gary Ashland was a loudmouth and a bully who had been arrested for two misdemeanor offenses. 'Buck' was the hero stopping Ashland from kicking people who were down on the floor. Ashland had started it. After a brief hearing, Michael was released on his own recognizance. Bail was never discussed.

Nick Marcus told the assistant district attorney that Mr. Buckley would request a jury trial if their office wanted to proceed with the assault charge—simple or aggravated. In addition, Hannah Turner and Keith Underwood were prepared to file an assault complaint against Mr. Ashland. By the end of the week, after all of the stories were sorted out, the district attorney concluded that no charges were in order. Gary Ashland agreed to withdraw his complaint if Hannah

Turner and Keith Underwood did not file a complaint against him.

Peg and Jack said nothing to Michael about the incident that week. The sailing trip with the Turners was postponed. Michael did not know that his parents, his sister, and Nick Marcus met on Tuesday to discuss what happened. They all agreed that Michael was not the same since he returned from Vietnam. Maude told her parents and Marcus, "He wanted to kill Ashland. I mean it. He wasn't going to stop. I've never seen him like that. He scared me."

"He did what he had to do," Jack said.

"Dad, you should have seen him. He was totally out of control. I'm not kidding."

Nick said, "Jack, from the stories I heard from the others, Maude's correct. Unfortunately, it's possible that Michael may have a serious problem. My concern is that it could be more than a broken nose and some chipped teeth in the future. Imagine if one of his kicks had ruptured Ashland's spleen."

"But it didn't."

Peg didn't say anything and let the discussion continue. Then, finally, she said, "He needs help. I don't know how to help him." She looked at Jack. "Neither do you. None of us do."

Maude asked, "So what do we do?"

Peg said, "I'm going to go and talk to Father Greenley."

"Seriously, Peg? What's he going to do? Tell him to go to Mass every day?" Jack said.

"Stop it. I don't know, but he's known Michael since he was a boy, and Michael likes him."

"Mom, do you think Mike will talk to him about what's going on?" Maude asked.

"I don't know. I want to talk to Father Tom first. If he thinks talking to Michael will be useful, I'm going to ask him to call him. I think Michael will talk to Father Tom if I ask him to."

Nick said, "I don't know what the best thing is to do. This is out of my league, but I believe that doing nothing could be harmful to Michael and possibly others. Jack, this was close. Slightly different circumstances, and Michael could have been facing jail time. I'm curious; neither of you has said anything about his future now that he's home. I've been wondering, does he have any plans?"

Jack said, "Not really, and we haven't pressed. He's been using my dad's old lobster boat and doing some fishing. At times he talks about looking for a job in Boston, one of the newspapers. It's always been his dream."

"He's not ready to do that," Peg said.

Nick said, "Perhaps work of some kind would be good for him. What if he got a job at one of the local papers until he had a chance to sort things out a bit. Might keep him occupied."

"He could come live with me in Portland. Get a job there," Maude said.

"It's up to Michael. We're not going to plan his life for him. He's a grown man," Peg said.

Reverend Thomas Greenley had wanted to be a Navy chaplain when he graduated from the seminary, but his mother became ill, and he felt he could not be away from her for long periods of time. Moreover, he didn't trust his father as a caregiver. "He's a good man but a dreamer who hasn't known a practical idea in his entire life." His two sisters had their own families to tend to, so it fell to the oldest, the unmarried priest, to assume the responsibility. The bishop, however, permitted him to apply for a position as one of the chaplains at the Veteran's Administration Hospital in Augusta. The hospital turned him down because he had not been a chaplain in one of the services. Every other year he would reapply. Finally, it was on his fourth try that he was accepted and went on to serve ten years at the Augusta VA. He would have stayed, but Bishop Daniel Paul Leavey needed parish priests, so Father Thomas Greenley eventually became 'the boss' at St. Mary's in Bath. When Peg Buckley called him to tell him about Michael's 'situation,' the priest said, "I heard something about it, but it didn't sound serious. Is Michael okay? And how are you and Jack?"

Three days later, Michael was sitting in Father Tom's office in the parsonage. Behind the priest were prints of John Hilling's paintings depicting the 1854 anti-Catholic riot in Bath. He saw Michael looking at them. "Easy to forget. Just a little over a hundred years ago. Do you know the story, Michael?"

"Yes. My grandfather told me. They burned the Catholic church down."

"It was more than that. It was a mob. They hated Catholic immigrants. Irish and French. It was not a good time to be Catholic in Maine. Up in Ellsworth, they tarred and feathered a priest. They blamed Catholics for everything wrong in their lives, including a state prohibition law."

Michael didn't say anything. He just sat looking at the three pictures. Finally, the priest asked, "What do you see?"

"The fire. The people must have been terrified."

"Yes. I'm sure they were. Probably wondering if their homes were next or whether they were."

Michael continued to stare at the paintings. The priest didn't say anything. When Michael looked away, he turned and stared out the window. Eventually, the priest said, "From what your mother said, I expect you've seen more than your share of horrible things."

"You mean like fire?"

"And terror?"

"I saw a lot of fire."

Greenley didn't respond. He let Michael be. The only sound was an occasional car going by in front of the parsonage. The two men sat that way, neither moving. When Michael took his eyes away from the window, the priest asked, "How're you doing, Michael? Really?"

"What do you mean?"

"You know your mom called me. Your parents are worried about you. It's why I gave you a call. I did want to welcome you home, but I thought we might talk a bit as well."

"About?"

"Whatever's keeping you up at night. Anything that's on your mind."

"You doing therapy now?"

The priest laughed, "No. But I talked to many vets when I was chaplain at the VA. Coming home isn't always easy."

It is more than an hour's drive from the Convey Farm in Georgetown to the Veteran's Administration hospital in Augusta, Maine. The hospital served veterans from WWI, WWII, Korea, and, more recently, Vietnam. In addition to the physical ailments and injuries of the veterans, the staff also treated the other damages of war: shell shock, battle fatigue, war neurosis. Each war gave a different name to the internal assault on the psyche. The priest had discussed this with Michael. Michael had dismissed it during their first meeting, but the sleepless nights continued, as did the nightmares. When he returned to the priest's office a week later, he asked if anything could be done about the night terrors. The priest said he didn't know for sure, but he thought it might be helpful for Michael to talk to someone who knew more than he did. He offered to drive Michael to Augusta if he made an appointment. Michael turned the offer down but said he would make an appointment.

In 1969 when Michael first visited the VA in Augusta, post-traumatic stress disorder was not recognized by the psychiatric profession. That didn't occur until 1980, and it wasn't until 1989 that the VA began to treat it. The doctor Michael met during his first visit assigned him the diagnosis of 'Adjustment Reaction to Adult Life.'

Unfortunately, the diagnosis was given to only three categories of trauma: Unwanted pregnancy with suicidal ideation, fear associated with military combat, and Ganser Syndrome, where a patient presented with fictitious ailments in response to a traumatic life event. Michael was sent to a psychiatrist who recommended psychotherapy with a social worker and an antianxiety medication, a relatively new drug called Valium.

When Father Greenley called to find out how the visit went, Michael told him about the Valium and his response to it. "I feel out of it, like I'm in another world. I hate it."

"Is it at least helping you sleep at night? What about the nightmares?"

"I sleep better, but I don't feel rested the next day. I walk around in a daze." Michael didn't say anything about the nightmares, and the priest didn't ask.

"Maybe it's not a good choice for you. Did they suggest any other options?"

"Just talking to a social worker. He gave me a name, but what's she going to be able to do?"

"Have you met with her yet?"

"No. I have an appointment next week."

"Why don't you keep it? Sort of like an experiment. Don't make any judgments until after you see her. Maybe give it three or four times and then evaluate whether or not you think it helps."

"Help with what? Talking to her is going to help me sleep so I can get off this damn Valium?"

"I don't know, Michael. What do you have to lose?"

When he got off the phone with the priest, Michael asked his mother, "Why does everyone think there's something wrong with me?"

"Oh, darling. You've been through hell. Of course it's left its mark. How could it not? At least you're starting to sleep at night with that medication they gave you."

"Yeah, and I'm a zombie during the day."

Hannah Turner and Michael Buckley exchanged five phone calls in late August and September. On the first, Michael called her to reschedule their sail on the *Redhead*. On the second, the day after the sail, she called to thank him for a beautiful day on the boat. On the third, Michael called her, at Maude's urging, to ask her about the job she had applied for. She said, "No word yet." On that call, she asked him if he had started to look around. He said he had not, but he was going to start. During the fourth call, Hannah asked if he had found anything he was interested in. Again, he said he had not. He didn't tell her that he hadn't started to look. Finally, Hannah called Michael at the end of September to tell him that she got the position at Bath Iron Works, when she would start, and wondered if he knew of any places to rent. This was their fifth phone conversation since the charges against Michael had been dropped. Hannah was moving to Bath.

Against his mother's wishes, Michael stopped taking the Valium he had been prescribed. Against his priest's advice, he stopped seeing the social worker in Augusta. He needed to get a job. Hannah had one, and she'd be working in Bath.

The *Bath Daily Times* was started in the 1800s. It was the newspaper Michael had grown up with. If Hannah was going to be in Bath, then the Daily Times seemed like a good place to begin looking for his first paid job as a journalist. Michael hadn't paid attention to any newspapers since he had been discharged. He knew one came to the house. When he dug one out of the basket next to his father's chair, he was surprised to see the masthead, *The Times Record*. His *Times*, the *Bath Daily Times*, had merged with the *Brunswick Record* in 1967 while he was in Vietnam. Now, Bath had no newspaper to call its own. He didn't know why, but he started tearing up the paper he was holding. It was a travesty. Brunswick was not Bath. He had competed against Brunswick in football. Brunswick was a college town. It was snooty. Even though he lived in Georgetown, Bath was also his town. His family had a home there. That's where his grandparents had lived, where he had gone to high school, and now where Hannah was going to work. Bath had to have its own newspaper. He kept tearing it up. He felt his rage grow. He threw down what was left of the paper and rushed out of the house. He started to run. He ran away from the farm towards Bay Point and the Kennebec River. He ran as fast as he could for a mile, and then, winded, he slowed into a steady jog. After two miles, he started to walk. He alternated between walking and jogging. With the short, steep hills, it was hard. He thought about turning back, but someplace along the way, he decided he was going to the end of the road, all the way to the Kennebec, to Bay Point. He kept walking and running until he reached the cluster of houses and the docks at the river's edge. He climbed down the river bank and sat on a boulder at the water's edge. The tide was going out. He watched it, staring at the ducks riding the tide out towards the Gulf of Maine. The ducks didn't move, content to let the tide carry them. He thought about jumping in and joining them.

    He heard noises behind him as people came and went in cars and trucks. He got up and climbed back up to the road an hour later. His legs were sore. He didn't want to walk the three miles to get home. He saw a woman climbing into a truck and approached her. "You going into town? I was wondering if I might get a lift?"

    "Mike? It's me, Julie Hoster's Mom. Sure, hop in."

    Then the woman asked, "How'd you get down here?"

    "Needed some exercise, so I ran and then walked. Afraid I bit off more than I could chew. I know it's only a couple of miles to get home, but…."

    "It's more than a couple of miles. That's a long way to come on foot. And you ran. On those hills."

"I walked some of it."

"Even so, you must be beat. Walking back. Could seem like forever when you're tired. And those hills. More up than down getting home. They'd feel like mountains."

"You're right. I really appreciate the ride."

"Glad I could help."

A week later Michael found a job, three days a week, at the *Boothbay Register* in nearby Boothbay Harbor. The editor was more impressed with Michael having recently returned from Vietnam than with his journalism credentials from Boston University. He told Michael, "Vets get preference here, just like the post office." Michael refrained from sharing his thoughts about that until he got into his mother's car to drive home. As he drove out of the parking lot he said, "Fuck you."

"It's not much of a job," he told his mother. I'll be covering meetings for the most part, but at least I'll be writing."

Chapter Sixty-Four: Ms. Fix It

When it came to her son, Peg divided time into BH and AH: 'Before Hannah' and 'After Hannah.'

'After Hannah' began precisely on October 5th, 1969. That was the day Hannah Turner of Brookline, Massachusetts, moved into a small garage apartment in Bath, Maine. Michael Buckley helped her to move in. The young electrical engineer began work at Bath Iron Works the next day when she joined an 'all boys' department and changed it forever.

Hannah used to say that she became an engineer because she liked to fix things. She liked problem-solving, figuring things out. Although her father was a physicist, Hannah said she was more like her mathematics teacher mother, where two plus two did equal four, and you didn't have to explore theoretical possibilities the way her father did. She liked certainty and control.

She struggled with this in the Peace Corps. The people she worked with in a small village in Honduras often didn't 'fix things' when the solutions were obvious to Hannah. It was well into her first year, and a new supervisor, before she fully understood what she had been taught during her training: cultural differences are fundamental and powerful. She told everybody about the day, the very day, it finally made sense to her.

She watched several of the village women go together to the river to wash clothes. It was a relatively long walk, and the baskets they carried were awkward to manage along the trail. It would have been much easier for them to get water from the recently dug well and do the washing in tubs at home. But they didn't.

Using her fast-tracked Spanish language immersion from her training, Hannah asked one of the women about it. Of course, Spanish in a Honduran village is different from Spanish on a college campus, but eventually, an understanding was reached. "Friends are at the river," the woman said.

"But it is easier at your home," Hannah explained.

"No socializer," the woman responded.

"Más eficiente a casa," Hannah said.

"No. Amigas femeninas."

Eficiencia versus time with amigas femeninas. Hannah 'concluida' she had made the right choice of career. She would not have been a good social worker or psychotherapist.

This was the first of several Peace Corps experiences that moderated but did not erase her "fix it" orientation. She liked plans and predictability. She liked Michael Buckley a great deal, but his moods were unpredictable, his flashes of anger scared her, and she hurt for him when his night terrors raised their head. Hannah Turner wanted to 'fix' Michael. She deemed him worth fixing. She told her parents and Valerie that she was going to marry him. "This is a good man. He's perfect for me." She would then go about listing Michael's husband qualifications. He came from a good family; he was down to earth, intelligent, and cared about people. Unsaid to her parents, she said in confidence to Valerie, 'He's not a stuffy academic, and he's sexy as hell."

On moving day, after all the boxes were carried up the stairs, into the apartment, and her parents left, Hannah went about giving orders as Michael helped her to unpack. She had taken pictures when she first saw the apartment and had drawn-out measurements for every inch of the space. She knew where every piece of hand-me-down furniture was to go. She knew which drawer the kitchen cutlery would go in and had purchased a perfectly sized garbage pail to go under the sink. There was no experimenting and trying things out in different places. Michael told Maude, "She never once said, 'Let's try it here.' This woman is amazing." Maude shook her head and laughed, "You got it bad, brother."

When they were sufficiently unpacked to where the apartment

was livable, it was seven o'clock in the evening. Michael said, "Let's go get something to eat. Where'd you like to go?"

"The Spindrift," Hannah said.

"The Spindrift? Are you serious?"

"Yes, the Spindrift. Bath is now my town, and I'm going to go anywhere I damned well feel like."

"Okay, if you say so. The Spindrift."

The Spindrift was practically empty when they arrived. They got a table away from the television set. It was Sunday evening, so there was no live music, and no one had fed dimes or quarters into the big Wurlitzer Statesman jukebox. The bartender came over with menus. He recognized Michael and Hannah but said nothing about their previous visit. "What would you like to drink?"

"Bourbon on the rocks."

"Pabst."

Once they ordered, Hannah said, "Drinking the hard stuff, huh?" Michael didn't say anything. "Not judging. Just an observation. I'm going to feed the machine. My kind of music, if they have it on their box."

They did. She put in a quarter for three songs: 'Aquarius,' 'Hair,' and 'Spinning Wheel.' When she returned to the table Michael asked her, "What'd you play?" She told him. "They had those?"

"Yep."

"You're probably the first one who's ever played them here."

"I doubt it."

"You plan on taking over the town?"

"No. But I live here, now. Do you mind?"

"No. I was just teasing. I'm glad you're here."

"What kind of music do you like?"

"Sort of everything. Not opera."

"Have you ever been to one?"

"No."

"Well, we'll have to remedy that. Probably have to do that in Boston, though."

On the phone that night, Hannah told her sister, "It was so weird. It was like a first date, but it wasn't. I don't know how to explain it. Emotionally it didn't feel like a first date, but we don't know much about each other. We spent hours filling in all sorts of spaces. It was like this giant crossword puzzle we were completing."

"So, what happened?"

"You're not going to believe it. I don't know how to explain it. But, again, it was just bizarre. We kept talking until the bartender kicked us out around ten. When we got back to my apartment, I was ready for him to spend the night, just to sleep with him. How's that for being weird? Here's this sexy guy I really like, and I didn't want to have sex with him. But I didn't want him to go home. I wanted him to spend the night. He's the one who said he should go home because I was starting a new job the next day and needed my sleep. What kind of guy does that?"

"Did he kiss you good night?"

"Yes."

"A real kiss?"

"Yeah. A very real kiss. There was no question we were going to kiss. It was like neither one of us could imagine not kissing."

"Oh, wow. Do you think you love him?"

"Yeah. Possibly. Maybe a lot more than possibly."

"So, what's next?"

"I've offered to go help him on the farm next weekend. His parents are going to Portland for a couple of days, so he has farm duty."

"So, you're spending the weekend together."

"Yeah, but it's not like we're going away to some romantic inn or something."

"So, you're spending the weekend on the farm together because you have to help him do farm things, whatever they are?"

"You're making fun of me."

They did make love that first night on the farm, but Michael didn't want to sleep together. "I don't sleep well," he said. "I toss and turn and sometimes have to get up. I don't want to wake you up."

"That's okay. I don't mind."

"Sometimes, I have nightmares. They can be pretty vivid."

"I do, too, sometimes."

"Hannah, trust me. It's not a good idea."

She relented, and it was at three o'clock in the morning on October 12th when Hannah realized something was very wrong. Michael was screaming. She had never heard anything like it before. She left Peg and Jack's bedroom where they had made love and where she was sleeping. She rushed into Michael's room. He wasn't there. She went downstairs and saw him sitting on the couch in the dark. He was crying, slapping his head, and muttering to himself, "What's wrong with me?"

She went over and climbed up onto the couch behind him, slid down, took his hands, pulled them away from his head, and wrapped her arms around him. She held him tight, as tight as she could. Slowly his crying stopped. That night is when the actual storytelling began.

She called her mother Monday night. After she told her what had happened, her mother asked, "What are you getting yourself into? It sounds like that young man has issues that you're not equipped to handle, and you shouldn't have to." Hannah told her about Father Greenley, the Valium, and the social worker.

Her mother said, "If he doesn't want to get help, there's nothing…."

"Yes, Mom, I can. I can do something. I don't know what, but I know I can do something. He's worth it, Mom. He's really worth it."

Her mother knew not to argue with her and said, "You've just started a new job. Don't forget to take care of yourself."

Where Peg Buckley's first instinct was to turn to her priest, Hannah Turner's was to turn to a college or university. So, she found Dr. William Murphy at Bowdoin College in Brunswick. He was new to Bowdoin. He had received his degree in clinical psychology from Harvard and done his internship at St. Elizabeth's Hospital in Washington, D.C. After his internship, he taught for three years at Georgetown University, where he worked part-time at the university counseling center. Eventually, he and his wife decided they wanted a small town and a small college. Bowdoin was perfect for them. He planned to start a small private practice in addition to teaching but hadn't done anything yet to make that happen when Hannah tracked him down.

Hannah didn't tell Michael she was going to meet with Murphy. She was in her 'fix it' mode, and she wasn't going to risk sending Michael on a mission that had no chance of success. He had been through enough of those already. She had listened to this man who consumed her attention. She had listened very carefully and backed off when he resisted answering questions. She had to meet Murphy first and assure herself that he would be a good match for Michael. Based on her phone call with Murphy, she knew he wasn't much older than Michael, and Murphy was an Irish name, but could Michael relate to an academic psychotherapist? Hannah had to meet Murphy to assess his suitability.

Murphy said that it would be best if she encouraged Michael to see him. When she described Michael's history and his experience at the VA, Murphy asked her what she hoped to accomplish by her coming to see him.

"I need help helping him. I don't know what to do. I don't know what to do when he wakes up in the middle of the night screaming or gets so angry over nothing. Then, of course, he apologizes, and I know he doesn't want to do it, but it's hard to live with, and it's unpredictable. That's the worst part." Reluctant at first, Murphy eventually agreed to meet with her without Michael.

When Hannah first met with Murphy, she walked in with three pages of notes and discussed Michael as though she were a physician making a grand rounds presentation. Murphy listened politely before asking, "How long have you known this man?"

When she said, "Really only a couple of months," Murphy said, "You seem to care about him a great deal." Ten minutes later, Hannah was in tears about the torment this man she loved was suffering. When she left Murphy's office, she had new notes about things she could do and say that might help Michael. She also had notes about what she might say to encourage Michael to see Murphy. William Murphy, PhD bought a 'do not disturb' sign for his office door a week later. Michael was his first patient.

Michael liked Bill Murphy's informality. He didn't sit behind a desk as the psychiatrist had at the VA. Instead, he offered Michael coffee and sat opposite him across a small coffee table. He leveled with Michael, "This may take some time. Let's start with what's bothering you most, and we'll go from there."

Murphy hunted around Brunswick and found a psychiatrist willing to work with him on Michael's case, Dr, Stuart Price. Soon they had a plan. Michael would start the Valium again at night, begin with a low dose, and continue to increase it until the night terrors eased off and he didn't feel sluggish during the day. Michael came to accept the idea that they were trying to find an optimal dose, but it wouldn't be perfect. He also liked the idea that they would slowly decrease it if things seemed to be getting better. Murphy used the word 'optimal,' as did the psychiatrist. Michael liked the plan; so did Hannah, who bought a small pill organizer for her boyfriend.

Michael also started spending more time at Hannah's apartment. At first Peg objected, "They're not married. They should wait." Jack told her to leave it alone. When she complained about it to Father Tom, she was surprised when the priest said, "God's love works in ways we don't always understand, Peg. Michael needs love, and he's receiving it. You like this young woman. Do you believe she wants the best for Michael?"

"Oh, yes, but...."

"I know they aren't married, they're having sex, and that bothers you. I understand. You think they should wait until they get married."

"Yes."

"Do you think you can have any influence over what they do?"

"No, but..."

Acceptance came slowly to Peg, but her awareness of Hannah's goodness and love for her son coupled with Father Tom's reluctance to condemn them eased the transition.

Murphy asked the Buckleys, all of them, to come in for a session with Michael. It took some convincing, but they agreed. Maude was the most eager; Jack was the most resistant. Hannah was not invited. She wasn't family yet. Michael objected. Murphy had Hannah come in for a separate session with Michael. Hannah did not fully appreciate Murphy's attempt to explain healthy boundaries.

One consequence of the two sessions with Hannah was the attention paid to Michael's irritability and outbursts of anger. They had been decreasing but were still present. In the session following the second one with Hannah, Michael described the episode when he ripped up a copy of the newspaper and ran down Bay Point Road to the Kennebec. They spent time dissecting what Michael thought and felt during the run, his exhaustion at the end, the recognition that he needed help to get back home, and his asking for it. Murphy repeated the phrase 'help to get home' several times during the session. The analysis of his run to the river and the good samaritan driving him home also yielded unexpected benefits. Michael did not feel as irritable the next day and started looking for a job which led to part-time work at the Boothbay Register. Murphy suggested that running might become part of his treatment. When he told Hannah, she said, "I'm going to come with you."

"Have you ever been a runner?"

"No, but I'll start. I need to get some exercise anyway. Get out of my work head."

According to Hannah, the newly developed running regimen, only feasible in the morning, was also a good reason for Michael to spend more nights at the apartment in Bath. In addition, it shortened his three days a week commute to the newspaper office in Boothbay. Michael offered his mother a multitude of reasons, and by Thanksgiving, he was living in Bath full-time but was available to help Peg out when Jack was away on a business trip.

Bill Murphy canceled his appointment with Michael Thanksgiving week because he and his family were traveling to be with his wife's family in New Jersey for the holidays. Hannah asked Michael to join her with her family in Brookline for the long weekend. It was his first Thanksgiving home, though, and Michael wanted to spend it with his family in Georgetown. He asked Hannah to join him there. She declined. "I haven't seen my family in over a month," was her response to his invitation.

Peg's family came up from Boston for the long weekend. On Friday morning, Peg's brother Tommy was helping his sister with breakfast in the kitchen and holding forth about the absurdity of sending young Black men to fight in Vietnam when Michael entered the room. When Michael came in, Peg motioned to Tommy to keep quiet, but Michael had already heard the conversation that was taking place. Tommy turned to Michael and asked, "What do you think, Mike? You were there."

"I try not to think about it."

"Do you think people should refuse to go, burn their draft cards, protest this fuckin' war? I do."

Peg said, "Can we drop it?"

Michael said, "Why drop it? Because Michael's here and he's all fucked up because he went to Vietnam and got his ass blown off? Because he's sick in the head, and you'd better walk on eggshells when he's around because he might blow up and rip your face off? Is that it, Mom? Drop it? Well, here's what I think, Tommy. It's a god-damned cluster fuck, and if I hadn't been so fucking gung-ho and stupid, I never would have signed up for ROTC, and if my name came up now, I'd be heading for Canada. That's what I think." I'm going for a run so you two can figure out what to do about the war. You can tell me all about it when I get back."

When he returned, he asked his father if he could borrow the truck. Jack told him sure and asked him where he was going. "Brookline. To see Hannah. I should have gone there in the first place."

For the next three weeks, Michael and his parents saw Murphy together. In and out of the sessions, they talked. Talk that was hard work; talk that feels like it will never end; talk that consumes and leaves the soul exhausted. Slowly, ever so slowly, a new normal emerged. Innocence, they came to accept, would never return. As his son began to reveal his woundedness, Jack discovered and uncovered the scabs that had formed over his years flying in the Aleutians two wars ago. Father and son began to talk to one another in a way they never had. As they talked, Michael began to see his mother differently. He understood her protectiveness and began to tease her for it when it became intrusive. It was hard, though, hard on all of them. Murphy saw Michael and his parents three times. Maude came once. Murphy also saw Michael with Hannah. When Hannah complained about being excluded from the family meetings, Murphy reminded her that some of the issues had a history that she was not part of, and those issues needed to be addressed by those involved. When Hannah said to Michael, "I don't want them to hurt you," he said, "They wouldn't dare. They'd have to face you."

Hannah and Michael started to spend weekends at the farm. With Maude in Portland, Hannah slept in Maude's room. They accepted that Peg would not bend on the sleeping arrangements, and no one asked her to. A new rhythm developed. During the week, Michael was in Bath with Hannah. On the weekends, the young couple was in Georgetown.

Christmas was a major logistical and emotional set of negotiations. Hannah was the negotiator with both families. Michael wondered at her persistence and skill. When the plans were finalized, she would spend Christmas Eve in Brookline with her family, and on Christmas Day, the Turners would join the Buckley family in Georgetown.

When Christmas Day arrived, Michael and Hannah's parents and Tommy and his family were surprised. After pie orders were taken and delivered, the kid sisters, Maude and Valerie, giggled and asked to be excused. They didn't wait for a response. They just got up and left the table. Finally, Jack asked, "What's with those two?" Michael and Hannah didn't say anything. Maude and Valerie returned a few minutes later and stood in the doorway between the kitchen and the dining room. They looked at one another, leaned over, and started drumming on their knees."

With that, Michael and Hannah stood up. No one was surprised at what they had to say. When they finished, Maude and Valerie reached behind them and picked up two open bottles of champagne.

Chapter Sixty-Five: The Bugle Blows

Laureen Cousins had worked for her father, Oliver, since she graduated from Barnard College in 1926. When he passed away in 1969, he also passed ownership of his eight newspapers to his never-married daughter rather than her brothers. Disengaged from the business, 'the boys' had little interest in journalism and certainly no interest in the work of running a group of weekly and bi-weekly newspapers in towns and small cities in Maine and New Hampshire. Boston's financial district was far more exciting, and 'the boys' made far too much money to consider changing careers.

Laureen had encouraged her father to expand the business. He had told her she could do whatever she wanted when she was the boss. So, she made plans to do precisely that. She had her eye on several possibilities in the three Northeast states: Maine, New Hampshire, and Vermont when he died. She went state by state and examined every town or city that had lost its daily through mergers, acquisitions, or had failed. Laureen believed each loss brought about a concomitant loss of local identity, and people didn't like it.

She planned to call each of her papers the *Bugle* because her grandfather was a bugler in WWI. She had adored him. She liked the metaphor of the bugle blowing to alert the town members and get their attention. The logo incorporating a bugle graphic and the city's name was easy to imagine. Each town would have its own *Bugle*. Its *Bugle* would let the world know that the city or town existed. Because the merger with the Bath paper was fairly recent, Bath was second on her list.

Laureen did her due diligence. She visited Bath several times and talked to potential advertisers, local politicians, school board members, and the clergy. They always knew what was going on in a small city. When she visited him, Father Thomas Greenley suggested she contact Michael Buckley, who had recently returned from Vietnam.

When the *Bath Bugle* launched in January 1970, it was bi-weekly, every Tuesday and Friday. Michael Buckley was one of the new paper's two reporters. With the permission of Ms. Cousins, Michael continued to work for the Boothbay Register on a part-time basis. He also began to write occasional articles for small area magazines and newsletters. He wasn't earning a great deal of money, but he was able to buy a used 1965 Ford Pick-up with a V-8 engine within a couple of months. When Hannah asked him why he needed a pick-up rather than a car and why such a big engine to boot, Michael answered, "Because I'm a reporter in Maine talking to Maine people."

"What difference does that make?" she asked.

"Oh, wow, girl. You are sooo 'from away.'"

The truck's previous owner had removed his rifle rack from the truck's rear window, so Michael picked up a second-hand one from a junkyard. Hannah asked him if the rack meant he was traveling incognito as a hunter when he installed it. He said, "You just wait 'til deer season."

Their engagement was compressed, a mere four-and-one-half months. They continued filling in the crossword puzzle of history and dreams that they started at the Spindrift the night Michael helped Hannah move into her apartment. Hannah would make up lists of things she wanted to know about her fiancée and his family. When Michael didn't have a list, she would just answer the list of questions he should have had. Eventually, with histories complete, Hannah moved them to the narrative they would write as a couple. Children were immediately agreed upon; the number was to be negotiated as long as it was at least two. When she mentioned 'four' over dinner one night, Michael said, " You're joking."

"No."

"No?"

"As in, 'no,' I'm not joking."

"How on earth do you plan on paying for four kids?"

"I don't. You're going to write the great American novel and handle that."

"Thanks a lot."

"I have faith in you."

"Jesus, Hannah."

"Mary and Joseph. See. I'm learning your mother's sayings."

When Hannah pointed out that they had yet to fill in the crossword square marked religion, the discussion was completed in fifteen minutes. Hannah's family members were nominal Congregationalists. In the Buckley family, Peg was very Irish Catholic; Jack was somewhat Irish Catholic, Michael was Irish and occasionally Catholic. Maude was Irish.

They agreed that being married in a Catholic church was necessary to maintain peace and tranquility with Peg, but, Hannah said, only if Father Tom could marry them. She had come to respect the priest whose understanding and compassion continued to support her husband-to-be. She also found the priest to be un-priest-like, even un-minister-like.

Father Tom got permission from the pastor of St. Mary of the Assumption in Brookline to marry the young couple. They were married on May 9th, 1970. His friend and summer neighbor since childhood, Judd Fishman, was Michael's best man; Valerie was her sister's maid of honor. Maude was a bridesmaid.

During the rehearsal dinner at the Union Oyster House, Jack asked everyone not to talk about current events for the entire weekend. "It's a time to celebrate these two. Let us not get distracted by that. He wasn't entirely successful in his admonition. The previous Monday, the Ohio National Guard had killed four students and wounded nine others at Kent State University. The day before their wedding, Friday, in New York City, five hundred construction workers attacked students from Pace University who were protesting the war in Vietnam. On the day they got married, in Washington, D.C., one hundred thousand people marched against the war. At brunch, Sunday morning, Jack Buckley and Charles Turner sat next to one another. Charles said to Jack, "What a week to get married."

"You're not superstitious, are you?"

"No, I just wish the world could have given them a better send-off."

Neither Michael nor Hannah had worked long enough at their respective jobs to be eligible for vacation time, so they asked for three days of leave without pay for their honeymoon. Hannah's father's colleague and close friend, Bernard Edwards, owned a modest home on a bluff in Wellfleet on Cape Cod. Since it was before the summer rental season, Edwards gave them the keys to the house as a wedding present. He and his wife also stocked the house with food and drink that the young couple was fond of, according to phone calls with the respective parents. Since it was still May, Edwards ensured an ample supply of seasoned firewood.

It was still chilly, but they walked Marconi Beach, huddled in a blanket one evening, and watched the sun set. Michael wrote in the sand, 'The Buckleys were here.' Hannah added, 'And they will return.' They chased one another. They dared one another to go into the cold water. Michael did, yelped, and ran right out. Hannah refused and ran away from her husband, who was dripping cold water. He caught her. "Warm me up." She held him.

June, July, and August, they spent weekends at Tír na nÓg. Because of his status as an Air Force Pilot who had been to battle, Michael provided the Erascohegan Yacht Club members a degree of shared pride. He had grown up here, they reminded one another. Older male members told him stories of their wars. Their wives doted on him and his new bride. At the other end of the island, Indian Pointers welcomed Hannah's war hero in subdued tones and wanted Hannah to tell them what it was like to live in Georgetown in the winter. She reminded them that she lived in Bath, and it was quite civilized.

Their jobs were new to each of them. It took months before the men in Hannah's department recognized that she could keep up with them. In October and November, they teased her. In December, they ignored her. Finally, they invited her to join them for Friday after-work beers in January. By the time she and Michael got married in May, they had all pitched in to buy a wedding present.

Michael overwrote every piece he was assigned during his first few weeks at the *Boothbay Register*. The editor, Joseph Broder, was old enough to be Michael's grandfather and enjoyed taking the young Air Force veteran into his office and going over the copy that Michael submitted. He kept asking Michael, "What would your father or mother want to know about this event or this person?" What's important to them?" Slowly at first, but with increased awareness, Michael learned to differentiate between his own interests and those of the readers of the *Boothbay Register*. By the time he started to work at the *Bath Bugle*, he felt he was beginning to understand the small city newspaper business.

The first editor of the *Bugle* was younger than Michael. He had been the assistant editor of one of the Cousins' papers in New Hampshire, a weekly with a paid circulation of just over three thousand. Raymond Ryan wanted desperately to make his mark in Bath. He wanted to win awards. He wanted a bigger paper, fast. Ryan insisted everyone call him by his single initial nickname: 'R.' R wanted flash, excitement. "Blow that bugle, Buckley," he would say to Michael. "Wake this town up. That's what I want you to do. Wake this town up. They need some excitement, and we're going to give it to them."

Hannah and Michael laughed about their jobs. They laughed about their lives. As night approached, Michael gradually stopped worrying whether or not he would have nightmares. His angry flashes dissipated to irritation, followed by quick apologies. He continued to see Bill Murphy, and together they developed ways of coping with memories. Memories became matter for sessions in Murphy's office. Michael learned to delay thinking about them when they popped up at other times because he knew he would get to them. Michael and Hannah continued to run every morning except Sunday. They became 'fit.' No one else they knew ran.

Michael's completely different instructions from his two editors amused Hannah. She encouraged her husband to delight in the absurdity and think of it as a challenge to his writing skills. On occasion, he was required to cover the same story for both newspapers. However, he knew he had mastered what the editors wanted when neither one made significant changes in the stories he filed.

He wanted to be covering national news. Important things were happening, and he felt removed from them, even when they struck close to home. In August, Hannah wanted to go to New York to join the Women's Strike for Equality. She said, "Next time, if I have any vacation time, I'm going." When William Calley went on trial for the My Lai Massacre, Michael was surprised. He never thought the trial would take place. He wanted to be there covering the trial.

The paper industry with its many mills reigned as the economic behemoth in Maine, but it was not on the Coast and so it was ignored by the papers Michael worked for. Tourism, however, was becoming the focus of coastal communities and the number of rooms for rent along Route 1 grew dramatically. Littering, inadequate septic systems, and traffic were only a few of the problems that Michael began to cover. But, according to his Boothbay Register editor, he was to always keep in mind the wonders of Boothbay Harbor even as he reported on problems. For the Bugle, though, 'R' wanted him to keep digging until he found a story that no one else had. "The Bugle has to surprise people, Buckley."

In Bath and Boothbay, he attended town meetings, reported on automobile accidents, and interviewed fishermen about lobster catches and the impact of government regulations on their ability to make a living. Developers and politicians greeted him with exaggeration, misdirection, and obfuscation when it came to tourism problems. Slowly, the cynicism of a newspaperman with its shell began to develop. He was a spectator on local events, and he did not object to the distance.

After a Thursday night board of education meeting that went on, in Michael's mind, endlessly and needlessly, he came home and woke Hannah up. He told her, "I can't do this for another year or two, let alone twenty or thirty. I'm going to start applying for jobs in Boston."

"You woke me up to tell me this?" she said.

"Yes."

"I'm going back to sleep. Can we talk about it this weekend?"

They did talk about it that weekend. He did send out resumes, but there was a recession, and no one was hiring. His resume as a reporter was that of a recent college graduate. Even if there had been openings, Hannah pointed out, it was unlikely that he would get a job. He needed to wait a couple of years. She was willing to move; she could always find a job.

Ruth Ann Buckley was born on March 11th, 1975. Michael wrote the birth announcement for his first child. The young couple was shocked when Hannah was informed that the shipyard would not hold her job open for her while she was out having a baby.

Peg and Jack were in Florida at their winter home for January and February. Peg had insisted that they come back in March for the birth and not stay in Florida until the beginning of May, which was their original plan. Jack came back with an announcement: "I'm retiring. I'm going to keep my hand in, but not full-time, and that's only going to be for a couple of years."

With Michael making too little to support a family and Hannah potentially losing her job, anxiety began to take hold. With it, Michael's irritability re-emerged, as did his sleeplessness. No matter how many times Hannah said, "We'll figure this out," he didn't believe her. Peg and Jack also could not imagine how they would get by. That's when they 'wondered' if Michael and Hannah might be interested in moving to the farm in Georgetown to raise their family. Jack and Peg would do what Will and Nell had done before them and move into the house in Bath. The Bath lease had already expired, and the people were just living there month to month. Peg said, "Taking care of the farm's too much. There's no mortgage on the place, and the taxes are low. We'll cover the taxes until you 'kids' get on your feet again. You'd be doing us a big favor."

They moved into the farmhouse on April Fools' Day. His interest in his daughter replaced Michael's interest in Boston and, as he told Hannah, "I can always write books." He also became the advisor for the journalism club at the high school. He wasn't paid anything, but he enjoyed working with the kids. He always told them the story of the 'teachers' room,' and how he almost got expelled when he was a student.

The shipyard did not replace her, and after a month, Hannah was dropping Ruth off in Bath, where Peg was delighted to take care of her only granddaughter. During her breaks and lunch period, she'd express milk while sitting in her car. Peg was there to take it and bring it back to the house where Jack would be taking care of Ruth.

That summer, the only Buckley who spent more than two weeks at Tír na nÓg was Maude. The remarkable novelty of the newborn saw the family through that summer, but as fall approached, everyone realized that more 'figuring' was needed. Hannah was already talking about wanting another child. She loved being pregnant; she loved being a mother; she loved living on the farm. However, she had to work. And, she was exhausted. Michael did a great deal, but he had to be away covering meetings two to three nights every week. "We can't ask them to stay home this winter and not go to Florida," Hannah said after Ruth settled down one night in early September. "We can't afford to hire someone."

"We should have thought this through more carefully," Michael said.

"Excitement. We were too fucking excited about having a baby. What were we thinking about?"

Peg and Jack had planned a trip to Ireland to visit Peg's relatives whom she hadn't seen in several years. They had put it off and put it off. Then, finally, Peg asked Maeve if she would come to Bath for a week to help out with Ruth so she and Jack could do a "…bit of traveling." Maeve was delighted to take care of her grandniece.

When Peg and Jack returned, they had someone new to the family with them. Orla was the first of several Irish nannies that would help raise the Buckley's four children.

Time is personal. Coordinated Universal Time (UTC) is derived from International Atomic Time (TAI) used by scientists and navigators. Still, most people's memory clocks have little to do with scientific precision, although some arguments suggest that they do: "Was that before or after we moved from Boston to New York?"

While Peg referred to the time before and after Hannah when talking about her son, Hannah's time measurement was geared to her children and the ships she worked on. For her, family time was measured before and after Ruth, Jesse, Joel, and Rachel were born. The ships came next, although she worked on so many over her tenure at the shipyard that ships became less critical and were replaced by measuring time in grandchildren.

Michael also separated time by children, but editors were markers for him as well. Harold was his favorite, but Josephine was up there. He didn't stay working for both papers for very long, and neither did 'R' remain long as the editor of the *Bath Bugle*, a mere three years. Michael would also remember in terms of books: "I was working on—he would supply a title—at the time."

For the children, it was nannies. Five nannies would appear between 1973 and 1985. Most stayed for the prescribed two years; one stayed for three. Orla reappeared for two summers. Fiona came every summer after Rachel was born. She said she missed the children too much not to see them. Hannah believed it was because she missed summers at Tír na nÓg and the young adults at the yacht club.

Over the years, Michael turned down three opportunities to become editor of the Bugle. Instead, he reported and wrote occasional pieces for various outlets in Maine. He published five books. Hannah worked on a series of warships at the Bath Iron Works. She learned one computer language after another as computers became smaller and faster. Children broke limbs and had them repaired; treasures were discovered and preserved in boxes in the attic as the family moved back and forth between the farmhouse and Tír na nÓg every summer. Boyfriends and girlfriends were collected and cast off. Peg died as a relatively young woman. Unable to defend itself because of the years of rheumatoid arthritis, her body succumbed to pneumonia. Two years later, Jack remarried a woman he had met in Florida and moved there permanently. The house in Bath was once again rented.

Every summer, the family would cruise for one, sometimes two weeks. Sometimes the older children, especially Ruth, had other, more pressing plans, but most of them looked forward to the annual cruise. They all went on the extended cruise to follow the Trade Wind route to Europe and back.

During one cruise, Ruth's last, Michael and Hannah sat in the cockpit of the *Redhead*, watching the sun set over the Camden Hills. The four children were below playing bridge, girls against the boys. Hannah said to her husband, "I miss your mother so much."

"So do I."

"I don't know what we would have done without her when Ruth was born."

"Although Dad was the one who offered it, I'm sure she was behind our getting the farmhouse."

"God, I miss her."

"She was a good lady."

The night was calm, and Pulpit Harbor was filled with sailboats. Anchor lights on the top of masts were stars of their own kind. They could hear people talking in low tones on other boats. Michael always brought 'the good stuff' with them when they cruised, and they were in the process of finishing the bottle of merlot they had opened before dinner.

Hannah said to Michael, "We have a good life, don't we? We've been very lucky."

"That we have."

Five summers later, Rachel, the youngest, fell in love with the steward at the yacht club. Many years and many traumas later, her daughter, Wendy, came to Tír na nÓg to work on a history paper.

Chapter Sixty-Six: Do Not Go Gentle

Michael remembered dates and kept them in his head, often for far too long. He remembered September 2nd, 2014. ISIS had just beheaded another journalist, Steven Sotloff. Michael said, "They don't give a shit about anything." When they went to bed that night, he added, "They're not human."

Hannah said, "I'm glad you never wanted to do that."

"What? Lose my head?"

"No, you know what I mean."

"No. What?"

"Wanted to be a war correspondent."

"I did. And a Woodward and Bernstein."

"Both of them?"

"Why not? Get more done."

"Yuk, yuk. I'm going to take a long hot bath. See if I can get rid of this backache."

"It's still bothering you?"

"Has been since Sunday. I'm too old to be helping you pull floats at the end of the summer."

"Nonsense. You're not even seventy."

"I wasn't raised to be an ox even if you were. It hurts, damn it."

"Want me to get out the heating pad?"

"Please. I'll put it on when I come to bed."

The following day Hannah could not get out of bed. She was in pain. She applied heat and cold, but it did not alleviate the pain. Two days later, Hannah was in the radiology department at Mid-Coast Hospital in Brunswick, anticipating a slipped disk diagnosis.

When the radiologist came out to see her, he said, "We did not find any evidence of a herniated disc. However, we found something that is more concerning. We'd like to do some additional tests."

Two weeks of 'investigations' and consultations later, Michael drove his wife to the Maine Medical Center in Portland for a second opinion about the diagnosis and treatment plan for pancreatic cancer. They carried a disc with them that showed, in digital format, the betrayal of her body and their retirement plans. The oncology surgeon to whom she had been referred confirmed the diagnosis and said, "The treatment plan they have suggested is appropriate: surgery followed by chemotherapy."

On the way home, Hannah said, "Good thing I helped you with those damned floats, or I would never have hurt my back and needed to get the imaging done."

"I guess that's one way of looking at it."

"You heard the doctor. Early is better, and most people don't know they have it until too late. Look at RBG. She was diagnosed in 2009, and she's still being 'notorious.' She's a lot older than I am. If she can carry on with the Supreme Court, I can sure as hell carry on pulling weeds and harvesting vegetables most of the day. She has to deal with Scalia, Thomas, and Alito. One of them would be bad enough. Poor woman."

"I don't know how she stands that Scalia. Can you believe they're friends?"

"Opera, Michael. They both love opera. They go together. I told you years ago, opera's magical."

"Well, we could use some magic right now."

Hannah reached over and put her hand on Michael's arm, "We've got it, my love. We've always had it, and we always will."

Siobhan O'Neil Putnam, Michael's Boston cousin, had outlived her twin sister by seven years and her husband by four. She lived in the Back Bay neighborhood of Boston, close to where she had spent her entire professional career, first as a phlebotomist, then as a nurse at Massachusetts General Hospital. Over the years, she became the resident health expert in the Buckley/O'Neil family constellation. Whenever something happened, the question was, "Have you called Siobhan?"

Siobhan told Michael to call her after their trip to Maine Medical Center. When he did, she said, "I want you and Hannah to come to Boston for treatment at MGH. You can stay here with me. I've got plenty of room, and I'd love to have you. This is too serious to stay in Maine for treatment. We're the best. We have a group dedicated to just pancreatic. So do not hesitate about this, Michael. I mean it."

"I don't know. I'll ask Hannah."

"No, this is not about asking. I know Hannah. She will do it if you insist. The only reason she wouldn't is because you didn't want to. Besides, Jesse, Naomi, and the girls are here, and you will need support."

Hannah and Michael became experts on surgical approaches during the next few days. Words that had meant nothing to them became common. Whipple procedure, distal pancreatectomy, and total pancreatectomy were researched on the internet. There was no pain much of the time, so Hannah was at her computer savvy best. At one point, she said, "I love the way PubMed is organized. I could get lost in there for days."

Siobhan did her homework. She chose the surgeon and made the appointment. She made sure everyone Hannah would encounter at the hospital knew that this was a very important patient who was to be treated with the utmost care and respect. Michael and Hannah moved into Siobhan's home in Back Bay, minutes from the hospital.

In the days leading up to the surgery, Michael and Hannah took long walks along the Charles River. During one walk, Hannah got teary and said, "I'm sorry."

"For what?"

"For waiting so long to retire. It was a mistake."

"You loved what you were doing."
"I could have left sooner. I should have. Now it's too late."
"What are you talking about?"
"I'm going to die, Michael."
"Yeah. Someday."
"No, not someday. I'm not going to make it through this year."
Michael stopped walking and turned to his wife, "Why are you saying that? It's early; they caught it early. And it's operable. You know that's good."
"Please. Can we not delude ourselves? Two years at best. If there are any damned metastases, it will be a year or less."
"You're always talking about Ruth..."
"Bader Ginsburg. I know. She's an exceptional case. I'm not her."
"You're going to outlive her. We're going to beat this."
"What's this 'we?'"
"You know what I mean."
"Michael, I'm sorry. Very sorry."
Hannah wrote lists. There was a list of essential documents. There was a list of due dates for bills and renewals of everything from AAA membership to car registrations. There was a list of passwords. Her Google contact list was purged and brought up to date. Then, they went shopping for stationery. "I'm going to start writing letters, Michael, in longhand. I've never done that, but I'm going to do it now. I'm going to write to everyone."

The surgery was successful. When Michael called his children, he reported, "Surgeon says they got it all. There was some difficulty with where the tumor had wrapped around a blood vessel, but he's confident he got it all. The chemotherapy is precautionary in case there were any metastases, but so far, no sign of any."
Hannah returned to Siobhan's with a chemotherapy port in her upper right chest to avoid using the veins in her arms or other parts of

her body. The chemotherapy would be administered through the port. Blood could also be drawn from the port to keep track of various markers, especially her red and white blood count and platelets.

She spent the next two months at Siobhan's house. Time was now measured in cycles of chemotherapy, days on and days off.

During the first weeks of Hannah's retirement, they added pigs and chickens to the sheep they already had. "I will be a gentlelady farmer," Hannah announced at her retirement dinner when her colleagues asked her what she would do now that she was retired. Michael went back and forth between Georgetown and Boston to take care of farm chores. Hannah had insisted. Michael didn't want to go and said he could hire someone to take care of the livestock, but Hannah said, "You need a break from all of this. Jesse, Naomi, and Siobhan are taking excellent care of me." Jesse's family cooked meals and brought them to Siobhan's. When Hannah wasn't too tired, they would stay and visit.

Michael would go back to Georgetown for a day, take care of whatever chores around the farm needed to be addressed, and return to Boston the following day. Finally, after a while, Hannah relented, and Michael hired someone to look after the farm.

All of the side effects that Hannah had been warned about materialized. She was nauseous. They gave her medication. It took the edge off but did not eliminate the nausea. She was exhausted. For Hannah, that was the worst part. After treatment, she would go to bed. She would sit up. She would go to bed. It did not take long for her hair to fall out. Her granddaughters, Natalie and Miriam, made different hats and caps for her.

Valerie called every day to check on her sister. She wanted to come to Boston, but Hannah talked her out of it.

As Christmas approached, Hannah decided she wanted to go home to Georgetown. Siobhan and Jesse argued against it, as did Rachel. Joel said she should go where she wanted to as long as she could get the care she needed. Ruth didn't have an opinion. Valerie thought it was a good idea and would do more good than harm. Michael vacillated. The treatment team was entirely against it. They wanted her to stay in Boston. Hannah said she thought it was because they didn't believe any medical people outside their Boston enclave were capable. She insisted, though, and she was home three days before Christmas.

Friends from Georgetown had gone into the attic and taken the Christmas boxes down. By the time Hannah and Michael arrived home from Boston, the house was fully decorated. Of course, not everything was where Hannah would have put it, and she had Michael do some rearranging, but it was done, and they both appreciated the effort.

There were also frozen dinners to last them for a month or more. One family had brought over an enormous chest freezer that they had used when they raised pigs for slaughter. The freezer was set up in the barn next to Michael's airplane.

Hannah was on a two-week break in her treatment cycle. Slowly, her physical strength returned, and so did her energy. Even Michael's spirits improved. When he was with Hannah, he did his best to remain upbeat. She chastised him for it. "Stop it. You're being ridiculous. This sucks; we both know it. You being a phony trying to act like you're not scared does not help." He insisted that the 'Christmas break' was good for him, too. They were home. His wife was 'up,' and so was he. It was Christmas; the house was decorated. His big concern was that he hadn't bought presents for people. Everyone got gift certificates that year.

People came for Christmas, family, and friends. Ruth and Harold did not come, but they arranged for a 'Skype' visit on the computer. Joel and his family did the same thing as did Valerie and her family. Jesse, Naomi, and the girls came on Christmas Eve and stayed until Christmas night, when all the clean-up was finished. So did Siobhan and Maeve. Tommy was in a memory care facility. Rachel and Wendy came and stayed overnight. Maude stayed for the week. Judd, Patty, and Rina came. On Christmas Eve, Hannah said, "Wall-to-wall beds, even with the addition. We should have made it bigger." Siobhan screened everyone for temperatures and runny noses. All passed and were allowed in.

By Christmas evening Hannah was exhausted and retired early. The week after Christmas, she rested, and by New Year's Day, she felt like her 'old self.' When Michael asked her what she would like to do, she said, "I want to go cross-country skiing."

"Are you out of your mind?"

"You asked me what I wanted to do. That's what I want to do. I didn't say I could or we should. Come on; you're the master of words. Ask a question, and you get an answer. I want to drive over to Vermont, go to the Trapp Family Lodge, and go cross-country skiing like we did that year when we wanted to get away from the New Year's Eve nonsense. That's what I want to do. I want to be outside in the snow. I am so tired of being inside I can't stand it anymore."

Michael mentioned it to Jesse. Jesse told Naomi. Naomi told Natalie, "Nanna wants to go cross-country skiing. She's amazing." Natalie told Miriam, and the two granddaughters started searching the internet and found a farm in New Hampshire that had horse-drawn sleigh rides. It was a two-hour drive. Would Nanna be able to handle that?

"You bet I can," came Nanna's response from Georgetown.

They did not like the idea, but Hannah's medical team at Massachusetts General Hospital agreed that she could receive the next cycle of chemotherapy at Maine Medical Center in Portland. One of the physicians at Maine Medical had trained at Mass General, so he was acceptable. Hannah wanted to be treated closer to home, but since Mid-Coast Hospital in Brunswick was only thirty minutes closer than

Maine Medical, Hannah somewhat reluctantly said, "Fine, we'll drive to Portland." The Boston team insisted that she come to them for her follow-up appointment and the next chemotherapy cycle. In response, she said, "We'll see."

She did, but only after a follow-up scan indicated "suspicious" lesions on her liver. According to her team, 'additional investigation' was called for, and within two weeks, the diagnosis was that the cancer had metastasized to her liver and lymph nodes. A more 'aggressive' course of chemotherapy was recommended. Hannah and Michael returned to their room at Siobhan's Back Bay home in Boston. When she was strong enough, and when the weather was cooperative, Hannah and Michael again took walks along the Charles River. Visits from Jesse, Natalie, and their daughters were more frequent. Maude came whenever she could. Joel and his wife Sharon came for a week. Ruth and Hal flew in for Easter. Rachel came periodically and stayed on the couch in Jesse and Natalie's living room. Valerie came and stayed with a college friend.

In May, Hannah said, "I'm going home. If I'm going to die, which I surely am, I will die in our bed at Tír." So, they went home. Her care was again shifted to Maine Medical in Portland.

Hannah did not die in the bed she had shared with her husband. That bed was broken down and moved to a corner of the room that Maude usually used. A hospital bed replaced it. A single bed stored in the farmhouse's attic was brought down to the cottage for Michael and erected next to the hospital bed where Hannah now slept. Although in different beds, Michael slept next to his wife.

Valerie came for another week. On 'good days' the two sisters drove out to Indian Point, where they had grown up. The 'Turner Camp' had been sold when their mother died. They were no longer members of the association, but Valerie didn't care. She brought folding chairs and helped her sister walk out the path to Sea Beach.

While Hannah watched, Valerie helped some youngsters build a lean-to out of driftwood.

Hannah finished writing her letters. Some had already been mailed, but there were some she had instructed Michael to send only after she died. There were six without addresses—one to each of her children and one to Michael. Finally, one was to be read at her memorial service.

Judd and Patty Fishman came early to their home on Heron Cove. Patty and Valerie spent hours with Hannah on the porch at Tír na nÓg. The three women recounted memories, laughed, and cried, sometimes from laughter, sometimes from loss. When they exhausted what there was to say, one of them would read to Hannah. Michael welcomed Patty's visits and would often nap on the porch swing while the women talked. Sometimes he would go for a short sail. Finally, one morning, Valerie said goodbye, and flew home.

Hannah interviewed the head nurse of the hospice care organization that would provide her with the services she wanted to have. She went over every aspect of her death plan with the nurse. Most of what she wanted was standard, and the two of them negotiated where it wasn't. Finally, hospice care began on June 19th.

The night of June 22nd, it rained very hard. The rain continued into the morning of the twenty-third. The metal roof seemed especially loud to Michael as the rain pelted it. The cold front also brought wind that shook the shutters of the old cottage.

When morning came, it came with a clarity that made Michael think he was seeing for the first time. The rain had scrubbed away clouds and haze. Houses glistened with the wetness of the rain. When he opened the door onto the porch, he could smell the grass he had cut around the cottage the day before. There was a chill in the air even though it was late June. He went back inside and got the coffee going. When the coffee was done, he filled his travel mug and went back into the bedroom to see if Hannah was still sleeping. Assuring himself she was still asleep, he went upstairs to where Maude was staying. He tiptoed into her room and shook her gently to wake her. When she stirred, he told her, "I'm going into town to get the groceries."

"Okay. Is there coffee?"

"Yes. Hannah's still asleep, so be quiet. She didn't have a good night with all that noise."

"Okay."

"You need anything?"

"No. Take your time."

On the drive into Bath for groceries, Michael was struck with the color green. June was always green, but the morning sun created shadows in the trees and bushes that somehow brought out shades of green he had never noticed before. Sun, shadows, and so many textures, and they were all green. He thought, "World, you had some bath last night. You are clean this morning." He pulled off the road before Back River just to look around. On the opposite side of the river, he saw an eagle leave its nest and fly off. He watched it circle and fly away. He continued across the bridge into Arrowsic.

Hannah Turner Buckley died in her sleep on June 23rd while her husband was driving into Bath for groceries. She had followed her death plan almost to the letter. Almost. Michael was supposed to be with her, holding her hand when she died, but even Hannah couldn't control that.

Her after-death instructions were followed as she had written them down. She was cremated. A small memorial service was held at Tír na nÓg at low tide. Valerie read Hannah's letter. In it, she said she was angry that she was dying. She loved her life, and she wanted more of it. She thanked the people who had made her life so rich that she didn't want to leave it or anyone, especially Michael.

Her ashes were placed on the shore in front of the cottage just below the high water mark. Three tides later, there was no evidence of her remains. A memorial headstone was erected in the family cemetery next to the one commemorating the life of Treasa de Burca Buckley.

November 19, 2010
HOME TOWN BOY by Michael Buckley

It snowed yesterday, a white Thanksgiving, which is not always the case. My Boston son and his family arrived in the middle of a flurry. When they came in, they told me to get my wife out of the kitchen and into the living room, which I did. The four of them began singing:

> Over the river and through the woods,
> To grandmother's house we go;
> The horse knows the way to carry the sleigh
> Thru the white and drifting snow, oh.
> Over the river and thru the woods,
> Oh how the wind does blow!
> It stings the toes and bites the nose,
> As over the ground we go.

The river, in our case, is the Back River which one must cross coming from Arrowsic onto the island of Georgetown. They sing the same song every year as they cross the bridge but this was the first time they could remember doing it in the snow, so the song deserved to be sung twice: once on the bridge and then again when they arrived.

I remember doing the same thing when I was a youngster and we would go to my grandparents' home in Bath for Thanksgiving. We also sang it twice. First, we sang while crossing the Back River; then Maude and I did more shouting than singing as we crossed the Kennebec into Bath.

I wonder how many other families sing this song on Thanksgiving Day? Anticipating Thanksgiving this year, I decided to do a little digging at the library. It turns out that the lyrics first appeared as a poem in 1844, in a book entitled *Child's Flowers for*

Children. The title of the poem is "The New England Boy's Song About Thanksgiving Day," and the poet is Lydia Maria Child. Now in the original version the destination was 'grandfather's House,' not grandmother's. Somehow along the way we grandfathers got replaced by grandmothers. Given who does most of the work on Thanksgiving, this seems appropriate. There are four more verses. How many do you know?

>Over the river and thru the wood,
>To have a first-rate play;
>Oh, hear the bell ring, "Ting-a-ling-ling!"
>Hurrah for Thanksgiving Day-ay!
>Over the river and thru the wood,
>Trot fast my dapple gray!
>Spring over the ground like a hunting hound,
>For this is Thanksgiving Day!
>Over the river and through the wood,
>And straight through the barnyard gate.
>We seem to go extremely slow,
>It is so hard to wait!
>Over the river and through the wood,
>Now Grandmother's cap I spy!
>Hurrah for fun! Is the pudding done?
>Hurrah for the pumpkin pie!

To confuse matters, these are not the original lyrics. Not only did grandfather's become grandmother's, with time the lyrics got shook up as well, especially in the later verses. Such is the nature of folk songs, even when they were written down to begin with. And, as a good folk song, no one knows where the music came from.

It turns out that Ms. Lydia Marie Child was quite something. She was an abolitionist, women's rights activist, and a Native American rights activist. She was also opposed to American expansionism. She was a novelist as well as a poet. In some of her stories her negative feelings about White supremacy and male dominance are revealed—in the 1800's. Ostracized at times, she kept at it. She had a very impressive literary career. Yet, this simple little Thanksgiving song is what made it into the public imagination, and most of us have no idea who the author was. So, Ms. Lydia Maria Child, thank you for this family tradition. I will take it upon myself to teach my family some new verses, perhaps one a year.

A personal note: This will be my last *Home Town* Boy. I have decided to retire. I have been at this newspapering business for a long time now, about forty-five years. Forty-four of those have been with the *Bath Bugle*. Given this longevity, if I ever decide to come out of retirement, the first thing I am going to put on my resume is "He knows how to keep a job."

I love this business and am grateful to the three different publishers and six editors who have given me the opportunity to practice my trade during my time with the *Bugle*. We have argued at times, but we have done a lot more agreeing and celebrating than arguing.

The business has changed dramatically during my years as a newspaperman, especially the technology. We are of the computer age. Next week I will return my Blackberry and computer to the *Bugle*. These are devices that a reporter could only dream of when I started in the business. It is amazing. I cannot imagine what lies ahead. Will all news be online? Interestingly, one thing has not changed. The QWERTY arrangement of letters on the keyboard remains.

Our need for accurate information about the world around us also remains. News people have always had the responsibility to get the news, communicate it in a way that is understandable, and to provide context so it has meaning. I like to think I have done this.

I don't know if I will be miss being a reporter. I do know I will miss the people I work with and the readers who have been kind to me over the years with their comments. Although retiring from full-time employment with the *Bugle*, I will continue to write pieces now and again as I am asked to do so by the editor or if I get so fascinated with a story that I just can't help myself.

So, this Thanksgiving I am grateful for having had a wonderful career doing what I love. I hope you had a great Thanksgiving yesterday. I know I did.

Chapter Sixty-Seven: Changing Colors

There are several maple trees between Tír na nÓg and the general store in Georgetown, but three stand out. Every year they let me know that summer is planning an exit. It happens in late August. Days are a bit shorter, nights are a bit cooler, and that is enough for these three. It's just a few leaves at first. They show a bit of yellow, no red. Each day, though, more leaves join them, and by Labor Day Weekend, red and rust make an entrance. As the season changes, at Tír na nÓg, whoever is up first builds a fire in the small kitchen woodstove.

I mentioned the yellow leaves to Wendy at dinner after returning from my meeting with Judy Reddin. She said, "I know. I can't believe it. Summer's over. I start classes next Monday."

"It's flown."

"Has it ever. It's been super."

"So, school starts next Monday? I'd forgotten it was so soon."

"Gramps, I've got an idea. I'd like to do something if it's possible. You know we never did get to fly this summer, not even once."

"I know. I'm sorry about that."

"What would you think about flying me back to school?"

"You want me to fly you to Burlington? I thought your mother wanted to drive you."

"She did, but we had a long talk earlier while you were having lunch up in Waldoboro. Mom's fine with it if you're willing to."

"What about your stuff?"

"Nathan. Remember Nathan? You met him when I took the motorcycle test. My friend from 'Brat' that goes to UVM. He said he had room to take my things in his car. Mom said she would pack for me. Besides, I already have a lot of my things with me. I leave my skis up there, so it's mostly winter clothes."

"Wow. I hadn't thought about it. Sure. Why not? I'd have to look at the weather and…"

"I already did. Supposed to be beautiful. All weekend. Here and in Burlington."

"I see. Okay. If it's alright with your mom, let's do it." My mind started preparing a checklist of everything I would need to do to get me and the plane ready to go. I asked, "When would you like to leave?"

"Saturday, if that's okay. Can't get into my dorm until Sunday night, but I can stay with a friend of mine who lives in Burlington. Already checked with her. She's the one who has my skis. Rina will take care of Charlie."

"Sounds like you have this all worked out."

"You sure it's okay?"

"Yes, I'm sure."

By car, the trip from Georgetown to Burlington is convoluted. First, you have to dip down into New Hampshire, almost into Massachusetts. Then, you drive across New Hampshire and finally head up into Vermont. It's a four-and-a-half-hour drive if you're lucky. Getting out of Maine on a late-summer Saturday can be torture, so you have to add another half an hour, at least. The Cessna cruises at a bit over one hundred and fifty miles an hour. Take-off to landing, and we'd be there in under two hours.

The plane was in good shape, but I spent Friday morning giving it a thorough going over. I contacted the airport in Burlington and made the necessary arrangements for parking and fueling. I gave them the estimated arrival and departure times. I also ordered a rental car. I told the August tenants at the farmhouse about our plans and not to be surprised when they heard the plane take off early in the morning and land in the late afternoon. Wendy was right about the weather. The prediction was for perfect weather throughout the day.

Saturday morning came without fog. It was dry, crisp. We loaded her luggage into the plane, I entered everything into the computer, got my flight clearances, and we were 'wheels up' at 0815. The sky was cloudless, and the plan was to fly direct to Burlington.

It had been a long time since Wendy had flown with me. She asked if we could do a little sightseeing. I suspected she would want to do this and had accounted for it in my flight plan. Once in the air, we went out over Five Islands and Heron Cove, circled, and came back over Indian Point and Sagadahoc Bay before climbing and settling on our course.

Automatic pilot on, Wendy brought out the thermos of coffee and the blueberry muffins she had baked the night before. We commented on the weather and how far we could see. Wendy was talkative. She had her face pressed to the window and pointed things out as we passed over them. She asked questions about places she didn't recognize. After a while, she settled back into her seat and was quiet. Then, when we saw Mt. Washington in the distance, she started to talk again. She said, "I'd love to climb that one."

"No reason not to."

Neither of us said anything. We just watched the mountain. After a few minutes, she said, "I talked to Mom about changing my name."

"Ohh. What'd your mother say?"

"She said she loved the name, Wendy. I tried explaining to her why I wanted to do it. She doesn't get it. She asked me if I could wait until I graduated. Just sit with it for a couple of years. Then, if I still wanted to do it, she'd help me."

"Good for her. How'd she react to the name you've been thinking about?"

"Chava? I told her all about it. She didn't say much about it. Said it had a lovely sound, but that's about it."

"So, are you okay with waiting until you graduate?"

"Yeah. I think I am. I may ask some friends to call me Chava. Sort of get used to it."

"Do you want me to call you Chava? I guess if I can be Gramps, you can be Chava. Chava."

"You're making fun of me."

"Ahhh, maybe just a little. You know, if you decide to do this, it's going take me some time to get used to it. I think you may always be 'Wendy' to me."

"I know."

We didn't say anything more. The only sounds were those of the engine and the voices of air traffic controllers and pilots in our headphones. When we crossed over into Vermont, she started to fidget. I asked, "You okay?"

"Yes. Starting to get a little anxious about school starting up."

"Why's that?"

"I want to do well this semester."

"I'm sure you will. Look how well you did on your paper this summer."

"Yeah, but that was at Tír. I could concentrate there. It's harder at school–too many distractions. Archie said I should just go to the library. Study there. He said that's what he did."

"Might work for you."

"I suppose. I want to do really well this semester."

I repeated myself. "You will." We didn't say anything more for another few minutes. Then she started with, "I've been thinking about something for next summer."

"Oh."

"It involves you and Tír, though."

"Oh. Go ahead."

"I've decided I want to minor in anthropology, actually archaeology."

"That doesn't surprise me. I sort of thought that might be coming."

"I can start taking courses spring semester, but I had an idea. I don't know if it's possible, or if UVM would approve, or if I could get in, but Orono has a summer field research course. I could apply for it next summer."

"The dig over in Popham."

"That's where I learned about it. There may be other sites, too."

"You seemed interested in it."

"And, if I can get in, could I stay at Tír? I checked with Mom. I also called Dad, and he said he'd pay for the course."

"Of course you can. I'd love it."

"There's one other thing. If I can't get in, would it still be possible for me to come for the summer? Get a job. Maybe pumping gas at the boatyard or waitressing, or something."

"Of course, honey. You can always come to Tír. You know that."

"It will be my last summer before I graduate."

"I know."

We bounced a bit as we crossed the mountains, but other than that, the flight was uneventful—the best kind. Airport services were excellent. Renting the car was easy, and off we went on a Wendy tour of the University of Vermont campus and downtown Burlington. Next, we drove out to Mt. Mansfield and took the toll road to the top. She pointed out some of the more challenging ski trails. We stopped at the Ben and Jerry's factory on the way back from Stowe village.

As we left Ben and Jerry's, she said, "What's up with this Grace person?"

"What do you mean?"

"Come on. I saw you with her…"

"For what? A minute."

"Yeah, but your voice was different. Are you interested in her?"

"No, honey, she's just a friend. Not even that. An acquaintance."

"You sure?"

"Yes, I'm sure."

We didn't say anything more about it until we got to Waterbury. Then she said, "You should start dating. Mom and I talked about it. You really should. You should use one of those senior dating sites. I'll help you write your profile."

"You'd just love that, wouldn't you? I can imagine what you'd say. Old geezer, goes by the nickname 'Gramps,' is interested in meeting—what?"

"No, I'm serious. You put yourself out there at your age, in good health, hot in your own way, and you'd have every divorced and widowed woman in the county responding."

"Hot in my own way?"

"Well, yeah. Rina thinks so, too."

"I think maybe we should end this conversation."

"Well, think about it."

I didn't respond, and we didn't say anything more about it.

After our tour, I offered to drop her off at her friend's house, but she insisted on going with me to the airport. She said, "I want to watch you take off." She made arrangements for her friend to pick her up after I left.

We said goodbye in the lounge. "Gramps, thank you for this summer."

"It was good, wasn't it?"

"It was the best."

"So, any chance I'll see you at Thanksgiving?"

"Uncle Jesse always invites us. I'm going to talk Mom into going this year. Time for her to rejoin the family. I mean, really rejoin it."

"I agree. Not sure I'll be at Jesse's this year."

"Why not?"

"Joel wants me to come to Texas. Do Thanksgiving with them, Ruth, Harold, and Hal."

"You going to do it?"

"Not sure. Still thinking about it."

"I'll miss you if you do."

"I'd miss you, too."

She hugged me, "I love you, Grandpa."

"I love you, too, sweetie. You know where I am. Maybe we can Skype sometime."

"Absolutely."

The day had remained clear. I was back in the air at 1630 in the late afternoon and landed at Buckley Airport at 1815. Back at Tír, the house seemed empty. I walked up to Patty and Judd's, where Rina was taking care of Charlie. I turned down a glass of wine and, with Charlie in tow, returned to Tír and a dinner of scrambled eggs with some leftover chicken. It had been a long day, and I was asleep by nine-thirty. I had to move Charlie to one side of the bed to make room for myself. Rachel called at ten.

"Dad, you up? Sorry to call so late."

"Everything okay?"

"Yes, it's fine. I just got off the phone with Wendy."

"She okay?"

"Yes, she was teary, though."

"About?"

"You. She said this was the best summer of her life. I wanted you to know."

"It was good for me, too. Good having her here."

"She said she forgot to ask you something and passed it on to me."

"What's that?"

"I planned on taking Charlie home with me when I come up but she wanted to know if Charlie could stay with you. She said you could use the company, and you had more time for Charlie than I do. I'm just passing this on, Dad. I told her I didn't want to be in the middle, but…"

"You got in the middle."

"Yeah."

"You know, it's not a bad idea. He's a good dog. Bit energetic. He gets along okay with Fire and Ice when they come, so, yes, I think it'd be fine. I'll text her and let her know."

"She's got you texting, now?"

"Only thing she responds to. I'm not sure she ever looks at her email."

"I know."

"She's a good kid, Rachel. You should be proud."

"I am."

"Be prepared. She may say something about going to Jesse's…"

"For Thanksgiving. She already has. I told her I'd think about it."

"Rachel."

"I will think about it. People will be drinking, and that's still hard."

"If you want to come, everyone will understand. Jesse and Naomi will simply say no drinking, and people won't. You know that."

"I know, but I hate to…"

"Don't be silly. It's not a big deal."

"I'll think about it."

"Good."

"Dad, thank you for this summer."

"You know she wants to come back."

"She will be back. I don't think that's a question."

"Good. You still coming up Labor Day for the week?"

"I am if you'll still have me."

I made a raspberry sound into the phone.

Chapter Sixty-Eight: Closing Up

I missed that red-headed granddaughter of mine. It was an ache that I couldn't get a handle on. I understood the ache of missing Hannah, but this was different, and it was new. Wendy had filled a hole that I didn't even know was there. I missed the chatter. I missed seeing her at the other end of the dining room table while we both worked. I missed seeing her excitement with Archie or Rina as they inhabited a world that I could observe but not enter.

Charlie adopted me. He'd come down with me onto the pier in the morning for coffee. He'd tuck me in at night. We had to argue a bit about lap or no lap when I was trying to read. He'd curl up at my feet while I continued to work on the book and sorted through copies of *Home Town Boy*. I still needed human company, though, and found myself rowing across the cove to the yacht club and hanging out on the porch when boats that had been out all day returned in the late afternoon. Crews and people doing pick up duty would stop and chat with me. It got me through the week until Friday and the start of the Labor Day weekend.

Maude arrived Friday afternoon with Fire and Ice. The three dogs tore through the house together until we let them outside, where they proceeded to chase one another and then redirected their energy to squirrels. Jesse, Naomi, and the girls arrived later complaining, as always, about the traffic leaving Boston. We went down to *Five I* and ate lobster dinners out on the wharf. Miriam and Natalie got *Code Name* out of the game box when we got home. Jesse, Miriam, and Natalie challenged me, Maude and Naomi. They won. Tír had come to life again.

Erascohegan members with school-aged children had already left for the summer, so the Beetlecats did not race over the weekend.

However, there were still enough members around for the 12 1/2s to race. Jesse was determined to get some firsts. He signed Maude on to crew for him. He wanted someone as competitive as he was. The rest of us decided to take the *Redhead* out and watch the races from a safe distance so we wouldn't interfere. At dinner Friday night, Natalie and Miriam proclaimed that sailboat racing was too formal. "You should have cheerleaders and cheers," Miriam said. They had a plan. Early Saturday morning, they went into Bath and bought poster board and magic markers. When they returned, the two of them made signs supporting their father and Maude: *Buckley Boat Beats All*. My grandfather always painted the 12 ½ white. When it was passed on to my father, he started painting the boat the same color green as the color for the Boston Celtics, whom he dearly loved. So, one sign was *Go Green*. None of us knew what they were up to.

I admit it. I was hesitant when the girls brought the signs out when we reached the starting area. No, I was embarrassed. Over the years, I had inhaled the yacht club's sense of propriety, and this was not it. Holding the signs up so everyone could see them, they started cheering: "Go Maude; Go Jesse; Go Fast, Go Faster' You can do it; we know you can." My two African American granddaughters, city kids, were challenging years of culture, and I don't think they had any idea they were doing it. When they started cheering, Jesse stood up in the 12 ½ and started pumping his fist in the air. The small boat started rocking, and he fell back into the cockpit. Skippers and crews in the other boats began laughing.

When the race committee posted the course, Jesse and Maude got serious. They huddled; heads close together so others couldn't hear them. I knew they were plotting tactics for the start. The ten-minute warning went off, and I could see Maude start the stopwatch that hung around her neck. When the five-minute blast from the air horn blew, the boats began to maneuver in earnest, each trying to get to the favored end of the starting line and hit the line exactly when the start blast sounded.

Jesse timed it perfectly, and he and Maude got off to a great start. They were first at the windward end of the course and held onto their position for the entire race. With one win behind them, lunch on the yacht club porch was celebratory. There was a lot of discussion about the cheers and the signs.

More spectator boats went out for the afternoon race to watch the start. People had been busy over lunch. Now signs appeared on other spectator boats as well as a few cheers. So much for my embarrassment.

Jesse and Maude did well in every race over the weekend and won the Labor Day series with two firsts, a second, and two thirds. To celebrate, Naomi bought champagne. Monday night. Maude insisted we have racks of lamb on the grill for dinner. "It's what got this family started, and we should never forget it." When I reminded her that it was granite and ice, she shushed me, "On land, it was sheep, and we aren't about to eat granite."

After dinner, Jesse's family packed up their car and waited until Rachel arrived before leaving. "I'm done," Rachel announced when she came into the house. "Summer is over, and I have a week of vacation. Thank the goddess."

After hugs all around, Naomi corralled her crew into the car, and they left. Maude said, "We saved you dinner and dessert. Do you want to eat here or on the porch?"

"Oh, the porch. I want to smell pine and salt air. It has been a shit summer, but I survived."

Maude became Mother Maude and got dinner together for Rachel while I helped my daughter bring her luggage in from the car. When I went to lift her backpack, I was surprised at how heavy it was. "What do you have in this thing, books?"

"And my laptop. I have to work this week. I'm taking two courses this semester, and they've already started." I had forgotten she was now back in school and working on her bachelor's.

While Rachel ate, Maude and I talked about the weekend, the races, and how mature Miriam and Natalie were when they were not corrupting the culture of the Erascohegan Yacht Club. When we told Rachel about their signs and cheers, Rachel said, "I would have loved to have seen that. You mean something actually changed around here?"

"It appears it did," I said.

"Good golly, Miss Molly. Will the yacht club survive?"

Maude left about ten o'clock with the prediction that traffic would have thinned by then. Rachel and I went back out to the porch. She handed me a folder, "This is for Charlie. It's got all of his medical records. You'll have to get him registered here. Thank you for doing this. With work, meetings, and now two courses, I am flat out and wouldn't have time to do anything but walk him." Charlie was sitting in my lap when she said all this.

"No problem."

"I hear you're dating."

"Who told you that?"

"Everyone. Text is a wonderful thing."

"Well, you can text everyone and tell them I'm not."

"Grace. Isn't that her name?"

"Just an acquaintance."

"Not what I heard."

"Well, you heard wrong."

Something in my tone of voice must have told her to drop it. She did. She asked, "Do you mind if I work at the dining room table while I'm here?"

"No, as long as you don't mind me working at the other end."

I told her about my meeting with Judy Reddin.

"A collection of *Home Town Boy* pieces is a great idea. I love it."

"I'm still going to do the book."

"You are? Even though…"

"I'm going to publish it myself if I have to."

"Good for you."

"I'm going to go back up there. I have different questions to ask now. More important ones."

"Like what?"

"I've been too focused on the externals of the chaos the strike created. I want to know how the strike changed people, their view of the world, and their view of themselves. That's what I have to understand. Unfortunately, I haven't been paying enough attention to that part of the story.

"I'm also going to talk to current workers up in Old Town. When you read all of the newspaper articles about this Chinese company, it sounds like they are the Second Coming. Maybe they are. Maybe they're not. I want to find out. That will be the last chapter. I'm not going to let this go."

"You're serious about this."

"Yes."

The two of us had a good week. Rachel was diligent. It was a quiet diligence that I had never seen in her before. It could have been Hannah or Wendy sitting at the other end of the table from me. We both worked on our respective tasks in the morning, and in the afternoon, we sailed, read, or sometimes play cards. She took out a puzzle and set it up on the 'puzzle table' in the living room. Both of us would add to it periodically. She told me more about her job and her sense that her boss would not last long because she didn't understand the community. She told me about her AA meetings and the community that had developed. She belonged. "First time since I was a kid, Dad. I feel like I belong someplace."

"I'm glad, honey. I'm happy for you."

"Can't tell you what a difference it's made."

"I'm sorry, Rach, that your mom and I..."

"Dad, don't go there. You and Mom gave me lots of chances. My staying away was on me. Not you."

"Still, it hurts when I hear you say..."

"I'm here now, Dad, and I want to be. As long as you don't interrupt me when I'm studying."

"You're as bad as your daughter."

The renters at the farmhouse left the following Saturday morning, and the two of us went up to check and make sure everything was in order. It was. We went back to Tír to clean and close up. We had just put sheets and towels into the washing machine at Tír when I got a call from Dick Tubbs. "Hey, Mike, you missing something."

"Good morning to you, neighbor. Not that I'm aware of."

"Perhaps a few sheep."

"Oh, shit. I'll be right up. Where are they?"

"One's in my yard, and it looks like there's a couple up near your cemetery. Want me to try and chase the guy back that's in my yard?"

"No. We'll get him. Thanks, Dick."

When Rachel and I checked everything out at the farmhouse, I didn't think to check on the sheep. The tenants must have left the gate open when they left, and I didn't notice it. "Rachel, some of George's sheep got out!" I yelled upstairs, where she was starting to vacuum.

She ran down; we hopped in the truck and headed up to the farmhouse. "I'll go count. You try and see where the ones Dick saw have headed. I'll grab some hay and ropes." All I could think of was somebody speeding and running into one of them in the middle of the road.

My count showed only three missing. I broke open a bale of hay from the sheep barn, grabbed clumps and some rope, and headed across the road to Dick's. I saw Rachel heading for the cemetery. Once I got the ewe from Dick's yard back where she belonged, I headed for the cemetery. Rachel had opened the gate and was trying to herd the other two into the cemetery and use it as a holding pen.

It was a good idea. When I arrived, I had something they wanted, and getting them to follow me and the hay was fairly easy. Once inside, we closed the gate, and the two of us sat on the granite bench that my grandfather had built for my grandmother. The names Convey and Buckley were inscribed across the top. "Well," Rachel said, "That was exciting. We have them all?"

"Yeah, I'm pretty sure. I did a quick count. But I think I got all of them. Most of them were down at the other end of pasture two, so it was easy."

Dick called on my cellphone, "Got em?"

"Yeah. Thanks again."

"No problem. That you two up in the cemetery?"

"Currently, it's a sheep pen."

"Let me know if you need any help getting them back where they belong."

"Thanks for the offer, Dick. I think we're okay. If not, I'll call you."

When I hung up, Rachel asked, "Dick?"

"Yeah."

Rachel got up and started strolling around. I followed her. "It's been years since I've been up here. Not since you put up Mom's headstone."

"I come up every couple of months. Clean things up."

"Who mows the grass?"

"Dick's son. For some reason, I don't want to do it."

"I'm always amazed there are so many headstones here without remains."

"All of the empty sites are Buckleys. Conveys had sense enough to die in their beds. Then your mom wanted to be cremated. She didn't want a stone. I talked her into it."

"I'm glad you did."

We kept walking. The original Convey who built the cemetery had taken a half-acre of land on top of a knoll to bury the family's dead. There were two generations of Conveys already here before Will Buckley arrived in Georgetown. Rachel walked over to the stone for James Buckley and said, "Jamie Buckley must have been something."

"From everything my grandfather told me, he was. But the one I would have liked to have known was his wife, Treasa. I have a hunch she was something like your mother. She sure broke the mold."

"Wasn't she a writer?"

"My grandfather said she was, but when I asked him, he didn't have anything she had written."

"Too bad."

Treasa's gravesite was empty because of the plague. Hannah's cancer felt like a plague. I felt sorry for my great-grandfather, losing his wife, and not being able to be with her when she died. I didn't get to hold Hannah's hand as we had planned. She was alone. I wondered for the thousandth time if she had awakened before she died.

Rachel had moved over to her grandfather and grandmother's graves. "I miss Grandma. Grandma Peg was something else. Sick as she was, she kept going."

"She did."

"This is probably terrible to say, but I wish Grandpa Jack had not remarried."

"Why?"

"I didn't like the new wife. None of us did."

"My mother was a hard act to follow."

"You, on the other hand, should remarry."

"Don't start that."

"Just saying."

"Enough. We should get going. Get these animals back where

they belong."

"Just a minute, Dad." She walked over to my grandparents' graves; the headstones for Brian Liam Buckley and Connor Walter Buckley were right next to them. "More empty graves."

"World War Two."

"I don't know how they did it, your grandparents. If anything ever happened to Wendy, I don't know what I'd do."

"I know."

"I'm glad Joel's coming home."

"Me, too. I'm glad he's stateside. We should get these animals back."

"How are we going to do it?"

"I'll put the stakes in the truck and bring it up here. We'll truck them down."

"I'm going to wait here if you don't mind. I want to sit a bit with Mom."

"Sure. I'll only be a few minutes."

I walked back down the hill to the farmhouse. I grabbed a few more clumps of hay and drove the truck out to the barn. I set the stakes up in the back of the truck so the sheep couldn't climb out, slid the ramp in, and drove back up to the cemetery. I backed the truck close to the cemetery gate, took the ramp out, and set it up. Rachel was still standing in front of Hannah's headstone. It looked like she was praying. I didn't say anything. I walked over to her. When I reached her, she said, "Dad, don't let anything happen to you. We need you. All of us."

"We need each other, honey, and I'm not going anyplace."

"Good."

"You ready to go?"

"Yes. You?"

"Yes."

We got the sheep back into their pasture and went back down to

Tír to finish cleaning and closing up. First, we loaded everything in the truck that needed to be brought back to the farmhouse. Some of the refrigerated items had probably made this trip more than once. How long does mustard last, and why did we have such variety? After we delivered everything to the farmhouse and put it where it belonged, we returned to Tír na nÓg to finish with the laundry and the cleaning.

When we completed everything, we went out and sat on the porch rockers. Rachel asked, "I forget. Who gave Tír its name?"

"I'm sure I told you. It was Jamie Buckley. The story is they were just finishing Tír when Jamie stopped on one of his trips back and forth to Stonington. According to my grandfather, he brought the *Treasa* into Heron Cove under sail, something I can't imagine trying to do.

"Grandpa Will showed him around, and—now this is according to my Grandmother—the old man asked her what she was going to name her bloody hotel. She said she hadn't thought about it. So, he said, "You should call it Tír na nÓg." Grandpa Will, of course, knew the legend, but Grandma Nell didn't, so she asked him to tell it to her. When he finished, she said, "Perfect, Tír na nÓg it is."

"I only remember parts of the legend. I remember Mom telling it to us when we sailed to Ireland."

"It's a great legend, sad and beautiful, typical Irish."

"Tell it to me again."

"Okay. You want it with a brogue?"

"No."

"Okay, no brogue.

"A long, long time ago, in Ireland, or Eire, there was a great warrior whose name was Oisín. Oisín was the son of Fionn mac Cumhaill—that was the original name for Finn McCool. Fionn was the leader of the Fianna. The Fianna were a group of warriors who protected Ireland. One morning the Fianna were out hunting deer on the shores of Lough Leane in County Kerry. A beautiful woman came riding towards them out of the mist on a magnificent snow-white horse. She was the most beautiful woman any of them had ever seen. She had long golden hair that came down to her waist. She was dressed in pale blue flowing robes and surrounded by this light that moved with her as she rode.

"She rode up to the Fianna and said, 'I am Niamh of the Golden Hair. My father is the King of Tír na nÓg. I've heard you have a great warrior named Oisín. I want to find him and ask him to come with me to Tír na nÓg, the Land of everlasting youth.' When he saw her, Oisín fell in love with the beautiful princess and said 'yes' he would go with her to Tír na nÓg. He jumped onto the snow-white horse behind her, and the two of them rode off with the light now shining on both of them.

"Over land and sea they rode, until, out of the mist, they saw the magical shores of Tír na nÓg. Niamh's parents, the king and queen, held a great feast in Oisín's honor when they arrived.

"Tír na nÓg was a magical land. During the day, Oisín and Niamh hunted and feasted together. At night Oisín sat and told Niamh stories about Fionn Mac Cumhail, the Fianna, and Eire.

"Oisín stayed in Tír na nÓg for three hundred years, but eventually he became homesick for Ireland. It wasn't long before his need to go home to the Emerald Isle was stronger than his desire for eternal youth. Niamh didn't want him to go, but seeing his love for Ireland, she finally agreed. She warned him that when he set foot on Ireland, he would never be able to return to Tír na nÓg.

"So off he went. When Oisín reached Ireland, everything had changed—to him it felt as though he had been gone for three years, but it was actually three hundred. His family was long gone, and the castle he had grown up in was a pile of stones. As he passed through Gleann na Smol, the Valley of the Thrushes, he offered to help a group of men who were trying to move a large stone. When he got off the magical horse, the horse ran away. Oisín, now on Irish land, became an old, old man who was getting older every minute.

"This scared the men he was trying to help, and they brought Oisín to St. Patrick. St. Patrick tried to comfort Oisín, but Oisín, having lost his family, was filled with despair. In his despair, he told the stories of the triumphs of his father, Fionn mac Cumhaill. He told stories about the Fianna and their hunts and feasts and how they protected Eire. He told stories about Tír na nÓg and his beautiful, golden-haired wife, Niamh. Oisín died from old age within days. Tír na nÓg was lost in the mist forever. Sometimes, though, when the fog is right, people claim they see a beautiful woman with long blond hair wearing blue flowing robes on a magnificent white horse riding in the mist."

Rachel asked, "Have you ever seen her?"

"No, not Niamh. Sometimes, though, when it's foggy, I think I see your mother down at the end of the pier."

"Would you follow her to Tír na nÓg?"

The question surprised me. I knew the answer, though. "I did."

We sat for a few minutes more before I asked, "Shall we go?"

"Yes. I'm cooking tonight. Nothing fancy."

We put the rocking chairs in the house, and I locked the door. As we walked toward the truck, Rachel said, "So five generations have been here?"

"So far."

"Dad, no matter what it takes, we can never sell it."

"Maude and I won't. Then it's up to your generation."

"We won't if I have anything to say about it."

"I'm sure you would."

"You know what Wendy told me?"

"What?"

"When she has children, she wants them to grow up spending

summers at Tír."

I stopped walking. "She said that?"

"She did."

"A land of everlasting youth."

Rachel smiled and said, "Come with me."

"Where we going?"

She took my hand and led me down to the end of the pier. When we got there, she said, "I just needed to have one more look before we leave." I put my arm around her, and the two of us looked at my grandmother's dream. Shadows had fallen across much of the house in the late afternoon light. The windows were dark with the shades drawn down. With all of the chairs moved inside, the porch looked empty.

Rachel said, "We're lucky to have this, aren't we?"

"Yeah. We are."

"She sure knew what she was doing. Thank you, Grandma Nell."

"Let's not forget Jamie Buckley."

"Thank you, Jamie Buckley. Tír na nÓg is the right name."

"It is. You ready?"

"Yes. You?"

"Yep. Let's do it. I want to get some writing done while you're making dinner."

Author's Note

I have gone to the Maine coast for a portion of every summer for fifty years, more or less. I am one of the 'summer people.' I have spent these summer respites in various places from Portland to Bar Harbor. I've driven the entire coast, read the literature it has inspired, and eaten at a lot of diners along Route 1. I have also sailed a good portion of the coast in everything from small day sailors to well-found cruising boats. I have relatives who live along its coast and have visited with them during every season of the year. Nevertheless, I am, and probably always will be, one of 'the summer people' who is 'from away.'

Tír na nÓg is a book of fiction. There is no Heron Cove or Erascohegan Yacht Club on the island of Georgetown. But there well might be. Geologically and sociologically, both would fit with the history and coast line of this beautiful island. There was never a "Convey Farm," but there were sheep farms. The artists did come to *Seguinland* and there was a devastating fire in 1934.

The history of the Irish famines is well documented as is the history of the schooners that were the boat design of choice to carry goods and people well into the early 1900's. World War I, II, Korea, Vietnam, and Afghanistan were as real as the men and women who fought in them. Once war planes entered the culture of the Buckley clan, the men flew into battle in the planes of these wars. Not all came home.

Today, when you cross the Sagadahoc Bridge between Bath and Woolwich you can look down and see the Bath Iron Works, still turning out vessels of destruction. Within a few miles you can find yards building wooden boats powered by sail.

The folks at the Georgetown Historical Society and Maine's Paper & Heritage Museum were very helpful with their time and suggestions. Peter Kellman provided first-hand knowledge about the strike at International Paper. His book, *Divided We Fall: The Story of the Paperworkers' Union and the Future of Labor*, was very helpful.

Richard Diller's journal *Firefly* is the basis for Michael Buckley's experiences in Laos and is a captivating account of that 'secret war.' I hope I have been true to the spirit of those who flew the A1 Skyraider.

E. J. Chandler's *Ancient Sagadahoc: A Story of the Englishmen Who Welcomed the Pilgrims to the New World*, Gene Reynolds's, *Images of America: Georgetown*, and *A History of Indian Point*, compiled by Sereno Sewall Webster, Jr. provided me with a wonderful introduction to the history of the island of Georgetown.

Louis B. Dorny's *US Navy PBY Catalina Units of the Pacific War*, and Mel Crocker's *Black Cats and Dumbos: WWII's Fighting PBYs* taught me about the iconic Catalina flying boat. Byron E. Hukes *USAF and VNAF A-1 Skyraider Units of the Vietnam War* and Wayne Mutza's *The A-1 Skyraider in Vietnam: The Spad's Last War* did the same for the A-1.

All of the errors and misunderstandings are, of course, my responsibility.

Made in United States
North Haven, CT
18 December 2022